The Great Devourer

More Warhammer 40,000 from Black Library

• **DAWN OF FIRE** •
BOOK 1: Avenging Son
Guy Haley
BOOK 2: The Gate of Bones
Andy Clark
BOOK 3: The Wolftime
Gav Thorpe
BOOK 4: Throne of Light
Guy Haley
BOOK 5: The Iron Kingdom
Nick Kyme

INDOMITUS
Gav Thorpe

• **DARK IMPERIUM** •
Guy Haley

BOOK 1: Dark Imperium
BOOK 2: Plague War
BOOK 3: Godblight

BELISARIUS CAWL: THE GREAT WORK
Guy Haley

SIGISMUND: THE ETERNAL CRUSADER
John French

VOLPONE GLORY
Nick Kyme

• **WATCHERS OF THE THRONE** •
Chris Wraight

BOOK 1: The Emperor's Legion
BOOK 2: The Regent's Shadow

• **VAULTS OF TERRA** •
Chris Wraight

BOOK 1: The Carrion Throne
BOOK 2: The Hollow Mountain
BOOK 3: The Dark City

WARHAMMER 40,000

The Great Devourer
THE LEVIATHAN OMNIBUS

GUY HALEY | JOSH REYNOLDS | BRADEN CAMPBELL
JOE PARRINO | L J GOULDING | NICK KYME

BLACK LIBRARY

A BLACK LIBRARY PUBLICATION

Valedor first published in 2014.
'Wraithflight' first published digitally in 2014.
The Last Days of Ector first published in 2014.
Deathstorm first published in 2014.
'Shadow of the Leviathan' first published digitally in 2014.
Tempestus first published in 2014.
Devourer first published in 2014.
'The Word of the Silent King' first published in 2014.
'Dread Night' first published digitally in 2014.
This edition published in Great Britain in 2023 by
Black Library, Games Workshop Ltd., Willow Road,
Nottingham, NG7 2WS, UK.

Represented by: Games Workshop Limited – Irish branch,
Unit 3, Lower Liffey Street, Dublin 1,
D01 K199, Ireland.

10 9 8 7 6 5 4 3 2 1

Produced by Games Workshop in Nottingham.
Cover illustration by Mark Holmes.

The Great Devourer: The Leviathan Omnibus © Copyright Games Workshop Limited 2023. The Great Devourer: The Leviathan Omnibus, GW, Games Workshop, Black Library, The Horus Heresy, The Horus Heresy Eye logo, Space Marine, 40K, Warhammer, Warhammer 40,000, the 'Aquila' Double-headed Eagle logo, and all associated logos, illustrations, images, names, creatures, races, vehicles, locations, weapons, characters, and the distinctive likenesses thereof, are either ® or TM, and/or © Games Workshop Limited, variably registered around the world.
All Rights Reserved.

A CIP record for this book is available from the British Library.

ISBN 13: 978-1-80407-423-7

No part of this publication may be reproduced, stored in a retrieval system, or transmitted in any form or by any means, electronic, mechanical, photocopying, recording or otherwise, without the prior permission of the publishers.

This is a work of fiction. All the characters and events portrayed in this book are fictional, and any resemblance to real people or incidents is purely coincidental.

See Black Library on the internet at

blacklibrary.com

Find out more about Games Workshop
and the worlds of Warhammer at

games-workshop.com

Printed and bound in the UK.

For more than a hundred centuries the Emperor has sat immobile on the Golden Throne of Earth. He is the Master of Mankind. By the might of His inexhaustible armies a million worlds stand against the dark.

Yet, He is a rotting carcass, the Carrion Lord of the Imperium held in life by marvels from the Dark Age of Technology and the thousand souls sacrificed each day so that His may continue to burn.

To be a man in such times is to be one amongst untold billions. It is to live in the cruellest and most bloody regime imaginable. It is to suffer an eternity of carnage and slaughter. It is to have cries of anguish and sorrow drowned by the thirsting laughter of dark gods.

This is a dark and terrible era where you will find little comfort or hope. Forget the power of technology and science. Forget the promise of progress and advancement. Forget any notion of common humanity or compassion.

There is no peace amongst the stars, for in the grim darkness of the far future,
there is only war.

CONTENTS

Valedor — 9
Guy Haley

Wraithflight — 219
Guy Haley

The Last Days of Ector — 233
Guy Haley

Deathstorm — 309
Josh Reynolds

Shadow of the Leviathan — 411
Josh Reynolds

Tempestus — 425
Braden Campbell

Devourer — 491
Joe Parrino

The Word of The Silent King — 565
L J Goulding

Dread Night — 585
Nick Kyme

VALEDOR

GUY HALEY

PROLOGUE

WAR'S CALL

The voidspawn creature clattered to a lifeless halt, the stump of its neck hissing. Prince Yriel of Iyanden landed lightly next to it in a crouch, head bowed, one hand upon the blood-slick firestone paving, the other holding his power sword out behind him in the posture of Death Brought With Precipitate Cunning. Before the last twitches had left the creature's six limbs, Yriel had artfully killed another, then a third, until there were none left within his reach.

Shuriken fire whistled behind Prince Yriel, massed volleys from the surviving Eldritch Raiders. Voidspawn shrieked as the rounds hit home. There were shouts and the cracking buzz of power weapons hitting chitin, the soft rattle of alien bodies falling. One last scream, and the plaza of Red Moon's New Birthing was clear.

'Yaleanar! Yaleanar! My shadow!' shouted Yriel. 'Secure the entrances to the plaza!' He gestured to the three grand archways leading into the square with his sword.

Yaleanar, a gaudily armoured warrior whose back was busy with pennants, snapped back a quick nod and ordered the remaining Eldritch Raiders into defensive positions. The last stragglers were running into the plaza.

Too few, how many have I lost? thought Yriel in dismay. His bold voidsmen were dying for him.

The archways opened onto an intricately decorated pentagon a thousand paces across. A clear-sided tower stood over the plaza, ten thousand paces tall, walled with transparent composites that afforded views of the stars and decorated with a thousand statues of Ulthanash. And on the far side, the forbidden shrine. The place he had sought. Or had it sought him?

He strode towards it, the tug of its call impossible to ignore.

None but those of the direct line of Ulthanash might enter the shrine, a number of eldar reduced now to Yriel alone. But Red Moon's New Birthing was for all. It had been a place for those new on the Path of the Warrior to come and meditate on Ulthanash's fate, to pray that they would not fall to Khaine as he had. So it had been for ten thousand passes, until five cycles ago, when Khaine had come calling upon the Red Moon in person, and offered up his own dedications.

Blood coated everything. Dead eldar lay in piles, the corpses of their mindless enemies around them. Shattered psychoplastics skidded across the smooth floor with every tremor of the war-wracked worldship. Broken wraithbone ribs bled light. The fighting had moved deeper into the craftworld long before Yriel had landed. The aliens they had encountered had been of the lesser types, a feeble rearguard, but still he had lost a quarter of his corsairs getting to the shrine.

Iyanden shuddered bodily, rocking the prince. Yriel nimbly redistributed his weight.

He looked up to the gate of the Shrine of Ulthanash, a shimmering wall of energy held between the arms of an alabaster arch set with runes of bronze and iridium. It was marvellous, this power of the ancients on display. Calamity strode the halls and causeways of Iyanden unopposed, but the shrine remained imperturbable.

Waiting for him.

Yriel had a grave choice to make. The Crown of Ulthanash, rendered in red gold and jade at the apex of the arch, seemed to glower down at him.

To walk under it, he thought, *is as good as placing that crown upon my head. I will crown myself with nothing but his curse, the king of fools, last scion of Ulthanash's line. That is not an honour I wish for.*

On the outside of the rippling field stood Captain Yriel, corsair: fickle, sometimes callous, always full of rage, lauded and feared in equal measure. On the other side, at the heart of the shrine, another Yriel awaited, and the manner of that Yriel was unknown to him. This Yriel, proud Yriel, Yriel the pirate, was free to make the choice between the two, as free as he had been to choose to return at his birthplace's time of need, as free as he had been to abandon the restrictions of the Path in the first place. To pass through the shining wall and enter the Shrine of Ulthanash, or to let his home die, turn away from those who had dishonoured him and remain the exile pirate king?

'Choose choice, or choose to relinquish choice forever,' he said. 'There is no departing this path. And it appears for all my efforts, there is no escaping the Path.' He laughed. 'How delightfully absurd, how dreadfully irritating.'

He remained where he was, lost in thought. Shouts came to his ears, more screeching. A wave of aliens tried to break through the Eldritch Raiders' defensive perimeter. There were not many of his voidsmen remaining, deadly warriors all who had followed him to the edge of the galaxy and back. They fought expertly. He was sure that no more would fall here, now they were in a good position. But they were ready to die for him.

To die, so that he might vacillate.

I am lost, he thought. *Lost is the word for it, in thought and in deed. I have been for a very long time.*

He pinched at his slender chin with armoured fingers, as if this were a choice such as those on the Path of Dreaming might make, a phantom decision to prepare him only for more phantom decisions, from which he would awaken excited but untouched by consequence.

He dithered. He, Yriel, decisive and bold, wavering in the face of responsibility.

Insight flashed in him like lightning, although in truth it was but the first strike of a storm that had been gathering for many passes. What if he had abandoned Iyanden not because of his wounded pride, but because of his inability to bear the burdens placed upon him?

This is what he thought: *For all my prowess, am I a coward?*

'My prince! You must hurry!' shouted Yaleanar. There came the loud, staccato banging of a scatter laser, multiple bolts causing the air to heat explosively. Another chorus of screeches, this followed by uneasy quiet.

Iyanden rumbled. The winds of far-off decompressions tugged Yriel's robes. A foul taint came fleetingly onto the air. The infinity circuit screamed in outrage as the hive mind assailed it. Crystal shattered somewhere distant, wild screams chasing after the delicate sound.

I have rushed here. Why do I delay? he thought.

Because I have not made this choice, another part of him countered. *I have not come here of my own volition. Coming here was not my choice to make. It never has been. The dead hand of Morai-Heg grips the threads of my destiny tightly, dragging me pace by painful pace to face the duties demanded by my heritage no matter where I hide.*

He shifted his posture.

I have been brought here by what is hidden within the shrine, but it cannot make me enter.

Yriel's mind was heavy. The pain of the embattled infinity circuit was his pain, the implacable wall of the Great Devourer's intellect opposing it threatened to crush his spirit. Through this psychic tumult still the shrine's ward had pulled at him. Freedom was not the lot of any eldar, not since the Fall. He realised that now.

They call me proud, arrogant, he thought. *So be it. I will not let fate take me on unequal terms. Coming to the shrine was not my will. Entering it shall be.*

'Yaleanar? Where is my shadow?' Yriel had lost two-thirds of his fabled Hundred Ships destroying the voidspawn's fleet. But faithful, deadly Yaleanar lived. A bad voidsman, but a great warrior. He ran across the plaza from the corsairs to the prince and saluted, armoured fist clacking upon his breastplate as he dipped his conical, tiger-striped helm. 'My prince.'

Yriel looked over the warriors crouched in cover by the plaza's entrances. 'A fine spread, my shadow.'

'We have lost no more. We are secure here.'

Yriel smiled sadly. 'What would I do without you?' He sheathed his sword.

'Die, probably,' said Yaleanar, the humour Yriel loved so much evident as always despite their circumstances. Yaleanar had such marvellously insolent body language that he had better-mannered persons simmering with outrage within the microcycle.

'Oh, do take away your helm,' said Yriel irritably. 'If yours is the last face I see, I do not want it to be the grille and eye-lens in my memory.'

Yaleanar complied, lifting the tall helmet off with both hands and shaking out hair coloured a subtle lilac. Intricate patterns were painted on his face.

'You are going to do it?'

Yriel shrugged, hands moving in gestures indicating equivocation. 'I am going into the shrine. If I take up the spear or not is another matter.' He trailed off, sinking back into his thoughts.

An explosion rumbled nearby. Alien shrieks closed.

'Yriel? I am sorry, my prince, to hurry you, but you must, well,' Yaleanar grinned, 'hurry.' He replaced his helmet.

'You will await me here?'

'Where else would your shadow be other than right behind you?' Yaleanar hesitated. 'If you do not return?'

High over them a flight of eldar attack craft sped through the void, their outlines rippled to fragments by holofields. Biological projectiles chased the fighters, green bio-plasma sending them on at speed. A fighter was caught and exploded silently. Bright light flared on the plaza. Guilt stabbed Yriel. He was losing his composure. Another death on his conscience. This would not have happened had he remained autarch-admiral.

'If I am gone longer than a tenth-cycle, do as you think best. Fall back to the ships, or fight on for unsung glories. The choice is yours, my shadow. Either way, the final death of our kind will be snapping at your heels when Iyanden falls. Fly to some forgotten corner of the galaxy, and still fate will find you, as it has found me.' He drew in a shuddering breath. 'I left the path, Yaleanar, in my pride and my arrogance. I came to see destruction's beauty. Dishonoured here, I exerted my will upon the stars, and for what? Who was watching me, who marked my cunning and my audacity but my own vanity? Is this my punishment, Yaleanar? Is this what my pride has wrought?' He lifted an ichor-stained hand and swept it around the dome. It was as heavy as stone, weighted with guilt.

'My prince,' said Yaleanar. He grasped his friend by the shoulders, an intimacy Yriel allowed no one else. 'We are all prisoners of the skein. What could you do but follow your own thread?'

Yriel was not listening to him. Tears streaked the filth on his face and dripped to the floor to mingle with the blood of his countrymen. 'My passion for adventure has gone. I left the path and lost my way.' He looked up at the gates again, determination entering his voice. 'The way has found me.'

With those words, he stepped through the shimmering curtains guarding the shrine. No one else could have done so and lived, but he was Yriel, last of the immemorial line of Ulthanash, who strode the heavens tens of millions of years ago when the eldar race was young and the numberless days of glory had not yet begun.

The exiled prince had come home.

Dynasties of silence reigned over the chambers of the shrine. Dust lay thick upon the floor. Yriel followed a single line of footprints – his own, made the first and only other time he had visited his ancestor's temple, over an arc before. No other eyes had lit upon the pre-Fall masterpieces that lined the walls in shadowy alcoves since; no heads had bowed to the mighty idols whose upheld arms supported the ceiling.

Dead gods with dead gemstone eyes, thought Yriel. Meaningless relics, the ephemera of a vanished civilisation, protected by stasis fields for no one to see. And yet, he had to admit, they represented something; something pure, something that he had the power to save, should he so choose. Yriel passed them all quickly; the compulsion of Ulthanash was on him again, drawing him deeper into the shrine.

Battle-sign had made no mark here, for the doom of the shrine kept war from its halls both in the material plane and on the mess of potentialities that made up the skein. Past sealed portals and the tattered banners of extinct houses Yriel went. In one place he found the footprints of another, smaller than his own. He followed these with his eyes, knowing he looked upon the last mortal traces of his mother, a woman he had barely known. There had been more such footprints on his last visit. Dust had blurred their outlines. In time, they would be gone.

He wrenched himself away. He soon found himself in the small domed chamber at the heart of the shrine. As he remembered, it was dominated by a circular dais. Twin statues of maidens, twice life size, knelt either side of a pedestal upon the dais, their faces covered by their hands. Delicately rendered tears seeped through their fingers as they wept an eternity for what had been lost.

A cone of light illuminated a wraithbone cradle on the pedestal. Resting within it was a long, leaf-bladed spear. Yriel's mouth went dry as, for only the second time in his long life, he looked upon the Spear of Twilight. Ulthanash's weapon, immeasurably ancient, trapped in a bubble of frozen time. Through the stasis field that held it, the spear's fell nature could be felt as an oily darkness on Yriel's soul. The air around it was somehow thicker, the light of a sinister quality. The weapon of Ulthanash was cursed: anathema to those not of Ulthanash's House, and slow death to those that were. It had filled him with horror when he had seen it as a youth. It filled him with horror again.

A voice spoke to him from the darkness of the shrine. Female, mocking.

'Why have you come here, Scion of Ulthanash?' A woman came forward, her outline blurred by a dathedi field as she walked around the dais. Yriel had the impression of a mirrored face mask beneath a bright cowl of yellow and purple diamonds. A Shadowseer, a mistress of illusions. One of the Harlequins.

Yriel found his voice. Her purpose here he could not guess at, but he knew his own. Confronted by the spear and the fate chosen for him, in freedom's absence his pride returned. 'I seek the means to deliver Iyanden from the Great Devourer. I will not be challenged here, not in the shrine of my ancestor. I come to take my birthright.'

'Is that all you seek?' Laughter ran through the voice, as bright as sunlight on rippled water, or on blood.

'You mock me?' he said.

Swift movement, a blur of trailing diamonds lost in the dark. The voice spoke from somewhere else. 'I am Sylandri Veilwalker, last of the troupe that came to the aid of the people you abandoned. All my friends are dead, and I laugh yet. Cegorach mocks all, prince and fool alike, and especially foolish princes,' she said. 'Answer me, last of the line of Ulthanash. My question is a fair one.'

Yriel paused. Was there more? Was sacrifice his only aim? He looked deep inside himself, past the veils of shame and guilt.

'No, it is not all,' he admitted. 'I have failed those whom I swore to protect. I would atone for my error, if such a thing were any longer possible.'

Laughter rang out. 'Then take up the weapon of your forebear. He too was led astray by pride, but found redemption in battle and, soon after, his death.'

Yriel took a step, stopping before he reached the dais. 'You are a seer. Grant me a boon and tell me: will I perish, as did he?'

'Would my answer alter your resolve?'

Yriel cocked his head and laughed in his turn.

'You laugh too, I see. A good tonic to all ills, even death.'

'I laugh because there is an irony to my situation, being pushed into servitude by the servants of the last free god.'

'The choice is yours.'

'I would fain it were not,' said Yriel. 'The hour is late, the time of desperate measures is at hand. I do not think knowing the hour of my death would change anything, for we must all die.'

'Then, young prince, choose your fate in blissful ignorance. The skein is not set. Can you not feel it? Here, all things are possible, just for a moment. A rare moment. You will experience no other like it in your lifetime. Here is your chance to decide for yourself.'

The weapon called to him, like to like. Both of them were poison to those they protected. For the briefest fragment of time, he did not move, allowing himself an indulgence, a last savouring of choice.

The spell broke. 'We are well suited to one another, you and I,' he said to the spear. He strode forwards, up the single step onto the dais, and into the cone of light. Without hesitation he thrust his hand into the stasis field. It slowed, and pain needled his skin as chronaxic dissonance set up and his arm was pulled into a different reference frame of time. He thrust the harder. His fingers moved so slowly, until his hand closed around the smooth shaft of the weapon and the field snapped off.

He lifted the spear, holding it up in front of him. The blade sang, the shaft vibrating. Raw power flooded through him, a remembrance of the untamed eldar psyche of the elder days. He had sought to recapture that vigour by abandoning the strictures of the path and living as a corsair. He saw he had only achieved a base caricature. More pain came with this epiphany, a snag at his soul, a cut that would never heal. A chill emanated from the spear along with the power and the hurt, one that in days to come would consume him utterly; of this he was as certain as he was that the heart beating in his chest was his own.

He cared not.

Another explosion rocked the craftworld. As if the shrine were no longer protected now the spear had been claimed, the lights went out. Yriel's face was lit from below by the blue lambency of the spear's blade.

'You are mine, and I am yours,' he said. He smiled, although his doom was upon him. He felt a sense of purpose he had never experienced before, and he knew without a doubt that this was *right*. He hefted the spear and then spun around, gauging its weight as he ran through a series of lightning-fast combat stances.

He stopped, arms outflung. The spear rang. He laughed; a raw, wild sound.

'It is time for us both to be about our purpose.'

The Fortress of the Red Moon was falling. Already the upper spires that stretched into the void had been cast down upon the craftworld, or infested and sealed off by forcefields.

At the feet of the fortress below the energy domes, where mighty bastions soared over once-beautiful wilderness, battle raged most fiercely. Iyanna Arienal stood behind a dyke of alien corpses that stoppered a breach in the wall. The bodies of fallen eldar not yet reclaimed lay tumbled at its feet, blood mingling with alien ichor, cracked yellow armour abutting shattered chitin. Iyanna tried to ignore the glimmers of unclaimed spirit stones still bedded into the psycho-plastics and mind-smithed metals of the dead's wargear. There had not been time to collect them, and she feared there never would.

The tyranids were upon them again: a horde of aliens as far as the eye could see, crashing over the blasted parklands that fronted the slighted walls of the fortress, swarming around the rubble of fallen towers. Smoke rose in the middle distance, a funereal column marking the position of the broken Avatar of Khaine. When the returning fleets of outcasts had destroyed the voidspawn's craft, Iyanna had felt a brief surge of joy, quickly doused. Their ships gone, the tyranids in the domes had fought with unbounded ferocity, and when the living idol of the murder-god had fallen before them, so had Iyanna's hope.

The tyranids charged, a seething mass of multi-limbed monstrosities of bone and red. They switched direction with one purpose, like a flock of birds in flight, the mind that was generated by them and governed them all a baleful presence of inconceivable magnitude upon the skein. It squeezed at her, making her mind, already weary from communion with the dead, feel as if cast from lead.

'Fire!' she called. She focused her mind, conveying what her eyes saw to the silent ranks of wraithguard arrayed alongside her. Now more than ever they needed her guidance. Earlier in the battle, the spirit stones of those freshly slain had been plucked directly from their bodies and melded with new, unfeeling forms. Not for them one moment of the infinity circuit's peace. The first ghost warriors roused had been fierce: those who had died while in the grip of the paths of Leader and Warrior, or outraged souls of sure purpose. These last were civilians all, innocents on the paths of gardeners and jewellers, poets, carvers, cooks and musicians, often slaughtered in terror. Their woe at their predicament was bitter in Iyanna's mouth.

'Fire!' she called again. The air rippled with the discharge of distortion weaponry. The wash of the weapons' energies, fatal to any living being that attempted to wield them, sickened her to her bones. She saw the wounds they made on reality vividly with her second sight, fleeting glimpses into the horror of the warp where She Who Thirsts glutted herself on Iyanden's disaster. She could not draw back from it, the ghost warriors needed her guidance, and so she faced the death of flesh and soul equally and unflinchingly.

Where the weapons' deadly beams terminated, pricks of light as bright as stars appeared along the line of voidspawn. They twisted in on themselves, expanding with flares of purple and green ghostlight, briefly lived portals opening up onto the hell-dimensions of the Othersea. Where the distortion weapons hit directly, voidspawn exploded, torn apart by the forces at work within them. Others were pulled off their feet and dragged wholly through the veil that separated this world from the next. Hundreds were sent into the world of nightmares this way. The sense of horror built until Iyanna thought she would collapse, and then the portals slammed shut. Iyanna could still sense the enemy on the other side of the thin veil of reality. Torn from their hive mind's great rope of being, the creatures briefly showed as feeble fibres on the skein, before winking out.

The distortion weapons whined as their power cells recharged. Iyanna brought new targets to the wraithguard's attention.

The aliens came on undaunted, as unafraid of the warp as they were of physical death. Ranks of Guardians atop the broken parapets opened fire, alongside the last of Iyanden's Aspect Warriors. Their fury raged unchecked. After cycles of ceaseless fighting, Khaine had taken most of them and they fought hard. But there were too few, so pitiful in numbers. The dead outnumbered the living many times over.

Iyanna dipped into the skein, seeking a future she could exploit. She was almost as skilled at this as the farseers, but could see no way to influence the battle. The consciousness of the hive fleet was a thread like no other, a huge, braided presence made up of billions of individual fates. Individually, the minds of the tyranids were nothing, animal spirits. But as a rope is twisted from many strands, and a cable twisted from many ropes, so the hive mind of the Dragon was made. Its presence dominated everything, smashing possible futures aside with its singular purpose, making psychic contact with the other seers all but impossible. The infinity circuit was tormented by it. Iyanden was under psychic as much as physical attack.

The tyranids reached the walls. Uncountable numbers of the lesser creatures clambered over their heaped dead, springing upwards on powerful legs. The greater species came close behind. In their midst was their leader, the vast hive tyrant that they could not bring low: the swarmlord. For the hundredth time, Iyanna looked into its fate. On the skein it showed up as a knotted ball, a confluence of lesser destinies. As much as any one of these monsters could be regarded as representatives of the hive fleet's collective mind, this one was the Dragon incarnate. Slay it, and the bindings of the hive mind's thread would unravel.

They had tried so many times to destroy it, and had failed at every attempt. Their last gambit had been to send Khaine himself in open challenge. But the hive mind had no concept of honour, no need to prove itself to its followers, in the same way that an eldar has no need to prove himself to his finger. The Dragon's living tanks had barred the way, a hand sacrificed to fend off the blow, and down the Avatar had been dragged.

Iyanna brought the attention of the dead to rest upon this creature, and willed them to shoot it down, but the dark energies of their ghost weapons were blocked once more by the swarmlord's towering guard of monsters. Where there had been a dozen of these titanic beasts, now only three remained, but this thinning of the swarmlord's living shield had come too late. When the Fortress of the Red Moon was destroyed, there would be no more organised resistance, and Iyanden would be consumed.

Wearied beyond comprehension, the eldar fought on. Weapon-beasts waded through the tide of lesser creatures, again to assail the main gates to the fortress or spitting boluses of bile laced with toxins into the defenders. From riven bastions high above, bright lances shot killing stabs of light, but for every creature dead, two more took its place.

The gate was long rent asunder. A new barrier blocked the way through its arch. A double wall of the dead, alien corpses heaped without dignity; and behind this redoubt of flesh the spirits of eldar fought on, rehoused in wraithbone. Against this barrier half a dozen giant beasts went. The wall of bodies collapsed, the corpses toppling in on obscene flood. Wraithblades stepped forwards, crystal weapons flashing. They attacked as one and in silence, psychically charged blades cutting through the bony armour and cartilaginous cladding of the monsters.

Then Iyanna's mind went elsewhere, calling upon her ghost warriors to open fire again.

There came a flash of terror as a spirit stone was breached and the eldar soul within sucked into the waiting maw of the Great Enemy. Iyanna would have wept, had her heart not been cased in icy fury. She would see as many of these creatures die as she could before her own soul perished. She directed her ghost warriors to rake the walls free of climbing aliens. The effect on the fabric of the fort was catastrophic, but there was little else she could think to do.

Focus. She had to keep focused, form, mind and being. Her soul was a pale candle suspended between the skein and the now, on one side the ravening terror of She Who Thirsts, on the other the blank malice of the Great Devourer. Focus kept her safe from the depredations of both. It kept her from slipping away and joining the dead.

A shout went up from throats hoarse with screaming. To the rear of the parklands a disturbance rippled through the horde, close by the broad tunnelway that had led to the Oceans of Ceaseless Tranquillity; empty like so much of Iyanden, the seas all boiled away into the void.

'Aid comes! Aid at last!' The tyranid assault on the walls faltered as the impenetrable mind of the hive fleet turned to regard this new annoyance.

Iyanna stared towards the source of the cries, her sharp eyes scanning the tumult. Jetbikes powered out of the tunnel. Weapons fire flashed. Bright banners flickered amid the bone and red mass of the aliens.

Another voice rang out. 'The Eldritch Raiders, it is the Eldritch Raiders! Prince Yriel is come, Prince Yriel is returned to the halls of his fathers!'

Iyanna cast out a desperate message from her mind in the obscure language of the seers. +The Great Dragon has many scales but a hollow heart. Pierce the breast and they shall fall away.+ She stumbled with the effort, the alien consciousness swatting aside her mind's assay.

The eldar upon the wall, dead and alive, fought with the mettle of hope and despair combined.

Yriel saw Iyanna's thought-sending as a single, burning rune hanging over the centre of the mass of aliens: the Dragon. The words of the spiritseer sang in his thoughts against the tuneless roar of the hive mind. 'That way lies the leader, it is him we must slay! Slay him and they will falter! Make a path, make a path!'

Yriel hung by one hand from the rear portion of a light sky-runner, pointing the Spear of Twilight at the heart of the alien throng. The spear's tip crackled with baleful energies, the weapon's spirit enraged by the presence of the aliens on the craftworld. Yriel drank deep of its hatred, its power lending him enormous strength. The impetus of their charge had driven them deep into the horde attacking the carnelian walls of the Fortress of the Red Moon, but his raiders were few and their assault faltered. 'Onward!' he cried. 'Onward for the House of Ulthanash! Onward for Iyanden!'

Yriel revelled in the fight. He had abandoned the path years past, allowing the extremes of life to soak his psyche. He did not turn from the horror of bloodshed, for he had long ago embraced his dark side. His soul was upon a knife edge, overbalanced further by the fell nature of the spear. Tottering over damnation's abyss, he laughed, the grimness of his home's predicament swept away by the glory of the moment, the romance of the final charge, the vision of the fortress saved. Both downfall and triumph were of equal value. His sharp eldar senses drank in the spectacle of carnage, and found it pleasing: the snap of his gonfalons in the wind, the poignancy of the eldar's final stand, the light of artificial stars gleaming from glossy carapaces, the smell of burning and flesh putrefying, the dusty scent of ruptured wraithbone, and over it all the thick, acerbic stink of the Great Dragon's beasts. Everything was cast in greater contrast through the medium of the spear, heightening already potent sensations. He was filled to the brim with the powers of his ancestor, intoxicated with new-found godhood.

'Onward, my brave reavers! Onward!' he cried. He held aloft the thrumming spear, and the sky-runner plunged on.

Open transports skimmed in the wake of his sky-runner. Corsairs, once of several bands but now wholly his, fired from the railed sides, their shuriken and las-bolts slaying many. Gargoyles attacked them and were driven back, the skimmers dodging their clumsy claws. Harpies and harridans flapped, too slow to catch them. The weight of living ammunition hurled skywards could not help but bring a few craft down, sending skimmers into the teeming infestation like great arrows, but not all.

Yriel's pilot ducked and wove. Sprays of sharp-toothed grubs and ichor splattered against the hull, the plating hissing as acid ate into it. Through the cockpit shield Yriel heard the urgent chimes of alarms. 'Onwards, Kalaea, take me to their heart! Do not fail me now!'

The sky-runner sped true. A serpentine monster reared up in front of its sharp prow, but the craft swerved, and resumed its course. It banked into a great curve, slowing just enough to allow Yriel to leap in safely. As he jumped, the stubby wings of his corsair's flightpack flicked out, decelerating him rapidly. He landed lightly upon the gory corpse of a fallen giant. Before him the swarmlord loomed, taller than a wraithknight and greatly more massive. Its eyes glittered at him with malign intelligence.

'Great Dragon!' Yriel called, holding aloft the Spear of Twilight. 'I come to slay you, as my forefather Ulthanash slew the wyrm Draoch-var with this very blade!'

Three huge creatures lumbered at Yriel, directed by the psychic command of the leader-beast, but he leapt aside from their swipes, the spear granting him unparalleled reflexes. One and then another fell, pierced by the pinpoint lance beams of the prince's followers as he bounded closer to his prey.

Roaring, the swarmlord attacked, driving down a claw twelve paces long at Yriel. He backflipped, the wind of its passing stirring his hair. The tip of the claw slammed down into a carcass, slowing the hive tyrant for the merest heartbeat as it tugged it free, but it was enough. The prince landed on his feet. Smoothly he drew back his arm and cast the spear of Ulthanash at the creature. The spear screamed a polyphonic wrath-song as it hurtled through the air, passing in an eyeblink to pierce the jaw of the swarmlord, drive up through the soft mouth into the swollen brain case, and emerge, gleaming, from the top of the armoured skull.

The swarmlord toppled, lifeless. Yriel yelled in exultation, feeling more alive than he had in many cycles. He had become jaded by his life as a corsair. But this! This was the theatre of life full in the round!

The niggling pain he had experienced when he had picked up the spear became more intense. The spear, lodged in the skull of the leader-beast, glowed brighter and brighter. Its hunger burning, the spear sucked greedily upon the limitless psychic banquet of the hive mind.

The spear-tip blazed, bright as a solar flare, the chill of its link to his soul turning to incandescent agony. A pressure built in his head, pain so acute he thought it would crack open. The world became a radiant tableau of hard whites and black shadow under the light of the spear's feeding.

Prince Yriel gripped his temples. Something gave in his left eye and a wash of liquid heat filled the orb of it.

Falling to his knees, he screamed.

The light ceased. The hive mind retreated, its oppressive presence becoming again a distant threat. With no other of the higher creatures remaining, and the hive fleet destroyed in Yriel's drive back to the craftworld, there was nothing to link the voidspawn to their gestalt soul, and the conjoined intellect of those upon Iyanden dissipated altogether.

The swarm faltered. The assault collapsed as the creatures lost their unity. Some milled about, some fell catatonic, many died at the sudden severance. Some, reverting to savage, simplistic instinct, attacked their fellows.

With one blow, the tide had turned. The hunters became the hunted. Iyanden was saved.

The Spear of Twilight stood proud of the swarmlord's blackened skull. For one hundred paces around was a wide circle of smoking bones and black earth. All soft matter had been atomised. At the centre of this circle, unharmed, Prince Yriel lay curled in the ash.

Yriel was upon a beach. A hot and merciless sun burned at his skin, a calm sea was in front of him. He wished to dive in, to cool himself even if he could not quench his thirst, but as he approached he saw the sea was not of water but of blood. He turned away only to find that he could not move: his feet were trapped in the sand. Bending to free his feet, he saw each grain was a miniature, screaming skull.

He stood again, perplexed. A long while he remained there, until a mighty wind whipped up a swell, bringing with it the rich scent of ripe meat. The sea drew back from the shore as a red wave rose over him, the thick, glistening face of it blood, the cap frothed with skulls.

The wave crashed upon him, and Yriel surfaced from his sleep, tipped from nightmare by a rush of fury. He sat up in his bed with a cry, silken sheets stuck to his muscled torso with his sweat. He kicked at them to free his feet, tangled while he dreamed.

His nightmares were becoming more frequent and more vivid. He growled in frustration when his feet would not come loose and he trapped himself further. The urge to rip at the sheets built, the wave about to break. He saw the wave still in his mind's eye, his dreams intruding into his wakefulness. He slapped his hands to his face; fingers clasping at his temples, he tried to grind away the image from his eyes with the heels of his hands. After a moment, it passed, and Yriel sighed raggedly.

He lay back on his pillows, forced his heart to slow, regained his poise. The seers had taught him meditative techniques to purge himself of his irritation and pain, and although not entirely effective, they helped. He let the rush of his blood in his ears soothe him, until it calmed, and the wave sank back into the churning seas of his emotions. He opened his eyes again, and saw from only one. His fury had become annoyance. Anger was his constant companion, though whether his own or that of the spear, he could not tell.

Shakily, Yriel unwrapped his feet and slid from his bed. He was weak. His limbs shook; this palsy upon waking was becoming a regular occurrence, following hard on his nightmares. Always, his right hand tingled.

He needed to calm his pains. He went to a delicate vanity table where he once kept his paints and pigment changers. His days of vanity were behind him: he cut a grim figure now, his hair, clothes and skin unadorned by eldar standards, and several decanters crowded the table instead of flasks of perfume and the devices of beautification. Yriel snatched at one, high-necked, full of deeply purple nightvine liqueur. He kept his head bowed as he poured the drink into a goblet, so as not to look in the mirror. He had subconsciously taken to avoiding his own reflection, some part of him not wishing to see his ruined eye, nor the sallow skin it glared from. An angry red sun in a sickly sky his eye was, too reminiscent of the beach of his dreams. His blindness was a reminder of the power of the spear, a lesson he had barely survived.

The glass of the elegant vessel rattled on the lip of his cup as he poured. Nightvine was potent, supposed to be taken in moderation, but Yriel served himself three fingers' worth and gulped it back, a thin trickle spilling from the corner of his mouth. He wiped at his face with the back of his trembling hand, and poured himself some more. The shaking in his arms and legs receded, and he sipped at his second drink with more decorum.

Yriel looked out through the double doors of his bedroom. On a stand in the drawing room of his private chambers the spear rested, lit within a cone of stark white light. Yriel slept always with the door open, for he could not bear to be out of sight of the spear. The weakness he felt grew the further he was from it. If it went from his sight, he was gripped by panic, sometimes murderously so. He would have slept with it by his side, but the seers had told him it would devour his soul all the quicker, and for the time being he retained will enough to heed their warnings.

The light was a stasis field, and the Spear of Twilight was dormant, but it was forged in the elder days of glory. It was not bound by constraints on time and space, and it never truly slumbered. Its regard was upon him, made sluggish by the time-inhibiting energies of the field, but vigilant still.

Yriel stared at it longingly for several minutes. He turned from it with a hiss of disgust. Not for the spear, but for his own desire to hold it.

The hour was late, his palace silent. Few were his living servants, vast his domicile. The breeze through his open windows was cool, and that helped. Feeling the need for further restoration, he followed it. Cradling his goblet, he passed through gauzy curtains to the curved balcony of his room, and let the perfumed winds of the dome of the House of Ulthanash dry the sweat upon his skin. Little sound came to his ears: the chirp of nightcallers and buzzing calls of darkmoths only, no song beneath the trees, no lights in the glades. The parklands were dark. The whole dome was quiet as a sepulchre. His people had suffered less than others of the Iyandeni, but they were cowed. Cowed by the Triple Woe, by their rejection of him, by the failures of his kinsman Elthrael to guard the craftworld, by death and the damnation of those they had raised to fall again.

But most of all they were cowed by the sombre presence of the ancestors who walked among them. The dead refused to sleep on Iyanden. Many ghost warriors remained at large even in peace. The flames of these revenant spirits' souls burned lower than in life, and yet the mightiest of them shone brighter by far than those of the greater part of the living. Ulthanash's House was much reduced in number and in vigour, and with the evidence of his people's dwindling standing right in front of them, it could not be denied.

Still Yriel enjoyed the quiet. Far from silent, the dome possessed a velvet soundscape made up of a million small things growing. He had missed that, during his exile; the monolithic presence of his ship was no substitute for the infinity circuit or the myriad elements of ecology, free of any purpose greater than to individually live, creating something glorious in concert as they did so.

The liquid in Yriel's cup rippled. A flock of birds soared from their roosts in the trees outside, calling in dismay. A tremor ran through the wraithbone skeleton of the worldship, bringing with it a flash of hot anger. An answering pulse of bloodlust came from the Spear of Twilight to tug at Yriel's soul.

'War is coming again,' he said. His tongue felt thick at its root, as though swollen. Although alone and speaking out into the night, he addressed his words to the spear. 'War is coming, the Avatar of Khaine stirs.' He looked over the parks. At the distant edge of the dome, the first light of artificial dawn glowed ruddy as blood. He gripped the smooth balcony rail, its semi-organic stone warm under his hand. 'And I am not sorry for it.'

Yriel could not decide whether to laugh or cry. In the end, he did both.

CHAPTER ONE

GRIM COUNSEL

The same night, in Iyanden's Dome of Crystal Seers, Taec Silvereye sat cross-legged. He winced as the tremor shivered the skein and material worlds alike, his scars creasing awkwardly around the orb of metal that had replaced his left eye.

He pulled himself back from the skein, and looked around the half-ruined grove. The leaves on those few crystal trees still standing here tinkled. Wrath hung heavy over Iyanden.

He had been correct, then. The Avatar stirred, war was coming, and sooner than he had hoped. The question remained, whence came the threat?

This problem had exercised Taec for the best part of three cycles, since the sense of foreboding had stolen up on him. He could not divine why, and it had only grown. He had come to this hidden grove near the edge of the dome alone, compelled by this sense of doom that he dared not share. Before the Triple Woe, Taec had been something of a maverick. His predictions were seen as obscure and alarmist and dismissed by the Council Elder, Kelmon Firesight. But he had been proven correct. Kelmon was dead, slain after pursuing a false future to the ruin of Iyanden.

Vindicated and elevated to Council Elder, Taec now had the opposite problem. His every word was hung upon and dissected for hidden meaning, his least concern about the skein provoked panic. He had ceased to say anything, but his posture and gestures were as diligently interpreted. He had withdrawn from society, going into seclusion willingly where before it was forced on him. Taec had become increasingly aloof, but with good reason. He would not bring his fears to the rest of the High Council and seer council until he was absolutely sure where the threat came from.

The Avatar stirred. He still did not have the answer. Time was running out.

Taec sighed heavily, and closed his eyes. He regained his focus, leaving behind the concerns of form. Glad he was to do so; he was old now, and the Crystal Transformation of Morai-Heg was quickening. He sank into the warm embrace of the infinity circuit, the source of Iyanden's power, its communications system and its compound soul. Made up of the millions of eldar who had died here over the arcs since the Fall, it was a spiritual refuge against the eternal torments of the Great Enemy.

The circuit spread out around him, as intricate as a circulatory system. The bright flames of the living moved along it. At the edges – a nonsense really, Taec's mind forced upon the circuit a form he could understand, the infinity circuit had no true edge – the circuit's capillaries and lacy vessels drew together into a handful of arteries that connected Iyanden to the greater eternity matrix linking all that remained of the eldar's fractured domains.

Warp spiders clustered around Taec's astral form and made their strange greetings. Further out crowded the ghosts of eldar gone before. Their shades were pictures made of flame; solid forms coalesced momentarily, before the dance of their energies attenuated or flared, wiping away any semblance of their lost bodies. It once was that Taec rarely encountered a spirit with cohesion enough to be aware of him. Since the Triple Woe, they dogged his footsteps always, petitioning him with their inchoate desires. The infinity circuit had swollen with the huge numbers felled in Iyanden's recent battles, and the world-ship throbbed with their power. They did not fade, their anger and multitude allowing them to cling to being where once they would have slept. The tranquillity of the circuit was gone. Iyanden was gripped by rage.

+This is not the way that it should be,+ he thought to them. +Return to your rest.+

They wavered, and drew back, but did not depart. Ordinarily they would have dispersed at his command, but these were not ordinary times.

From a pile of runes by Taec's side in the dome, five rose into the air. They presented themselves in a line before the farseer's face for approval. He did not open his eyes, but saw them nonetheless.

He nodded at the first four in turn, consenting to their selection. The first was his name-rune, his power focus. Two syllables combined into one ideograph to spell out his first name. Worn by use, its wraithbone was grey with age. Through this he could draw upon the power of the Othersea with little risk to his eternal essence. The other three runes were specific aids that would help him in divining the truth of his foreboding. The Scorpion, the revealer of hidden secrets; the Seeking Shaft, Kurnous's arrow; the Flame of Asuryan, the world-rune of Iyanden itself. His name-rune stayed in front of his face, rotating gently. The other three lifted up to circle his head.

The fifth rune he regarded with his second sight for some time. The Bloody Hand, the rune of Kaela Mensha Khaine himself. He had not wished to employ this rune, but time was short and he had exhausted all other options. Khaine's sign glowered at him, filling his mind with the stink of blood and hot iron. He decided to let it hang there, out of synchronisation with the others. He would not deploy it yet.

Taec looked past the shades in the circuit, past the traceries that linked the living and the dead of Iyanden, out beyond the eternity matrix, and onto the skein. The warp spiders were seemingly aware of his task, and corralled the dead, keeping them back so that they would not obscure his view. He watched the future, ignoring those who had passed before their time.

The beauty of the skein never failed to move Taec, and now, when the burning hand of Khaine hovered in his mind's eye, it moved him all the more. The threat of destruction added to his appreciation. The skein defied description. The eldar tongue, for all its complex shades of nuance, could not encompass it. Even psychic communication and shared recollection could only hint at the skein's glories, for all that was passed over was the seer's subjective impression of it. Only pure mind could comprehend it, and then only while it was upon the skein, for when form and mind were one again, memories of the skein became flat.

But to be in it! All of reality was laid out before him. Threads twisted into yarns woven into tapestries depicting universes of possibility. Shards of infinitely shattering mirrors, each fragment showing the same event in different perspective; ripples alive with images on the surface of a lake, its depths also ablaze with scenes that were, could be, and had been. There were many ways of seeing the skein.

He deployed his first rune: the Scorpion. In the dome, it spun a little higher over him, breaking orbit with its fellows. The Scorpion had been the mainstay of his scryings these last cycles. It revealed nothing new to him. If anything, the skein grew more complicated. He had had no vision, seen nothing. His instinct was unerring, and had brought him here, but it was precious little to go on.

Next, the Flame of Asuryan.

Currents of potential ran crosswise, breaking the lines of fate, causing eddies and causal loops that twisted smokily and died. Under the influence of the rune, new threads forked at weaknesses in Iyanden's destiny, each one branching and branching again, some heavy with the promise of destruction. All these fates were weak, improbably distant, and most collapsed as Taec regarded them.

He thought out for the wraithbone shapes of other runes, among them Vaul's Anvil, the Tress, the Humbling Silence – half a dozen all told. With these he would weave a cage about the Bloody Hand, to direct its energies to his own ends. Khaine's rune demanded precision, or it would show only what it desired to show, and that was mostly the seer's own demise.

Taec spent several minutes crafting his runic binding, a dancing pattern of runes that circled a central point over his head, orbits stately as an orrery. Satisfied, he allowed Khaine's rune to take its place at the centre of his creation.

Released rather than psychically impelled as the other runes had been, Khaine's mark blazed upwards. Upon the skein it threw a fiery, sanguinary light. Taec was surprised that rather than shrinking back from it, the angry ghosts on the circuit beseeched it for vengeance. In the crystal dome, the rune glowed red-hot at the centre of its runic prison, raging against Taec's entrapment of its energies.

Brought by Khaine's hand, a thousand images of war flickered before Taec. He picked over them, examining them, bringing one into focus with the aid of his runes, dismissing another. Several frayed to nothing, banished from possibility by his scrutiny. His sense of impending disaster intensified, but nowhere could he find the cause.

Frustrated, he pulled back, letting time run on, seeing the skein break and reform under the influence of a trillion unremarkable events.

He listened to the ghosts. Their clamour for vengeance was unprecedented.

As if in reply to their petition, another psychic pulse perturbed his meditations, sending through the skein a slow wash of disturbance. New possibilities erupted all around Taec, none the ones he sought.

Vengeance, he thought. The ghosts call for vengeance.

He called up Anaris, the Prize of Vengeance. The rune was a stylised miniature sword, depicting that with which Khaine slew Eldanesh. Another dark symbol, a portent of revenge. In the dome it orbited the world-rune of Iyanden, spinning on its axis, point down.

A twitch in the skein, or in his soul. Manifested as pure mind on the skein, there was little to distinguish Taec from the fates he observed: they were one. His attention focused on Anaris intently, and the point swept up away from him and shot off ahead, hurtling into unknown futures. He followed hard, travelling the darkest of fates, those that saw his depleted home aflame for a fourth time; and the influence of the Bloody Hand brought many that saw his own end. Taec felt some of the pain at the deaths of these shadow selves as he chased Anaris down his chosen thread of destiny. Elation built. For all his poise, Taec was as excited as any huntsman who spies quarry.

Anaris slowed, point quivering, at a pulsing nexus where many lines of possibility converged; an inevitability, then. As he approached, Taec saw a red world in the throes of death.

A glimpse, deep red and bone white, alien armour grown not worn. A thick skein woven from many braids whipped into view on the far side of the nexus.

He had seen such a thing before.

With mounting trepidation, Taec pulled Draoch-var out from the bulging rune pouch by his meditating form. The Dragon. The rune had accrued many meanings over the arcs, and had gained a new one recently. It stood for the Great Devourer, the Star Ravener, the Hunger from the Void. The tyranids, which the eldar called the Great Dragon.

With Draoch-var he brought the Parting of the Ways. Modified by the Parting of the Ways, Draoch-var represented the hive fleet Far Ranging Hunger, the one the humans called Kraken.

Well Taec knew the signs of the beast: a tendril of Far Ranging Hunger had almost destroyed Iyanden seven passes before. This was the second incident of the Triple Woe, and – in denying Taec's prediction of it – Kelmon Firesight's greatest folly. The skein was still scarred with that happening. Iyanden's population had been reduced by seven-tenths, and its physical form had not yet recovered. It might never recover.

Khaine's Bloody Hand rotated over scenes of swarming aliens.

Crowding behind him, the ghosts of Iyanden saw what Taec saw, and they were further enraged.

Taec irritably demanded their silence, for he had seen something new and troubling. Amid the bone and red of Far Ranging Hunger's weapon-beasts he caught flashes of white and purple.

More voidspawn, those the eldar called Starving Dragon and the humans Hive Fleet Leviathan.

Taec looked closer, subtly manipulating the skein, but could see little more. The great mind of the tyranids blocked his sight, the psychic roar of it hampering all attempts at divination. He saw, again and again, the same scene, hordes of horrific beasts bounding over a dusty plain. An echo of beauty clung to the planet's dead world spirit. An eldar world, an old one. A name, Dûriel, came into his mind, and then another – Valedor, given to it by the trespassing mon-keigh. A True Star system despoiled by human usurpers, then despoiled again.

Taec looked through funereal smoke, black and thick with death. His body twitched in recognition of the bone and red, so deep was the horror at the loss the latter had inflicted upon Iyanden. It leaked through his trance, bringing with it a memory of a swiping claw, agony, and the loss of earthly sight in his left eye.

He suppressed the echoes of pain, concentrating his mind on this future. On a whim he modified his cycling rune pattern with the Twin Birds. It joined the others circling his meditating form. On the skein, its component parts Hawk and Falcon split, becoming aethereal, and headed off along the tangled futures. Even here, at this nexus, time was a confused jumble, many paths crossing and ending. The thunder of the hive mind, a billion billion alien voices shouting simultaneously, obscured all.

Hawk and Falcon rejoined, and he followed. A coming together.

The Avatar bellowed, his fury dancing across the timelines. A wall barred Taec: the Shadow in the Warp was directly before him. He wondered if it could sense his probing, if it had any inkling he was there. The strands balked at the dense alien being, ran around it, as if these lines of time and space were in fear of it. The skein twisted, went within the nexus; few strands escaped.

Taec was not to be denied. Summoning all his will and channelling it through the rapidly orbiting runes, he looked deep into this pivotal moment of time, smashing aside the blankness of the hive mind.

What Taec saw froze him to the core.

Two breeds of voidspawn came together as a world died; they fought in savage mating, Dûriel's dying lands fertile fields for their joining. Hive fleets merged and new forms of death were their get.

'Far Ranging Hunger joins with Starving Dragon, two become one, two become one!' he half-sang to himself. Taec watched as the immense minds of the two fleets reached out towards each other, groping blindly across the streams of probability. The components of the hive minds were spiritually puny, whisper-thin lines generated by bestial minds. But with so many twisted together, they made a mighty cable of fate, dwarfing all other threads on the skein.

As the twin cables of the hive fleets' consciousnesses drew near to one another, their strands unwrapped. Their writhing tendrils reached, grasped, and the two pulled into conjunction. As one they were monstrous. Taec had a glimpse far back along their ancient path. As Far Ranging Hunger's fleets made many splinters of one larger consciousness, so the wholes of Far Ranging Hunger and Starving Dragon were themselves only tendrils of something so vast it was beyond Taec's scope to comprehend.

The psychic shock of the joining reverberated down through time. Sudden visions of many world-deaths crowded near-past, present and future. With a vertiginous rush, the ultimate doom of the eldar loomed into view over Taec, as a black and impenetrable mountain. This certainty of extinction was pricked by few lights of unreadable hope. Behind the black walls of the race-death lurked the pervasive presence of She Who Thirsts. Her lusts washed at Taec's wards as the sea washes at the feet of cliffs, seeking to erode their foundations and bring them down.

Taec blocked the Great Enemy, muttering verses of focus to bring that part of his mind tasked with guarding his essence to greater alert, pushing the soul-threat from his mind. She had not taken him yet, and would not do so today.

No, what concerned him here was not the doom of the soul, but of the flesh.

He followed the eventuality of the hive fleets' merging, watching the landscapes of possibility unfold through his third eye. Images flickered, the multiple paths of fate layered atop one another. He fought his way through confused futures, to discard the middling and inconsequential differences that clouded the truth, looking for a clearer vision.

Many futures sprang from the nexus, all dire. The psychic backwash was intense. Blood and war. Creatures made stronger by the genetic inflow of ork, human, and eldar, perfectly forged for the death of not only Taec's kind, but the entire galaxy. The stars of hope in the black doom winked out one by one, the few threads of the skein stretched out to them unravelled. There was nothing beyond the blackness but the laughter of his people's twisted daughter. The shades of the dead clamoured, pushing at the warp spiders. Their minds brushed his like cobwebs.

Another tremor rocked the skein and physical world both, bringing with it a tide of hatred and anger. The dead were invigorated by it. Taec despaired. So much rage was in the circuit now – where was the noble Iyanden of the past?

The hands of the departed grasped at his astral form. They meant him no harm. They would speak. Long practice as a farseer kept panic at bay. He redoubled the guard on his soul, but let the energies that touched him pour through the crystallising flesh of his earthly form. Around his body in the dome, more runes shot into the air from his pouch, burning with sudden heat. The orbits of those runes already airborne became faster. Each burned brighter and brighter, until a constellation of miniature suns circled him.

Taec suppressed his anguish as his mouth opened without his volition, driven by the necromantic energies of Iyanden's overfull otherworld. The words of the dead seared his tongue, each one molten with the fires of wrath.

'The Voidspawn shall be cast into the abyss,' he said, and the voices were of many, and none was his own. 'To a dying flame shall the hungry ones be drawn.' His body spasmed, learned though he was in the ways of the skein. His skin crawled. 'There to meld with their kin. There to quicken the Great Change.'

A final flash, glimpses of many things. A lone eldar stood in silhouette before a red sea. A second red sea of molten rock. Two hearts, one consumed by fire, the other emitting cleansing flame.

A blazing pillar roared up in front of Taec. He stood upon a shaking mountainside. A world burned around him. Taec reached for a giant's hand and slipped. Plunging into searing lava, his body and his waystone were destroyed together.

He fell into the next life, a third sea of maddening energy. There the fires did not go out.

The Dark Prince laughed as Taec's soul slipped into his grasp. The Bloody Hand of Khaine turned.

Psychic energy blasted out from Taec. He gasped, coming out of the skein quickly. Vitreous leaves rattled in the grove, setting up discordant, tinkling melodies in the aftermath of his scrying.

The runes orbiting him flared, then clattered upon the clear stone.

Peace returned.

Taec swallowed. His limbs shook. His thin, ancient skin burned. He looked down.

Five runes were before him, smoking and black, the Dragon Draoch-var at their centre. The Flame of Asuryan lay some distance from it, and between them was set the world-rune of Biel-Tan: the Rebirth of Ancient Days. At the end of the line was the Dying Fire, and a last rune, obscure and dark in portent – Llith'amtu Khlavh, the Knife That Stays The Blade.

A sixth caught his eye, away from the quintet of principal runes, but lying within the measure of influence. The Balance of Asuryan, canted. It lay on its side, imparting ambiguity to all. He looked for the other runes. They were all around him; some he had chosen, some he had not. They added inflection to the others. *Perhaps.* Most had come down too far for a sure reading. The crude rune denoting mankind, the Asurya, the Broken Tree Of Paradise Lost, and more.

Taec swept the first up, holding it in his hand. Draoch-var. This, at least, was clear.

'The Great Devourer is not done with Iyanden,' he said. Sorrow welled in his breast, of an intensity hard to bear.

A voice came to him, as from a great distance. The crystals of the dome thrummed as the soul of Farseer Kelmon Firesight whispered in his mind.

+Or Iyanden is not done yet with the Dragon.+

Taec nodded his agreement. Wearily, he pushed himself to his feet. He saw what must be done, but the others might not. The last century had been hard on his people. Three times had Iyanden been directly attacked: the Triple Woe. First, the Battle of the Burning Moon against Chaos, which had led to the destruction of House Arienal and the shaming of Prince Yriel, then the ravages of Far Ranging Hunger, finally war against the orks and another invasion of the craftworld's sacred ground. Iyanden's fleets were all but spent in wars with humans, orks, necrons and the infernal beings of the warp. Despite the great sorrow and fury of the living, there was little further appetite for conflicts far from home. In such times they did not seem... *pressing.*

Convincing Prince Yriel to fight on the far side of the galaxy would be easy; he remained wild and warlike, despite taking to the path again. The rest of the High Council might be difficult to convince. Iyanna certainly would not be lightly turned from her occult quest. She teetered on the brink of obsession, that one, and was becoming dangerous.

He needed a clearer reading. He needed aid.

Taec moved awkwardly as he pulled gloves over hands greying with the early signs of crystallisation. His limbs were stiffening. His time was drawing to a close. Soon he would set root here, amid the broken statues of his predecessors. He reached out his hand to his staff, floating some metres away. At his bidding it flew across the room to him, slapping quietly into his palm. He leaned on it, letting it draw him strength from the soul of Iyanden; quieter now its message was delivered, though heavy with expectation.

Unchecked wraithbone extrusions surrounded him, the product of the overcharged infinity circuit, swollen as it was with the souls of so many million dead. Throughout battered Iyanden the bonesingers coaxed the growths back, but here at the interface between Iyanden's spiritual and physical aspects they would not be tamed. The signs of war were everywhere in the Dome of Crystal Seers, even as elsewhere they were smoothed away. The vitrified bodies of ancient seers were smashed, their pieces left where they had fallen. In places the stumps of shattered crystal trees outnumbered those whose branches still spread to frame the stars. The floor was pitted and cracked. And in this part of the forest the signs of destruction were not so pronounced; where Kelmon had perished the crystal had turned black, and no scrying could be made there. In the Dome of Crystal Seers the desolation of the worldship was plain for all to see and so it would remain forevermore.

'And yet war has not done with Iyanden,' he said.

As if in answer, another tremor rolled out.

'The Avatar stirs.'

Taec took a sky-runner across Iyanden. His celebrity was such that he was noticed wherever he went. He was so shaken he could not bear the eyes of his fellows on him, and avoided the public spear-cars and transitways.

House Haladesh was close to the Dome of Crystal Seers, both being towards the aft of Iyanden, but the way between the two had become as crooked as that of the skein. Many of the lesser domes were still without atmosphere. Perhaps in less troubled times their like would have been let loose to float away into space, and new ones raised in their place. But Iyanden in flight was far from any star that might consume them, and the council were wary of leaving a breadcrumb trail for the Great Dragon to follow. Furthermore, so great had the damage been to the craftworld, that those bonesingers who oversaw the skeleton of Iyanden feared that to lose so much mass from the remainder at once could lead to unforeseen gravitic stressing. And so the broken areas of Iyanden remained attached, grim reminders to a people who needed no reminding of their suffering.

In places where many had died, bizarre wraithbone forests had sprung up, the uncanny trees each seizing an unclaimed spirit stone. These were haunted areas, where spirits had turned wicked in their pain. Taec avoided them. Transit tubes were broken, doors healed shut with thick growths of wraithbone like scars upon wounds. In parts, power was erratic, and the fluctuating artificial gravity of the craftworld tossed his skiff about as if a tempest raged. In other places too much energy was expressed, and those lights that had not exploded shone like the trapped suns of the domes.

And everywhere there was ruin. House Arienal was a blasted wasteland, scorched lifeless by cyclonic torpedoes in the Battle of the Burning Moon, first of the Triple Woes. The psychic shock at so many deaths had been of such magnitude that all but one of the Arienalani had died, their spirits fleeing into their waystones the instant their kin perished.

Taec sped over blackened remnants of palaces and parks. Twilight reigned here, light coming only from the stars and from cracks in the fabric of the worldship wherein the raw infinity circuit sparkled. In the ruins of a palace he saw a gathering of wraithkind, but no other movement. Even the walking dead of Arienal were few in number, and the whispers of unquiet spirits were all around him.

How Iyanna Arienal had not been driven mad with grief was a mystery.

Talks on the restoration had begun shortly before Far Ranging Hunger had attacked. The seals had been reinstated in preparation, but now, in all probability, the dome would stay ruined.

He left the shattered house by the forward tubes, thrusting down a highway that once was full of bright, darting craft, but was now traversed by only him. He passed into the Endless Forest, seven great domes run one into the other to create a huge wilderness. The forest harboured artful ecosystems engineered from the life forms of a hundred thousand worlds. The Great Dragon had fought hard for this delectable morsel, and the scars of its assault were to be seen everywhere, the earth scraped down to the raw wraithbone core in places. The bonesingers and wilderers would be occupied for many arcs to come.

The signs of war became lighter as Taec entered House Haladesh. The council, with him as its reluctant head, had directed restoration efforts to be concentrated where the most eldar still lived. He flew over rebuilt villages empty of people, through domes whose biomes were being laboriously reconstructed. Eventually he saw other eldar, small groups at first, and then in increasing numbers. If anything his sense of isolation grew as he came across them.

Taec came to Urhaithanalish, House Haladesh's main city, set in its own dome at the junction between nine others like the heart of a flower. Near its centre he alighted from the sky-runner. He strode with purpose through an empty tunnel from the landing site. All was pristine, no mark of war in these parts. House Haladesh had been spared the worst of fate's caprice, and what damage there was had been largely sung away. But there were no scions of that house abroad here. Always populous, the numbers of Haladesh's folk were still great compared to the others of Iyanden's peoples, but many had died, and lesser roads such as the one he trod were oftentimes free of traffic.

Taec reached a wider way that took him to a market square, and there something of Iyanden's old glory was evident. Eldar of all ages and paths went on their business, in thinner crowds than before the Triple Woe to be certain, but the hum of conversation settled Taec's troubled spirit after the ominous silence of the desolation. Underpinned though it was by sorrow and less vital than of old, there was cause for hope in the chatter, and in the wares displayed in the square by those on artisanal paths.

He found it hard to admit to himself, but he was unnerved. He told himself that the terrible fate that awaited him was by no means a certainty, and that all the runes of Khaine delighted in showing their users' vilest ends. Somehow, he felt that this was different. Ever heedful of his inner feelings, Taec was greatly perturbed. He desired to halt, to take wine and engage in talk of something other than dark destinies, but he did not. The other eldar did not bother him, but he knew they saw him, and that many itched to approach him.

And so the single indulgence he allowed himself was to proceed on foot at brisk pace. Time was of the essence, but he required time to think, to calm himself, and to formulate his words well. He drew upon his experiences upon the Path of the Playwright, dim though his recollections were, as he pushed on through Haladesh. Simplicity, he thought, not adorned phrases. One had to be direct when speaking with the dead.

He passed from the city into Haladesh's lake and woodlands. As blessed as it was, in Haladesh too there were domes laid waste by the wars, although here most had been restored to bare spaces awaiting restocking. He went across arching bridges over deep fissures in the craftworld, protected from the void only by thin energy sheaths. He walked through the tightly packed streets of lesser townships. Thousands of homes were empty in Iyanden; every eldar living could have claimed a palace should he have wished, but many desired close proximity to one another, needing the buzz of life after so much death. Crammed settlements were much in vogue. The echoing halls and domes left empty were wastelands of the soul.

On he went, taking up another public sky-runner to cross Haladesh's large central desert. He swooped over the grasslands at its edge, putting herds of scarlet ungulates to flight, then ran with the birds out over the sands. He passed over the Hidden Gorge, that jewel in the desert's heart, a chasm that split the sands as far as the crystal bedrock of the craftworld. Cliffs of bright rock made up its upper reaches, a wide lake at their head. The thunder of waterfalls pouring from the lake boomed, and Taec looked down into the canyon, misty and broad, thick with the verdure of uncounted star systems. In the deeps a wide river glowed with the light of the exposed infinity circuit at its bed. Then he was over it, and the thunder receded as if it never was, and the sand glared at him. The dome was hot, its beauty was a hard one. In the sands he saw the tents of those who had withdrawn from community, following the Path of Solitude.

Mourning, Solitude, Wandering, Lament, Eulogy, Forgetting, Remembrance, Dreaming; many eldar of Iyanden had taken to these paths in recent days. Others flocked to the aspect shrines, their rage unsleeping after their participation in the craftworld's battles. Aspect shrines long-dormant rose again, and no bad thing. The wisdom of their exarchs was required lest the kindled fury of the Iyandeni send them off down the dark road of their ancestors, a worrisome future that occupied much of Taec's thoughts.

Taec left the sky-runner by a tether at the dome's edge, and walked from blistering heat into cool galleries. Tiered and dimly lit, they looked out over the void. Iyanden was far away from any system, making all speed across interstellar space from the tyranid-beset Eastern Fringe. The stars shone coldly upon the craftworld, flintily unsympathetic to its fate.

The galleries ran on for several thousand paces. Taec passed lovers whispering in the dark, small groups staring into space, sole eldar weeping in secret nooks. He ignored them all. He listened, form, mind and being, for further stirrings of the Avatar, but the shattered god offered no more disturbance.

'Hoi hoi!' a voice called him. Taec glanced over. A young eldar was sat in a drinking den recessed into the worldward wall of the galleries, a dark place serving bitter wines to doleful drinkers. His voice was mocking, his body language spoke of callowness and cynicism. 'Taec Silvereye is abroad in House Haladesh! What business has he here? With whom will he speak – the living, or the dead?'

The youth laughed, as if he had made an outrageous jest. His laughter was tinged with hysteria. It was a sound Taec had become too accustomed to of late.

As Taec passed, a young woman hushed the youth. Their souls were bright fires, wrapped around each other. Twins, a rare beauty in these times. The other drinkers, the flames of their essence darker, looked on unamused, disturbed from their miseries. Taec hurried onwards into areas empty of the living.

By this way Taec came at last to the Mistmaze Spire, the Ghost Halls of Haladesh.

Wraithblades, their helms marked with the runes of House Haladesh, stood guard over the spire's sole remaining gate, a small portal large enough for a wraithlord to pass through but no more. All other gates were closed over with wraithbone at the behest of the dead.

The wraithblades faced forward, arms out at their sides so that their sword tips crossed and barred the way. This position a living being would find hard to maintain for any length of time, but the wraithblades were still as statues.

Taec reached out to the wraithkind with his mind. Their souls were dim, flames turned low; watchful nonetheless.

A dolorous voice reached into him, dry and quiet as wind in a tombyard. Taec's soul chilled at its touch.

+What business have you here, here in the halls of the dead?+

'I seek counsel,' Taec said aloud. 'I wish to speak with Wraithseer Kelmon Firesight. War comes again. The final doom of all the eldar is upon us. I would avert it.'

No response came. Taec waited patiently, for the dead are beholden to no clock but their own.

'You may pass, Taec Silvereye,' they said as one. Their swords lifted, crystalline blades rasping on one another. The blank wall of the gates developed edges and its petals drew back.

And so Taec passed from the lands of the living into the realm of the dead.

In appearance, the Ghost Halls were as any other hall within the houses of Iyanden, complexes of interlocking domes and chambers, some small, some vast. Ecospheres of many kinds were found within, as were towns, workshops, great palaces, apartment spires and humble homes. In manner, they were unlike anything that had ever been seen upon Iyanden before, or any other craftworld for that matter. Within the ghost halls dwelt not living eldar, but the revived dead. Drawn back into their waystones and plucked from the infinity circuit, the dead were placed inside wraithbone bodies to bolster Iyanden's reduced armies. It was an ancient, if distasteful, practice. The wraithkind ordinarily returned to their sleep once their task was done, but sustained by the overcharged infinity circuit, many refused to return to their slumber, and this truly was unprecedented.

The wraithkind walked the halls of the craftworld, unnatural things neither of life nor of death, the numinous caged by wraithbone artifice. In battle the warriors of Haladesh gave as selflessly in death as they had in life, but their sense of purpose ceased with battle's silenced clamour. They were caught between the two worlds, and in Iyanden's fleeting moments of peace they spent the cycles endlessly re-enacting what little they could remember of their past existences.

Taec saw this shadow play of life all around him inside the Mistmaze Spire. The utterly silent forms of wraithguard trod its ways. The wraithlords, the greatest of their number, remembered well what they had once been and moved with purpose. Many were abroad in the craftworld, reassuming the roles death had forced them to lay down. Outside the ghost halls they were treated as equals, albeit coolly. Even the greatest souls still had one foot in the infinity circuit, for all their vitality.

The minds of the lesser wraithkind were but collections of compulsions, barely perceiving the world around them. Their eyes looked upon vistas of mind, not of form.

The dead were not as the living.

Taec walked past an audience of wraithkind silently watching a stage upon whose boards giant, robotic players did not move. He saw the huge hands of the resurrected cup empty glasses and eating utensils. They knocked them carelessly against the long heads of the units that imprisoned their souls as they attempted to eat and drink. In bio-domes, crowds of wraithguard stood stock-still in fields of many-hued grasses; others walked to and fro, wearing grooves in the soil as they repeated over and again some small action that the soul recalled perfectly, but in which Taec saw no meaning.

Most of the dead he saw were of the lesser kind. The handful of wraithlords abroad in the Mistmaze Spire spared him no thought whatsoever. All but one. Taec was acquainted with him: Teradryan the Lyric. The farseer was wise enough not to disturb him. For his part that exception only turned his great, eyeless face to look at Taec to follow his progress as he walked by, and then returned to whatever occupied him.

The spire was dimly lit. A cliche almost, thought Taec, but there is no cliche without truth, and the dead had little need for light. However, where infinity circuit nodes, the touch interfaces the eldar used to commune psychically with each other and the craftworld, were set into the wall, the space around them glowed with hot light. Ghosts flocked to their ancestral homes rather than accepting forgetfulness in the lethe of the circuit. Through these interstitial points the bodiless looked outward, the power their spirits contained overloading the devices they touched.

Taec had sympathy for Kelmon. This state of affairs was so unnatural no one should be surprised he misread the skein. No one could have predicted this.

War had come and war had gone, and the dead walked. All remained in order. The mechanisms of the craftworld kept the Ghost Hall pristine, aided by the living servants of the wraithkind, those who had taken a new branching upon the Path of Service as the Tenders of the Dead. As the dead served the living in war, so the living served the dead in peace. They cleared away the shattered objects the wraithkind left in their wake. Eyes ringed with ritually streaked make-up, heads shaved and expressions dead, they were as silent as their charges.

The atmosphere was heavy. If that outside the ghost halls was sorrowful, within melancholy reigned unopposed. Taec's mind was suffused with it, and it would not be shaken off.

In a dome of purple vegetation, beneath a permanent twilight, was a grand palace of soaring roofs and unlikely minarets. There Taec found Kelmon.

The dead farseer's wraithlord body was seated upon a throne carved from a single giant pearl. Seven large skulls were set above it – those of the serpentine voidspawn that had slain him. Wraithbone runes, enormous in size, were scattered over the floor. Kelmon was surrounded by dead courtiers who prosecuted their repetitive business in total silence. Living there were also – three on the Path of Service stood on Kelmon's left, a spiritseer in full mask to his right. The spiritseer was deep in conversation with Kelmon as Taec arrived, the wraithseer's enormous head dipped towards her, a giant listening to a child. She stopped talking immediately she sensed Taec, and all four living eldar bowed their heads to their leader and withdrew.

'Welcome, my friend,' said the wraithseer. His voice was sonorous and somnolent, almost free of inflection. Nor did he move as he spoke. Shorn of all nuance of gesture and tone, the words of the dead were unlovely. 'You have come, as I foresaw.'

As he had earlier decided, Taec did not wait upon ceremony. The dead maintained focus on the affairs of the living for such short duration, even ones so mighty as departed Kelmon.

'The Avatar stirs,' he said plainly.

'A tremble in his slumber. He sleeps again,' countered Kelmon.

'Once his sleep is disturbed, it is over. He will come to full wakefulness soon,' said Taec.

'That is so. What is it you would know, Taec Silvereye of House Delgari?'

'You have seen what I see?'

A long pause. Silence was a province of death, and Taec had strayed deep into it. The courtiers continued their ghostly rituals, over and over again.

'Yes,' said Kelmon. 'I have seen. A red world, Dûriel, a maiden ravaged and now devoured.'

'Then I would know this, wraithseer, you who were once my colleague and friend. Can we afford to act? I fear not to, but I equally fear action. What see you? Can we afford to wait and hope for a better turn of events? I hope fervently that it is so, but doubt very much that I will receive the answer I long for. You, mighty Kelmon, you have seen what I have, doubtless more clearly. You eyes are not clouded by the world of the living, your view is unimpeded by flesh. Tell me that I am right, that my castings do not lie, and so I might go forward along this skein without guilt.'

Kelmon sat forwards. The arcane technologies of his body were silent, and that underscored his eeriness. 'There is always guilt, farseer. No path can be taken without it, nor without regret. You call me friend. I was never your friend while alive, and I regret it mightily,' he said. 'I ignored you, ridiculed you, and was a fool to do so. If I could change what was, I would, but I cannot. I cannot offer my friendship now, for what use is the friendship of the dead? No warmth and laughter will you find here, no support or timely rebuke. And what is friendship to the dead? All is dust and eternity, with a gaping maw at time's end.'

Taec bowed his head.

Kelmon waved a slow hand. 'Your respect is not necessary. I can grant what you request, a second reading of your own vision.' A number of the runes in front of Kelmon's throne lifted off the ground. He looked at them as they turned in the half-light of the hall. The silence went on for a long time.

Said Kelmon eventually, 'I see war, and ruin. The mating of two dragons brings the birth of a new and greater. The legions of steel rise in number, She Who Thirsts follows in the wake of the young races. The time of ending is at hand. All this you have seen.'

'What can we do?' asked Taec.

'What we always have done – scry, foresee, avoid, survive.'

'And in this instance? What is your specific guidance, Kelmon? Is my vision correct? Do we risk all for Dûriel?'

'You ask the wrong questions, as I once did. Do not do as I did.'

Taec thought, formulating his next words with care. 'What if we act? I cannot foretell, the mind of the Great Dragon obscures all. Doom and death is all I can perceive.'

Kelmon's long head swung slowly to and fro, as if his smooth faceplate had eyes and he could see as the living see. 'The bonesingers have done their work well here. This hall was ruined, and you would never know it. It is unmarked, seemingly unchanged. But it is not. It was destroyed, and the psychic shock of its destruction is still there. That is the hall I perceive, not this phantom. For all our arts, we cannot sing the living back to life, try as we might.' The wraithlord gestured at his slender body. 'In other halls the dead preside in airless sterility. I am fortunate indeed.' Kelmon laughed bitterly. Taec shrank involuntarily back;

the laughter of the dead is not a thing to be heard by the living. 'Time heals all, they say. It heals nothing, I say.'

Taec leaned on his staff. 'I remember how, before the Triple Woe, that even at this late hour the corridors of the Mistmaze would echo with song, I mourn its loss, Wraithseer Kelmon.'

'Your sympathy is noted.'

'How can I not sympathise? Your people are mine, even if you never were aware of that.'

Kelmon dipped his mighty head in acknowledgement. 'I say I was a fool. What do you think, O greatest of our number? Tell me, Taec. You are no fool, not as I was.'

Taec stood tall. Boldness was required, and honesty. And Kelmon in death was not the same eldar as Kelmon in life. 'If we do not act, no matter the risk, then the stars will be emptied of the eldar race as surely as Iyanden has been emptied.'

'Great is my shame, greater than the pride I bore and that brought our home to ruin. I will not make the mistakes in death I made in life. Thankfully, yes, my vision is clearer than yours.' He pointed a long finger at Taec, an oddly direct gesture for the unliving. 'This cannot be allowed to happen. You are correct in your words, action is our only recourse.'

Taec sagged, relieved and terrified in one.

'But I cannot see as well as you might like.' Kelmon stood, his blank helm-face, emblazoned with the infinity rune and the sigil of House Haladesh, staring down at Taec. 'I will say this, Taec Silvereye. If we ignore this fate and turn aside, many are the Iyandeni lives we will save, but in the short term only.' He pointed at the runes orbiting his great head one after another. 'A thousand more passes we might persist, until the Great Dragon withers the galaxy unto desert, and the young races be consumed. Long before then, the Eye will open wide. The Womb of Destruction will give birth to countless foul children, and the great doom of the eldar will feast upon all our spirits. Chaos will corrupt the remainder of the sentient, before passing on as all wildfires must. The threat spent, the soulless ones will rule an empire of dust until the stars die. Know this – the great war finally we shall lose, and all will have been for nothing.'

Kelmon looked off into the distance, over the heads of his dreaming courtiers. 'The Avatar has stirred. Kaela Mensha Khaine thirsts for further battle. This is our cue – we ignore it to the peril of all eldar. We must act, you are right. We must act.'

'How, what course must we take?'

'I cannot see the full truth,' said Kelmon, and for a moment his voice took on some of the pride and power he had had in life. 'Not past the wall of thought that surrounds the Great Dragon. I am blinded by its mind as much as you. If it is as you fear, that Far Ranging Hunger is abroad once again, then let the spiritseers help. The dead taken by the Great Dragon are not gone, not entirely. A trace of them remains, a patina of horror on the animal souls of the Great Dragon's voidspawn. This can be followed. If our prophecy is true, then so guided by the suffering of our dead shall we see the future we have glimpsed entire.' Kelmon became strident, his voice taking on many of the characteristics he had possessed in life – over-confidence and pomposity might have been among them, but there was no denying his wisdom. 'We require a conclave. Many seers, acting in concert, the Athelin Bahail – the Mind Choir. That will see us to the truth of the matter, and open up the skein so that we may draw our plans. The Mind Choir will set our course, for good or for ill.

'You are head of the seer council, Taec. You must summon them.'

'Then you must come with me, be a part of it.'

'The living no longer listen to me,' said Kelmon.

'I am living, I listen. They will also. Come, I need your aid.' Taec held out his hand to Kelmon, a reflection of what he had seen in his vision.

This time, their fingers met.

CHAPTER TWO

THE FATE OF WORLDS

Silk robes whispered so gently Neidaria caught the sound of them after her brother; his ears had always been the sharper. She turned to follow his gaze, and saw a regal figure stride past where they sat in the Oasis of Tears.

'Hoi hoi!' Ariadien shouted out. 'Taec Silvereye is abroad in House Haladesh! What business has he here? With whom will he speak? The living, or the dead?'

'Ariadien!' Neidaria gasped, scandalised. 'Have respect, that is the Silvereye. I cannot bear the shame of you.'

Her brother, slightly drunk, shook off her hand from his arm and drained his goblet of wine. The Silvereye ignored them, and passed on. Ariadien smiled and poured himself more wine from the jewelled flagon on the table.

'And why should I not shout out, sister? Our woes stem from them, from all the seers and their councils, or should I say the lack of their good counsel!' He toasted his own wit to the occupants of the dark bar. They ignored him.

'What do you know of it?' said Neidaria, hunkering down to the table. There were few other eldar around them, and they glowered at Ariadien.

'Know?' he said, far too loudly. 'Know? As much as any eldar, as much as you. Better to have followed the path Yriel set, break the progress of war with war, as the courses of fires are broken with fire. He delivered victory against Kallorax at the Battle of the Burning Moon, and they drove him out for his troubles, and then we had trouble aplenty. The first of the Triple Woes was the prince's doing, they said, and the second caused by his absence. Nonsense! Do you not see, sister dearest? Kelmon Firesight led us, and Kelmon Firesight was wrong.'

What Ariadien said was common opinion enough, but Neidaria had little interest in the politics of drink. 'I would rather not know war,' she said. Ariadien cupped her chin and tilted her face up to look at him, a gentle gesture, and though drunk his face was full of kindness.

'Aye, but we must fight, must we not, you and I? Because the council chose our path for us, not we our own. And why?' He took another drink of wine. 'Because they would not listen to sense, and sent away the prince, then revelled in the follies they ascribed to him and set our path for greater conflicts than he ever brought. Today, the Avatar stirs again, his war-drums opening a new movement in the symphony of their follies. Have you not felt his rage boil in the infinity circuit? Tell me sister, if our kind were greater in number, would we be upon the path we have been set? I do not think so. And why are we Iyandeni so few in number now, why?' he hissed. 'Why of course, 'tis the council.'

Neidaria said nothing. She had often thought this herself. The whole worldship was in the grip of martial mania; all eldar were required to drill and practise with the weapons of war, not only those eldar bound to the paths of the aspect shrines. Many others could set aside their guns and their swords for most cycles of the pass and still proceed along their chosen path. Not she, not her brother. Titan Steersman was a path as complex as any other. Piloting a pair of Revenants in perfect synchronicity required endless exercises. There was no time for other things for them, as they had been repeatedly told. It was duty, their teachers said. It was slavery, she felt.

'You are more accepting of our fate, brother. When the path we have had forced upon us suits you far better than I, why complain? You want to fight. If not for me, you would be a pilot, I am sure. A pilot you are, steersman of a great machine, not so distant from your heart's desire,' she said sullenly. She hated to be so surly, but denied her chosen vocation, an ennui had settled into her that she could not divest herself of.

'True, true,' said Ariadien. The light was so dim in the bar that his face was ghostly white. She thought a moment of the Dark Kin, and was revolted with herself for comparing her brother to them, no matter how tangentially. 'I do not like being told what to do any more than you, dear sister.' He put his goblet down unsteadily. The truth was that he worried for her. On one of his less bitter days he would have said so. Today was not one of those, and only their close link allowed her to feel what he felt. 'Far they are supposed to see, but did old Kelmon spot the Triple Woe, or even the start of it? The merest part, the first? The Battle of the Burning Moon, where Kallorax destroyed all poor House Arienal and our saviour was sent away in shame.'

'The Great Devourer was not the merest part, but the greater,' said a voice from the darkness.

Ariadien turned around in his seat. 'And so I said. Who cares for orks or reavers when the jaws of the Dragon are snapping closed? Unstopper your ears so you might eavesdrop more effectively. Who are you, to speak to me so?'

'Your elder, child. I have walked a dozen paths. You? On your first, I think. You should ask yourself, who are you to speak to me so?'

Ariadien was not cowed by the stranger's words. 'Marvellous,' he said, using a particularly insolent form of the word, his shoulders set in a way to rile the calmest eldar.

'Don't provoke him!' said Neidaria.

The stranger tipped his glass towards Ariadien. 'Listen to your sister, she is wiser than you. I am Gelthelion the Wave Shaper, although I leave that path soon. Khaine calls me to him. I try to wash away his blood here, but wine will not do. I know, the stars know, and now you know. Tomorrow I go to the shrines, to see which will choose me. I will take up arms again and revel in killing.' Far from looking imbued with fury, Gelthelion appeared thoroughly miserable at the prospect.

Neidaria was suddenly afraid. 'Should you not be in a shrine already, to keep your dark impulses separate from...'

'...you?' Gelthelion snorted and leaned backwards.

'How are you here, then?' said Ariadien, having the same thought as his sister, as is the way of the twin-born.

The older eldar, a grey smear in the purple gloom of the bar, stared at them with eyes like black pits. 'Because it is not the first time. You have nothing to fear. I have my war mask already, and Khaine's pleasures are shut behind, keeping me from striking you down for your impudence. I will not put it gladly on again, and yet I must. I must.' He did not say why, but his manner revealed loss he could not speak of aloud. 'You should leave, leave all who come here to the quiet that will fall in your absence. This is no place for you. Leave us to our sorrow, there are better venues for gaiety. Come back when Khaine takes your heart too, as he surely must, then we will welcome you. All Iyandeni will fall to wrath in the end, now that death has come to claim us all. But not now, young one. Be gone.' He turned his head away, face down: a sign of obvious dismissal, laden with threat.

Neidaria yanked her brother to his feet before he could come out with some idiotic reply and dragged him out of the drinking room. When he made to complain, she kicked him hard. The subtle expression on her face told him all he needed to know; they were in danger. At his sister's prompting, he glanced around without moving his head, looking into booths with his peripheral vision. There were several such as Gelthelion lurking in the dark, trying to damp down Khaine's fires with wine and darkness.

Judging by the sparks in the eyes of the older eldar, they were failing.

Within the Dome of Crystal Seers, Taec took his place amongst his fellows. The forty-strong seer council of Iyanden were gathered together in three concentric circles. Not often were so many worthies gathered at once. Both the living and the dead attended; the circles were set so that the crystal forms of eight seers gone before were incorporated. Their spirits had been coaxed from deep in the circuit, and the statues glimmered uncannily.

Seven of the most active of the wraithseers had left their ghost halls to lend their strength to the seeing. Kelmon was among them, and Ydric the Wise, as was gifted Teluethiar, dead many arcs since. Their powers had diminished as their connection with the world had diminished, but with the blinds of life removed, their witchsight was far clearer than that of the living. These seven, all within the towering shells of wraithlords, formed the innermost circle. The nineteen greatest living seers sat in a circle around them, spiritseers and farseers alternating, some places occupied by the crystal statues of those ancestors that yet remained whole. In this circle, Taec sat.

The remainder of the seers formed a broad circuit outside. This third circle would shape the seeing, but would not see. They were younger seers, and those of paths less concerned with foresight: warlocks, wayseers, dreamsingers, bonesingers, Isha's Maids and those fresh on the witch path sat in small groups around the periphery, sinking into trances and readying themselves should their psychic gifts be needed to shore up the efforts of the council. At a discreet distance, the autarchs, princes and other potentates of the Iyandeni watched the ceremony from a raised pier of wraithbone.

Yriel was among them, the doom about him so thick that all eldar, whether seer or not, could taste it. As one of the High Council with Iyanna and Taec, he had been apprised of the situation before all others. Already decided on the fight, he impatiently awaited the seers' judgement to sway those of his peers less eager for conflict.

Below the pier stood another wraithlord, this one unlike any other, its body a deep orange detailed with yellow. The head, limbs and tabard were emblazoned with the runes of an extinct aspect shrine: the Fire's Heart, smashed to flinders by the cyclonic torpedoes of the Chaos raiders Yriel had so singularly failed to stop. This spirit was Exarch Althenian Armourlost, bodyguard and constant companion of Iyanna Arienal, the Angel of Iyanden.

Iyanna left her consultation with Althenian, and walked to her place by Taec. She did not sit. Like all the seers, she wore ornate robes, over which were laid the delicate, geometric patterns of rune armour. An eldar maiden on the Path of Service stood behind her, carrying Iyanna's ghosthelm. Iyanna was as beautiful as the songs said, but her face was cold, carved from frostmarble. Unassuageable grief had frozen her heart.

'Taec Silvereye is our most gifted seer, the greatest of the Iyandeni, if not of all eldar,' she said. Her voice was quiet, that of one who is used to dealing with the dead, but her manner was forceful, and all present listened intently. 'He has seen that which we have not seen. Wraithseer Kelmon has seen it also, a message from our dead kin – slaughter and blood, the time of our ending brought upon us quickly. We, together, will set free our minds from the cages of flesh and seek the truth of what is said, to see what the dead would warn us of. Much we have suffered, we sorrowful few of Iyanden. We will not suffer again, not while it is within our power to predict and prevent.' She took her helm, and held it in arms outstretched above her. 'Today we gather as if girded for war, for to look through the shadow of the Dragon is to go into battle.' She placed the ornate helmet over her head. It hissed as its seals moulded themselves to her flesh. 'We begin.'

Iyanna sat down beside Taec. Runes rose up all around the circles – a hundred, two hundred. They sailed gracefully to their stations above the seers, orbiting one another in the complex minuets of fate. Under the stately precessions of the runes, the seers within the second circle joined hands. As one, they slipped into the world of the infinity circuit.

The infinity circuit was in spiritual tumult, full of so many recent dead, many of whom were vibrant with rage at their deaths. It throbbed with power; a bitter irony that Iyanden's halls were so empty, and yet the world itself had become so potent. Many centuries would pass before the dead's energies would fade and they passed into peaceful slumbers. The dead clustered around the seers as they sank into the skein, phantoms who glowered at them, demanding action, release, vengeance! Taec was aware of something half-formed moving in the depths. Iyanna insisted this to be Ynnead, her new god and the salvation of the eldar. Others were sceptical.

+Make way, make way!+ Iyanna's soul-voice called, as beautiful as she. +Clear a path, O dead, let us see what you would show!+

The throng of the dead paid heed to her, for she was known to them, and they parted. The skein opened before the seer choir.

+We seek the spoor of the Great Dragon. We seek those who were taken,+ said Spiritseer Hestarlia. One of the fifth rank, as the spiritseers reckoned such things among themselves.

Taec felt sorrow as they groped through the void, seeking the residual psychic anguish of those eldar who had been absorbed by Far Ranging Hunger during the Battle of Iyanden. Sensitive to all things beyond the veils of the dead, the spiritseers found the trail quickly, when Taec, counted amongst the greatest of farseers, could sense nothing. So the path differentiated those of talent into the roles best suited to them.

Taec let himself be carried by the minds of the spiritseers. Across vast distances they travelled, cutting through the warp where the bounds of reality have no meaning. Taec saw the world-as-is – that of the material realm – sweep by. Stars, planetary systems, clusters of light where stellar nurseries clotted gas into new life. After a time that could have been a pass or a cycle, he caught the trail that the spiritseers followed: the pain and sorrow of eldar souls drawn thin, warped to fit new bodies. The implacable presence of the Dragon's shadow hung over it all. A rush of anger at this sight buffeted his soul, Iyanden's fury finding an outlet through him.

The seers followed this slick of pain ever quicker, until starlight streaked and the blackness of space coloured with stretched light.

They stopped. A collective cry went up from the spiritseers. One by one Taec felt their presences drop away.

In front of their warp senses, a world spun, and it was dying. The fleets of the Dragon had converged here. As in his vision, the world was red with death, the creatures who feasted on it pale and purple coloured. Beyond the curve of the planet's nightside was another fleet, another aspect of the Dragon. Smaller, swifter, more dispersed, these vessels too made their way towards the beleaguered world. With the heart of the perturbation in the skein before him, the blocking of the hive mind had a lesser effect. Taec, bolstered by his comrades, saw clearly.

+The mating of the Dragon,+ he said, and the chorus of seers moaned in horror. +Two become one, to destroy all in their path.+

Taec led the seers back down Dûriel's thread, and there they saw the past. A verdant world, lovingly brought to life by their ancestors, a sun tamed. A system of beautiful garden planets, inhabited by the eldar of the days of greatness.

A True Star yet far from the hub of the empire, the eldar of Dûriel were untouched by the depravity that grew in the eldar heart, but they were not free of the consequences. Taec flinched at the echo-memory of the Fall, eldar dropping dead where they stood as the birthing of Slaanesh wrenched their souls from their bodies.

Its people consumed, empty cities stood eerie, much like Iyanden now. +So the cycle repeats,+ thought Taec.

+Its name was Dûriel,+ came Iyanna's voice, many others speaking with her.
+Lambent flame,+ said Kelmon.
+To a dying flame shall the hungry ones be drawn,+ spoke Farseer Teuthis.
+The prophecy, the prophecy!+ said Wraithseer Ydric.

Time moved swiftly. The rude ships of mankind came to Dûriel. They settled. Doggedly, they set about the ruination of the world's beauty, tearing down the ever-living cities of the departed eldar, tipping the balance of nature with their ugliness and filth. Billions dwelled in the system, each verdant world polluted unto death, and still mankind swarmed in verminous multitude, crowding their ugly cathedrals, raising praise to their corpse-god.

War, death, disease – the cruelties of man inflicted on his fellow men. Seas dried, forests died, mountains were toppled. And now this. Leviathan came, a terrifying swarm of ships grown fat on the life-codes of orks and men.

The scene flickered, ripples from the pain of Iyanden. Taec saw himself and the others not long after the battle, when they were pursued still by Far Ranging Hunger's vessels. The hive fleet pursued the crippled craftworld doggedly, until he and the remaining seers had channelled the rage and the pain of their world through their minds, ripping the fabric of space and time and casting this second tendril of Far Ranging Hunger into the hell-dimensions of warp space.

Taec saw himself, he felt his own satisfaction. He, like the others, did not think it an unjust punishment for Iyanden's suffering. Pride. It always began with pride.

+Here, we will start here,+ said Taec.

Seer voices mumbled over one another, each scrying as best they could, an overlaid babble, mingling with the thoughts of Iyanden's unquiet dead.

+Consequences, always there are consequences. Move here, the skein will ripple there,+ Farseer Ukallior spoke. As he did so, the skein quirked, multiple futures leaping into life before settling back into the one Taec sought.

From out of the warp Far Ranging Hunger's tendril came, the last of their kind, cast out far into the galactic south by an intermittent warp phenomenon on the edge of the Dûriel system: one the humans called the Vortex of Despair.

+I sense the hand of the Great Enemy,+ Taec said grimly. +This was no chance ejection.+

Taec guided the others, the majority of them working to keep the Great Dragon's shadow clear from the seeing. He looked forward. +Far Ranging Hunger comes from out of the tides of the warp. First it fights, and then it merges, as I have foreseen,+ said Taec. He relived his vision of death and destruction, sharing it with the company, although his own fate he kept hidden.

Further forward into the future. Tyranids of new and terrible kinds rampaged through the stars, unstoppable, growing stronger with every conquest. +The genius of Iyanden, the mental power of our kind, wedded to the resilience of the ork, fed by the seething mass and vitality of humanity.+

+Doom,+ said Kelmon.

+Disaster,+ said Jaekherian Castdart.

+Extinction!+ said Iyanna. +It is not yet time! The new god is not ready. This cannot come to pass, or all will be lost.+

Dissent clouded their conjoined minds. Not all believed in Iyanna's obsession.

+It will not,+ said Taec. The council decided unanimously. The skein immediately rearranged itself, the super-tyranids dissolving back into a sea of possibilities as something else took their place. War, such as had not been seen in long ages; the green and white of Biel-Tan beside the yellow and blue of Iyanden. A host of resurrected warriors. A fiery end.

Taec gasped as fire burned him. He alone saw this, that he was at the heart of Dûriel's end. In terror, he watched his spirit stone crack and heard again the triumphant howl of She Who Thirsts.

They came out of the skein, the third circle seers singing them home. Taec rose and turned to face the pier whereupon the war council stood. Yriel leaned forwards onto the railing. Hollow-eyed and wan, there was a fell look to him, his red eye sinister. He held a fruit in his hand, and he bit into it nervously. Juice dribbled from his chin.

'What is our action, what does the council decide?' the prince said.

Even as the memory of agonising death and his damnation threatened to overwhelm him, even as he knew their decision could bring his vision to pass, Taec spoke decisively. 'The seer council is unanimous. Iyanden will fight.'

Yriel nodded, a small movement. 'And the Lady Iyanna? You and I have been at odds often. What say you? Will you support me in this war?'

Iyanna got to her feet elegantly, and unclasped her helm. She shook out the long braid of her hair and stared her rival in the eyes. 'Unanimous means unanimous, Prince Yriel. You will have your war.'

Yriel clenched his fist in triumph. 'Ready my fleet. We strike now.'

'Wait!' called Teuthis, also rising. The rest of the council followed suit. Standing with a rustle of robes, the seers and wraithseers all turned to face the pier. Runes criss-crossed the air around them still. 'The danger is far from here. Dûriel the world is known by the human usurpers as Valedor. It is not our fate to strike the first blow. It is too far. Even were we to depart now, we would not arrive in time. We must call for aid.'

'A play for time? Who? Who will aid us? The times of our mastery of the stars are long gone, or have you forgotten?' Autarch Yaleanar spoke, Yriel's chief lieutenant and also of the House of Ulthanash. Yriel's shadow, he was called. His words were often hard; it was no wonder he had left the craftworld to pursue the life of a corsair. Wild as his master, thought Taec, and still not fully tamed by the path.

'Biel-Tan. It is to Biel-Tan we must turn,' said Iyanna. 'They are not far from dying Dûriel.'

Yaleanar snorted. 'The warmongers? Allies they were once to us, but they long ago eschewed our wisdom in favour of spending their lives and blood freely.'

'And yet it is they who persist, and we who teeter upon extinction,' said Iyanna.

Yaleanar leaned on the railing next to the prince. 'They are so bloodthirsty, my lady, that my lord Yriel appears restrained by comparison. If it is to them we go, then we truly are without all hope.'

As Yriel moved to talk, a great howl of rage interrupted him. On and on it went, a roar of terrifying magnitude, lengthy as the waning of the stars, furious as their birth. Every eldar on the craftworld felt it, no tremor this time, but a full-blooded, atavistic shout that touched the hearts and souls of them all.

Lights coloured red. The craftworld shook. The fury of Khaine pounded in the temples of every Iyandeni; an undeniable call to war.

The roaring stopped, leaving in its wake a more terrible silence. The eldar looked to one another, shocked.

'The Avatar awakens,' said Yriel, when the shockwaves subsided. He took another bite of his fruit, uncouthly talking around the pulp. 'We have no choice but to fight.'

All present saw that he rejoiced. 'The fleet will depart,' said Yriel, cruel pleasure in his eyes. 'Getheric, Ybrann, Doloroana Startreader! Go ready your crews and your squadrons. We will leave before the cycle is done and make all haste to Dûriel.'

The three commanded bowed. 'Yes, my prince.'

Yriel spoke further, giving orders to the rest of the war council, and sent word that the exarchs of the shrines should gather in the Hall of Autarchs. 'A full third of the autarchs will remain behind, to prepare defences in case of an assault upon Iyanden in my absence.'

'Who?' asked one.

'We shall draw lots,' said Yriel. 'It is the only fair way. I would deny no Iyandeni the opportunity for vengeance.'

'Twice now has Iyanden nearly been overrun while our armies were elsewhere. Even once-reckless Yriel has learned his lesson,' murmured Iyanna.

Yriel was sharp-sensed and heard her.

'I have learned my lessons, angel. Have you?'

'I support your cause, do I not? Let us be allies. We are successful when our blades are uncrossed and pointed in the same direction.'

Yriel gave her a curt nod. 'Away, autarchs! Away to battle!'

He and the rest of Iyanden's war-leaders strode along the pier and out through an opening that led from the Dome of Crystal Seers.

Taec's anxieties grew with the passing of the cycle, fearful of the consequences of failure at Dûriel to the eldar race, and fearful of the cost of success to himself. A psychic message was sent out by the seer council to Biel-Tan, courtly worded in the old eldar tongue known before the Fall. As Iyanden's artificial night approached, the reply, faint and disrupted by the Shadow in the Warp, came: the war council and seer council of Biel-Tan had gathered immediately, but had fallen at odds, and no decision was forthcoming.

'Biel-Tan will not throw its lot in with Iyanden easily,' said Teuthis.

'I did not expect them to,' said Taec.

'Still, you are perturbed that they do not,' said Teuthis. 'I sense it.'

Taec did not reply.

After further discussion, Iyanna sent a message of her own. The psychic impression of a single rune: Kurane Dullae. Extermination.

'Ours, or theirs?' asked Teuthis wryly.

'Both,' said Kelmon before Iyanna could speak. 'She seeks to stoke the fires in the warriors' hearts. Ever it is the way of the Biel-Tanians to seek the utter destruction of their foes. This will work in our favour.'

'And equally I seek to drive home Taec's message, that this mating of the Dragon will spell disaster for all eldar. They are belligerent, but do not lack for wisdom,' said Iyanna.

The message had some effect. Taec felt the skein shift as new possibilities opened up. He cast a handful of rune-forms in the air, and watched them morph into distinct shapes. He studied them closely. 'Do they accept, I wonder? The runes' orbits are uneven, their meanings clouded.'

'I have a similar reading, Silvereye,' said Kelithia, a female farseer almost as old as Taec.

'And I too,' said another.

'The skein twists, it will not be read,' said Kelmon. 'As it always does when matters of great import are at hand.'

'Then we must wait for Biel-Tan to reply,' said Taec. The runes settled in the open palm of his hand. He put them into his pouch.

They waited until the dawn began before departing.

Biel-Tan still had not replied.

Iyanna entered the causeway to find her companion Althenian waiting. He stood in the near-dark, arms folded. Unlike so many of the other wraithlords, Althenian's movements had a certain vital energy, his voice a wry humour and quick anger. He was dead, and yet not dead, a peculiarity of his exarchhood. She hurried to his side.

This part of Iyanden was recently rebuilt, and none of the living had yet returned. The spiritseer's constant sadness intensified; this area, unrecognisable now, was not far from where her family's house had been. All had died bar her during the Triple Woe, incinerated by the torpedoes of the Chaos fleet.

'It is ordinarily I who issues the summons, Althenian,' she said. She rarely made light these days. Only Althenian ever heard her attempt levity.

'Glory to see,' he said. He came down to one knee so that he could better address her. Althenian was kind like that, at least to her. Perhaps his engagement with the world of life came from the fact that, as an exarch, he was a warrior foremost and invested in the life in the fight. Or perhaps it was because his soul was made up of many souls, a spirit pool of all those who had been him since the original Althenian's birth on some forgotten world, millennia ago. The presence of so many souls as one, those that had never been merged with the peaceful afterlife of the infinity circuit, meant that Althenian rarely needed her guidance.

She thought that if anyone could see them, they would be amazed. Althenian was notoriously fiery of temper, even for an exarch, but such tenderness from one in the grip of the murder-god was surely a sign of the bond between them. Althenian never ceased to amaze her; he was a stack of impossibilities wrapped in wraithbone.

There had been other exarchs temporarily dressed as wraithlords, those from dormant shrines. Now there were no dormant shrines, but Althenian's would not rise alongside the others. Althenian's shrine had been destroyed and his armour – his immortal body – had been lost. His long sojourn in wraithbone had changed him, of that she was sure.

Hesitantly, she nuzzled his giant thumb with her cheek; a brief action that could be construed as accidental.

'I show you, something here please follow this way, O great lady.'

'You are a strange one, Althenian,' she said, the ghost of affection warming her cold words.

'Strange? Unique,' he said. 'Few like me in all of time, now not one.'

'You are proud of that.' She smiled tightly. She sensed that whatever Althenian wanted to tell her, she was not going to like it. 'What is it you want to show me?'

Althenian reached out a massive, sculpted hand and rested it upon her shoulder. His fist could have crushed her to a paste. She had nothing to fear. Althenian's control of his tomb was beyond that of other wraithlords.

'You are like no other, it is true,' she murmured.

He stood soundlessly. 'Come this way,' he said. 'There are real wonders to see, a promise.'

She followed after him as he walked down the oval corridor, the pale blue of its minimal lighting glancing from the fire-dragon crest mounted upon his head.

As they proceeded, the corridor took on an unfinished look. Where lights should be were only depressions. Nobbles and burrs protruded from unsmoothed wraithbone. She felt a soft push of psychic energy, different to that which she employed. She called and shepherded; this was the sensation of careful hands deep in soft clay. A singing came, sweet and mournful.

'Bonesingers,' she said.

'Bonesingers, there are many in these parts, all working,' replied Althenian.

They approached the singing. Bright white light bathed the next section of the corridor, and there they came across seven female singers from whose soft lips the songs of making emanated. They were lost in their work, deep in the trance of the path. Iyanna turned from the bonesingers' work as Althenian's torso twisted so he could look at her.

'Beautiful, but this section is not yet done, a thousand paces, the way ends, abruptly stopped it grows, all grows. To the end, we must together proceed, there to see.'

Iyanna moved closer to her guardian's towering form. 'I do not know this area well, even though I grew up close by.'

'No reason, to venture here I suspect, and made new. Here service, a few surface access points, aspect shrines.' He paused. 'Five of them, the shrines of House Arienal, no child's place.'

He stopped before a nondescript door.

'We are here, within is my new destiny, come see it.' He placed his mighty palm flat against the door panel. It was barely tall enough to permit his entry. 'I allow you, rare and unusual honour. Few may pass. Portals of Khaine, sanctuaries of war, for those called. I take it, you understand me clearly, Iyanna?'

Of course she understood. Althenian was ancient, and in the habit of patronising her. It was the one thing that annoyed her about him, but her annoyance was swamped by a surge of apprehension. Her heart beat so quickly its pulses blurred into one. She nodded.

'Very well, the door opens for me, not to close.' The door reacted to his spiritual signature, wraith-stuff parting on an invisible seam and rippling back. 'Was my shrine, or "is" as it is new, old also. Exarchs reborn, the flesh of new worshippers, Khaine's pure fury.' He shook his head. 'Unexpected, that my shrine undergo the process, strange these times.'

He ducked his head to pass through. Iyanna followed, her cheeks hot.

Inside was an endless space, a huge habitat dome whose edges were so distant they blended with the floor in a hazy band of off-pink, unfinished psychoactive plastics. Far off in the distance was a towering monolith of black stone, the dome's only feature. 'Welcome lady, to the Shrine of the Fire's Heart, unfinished,' he said. 'Life empty, needed again and reborn, Isha's grace. Khaine's desire, the workings of Iyanden, destiny. Soon rebuilt, water and of life to return, warriors. Fire burns, the sea-drakes are to return, I return. Fire's Heart slays, the enemies of our people, with heat's fury.' He sounded eager, if such a thing were possible for the dead. 'One more thing, that you must see in this place, Iyanna.'

Iyanna nodded, feeling faint. She knew what that might be.

They walked to the monolith, a long way across the spongy, unfixed floor. They talked a little of the coming war, Althenian grimly delighted at the prospect of wreaking vengeance on the Dragon that had devoured their kinsfolk. 'Fitting be, one dragon slays another, right this is,' he said. Iyanna's answers became shorter and shorter as they approached the ziggurat. Their conversation died away. The dome was wide and high, the sides of it of translucent orange panels arranged in seemingly random patterns, the top third a shimmering energy field also of reddish hue, but to Iyanna the place was oppressive. The spirit of Khaine had already begun to seep back in.

'My chambers, sanctum this was and will be, all made fresh,' said Althenian. 'I did not, think to see return again. We enter.'

The temple was finished. In stark contrast to the reborn dome that housed it, it had an air of great antiquity, although Iyanna knew that it had not been here a pass ago. The pattern of it had been retained by the group consciousness of the craftworld, and under the prompting of the bonesingers, remembered back into being.

'Inside here,' the wraithlord said. 'In here you will see something, noteworthy.'

It grew hotter as they went deeper, until Iyanna's skin glowed with sweat. Ruddy light bathed them as they reached the temple's heart. They went into a square room with sides that sloped upwards to a sharp point. In the middle of the floor was a pool of molten metals. From this something like a statue, also of red-hot material, was being extruded. It had the look of a rough mannequin, perhaps a deliberately primitive sculpture; there were schools of art that followed that style, after all.

Iyanna realised it was not. There was a crested helmet. Once that was noticed, the other elements fell into place like the image in a thought puzzle.

Armour.

'I have never seen the likes of this,' she said. 'The activities of the dead are pronounced here.'

'Dead smiths work. As my shrine is reborn anew, so my garb. Iyanna, armourers and artificers, slain together, work together, directed by our craftworld, to remake. See yourself, that is my sole intention, and know first. This will be, my last battle in this form, I am free,' said Althenian. 'Not long now, I will tear forth the waystones, from this body. Replace them, in their proper mounts again, I shall live!'

Iyanna stared at the suit of exarch armour, growing from the very flesh of the craftworld. She tried to maintain her composure, but could not. Her own emotions were buried deep, a place she could not look, for to open the lid on the portions of her mind wherein dwelt the deaths of her entire house, her mother, father, siblings, everyone... She could not face it. Other parts of her had been trapped there, making her seem cold-hearted and distant to all others. There was only one exception, one being with whom she felt herself. Never could she hide her feelings from Althenian. Their bond was too strong. 'But...' she said. 'I need you.'

Althenian looked from her to the armour. 'I know this, since you called me from slumber, our link is strong, a good thing. Iyanna, it sorrows me to leave you, fate calls loud. This must be, Iyanden's need is great, it is fate. Many old shrines, long-dormant, are awakening, mine also. Ynnead stirs, Iyanna thanks to your strength, battle calls. The final war, survival or death's hard choice, is coming. I must serve, and this form will not serve me, to this aim. This is truth, before the greater rebirth, I must too, be fresh reborn, it is the truth and the way, Khaine wills it.'

He knelt down again, his head slightly inclined as if he were looking into her eyes. The stylised dragons on his face screamed silently at her. 'I have much, to thank you for my lady, please know this. When my shrine, my armour were lost to me, you saved me. This body, crafted for me at your command, was your gift. You called me, back into the light of life, I fought on. Eternity, I thought to spend powerless, but not so. Life's sense gone, a small price to pay to fight, at your side. The wrath of Khaine, dimmed by death and made light, peace for me. You brought it, and although wracked still by war, peace was mine. Thanks to you, these have been good times of joy, pleasant time. No longer. A candidate approaches, a new soul. One of Khaine's, who burns with vengeance's fire, fate provides. He comes here, soon he will don this armour, to serve Khaine. I with him, in flesh shrouded Khaine will work, through us both. More will come, I will gather followers, to my side. A hot bane, we shall be of all our foes, as is right. Iyanna, I thought to say this to you, one to one. As a gift, for once I am restored, I will change. This old soul, will not be as he is now, I regret.'

'I will lose you,' she said.

'That is so. We have all lost much lately, all of us,' he said. 'Fate decrees, you lose more than most, Iyanna...'

A change came over Althenian's voice, the rhythmic, ritual pronouncements of exarchy giving way to something approaching normal speech.

'I do not know what to say.' He enfolded her in his long arms and held her to his unyielding chest. 'I am sorry, but it must be this way.'

Unseen by all others save Althenian, at the heart of a shrine dedicated to endless violence and embraced by a dead killer, Iyanna Arienal wept.

'No, no, no!' shouted Uskariel-Iskarion, his twin voices, subtly different to one another, layered one over the other. The wraithknight strode across the combat dome to stand between the *Silent Scream* and the *Sound of Sunlight*, the mounts of Neidaria and Ariadien respectively. The motile plastics of the practice drones came to a halt, losing some of their shape as they half-melted back into the adaptive floor. 'You must think as one, be as one. Only then will the complementary aspects of your Revenants be in accord with one another, only then can you perform the dance of destruction. Again! You must do it again.'

'Testy today, are we not?' said Ariadien.

The wraithknight's blank helm swung sharply to regard the *Sound of Sunlight's* cockpit. Ariadien got the uncomfortable impression of eyes staring straight into his own, although the wraithknight had none, and his own face was hidden behind the Titan's faceplate. He dropped his gaze instinctively, his Titan shifting under him as it mirrored his discomfort.

'You are twins, the bond between you is like the bond between no other eldar. Only you can follow the Path of Warstrider Steersman, only you! It is an honour, a great one, but you mock it, Ariadien. There is cynicism and arrogance where there should be duty.'

'Am I not to be proud of this honour?' said Ariadien.

'Of course!' snapped the wraithknight. A dissonance crept into its voice as its living and unliving pilots fell out of synchronisation with one another, vexed by Ariadien's attitude. 'But such outright disrespect is a disservice to your house and your ancestors.' The wraithknight's anger abated, and it strode around the war machines. Its head came up to the chest armour of the twins' Revenants. From his vantage, Ariadien saw it as being small, almost comically so, although in actuality all the war machines would have dwarfed an eldar on foot. 'You have no choice on your path, I appreciate that. So it was for us also. Do not wallow in despondency. There is glory on this path, and satisfaction. Is that not what the path gives us all, however we select its routes? Embrace your fate for the survival of our home.'

'I will try,' said Ariadien.

The wraithknight made a noise of irritation. 'We do not understand, Ariadien. You are proficient, and joyous in your battle. Why do you chafe under our authority?'

Ariadien's mind strayed to the crystals in his sister's rooms, those containing her poetry. He walked the path willingly, she did not. He could not tell this to Uskariel-Iskarion, that his anger stemmed from the pain his sister suffered at being denied her chosen path. They would probably have understood; they too were twins, after all. Ariadien was ashamed, as annoyed with his own attitude as the wraithknight was. His tutor was correct, he did enjoy being a steersman. His feelings – anger at himself, at the path, at his sister for stopping him enjoying their role – were complex and not easily untangled.

'You will not answer? So be it. You have one cycle until you must depart. You will soon face the monstrous children of the Dragon in open combat for real.' The wraithknight flung out a fist, sweeping it to encompass the active plastic representations of monsters, ugly things all. 'They will not be as forgiving as we. Now, again!'

At a thought impulse from Uskariel-Iskarion, the pseudo-aliens came alive, and with a pang of guilty pleasure, Ariadien's pulsars swept round to target them. His sister, her form splintering into a bewildering parade of doppelgangers as the *Silent Scream*'s holofield engaged, sprinted forwards.

'Better!' said Uskariel-Iskarion. 'Much better.'

CHAPTER THREE

THE ROAD TO VALEDOR

Taec did not sleep that night. With Biel-Tan silent, Taec and Kelmon were hurriedly appointed to lead a delegation to the craftworld. Biel-Tan plied the void in the galactic south, much closer to Dûriel than Iyanden, and such a journey took time. He and Kelmon would take a swift void-runner through lesser conduits to Biel-Tan, to arrive cycles before the Iyandeni would reach Dûriel. With luck the Biel-Tanians would join with them, and be in time to aid their Iyandeni cousins. But of a holding action to buy Iyanden time ahead of their arrival, Taec had little hope.

Taec spent the time leading up to their departure in a glass-walled observation lounge at the very pinnacle of the Chambers of Starlight, the silent form of Kelmon beside him in the gloom. They watched as the shoals of ships that accompanied the craftworld manoeuvred themselves towards the Spider's Gate. This was Iyanden's main webway entrance, a sphere of swirling energies towards the stern of the craftworld held in place by ancient machineries.

The *Flame of Asuryan*, Yriel's flagship, had already left its dock. Resplendent in blue and yellow, the battleship was of sleek line and great length. Three sets of enormous solar sails swept back from the rear of its hull; a twinned pair above, two mounted dorsally at steep angles to either side. Despite its great size, the Void Stalker was nothing compared to Iyanden, and seemed toy-like in comparison to the worldship. Sails billowing with aetheric energies, it waited with its prow towards the webgate, charging its engines from the meagre starlight of interstellar space. Taec sensed the impatience of the vessel's spirit core to be away.

There were many ships, their numbers bolstered by the Wraithborne, a squadron of vessels crewed entirely by wraithkind and spiritseers from the House of Valor. The docking towers of Eternity Gate, Long Swift Voyages with Fortuitous Endings, Lost Wandering and the others were crowded with transports taking on the army of Iyanden. Periodically the gate flared as fast-running scoutships and ranger craft departed, or reinforcements arrived from distant outposts.

'Yriel must take the long road to Biel-Tan,' said Taec. Following in Kelmon and Taec's wake, Yriel would come to Biel-Tan and pass through their webgate into real space. Yriel's fleet would then traverse the void to attack the hive fleet of Far Ranging Hunger in orbit around the stricken world. The army was to press on by yet wider routes. 'He will arrive after us. The fast ways are too narrow. The army will continue on without him, directly to Dûriel's terrestrial gates, there to await the Biel-Tanians, if they are to join us. With fortune on our side, we will ensure Yriel has a warm welcome when he docks at the Rebirth of Ancient Days.'

'We can only hope, the skein is obscured,' intoned Kelmon in his funereal voice, the first time he had spoken for half a cycle. 'All over Iyanden, we prepare for war. The ritual to bring the Avatar of Khaine to full wakefulness has already begun. His ship awaits his coming.'

'Will the ritual conclude in time?' said Taec, surprised. 'The last time the Avatar was roused, three cycles were required.'

'So great is his fury, he will not wait. A young king has been selected, the exarchs chant their songs. I feel his urge to depart. He will set out with the last of the fleet.'

Although high up in the spire and away from the mass of the population, Taec could feel the passions of the eldar provoked by the Avatar's stirring. In aspect shrines, eldar set aside their compassion and revelled in their bloodlust. Guardian hosts headed to the public armouries, the numbers of volunteers far outstripping the equipment available. There, they were put into lesser war trances by the autarchs to shield their psyches from the extreme emotions of battle. Hot blood painted on their faces, their more delicate sensibilities were disengaged by many tenth-cycles of meditation. Taec was troubled by this.

'I fear many of the people, exposed to the full force of war, will fall under Khaine's spell. The aspect shrines will be swollen with recruits and the streets emptied, ere this conflict is done.'

'These are deadly days,' said Kelmon. 'Iyanden requires such sacrifice. Better fight as a warrior than a gardener. The proper time for peaceful activities will be when peace returns.'

Taec shivered, mindful of his own vision. How many others faced a similar fate as he?

'We will still need gardeners, Kelmon. And artists, poets, servers and the rest. If we are to dedicate ourselves wholly to slaughter, what hope is there for our people? One cannot live on blood alone. Death is but one part of life. We must not neglect the other paths.'

'With the Dragon perfected, there will be no art to make and no fields to plant,' said Kelmon. 'Listen! It is not only the living that thirst for vengeance.'

Taec followed Kelmon's psychic impulse. They dipped into the infinity circuit. Small bursts of pain resonated from the Chambers of Resurrection as the dead, called forth by spiritseers, returned to their spirit stones. The doors to sealed ghost halls cracked asunder from blows within and the wraithkind strode out to take their place in the armies of Iyanden once more. Taec was saddened by this, but the dead appeared unworried by the concerns of the living for their souls' welfare; they came gladly.

Taec shifted his stance, the curve of his legs and spine expressing sorrowful disapproval. 'How times change,' he said, 'and not always for the better.' He stared out at the vast expanse of the craftworld, so huge that even from the top of the spire the edges were indistinct. Iyanden was vaguely kite-shaped. A long prow swept back to the broadest section two-thirds along its length, the worldship's lines then turning back abruptly to the rearmost point. The stern was capped by the Dome of Crystal Seers, hanging out over the void. As the craftworld's beam broadened in the centre, the overlapping domes, palaces, monuments and bubble habitats piled atop one another in increasing height to make a sculpted mountain range of bold curves and artful blisters, everywhere adorned by the glorious artifice of its people. There were few structures in the galaxy larger than the craftworlds, and Iyanden was among the largest of its kind. A marvel of eldar technology, a defiant statement of hope's triumph over despair, of order over anarchy. And still it was but the dimmest shadow of the eldar's ancient achievements, and a broken, war-scarred one at that.

'The last time I looked out from the Chambers of Starlight, Iyanden was perfect. Now look at it,' Taec said. 'Mankind, the forces of Chaos and tyranid alike have had their way with it. Iyanden is a maiden ravaged, her beauty despoiled.'

'The bonesingers will heal her,' said Kelmon. 'All we need is time.'

'Ah,' said Taec wearily. 'But who will people it?'

'Time again will fill its halls. Are you not tired, old friend?' said Kelmon. 'Perhaps you should rest.'

Taec sighed, a mellifluous exhalation that carried within it the music of his own despairs. 'You call me friend now, and I am glad.'

'When you spoke of the danger presented by the Dragon, I would not listen, nor would the council. The runes showed me pride and destruction, but I was too proud to recognise destruction brought down on us by my own pride, so convinced was I of Yriel's arrogance. I was in the wrong. I should have listened to you. Friends we are now, united in joint enterprise.'

'Do you not grow tired of repenting your mistake, wraithseer?'

'Why should I? The dead have no regrets. Anger, hatred, love, joy, pale remembrances of these survive the transition, but something as shaded as regret does not – not undiluted. It is easier to admit my errors now.'

Taec looked up to the towering wraithseer, the blue domed head that housed the eldar's soul, the wraithbone runes that hung in rich profusion from his slender limbs. 'Does pride not survive death either?' he asked.

'It does, it is not solely a vice of the living,' said Kelmon, and turned away. 'But I have little to feel proud of.'

'At least you do not become tired, I suppose,' said Taec ruefully, for Kelmon was right, he was weary.

Kelmon made a strange sound, like the waterfalls in the Hidden Gorge. 'You are wrong. I am always tired. Death is weariness, death in life is toil, but death's sleep... That is the rest that none desire. I remain awake.'

They maintained their vigil until morning came and, assembled, the main body of the fleet began passage through into the webway.

* * *

As soon as the call to war went out from Prince Yriel, the army began its muster at the Starward Towers, the dockyards of Iyanden. Neidaria and Ariadien were among them, riding the *Silent Scream* and the *Sound of Sunlight*. They flanked the Phantom Titan *the Curse of Yriel*, a new name for an old machine. Upon Yriel's return, the spirits of the Titan had taken this title in honour of the prince and his victory. The Lariani, its triplet exarch pilots, had agreed a little too enthusiastically for their decision to be tasteful. A display of sycophancy, thought Ariadien, or maybe not. Perhaps Uskariel-Iskarion was correct, and he was growing cynical.

+Perish the thought.+ Neidaria's voice came to his mind with great force, their natural psychic sympathy boosted by the infinity cores.

+Ow! Not so loud,+ he shot back, then rallied himself. It would not do to appear anything other than insouciant to his sister. +I wonder if their votes really count? Do you think they bully the triplets, the ghosts in the machine? The spirits of the Phantom are more numerous and more vociferous than those in ours.+

+Stop it, Ariadien. Your levity is infuriating!+ Which was his intended effect, and his juvenile satisfaction enraged her further. +You know as well as I they think as one.+ She was silent a space. +I do not think I would like it, to be entrapped so.+ Ariadien felt her fear over the link. +We can come and go, at least.+

+Oh, they can leave,+ said Ariadien. +But choose not to, that is all, sister. They are like the knights, free to do as they please, but, not desiring freedom, staying locked within their machines, supping upon the sweet, poisonous honey of the battle-trance.+

A round dozen wraithknights formed an honour guard to the Titans, all such of those rare machines that Iyanden had to offer. It was to these that Neidaria really referred, not the *Curse of Yriel*. As Ariadien had said, the living pilots of those machines rarely walked abroad outside their armour. It was as if, forever sealed into the chest cavities, they were eternal co-pilots with the souls of their dead twins, and would not willingly leave them. Uskariel-Iskarion, twin brothers and once pilots of their own Titans before Iskarion's death in battle, were of that kind. Neidaria never referred to them directly, but she had a horror of ending up like them. The bars of a prison are far worse when forged by oneself, she often said. Ariadien sought to distract her.

+See, Neidaria, look at the assembled host of Iyanden. Isn't it beautiful? Surely worthy of a song or three.+

She had to admit that he was right. He felt that too, and was relieved as her emotional state turned to amazement and her mind to composition. The serried ranks of golden-yellow armoured warriors, their helms deep blue and emblazoned with the marks of their houses, was an uplifting sight. It was cathartic, thought Ariadien; here was a sign that Iyanden was not beaten, and that it would have its revenge.

Grav-tanks by the score hovered slowly forwards, moving off to this ship or that as directed by the marshals of the docks. Four thousand Guardians marching in blocks followed them, peeling away to board the ships owned by their houses. Nine hundred Aspect Warriors marched behind them. Fully two-thirds of Iyanden's remaining martial might went out to war.

There was sorrow in the spectacle. The Guardians were arranged by house, and it was pitiful how few members some groups contained, especially as the eldar of those houses worst affected by the Triple Woe were most likely to have volunteered. Ariadien did not doubt that some of those groups of warriors represented practically every living adult member of their kinband.

The aspect shrines too hid pain in glory. There were many warriors, each shrine was swollen by new recruits, and many older shrines, long-dormant, were recently reborn. That so many eldar had succumbed to the rage of Khaine was a terrible thing.

+It is a temporary damnation,+ said Neidaria, catching her brother's thoughts. +They will purge themselves of rage in battle, and emerge purified.+

+Not so temporary for some,+ replied Ariadien, glancing at the exarchs in their elaborate armour. +See them walk so proudly at the heads of their shrines. They are too blinded by glory to see their own damnation.+

Most tragic of all were the ghost warriors. Nigh on three-score wraithlords strode with the army, and many times more wraithguard and wraithblades, their long heads swaying in eerie unity as they followed the lead of the spiritseers. Ariadien had his Revenant zoom in on Iyanna Arienal, the Angel of Iyanden. By her side strode a wraithlord, coloured in flaming oranges and deep reds, a pair of dragons facing each other upon his helm. The exarch Althenian Armourlost, a rarity among rarities.

+A monster among monsters,+ he caught his sister think.

Ariadien barely noticed Althenian, staring at Iyanna through the eyes of his Revenant. He freely admitted he was enraptured by her beauty. She was so perfect it stirred something visceral within him, even though her face was hard and her aura – picked out by the psy-amplifiers of his mount – dark with melancholy. She was the warden of the dead, and to her the ghost warriors looked for guidance. +There are so many of them,+ he thought to his sister. +Think of the burden!+

The serried ranks of wraithkind were not the full number of Iyanden's dead. With each cohort of ghost warriors came caskets floating on anti-gravity fields. Elaborate script covered each one, proclaiming the names and deeds of the spirits contained within; nine spirit stones inside each. What was intended for the stones, Ariadien did not know.

+Nothing good,+ said Neidaria. +There is nothing good left at all any more.+

Finally, it came the turn of the Gemini squadron, the Phantom and their escorts to board their transports. The wraithknights each went off to the ships of their houses, but for the Titans a special vessel awaited: a cruiser, into which went also many of the army's leaders by lesser doors and ways. For the Titans the rear of the ship was open, revealing a womb-like cargo bay with transport cradles for the three of them.

The *Curse of Yriel* went in first. Moving gracefully, it sat itself into its throne-cradle, back to the prow, the shield vanes projecting from its shoulders sliding into recesses in the wall behind. These closed tightly, holding the Titan firm. Elegant wraithbone arms came forward, taking the Titan's weapons from its hands and stowing them either side of the cradle. Hands freed, the *Curse of Yriel* gripped at its throne's arms as straps worked themselves out from the wall to hold it in place.

Neidaria and Ariadien followed, taking their places either side of the Phantom. Facing each other, they too were restrained in similar manner, and the doors to the vessel shut. Darkness came, then soft blue light. Ariadien sighed, and began the deactivation process, passing his hands over control studs and jewels.

+What now, brother?+ thought Neidaria.

+It's a long trip, sister,+ said Ariadien. +I'm going to get a drink.+

Before Neidaria could reply, Ariadien slipped off his command circlet and placed it within its dedicated recess where it was whisked away. The psychic amplifier removed, the telepathic contact with his sister dulled, going from clear thought to the simple awareness of her presence and mood he had experienced since they were born. He caressed the final runes; the giant fell dormant and its face mask slid upwards into the helm, opening the cockpit.

He walked down onto the steps reaching out from the wall before they had engaged fully with the Titan.

For the time being, Ariadien was free.

Taec paced impatiently back and forth across the bridge of the void-runner *Imbriel's Embrace*. The ship was designed to travel narrow tunnels in the webway, a small ranger vessel with capacity only for two dozen passengers, but it was quick.

'Our voyage will last over two cycles, farseer,' said the captain from his cradle. 'Why do you not rest yourself? You have much toil ahead of you.'

'We have so little time!' snapped Taec. The steersmen, the only other two eldar on the bridge, glanced back at him with undisguised surprise. Taec composed himself. 'I apologise, captain, my way of speaking has become short. I spend much time in the company of the dead.'

'I understand your impatience, farseer,' said the captain, his masked head cocked to indicate both compassion and irritation. '*Imbriel's Embrace* is the fastest craft in the fleet, and we take the most direct path to Biel-Tan. I cannot make the passage any swifter.'

Taec halted and gripped his staff, leaning on it for support. The crystallisation was not painful, and did not inhibit his movement directly. Rather, it was the sensation of numbness that afflicted his limbs that made him awkward. A tingling coursed through the glassy areas of his transforming flesh, but otherwise he felt nothing.

'I am distracting you,' said Taec, his words inflected with the forms of profound apology. 'I beg your pardon once more.'

'There is no need, I assure you.' The captain turned back to his displays, passing his hands over glowing instruments like giant opals when the ship required adjustment.

Through the ship's eyes, they watched the endless, undulating tunnels of the webway projected in a space to the front of the bridge. Golden energy delimited the labyrinth, burrowed through the membranous non-space that separated the material world from the warp. Branches led off from the tunnel, some large enough to accommodate the ship, others so small only those on foot could pass. In places wraithbone gates closed tunnels, dire warnings written upon them, or walls blocked sections entirely. Taec's sensitive mind felt the pull of the warp on the other side of those fragile limns. The wicked presence of She Who Thirsts was forever beyond, peering in at morsels she could not take as a gyrinx peers into an ornamental pond full of fish.

Taec stared into the tunnel a while, lost in the rolling procession. 'I will leave you to your task, captain,' he said. 'I will not trouble you again. Please inform me when we approach Biel-Tan.'

'As you wish, farseer.'

Taec rejoined his party, sat in sombre mood in the ship's simple lounges. Fifteen others accompanied him and Kelmon. Autarch Yaleanar and his aide Herethiath stood for the war council of Iyanden. The rest of the autarchs travelled with Prince Yriel or with the army. Three spiritseers also came with Taec's group. Away from the thrumming infinity circuits of Iyanden, Kelmon grew sluggish. His mind wandered from the world of the living. Without the ministrations of the spiritseers, Taec struggled to keep his dead colleague focused upon the matters at hand. The rest of the group was comprised of a party of rangers, eldar who had chosen to become outcast. Taec heard the dialects of several craftworlds and Exodite colonies when they spoke, but they did so rarely. There was no conversation besides the infrequent talk of the rangers. The frivolity that characterised eldar at rest was absent.

Taec spent the remainder of the journey reliving his vision, going over every fragment of imagery. Each time he thought on the fire of his demise, he quailed within. But he could not discern how this came about, nor what it truly betokened.

And so it went, one cycle, then two, then three. Days spent in frustration, nights spent sleepless. Food was ash in his mouth, conversation irritating and frivolous.

On the fourth cycle, the captain called Taec to the bridge.

'We approach our destination. Behold,' he said, 'the Nexus of Remembered Supremacy To Be Regained, the primary gateway to Biel-Tan.'

Imbriel's Embrace emerged from their small tunnel into a cavern wrested from the membrane twixt the worlds. Its sides were full of tunnel mouths, the exit points of other ways into the webway. Other craftworlds kept the way to them secret; not proud Biel-Tan. The portway to the craftworld sported a massive gate, thousands of lengths in height and breadth, and coloured bold green and white. Two gargantuan wraithbone statues faced one another: on the one side stood howling Khaine, sword clasped in both hands upright in front of his face. On the other was Asuryan, his proud head bowed in sorrow. He held aloft his scales, their balance off. It was said that the balance moved, and that when the time had come for the eldar to reclaim their empire, it would be level once more. That time would be a long time coming, looking at their cant.

The gateway's frame carried on over the figures, flowing from their backs to form an ostentatious arch scored by hundreds of thousands of runes. It bristled with weapons emplacements, cunningly incorporated into the design. At the very top stood the world-rune of Biel-Tan, a heart in a Y-shaped cup: the Rebirth of Ancient Days.

Dozens of ships plied the space in front of the gate, sleek traders, far-runners and void ships. The tunnel appeared to go on indefinitely behind the gate, vessels coming through from the real space side suddenly appearing as if from nowhere.

'I see no warships,' said Taec with a heavy heart. 'Biel-Tan does not ready for war.'

The captain ignored his indiscretion. 'I have a docking berth assigned, farseer.'

'Proceed, then,' said Taec. 'We shall see what the Biel-Tanians have to say for themselves.'

Imbriel's Embrace went through the gate, tiny in comparison to the massive structure. One moment they were in the webway, the next in the void, Biel-Tan passing under their keel. Where Iyanden was kite-shaped, Biel-Tan was a long, sleek dart, its stern split in a swallow tail. Iyanden's form owed much to personal expression, Biel-Tan's everything to symmetry and the prosecution of war. Everywhere there were statues of Khaine and the other gods' warlike aspects. Massive fortresses studded its length, the weapons they bore not hidden as on other craftworlds, but exaggerated proudly. Biel-Tan was a world that spoke of reclaiming a lost empire at the point of a sword. Taec could hear its warlike soul shouting defiance at the stars.

The captain spoke to the dockmasters of the craftworld, and presently *Imbriel's Embrace* pushed through a forcefield to approach a docking tower equipped with thousands of quays.

Taec and the party from Iyanden disembarked, leaving the long ramp of *Imbriel's Embrace*. Shockingly, they were met by the guns of three aspect shrines, a single farseer at their head.

'What folly is this?' said Taec. The rangers accompanying them brought up their own long rifles, their outlines fading as the cameleoline in their cloaks engaged.

The farseer addressed them in the curt accent of the Biel-Tanians. The movements of his body underlined the character of all his kind, curt, imperious and aggressive. 'Folly? Wisdom! Here you come, and no further will you go.'

Taec narrowed his eyes. He recognised the psychic imprint of this seer. 'Do I speak with Farseer Altariec?'

'You do.'

'We have conversed many times before in amity. I protest! This is no fitting manner to receive our embassy.'

'This is the manner in which we greet those we cannot trust,' said Altariec baldly. He addressed the Aspect Warriors with him. 'Iyanden calls us to their aid, do they forget our alliance is a thing of past times? Broken, so I recall, by their own unwillingness to commit to the struggle to restore our people's glories.'

'You were too aggressive, too soon. We share the same purpose still, I assure you,' said Taec. 'The time will come when we will march onwards to restoration together, and all the other craftworlds besides.'

'Your assurances are worthless. How many enemies will they fell? There are wars that should have been fought from which you turned, and yet wars that should have been avoided that you fought.' An unpleasant sense of bitter amusement passed through his posture. 'Those you seem to have suffered greatly from. Why should we listen to you?'

'A confluence of probability has formed. Now is the time to act in concert,' said Kelmon. 'Put up your weapons and let us pass.'

'You would have us fight, Wraithseer Kelmon, engage that which threw down the bastions of Iyanden, the greatest of all the craftworlds?' Altariec said this disdainfully. 'Reckless.'

'It is my shame to have counselled war whilst I lived. The result is all around you. Shame binds my soul. I am shaped by it,' said Kelmon. 'I repent my pride, and bring only wisdom to you.'

'You remain reckless in death then, if you still preach war. Where is your shame? This world of Dûriel was lost to us long ago. Let the Great Dragon complete our task for us, and remove the human blight.'

'The dead are not reckless. What you have seen cannot come to pass, you know this,' said Taec.

'And you come here, the Silvereye, come here and beg for our aid in your struggle. Great as Eldrad Ulthran, they say. Greater, perhaps. No!' Altariec slammed the butt of his staff hard onto the floor. 'What trust there once was between us is gone. You and we, the greatest of craftworlds, together we could have stayed the slow death of our kind. It was foreseen!' He levelled the point of his staff at the Iyandeni. 'Scried on the skein by the minds of the seers of both craftworlds, and yet your kind turned aside.' His voice grew dark, the air grew thicker with his wrath, the light bled away by his displeasure.

'I know of those seeings,' said Taec calmly. 'I was told of them by Uriethaniel Goldenhand, he who instructed me upon the Path of the Seer, now passed. He told me the reading was not so clear cut, that glory could have been the result, it is true, but that suffering to both peoples would be the more likely result.'

'Your seers were wrong,' spat Altariec.

The wraithseer spoke. 'Kelmon the Admonished I call myself, not the far-sighted but the short-sighted. Yes! Even Kelmon the Fool. I was proud, and I was wrong. I have sworn never to be so again. We must act now.'

'You are wrong again, once-Kelmon,' said Altariec. 'My own foresight has warned me. This battle cannot be won. We will lose many warriors. Who can afford to, when each life is so precious and each fighter needed?'

'Prince Yriel does not think it unwinnable.'

'The pirate king?' scoffed Altariec. 'Pride brings ruin, no one is better placed to know this than the Prince Yriel, for his pride ruined you all.'

'I know this better,' countered Kelmon. 'Even more than the Exiled Prince. It was my pride, not his, that proved Iyanden's downfall.'

A figure hurried onto the dock, elaborately garbed, one far along the Path of the Seer. He took in the scene on the quayside, his dismay palpable.

'Farseer Taec Silvereye?'

'I am he.'

'I was not informed of your arrival. Altariec, as the elder farseer on Biel-Tan at this time, why did you not tell us?'

'I wished to deliver my displeasure to them myself,' said Altariec.

'Then it is good the infinity circuit told me you were here. I am Farseer Dahtarioc.' He turned to regard Altariec's guard of Aspect Warriors, their weapons levelled at the visitors. 'Why do you berate our kinsfolk so? This is most unbecoming, unforgivable, for Altariec to greet you in this manner! Are we the brawlers of Commorragh? Stand down your arms, warriors of Biel Tan! You have our hospitality, O Taec Silvereye of Iyanden.'

The Aspect Warriors, two shrines' worth of Dire Avengers and one of Fire Dragons, looked to their exarchs. These held up their hands flat, fingers spread. The weapons dipped.

Taec hid his relief in courtly words. 'And we gladly accept it.'

'You have come alone? We expected your armies,' said Dahtarioc.

'Our warhost makes its way to Dûriel directly. Prince Yriel comes here, to take the star-road to Dûriel where he will destroy the voidspawn in space. We will attempt the attack even if Biel-Tan will not stand beside us.'

Dahtarioc was taken aback. 'What makes you say this?'

'We received no reply to our plea. I see no warships.'

'It was sent, farseer, it was sent. We decided in majority, the seer and war councils both, to aid you. Only Altariec here and his followers disagreed. We move with all haste towards Dûriel.'

Taec slumped a little with relief. 'Do not allow Biel-Tan to approach the Dragon itself, that was Kelmon's error. I pray you will not make it yourselves.'

'No,' said Altariec. 'The fools are not that foolish. Biel-Tan moves nearer so as to close the distance, nothing more.'

'The craftworld will be in no danger,' said Dahtarioc.

'We cannot be sure of this,' said Altariec.

'We can be sure of nothing, the shadow is on everything! It has been decided, farseer,' said Dahtarioc. He spoke more civilly to Taec. 'Perhaps the shadow of the Dragon consumed our reply? We have had much trouble with our communications, so strong is the alien mind-voice now that it casts a pall over the webway and warp together.'

Taec nodded hesitantly. 'Perhaps so. I sense the shadow, it is deep and dark and clouds all thought. We were forced upon an astral journey before we could start our scrying. This means then that you will aid us? If that is so, I come to press you still, for Biel-Tan to attack immediately. The chances of success if we wait for the Phoenix Host are slim.'

The word *phoenix* carried many complex meanings, and Taec chose to reveal the name of their army purposefully. It was a concept that lay at the heart of Biel-Tan's philosophy. Dahtarioc smiled.

'Ancient days will be reborn. It is good to hear it from the lips of the Iyandeni once again.'

'Yes, even if the fire of Asuryan's shrine is doused.'

'It will burn again, farseer. We will light it with the bonfires of war. Come now, rest. You have no reason to press us.' He reached out his arms and performed a complex bow of true greeting. The physical nuance it added to his words appeared odd to Taec, but its meaning was clear. 'The assembled warhost of Biel-Tan departed for Dûriel half a cycle ago under the command of Autarch Aloec Sunspear,' said Dahtarioc. 'We go to Dûriel with all speed.'

Taec was aghast. 'You attack alone?'

Altariec slammed his staff upon the floor. 'And there you have it! Idiocy! Poor counsel! No good will come of this, you will see.'

CHAPTER FOUR
THE SWORDWIND STRIKES

The Shrine of the Patient Blade lived up to its name. Aspect Warriors of all kinds gathered on the plateaus surrounding the valley slopes, but the Patient Blade, led by Exarch Thurliarissa, had been first to descend into the den of the enemy. A half of this planet's cycle they had hidden, awaiting their prey under the spore-choked skies of Dûriel. A parade of alien monstrosities passed them by, and they had not stirred. The squad felt the awful touch of the hive mind as much as any eldar, their psychically sensitive minds open to its terrors. But death was their ally, her presence palpable, and their faith in Khaine reduced the warp shadow cast by the fleets' minds until it was as threatening as a cloud in front of the sun.

A signal. Tulian had their prey in sight. Thurliarissa pulsed the command to move and they slipped carefully through the boulders and scrub of the valley sides. They had all memorised the shape and the thought forms of the creature they had been sent to kill, and wisely so. A Dragon in Shadow was a difficult prize to track. It moved as stealthily as they moved, a ghost, its chameleonic skin making it a little more than a shimmer on the land. The exarch had deep respect for this creature; its genetics were artfully engineered, perfectly adapted for its role as scout, sentry, and terror weapon. A lictor, humans called it. A superlative hunter, this cycle it was the hunted. Thurliarissa was intent today's rising sun would be the last it ever saw.

Her Aspect Warriors broke cover, emerging from hollows in the rocks. Following the wavering outline of the lictor, they ran over the scrubby hillside in the stance of Death To Giants, for giants they sought.

'Strike swiftly and hard, the claw closes on our prey, bring death mercilessly,' Thurliarissa spoke to the squad. The crystal psychic pick-ups in her helm were useless, for all but the strongest psy-signals were blocked out by the flat, raging presence of the hive mind, and she was forced to speak over radio. Silently, they spread out into the form requested, nine of them in a curved U – a moving pincer preparing to snap shut.

The lictor caught wind of them just before the trap was sprung, the tendrils on its face twitching, somehow tasting their presence despite their armour's sophisticated baffles. Thurliarissa had heard they could sense electromagnetic radiation, and cursed the psychic roar of the hive mind for forcing such crude communications on them. It spun around to meet them, shedding its camouflage and rearing up to its full height, four times that of an eldar. Scythed talons five paces long arched over its back, a mockery of the curved sting of the scorpion. These were all too ready to meet the blade of Dariathanar as he leapt and struck.

The Dragon in Shadow caught Dariathanar's whirring chainsword on the armoured upper surface of its claws, turning its torso up and back to pitch him off-balance. It smashed at the Striking Scorpion with its lower hands, slamming him backwards half a dozen paces. Dariathanar clattered against the stone and lay still. In her helm Thurliarissa caught sense of his injuries: not grave, but he was stunned. Seven of her Striking Scorpions remained. She would chide Dariathanar for his rashness when they returned to the shrine.

Wordlessly, she signalled her warriors to attack as one, not alone. They moved swiftly around the creature, sending artful fusillades at it, their chainswords swirling through the air in complex death patterns. Quick as they were, the warrior beast was swifter, moving with speed that was breathtaking. Wherever their weapons went, a claw moved to intercept them and turn them away. Shuriken embedded themselves in the mountain's rock where a short instant before the lictor had stood. Embattled on all sides, it was on the defensive, but they could not slay it, no matter that they outnumbered it.

Thurliarissa saw an opening and moved in, her warriors parting in their deadly dance to allow her through. She ducked under a claw that chopped towards her, switching postures. Stances that looked ungainly and uncomfortable away from battle enabled her to slip around the lictor's blows. Ferion got too close, the lictor reacted, and the point of its claw buried itself in his chestplate. Ferion struggled upon the spike, his waystone's light brightened, and he hung limp.

Ferion's death bought Thurliarissa victory. She opened up with the shuriken pistols built into her chainsabres. Twin streams of sharp discs smacked into the creature's heavily armoured thorax. It screeched as they penetrated its chitin, finding their way into the soft organs beneath. Thurliarissa bounded forwards as it staggered back, arms apart in the stance of the Claw's Embrace. She swung her forearms together with force, targeting the Dragon in Shadow's knobbled neck. The teeth on the ancient weapons screamed as they cut through the creature's spine, and its head rolled from its shoulders and fell into the dust. The Scorpions moved aside as it died, the tall, lanky carcass spouting bright fluids as it collapsed to the floor.

Thurliarissa panted, praise to Khaine on her lips. She communicated the squad's triumph to Inner Command. It was her great pride that Sunspear had once fought under her, in an earlier life. 'The Patient Blade fights well, the scorpion's prey is dead, this zone is now clear.'

Praise came from Sunspear, then new orders.

She stopped to pluck Ferion's waystone. Marking the position of his corpse for later retrieval, she led her squad onward, down into the reeking forests of the valley.

* * *

The Godpeak was Dûriel's highest mountain, and the site of the world's ancient webway portal. From his command position upon the cliffs fringing the summit, Autarch Aloec Sunspear of Biel-Tan sent his thanks to the Patient Blade. He consulted his viewing orb's map of the Godpeak and the valley stretching out from its southern side. Faint shimmers showed the positions of eldar hunting squads, and he nodded in satisfaction. Ever since the Battle of Iyanden had reduced Biel-Tan's erstwhile ally to a haunted ruin, Sunspear had studied the Great Devourer, certain that its attention would one day fall on his own craftworld. He had determined that the Dragons in Shadow operated as an early warning system for the swarm, among other things. He was confident that with the lictors dead, his force would be able to move in unopposed and take the creatures of Far Ranging Hunger by surprise.

So confident was Aloec Sunspear that it would never occur to him that he might be wrong. After all, he so rarely was. Sunspear was not arrogant, nor was he afflicted with hubris. His expertise was a simple fact.

This steely self-belief was the core of an unbending personality. Aloec was a commander without compare, determined and ruthless on the battlefield, some would say humourless off it, as he found laughter in few things other than victory. Mocked by his more flippant colleagues, he would retort, 'And what is there to laugh about, in these dark and dismal days?' Although like most Biel-Tanians, he believed with utter conviction that the eldar's time was coming again, he harboured no doubts as to the odds that they faced.

His mouth was therefore permanently downturned, his eyes flat and calculating. It was whispered that he should not be upon the Path of Command at all, but was marked by fate to be an exarch, and that Morai-Heg's ghost would make him pay for his defiance of her intentions. Three aspect shrines he had passed through, the Patient Blade, Regrets Rendered Molten, and Flickering Extinction, and the exarchs of them all said differently. He had endured the ritual of Rhaan Lona in each without incident. No matter what his peers thought, Khaine had deemed him worthy.

Sunspear wore a tall scorpion helm. His armour was the white of Biel-Tan, and a rich green cloak patterned with thorns of gold hung from his shoulders. His stern demeanour was hidden by the helm, and his exceptional height – he was tall by the measure of his people – made greater by his towering crest. A grey sash hung with the runes of Dire Avenger, Striking Scorpion and Fire Dragon crossed his chest.

'The eyes of the Dragon are put out.' His words were conveyed to the whole of Biel-Tan's army over radio. An inconvenient consequence of their foe's nature. If he was affected by the crushing horror of the hive mind's psychic roar, his followers could not perceive it.

The autarch turned from the swirling clouds of pollutants and spores that obscured his view of the valley. His command post occupied a flat shelf of rock several thousand paces below the summit of the Godpeak. The rest of the Inner Command were with him – the farseers Forlissiar, Kellian and Serriestalor, the quartet of warlocks that accompanied them, working hard to shield the farseers from the collective psyche of the swarm, and Autarch Hethaeliar the Fourth-Blooded, his second-in-command.

Sunspear's personal transport floated several paces away, the Inner Command standing around it, all utilising gestures that suggested deep communion with the army's various elements. Autarch Hethaeliar hailed him, her languid voice intimate in his ear-beads. 'Lord Sunspear, the Vyper squadrons are reporting in.'

'I open my ears to you, swift hunters,' said Sunspear in the formal mode.

'Autarch, creatures of both swarms are present in large numbers.' Images flashed up on Sunspear's viewing orb. The orb was projected by his helmet lenses directly onto his retinas in such a way as to make it appear as if it were in the air in front of him, a useful illusion. Flawless pictures of tyranids and broken cities paraded past his eyes. A smattering of the aliens were of red and bone; in the main they were purple and an unhealthy white. 'The majority of Far Ranging Hunger are to our north, heading at speed towards your position.'

'They have detected us?'

One of the farseers, Serriestalor, moved his head sideways, one hand up, the other palm down and descending. Not yet.

'Starving Dragon roams the plains and the dead seas to the south, with greatest concentrations around the human cities and other population centres,' continued the Vyper pilot. 'Far Ranging Hunger moves towards them. It is incidental that you are in their path. As far as is discernible by us, you are undetected, my autarch.'

'The humans, what was their fate? How fare the first despoilers of twice-despoiled Dûriel?'

'You seek allies, autarch?' interjected Forlissiar. Of all the seers in Sunspear's Inner Command, he had been most opposed to the plan. He was firmly of Altariec's camp.

Forlissiar wished to goad him by suggesting that the lumpen humans could aid them. Sunspear ignored his mockery. The Vyper leader continued his report.

'There are no signs of the humans anywhere remaining within five hundred thousand paces of the Godpeak. They have been destroyed and are being devoured. The majority of this world's biomass was concentrated within the settlements of the humans. Our outrunner squadrons passed over three of their smaller cities. They are deserted of inhabitants.'

'This area, it is free of their activity?'

'There is a crude geothermal power station to the north-west of our position, that is all.'

'What is its status?'

'Empty but for blood, autarch. The Godpeak may be extinct, but the area remains volcanically active. The plant's systems, though primitive, appear to have gone into failsafe shutdown. A fleet of humans flees the system from the world they call Ector, they will pass near here in half a cycle's time.'

Sunspear tensed. He would have dearly liked to scatter their remains to the stellar winds for their crimes in this system.

'They will have to wait for their punishment. We have no time, nor the strength to destroy them,' said Kellian softly.

'Show me Starving Dragon,' Sunspear said. The images projected by his helmet changed to show concentrations of the purple aliens.

'As yet it is unaware of us,' continued the Vyper leader. 'Resistance has been quashed, the tertiary phase has begun.' Fat creatures that were little more than bags surrounded by legs vomited torrents of bile into shallow pools excavated by strange, shovel-faced drones. Spines grew out of the ground, and from his studies of the Great Devourer, the autarch knew they would be sucking the mineral and organic wealth from the soil and rocks. The spines would grow throughout the next dozen cycles, to be milked and then devoured towards the end of the consumption phase. Others, those around the digestion pools, would grow into immense capillary towers, the means by which the biomass of the planet would be assimilated by the hive fleets. Swarms of small leaping creatures picked up every scrap of biological matter and devoured it, while larger workers stacked corpses in front of the smoking cities of mankind to be consumed by immense eater beasts.

'They prepare to concentrate planetary resources,' said Sunspear. 'We must strike before the swarm begins to consume itself and returns its matter to the hive fleet. That is the point of danger for us. Far Ranging Hunger's creatures will be swept up by the greater swarm of Starving Dragon and our own life codes added to bolster the arsenal of the Great Dragon.' He pursed his lips, then lifted a hand, fingers fanning out. This gesture of confidence-in-knowledge would be visible in the squadron leader's own visual feed. 'Now tell me, what news of our own cities? I am curious.'

'See for yourself, my autarch.' The orb showed weathered stumps of wraithbone. 'The usurpers demolished them, and those few ruins that stand still have been abraded by time's passage.' More pictures clicked by, dry seabeds, desert where there had once been rich grassland. Dûriel's forests had survived, including those in the valley and hills below the Godpeak, but in a sorry state. Dead trees, felled by pollution, leaned drunkenly on one another; in places all were dead, nothing but rotting stumps and weed species remaining. Everywhere the vegetation was sickly, ravaged by off-world diseases and the salt blowing in from the dried-up sea beds. This was not the work of the Great Devourer, but of mankind. 'The human squatters have managed our property carelessly. There is nothing but despoliation here. They were unforgivably thorough.'

Anger quickened Aloec's heart. The seers, Altariec chief among them, had warned him his gambit was unfavourable, but he had nurtured a hope that once the voidspawn had been driven off, Dûriel could be saved for the future of his people. The seers accompanying him saw his disappointment and sorrowed for it, although they had known it could be no other way.

'Their rapaciousness disgusts me. They take a paradise and make it a wasteland,' said Aloec. 'It is a mercy that they fell before the Great Dragon, for my revenge upon them would have been a hard one.'

Sunspear looked upwards to the pinnacle of the Godpeak, periodically obscured by the shifting red clouds of spores. Upon the very top were the broken remains of webway pylons, so ancient that the fragments of wraithbone looked indistinguishable from weathered stone. 'They may topple our monuments,' he said grimly, 'but they have not the faintest understanding of our mastery. Final deployment may begin!' he proclaimed. He unsheathed his chainsword and raised it high.

Above the shattered summit of the mountain, the clouds glowed bright as the chief webway gate to Dûriel opened. A slash of light swelled, then dilated into a sphere. Swarms of grav-craft shot through it, soaring off to hide themselves among the clouds. Dozens of smaller portals – temporary gates off the main conduit brought into being by wayseers – opened one after another where webway beacons had been secreted by eldar scouts, disgorging the armies of Biel-Tan unseen to positions all over the mountain.

'You have lain dormant!' said Sunspear to the gateway. 'Too long you have waited for your true masters, for one hundred arcs! Today, your masters have returned!' Sunspear looked again to the valley. 'And we are too late.'

'Autarch?'

The eldar who had spoken was a ranger, swathed in the heavy coat of his kind despite the sultry heat of the dying world. He wore no insignia, save a small badge depicting Iyanden's world-rune. No marking told of his path, for his clothes told all. Sunspear smiled unkindly under his helmet. He knew the values of the outcasts well, but it never failed to amuse him that for all their rejection of the restrictive eldar way of life, they all affected exactly the same dress.

'You say we are too late.' The ranger shrugged. His topknot quirked with the motion. His helmet was off, his mouth covered with a filter mask, his eyes hidden by dark glasses. 'There are thousands more virgin worlds awaiting the eldar, autarch. I have seen many of them.'

'The loss of even one shames us all,' snarled Sunspear, and he turned from the outcast to watch the might of his craftworld arrive to reclaim the wreck of Dûriel.

From a dozen webway gates, sleek eldar grav-vehicles poured forth. Delicate yet deadly Falcon grav-tanks, Wave Serpents, super-heavy Cobras, Vypers by the dozen and jetbikes by the score. Their engines were so hushed, the sound of the spores hissing down onto the rock of the mountain drowned them out. At the Inner Command's order, the tanks took up formation in the boiling clouds, hidden from eye and mind alike.

On the flanks of the mountain, Dark Reapers took up station. Teams of Guardians guided heavy weapons mounted on grav-platforms into place. Aspect Warriors of close-combat shrines moved down the slope, preparing to blunt Far Ranging Hunger's inevitable counter-attack. War walkers, nimble as mountain grazers, sprang from rock to rock as they moved into advantageous positions from where they could reap the greatest tally of the dead.

Sunspear watched all this on visual projection, listening in on the minimal radio chatter of his army. It gladdened his heart to see so many fine warriors, even if they were several thousand years too late to save stricken Dûriel.

The streamers of spores and pollutants blew away for a moment, revealing the vista to Aloec's eyes unaided. From his vantage point, he looked down upon a karst landscape, a range of dumpy, round hills like blisters on the land, deep caves, and sudden gashes in the ground. All was swathed in sick forest, broken up by expanses of bare rock and scrub. The hills spread either side of the Godpeak to frame a shallow valley that once, so he had read in the records of Biel-Tan, had been a most beauteous place: the Valley of the Gods. Its statues and gardens were not even memories, levelled by mankind in unthinking destruction. Only the plants of dozens of worlds growing in weedy profusion hinted that once upon a time things had been different here.

What maddened Sunspear was that men had not even deigned to settle in the valley. The glory of the gardens ruined, they had withdrawn, perhaps unnerved by the atmosphere of the place; the main cities of men had lain some distance away from where the eldar's old haunts had been, and the nearest lay well away from the valley. Senseless, thought Sunspear. They destroy for the sake of destruction.

All around the Godpeak, plumes of dust rose upwards, thrown into the air by the sharp hooves of hundreds of thousands of voidspawn racing towards the south; deep red and bone, the children of the Kraken.

To the east, the valley opened out to a plain that sloped down to the site of Dûriel's evaporated oceans. The stubby forms of ex-islands poked up from dry flats in the far distance. Where the sun penetrated the cloud to shine upon the flats, there blazed the dazzling white of extensive salt deposits. This wound on the world bore injuries of its own: long, parallel rectangles had been scraped out by human mining machines.

To the south, glinting slicks of liquid could be spied, tiny shapes around them. Organic towers grew like plants, though many thousands of times bigger. These were the digestion pools his Vypers had shown him.

'See, Forlissiar,' said Sunspear. He asked for his guidance deliberately. 'The tyranids of Starving Dragon have begun upon their digestion of the world's remaining bounty. There, the capillary towers have taken root and grow. We have little time. When will the swarms combine?'

Forlissiar's voice was strained. All the eldar felt the crushing intellect of the hive fleets pressing down upon them, a formless horror wracked by unspeakable hungers. Terror was yet another of its weapons, projected into the minds of its prey. For the likes of Forlissiar, whose psychic abilities were fully developed, the effect was amplified a thousand-fold. Only the coterie of four warlocks, lending their own psychic might to that of the farseers, allowed them to see into the future at all, or indeed to remain sane. 'As far as I can judge it, in the afternoon of tomorrow, autarch. The threads of fate are obscured in many places, but we have persevered. You must strike before then. Eradication will take some time, if it is possible at all. Kellian, Serriestalor?'

The other two seers of the Inner Command joined them. 'Starving Dragon will yet be unaware,' said Kellian in the sing-song voice of a half-trance. 'In this its dominance of the skein will be a blessing, for its ignorance will be plain to see.'

'The dragon will feed, bent to the table, it will see its brother not,' said Serriestalor.

'Good,' said Sunspear. 'Good.'

'Be wary, autarch,' said Forlissiar. 'Your opportunity is slim. Destruction of the Swordwind is the outcome of many threads, as Altariec warned you. You must be careful. Strike quickly, and withdraw.'

'We have time,' said Sunspear. 'Altariec is too timid. We will wipe out all the creatures of Far Ranging Hunger and depart. I decree it will be so.'

A stream of information came to Sunspear and the Inner Command, squads moving to rendezvous points or emerging from the webway, wings of Crimson Hunters calling ready, status updates on the deployment. The farseers consulted the runes and each other, Forlissiar voicing concerns all the while, the three of them passing direction on to Sunspear who relayed it to his warriors. He trusted the seers would find the most fortuitous positions for his forces.

The sun sank below the horizon, and still the eldar army came through the webway. Hidden in the cloudbanks, they spread over the continent, taking up position over Far Ranging Hunger's beasts. Vypers criss-crossed the planet at speed, marking out the locations of Starving Dragon's main digestion pools. Most of these were outside the human cities. Grisly images of thousands of corpses dumped into steaming acid became commonplace on Sunspear's display. Starving Dragon's creatures on the world were vastly in the majority, even if they were only a part of the greater swarm in orbit. Sunspear was not complacent. If even a handful of Far Ranging Hunger's higher creatures were absorbed by Starving Dragon, then the terrible future foreseen by Taec Silvereye of Iyanden would come to pass.

The night wore on. Lightning cracked in the distance and a mighty storm sprang up. Wind blew strongly over the peak, dry at first. Later in the night veils of coloured rain washed the landscape. Sunspear wondered idly if, now men were gone, the planet's balance would reassert itself; if over time the rain would fall to fill the seas again.

Sunspear waved away his aides when they suggested he rest. 'I will oversee the deployment of the last Guardian,' he said. And he did.

The sun rose over clearer skies, the rain having cleared the lower atmosphere of spores, although the higher altitudes where the eldar waited were still thick with them. The last few messages came over the communications network. A Gemini squad of Revenant Titans, the last of the force's heavy elements, emerged from the main webway portal bent double.

The army assembled, Sunspear took stock. His army was the fastest elements of the Swordwind, all that could be gathered and moved quickly through the webway, and was ready for battle. He made a silent prayer to Khaine and Asuryan that it would be enough. 'We come in answer to Iyanden's call,' he said, 'as is right. Now, let us announce our presence to the voidspawn, and redirect the flow of fate.'

During the night, the creatures of Far Ranging Hunger had made good headway. Coming down from their planetfall in the north, they filled the Valley of the Gods, their red and bone bodies lapping around the feet of the Godpeak in parody of the dead seas of Dûriel. Several hundred thousand paces east and west they stretched out, a tidemark on the landscape. Unsuspecting of the eldar craft hidden in the clouds, they pressed on, instinct driving them towards Starving Dragon.

How fitting, thought Sunspear, that their own spores mask the instruments of their destruction.

'Attack,' said Sunspear calmly. 'Scour them from the skein.'

Immediately, several hundred craft plunged from the turgid skies over the swarm, spitting shuriken, las-bolts and the plasma packets of suncannon at the teeming mass of tyranids. Upon the mesas and hills around the valley, Aspect Warriors and war walkers opened fire, targeting the swarm's leader-beasts. The Revenants ran towards the edge of the rock shelf where Sunspear's command post was situated, and leapt into the air. Jump jets flared blue-white and they hurtled down the mountainside.

All the eldar felt the shock of the hive mind as it was ambushed. As oppressive as they found the psychic entity, the eldar drew satisfaction when they felt it snap and snarl, Sunspear above all others. 'Shaft of Sunlight, proceed to the dawnward edge,' he said. A flight of nine Vypers shot towards a group of monsters scrambling up the valley sides in the direction of a group of Dark Reapers. He made many similar adjustments, reacting to the hive's reactions. Forlissiar, Kellian and Serriestalor were beside him, whispering advice in their cryptic trance voices as they peered down the skein. The swarm moved as one organism, spaces opening around areas of intense bombardment. Sunspear had accounted for this in his plan, laying out fire patterns that would force the aliens into certain groups, then engulfing these bunchings as they occurred. And so the voidspawn fled from the impact of missile swarms straight into clouds of monomolecular wire spun by deathspinners. Caught in the strands, their own struggles saw them sliced into bloodied chunks.

Sunspear picked out weapon-beasts and leader creatures, channelling fire onto them in merciless salvoes. Where they fell, the hive mind weakened. He felt the attention of the alien consciousness turn to him, a crushing sensation – Serriestalor, his mind more attuned to the currents of the Othersea than Sunspear's, cried out in pain. But there was little it could do. Leader-beasts toppled throughout the swarm, the twisted vegetation of the valley forest offering scant cover against the eldar's sophisticated targeting matrices. By the dozen they died, chitin plates full of smoking holes. As they fell, the grip of the hive mind on its lesser creatures diminished, and slowly the swarm's coherency began to disintegrate.

Overhead, Crimson Hunters duelled with the few airborne elements of Far Ranging Hunger's swarm. Winged shapes fell from the sky, wings shredded. They crushed their kin by the dozen where they crashed. The skies were swept clear quickly, and the fast craft turned their guns upon the creatures on the ground.

'The reach of the Great Dragon's mind is much reduced,' said Kellian. 'Your strategy is working.'

'We shall see,' said Forlissiar. 'This opening act to the dance will not go unopposed. The swarm reacts again.'

He pointed out an area towards the valley mouth, where a line of sharp karsts broke through the trees. Enhanced images showed tall warriors marshalling the lesser creatures. All over, the tyranids were turning back to attack their attackers, converging on the valley.

'An element of my plan, farseer,' said the autarch. 'If they do not concentrate themselves here, how shall we annihilate them?'

Sunspear made a sharp gesture, hissing into his helmet pick-up. The warriors were cut down by a unit of Dark Reapers, the trees where they had been billowing with sudden flame.

'The Great Dragon can react all it wishes, we have the advantage,' he said. 'We are the superior species.'

Exarch Thurliarissa dodged a claw strike, disembowelling the creature with a double-handed cross-strike of her chainsabres. The Shrine of the Patient Blade fought around her, chopping down leaping, scythe-armed creatures in droves. The aliens fought without thought, snarling and chittering. No matter how many were slaughtered, they did not fall back. The quiet discharge of the scorpion's sting, the whirr of the chainblades, the shriek of shuriken competed with the clicks and whoops of the lesser warrior beasts. This was Khaine's music, and Thurliarissa danced to it. The Patient Blade fought melee specialists like themselves, and outmatched them effortlessly.

Explosions rocked the forest. Fires set by the stellar heat of starcannons burned fitfully on rotten wood. The screams of the aliens sounded from every quarter. The last leaping beast died, its bladed forelimbs knocking together manically as Jolarithel cut it in half with his chainsword. Then they ran onwards, following orders sent to them by Inner Command.

They passed a roaring giant, a hideous thing bent double, a giant pulsing sac held beneath its belly. Smaller creatures surrounded it, similar to the ones they had slaughtered moments before, but with bony guns in place of bladed forelimbs. Squirming bugs drenched in acidic ichor spattered on the Aspect Warriors' armour as the Patient Blade drove into their enemy.

The giant brood mother of these beasts rounded on the Scorpions. It lurched forwards, shouldering trees into rotten mulch. Apertures on its carapace sent a spray of barbed spines as long as an eldar's arm arching towards them. The Scorpions dodged, loosing volleys from their pistols at the smaller beasts. Rihanarisal was hit by a spine, staggered by its impact, but his armour remained whole, and he fought on.

Thurliarissa made for the beast, cutting down three of its children. Its sac pulsed, a wide orifice opened at its front, and a dozen more creatures tumbled out, their white and red carapaces dripping with fluids. They attacked immediately, and Thurliarissa was driven back. The mother-creature roared, the ground trembling as it came at the Patient Blade. Thurliarissa went into a frenzy of cuts and slashes at the offspring. The beasts somehow sensed that she was the leader and attacked her en masse, but the others came to her aid, dispatching many of the aliens.

There came a hissing, then a loud whoosh and a wash of heat. The mother-creature howled in pain, black smoke gouting from the side of its birth sac. Yellow ichor gushed to the ground, carrying the stiff corpses of unborn broodlings with it. Thurliarissa was occupied with her foes who, though poor fighters, were numerous, and only registered her allies as flashes of orange in the trees.

More blasts – fusion weaponry. Six burning craters appeared in the brood mother's flanks. It reared up shrieking, then collapsed forwards, tried to heave to its feet, and died.

Immediately the lesser beasts fell to writhe on the floor. They keened as they convulsed, their weapons discharging involuntarily. Those that did not die from the shock of their mother's death were executed easily by the Patient Blade.

Quiet fell, the sounds of battle moving away from them. Thurliarissa panted hard.

Warriors came into the clearing made by the creature's death throes. Their armour was lividly coloured, no camouflage for them: the Burning Rebuke, Shrine of the Fire Dragon.

'Sister exarch, I greet thee heartily, in time we come,' said their leader, Oskirithil of the Sorrows, a lugubrious being who seemed to take no joy in being an exarch. 'Might I advise, slay the largest first, they are the Dragon.' He inclined his head at the smouldering brood mother. 'As you can see, this one is the mother, dead the threat dies.'

Thurliarissa nodded her thanks, and gestured for her warriors to follow her into the trees.

CHAPTER FIVE

THE SERPENT BENEATH

Sunspear watched the tyranids pressing their counter-attack. On the eastern side of the valley they swarmed up the cliffs, attempting to attack the Aspect Warriors and war walkers firing on them from above. To the west more of Biel-Tan's close-quarter warriors had come down to the valley floor to drive the beasts onto their comrades' guns. Sunspear's viewing orb showed the various aspect shrines as glowing runes, his helmet lenses zooming in to their positions at a thought, the individual warriors outlined in bright reds and oranges. Above them flashed jetbikes and Vypers, strafing the ground.

'The Swordwind does its job well,' said Serriestalor, who, as the leader-beasts of the swarm had dwindled, had recovered somewhat. 'Your plan is working. Many are dead at little loss to our own. Perhaps Altariec was wrong.'

'I see nothing to suggest this,' said Forlissiar. 'Autarch, the warriors' might is their weakness, they advance too quickly and are overstretched. Observe.'

Sunspear followed Forlissiar's fingers as they danced over the viewing orb. This one was projected into all their eyes, a shared illusion.

'See here, the piercing arrow digs deep into the flesh of our prey, but the further it penetrates, the more likely the jaws are to shut around it.' He indicated the narrow column of Aspect Warriors. As he described, their formation was like a hunter's arrow. As its flanks grew longer, tyranids massed either side. In the valley, ragged treetops shook with their passing.

'I concur,' said Serriestalor.

'I too. The creatures will fall upon the wind of falling leaves, and shiver the blade. The skein shows it to be correct,' said Kellian.

'The Great Dragon attacks where I desire, this is part of my strategy. But you are correct. It is time to pull back those of the shrines, they have done their work,' Sunspear said to the farseers. 'Group of the Sun's Setting, fall back to your transports and redeploy to the following coordinates,' he ordered. 'Group of the Sun's Rising, intensify fire, hold the cliffs and prepare for reinforcement. Group of the Sun's Anchor, cover the retreat of Sun's Setting.'

Instantly, the flow of battle changed as the Aspect Warrior formation fell back in good order, the column of them growing thicker as the foremost elements rejoined those shrines behind them. Support weapons batteries on the cliffs trained their armaments on the voidspawn massing on either side, and the distance filled with glittering energy beams.

'Flawlessly done,' said Forlissiar dryly. 'I believe you will not lose a single one.'

'That is an exaggeration, farseer,' said the autarch. 'But by all means, please convey your sentiments to Altariec. Seers,' he said, his tone changing to one of more respect, 'do you yet have an inkling where the spear of Khaine should be thrust?' He touched at a webway beacon hanging from his armour. 'This is one task I will leave to no other.'

'As yet no, autarch,' said Serriestalor with a humble bow. 'I... Wait!'

Frantic shouts and battle-crazed laughter came over the communications web.

'Sun's Rising has encountered something... unforeseen,' said Serriestalor.

'Where? Show me.' The mind-map moved over to the west. The cliffs on that side of the valley were shallower and less heavily forested. From here the aspect shrines had descended, and at the cliff tops waited their Wave Serpents and Falcons to bear them away to the eastern battlefront. But something blocked their way.

The seers conveyed impressions to Sunspear – earth heaving upwards, the ground boiling with snake-like forms, creatures pulling themselves from the earth.

'This will happen in moments. The Hidden Serpent,' said Serriestalor. 'It has been actively obscured, kept from the skein. The mind of the aliens is powerful.'

'More powerful than we expected. We are duped,' said Kellian.

Forlissiar said nothing, but his posture conveyed his thoughts well enough; that of an eldar whose case has been proven.

As Serriestalor predicted, an ambush was sprung. The Swordwind reacted instantly, masses of fire erupting at the point of the creatures' emergence, the tanks and artillery covering the Aspect Warriors cutting the forest to shreds directly in their line of retreat, but the serpents were many, and they fell upon the Aspect Warriors falling back. Behind them, the greater mass of voidspawn moved in for the kill.

'My question has been answered,' said Sunspear. He called for his weapons, his fusion pistol and his diamond-toothed chainsword. He took them from his aides, and girt himself with his belt. He gestured to the four warlocks waiting by the Wave Serpent's open ramp. They bowed their heads and went within.

'Let us join the fray. It is time we took an active hand.'

Sunspear's Wave Serpent rose from the mountain shelf and flew down the flanks of the Godpeak. The rocks blurred as they sped on, arrow-sure. As they descended from the peak, the air grew clearer, the bow-wave energy field sparking as minuscule examples of the invading ecosystem's creatures were annihilated. The pilot, Durantai-Bec, one of Biel-Tan's very best, jinked around formations of pockmarked quartz, skimming so close to the leaves on the dying trees they bent in the Wave Serpent's slipstream. Tyranid fire, vicious and messy, sprayed upwards from below, but Durantai-Bec danced past the worst of it, the weapons grubs that hit them shattered to atoms by the power field of the craft.

The Wave Serpent cut into the forest, taking gaps other pilots would think twice before chancing, bringing the autarch and his seer council down undetected near the raging battle at the foot of the western valley cliffs.

Sunspear bounded from the craft, the seers close behind, their psychic weaponry crackling with witchlight. The Serpent rose into the air, the hatch closing, starcannons swivelling in its turret in search of immediate threat.

The direction the melee lay in was unmistakable. The roaring of the voidspawn and the delicate chatter of eldar weaponry came from the south.

'Follow me!' shouted the autarch. Breaking into a sprint, he leapt surefootedly from slippery branch to rotting trunk without error.

A whirling combat greeted them. Snake-bodied monstrosities of various breeds assailed a broad front of Aspect Warriors. Squads were falling back to their transports as ordered, a large group of Dire Avengers and Howling Banshees holding the creatures in place. The guard served their purpose well, but their numbers were being whittled down despite their skill. Howling Banshees leapt all over the creatures as the Dire Avengers riddled them with shuriken fire. Although the smaller creatures were felled by the discs once sufficient had found their mark, the larger serpents seemed impervious to their edges. Worse, the psychic shock masks of the Banshees seemed to have no effect upon any of the creatures.

The autarch levelled his fusion gun and vaporised one of the smaller worms without slowing. He headed for a trio of giants, each several eldar in height. Forlissiar, Kellian and Serriestalor strode forwards, runes circling them. Kellian cast his singing spear into the fray. It looped around, taking three lesser serpents to their deaths in turn. Witchlight blazed from Forlissiar's hands and lightning arced over the bodies of the beasts, leaping from creature to creature and erupting through their chests, felling more.

And then the hive mind turned its attention upon the scene, and the eldar screamed. Sunspear staggered, his spirit crushed. For just a second, he wished to flee and hide from the scrutiny of the terrible being staring at him. He became aware of his own insignificance, he was no more than a particle of food. The hive mind's ancient intellect was as wide as the void, its examination of him was a cold spike through his heart, and his mind was swamped by endless horror.

One of the warlocks collapsed, light pouring from his eye-lenses. He babbled nonsense in a hard alien tongue, and died. Serriestalor screamed and screamed, clutching his helmet. The other psykers rallied themselves, redoubling their psychic defences. It took all their effort just to keep the pressure of the hive mind at bay, and their offence died to nothing.

The Aspect Warriors, their own psychic natures buried deep, were less affected. A few of them faltered under the assault; two were swept up by the spiked limbs of a writhing beast as they stumbled, another swallowed whole by a broad-mouthed horror.

'We can do nothing more here!' said Kellian. He shouted as if his voice were battling a great noise, but the roar was in his mind. 'The skein is hidden from us, we can offer no further aid!'

Sunspear nodded. 'Withdraw!' he shouted.

'I remain with you,' said Kellian. 'Someone must.'

'As you wish,' said Sunspear, then dived into the fight.

His chainsword sang. Only a handful of the smaller serpents remained, but the three giant beasts were unharmed. He attacked one directly, slicing a gash down its side. He sought nearby support, ordering the fire of the tanks atop the cliffs into the animals. The machines locked him into their targeting matrix. Laser bolts and lance beams followed an eyeblink later, hammering into the rearmost serpent. It rose up to a terrifying height. Tail sweeping, it swatted trees and warriors alike aside.

Sunspear sighted his fusion gun at its head and gave fire. The air shimmered and roared in a line between gun and beast, atoms agitated by high-frequency electromagnetic waves. The monster thrashed all the more as its brain was cooked. Sunspear calmly tracked its head, not letting the beam be broken. He leapt over its tail as it swept at him. A scorched hole appeared in the creature's skull, and it crashed down, dead.

Sunspear dashed onwards. He sent a command pulse to silence the bombardment as it threatened the Aspect Warriors still fighting. He leapt nimbly from tree trunk to tree trunk, pushing off from two close together to gain height. As he leapt from the trees straight at a second trygon, he tossed his sword upwards, snatched it back out of the air in a reverse grip, and buried it in the belly of the creature.

The beast howled, its long body whipping madly. Sunspear lost his fusion gun. He deactivated his chainsword's teeth with a thought and clung on to the embedded weapon for grim death. He grabbed at it with his free hand, and planted his feet firmly on the beast's flesh. Bracing himself thusly, he shot his scorpion's sting repeatedly into its side. The monster swung its head back, trying to snap its jaws around the irritation riding it, but Sunspear ducked, activated his sword again, pulled it free and pushed off backwards. He executed a somersault in the air, landing heavily, recovering just in time to leap aside as six bladed limbs hammered into the ground where he had been standing.

The beast was weakening. Banshees took advantage of its distraction to attack its exposed belly, power swords crackling with every impact. The gut wall gave way under the flurry of blows. There was little viscera; this was a fighting creature, short-lived. Strange organs revealed themselves to the Banshees, who riddled them with laser bolts.

From somewhere behind Sunspear, Kellian's singing spear soared over his head and took the creature in the throat. The serpent flopped over its dead companion, and lay still.

Sunspear caught his breath. The third beast, the wide-mawed one, was dying under a barrage of fusion gun fire coming from a squad of advancing Fire Dragons.

He signalled the Banshee exarch. Unusually, a male. 'Aseterion, where is the rest of the battle group?'

'Delayed, Autarch Sunspear. The ambush slowed our withdrawal, they are under attack.'

'The Great Dragon turns its attention that way, autarch,' said Kellian. 'We have our chance. Bring forth Khaine now!'

Sunspear retrieved his fusion gun and allowed the exarch and warriors to guide him, leaving his map dormant for fear of its distractions.

They came to the edge of a low rise; below them an arc of Aspect Warriors were embattled by dozens of large tyranid creatures. The hive mind was particularly strong here, the density of its synaptic web apparent to the sensitive eldar.

'Here,' said Sunspear. He pulled his webway homing device from his belt. Kellian leaned heavily upon a tree and inclined his head slightly in affirmation.

'Khaine will wreak much havoc.'

'Then this is the correct place,' Sunspear said to the warriors. 'Come, we will aid them, and bring the wrath of Khaine down upon the enemies of Biel-Tan. The Avatar will lead us into battle.'

Sunspear circled away from the fight at the base of the hill, taking his group of Aspect Warriors with him. Kellian remained behind; the might of the hive mind was taking its toll upon him, but he shielded Sunspear and his warrior band from its psychic senses as best he could. They went through the trees undetected, gained the level ground without incident and ran into a clearing floored with hard stone. The forest was unexpectedly still, though the combat rumbled on out of sight. There were no voidspawn present. All had been drawn off in the swarm's attempt to destroy the Aspect Warrior force.

Sunspear tapped at the floor. What at first looked to be a natural stone pavement was in fact made up of shattered paving slabs. He looked around, at moss-covered boulders and lumps in the understorey. On second inspection, many looked formed by sentient hands.

'A garden of the old empire. A fitting place to call forth our wrath,' he said.

With a flick of his thumb, Sunspear activated his webway beacon, casting it into the air. It hovered, spinning, gentle light emanating from it. The light intensified, glimmering like a star as the device was consumed, its power generators forcing open the skin of reality as they burned out.

A long slit appeared in the air, and widened, peeling back the forest scene as if it were upon painted cloth. A nebulous shape of light hung there.

A tremor passed through the ground. Sunspear's heart quickened, his war mask surging to the forefront of his consciousness and threatening to drown his reason in blood.

'The Avatar of Khaine! Blood will flow freely by his hand, death approaches and we serve,' Aseterion whispered, joy in his voice. His mostly female shrine set up an ululating cry, while the Fire Dragons and Dire Avengers with Sunspear declaimed their own complex war chants.

An outstretched hand the size of an eldar's torso emerged from the portal. Hot blood dripped from it, hissing when it hit the mossy paving. The Avatar stepped through the rent in reality, and onto the surface of Dûriel.

The Avatar resembled a stylised statue of an eldar warrior, many times life size, its roaring face crowned with a regal helm. A core of white-hot metal was its body, iron plates that glowed red with heat its armour. In its hand it held a long spear, the Suin Daellae, the Wailing Doom. The weapon sang its wrathful song, and it fired the eldar's hearts with battle lust. The warriors whooped louder as they gathered around it, hands tightening on weapons in their eagerness to spill blood.

'Now,' said Sunspear, his voice hard and savage, 'let us sever mind from flesh, and destroy the ability of our foe to control its body. Onwards, to glory and the restoration of our kind!'

'Biel-Tan! Biel-Tan! Biel-Tan!' the Aspect Warriors chanted.

The smouldering figure of the Avatar leading the way, the eldar fell upon the concentration of tyranids.

Thurliarissa and the Shrine of the Patient Blade killed and killed, and the tide of voidspawn did not abate. Four great creatures directed the horde of red and bone beasts, guarded by squat, dome-headed monstrosities. At their command, waves of shrieking monsters crashed into the Aspect Warriors. Raw terror emanated from these leader things, battering at the minds of the eldar, causing them to falter and sapping the strength from their blows. Even so, many of the eldar had managed to withdraw, breaking free to go back to the transports and reinforce the eastern front. Wave Serpents rushed overhead, heading for the spore-hazed cliffs on the far side of the valley. That was good.

Thurliarissa was lost in her art, the five minds that made up her personality working as one, drawing on dozens of arcs of experience. Although the Great Dragon was a new foe in the galaxy, many savage beasts and psychic horrors had fallen to her blades over the aeons and she was not afraid.

She slashed and cut, severing weapon-limbs at the elbow, ripping open hardened thoraxes, blasting shuriken from the pistols built into her chainsabres into vulnerable eyes and mouths. Not all weak points could be engineered away.

She bent over backwards as a crackling sword of bone swept over her. The creature that wielded it did not hold the weapon; rather the hilt was melded to its hand, ribbed tubes going from the sword into the arm. Thurliarissa caught sight of dark eyes near the base of the blade, vestigial legs fused to the fingers of the warrior beast wielding it. It too was alive. A claw came after the sword, then another, weaving a cage of talons around her. She saw the sword coming again, and did an elegant cartwheel away. She spun on her heel, driving her chainsabre into the hilt of the living weapon and cracking its shell. The sword squealed piteously; the creature carrying it roared, sharing its weapon's pain, and she took her chance. Dodging under its other arms, she raised her fists and decapitated the creature with a hail of shuriken. It staggered forwards, arms waving, the body perhaps under control of its symbiote-sword, but its mind was evidently not strong enough, and it jerked spasmodically before crashing down.

The Shrine of the Patient Blade was down to five. Four of her warriors had been killed, including rash Dariathanar. He had lost the opportunity to learn his lesson of earlier in the day.

Her warriors fought well, working in pairs as the scorpion's claw works with its sting, pinning and then destroying alien after alien. Not far from her position, Dire Avengers of the Diligence of the Argent Fault Forgotten cleared a wide arc with the endless firing patterns of their catapults. The ground before them was littered with shattered flesh, and sodden with alien life fluids.

The Burning Rebuke fought again alongside the Patient Blade, Oskirithil of the Sorrows directing his warriors to vaporise those creatures too mighty for the Striking Scorpions' weapons. And so, as each eldar was deadly in his or her own right and was made deadlier by fluid cooperation within the squads, the multipliers of force where several different elements worked together were astounding. This is art, Thurliarissa thought, the greatest art known to our kind. She revelled in her exarchhood; a fate terrible to most eldar was to her the finest of all things the galaxy had to offer.

Yet deadly as they were, still battle's tide turned against the aspect shrines.

Fully half of the taskforce's Aspect Warriors had been trapped in the valley, attacked by voidspawn drawn to the Swordwind's initial thrust. Such was the way of the Tempest of Blades, to strike and withdraw and strike elsewhere. The greatest danger to its warriors was to become bogged down and lose their formation's fluidity. This had happened in the valley. Slowed momentarily by the ambush, they had been caught by their pursuers. Two hundred Aspect Warriors of many shrines battled the horde, but deadly as they were, they were ill-equipped to fight such a war of attrition. The eldar slew the voidspawn by the score, but every rare death they suffered in return was calamitous.

Thurliarissa glanced to their flanks and saw the Aspect Warriors were being pressed back. They were surrounded. Some kind of munition like a large fruit blurred through the air, landing in the middle of Diligence of the Argent Fault Forgotten. The seed pod erupted in a frenzy of tentacles, whipping out and tearing the Dire Avengers from their feet. Its activity reached a crescendo, ripping limbs from fragile bodies, and the tentacles fell limp, their energy expended. The Diligence of the Argent Fault Forgotten was no more.

Jetbikes and Vypers streaked overhead, strafing the horde and bringing down the living tank that had fired the strange munition, but heavier weapons were not being utilised, probably for fear of hitting the vastly outnumbered eldar in the maelstrom. The remaining three great leader-beasts, a massive swarmlord at their head, suddenly pushed forwards. No readying themselves, no sign of preparation, no signals, no warning, they just *moved*. Three-score of the large warrior organisms came with them, heading for the weakened centre of the line.

They were going to lose.

Thurliarissa vowed to sell this body's life dearly.

A bellow from the north, from the trees. The voidspawn there turned their heads as the Avatar of Khaine strode into their midst. Its green and white plume whipped in the convection currents coming off its glowing body, its green cloak streaming behind it. It cast the Wailing Doom hard. The spear sped through the air, leaving fire in its wake, and plunged into the side of one of the leader-beasts. The voidspawn crashed down, eyes smoking, its internal organs burned out from within. Before the spear flew back to the Avatar's hand he had smashed several lesser creatures down with his fists, their touch setting the broken corpses ablaze. Behind him came the Autarch Sunspear, greatest of Biel-Tan's generals, and a portion of those eldar who had earlier withdrawn.

Suddenly, explosions rippled in the forest. Thurliarissa consulted her viewing orb; Dark Reapers had been brought down from the cliffs to the east. Guardians protecting them, they fired from the trees into the rear of the alien force.

The Avatar roared, hatred emanating from it so powerfully that the hive mind shrank back as dry grass shrinks back from fire. Smoke pillared in the distance, evidence of grav-tanks scouring the valley floor with high-energy weapons.

The autarch's voice came through to her helm's ear-beads. 'We have them trapped. Destroy their leaders, let Khaine bathe in their blood, for Biel-Tan!'

'Biel-Tan! Biel-Tan! Ancient days reborn, our time comes again!' came the shout from the Swordwind, and Thurliarissa's heart sang. With laughter on her lips, she danced back into the fray.

Night came again to Dûriel. From the shelf on the mountainside the Inner Command watched the fires burn unchecked in the forests.

'Every one must be slaughtered,' said Sunspear.

'They have gone to ground, autarch, it will take some time,' Autarch Hethaeliar the Fourth-Blooded said.

'It is to be expected. Their leaders slain, they will revert to animalistic impulses. At the least they will stay put and await their end. Seers?'

'The mind of the Great Dragon is in disarray,' said Kellian. 'Its presence is upon the skein heavily, yet here it has little influence. We have rooted out the greater beasts of Far Ranging Hunger, rupturing its synaptic web. The integration between Far Ranging Hunger and Starving Dragon has yet to begin. The lesser creatures of Far Ranging Hunger will be easy prey to our warriors.'

'Do not be so certain, Kellian, it ever was your weakness to see invincibility in Biel-Tan's greatness,' Forlissiar said. 'As it is our autarch's.'

Kellian bowed his head in acknowledgement of the older seer's rebuke. 'And yet you have thus far been wrong.'

'Autarch Sunspear has fought a masterful engagement, it is true, and flawlessly exploited fate. The fact remains that we are pressed. As you yourself say, autarch, we do not have much time. We have kept the swarms apart, but to what end? Can we annihilate them all? I think not. The joining has yet to commence, but it will not be long before the fleets' minds merge and then we will have a far more numerous foe to contend with.'

'But how long will that take?' said Kellian. 'I see much confusion.'

'It is a mistake to think of them as separate entities, they are one and the same,' said Forlissiar. 'I see a great chance that their bonding will go quickly. Once the two fleets are of one psychic accord, it does not matter how stealthy we are, the greater numbers of Starving Dragon will fall on us. And what of the creatures yet in orbit? There are several hundred of their hive ships, no doubt greatly equipped with more monstrosities to unleash upon us. One spore fall, and our work will be undone. We will have achieved a worthless victory at great cost in eldar lives.'

'I have the night,' said Sunspear.

'You do, but it will not be enough. Daybreak will bring more death, and defeat,' said Forlissiar. 'This I foresee.'

Sunspear turned away from the flames in the valley and stared at the farseer. 'That is as may be. We have bought Iyanden time.'

'Ah, so you retreat from your initial aim of victory alone?'

Sunspear twitched with annoyance.

'And this time. Time bought for what?' said Forlissiar. 'Altariec saw this clearly also. They have no means of preventing this merging. Even together, the two craftworlds are outmatched.'

Sunspear shook his head. 'You are wrong. Kellian does not agree with you, nor did Serriestalor.'

'Serriestalor's mind is greatly ravaged, a direct consequence of his taking part in this battle. His personal experience indicates that, just perhaps, his opinion was incorrect,' said Forlissiar mildly.

The autarch looked out from the mountain again, across the fires, to where, in the distance, the bioluminescence of the feeding Starving Dragon glimmered in the night. 'Time is all we need, and time I have secured. Between us, Iyanden and Biel-Tan have the might. We will not be denied victory. I can feel it.'

Forlissiar moved dismissively. 'You are no seer, autarch. Vague feelings are no match for the skein.'

'And the skein is nothing without will and the sword's edge to make it,' countered the autarch. 'You are timid. We will scour this valley of Far Ranging Hunger's creatures, and be away.'

In the valley, the slaughter continued.

CHAPTER SIX

LEVIATHAN AWAKENS

The next morning came swift and sultry, the carefully engineered climate disrupted long ago by the carelessness of the human interlopers. The sun was a bloated orb, its light dispersed by the thickening of the atmosphere. Angry red clouds striated the sky, and there was a sharp scent on the air that, although faint, induced a sensation of queasiness in the eldar if breathed too long without filtering. Far to the south, a thick black band of cloud cast shadows upon the dying planet, shafts of sunlight stabbing through to impale the scarred lands below – sunspears. The autarch thought this a good omen.

Sunspear stood on the lip of the rock shelf, staring out at the ravaged world. His helmet was off, his topknot blowing in the stiff, hot wind. He let his body relax, allowed its sensations to engage his mind; the feel of the airflow over the runes of dried blood painted on his face, the way his feet made tiny adjustments to keep him steady, the grit under the soles of his boots, the clasp of his armour, the drag of his cloak as it billowed. The light sparkling from the salt in the dried seas arrested him, his heart swelled with profoundly sweet melancholy, and he allowed himself to enjoy the ruination of a world.

'It is beautiful, is it not?' said Forlissiar, coming up behind him. Kellian was there too. Both were fully masked and robed.

Sunspear nodded. 'Our ancestors saw the beauty in destruction, but it is unwise to appreciate it for too long.' He turned his attention to the valley. Smoke, trapped by temperature inversion, formed a bluish pall over the trees. The sun had not yet cast the full force of its light upon the ground there, and through the haze bright points of smouldering forest twinkled like dying stars. The eldar's weapons were generally too quiet to be heard at such a distance, but the occasional crack as a laser beam superheated and displaced the air and the thin roars of dying creatures came to their ears frequently.

'How fares the hunt?' asked Sunspear.

'The psychic presence of the hive mind remains strong,' Kellian said, gesturing upwards. 'The fleet of Far Ranging Hunger remains in orbit, and moves towards that of Starving Dragon.'

'We inhibit this fate in one theatre, another remains,' said Forlissiar. 'The beasts of the earth may be prevented from merging, but the Great Dragon sails the void unopposed. You have led well here, autarch, but it was ever a fool's errand.'

Sunspear scowled. 'And I say no again. Iyanden will be here soon. With our fleets combined, we shall scour the voidspawn from space as surely as we have from the ground.'

Forlissiar assumed the posture of extreme disagreement, shoulders back, one fist upon his hip. 'That is a–'

A frantic communication interrupted their argument. A Vyper patrol. 'Autarch! To the south!'

'Manifest the image,' said Sunspear, cutting through the pilot's panicked voice. He placed his helmet on.

When his helm activated, the viewing globe came to life in front of him. The storm clouds to the south leapt into tight focus, a Vyper banking round in front of them.

'They move against the wind,' said Kellian.

'Those are not clouds,' said Sunspear.

The image zoomed in. What appeared to be storm clouds was a wall of winged tyranids, thousands of paces across. Not red and bone, but purple and ghostly white.

'Starving Dragon has awoken, as I predicted,' whispered Forlissiar. 'We are discovered.'

'Why was I not warned?' said Sunspear. Dread gripped him.

'The skein is clouded, autarch–' began Kellian, but Forlissiar interrupted, his voice hard.

'You were warned, autarch. We told you, Altariec and I, that this venture was doomed. And behold, your doom approaches. If we survive, I pray our counsel will carry more weight next time you march to war.'

Sunspear dismissed the image.

Forlissiar dipped into the skein. 'You will withdraw, and you will salvage your reputation.'

Sunspear looked into the valley. His warriors, unaware of what approached, continued the hunt. 'No. The task is almost done.'

'You will withdraw,' repeated Forlissiar.

Sunspear's pride overwhelmed him. He would not add defeat to his unblemished tally of victories. 'No!' he shouted. 'We need only a little more time.'

For the second time in two days, Thurliarissa found herself retreating. She fought as if possessed by Khaine himself. Screaming hordes of winged aliens fell from the skies, swooping low to discharge their vile flesh weapons at the Aspect Warriors. The sky was black with them, numberless pairs of wings blotting out the sun. The aliens' composite mind was a crushing presence. A cold intelligence regarded her through a million eyes, staring at her with an indifference that made her feel small and afraid, ancient and powerful though she was; prey for an infinitely superior being.

'Starving Dragon!' came the cry over the communications network. 'Starving Dragon has awoken!'

First was a shadow on the sky, a swirling mass that could have been mistaken for smoke driven into frantic curls by some inferno. As the eldar paused in their hunt for Far Ranging Hunger's creatures to look up at this new occurrence, the reddish sun went dim.

The swarm had fallen upon them, and the fight for survival had begun.

Leathery wings flapped at Thurliarissa as small beasts scrabbled hard claws against her. Guns and mouths ejaculated searing acids onto her armour that pitted its ancient surface. Under such pressure, her personalities coalesced into near-perfect unity, each one of the souls which made up Thurliarissa supporting the others.

She swiped her chainsabres through delicate membranes, sending creatures crashing down. She stepped and whirled, ending the lives of crippled voidspawn with controlled bursts of shuriken fire, or blasting away their faces with her scorpion's sting. Metal splinters shot from her mandibles; atomised by high-intensity laser blasts in the air, they burned flesh from the creatures with ease.

The shouts from her squad were losing their joy, becoming those of alarm rather than exhilaration. She ducked as a warrior variant swooped low on broad wings, claws outstretched. It missed her, only to jink sideways and snatch away Raelian. He struggled in its grip, blasted at its underside with sting and pistol simultaneously, but it bore him away into the flapping maelstrom and she did not see him again.

Her shrine was down to three members besides herself. They worked their way together, fighting in perfect concert, each blow powered by desperation. The swarm whirled around them, crashing through the thin trees of the forest. They caught glimpses of aerial combats: Swooping Hawks mobbed by dozens of creatures, jetbikes moving at insane speeds, far faster than the winged beasts could fly, dodging artfully only to be dragged down by the sheer density of the creatures. A constant rain of squirming bugs and weapon fluids spattered the ground, spent ammunition fired above them. A Crimson Hunter flight screamed overhead, spitting rapid death from its wingtips, but the skies were clogged, and one suddenly lurched to the side, flames spewing from its port engine, the result of an alien being sucked into its air intake. It plummeted, winged horrors bouncing from its fairing, going down somewhere to the south-west.

'Exarch, I fear we are overmatched,' said Ulieneathar, one of her last remaining warriors.

'We shall fight on, we kill as many as we can, we die with pride,' said the exarch, leaping high to eviscerate another large beast. It slammed into the ground. Creatures were falling from the sky, crashing through the trees. The noise of the swarm was tremendous, as overwhelming to the ears as the hive mind's presence was to the mind, a hideous cacophony.

Falcon grav-tanks drove overhead, turrets swivelling. 'Even the poorest marksman cannot hope to miss!' said Ulieneathar, and laughed.

A scream to the left. Hadirel went down, clawing at his shattered faceplate. Blood spurted as writhing grubs pushed through the fingers clutching the wound and into the soft meat beneath. Three of them left in total.

The gems of Thurliarissa's communications suite coloured red. A command pulse, broadwave broadcast. A voice spoke solemnly in her ear-beads.

'Retreat, retreat. The day is lost. Retreat, retreat. We return home to mourn our dead.'

Maps sprang up in her lower visual field – fallback points.

'We must fall back,' she said coldly. 'The fight is done untimely, home awaits us.' What did she have to fear, who had lived lifetime after lifetime? Her last two warriors, Ulieneathar and Ralitheen, signalled their understanding. They turned and ran.

Foliage whipped across their faces. Creatures came at them from everywhere. Thurliarissa threw herself aside as a pair of Swooping Hawks crashed into the ground directly in her path, mauled flesh bloody through their broken armour. Something exploded in the sky, and burning debris pattered down. Slow-moving creatures, large as young void whales, had joined the swarm. Hundreds of the smaller beasts detached from these aerial brood mothers. Wings sharply folded, they swooped upon the fleeing eldar like eagles.

Other warriors joined the Patient Blade, far-spread squads who had been engaged in the hunt for Far Ranging Hunger's remnants converging on the evacuation point. Thurliarissa snapped off shots as creatures lunged for her. Their death screams, she fancied, were more of frustration than pain. Ulieneathar killed a couple of the lesser types with his shuriken pistol. Ralitheen chopped in a controlled frenzy about herself, every blow severing a wing and tumbling a screeching monster to the ground. Fist-sized beasts bounced from Thurliarissa's armour, tiny mouths lined with rows of diamond-hard teeth snapping at her. She crushed them underfoot, where she could.

There were several dozen eldar Aspect Warriors streaming back. Their shrine markings were familiar to her from long association; Burning Rebuke, Hail of Tears, the Edge of Silence... They were all depleted, most under half strength, and they were still falling, plucked from the forest floor or smashed to the ground as multiple creatures mobbed them.

Calm instructions came to them over the communications web, directing them slightly to the west. They went up an incline. The noise of engines reached Thurliarissa's ears, then heavy weapons fire.

A dozen grav-tanks were arrayed in a circle in a break in the trees, guns blazing at everything around them. Laser light and actinic bolts of plasma lit up the clearing, large-diameter shuriken scythed the sky of monsters. It rained burning tyranids, and the assault on the group grew less ferocious.

Guardian squads aided by the Shrieking Havoc shrine swept the evacuation zone free of voidspawn. Thurliarissa was a warrior first and foremost; death held little fear for her, for she was unlikely ever to truly die. If she did, another would come, don her armour and add their soul to those who had gone before.

But even she felt relief.

Eldar were emerging from the trees, pursued by warrior beasts. The monsters, intent upon their pursuit, ran straight into the barrage of cannon fire streaking from the tanks, and the eldar broke free. By order from the Inner Command, some joined the firing lines of eldar, others ran up the boarding ramps of the tanks. When full, the tanks closed up their doors and shot off into the sky, using their greater speed and agility to evade the swarm. Thurliarissa saw the flare of webway gates on the mountaintop, another storm of weapons fire there clearing a way for the tanks to drop off their passengers. Other tanks landed, empty, their doors hissing open and turrets adding to the aerial barrage around the clearing.

The tanks were several hundred paces away. Thurliarissa shouted for her last warriors to run. They were nearly there.

A roar split the air. A giant creature landed directly in front of her, the ground shaking with the impact of its taloned feet. A hive tyrant, a general of Starving Dragon. It bellowed again, raising its high-horned head to the heavens, wings spread wide. Thurliarissa took this as a challenge.

The creature was three times her height, heavily built, and surrounded by an aura of utter malevolence. Below the wings, two enormous weapon arms were held up in front of it, similar to those of a praying mantis, but broad and flat, the deep purple carapace on the front full of tiny holes. The creature shook, and these arms twitched, shooting a shower of sharp-toothed organisms at Thurliarissa. She dodged, but some caught her. The impact was phenomenal, the velocity of the creatures equal to that of solid-shell bullets. One of the things found a chink in her armour, and pain flared as it burrowed manically into her flesh. She ripped the grub out, crushing it between armoured fingertips.

The creature charged, horned head down. The psychic horror it projected had little effect on Thurliarissa. She had in her time fought the daemonic servants of She Who Thirsts, and the perils of the flesh held no fear for her. But it was big, and fast, and her battle skills were sorely taxed by its prowess.

The club-like weapons limbs flicked forwards. The air they displaced buffeted Thurliarissa as she pivoted on her back foot, bending her lithe body around the arms. As they passed, she saw the rear sides were lined with hundreds of triangular plates like teeth, each serrated and deadly sharp. She responded with a volley of shuriken at the creature's eyes. The disks embedded themselves in its armour, only one finding its way through to the soft flesh beneath. The tyrant blew out air from its nostrils, and slammed its curved arms forwards again, whipping them back as fast in an attempt to snag her on their rear-facing blades.

Again she twisted, avoiding the blades by a hair's breadth. She dropped to the floor, and slashed with her chainblades. The diamond teeth of the weapons caught at the horny plates covering the creature's legs, jolting her arms, but did not cut through. She was forced to roll away as a foot descended, the sharp hoof and subsidiary claws upon its ankle biting deep into the ground.

Then Ulieneathar and Ralitheen were there, chainswords purring, raking the beast with shuriken fire from both sides. Through its pounding legs, she saw the flashes of colour as eldar sprinted past. Time slowed as her mind was filled with the memories of a hundred similar combats, each aspect of her composite soul appreciating the recollections in its own, subtly different way.

She pulled her knees under her. Pushing off from her feet, she leapt between the creature's legs as it slammed Ralitheen to the side with its clubbed forelimbs.

Ulieneathar drove his chainsword into the back of the creature's knee joint. It stumbled forwards, wrenching the weapon from his hands.

'Run! Run! This foe is too great for us!' Thurliarissa called. Ralitheen was up and into a limping run, Ulieneathar sprinting ahead. The hive tyrant lumbered in pursuit. Building up speed, it spread its wings, gliding after them.

A crack of superheated air had Thurliarissa's ears ringing as a lance beam snapped out from a Guardian support platform. It caught the tyrant square in its wing joint. The spread limb furled awkwardly, and the tyrant came down. As it got to its feet, other weapons came to bear on the giant beast, hammering into it mercilessly. Its chitin cracked, luminous ichor spilling down its exoskeleton. It roared weakly, and sank forwards.

Thurliarissa and her remaining warriors made it into a waiting Falcon grav-tank. Three more eldar leapt in after them. Warriors jumped into three other transports alongside their own, and the doors began to close.

The voidspawn were not done with the Patient Blade. With the tanks concentrating fire on the hive tyrant, a sudden surge of beasts flew in over the evacuation zone. Shuriken whistled at them in an upward hail, felling dozens. Scores got through.

As one, they opened fire, sending a tide of living ammunition streaming into the holds of the grav-tanks. The door to Thurliarissa's transport hissed shut, sealing the warriors into the craft with thousands of squirming weapons grubs.

The creatures spasmed violently, expending what little life they had to destroy the eldar. First to fall was Ulieneathar, shrieking horribly as the beetle-like constructs burrowed through the weaknesses in his armour and through the hardened bodyglove beneath. Then Ralitheen. And finally Thurliarissa. They all swatted at their limbs, fingers digging frantically at flesh to pull the creatures out, but there were too many.

Pain of a kind Thurliarissa had never felt overwhelmed her as the creatures chewed through her soft tissues, their barbed bodies scraping against her bones. Acidic secretions burned her nerves. The strength left her legs. She collapsed to the floor, and was engulfed by the grubs.

The last thing Thurliarissa heard in this life was the screams of eldar in many transports being devoured alive.

All over the Valley of the Gods and the Godpeak, eldar were withdrawing. Craft fell from the sky as they were overwhelmed. Grav-tanks were chased by shimmering clouds of living ammunition. Webway portals burst wide as squads and vehicles fell back. Here and there, daring seers dropped webway beacons, and temporary doors opened into the network, allowing the evacuation of isolated units who otherwise seemed trapped.

It was as close to a rout as any withdrawal Sunspear had overseen. Screams filled the airwaves, adding to the insidious terror projected by the hive mind. Purple and white tyranids broke like a wild sea upon small islands of eldar resistance.

Sunspear remained to the end, directing the heavy weapons fire of his weapons batteries and tanks to aid the evacuation as best he could. To the west, on a crag below the command post, his Revenants fought with three gigantic hive crones, the bladed tips of the tyranids' limbs slicing curls of wraithbone from the Titans' armour. He clenched his teeth as he watched a giant winged creature knock a war walker from a cliff, snatch up a second in its claws and drop it onto the rocks below. In the valley, the Avatar of Khaine battled on, its giant form reduced to a glow surrounded by darting shadows by distance. Sunspear watched as its fires were gradually eclipsed by the creatures attacking it.

He could not save it. Shame filled him.

'The heavier elements of our force have withdrawn from the valley, Autarch Sunspear,' said Hethaeliar the Fourth-Blooded, her sing-song voice as empty of emotion as ever.

'What of Guardian group Whispering Aid?'

'All dead, autarch. As with so many others, their waystones remain where they have fallen. It is something of good fortune that none, as yet, have been destroyed.'

'How many dead?' said Sunspear quietly. A Crimson Hunter exploded in the valley below. To his left, a range of support weapons intensified fire to the front of the rock shelf, battering a rearing harridan out of the sky. Its cargo of gargoyle children shrieked as they burned.

'Four hundred and eighty-seven,' she said. She shrugged. 'None damned. That is a thing.'

'It is a thing,' agreed Sunspear without conviction. 'Sound the final retreat.'

'What of the Avatar, autarch?' said Hethaeliar.

Sunspear turned away from the battle below, refusing to look at the place he had last seen the god-fragment. His posture told Hethaeliar all she needed to know. Sunspear looked at the farseers by his Wave Serpent, entirely occupied with keeping the morale-sapping presence of the hive mind at bay. His heart was like lead, his tongue ashen. 'I will inform the farseers myself.'

Hethaeliar the Fourth-Blooded dipped her head. 'As you wish, Autarch Sunspear.'

Her words were bland. Hethaeliar seemed entirely emotionless outside of combat, but within the carefully phrased statement, Sunspear detected her censure.

The eldar left Dûriel. The last to leave were the great Revenants, the rearmost covering his sibling as the webway portal gaped wide to allow his entrance. Stalking backwards, pulsars blazing, the second Revenant left the plateau below the summit of the Godpeak.

Within, wayseers hastily performed the rites of closing, sealing shut that which had been shut for ten thousand passes, but they worked under great pressure, and the hive mind battered at them as they sought to lock the way. Thinking their task done, these eldar returned to their ships with heavy hearts, not knowing that the doors had not been closed.

* * *

Deep in the forests of Dûriel, a pile of corpses stirred. An eye opened underneath a tangle of limbs. With a snorting grunt, a leader-beast stood tall.

A four-armed creature, a great swarmlord possessed of deadly and sure purpose. The eldar had been thorough, but the creature's cunning was depthless, with a sharp mind of its own, and able to draw upon millions of years of the hive mind's experience. Red and bone was its armour, the colours of Far Ranging Hunger. It roamed the mountainside, gathering to it those of its kind that had survived, burrowed in the ground, hidden in cracks in the earth, or lurking under mounds of dead warrior beasts. As the hive mind, focused through this leader, made contact with the primitive cortices of the creatures they ceased their basic behaviours, sharpness returned to their eyes, and they moved with surer purpose. Those of Starving Dragon fell under its influence also, quickening in infinitesimal steps the merging of the two branches of the hive mind present on Dûriel.

All over Dûriel, Leviathan calmed, going back to its feeding. But Kraken did not. Scouring the site of the battle, the tyrant at last came to the peak of the mountain. There, through unearthly senses, it spied an emanation of energy suspended above the ground.

Driven by the limitless malice of the hive mind, it went to investigate.

CHAPTER SEVEN
STRANGE AMBASSADORS

There was no joyous welcome for Sunspear's force. The ships exited the webway and slid into the docks of the Tower of Bloodied Knives without fanfare. A semi-circle of seers awaited him, heads bowed and expressions grim.

+They believe he has failed,+ mind-whispered Taec to Kelmon. The two of them were on a balcony overlooking the quayside. Crowds of silent eldar looked on with them, lining the walkways and viewing platforms that jutted over the quays. Many cast their eyes askance at the Iyandeni. Kelmon's presence elicited abhorrence in the Biel-Tanian civilians already, and Taec was uncomfortably aware that they were held accountable for Sunspear's defeat. Their staring annoyed him.

He was feeling wearier than usual today. That morning he had noticed crystal strands shining in his hair, fascinatingly supple, yet not of his earthly body. The tingling in his crystallising limbs was stronger. He had an urge to return to the Dome of Crystal Seers on Iyanden and sit, never to rise again. He put the call from his mind. There were more pressing matters to hand before he could take to his rest.

+His chances were never great,+ said Kelmon. +And yet I believe although he may have failed in his aims, he might yet have succeeded in ours.+

'Time has been bought,' said Taec aloud.

'Time has been bought,' agreed Kelmon. 'With eldar blood, but yes, time has been bought. We may yet be successful in preventing the joining, if we can persuade them to venture to Dûriel one last time.'

'Lose one battle to win the war. If only it could have been achieved in another way.'

'You of all people know well that sacrifice is demanded if we are to survive as a race,' intoned Kelmon, his deep, dead voice well-suited to the solemnity of the occasion.

Taec thought of the vision of his own demise, and he shuddered.

They watched as floating biers bearing eldar corpses were brought from the ships. Those on the Path of Mourning wailed at their sides. A group of spirit-seers fell in with the first of the biers, leading them to Biel-Tan's Catacombs of Repose, where their waystones would be ritually removed. Waystone caskets were interspersed in the funeral procession, carrying the gems of those whose bodies could not be retrieved.

Sunspear, his helm under his arm, went before the semicircle of seers. The three farseers with him joined at the horns of the group to face him. Sunspear was renowned as a haughty figure, self-assured, but the eldar Taec saw moved stiffly, keeping his eyes from the line of the dead and bodiless moving slowly past him. A gasp went up from the silent crowds as he knelt before them, an unusual mark of humility. He cast his arms wide, head bowed.

'An act of contrition, but for what?' asked Taec. 'What has befallen Biel-Tan?'

An iron throne was led out from the ship's wide doors: gravitic motors humming, surrounded by an honour guard of exarchs, empty of its god-fragment.

'He has lost Biel-Tan's Avatar,' said Kelmon. 'That is why he kneels. Troubling, most troubling.'

Taec glanced at his one-time rival. 'The skein grows ever more tangled,' he said.

'We said that a conventional strike would avail us nothing!' said Altariec angrily, his staff levelled at Sunspear's chest. The autarch had changed from his armour, wearing robes coloured the white of mourning. 'The skein was clear on this – the swarm of Far Ranging Hunger would be too numerous to extirpate from Dûriel by the Swordwind's efforts alone, it was said, and so it proved to be. What have you achieved, O vaunted son of Biel-Tan? Nothing!' Altariec slammed his staff hard upon the floor. 'Nothing I say, save death and the loss of eldar souls to our ever-thirsting enemy.'

'The thirst of one enemy is tantalised so the hunger of another might be blunted,' said Sunspear. He held his gaze level on the farseer. 'We have traded life for time.'

'And for what?' said Altariec. 'So that the mating of the Dragons might take place two cycles later than at first fate decreed? Oh, a fine bargain you have struck for the children of Biel-Tan. We thank you, great and mighty autarch.' Altariec gave a deeply mocking bow, causing a flurry of shocked chatter to fly around the chamber.

'Iyanden's warriors are coming,' said Sunspear, raising his hand in Taec Silvereye's direction. 'We are honoured by the presence of the current head of the seer council, as well as the presence of the former.'

They debated in the Chamber of Seers, an ornate spherical space ranked with many podiums that eldar stood upon, each encased in his own column of light. Many dozens of eldar psykers were there, not only those tasked with guiding the craftworld's fate, but warlocks, senior bonesingers, wayseers, pathmasters and more; all had a say in the affairs of the seer council of Biel-Tan. The craftworld's numerous autarchs were there in force, nearly twenty of them, stood in a block of seats of their own. Not all of them supported Sunspear's efforts, and those minority that did not stood apart from their fellows, a line of empty podiums dividing them cleanly.

The debating floor was a mosaic composed of giant gemstones, paving slabs of diamond, emerald and star sapphire, interspersed with panels of red grasses, different species artfully planted and cut to form intricate patterns. Altariec and Sunspear faced each other over it.

'And they are welcome here,' said Altariec, in breathtaking opposition to his actual welcome of Taec and Kelmon, 'but they are but two, while the children of Far Ranging Hunger and Starving Dragon are effectively numberless. The warriors of Iyanden are many cycles away. And how many, we do not know – they are in the webway, and our communications to them are delayed or dispersed by the mind of the Dragon. We have had no reply from them, as Iyanden did not receive our reply to their petition for aid.'

Taec was troubled by this, for he too had been unable to get through to the Phoenix Host. It was as if the Great Devourer had cast a shroud upon the eternity matrix; that, or darker forces had. It was a possibility that troubled him.

'The council voted to approve the mission,' said Sunspear coldly. 'You, the elder of the council, may not have agreed with the decision, but the vote was a clear majority.'

'We approved a limited strike! You exceeded your remit, autarch, and provoked a sleeping giant. Our children paid the cost for your arrogance,' said Altariec.

'I saw a chance to further the future of the empire.' Sunspear threw his hands up, and turned slowly on the spot, addressing the entire chamber. 'The skein is shrouded, the mind of the Dragon blinds you, you all say so. At times like this, we must look to other means of decision-making. Would you have me hold back, only for unseen opportunities to slip away to our detriment? Would you look back, and see in retrospect on a clear skein how things might have been, and weep? No! I did what had to be done.'

Forlissiar stood to speak. 'It is true that Autarch Sunspear performed magnificently under the circumstances.'

'Thank you, Forlissiar,' said Sunspear.

Altariec sneered.

'I did say under the circumstances, autarch. My blandishments are not without caveat. But blandishments they are. Even I admit this, Altariec, and I am one of your chief supporters. You ever were the voice of caution, and we respect you for it. Indeed, in a craftworld such as ours, circumspection is to be valued, lest hotter heads drag us all down with them. But whether Sunspear was right or wrong in his attack, the problem remains. If the fleets combine, then doom will fall upon us all heavily, whether we spend the blood of our children with profligacy, or hide our warriors from harm. Our visions were quite clear on this also, were they not?'

Altariec sighed, and leaned on his staff. 'Yes, yes. It is an impossible position. I see fire and death should the Dragons merge, but the immediate future for Biel-Tan should their merging be prevented is grimmer still – seriously weakened, we will be easy prey in the arcs to come. And this is my objection, as well you know. Success is so slender a chance, no matter how we manipulate fate.'

'Should they merge, the arcs to come will be the last arcs of our kind,' said Sunspear. 'Surely you must see this?'

'You would give up?' said Taec. 'Might I speak?' he added, imploringly from face to face. Haughty Biel-Tanians looked back, their approval or lack of it masked by courtesy. 'I am a guest here, and will not unduly influence your deliberations.'

Altariec waved his hand. 'Very well. You are here. You are well respected. You may address us, Taec Silvereye of House Delgari of Iyanden.'

'My thanks to you, father of seers,' said Taec humbly to Altariec. He addressed the rest of the council. 'I understand your fears, the fate of my own people is not one I would wish upon yours. But you have seen the consequences of not acting. You all have.'

Muttered conversations sprang up in the ranks of seers and autarchs, some agreeing, others in angry dispute.

'For many arcs we were allies,' continued Taec. 'We achieved much.'

'And then you turned your backs on us,' said Altariec. 'Iyanden's aims are Biel-Tan's when it suits Iyanden, and not when it suits the future of all our people, it appears.'

'Now is not the time to argue on past disagreements,' cut in Sunspear. 'What is to be done now, that is the matter at hand.'

'Scour the planet with fire,' said Forlissiar. 'Wipe them out.'

'Crude, human almost, but feasible...' said Geraintheneth, one of the autarchs of Sunspear's camp.

'I have seen such a future,' said Taec. 'Dûriel erupting, its inner fires worn upon its skin.'

'Atmospheric ignition, that would be an effective manner of destruction,' said Hethaeliar.

Taec shook his head. 'The voidspawn will hide in the earth, and emerge after the fires abate. Not many, perhaps, but if only a few dozen of Far Ranging Hunger's beasts are taken into the embrace of Starving Dragon, we will have failed. The bio-constructs of the Great Devourer are resilient, and the mind that rides them cunning. We would have to destroy the planet from the inside out to be sure.'

'Such a thing would have been a simple matter in the elder days, but now?' said Forlissiar. 'We lack the capability. Even if we were to bring Biel-Tan itself into the system and attack with every weapon we possess we would not fracture the planet, and we will not put our home in harm's way under any circumstances. Kelmon's error is a grave lesson to us all.'

Kelmon bowed his long head in acknowledgement.

'There are still such weapons...' said Sunspear quietly, almost to himself.

Altariec ignored him. 'What then?'

'Allies,' said Forlissiar flatly. 'The threads of the skein indicated allies and a joining of purpose. It is why the council voted approval in the first place. It appears that we must gather more.'

'Allies are in short supply in this dark age,' said Altariec grimly.

'We must meditate on it,' said Taec. 'And then decide upon our course of actions.'

More talk flared up around the sphere.

'How?' shouted one. 'The skein is draped all in shadow! The future is hidden to us!'

'The Mind Choir. As we did upon Iyanden to good effect, let us do here also,' said Taec.

More talk, more arguing. Shouting erupted. The Athelin Bahail had not been attempted on Biel-Tan in some passes.

'For seers they are a fiery breed,' said Kelmon quietly as the debate raged.

'We will be thankful of that, before the end,' said Taec.

Whereas large parts of Iyanden's Dome of Crystal Seers were fashioned of crystal, showing the veins of the infinity circuit to all, much of Biel-Tan's was a series of beautifully tended gardens and lakes housed in twenty-three interconnected habitats, the infinity circuit emerging into the world but coyly, where it was not easily observed. The bodies of their crystal seers were not concentrated in one place, as was the way in Taec's home, but dotted all over the dome's parklands, so that one might walk through a peaceful copse of trees and come quite unexpectedly upon a crystal-bodied seer rooted to the ground. Warlike in life, the expression on the crystal seers' faces suggested they reached a certain peace when they joined finally with their ancestors.

The seers made their way to the central dome in ones and twos from various places, emerging from forest edges or coming in from other domes, many having withdrawn for private meditation before the group scrying. Most of the senior seers were attending the Athelin Bahail, no matter their path.

Kelmon and Taec followed Dahtarioc over rolling hills of springy turf. They walked for some time, the exercise clearing Taec's mind as much as his meditations had. At length they came to a stone amphitheatre cut into a hillside. A hundred semicircular rows of seats surrounded a glowing circle fifty paces across. There, the infinity circuit was exposed to the air. Many small groups of seers came, winding their ways over the hills. Taec felt a sudden grip of sadness at their numbers, reminded of what Iyanden had lost in its earlier battles with the Great Dragon. More than the living seers, his heart was moved by the sight of a dozen or so crystal seers sat on benches in the amphitheatre, as if they enjoyed a play after long, troubled cycles. The crystallised bodies of Iyanden's own heroes were smashed, her living seers much reduced in number.

Close to a hundred psykers of all kinds gathered in the amphitheatre. Virtually all wore robes in the green and white of Biel-Tan. There were patterns of thorns in various contrasting colours, and a number of different designs executed in differing materials, but as Taec had noted before, in Biel-Tan there was a great deal of uniformity as to how the citizens dressed. An expression of their militaristic nature, Taec supposed. Despite the gravity of the occasion, and their supposed belligerence, their spirits were light, and many laughed easily with one another as they took their places.

Taec was to take part in the scrying, and was given a place by Altariec, whose froideur towards the Iyandeni had warmed somewhat. Taec thought Altariec had acted the way he did through fear, and the prospect of being able to see clearly again removed much of this anxiety. His initial hostility towards Taec had dissipated, now that he had presented the Biel-Tanian eldar with a solution.

After Taec had been sitting for a few moments, Altariec turned to the Iyandeni. 'The path is set now,' he said. 'There is little honour or profit in opposing you, whose thread is so similar to mine. I will not apologise for my welcome, because I believe that my course is the right one still, but I have no reason to go against the rest of the council when their success would be better assured by my aid rather than opposition. I extend the palm of friendship, see it is free of weapons and ill intent.' He recited an ancient greeting, not often employed.

'I see and reciprocate, see also my hand is empty,' said Taec, somewhat taken aback by Altariec's change in mood. His friendliness made Taec like him less rather than more, as it betrayed a certain cowardice and fickleness of character that doubtless accounted for his invidiousness. Taec resolved to watch him carefully.

Altariec looked to the glowing centre of the amphitheatre. 'No doubt you think me mercurial.'

'You are of lusty temperament for a seer, it is true,' said Taec tactfully.

Altariec laughed. 'I am the son of my father, although our final paths are different. All we of Biel-Tan are warriors, but he is mighty.'

'He lives still?'

'In a manner of speaking,' said Altariec sadly. 'It seems strange, does it not? I am almost as old as you. My father fell to Khaine,' he explained. 'His body inhabits the armour of the Exarch Suilin-Kraitharath, and Suilin-Kraitharath's spirit inhabits him. In all probability not for much longer, for his body is ancient now.'

Taec nodded. 'Now I see.'

'Why I shy away from combat?' Altariec became short again.

Taec stifled an irritated sigh. 'I mean no offence. I mean only that you are less set upon it than your fellows. Did not the Asurya through the path seek to instruct us that balance is paramount in all things?'

Altariec was mollified by this, making the gesture of offence-swept-aside. 'That is why I am council head, for the little good it does me...' He trailed away and looked around. 'I see we are all gathered. We should begin.'

Kelmon was kept away from the Mind Choir. The Biel-Tanians were not forced into such close acquaintance with their dead often. The majority of their departed farseers were within the infinity core, not caught in living tombs of wraithbone armour. Kelmon was a distasteful oddity to them, no matter how much respect they bore him.

Altariec stood and addressed the seers. His introduction was to the point, and the seers slipped quickly into their trances. In the uppermost tiers of the amphitheatre, the lesser seers worked hard to push back the hateful presence of the hive mind.

For Taec, the experience was a telling one. Rarely did he join with seers of another craftworld, and he found the techniques of Biel-Tan subtly different to those of Iyanden. War and supremacy dictated the choices they made upon the skein more than any other, and their choice of rune patterns held surprising lessons for him. Taec wondered, as he had wondered before in his long life, if the temperament and character of each craftworld unduly influenced the scryings of its elders. The seers, for example, were supposed to exemplify the wisdom that the path could bring, in the same way exarchy exemplified aggression and prowess in combat, and yet he watched as they discarded threads rapidly for not according with their own view of what should be. Taec would also have discarded the majority, for the choices open to the eldar regarding Dûriel were a slender group, but he would have done so after more deliberation, and some he would have more thoroughly investigated. Perhaps, in less straitened times, he would be well instructed by scrying alongside seers of other worldships.

He tried his hardest to forget that there would not be a later for him, should all he wished for come to pass.

The skein was as before, turbulent and beset by the hive mind, although here at least he was untroubled by restless dead, Biel-Tan's being properly quiescent. Worryingly, he saw that the twin cables of the hive minds' multiple threaded destinies were already joining as the seers' minds sped over the present, and would become one not far into the future. To this outcome there was no exception. Taec wondered if all of them had fallen into the age-old seers' trap, panicked into rash decisions that would bring about precisely the outcome they desired to avoid. Sunspear's attack might yet prove to be the catalyst for driving the two minds together, and that mental joining would in turn guarantee the physical joining he so feared.

Somewhere, Taec swore he could hear laughter. +There is a fell hand at work in all this,+ he thought out. +Beware.+

One by one, the farseers broke away from the conclave, each employing their favoured rune patterns to focus on particular threads of the skein. The world-runes of all the major craftworlds and many minor ones were produced, in some cases many times over. Others gathered up the lesser runes of maiden worlds, renegade settlements, corsair fleets and others who did not follow the teachings of the Asurya, or who had abandoned them.

The Biel-Tanians' minds were glowing sprites leaping from thread to thread in arcs of bright thought-energy. Runes glowed over various destinies. He followed the track of Iyanden many times over, until he was satisfied that his countrymen would arrive upon Dûriel in time. He skirted his own fate. Where he glimpsed his death, he was at least surrounded by the yellow and blue colours of his kinfolk.

Taec withdrew a little from the skein. Runes orbited in multitudes around the entranced seers, somehow avoiding collision. Daytime in the dome was pleasant, warm light from a tame sun shining upon the parklands of the Dome of Crystal Seers. He took the opportunity to think on his initial visions, recalling the runes the dead had showered around him in Iyanden's Dome of Crystal Seers.

He slipped back into the skein. He thought up the Llith'amtu Khlavh. Allies they looked for, perhaps their allies would be of a darker kind. One of the lesser associations of the Knife That Stays The Blade was with the Dark Kin of Commorragh; perhaps that was where they should look for aid. As a balance to its darkness, Taec brought out the Dawn rune, sign of hope and warm satisfactions. He set the two in the position of the second opposition, not quite diametric, but subtly supportive of one another. With this as his focus, he fixed his mind upon the future.

New possibilities opened up, a new possible future rushed towards him. Many kindreds of eldar fought on the blasted surface of Dûriel. Bladed attack craft flew in close formation with the elegant ships of the craftworlds.

+The craftworlds will not stand alone,+ he thought out, then, +I have it.+

Khaine's rune blazed bright over the skein, the Knife That Stays The Blade beside it.

+This is the path to victory.+

Biel-Tan's seers abandoned their own readings and flocked to his side, to see what Taec Silvereye of Iyanden would see.

The farseers delivered their verdict to the war council in the Chamber of Seers.

'Commorragh,' stated Sunspear in bald disbelief. A susurrus of whispers set up from the autarchs around him.

'It is certain,' said Altariec. 'Farseer Taec led the way. Only as a united host can we vanquish this threat.'

'The Dark Kin are our only aid,' said Forlissiar. 'The portents are quite clear. I trust this time you will listen to us?'

+I do not like this,+ thought out Kelmon to Taec.

+It is fate, and as good as done,+ he replied. They returned to the conversation of the Biel-Tanians.

'But how to contact them? Any message we send will doubtless go unheard, consumed by the Shadow in the Warp cast by the Great Dragon,' said Kellian.

'What then?' said Altariec.

'An embassy will be required,' said another seer, old and with milky white eyes.

'We are aware that you, Autarch Sunspear, have trodden the streets of the dark city and survived,' said Forlissiar. 'Perhaps you could go again?'

'It was a long time ago,' said Sunspear gravely. 'I recall the pathway there, but I do not wish to repeat the journey.'

Altariec gestured irritably. 'Doubtlessly they sealed it long ago. They are jealous of their privacy.'

'Murderously so,' said Forlissiar. He raised an eyebrow to indicate that it would be permissible to laugh, despite the gravity of the situation, and the others duly did.

'I find them tediously bloodthirsty, and without finesse,' said Hethaeliar. She was bored by the talk, her mind wandering. 'Can we not concoct some other plan?'

Sunspear twitched with annoyance. 'You were there on Dûriel, there is no other plan. It is numbers we lack. The voidspawn are too many.'

'The Dark Kin are our only hope, nevertheless. Taec has seen it,' said Forlissiar.

'I do not like it. But the Dark Kin hold devices we have forgotten. Such a thing as might burn a world. With the Dark Kin at our sides, Biel-Tan and Iyanden will stand at least a chance of preventing the merging,' said Sunspear.

'That thread ends in fire and the death of the world,' said Altariec.

'Our preferred result,' said Kellian. 'You see it now, don't you, Altariec? Your mode of speech suggests you do. Why trade in ambiguities? Be of one mind with us.'

Altariec leaned his staff out at an angle from his body. 'This thread has only one favourable conclusion, the one that Taec has seen. I have no choice but to put my support to your proposals, the time to avert disaster to Biel-Tan is past. We must follow the path of fate we have chosen. Or that has been chosen for us.' He stared at the others with hard eyes as he spoke.

'I am entitled to change my mind. This path offers the faint possibility of averting the crisis Taec Silvereye has seen. You will recall that my objection was to Autarch Sunspear's plan, and I was proven correct in that instance. His attempt to purge Dûriel of Far Ranging Hunger's beasts was a disastrous failure, as I predicted.'

'Taec Silvereye has made a convincing prediction,' said Kellian.

'As did I, if you will recall, Farseer Kellian. You did not pay me much attention.'

Hethaeliar's focus returned sharply. 'Taec is not of this world, with all respect, farseer,' she said, tilting her head in his direction. Taec acknowledged the potential insult, and indicated his intention not to be insulted by a delicate flaring of his nostrils.

'He is second only in ability to Farseer Eldrad Ulthran of Ulthwé,' said Kellian. 'We all acknowledge that.' He too bowed at Taec. Altariec snorted derisively. 'If he says it is so, then to the Dark Kin we must go.'

'It is not so easy, my friend,' said Sunspear. 'If we were able to retrace my steps, we would most likely be hunted down and killed. Even if this did not come to pass, and I somehow managed to communicate this portent to them without having the tongue ripped from my mouth, and they then agreed to aid us, that aid would be too late in the coming. Fearful of revealing the path to their domain, the Dark Kin would take a torturous route. As they delay, Dûriel will beget its abominations, and the galaxy will fall.'

'Quicker rather than sooner,' Forlissiar reminded them. 'The second fall comes what may.'

Sunspear flicked his hand out at the farseer. 'No, I do not agree. We shall rise again.' He made a complex salute. 'The rebirth of the light of ancient days.'

The war council and seer council murmured the same words in response.

Altariec sighed. He seemed frail all of an instant. 'They will aid us. Taec Silvereye of Iyanden has indicated to us that She Who Thirsts makes a play against us all. The ejection of Far Ranging Hunger's remnant from the Othersea hard by Dûriel was no accident. The taint of the Dark Prince is on this thread.'

'And how shall we reach them?' said Kellian. 'If, as you say, the way to Commorragh is barred to us, the more evil fate we have all now witnessed will come to be. There is nothing to be done!'

Sunspear stood stock-still, his hands clenched. He turned abruptly on his heels, and walked from the dome. 'I said the way is barred to us, but not to all,' he said as he left, his head held high. 'There are others we may call on, those who know the webway like none other. Although their aid and that of the Dark Kin may cost us dear, there is another way.'

The seer council looked to one another. Urgent whispers mingled with the rustle of robes as the farseers argued by voice, gesture, and telepathy. The autarchs argued more vociferously.

Kelmon held out his mighty wraith's hand. Silence returned. 'The Biel-Tanians did not allow me to speak at their council, but they said nothing of following their autarch. I suggest we go after him, Taec.'

The Iyanden farseer nodded sharply. The Iyandeni departed, and the seer council of Biel-Tan looked to each other. Several, and then all, hurried after Taec and Kelmon, the autarchs falling in behind.

Sunspear proceeded slowly and with great dignity, stepping out from the Chamber of Seers into the parklands of the Dome of Crystal Seers. Thence he went into the greater body of Biel-Tan, taking a short, wide corridor onto the Avenue of Lost Glories Remembered to be Recaptured, the giant arcaded space that ran just over half of Biel-Tan's length. Five hundred paces across it was and three thousand high, with many galleries and open walkways rising up its either side. Giant statues of historic Biel-Tanian heroes graced its length. Immense archways shimmering with energy fields separated the arcade from the discrete environments of various bio-domes housing ecosystems from across the galaxy. Vast wraithbone pillars, sung to resemble trees, interlinked spreading branches to make of the roof a tracery of breathtaking artifice. Between sky-runners, grav-skiffs and transport discs, aerial creatures flew on the avenue's artificial thermals, nesting in the thousands of living trees and plants that grew in ornate pots between the statuary and all up and down the galleries to create a cascading, vertical garden.

Taec snagged the arm of Kellian, who, being several arcs younger than most of the other farseers, had caught up easily with the Iyanden seer. 'Where is he going?' asked Taec.

'We shall have to wait and see,' said Kellian. 'Your guess will be as good as mine, and I see nothing on the skein but confusion. He spoke of the Harlequins.'

'Doubtlessly,' said Taec. 'They treat with the Dark Kin equally as with us. But I fear his sudden action.'

'I also,' said Kelmon gravely. 'This is no time to be rash.'

Kellian laughed, an unpleasant edge of offence to it. 'Then you have spent precious little time on Biel-Tan.'

Autarch Hethaeliar also joined them, as in time did others. A knot of high-ranking Biel-Tanians formed around Taec, keeping a respectable distance from Sunspear.

'I am interested in finding out, are you not?' said Hethaeliar. She had a detached manner that disturbed Taec. A permanent expression of snide amusement played around her lips, and her eyes were cruel and calculating. Taec could not tell if she were being genuine in her statement or not, for she used her words playfully in a manner that suggested she thought it all a joke, while her dreamy body language said something else entirely.

Taec glanced at her, watching her full lips quirk further with unpleasant amusement, and she drifted away.

+Be wary of her,+ Kellian thought over to him. +She sees all as a game, its sole aim to allow her to exercise her power and lust for conquest. War is all to we of Biel-Tan, if it restores us to our rightful place. To her, enjoyment of the means outweighs the sanctity of the end by far.+

+Such you have on the Path of Command here,+ Taec thought back.

'Heroism is the pleasant distillation of many noxious ingredients,' Kellian said aloud.

'Indeed so,' said Kelmon.

Eldar thronged the avenue, engaged in the toils of their path or walking with friends, all of them wearing variations on the craftworld's green and white heraldry. Once again, Taec noted it, thinking on how their militaristic sensibilities bred in the eldar here a certain narrowness of being, tighter even than that decreed by the Asuryan path. He did not think it healthy.

The eldar in the Avenue of Lost Glories Remembered to be Recaptured were subdued, for the news of the failed expedition to Dûriel had by now been passed throughout the entire craftworld. What conversation went on was hushed, and fell away to silence when the eldar spied their greatest living hero striding down the centre of the avenue. The crowds parted to let Sunspear pass, and turned to watch his unhurried progress. They shied away from Kelmon when they saw him, but when the seers of the seer council came hurrying in the wake of the autarch, many eldar fell in behind them out of curiosity. Soon Sunspear was trailing a crowd of eldar many hundreds strong, dragged after him as surely as iron filings are dragged by a magnet.

Sunspear eschewed transport, walking to wherever he was going with a measured stride that, though processional in manner, conveyed him swiftly along the arcade. Seven thousand paces from the Dome of Crystal Seers, the avenue was crossed by a second, similar way that went from one side of Biel-Tan to the other. Where they intersected, the avenue opened out into a true dome. The pillars reared up, doubling their height, and many habitation towers and other buildings were contained under the glass vault, forming a small town. At the centre of the town, where the narrowed avenues crossed, was a lesser dome, roofed over with solid wraithbone.

'Ah!' said Kellian with a smile. 'The great amphitheatre. What does he want there?'

The skirts of the amphitheatre were pierced by many arched doorways allowing ingress to its audiences. One, aligned precisely with the centre of the arcade, was bigger than the others, the height of five eldar rather than two. A thick border surrounded it, bearing an inscription that glowed faintly with the light of the infinity circuit. At the apex was a delicate mask, set into a depression: the mask of masques, an exaggerated eldar face divided into two, one half a weeping face coloured the deep red of misfortune, the other a laughing face the bright white of death. Sunspear stopped in front of this amphitheatre's main archway, and regarded this mask purposefully.

Without warning he sprang from the ground and, using the theatre's inscriptions as handholds, he swung himself easily the ten paces up to the top of the arch, snatched the mask from its recess in one hand, somersaulted and landed nimbly upon his feet.

'He would not dare...' said Kellian.

'What?' said Taec.

Kellian only stared at him, his face shocked.

A murmur went up from the crowd. Eldar within their apartments had come out onto their balconies and watched from above. A flotilla of sky craft hovered over the amphitheatre. All were silent. Biel-Tan held its breath.

Sunspear turned to the war council.

'Come,' he said, and strode through the archway. The seers and autarchs followed after him. By unspoken agreement, the common citizenry of Biel-Tan remained outside.

The interior of the theatre was dark and cool. Within the arches, a walkway ran around a deep bowl set into the floor of the craftworld. This was filled with descending rows of seats broken up by sinuous stairways. A round area at the centre of the bowl held a crescent stage large enough to present a small battle on. Wraithbone ribs held the soaring dome up high over it. The stage was bathed in light. Superficially white, subtle spectrum shifting made it glow with captured rainbows to the eldar's eyes, and the soft blue uplighting to the rest of the dome seemed an uncanny shade by contrast. The group followed Sunspear as he made his way down one set of steps. Every tiny noise made by the eldar was amplified a thousandfold, and in the susurration of moving cloth and breathing thus magnified Taec fancied he could hear teasing voices.

Sunspear stepped onto the stage. The war council and seers halted at its edge.

The mask tumbled from Sunspear's fingers, not as if he had deliberately dropped it, but as if his nerves had ceased working. Such clumsiness was highly unusual to the eldar, and a gasp went up from the assembled seers. Hands flew to mouths. Some turned away in grief.

The mask seemed to tumble in the air for longer than it should. It met the hard firestone of the stage and shattered, sending splinters out in a broad fan before Sunspear's feet. They skittered everywhere, and the breaking of the mask and the sound of the splinters skidding hither and thither made a harsh music that took an age to die away, transmuted by the acoustics of the dome to distant laughter tinged with madness.

As the last rasping note faded, Sunspear stepped back.

The light over the stage went out. More sounds of surprise from the farseers among the watchers. Several of them slipped in and out of the skein in an attempt to see what would occur. Their muttered ritual forms and frustrated exclamations evoked more mocking laughter, and this time it was louder and free of ambiguity.

New lights flickered on the stage, one emanating from each shard of the mask. The lights unfolded, each one becoming the graceful figure of a Harlequin: a hundred of them, a Great Troupe, a sight not often seen. Of all kinds they were, Death Jesters, Mimes, Shadowseers; only a Solitaire, who travelled alone and whose presence was rarely revealed, was missing from their number. At their head stood a Harlequin King, the greatest of the Great Harlequins. By his side was a Shadowseer, her faced masked with a blank silver bowl, her cowl yellow and patterned with purple diamonds. At the sight of this Shadowseer, Taec's eyes narrowed. The skein was blank to him, the presence of these strange images of the wanderers destroying his ability to see it. But there was a psychic echo to this seer, something familiar. Like a scent one does not notice at the time of first experience, but which triggers maddeningly elusive recollections when next encountered.

Sunspear kneeled, one knee on the floor, the other raised, his fingers splayed, their tips pressed to the stage surface. He bowed his head, and spoke.

'Wanderers in the webway, hear my plea and my call for help. A great danger awaits us, a terrible changing of the ways that will bring disaster upon the eldar race and all the galaxy besides.'

He spoke in an archaic form of Eldar not heard upon Biel-Tan since the years after the Fall. Old Eldar was indulgently phrased and sensuous, attributes that had been shorn from the common eldar tongue when the path had been adopted to save the speakers from the temptations inherent in its form. Taec, oldest among them bar dead Kelmon, found the words hard to follow, and yet their meaning was clear.

Sunspear detailed Iyanden's dilemma. The Harlequins were totally stationary, but as Sunspear described Taec's visions, he felt their attention on him – from somewhere far away, but penetrating nonetheless. Sunspear wept as he described his own defeat on Dûriel, gripped by a shame so intense the seers shared it.

'Already the Phoenix Host of Iyanden makes its way to Dûriel. It is to you we turn in desperation, walkers of the void. Aid is required. The runes of the Dark Kin loom large in the scryings of our seers. Without their alliance, delivered swiftly, a great and terrible threat will rise to engulf us all, the Dragon's hunger will exceed Draoch-var's worst ravages, and the galaxy will be stripped of life. Aid us, we beg of you.'

There was no reply. The regal Harlequin at the throng's front cocked his head in exaggerated mime of consideration, then executed a complicated bow.

The figures exploded into showers of multicoloured diamonds, the lights collapsed into bright points, then winked out one by one.

Sunspear stood and turned to face the astonished war council. His voice trembled at first, but regained its commanding strength.

'We must prepare,' he said. 'Call the fleet, muster the host again. We return to Dûriel with not one, but two new allies at our side. If the mating of the Dragons cannot be prevented with their aid, then it cannot be done at all.'

CHAPTER EIGHT

LORD SARNAK

The *Flame of Asuryan* arrowed out of Biel-Tan's main webway portal with a flare of rainbow light. Its pilots manoeuvred deftly between the multitude of ships gathering alongside the craftworld, the nimbleness of the ship belying its size. Further bursts of light painted Biel-Tan as the remainder of Yriel's warfleet exited the webway and came in fast to fly alongside the craftworld.

The voidway was crowded with eldar attack craft at high anchorage, there being insufficient room for them all at the docking towers. The craft were mainly of Biel-Tan, but there were many ranger craft, corsair vessels, and the occasional warship bearing the colours of other craftworlds. Most surprising to Yriel, however, were the bladed vessels of Commorragh sailing in great profusion around the others.

'What transpires here?' he called from his command pod. 'Why is the void crowded with the blade-ships of the fallen ones?' He gripped at his throne to stop his arms from shaking. The ague of the spear was hard on him, his fingers stiff within their gloves, his teeth clenched so tight his jaw hurt.

'No word, my prince,' answered his master of communications. 'All are emitting the signals of peace, Dark Kin and Biel-Tanian both.'

'An alliance?' said Yaleanar. 'They have come to our aid the second time.'

'I do not trust this,' said Yriel darkly. 'That the Commorrites came to our aid at the time of the Third Woe and now do so again...' He trailed off. A hand went to his mouth. He worried the soft leather of his glove with his teeth for a second and suddenly snatched it away.

'Biel-Tan will speak with us,' said the master of communications. Yriel thought out his approval. A viewing orb came on above the forward portion of the bridge.

'Prince Yriel, your arrival is welcome. I am Autarch Aloec Sunspear of Biel-Tan, commander of this effort to thwart an ill fate. We invite you in the spirit of brotherhood to join us in a council of war.'

Commander. Is that so? thought Yriel to himself. Anger twisted in him at Sunspear's presumption. 'I am Prince Yriel, Admiral, Last Scion of the House of Ulthanash, Autarch and High Lord of Iyanden, late of the Eldritch Raiders. I thank you for your welcome, and return it. Tell me, Autarch Sunspear. What is the business of the Dark Kin here?'

'They aid us, Prince Yriel,' said Sunspear. He was unsmiling. Yriel sensed unbending arrogance almost to match his own. A slight smile tugged at the corner of his lip, and the autarch noticed. His brow creased in response.

Yriel stood, and walked towards the display. 'The Dark Kin aided us not so long ago, in our struggle against the foul orks. They did so for the opportunity to mock our pain. What is their price today? Be on your guard, autarch, this is a situation I am wary of.'

'You lecture the cognoscente. I have been to Commorragh itself. I have supped with Vect. I know their untrustworthiness, prince of pirates.'

Yriel smiled. 'Then you are better informed than I. Forgive my impertinence, far-travelled one.'

'Follow our impulses to your berth, Prince Yriel. We shall meet soon enough.' The display went out.

Yriel fidgeted with his topknot, pulled off his glove, and slapped it in his palm. A number of emotions played over his face. 'Be on your guard, my brave warriors. There is more here than meets the eye.'

'Docking impulse received,' announced his master of communications.

'Allow the *Flame of Asuryan* to respond,' he said, some of his old energy returning to him, his mind and body invigorated at the prospect of intrigue. 'Let us be drawn in.' He set off to his throne, then spun on his heel, pointing at the viewing orb. 'But let us not be caught.'

'Yes, my prince,' said the bridge crew as one.

Yriel stared intently at the Spear of Twilight, hanging in the air by his command pod. He trembled with resurgent weakness and went to stand close by it, then settled back into his chair to be closer to it still.

His crew pretended not to notice.

The *Flame of Asuryan* pierced rippling energy fields to slide into dock, its weapon-studded sides coming to a rest against a four-levelled quay. Walkways on all levels reached out for doors in the side, but only the chief entrance, tall and imposing and framed within the world-rune of Iyanden, opened. Yriel stepped out alone, the Spear of Twilight in his hand. The crescent of farseers there to greet him took a step backwards as its fell energies touched their minds. Seeing their discomfort, Yriel whispered to it, and the sensation retreated.

One of their number came forward again. 'Your highness, Prince Yriel, I am Farseer Kellian,' he said, employing the full range of formal greeting postures. 'On behalf of the council of seers I welcome you to Iyanden.'

'I thank you for your welcome, but I will not be staying long,' he said. 'The fleet needs resupply, and I would speak with Taec Silvereye.'

'You shall, and our autarchs as Autarch Sunspear requested. Our council of war is in session now, Farseer Silvereye with them.'

'Then I must join them immediately.'

Kellian bowed his head in agreement.

'What of the Dark Kin?' he said. Sunspear had already told him of their alliance to Biel-Tan, but Yriel was curious to see what the farseers thought. 'It is ill-starred to see so many of their slaveships in close proximity to a craftworld.'

Kellian's tone was deliberately measured, and that in itself told Yriel how the farseer felt about their presence. 'They are allies, summoned by Autarch Aloec Sunspear.'

'The combined hosts of Iyanden and Biel-Tan are not enough?' he said, feigning surprise.

'Desperate times, prince, call for desperate measures. Autarch Sunspear's initial foray to Dûriel was... unsuccessful,' he said, declining the word to show his regret and slight embarrassment.

Yriel's eyebrow arched over the Eye of Wrath, the powerful relic that covered his ruined left eye. 'There was an attack? We heard nothing.' Which naturally, he had as soon as he had come alongside Biel-Tan, but he saw no reason to reveal the full extent of his intelligences.

'Biel-Tan draws closer to the wave front of the Great Dragon's mind. Our messages to Iyanden vanished into the Shadow in the Warp. We struggled alone.'

'Alone no longer,' said Yriel. Kellian bowed.

The Biel-Tanians took Yriel to the Chamber of Autarchs. Yriel was weary to his bones, and the spear dragged on his soul like a hooked, weighted net. He paid scant attention to Kellian's conversation as they progressed by transport disc from the docks of the Tower of Bloodied Knives, and Yriel had the vague impression that Kellian became offended by the lack of Yriel's response. Biel-Tan passed by in a blur. Yriel sank into the fugue of the spear. His mind was filled with the comforting wrath of the weapon, and he drifted in his mind to the beach of bone where red waves pounded in relentless procession.

Many times aboard the ship, in the breakneck flight through the webway to Biel-Tan, he had felt a febrile energy, and had been at times voluble as if intoxicated. His crew were used to his moods, the way he would swing from intense chatter to brooding, but for Yriel these more engaged phases, although he still felt ill while enjoying them, loaned him time. At Biel-Tan, at rest – or rather, he thought to himself, at a point of fulcrum in time, where the next dipping of the scales had yet to begin – he was tired, almost bewildered, and said little. Biel-Tan struck him as remarkably uniform, its people regimented, and its architecture, although as billowing and sinuous as that of any craftworld, suffocated by conformity. He saw many eldar under arms, and many training fields, and far fewer places of contemplation and art than he had when aboard the worldships of other kin branchings.

Within the Chamber of Autarchs, his wits sharpened again. The sense of militarism was strongest there; the council met, the exarchs had blooded their warriors. Surrounded by such a concentration of controlled rage, the malign soul of the spear became interested in the world of the fleshly senses once more. Yriel followed its interest, and the scene about him came back into focus. The aspect shrines had gathered about on their stands, the armoured warriors beneath runes woven of light that rotated slowly in the air. Yriel noted how few they seemed in number; their ranks were thin. Sunspear's defeat had been costly.

The Chamber of Autarchs of Biel-Tan was larger than that of Iyanden. Whereas Iyanden's was dimly lit and soberly appointed, in acknowledgement of the bleak realities of warfare and the toll it took upon the eldar mind, that of Biel-Tan was celebratory. The walls, where not pierced with fretwork or curved with decorative embrasures, were richly decorated with coloured bas-reliefs of victory. In alcoves all round the room's circumference, trophies of barbaric lesser races were displayed under bright lights. The dome over the chamber was made of a billion coloured crystal panels, set into a wraithbone tracery of hair-like delicacy. By great art alone, they made an image of Kaela Mensha Khaine's roaring face that glared down at the assembly. The flames wreathing his eyes and mouth seemed to flicker as Yriel passed under the face, and its burning gaze followed him across the room. This was a craftworld that pursued war with enthusiasm.

He could grow to like it here, he thought, if only he liked green and white more, but the combination did little to please him.

The autarchs and farseers were gathered in a golden bowl at the centre of the room, projected viewing orbs cluttering the air showing various tactical plans. Yriel was gratified to see both Taec and the towering form of Kelmon in deep discussion with those of Biel-Tan. If they were included directly in the war council, the alliance was closer than he could have hoped, and some of the worry he had experienced on the voyage at Biel-Tan's lack of reply disappeared.

Sunspear was at the centre of the gathering, stood in a floating pulpit that turned as he conversed, directing his face to those who addressed him. Household badges upon his cloak proclaimed a rich ancestry. He was a hawkish eldar, with a dour demeanour. On first impressions, he was even more unsmiling than Yriel himself had become – Yriel fought down a bitter laugh at that. The prince had been told some passes ago that the autarch bore him a grudge for his activities as a void-reaver, for in his wildness he had not been beyond attacking the merchant ships of fellow eldar, and he resolved to be on his guard.

The assembled eldar debated in calm, formal style various forms of attack and defence, exarchs around the golden bowl asking questions or seeking clarification in their role. Now the thread had been seized, it was time to scry for detail, seeking out those junctures in causality where victory might be assured or defeat delayed. Layers of plans within plans were proposed, checked upon the skein and set into order patterns, a counter for every eventuality. Yriel was impressed by their methodology, until he realised that their calm air came not from certainty, but rather from forced composure in the face of a lack of sure path through the battle.

Yriel dug deep into himself for strength, drawing upon the dark energies of the spear. In return, he felt the edge of his soul fritter away a little more. Sometimes, he felt there was not much of him left to be devoured, but he was needed and so he took freely from the spear's dark gift. To appear weak in front of an eldar such as Sunspear would be a mistake.

Kellian strode into the throng of debating eldar and proclaimed, in mind and voice, 'The Prince Yriel of Iyanden.'

Yriel came forward, the Spear of Twilight held lightly in his hand.

'Greetings, kinsfolk. I have been informed of your efforts on our behalf, and I give you the gratitude of all Iyanden in return.'

Sunspear's platform hovered closer to the prince. The autarch looked down on him imperiously. He stared long at the cursed weapon of Ulthanash, so long that other eldar unconsciously shifted into postures of disquiet. The spear thrummed in his hand at Sunspear's appreciation. Through the weapon, Yriel heard the autarch's mind, felt his covetousness. With such a weapon... he was thinking. What might be... He saw fantasies of victory, and felt the autarch weighing up the risks of damnation against those of glory, felt too the burning disapproval of what Yriel had done with his talents. Yriel had to exert all of what remained of his will not to pull the spear in towards his body protectively.

The moment passed, and Sunspear locked eyes with Yriel.

'Well met,' said Sunspear. There was little warmth in his greeting, and the form was of the lesser third degree of politesse. 'It gladdens my heart that such a leader has rejoined his folk, and makes petty war no longer. The likes of the last heir of Ulthanash should not be harrying the spaceways, but acting as a leader to his people.'

Yriel dismissed the jibe with a smile, and bowed. 'I returned when occasion demanded, and serve now as I should. All else is in the past. I fight only for the preservation of Iyanden, and the resurgence of our kind.'

'Is that the case?' said Sunspear. He placed his hands, richly decorated with rings of rank, upon the fluted railing around his platform. It sank lower, nigh to the floor, but his native height alone was greater than Yriel's, and the disc ensured he still towered over him.

'I came swiftly,' said Yriel. 'From here, I will debouch into real space and make the void-voyage to Dûriel. The fleet of Far Ranging Hunger needs destroying, and that is a task in which I have some expertise. I remain here but briefly. I have with me also the Titans of our craftworld, for they were too large for the swift passages to Dûriel. Once they are landed, I will engage the hive fleet.'

Sunspear held his eye, then nodded. 'As it should be. We will be present on Dûriel for longer than I had hoped. If we do not destroy the space swarm, then no matter how many we kill on the surface, it will not matter.' Sunspear turned from him, and spoke with one of his own autarchs. Yriel felt the strength leave him, and he had to clutch the spear for support.

'You are well?' enquired Kellian, solicitous again. 'The spear is a heavy burden. You feel Sunspear's disapproval keenly.' Kellian regarded the spear carefully. 'They say it enhances the gifts of the mind.'

Yriel leaned upon his curse and his crutch, the Spear of Twilight. He pinched the bridge of his nose between armoured fingertips. 'It does so, potently. I feel the emotions of those whose attention is directed upon me clearly, and I often hear their very thoughts.'

'Ah, as our people of old all did, before the Fall necessitated their powers' suppression. An equally onerous gift, for those not attuned or trained. To have the fullness of psychic power thrust upon you is no small thing, safe only for seers and twinned siblings, or to be mediated by machine. You must languish under the gaze of She Who Thirsts. I feel for you.' The farseer motioned the gestures of sympathy genuinely meant.

The spear vibrated in Yriel's grip. He nodded, gritting his teeth together. All he wanted to do was scream in Kellian's face, spurning his pity. Unbidden images of the spear driven through the farseer's body came to his mind. He swayed on his feet. He wished to flee the room, to get away from its incipient bloodlust, imbued into the fabric of the chamber by long millennia of war councils and the very nature of the Biel-Tanians. The spear twisted, eager to be free. Yriel held it tightly. He thought of the beach of bone and the sea of red, the hot sun merciless on his face. It was an unkind place, the beach, but there the malice of the spear was ever behind him and not within him, and he knew something of equilibrium on its bloody shore.

Thus centred, he thanked Kellian, attempting to convey with the posture of his body and the movements of his shaking limbs that he was sincere, and sorry for his earlier distraction. 'I am free of the Dark Prince at least – the spear is death to her creatures, and her whim does not affect me. Tell me, Kellian, might it be possible to obtain a drink?'

Kellian nodded with understanding. 'Of course,' he said. Kellian had a chair brought also, lifted on gravity cushions so that Yriel would remain on eye level with his peers, but Yriel sent it away, once again with his thanks.

As Sunspear spoke with his generals, Taec and Kelmon made their way over to the prince.

'It is good to see you, prince, how do you fare?' said Taec. His smile, rich with concern, turned to a frown. 'You appear ill.'

'It is nothing. I am tired, a long voyage under testing circumstances.'

Taec was unconvinced.

Yriel assayed a smile. It was brittle on his face. 'Why has the war council proper not begun?'

'The Dark Kin,' said Kelmon. 'They arrived not long before you, but have not spoken with us other than to confirm that they are to offer aid, as brokered by the followers of Cegorach.'

'What goes on here, that Biel-Tan allies with the Commorrites?'

Taec shrugged slightly. 'One should not examine a gift too closely. Without them we will fail.'

At that moment, as if they were listening in, the Dark Kin chose to engage with the craftworlders.

A face appeared enormous over the Chamber of Autarchs floor, the transmission overriding the Biel-Tanians' technology and swelling the viewing globe to ludicrous size. The eldar within was of singularly awful appearance. His bone structure was perfectly sculpted – it probably *had* been sculpted, for the Dark Kin of Commorragh were both vain and adept at manipulating the flesh. But his skin was taut and drawn over it as that of a desiccated corpse, of greyish pallor, hinting at a sickness of more than the body. His eyes were large, the whites very white, the pupil and iris the same coal-black; alluring, seductive eyes, but set in that ruin of a face they accentuated the cadaverousness of it. The eyes were not the worst his visage had to offer. By far the most unpleasant feature was his smile: a broad grin fixed by some form of rictus, it displayed overly long teeth and had nothing to it of humour. Contempt, disregard, callousness, cruelty, and an unholy joy were combined in its unmoving architectures. Laughter, especially of a wholesome kind, there was none.

'Greetings, cousins of the craftworlds,' he began, his voice booming at unnecessary volume across the speaking-stage, causing the craftworlders to wince. 'I trust you are well... Oh!' he said, as if he had misspoken. 'Oh, I forget myself. You are not well, not well at all. And I thought that the tedium of the path was affliction enough for you, now you find yourselves embroiled with this ravening monster from beyond the black gulf. How terribly awful.' His smile, although it did not change, contrived to become a sneer. 'Of course, that is why we are here, that is why you shattered one of our historic baubles to summon the laughing ones to come on your behalf. I would tell you to be more careful with what little shared heritage we have remaining to us.'

He leaned in closer. 'But a wise choice. Had you come begging to Commorragh, you would have left this life begging also, for a quick end. No aid would have been forthcoming.' He inspected long, manicured fingernails. 'Ah well, who are we to deny our kinsmen aid in times of need? Lord Vect, Ruler of the Eternal City and rightful inheritor of all the eldar's legacy greets you, staid Biel-Tan, weeping Iyanden. One-fifth of the fleet of the Kabal of the Black Heart stands here to fight beside you, and a full half of the Wych Cult of Strife, including Mistress Hesperax herself.' He paused for dramatic effect. His body language was hard and offensive to the craftworlders, worse than his verbal tone. No one moved or spoke.

'Don't all thank me at once!' he said with undisguised glee.

'With whom do we speak? Announce yourself!' said Sunspear.

The dark eldar looked taken aback. 'You do not know me? Truly? How terribly provincial of you. Worse than the mud-pilers of the maiden worlds mighty Biel-Tan has become!'

'I know you,' said Sunspear. 'But courtesy demands you announce yourself.'

'Oh, very well. I am Lord Sarnak, one of the five prime archons of the Kabal of the Black Heart. The prime of the primes, if you would.' He peered about expectantly. 'Anyone? Know me now? Dear me. I will accept your gratitude and amazement later, if you will. Now, in return, let me see who would treat with the Black Heart. Who do we have here? Taec! Is that Taec Silvereye? Doleful seer! And your dead friend. How nice of you to keep up contact through the veil. Sunspear? It is on your behalf the court of the motley king came and dragged us into the Great Wheel for this fight, no need to look so dour, and... Wait! Wait!'

His hand shot up, palm flat outwards, and he peered into his imaging device, his eye becoming magnified to monstrous proportions and his wizened face distorted. 'Now, now! Prince Yriel himself.' The eldar bowed with great insincerity. 'My lord! A pirate no more, they say. A shame, you were so amusing as a buccaneer, so very... earnest.' Sarnak tittered, and held an intricately embroidered handkerchief to his lips. He took it away with a flourish. 'A beautiful eyepiece you have. It matches your spear.'

'The Eye of Wrath,' said Yriel sternly. 'I took it from the Shrine of Ulthanash, of whose descendant Karathain Starstrider it is a relic. As last prince of the Ulthanar, I am entitled to carry both eye and spear.'

'I am sorry, where are my manners?' said Sarnak. 'We are kin after all. You have my apologies.'

Yriel's eyes narrowed. 'That is not true. There is no kinship between us.'

'Oh, I'd say there is. On your father's side, wasn't–'

Yriel snapped, 'A rumour! Nothing more.'

'Is that so? I rather thought not. If you truly are as sure of your parentage as you insist, then might I suggest that your royal house be a little more careful with its princesses? Although between you and I, it would be a shame if you were to be so. Your mother's ways demonstrate that there are some on the craftworlds who yet have a modicum of spirit, and it would be a sorrowful thing to cage them.'

Yriel snarled. The Spear of Twilight whooshed around, its blade pointing at the image. 'Hold your tongue.'

'Is this the welcome you give your allies? Tsk tsk.' Sarnak yawned theatrically. 'Perhaps I will start to feel unamused by you. Maybe I shall take my ships and warriors home and report to Lord Vect that you did not wish for our aid, after all.'

The atmosphere in the Chamber of Autarchs thickened.

'No?' said Sarnak provocatively. 'Good. Because now I can give you your present. Isn't that nice?' He leaned back from the viewing orb's capturing mechanisms on his ship, and assumed the pose of a poet about to declaim verse. 'I have in my possession a weapon of immense power. We of Commorragh make of it a gift to you, our benighted cousins who cling so bravely to life here in the Great Wheel on their tedious, joyless path. I would say that we derive no entertainment from your plight, but that would be a lie, and to lie in good company is simply unforgivable.'

His impossibly wide grin grew wider. 'Well, unless circumstances necessitate. Anyway, the nature of the problem was presented to us by the dancing fools, that you lacked a weapon of sufficient potency to incinerate the planet properly. My Lord Vect, in his infinite wisdom, proceeded directly to his grand armoury and produced this.' Sarnak's awful face disappeared, and a monolithic device, tall as a Revenant, took its place. Gems studded its sides at regular intervals, one of great size mounted on its summit. 'Behold!' he said pompously. 'The Fireheart. A device of the elder days, when our kind strode the Great Wheel as masters over all, and didn't live such dreary, funless little lives on boring worldlets. It's in the hold of my ship, waiting just for you. Aren't we *nice?*' He giggled.

'I have seen such as this before,' murmured Taec.

'I also,' said Kelmon. 'It is a relic, powerful. Used by the planetshapers of distant arcs in the sculpting of star systems. It can collapse a dust field into a world in the course of passes, or the resonance it can create in an existing planet's core will tear it apart in mere tenths of a cycle. I believe many were used in war.'

'Imaginative, those of the empire, wouldn't you say?' Sarnak's grinning visage reappeared. He affected an air of sorrow. 'Unfortunately, it is, like so much of our people's inheritance, psychically activated, and the ban on the use of the abilities of the mind precludes we of the Eternal City ever using it. Of course, you, our most excellent cousins, have no such ban, and as I see, there are many of you here skilled in the arts of such sorceries. A foolish taunt to She Who Thirsts, but what would life be if we were all the same? Boring, I say. So bravo. You goad the Dark Prince. Well done you.'

Sarnak was grinning wider and wider now, as if he were reaching the punchline of an enormous joke.

'The Shadow,' said Taec bluntly. His vision flickered through his mind's eye, he on the surface of a world tearing itself apart by a monumental device, and falling to be burned, his soul consumed. 'It will prevent remote activation.'

'He has it! Oh, he has it!' Sarnak pointed his finger at Taec, deformed by foreshortening. 'You will require a powerful conclave of seers to activate the Fireheart, and because of this "Great Dragon" and its "Shadow",' he said scornfully, 'they will have to be on hand to do so.' He put on an outrageous caricature of sympathy around his rictus smile. 'I am so terribly, terribly sorry about that.' He laughed sadistically.

The Chamber of Autarchs erupted in shouts. 'Treachery!' said someone. 'The Dark Kin trick us!' said another.

'It is no trick,' Sarnak said gloatingly. As he drew in the dismay of the assembled eldar, his skin smoothed, his hair darkened and he drew in a sibilant breath of pleasure. The effect lasted but a moment, his features returning to their repellent state of decrepitude as the Biel-Tanians watched. 'You are pleased with our gift!' he said sarcastically. 'How delightful. I cannot wait to inform Lord Vect.'

Sunspear motioned for silence. Those who knew him well saw a storm of emotion flicker across the stony angles of his face. The desire to shut off the holofield and blast Sarnak's fleet from the heavens was strong in him.

'It is indeed unfortunate. Perhaps you will mourn our losses alongside us?' said Sunspear, his head cocked expectantly. 'No? Very well, as you wish. We thank our Commorrite cousins for their gift, and invite you to our council of war.'

Sarnak hesitated. The Dark Kin were suspicious to a fault, and to walk into the lair of an enemy in Commorragh was foolhardy. All listening were almost sure he would not come onto Biel-Tan itself. 'I shall send my best dracon,' he said eventually, 'along with several of my senior captains.'

'And Hesperax?'

Sarnak frowned. 'Oh no, no, no. She is away on her own business. But do not worry, you will not need to lecture her on your tedious battle-plans. She will be present when her blades are needed, she always is. In fact, there's no need to lecture me further, for that matter. Askar-vaq will speak with my full authority and tell me the interesting parts.'

The holographic projection winked out, leaving the chamber feelingly momentarily empty.

'I am sure he will be watching through this Askar-vaq's eyes,' said Altariec. 'Why must we treat with these monsters?'

'You well know why,' said Sunspear.

Altariec nodded glumly.

'What must be done will be done,' said Taec. 'Fate decrees it.'

As they awaited the eldar of Commorragh, refreshments were served to the assembled warriors and seers. Within a quarter-cycle, a group of pale-skinned officers dressed in ostentatiously ornamented armour were escorted into the chamber. They looked upon everything they saw with snide amusement.

A lesser dark eldar strode arrogantly into the midst of the hall. 'I am Borhu'Q, captain of the Glowing Pain. I present to you Askar-vaq of the Black Heart.' He gave a curt salute, and bowed.

Vaq swaggered forwards, razor-sharp hooks rattling on his armour plating. His face was luminous and beautiful, coloured with a purplish hue to match his bone-threaded hair, his eyes darkened with protective lenses against Biel-Tan's light. 'I demand to know why we were brought here under armed escort,' he said, jerking a razored gauntlet behind him at the Aspect Warriors surrounding him.

'Your honour guard?' said Sunspear innocently.

Askar-vaq laughed, and though the sound was beautiful, his expression was ugly. 'I have followed your campaigns, Sunspear. You are bold and decisive in battle, but I had not expected the slightest modicum of wit from one raised among the po-faced miserablists of Biel-Tan.' He clapped his hands softly. 'Why, another like that and I may mistake you for a trueborn.'

'An insult disguised as a compliment that feels like an insult.' Sunspear raised his arm. 'You do not disappoint. Join our deliberations. Despite your nature, you are welcome here. For now.'

Askar-vaq looked over the food and drink presented him with distaste. 'Why do we wait? Let us get on to the business of the day. My patience is thinning. The sterility of this environment is unpleasant to me. How do you live like this? Our ancestors would be most discomposed.'

Altariec spoke up. 'Some of the Iyandeni are to deploy on the planet Dûriel with we Biel-Tanians and the warriors of your kabal, among them Iyanden's Titans. These ships are slower than the Prince Yriel's vanguard, but will be here soon. The rest of the Phoenix Host will join us via the webway on the surface.'

'Ah, yes! The bold admiral. Yriel! There's an eldar almost worthy of the name.' Vaq snatched a glass of darkvine wine from the tray of a server and held it aloft, and shouted out a toast to the prince. 'To you, daring pirate! Your exploits generated much mirth in the Eternal City. A shame you did not come to us, you would have received a royal homecoming.'

'I am home,' said Yriel. 'I am prince of Iyanden, last of Ulthanash's line. It is my shame that I left it.'

A slow smile split Askar-vaq's perfect face. 'As you wish, but mother's home is a haunt for milksops who will not reach for father's sword.' He pointed one finger at Yriel, swirling his wine around in his glass. 'Remember that, O prince.'

Fortunately for the peace of Biel-Tan, one half-tenth of a cycle after Askar-vaq arrived, the Naiad-class cruiser *Vaul's Caress*, bearing the Titans *Sound of Sunlight*, *Silent Scream* and the *Curse of Yriel*, arrived in the orbit of the craftworld. A number of lesser troop transports came with it. The autarchs, Titan steersmen, exarchs and ship captains borne by them were called in, and the Chamber of Autarchs became crowded with eldar of all kinds. Only the servants of the Laughing God were absent, but Sunspear gave assurances that the deal they had struck included the Great Troupe's involvement in the fight, and that they would be present when battle was joined.

Finally the business at hand was discussed in earnest, and in depth. Dark Kin in bladed armour rubbed shoulders with the green and white clad Biel-Tanians and the warriors of Iyanden. Rangers and corsair captains spoke amicably with those bound to the path. Petty rivalry was put aside as talk moved on to discussions of strategy, excitement grew from talk of battle, and for a precious cycle it was as if the empire of old had been born again.

Yriel was to take the entirety of the Iyanden fleet, along with large elements of Biel-Tan's and the Black Heart's ships, and strike for Dûriel. 'We will destroy Far Ranging Hunger in space, denying its ground swarms reinforcement, and preventing a later merging,' he explained. 'We shall deliver the Fireheart and Iyanden's Titans while Lord Sarnak holds the main body of Far Ranging Hunger's swarm, then we shall attack and crush them between our armadas.'

'What is to prevent a merging elsewhere?' asked Hethaeliar the Fourth-Blooded.

'Indeed,' said Gurieal, her autarch-companion, a male almost as reserved as she. Unusual to see pair-bonded autarchs, and Gurieal's expression told Yriel he did not much like the manner in which Hethaeliar looked at the prince; her interest was poorly disguised. 'Far Ranging Hunger attacked the galaxy across a broad front, how do we know it will not arise again?'

'How entertaining!' said Askar-vaq, who evidently shared many of his master's irritating traits. The craftworlders ignored him.

'We cannot know,' said Taec. 'The skein is as blocked there as it is elsewhere by the Dragon's shadow. We can but trust, and if the occasion arises again, we simply must react again.'

Yriel waved Taec's concerns aside. 'There are few elements of Far Ranging Hunger remaining in the galaxy. Most were destroyed by the mon-keigh, others we have hunted down ourselves. Those that remain are easily dealt with, as the Great Dragon requires a certain density of numbers within its swarms. Should this critical mass not be reached, the swarm functions poorly. I feel it in my very core that this will be the last threat we will face from Far Ranging Hunger.'

'That just leaves the other swarms,' said one of the Dark Kin. 'They are only few. You should not need our aid to destroy those!' The Commorrite eldar laughed unpleasantly.

'Then we shall all have to become dragon slayers,' said Aloec.

As soon as the meeting was over, Taec, Kelmon and Yriel rode a sky-platform through Biel-Tan to the Tower of Bloodied Knives. There the *Flame of Asuryan* and the fleets of the eldar were readying themselves for battle. It was not to Yriel's ship they went, but to *Imbriel's Embrace*, for Taec Silvereye was leaving Biel-Tan.

'Must you go, farseer?' said Yriel. 'The Red Eye needs the Silvereye. Once I was happy to follow my own guidance, but I realise a firmer hand is needed to tame my wildness. Come with me and grant me your rede.'

'Is age bringing wisdom to you, Lord Yriel?' said Taec.

Yriel moved his head a fraction. 'It has been said. It is not mine, however,' he said, his mood turning grim, 'but the spear's wisdom.'

Taec's own smile disappeared. 'It has been determined as best as we could discern upon the skein, I must depart. I must rejoin the Phoenix Host. Our communications are not reaching them, thwarted by the complexity of the webway and the shadow of the Great Dragon's mind upon the Othersea. If they progress as expected, they will be upon Dûriel soon. If they attack without us, they will fall alone and unsupported, not knowing that a greater host comes to their aid mere tenths of a cycle behind.'

Yriel, who had been watching the architecture and crowds of the worldship pass by, looked to the farseer.

'There is more. I sense you are keeping it from me.'

Taec raised his eyebrows.

'The spear.' He bared his teeth. 'I am become a seer also, it seems.'

Taec nodded. 'That makes a breed of sense, prince. Little is known of the Spear of Twilight's true nature, for it consumes those who probe at it with their minds, and its bearers have been few. The spear was crafted at the birth of our race, when our minds were unfettered and we did not live in fear of She Who Thirsts. It is natural, I suppose, that your mind, a blood echo of Ulthanash's own, should respond to its spirit so powerfully.'

'It is burdensome,' said Yriel. 'And it is a burden I cannot set down.' He looked at the shaft clasped in his hand with a mixture of love and hate.

'We all must make sacrifices if we are to survive as a species,' Taec said, remembering Kelmon's words to him.

Yriel looked away. 'For what, sometimes I wonder. For Iyanna's god to stir? Or so that successive generations can suffer even more greatly than we have already? Perhaps our time is over.'

'Do not discount Iyanna's prophecies,' said Taec kindly. 'They might seem the stuff of myth, but these are great times in their way – times of myth – when the fate of everything could well be decided. Despair will avail you nothing.'

'You think this will avail me where despair will not?' said Yriel, hefting his spear. 'Do not trust. It is despair wrought in steel.'

Taec put a hand on the prince's shoulder. 'You bear it well.'

'Look at us,' said Yriel weakly. 'A dying prince, a repentant revenant and a vitreous seer. Are we the great champions of our days? If so these are no mythic times, and you are wrong. Our kind has come to a sorry pass. Our light flickers dimly.'

The platform passed over a sparkling pink ocean, its expanse punctuated by islands fringed by grey sand, and grown over with exuberantly coloured vegetation.

'You do yourself a disservice. The heroes of old were just as flawed as you, and far less flawed than those who came after. You have borne the spear longer than any other save Ulthanash himself. You are of purer heart than you think, Prince Yriel, and mightier than you believe.'

They went into a transit tube bored into wraithbone cliffs rising high over the pink water. The sunlight became an oval behind them, their way ahead lit by coloured running lights, other discs moving ahead of them, joining or leaving the tunnel at its many junctions.

'My heart? Before I took up the spear, I set aside the cares of the heart, and became as careless with violence as a Commorrite. In my dreams I look upon an ocean of blood that pounds upon a beach of bone. The foam of this sea is purest white, but each bubble therein contains a death's head, one for each of the thinking creatures I have slain, I am sure. The sun never sets, nor moves in the slightest. Behind me, a dark presence waits, I feel its eyes upon the nape of my neck, and I dare not turn to face it. There is a peace to this place nevertheless, the peace of endless victory. My heart is not pure, seer, it beats to the pounding of the thick surf. I am lost, lost to Khaine. I am an eldar who should never have been. If I know one thing, it is this – Dûriel will be my final battle. The portion of my soul dwindles, imbibed by the spear. If this must be so, it must be so, but I still do not know who I am.' Yriel looked Taec dead in the face. The Eye of Wrath glittered dangerously. 'Who was my father, Taec?'

Taec refused to answer. He squeezed the prince's shoulder, and let his hand drop. They ceased speaking, and became lost to their own thoughts: Yriel to his bloody sea, Taec to his terrible doom, Kelmon to whatever occupies the dead.

The disc passed over a plaza, picking up speed. It entered another tube, and emerged in the grand lounges at the feet of the Tower of Bloodied Knives. Through crystal panes and energy walls they could see the bulk of the tower cantilevered out into space, cluttered with a thousand warships. The lesser docks and quays were crammed with eldar and machines supplying the vessels. It was surprisingly quiet, the Biel-Tanians intent on their tasks.

The disc floated downwards, heading for a final tube only broad enough for one. It ran out along the foot of the tower, and the starward side of the wall was of clear resins, affording them a better view of the fleet.

The disc came to rest at a small quay. The sleek hull of *Imbriel's Embrace* occupied the dock. Rangers sprang to their feet from where they had been waiting when Kelmon and Taec approached.

Taec stepped down stiffly from the disc, Kelmon by his side. The seers turned to face Yriel. Kelmon made the passes of sorrowful partings in front of his chest, the gestures given great force by the size of his hands. Taec looked up at the prince, his face still sullen at Taec's refusal to tell him what he wished to know.

'Farewell, prince.'

'Farewell, seers.'

'Prince,' said Taec. 'Do not fear the red sea. The thread of your destiny is still being woven by Morai-Heg, and she will not cut it yet.'

The disc rose into the air, and Yriel shouted over its rising hum. 'Have you not heard, Taec Silvereye of House Delgari? The gods are dead!'

Taec watched the prince depart. His shoulders sank a little. The tingling in his crystallising limbs redoubled.

'Aye,' he said softly. 'We are all the authors of our own dooms.'

CHAPTER NINE

THE GREAT TROUPE

'Ariadien, I am cold.' Neidaria shivered. Ariadien pulled her closer and moved her to the side of the pathway, out of the way of yet another squad of fully armoured Guardians jogging past. He held her in his arms. As they were identical in so many ways, they were of the same height, yet she huddled into him and became so small he could rest his chin on the crown of her head.

'It is this place,' he said. 'The Biel-Tanians have a cold world to match their cold hearts.'

'I was practically shaking the whole way through the gathering in the Chamber of Autarchs. Is there nowhere we can go to warm ourselves? I do not wish to spend the last night frozen to my bones.'

'I saw a pleasant enough drinking–' began Ariadien.

'Must we?' she snapped. 'Must we spend the last night with you in your cups, so I may watch you become bitter and sharp-tongued? I would rather freeze.'

Ariadien was taken aback by his sister's outburst. She rarely exhibited any aggression, even in war practice, where she was instead dispassionately efficient. But here she was, face twisted and teeth bared. He took a step away from her, his hands upheld. 'Sister,' he said, attempting a joke, 'pray do not bite me!'

'You are impossible!'

She turned away, her thoughts bright with her annoyance at him, with sorrow at the deaths that would come tomorrow, at being far from home. Her emotion flooded him. He reached out to her, mind and body. She recoiled for a moment, then accepted his touch upon her back.

'I am sure there are habitats, warm ones, like at home. Perhaps a sea, or a desert we might explore to while away the night. We have nearly a full cycle before the fleet will be ready to depart.'

'Prince Yriel is already aboard his flagship,' said Neidaria.

'He has his own battle to plan for, we ours, and we are not needed as yet,' Ariadien said gently. 'So, a desert dome? We can guarantee the heat there...'

She shook her head. 'I wish to see the ocean,' she said.

Ariadien bowed with courtly extravagance. 'As my lady wishes.'

She laughed through her tears. 'You are a fool, Ariadien. You always make me laugh, always. How can I stay angry at you for long?'

He grinned. 'I suspect that if I were to suggest a session of good wines you would be angry with me again.'

She blew a strand of hair from her eyes with a puff of breath. 'Don't taunt me.'

He became serious. 'When was the last time I made you laugh? You have been sorrowful of late.' He took her upper arms in his hands.

'Too long,' she said. 'There has been little amusement in life.'

'Then I promise, when this is done, I shall endeavour to make you laugh again – every day! – until you find a bondmate, and then, I solemnly swear, I will spend my days teasing him for your entertainment.'

'You mean yours.'

He waggled his head and smirked. 'Well, yes. But it's almost the same thing, is it not? You and I are the same.'

'One and one is one,' she said, the words they had spoken to each other every day since they had been children, when their minds had gradually divided from each other's as they had grown and they had become as individual as they ever would be.

'One and one is one,' he repeated, resting his forehead on hers. 'What is to be done with us?'

Neidaria smiled sadly, a mirror image of his own face cast in female form. 'Survive, until these wars are past memories and our service to Iyanden deemed complete.'

'I will be by your side until that is so.'

'I know you will. I love you, my brother.'

'And I love you too, my beautiful sister,' he said. Their combined affections overwhelmed them, and they stood in silence, one soul in two bodies, as the warrior-folk of Biel-Tan rushed gladly by them to their next war.

Ariadien found a suitable dome through the infinity circuit of the world. He melded with it at a public terminal. If he were truthful, it was not an entirely pleasant experience, being at once familiar and alien. The infinity circuit of Biel-Tan did not rage with angry spirits as did Iyanden's, but that was not to say it was the same as Iyanden had been before the Triple Woe had filled the circuit with the early dead. Biel-Tan had a cold soul. There was little of kindness to it, it had an iron certainty tempered with nervous frustration, as if it had bided its time through long night and was impatient to see the dawn. War seemed its main preoccupation, and as Ariadien interfaced with it his soul inadvertently touched upon the multiple domes, shrines, and groups dedicated to the prosecution of Khaine's bloody arts. The infinity circuit's gestalt mind regarded Ariadien as the Biel-Tanians regarded him. It was obvious he was a foreigner to both. There was a mild indifference and superiority in the infinity circuit's regard that bordered upon hostility.

He found what he was looking for within the circuit and withdrew, then led his sister to a transport hub where they took a disc and soared away over Biel-Tan's spires.

Half a tenth-cycle later, they were walking barefoot along the shores of a vast sea of cerise water, warm sun upon them. He sighed in happy sorrow, his heart carried to sad, comforting places by the pounding of the waves on the grey beach. Large aquatic animals of a shocking pink played out in the bay, double tails slapping at the water as they breached and came splashing down. Seabirds of types Ariadien had never seen wheeled in a simulated sky, and strange shells littered the sparkling graphite of the sand.

Other eldar paced the strand, but they were infrequent adornments to the beach. Ariadien could not see the end of it, and the sea seemed to stretch on forever.

They walked in companionable silence for a time, until music interrupted their shared reverie. Neidaria grabbed at Ariadien's arm, and pointed away from the sea to where a line of dunes fronted a red-leaved forest. An eldar sat upon a tree trunk bleached a light red by the salt and sun, beyond the line of tidewrack.

'A musician! Let us go to him!' said Neidaria, her face lighting up. She ran from him before Ariadien could grab her, and flew some way ahead, sprinting lightly. He could not muster the enthusiasm to go and converse with a stranger and so did not run, but despite his reluctance, he tramped wearily through the hot sand after her.

By the time Ariadien had caught up his sister was in conversation with the eldar, laughing at something the other had said while he was out of earshot. Her happiness at this distraction infiltrated his mind, and he could not remain angry with her any more than she had remained angry with him.

The eldar was shading his face from the sun as he looked up at Neidaria. He was dressed in rich clothing of simple cut, and his face bore the signs of great age: fine lines around his eyes, a certain parchment thinness to the skin, and an attenuation of the cartilage in his nostrils and the tips of his ears.

'Ah! The brother,' said the musician. 'Well met.'

'Well met,' said Ariadien cautiously. 'You are no Biel-Tanian.'

The eldar followed Ariadien's eyes up and down his clothing. There was not a patch of white or green anywhere upon it. 'No, it appears that I am not.'

'And you are old!' blurted out Neidaria. Ariadien cringed inwardly at his sister's gaucheness, but the old eldar was unruffled.

He dipped his head. 'I am.'

'How old are you?' asked Neidaria hesitantly, picking up on Ariadien's embarrassment.

The stranger laughed. 'Older than most you have ever met or will ever know, but does it matter?' He gave a cheerful toot upon his pipe, a summer-flute as long as his arm. 'I am here, and you are here. Location and position in time, and yes, I include age in that – these things are unimportant. Strangers meet in a moment, strangers part in a moment. Let us enjoy the moment together.' He gestured to the bleached log. 'Please, sit with me a while. I would be glad of the company.'

Neidaria looked to her brother. +Shall we?+ she thought to him. They were close enough to speak mind to mind without mediating equipment.

+I don't know,+ Ariadien thought back, caution underlining his words. +There is something a little... off, about this one.+

Neidaria burst out laughing. 'Oh truly, Ariadien!' she said aloud and clapped her hands together. She sat herself down with an abandon that was almost inelegant. 'I am Neidaria, this is my brother Ariadien.'

'Twins,' stated the eldar. He fixed Ariadien with eyes filled to brimming with the weight of many arcs, and Ariadien's spirit buckled under their examination. 'A sad rarity now. You are luckier than some in some ways, unluckier than some in others.' He played a brief tune on his flute.

'What do you mean?' said Ariadien, who would not sit.

'What do I mean? I mean this – you are close enough to communicate mind to mind without fear. Such a bond is so tight even She Who Thirsts cannot slip a blade between you to sever Morai-Heg's cord. You experience something few others in these times can, and naturally so, as it was meant to be. Machine shielding, or the Path of the Seers... these are poor manners by which souls should commune. You are lucky in this, as much as you are in your deep love for one another.' He played again, a mournful sound, then stopped. His musical interjections were unselfconsciously done; he tooted a few notes or bars, a musician looking for a song to play. 'Look to the sea, how it appears infinite here. Purposefully so.'

'How so?' asked Neidaria. She still wore an expression of gaiety, but she shuddered despite the heat of the bottled sun.

'It was designed by its architect to be that way, in recognition of a past so distant it is no longer even myth. The emotions of our kind are as the sea. Did you know that many of the first of those born from Asuryan's grace chose to live by the oceans of their home world, regarding them as the finest of Isha's gifts? Oceans and seas were beloved of our kind long before we first stepped into the void, for we share affinity with them. As our emotions, they appear infinite, they are of plumbless depths. They can transform in an instant from calm to fury, they are possessed of boundless beauties.' He pursed his lips, and there was contemplative sadness in his expression. 'Only those of the old empire discovered that nothing is infinite, and that no depth is too deep to be plumbed. All oceans are only smears of water lost in the night, and the vastnesses of the true oceans – the void and the Othersea – are not to be lightly sailed.' Another burst of music.

'You said unlucky also,' said Ariadien.

'Did I?' he said, seeming genuinely surprised. 'So I did. Unlucky, young Ariadien, in the same depth of that selfsame bond. For if one suffers, so does the other. If one dies...' He shrugged. A smile wiped his grave expression away. 'Serious matters. I am sorry. Enjoy what you have. It is in the moment that we truly live, and this is a pleasant moment and should be lived as such.'

'Serious matters for serious times,' said Ariadien. 'Death may greet us soon, we go to war tomorrow.' He squatted down beside the log, picked up a fistful of sand and let the grains run through his hands.

'Steersmen?'

They nodded simultaneously.

'Ah.' He looked at them both. 'And if I am not mistaken, a path not freely chosen. I am sorry.' He lifted his flute, then lowered it as a thought crossed his mind. 'You seek distraction?'

'Yes. Ariadien brought me here to take my mind off the war.'

'Then be advised, young eldar, that tonight a Great Troupe of the wandering folk has gathered in such numbers that none can remember the like. They come to aid the Autarch Sunspear, and will fight alongside you tomorrow.'

'That is good news,' said Ariadien.

The eldar smiled widely, his eyes twinkling with mischief. 'But it is not the best! Tomorrow they fight, tonight they dance.' He leaned forwards, his voice dropping, and he looked from one sibling to the other in conspiracy. 'There are rumours that a Solitaire is aboard Biel-Tan, and so they shall perform the Dance Without End! A rare occasion, one that must be grasped with both hands, Neidaria, Ariadien! Such an opportunity may never come around in your lifetimes again.'

Ariadien grew excited, and he felt his sister's interest building too. 'Truly?'

The eldar nodded seriously. 'Truly.'

'I have always wanted to witness the Dance!' said Neidaria.

'Every eldar should.' He held up a long finger. 'And tonight you shall.'

'Thank you, stranger, for your words and your advice.' Neidaria bowed her head in respect. 'But what is your name?'

'They call me Lechthennian,' he said, dipping his head, his ancient face alive with a glee that the twins found infectious. 'I will play awhile now, before attending the performance. We have plenty of time. You are welcome to remain with me and listen, if you would. Speak no more of war, let the sound of the sea and this simple flute soothe your fears away.'

'We would very much like to,' said Neidaria before Ariadien could speak.

Lechthennian looked to her brother. 'Very well,' Ariadien said.

Lechthennian winked and held the summer-flute up to his lips. 'Then listen,' he said. 'And know gladness.'

What Lechthennian played was far from simple, a long and haunting melody of such power that Ariadien found himself weeping and laughing at once. He could not look at Lechthennian as he played, afraid that the sight of his ancient eyes and the music combined would overwhelm him. He and his sister stared out over the sea, the music stirring in them images of times a million years ago and more, when simpler folk than they dwelled by the sea and looked out onto it with joy in their hearts and minds.

They fell asleep to the music, and dreamed of peace.

When they awoke, Lechthennian had gone, and the bottled sun was sinking slowly below the ocean's horizon. Mindful of Lechthennian's words, they gathered themselves quickly, and set out to Biel-Tan's great amphitheatre.

Tonight they would witness the Dance Without End.

News had spread of the performance and many thousands of eldar were converging on the amphitheatre. Despite the crowds, Ariadien and Neidaria found seats quickly. The excitement of the throng filled the space. Swept up in anticipation, the distance the Biel-Tanians had regarded the twins with had gone, and they found themselves surrounded by eager, welcoming faces. They were two eldar among many, distinctions of kindred gone.

The amphitheatre took a tenth-cycle to fill, so huge it was. The conversation of the eldar, reflected back upon them by the dome's peerless acoustics, became the rushing of the sea, and the twins clasped hands, the memory of Lechthennian's powerful music still fresh in their minds. They searched the crowds for him in vain; there were so many eldar in there and such were the angles when looking up or down the stepped rows of seats that it was impossible to pick out a single face.

The noise of the crowd eventually abated, their chatter giving way to anticipation. The air became pregnant with it, and Ariadien experienced a larger version of the sense of unity he shared with his sister. The crowd thought with one mind, breathed with one breath. Within this joining, the twins wondered to each other if this was the way it had once been, when the eldar were mighty and not afraid to enjoy their senses to the full.

When the last whisperer had ceased his whispering, the lights dimmed to a level just above blackness. Faces and hands were visible as luminous blobs, blue as deep sea fishes, the eyes in the faces moist jewels, all fixed upon the stage.

A sweet smell wafted over the twins, and they felt their minds sharpen.

A spear of white light snapped on, illuminating a figure dressed in the motley of the Harlequins. He was a hundred paces away from the twins, but every lozenge upon his multi-hued cloak was visible to them. His mask was alabaster white, fixed with a caricature of a smile that could have been a sneer, a single sapphire tear on the left cheek. He wore a tall brush of hair of constantly shifting colour, curving almost over to touch his nose to the front, running to long tails at the back.

He said nothing, but bowed artfully. The light went off.

'Tomorrow we fight,' said a female eldar's voice; a breathy whisper alive with joyful humour, it filled the auditorium wall to wall. 'But tonight we dance. Tonight we dance the Dance Without End, tonight we dance it as many, and in full.'

The lights came up. Forty-nine dancers were on the stage, frozen in poses suggestive of might and wisdom – these were the eldar of old. Music struck up, a skirling of pipes, underpinned with deep and sombre bass. A dozen eldar of noble bearing strode among the others as they slowly came alive. Their masks marked them out as the gods – Asuryan, Vaul, Khaine, Isha, Morai-Heg, Kurnous, Lileath, and more, each baiting, gifting or dancing with the eldar as to their own imperative. For the most part, these interactions went unseen by the dancers playing the eldar, for the dance showed the race of Eldanesh at their height of power, when the gods had been set apart from them by the will of Asuryan and their influence on the eldar was subtle.

The Harlequins playing the eldar danced nobly and with strength, various movements within the dance alluding to legendary happenings, some well known, but many leaving the twins feeling ignorant. Over time, a note of discord crept into the music. The gods' movements became halting, concerned. The eldar moved ever more twistedly, and one by one their dances became darker and darker, until they were acting out depravities in groups all around the stage. The music grew unpleasant. Stealthily at first, then with brazen openness, others came and joined the dance. They wore black body-suits, their masks projecting snarling faces that whisked into the audience and peered into their eyes, causing them to shrink back and cry out. The servants of Chaos.

The sweet scent grew stronger, and the dancers grew in stature, becoming giants. The black-suited creatures moved among the eldar, dancing obscenely. They drew them into grotesque pairings, and when they touched, the dancers representing the eldar took on the dances of the servants of Chaos, their bodysuits losing their colour, their stances losing the cast of nobility they had previously displayed. The gods recoiled as more and more of the Harlequins dancing the dance of the eldar were corrupted, and then they too were assailed. Prancing Death Jesters came swarming on stage, somersaulting over the writhing dancers. They attacked the gods, fighting mime battles with them, until one by one they were felled, their corpses thrown through the air to land in a pile. Only Khaine remained, battling skilfully with numberless opponents.

There were three eldar left untouched by the lusts of Chaos. One turned his back upon the depravity early, and left the stage. Another waited longer before he, too, turned and left. A third remained. As the frenzied dancing reached a crescendo, the last unaffected hid himself in a cloak of black, and disappeared with a vicious laugh. The rest collapsed as one, dead.

The tune ceased. A fresh began.

A new dancer entered: the Solitaire, his suit projecting beauteous images of pleasure interspersed with those of horror. The figure at their core was inconstant, seemingly male one moment, female the next. This was the Dark Prince, She Who Thirsts – Slaanesh. He danced around Khaine, enticing him, while off the stage the audience felt a great wrath build. The unseen source of this fury pulled at the god, and he was dragged to and from the edge of the stage, almost into the arms of Slaanesh, then back to the edge again. Finally the war god fell, the dancer playing him somehow becoming many dancers, and they rolled away. Slaanesh pranced in victory over the corpses of the slain, seeking when he could for those who had eluded him. A terrible scream built, drowning out the song. It grew beyond bearing, projected into the minds of the eldar audience, it tortured ears and souls alike. Laughter resounded within the scream, mad, despairing and exultant.

Another figure came onto the stage as the audience reeled. New laughter, laughter that parodied the first and took on an ironic edge, pure and cynical. The Great Harlequin. He wore the same garb as before. No costume for the one who represented Cegorach, for the clothes of the Harlequins were reflections of their god, those of the Harlequin King most of all.

Cegorach strolled around the stage, laughing at the fallen and provoking the daemons of Slaanesh before darting away from their clutches. The Dark

Prince grew angry, and sent his minions to catch him. They danced around the Laughing God until they brought him low, but he burst forth unharmed, his bright clothes shining brighter. On and on this went. As it did so, the three eldar who had escaped the Fall crept back onto the stage and took up the dance of their forebears in muted form, hiding away whenever Slaanesh glanced in their direction. This attention came seldom, for the Laughing God held She Who Thirsts's eye, sending her into furies with his antics. Once or twice, the Dark Prince snatched at the eldar, but they escaped again and again, and Slaanesh grew furious. He threw himself at the Laughing God, and they fought, the two Harlequins performing a breathtaking dance duel of high leaps and somersaults.

It was at this point that the Dance Without End traditionally ceased, the Solitaire and the Great Harlequin leaping around each other without conclusion. Every eldar knew this, for the Harlequins were much discussed and the ritual of the Dance Without End was well known.

That night, the great dance did not stop.

A new movement began.

As the Laughing God and the Dark Prince danced, one of the fallen stirred. Their costume flickered, the blackened images of perverse lusts and violence giving way to skulls and bones of pure white, studded with jewels clearly intended to resemble waystones.

The figure rubbed at her head, as if waking from a long sleep. She stood, the waystones upon her exposed bones flaring brightly.

She looked at her hands, and they clenched. She became huge, her size magnified in the audience's minds by the arts of the troupe's Shadowseers. She swayed from side to side with the music, arms of shadow sweeping over the audience and back with dire whooshing noises. The Laughing God laughed at this apparition, but leapt away from it, the movements of the Great Harlequin depicting him conveying defiance, humour, hope and fear.

The Solitaire, playing the Great Enemy, stumbled in the act of snatching at one of the three remaining eldar. The dancer representing his victim fell away shrieking, but was not dead. It crawled away, a broken thing of half a soul, to lurk in the darkness. He dived again at the Great Harlequin, and the dance became more and more frantic. The audience were spellbound, unable to move, the breath stopped in their mouths. The Laughing God leapt back and forth, keeping Slaanesh's attention from the being growing to power behind it.

At the last, Slaanesh tripped the Laughing God. Standing triumphantly over her prey, she reached for him, but Cegorach laughed, staring over the Dark Prince's shoulder.

Slaanesh looked around. The new god reached for She Who Thirsts, limbs burning with the light of borrowed souls. Slaanesh's face cycled rapidly through numberless visages of terrible beauty. Inconceivably, each displayed fear, and the Prince of Chaos shrank back.

The lights went out before the new god could grasp the daughter of the eldar, leaving the conclusion unresolved.

The lights came back on. The stage was empty. The crowd members looked to their neighbours, disbelief on their faces.

'Ynnead?' they said.

'Kysaduras's fable!'

'The god of death awakens.'

'It is a myth, a parable, that is what we have seen. It is all a parable. Isn't it a parable?'

'This is an ill omen.'

'What do the seers say?'

Ariadien blew out a long breath. He was emotionally overcome. He looked at his sister. She fixed him with a serious eye, and gripped his hand more tightly in hers.

+The Dance Without End has a new ending, it seems,+ she said.

CHAPTER TEN

THE MARCH OF THE PHOENIX HOST

Iyanna watched the boneseers at work. They wore their strange armour, rarely brought out for a bonesinger did not lightly go to war. All were helmed and masked, with tall antlers either side of their helmets and a stubby projection on the chin in the manner of an alien's bound beard. They danced while they sang, in a slow, languorous manner, bringing their hands around in wide passes, their arms at full length.

Several of them played instruments – pipes, cymbals, tiny gongs, flutes and harps. It was an otherworldly melody, not meant for entertainment, but possessing a profound loveliness despite its discordance. The melody of instrument and voice intersected in the centre of the ship's hold where light glowed brightly, wisps of it revolving around a bright core to make a galaxy-like tissue.

The song changed, the light coalesced, forming matter. Wraithbone.

Iyanna was spellbound by the creation of matter from nothing.

'Look at them, Althenian,' she said. 'I love to watch the bonesingers.'

'It is dull. I am unmoved by it, war is art,' said her hulking companion. 'Mine is death, not the act of creation, war is all. I will fight, battle's music is my music, not this din.' His voice was that of Jeleniar Death-bringer, the fourth Althenian. Only Iyanna could tell them apart. Guessing which aspect of Althenian spoke had been a game she played with herself, one of her last pleasures, until the psychic signature of each soul and the minor quirks their temporary dominance brought to the exarch's personality had become totally familiar to her and the game had lost its fun.

She rested her hand on his huge thigh, spindly in proportion with his mighty frame, but three times thicker than her arm nonetheless. The psychoplastic was warm to the touch. 'And without it? How would you make your war music, Althenian?'

'I would not, this is the full truth of it, you are right. Even so, I will remain unmoved, Iyanna.'

She tapped at his limb with her nail. 'It moves me. It demonstrates how superior a way of being the path is. The bonesingers are not so different to me, we both follow paths of the mind. They use their gifts for the manipulation of the physical, I for communication with the immaterial. Without the path, how would one reach such a height of mastery? We would wander from one vocation to the next, tasting each and never drinking deeply of their wisdom. Our way is the best way.'

'Perhaps so, what do I know of other paths? I am trapped,' said Althenian. 'More than that, I am twice trapped on mine, so I hold.'

'Watch and learn, dear Althenian.'

The wraithlord growled, an affectation that made Iyanna smile to herself. 'War is all. War is my only pursuit, that is just.'

'And you will have war soon enough!' she scolded.

The light at the centre of the chamber was dimming as more wraithbone solidified from intangible plasms. The product of the song was luminous, but no more than that. It had crossed the threshold from the *might-be* to the *is*.

Having judged there to be sufficient raw material for their purposes, the bonesingers changed their tune, picking up speed. Under their influence, the wraithbone moved, melting and reforming into recognisable shapes – an arm, a foot, a high-crested helm. For nigh on a full tenth-cycle they worked, until as if by some sleight of hand the wraith-stuff was gone and a tall, sculpted figure was at the centre of their circle: a freshly made wraithguard, its long helmet open and revealing the setting for a spirit stone. The song abruptly ceased, and the bonesingers stepped back. Eldar on the weaponsmith and pseudo-life branches of Vaul's Path moved in, fitting the construct with the parts that were not of wraithbone. They too worked quickly, a team of them chanting in the smith cant. They moved easily, always on the verge of colliding with each other, always avoiding their comrades' limbs.

They stepped back, another half tenth-cycle gone. Now it was Iyanna's turn. She turned to the two lesser spiritseers by her side, who presented her with a spirit stone. Small enough to fit in her gloved fist, it glowed with striated light of a soft yellow and was hot to hold. With reverence she walked to the newly minted ghost warrior, bearing the stone in cupped hands in front of her.

'Return to your children, honoured ancestor,' she said. 'We call you from your slumber and we are sorry for what we ask. Our hour of need is upon us, and you must wake awhile.'

She placed the stone into the setting and stepped back. It shone brilliantly in the shadow of the closing helm. The long face of the wraithguard snapped shut. The warrior sagged, lumbering three steps to the left as the spirit within tentatively inhabited its shell.

Iyanna shut her eyes and reached out with her mind, calming the spirit within. The spirit was in confusion, as they nearly always were. The final mortal thoughts of the spirit shook its being, memories of the warmth of the infinity circuit at odds with who it remembered being in life.

This one, like so many recently resurrected, had died during the voidspawn invasion. A potter, caught in his workshop and hunted through his art by a pair of hissing creatures. As he died, his dismay had been greater for his broken pottery than for his lost life.

Iyanna focused on this horror, bringing it into sharp relief. Shards of ceramic sharp in his mind, red with his own blood. She turned these thoughts of his into sword blades.

'Never a warrior in life, Hetherion of Divinesh, that time is upon you in death. Take up your arms, drive forward your armour and avenge your art and your life against those who took them from you.' She insinuated images of the voidspawn into his mind, a mental picture of ravaged Dûriel, sorrow at the fallen eldar race falling further. Hetherion of Divinesh's terror at reawakening turned to resolve.

'I...' he said haltingly, his wraithbone voice a monotone. 'I will live again to fight for Iyanden.'

She led him gently to more artificers, who presented a wraithcannon to the ghost warrior. With hesitant hands, Hetherion reached out and grasped the gun. He became steady. Iyanna was satisfied. She led the wraithguard to join several ranks of them already standing in the hold. She closed her eyes again. Under her mental influence, the pale bone colour of the psychoplastic blushed, turning yellow and night-blue. She caressed the potter's soul again, turning over his memories like seashells. From them she selected a rune, and this manifested itself on the cowling of his helmet. A simple rune – artful vengeance.

'Rest now, Hetherion,' she said. 'Grow accustomed to your new body. We will need you soon enough.'

She rejoined Althenian.

'A potter,' she said.

'A potter? He will find no clay to throw, in this war,' said Althenian.

'Do not scoff. He is one who will fight without much prompting. If only that could be said of more of our honoured ancestors.'

'You say so, there are many more to come, volunteers.'

'Yes, but not all,' said Iyanna. Her eyes lingered on the rows of caskets regretfully. Elsewhere in the fleet her brothers and sisters on the branch of the spiritseer performed the same rituals, placing spirit stones into new-grown wraith bodies for war. 'Were it not so,' she said. 'A necessary task, but after all this time, still distasteful to me.'

Althenian did not reply. He knew when to hold his tongue and when to tease her.

She oversaw the resurrection of seven more spirits and was about to retire to rest, when news of Taec Silvereye's arrival at the fleet reached her.

Taec was frailer than when Iyanna had last seen him. He leaned on his staff during their conversation, and was distracted when she spoke. They stood in the *Pride of Haladesh*'s observation lounge, watching the infinite involutions of the webway wall scroll past the port side.

'You have made good time,' said Taec. 'It augurs well. It is imperative that the Phoenix Host arrives simultaneously with Prince Yriel's grand fleet and the Swordwind of Biel-Tan.'

'We go the shortest way,' said Iyanna. 'To travel the larger passages to Biel-Tan would have taken too long, and to risk planetfall from orbit would have been foolhardy in such ships. We will leave the art of void war to its pre-eminent artist, Prince Yriel. We head to a nexus where we may disembark and make our way with haste to the main gate-point of Dûriel. Such is the nature of this route that even on foot we will arrive before Sunspear's second invasion can emerge.'

'Good,' said Taec. 'We must hold back until we are sure they are on the surface. If we leave the labyrinth too early and engage the voidspawn piecemeal we will be overwhelmed.'

'As the Autarch Sunspear nearly was,' said Iyanna. She frowned. 'Sunspear was brave.'

'There are few who would disagree, but it was not his bravery that led him along that thread. He is proud, he wished for outright victory, and although fortunate for our plans, that was nearly his undoing. His arrogance approaches that of Prince Yriel's, but even so, he was close to successful on his own terms.' Taec sighed. 'Victory eluded him. Still, a success for us, if a near disaster for them. For his failure he has had a hard time of it on Biel-Tan,' added Taec. 'We are not the only seers to treat our autarchs harshly, it appears.'

'And the council of seers is behind the Biel-Tanian war council now?'

'Fully,' said Taec. 'There is one seer among them, Altariec, who was against the invasion initially. However, your message swayed all but he and his followers. Now his hand is forced, he complains loudly that Sunspear's actions precipitate a doom for Biel-Tan that could have been avoided, but he is beginning to admit that a greater peril awaits Biel-Tan should the first be dodged.'

'That is good.'

'It was not a point of view that was easy to foster,' said Taec. 'We were greeted at gunpoint.'

Iyanna raised her eyebrows.

'Indeed,' said Taec.

'I am most relieved, farseer, that the Biel-Tanians march at our side. We feared the worst when we heard naught from you,' she said.

Taec began a slow walk down the lounge, the high windows to his left. Iyanna followed. 'Biel-Tan is closing on Dûriel, albeit to a safe enough distance to avoid attracting the voidspawn's direct attention. The presence of the hive mind there is very strong. Biel-Tan has received no message from any quarter for several cycles, and if our experience is the norm, then none they have sent have reached their intended recipients either.' He paused, and looked at her earnestly, leaning on his staff again. 'You have not felt the like, not even when Far Ranging Hunger nearly destroyed us. The strength of the mind... It is...' He trailed off. 'It is impossible to describe. You must arm your mind against it. I will spread the word to the seers in the fleet that they must take special care of their runes of warding. Psychic communication, even projected by devices, is impossible in the face of it. Sunspear was forced to rely on electromagnetic means to direct his army.'

'How primitive,' said Iyanna.

'There is more – the eye of She Who Thirsts is fixed upon the place. I grow ever more certain it was her caprice that cast the splinter out of the warp into the Dûriel system.'

'Crystal father...' began Iyanna.

'How many times have I said that you need not refer to me as such, Iyanna? Your days as a warlock are long behind you, your might is equal to mine, though different.'

'I speak respectfully because I must say a thing of some dreadfulness.'

'Then say it.'

'This war... It is a trap, designed by the Dark Prince solely to snare you. I feel this.'

'And I know it,' said Taec darkly. 'I am thoroughly caught. My doom awaits me there on Dûriel's dead surface, there is nothing to be done for it.' His eyes were tired and sad, and he spoke frankly to her. 'I will die and my soul will be forfeit, but what other choice do we have? She Who Thirsts will take me, but I go willingly. It is the only way.'

'You could flee, you needn't go. Let others work in your stead.'

'What, child? Such as yourself? And then your soul will be lost, and not mine. Whichever way the die is cast, the numbers are not in our favour. I have scried again and again and there is only one future that leads to total victory, and that is one where I perish.'

He sighed again. There was a tremulousness to it that Iyanna could not miss. He was afraid. 'There is nothing for it. Think of the sacrifices you have made, Iyanna Last-of-Your-House, that we all make. I will not be alone in falling into the Dark Prince's clutches. Many will feel the true death and the torment that follows. But if not, what? We all die, we all suffer for now and evermore? If I die, Iyanna, at least you,' he gestured at her elaborately with his hand, a mark of deepest respect, 'will live. And you are the most important of us all. I was never convinced by the words of Ulthran, his relaying of the visions of Kysaduras, but I am now. It is you who have convinced me. I would die a thousand deaths to see you succeed, and I will. Do not think you have the easier path, for upon you the hope of all our salvations rests. You must triumph, Iyanna. Bring forth the goddess of death and restore equilibrium to the souls of our people. Dying is the easy part, and it is not for you to travel that road.'

A half-cycle passed. The webway yawned wide, becoming a glowing funnel half a million paces across. The ships flew down it, coming into a junction of staggering proportions. Many conduits came together here, giving it the appearance of a great, golden heart viewed from the inside.

If a heart, it was dead, the walls of it plaqued with broken wraithbone structures, the ash of the sun fragment that once lit it hanging dark in the centre. The ruins of a port city, cast down perhaps at the Fall, perhaps later – for in the uncertain light of the webway, one could see that the spires were blackened by flame, and walls scored with the telltale marks of lance fire. Whatever its name was had long been forgotten.

The ships – a fleet of twenty-three in all – went for the centre of the chamber, shoaling by the dead sun as lighter vehicles sped from apertures in their sides and swooped down to the distant city.

The scouts were gone a long time, for the nexus was broad as a world's orbit around its sun, and the ruins were vast. Eventually they reported in, each vessel's captain declaring his assigned quadrant clear of danger, and the ships of Iyanden sank in streams to an area of crumbling docks where seven major webway tunnels pierced the city floor.

Aspect Warriors deployed first, taking up position in cracked towers around the piers extending towards the centre of the nexus. Flights of Falcon tanks swept overhead, turrets tracking back and forth.

The word was given, and the sides of the Iyanden ships opened. Out strode the Phoenix Host, hundreds of tall wraithbone shapes disembarking onto the ancient quaysides. Iyanna was at their head, Althenian as ever by her side. She and all the other eldar wore their helmets, for the atmosphere of the dead city was not safe to breathe.

'Fitting place,' he said. 'The dead walk in the dead lands. Homecoming.'

Iyanna, distracted by the sinister ruins all about them, replied, 'This is as close as we can come with our ships to Dûriel. We go from here on foot.'

'I will march,' said Althenian. 'I do not tire and will not, nor can I.'

Rank after rank of wraithkind tramped down the ramps into the dead city. A flight of Vypers sped overhead, looped and flew straight at the ground – an illusion, as they were scouting webway tunnels. The whole inner surface of the webway held gravity, making the chamber a giant world turned inside out, the broken towers of its bottom reaching out for their kind, lost to distance's caprice, on the opposing side. The world-city was so large that on the ground the curve of the chamber was imperceptible, and webway portals opened directly into the plazas of the place, appearing as glowing, smooth-sided pits.

All was lit by the lambency of the webway, a shifting light that made every shadow a trickster. In this dimness, the yellow and blue of Iyanden were sinister brown ochre and midnight black.

'In this place, the ghost warriors are as ghosts,' said Taec, walking to join Iyanna and her companion. He glanced up at Althenian with idle curiosity, but the giant exarch's attention was elsewhere.

'They are not the only ones,' said Iyanna. 'I sense dark shades, the spirits of those who dwelled here. Not many, but dangerous. We should not tarry. There is a hunger on the skein that I do not like.'

'We are done. The Phoenix Host is all ashore. All await,' said Althenian. 'Do not fear, with such might at your command, no danger.'

Iyanna shivered, as if touched by cold, and her face, a pale grey shape in the perpetual dusk, took on a seriousness mirrored by her gestures and the sense of her soul. 'Ghosts will fight ghosts, a waste of time. We must be away.'

As if to deliberately accentuate her concerns, the sound of laser fire cut through the sepulchral silence of the city: the whining of powercells, the crack of stale air heated explosively, the thump of impact explosions.

'From afar,' said Althenian. 'The sound of war in dead lands. Bad omen.'

The captain of the frigate *Lileath* spoke to the High Council through their helmet crystals. +We have movement in an area twenty thousand paces to the left,+ she said.

+There are worse things than ghosts in these places,+ said Taec via the same psychic link to the force's commanders. +Iyanna is right. We should not stay overlong here. We have the numbers and the might to overcome most threats, even that of fell spectres, but in doing so we will waste valuable time.+

Signals of assent came to them over the communications web. Columns were forming up alongside each of the five major transport ships, phalanxes of wraithguard at the front, their guiding spiritseers protected in their midst. Wraithlords went with them, three or four to each group of one hundred, those who were once seers aiding the spiritseers in directing the march of their lesser fellows. Wraithknights walked up and down the lines, weapons ready in delicate fists. Falcon grav-tanks rode by. A blast of air pushed at Iyanna's and Taec's robes as a Cobra floated onward to the front of their group.

Behind them came the Guardians of Iyanden, pitifully few of the living to fight alongside the dead. War walkers were gathering in number in the open spaces by the piers, waiting to go ahead as vanguard.

'You should take a transport, Silvereye,' said Iyanna kindly. 'The crystal grows apace within you, and you are venerable. I must walk with the wraithkind, to ensure their minds remain clear.'

Taec bowed stiffly. He was glad Iyanna had given him the excuse to withdraw. As head of the seer council, he was senior to her both there and in the High Council, but to have withdrawn to a vessel without prompting while the rest marched would have been unbecoming.

A Wave Serpent flew down to the broken square they waited in, and with a touch of his hand to his forehead, Taec took his leave of the spiritseer.

Only one warrior remained to join the column.

The army fell silent as the last door opened, a wash of fury coming with it. With steps like the ringing of a dolorous bell, the Avatar of Kaela Mensha Khaine strode down the gangway to the quayside. Aggression rose within every eldar present, living and dead. The thrill of it rose within Iyanna, starting deep in the pit of her belly and rising up her body to flush her face with heat. The power of it took her breath away. Her eyes slid closed, and when they opened again, she looked upon the world very differently. Fury; she felt it coming from all the others. Her sadness at war retreated, and became anticipation.

The Avatar halted, breathing fire, fire wreathing it from iron joints, fire streaming from its eye sockets, blood hissing from its perpetually dripping hand to the floor. Whatever spirits watched them shrank back into the dark. They feared the god-fragment greatly. It swung its head back and forth over the host, inspecting its followers. The roar of its furnace body was mirrored in the heartbeat of every eldar.

Abruptly, it walked ahead, eldar parting to let it through. Its heavy treads receded, taking with it some of its boundless anger, but not all.

The disembarkation was complete. Iyanna signalled the group of rangers who were to guide the force the remaining way to Dûriel.

+We are ready,+ she said. +You follow no path but your own, now show it to us.+

+This way,+ their leader said. Small groups of them joined the head of each column.

Iyanna held up her hands. With complex gestures denoting hope for victory, she signalled the army to move out, simultaneously emitting a psychic command pulse that galvanised all to motion.

The effect was, in its own way, shocking. The wraithguard of the first column suddenly lumbered into life from total stillness. The wraithkind did not move at all when not in motion, unlike living creatures, and their sudden transition from immobility made even Iyanna start. They marched in perfect unison, each one placing its feet exactly where the one before it had trodden; left then right then left again. The first column cleared the dockside, war walkers falling in to stride in front, and the second column joined it, then the third, until all five columns had merged into one to snake through the nameless port city towards the glowing way to Dûriel.

Iyanna and Althenian fell in behind the first group to draw off. The dead marched tirelessly, but slowly, and Iyanna thought she would have little difficulty in keeping pace with them.

+How far to Dûriel?+ she asked of the rangers' leader.

+Four cycles' march, my lady,+ he said. +An unusually long way to walk, but this part of the webway is seldom traversed, and has fallen into disrepair.+

She nodded. She knew this anyway, but asking again reassured her in some way she found hard to define. Perhaps it was simply the touch of a living mind upon her own when she was in constant communion with the dead.

The city shook to the stamp of the ghost warriors' feet. They were agile for such large machines, but still heavy, and the sheer number of them generated a certain noise. Their march was unlike the marching of other creatures: they planted their feet firmly but quietly, and the resultant tramping was loud but stealthy seeming, if not stealthy in actuality. The city was so silent that the slightest noise sounded like a crack of thunder. No living creatures had come this way for a long time, and why would they? A nexus point for the southern True Stars, all the inhabitants of those planets had been swept away by the calamity of the Fall, and there had been no eldar to come here for many generations.

Something stirred at the back of Iyanna's mind, the sensation of being watched again. Shielded by the webway from the fall of the empire, other port cities and worldlets had survived. Some had even been built since. Many had become satellites of Commorragh, but not all. What had happened here? she wondered. Where was the sun that should light it? Where were the people? Shielded from the warp, those in the webway had famously avoided being consumed by Slaanesh.

She looked up, at elegant windows piercing the sides of soaring towers. Most still held their glazing. The damage here was superficial, many parts of Iyanden were in far worse state, but Iyanden yet lived, while the dead nature of this place was unmistakable. Sure she was being watched, she looked around her. Some of the spires were tens of thousands of paces tall, impossible architecture in an impossible realm.

She saw nothing, felt nothing more than the unease she had felt since debarking. The glass reflected only the shifting light of the webway, empty windows like the eyes of the dead, but the feeling persisted until the Avatar walked past the building, when it abruptly ceased.

Iyanna pressed her lips together, and refused to look up again. Even for one such as her, for whom necromancy was life, this place carried too great a burden of death.

Iyanna breathed more easily as the roadway opened out. The remains of a park girt the trumpet-mouth of a webway tunnel. Air- and grav-craft peeled away from the column on the ground, soaring vertically, then coming down at a steep dive and passing down the funnel into the webway. The Phoenix Host marched directly for the lip of the tunnel, through ancient trees that crumbled at their touch and grass, held together by nothing more than the memory of its shape, that puffed into dust.

They went on without pausing over the edge of the tunnel. As Iyanna came to it she experienced a brief surge of vertigo. The mouth of the tunnel was like a slope that turned into a sheer drop and a pit that went on forever. But as she passed its edge, the wall became the floor so that she was perpendicular to the horizontal planes of the city. When she glanced behind, she saw the spires were now on their sides. Framed by the tunnel mouth, the ships were withdrawing to take up station at the centre of the chamber to await their return.

If they returned.

Grav-craft humming overhead, the Phoenix Host marched on in silence. Iyanna strained her mind to keep the huge number of wraithkind focused on their purpose. So much vengeance was hard to bear, but she summoned up her own pain, remembering the terrible psychic burst that had killed all her house but her, and drew her own determination from it.

She drew power too from Althenian. He marched alongside her, long limbs swinging easily. He had been there for her for so long, Althenian the Thrice-Dead, but not dead yet.

And soon he would be gone.

She drew strength from this sorrow too.

CHAPTER ELEVEN
WAR IN THE WEBWAY

Gateways of light irised open over a low mountain once known as Kurnous's Seat, ancient webway gates that had remained hidden, unseen beneath the skin of reality for ten millennia. Reaver jetbikes came through at supersonic speed, the wind screaming through the holes punched into their bodywork. They performed a wide sweep, then set themselves into a protective pattern. One of their number re-entered the webway. Within moments, it re-emerged, two dozen Venom transport craft streaking behind it. Behind the graceful fairings of the Venoms, each emblazoned with the emblems of the Cult of Strife, were fighting platforms crammed with wyches. Seven Raiders likewise full of warriors, and five more carrying collapsed hex cages, came behind. Scourges leapt from Raider fighting decks, wings spread, as keen-eyed wyches swept the muzzles of dark lances and splinter cannons across the angry sky. All were visible only to the other eldar, sophisticated field devices hiding the presence of the Commorrites from eye and mind alike.

A final flaring. Alone on a jet-black Venom came Lelith Hesperax, framed by pennants streaming from a dozen trophy poles arranged in a fan; the greatest of all Commorragh's wyches, mistress of the Cult of Strife.

Like her followers, Hesperax wore a half-armour, presenting more skin to the world than was covered. She was astonishingly beautiful, her long red hair tied up in a tall ponytail, her limbs long and well-proportioned, her body curvaceous even by the exacting standards of Commorrite convention. Hers was a deadly beauty; a great many males had paid with their lives for lingering upon it for too long.

The wyches of her cult were armed with all manner of exotic weaponry, most fit for the melee they preferred – agonisers, splinter pistols, razorflails, shardnets and impalers. All Hesperax carried was two long knives. They were forged from the finest metals to the very highest standard, but aside from that they were entirely unexceptional. No poison coated them, no disruption field generators lent their edges might. Lelith Hesperax would use no other weapons in close combat – her pride would not allow it, and her skill was such that anything more than a keen edge was entirely unnecessary.

The clouds were an angry red; the sun, when it appeared, tainted similarly by the density of spores in the atmosphere. There was a pungent stench to the air, acid, bile and rot, worse than that in the slave pens of the Eternal City. When the clouds broke to reveal the poisoned sky, the fiery descent trails of landing craft – or pods, or whatever the voidspawn used to further their endless interplanetary buffet – slashed across it in regular diagonal lines.

Hesperax glanced at the display floating over the Venom's rail. Dark purple blotches pulsed, indicating concentrations of the creatures. 'That way, and swiftly,' she shouted over the wind, pointing to the Godpeak.

Her Venom was piloted by her current favourite, Khulo Khale. He turned in his seat to look up at her, his pale face artfully marked from their last encounter.

'Mistress!' Khulo Khale had a deep voice, sensual. She liked that about him, and he had not yet bored or offended her. It was only a matter of time until he did. She smiled at the thought of that day, a pleasant thrill shivering her belly. She had the habit of deciding how to dispose of her lovers the moment they came into her arms; it made their couplings all the more erotic. The best had much time and attention lavished on their love-deaths. Each one, she was sure, came to her certain that they would be the one to survive her attentions, that somehow they would tame her. They were resurrected as wiser beings, if she allowed them to live again.

Khale was an exceptional pilot, a one-time Reaver champion, and he flew the Venom with consummate skill. Their craft banked to the north, following the Reavers. Terse reports came in from her followers, reassuring her that they had not attracted attention. The aliens were busy demolishing this world, eating it up like the mindless beasts they were. Hesperax stared through breaks in the streamers of red cloud. Already the industrious aliens had scoured much of the surface clean. Biological towers, weirder even than those created by the haemonculi, were growing from the cracked earth, many clustered around lakes of acid.

The creatures too were not dissimilar to those made by master haemonculi, she supposed, although they lacked any imagination, being brutishly utilitarian. She shouted a series of clipped commands, wyches' battle cant, the pick-ups in her armour conveying her orders to her followers. Twelve Reavers peeled away from the front of the formation, and dropped down to the remnants of forest in the valley before the Godpeak.

'Be sightful, my swift hunters. We seek the biggest warrior creatures alone, these eater beasts are of no use,' she said.

'Yes, mistress,' they said.

The consumption of the planet was well under way. Hesperax knew little about the tyranids, other than that which she needed to know: that they were formidable fighters. Hidden in the webway, the true eldar had little to fear from the threat the Great Dragon posed to the Great Wheel. The havoc they brought down upon others was mildly amusing, but it was as creatures for the arena that the aliens appealed to her. Novelty was the key to the games, and she owed her position to her inventiveness as much as her skill at arms. The voidspawn were devoid of fear and the capacity to suffer, but the terror they evoked in other species was particularly piquant. 'And here there are two colours to be harvested. How marvellous,' she said to herself.

The wyches sped on, invisible to the tyranids. Hesperax felt the hive mind as a dull pressure, for the true eldar were still psychic creatures, even if they repressed that side of their being. It was giving her a headache, and that made her irritable. Someone was going to regret upsetting her today.

'Mistress! We have sighted the prize!'

Hesperax manipulated the viewing orb with a swift motion of her hand. There was a large gathering of warrior beasts on the flank of the Godpeak. The red and bone coloured ones.

'A delightful find! Fifteen fresh slaves to the one who gets the largest!' she shouted. Whoops and laughter greeted her over the comm-net. On the backs of the Venoms, shardnets were readied. Wyches leapt to their feet, bringing large splinter cannons around. The weapons had been loaded with ammunition intended to incapacitate rather than kill. Ordinarily this was done by the infliction of excruciating pain, but the voidspawn felt little pain either, so she had had all her venom weapons charged with potent sleeping drugs painstakingly designed to affect the aliens' extra-galactic physiology. It was a dull way to reap one's harvest, and they would get no sustenance from the suffering of such animals, but the Ebon Sting haemonculi had assured her it was the most efficacious way of delivering the prizes intact. She yawned. The fight would be technically engaging, but there would be no feast of dark energy. Boring.

They worked their way up the valley, picking choice specimens, bringing them to bay and felling them with their tranquilisers. Soon, three of the five Raiders' cages were crammed with slumbering specimens. The day was going well, if tediously.

Her perfect brow creased as they approached the mountain. The air was clearer around its bulk, and she saw the majority of the craft were coming down to the north where her scanners indicated the greater part of the red and bone aliens to be congregating. There was a steady stream of them ascending the mountain. They formed a line that initially appeared chaotic, but on second inspection had the manic order one sees in social insects.

'Vespah told me that this would not be happening, that the war phase is over. What goes on here?' she said. No one answered, because none of them knew.

'Mistress...' said Uriqa, a pilot and succubus, with a servile mixture of caution and deference.

'Speak, Uriqa!' Hesperax said.

'The webway is open,' she said, and sent a visual of her proof.

For the first time in long arcs, Hesperax's stony heart twitched with fear. It was swiftly overcome by outrage.

'The webway! Those fools! The mewling craftworld flagellant fools have left the door ajar!'

The flotilla of wych craft dropped low, spiralling down over the horde of creatures. Sure enough, between high, fluted backs and chitinous limbs, the glimmer of webway energy could be seen.

'We shall have to abandon the hunt!' she snarled. 'We cannot allow this, the sacred grounds invaded so.' Thoughts of the hive fleet flooding into Commorragh filled her mind with dread. 'Soltarun!' She called for her lieutenant.

His face appeared in the viewing orb, maskless, face painted with blood-runes, eyes calculating. 'This one is ready.'

'We have the coding for this gateway?'

'This one has,' he said.

'Then open it fully. We will have to fly in, shut the gate behind us, and annihilate those beasts that have infiltrated. The fools!' she shouted, slamming her fist into the railing. 'They are children, puritanical fools!'

The dark eldar flotilla banked around. Soltarun had his transport broadcast the webway code into the ancient network, the machine mimicking the thought processes of the eldar to engage with its psychic matrices. The gate split wide, tall enough to allow a light Titan out. The aliens immediately surged forwards.

'Now!' screamed Hesperax.

The flotilla sped on, the wyches crouching low as windrush battered its way through their craft's streamlining energy fields. They whipped over the stampeding voidspawn. Hundreds were thundering through, kicking up clouds of dust as they disappeared into the bright light.

The wyches emerged on the other side. Hesperax cursed loudly. This was a main webway conduit, designed to take transports, even small void craft, and it was full of aliens.

She grabbed at the splinter rifle mounted on the Venom's rail. 'Drop the captives,' she said. 'I will need everyone to fight.'

'Mistress...'

'Do it! And shut the gate, Soltarun!'

Hex cages detached from the undersides of the transports, spinning as they fell. They hit the glowing bottom of the webway, squashing dozens of tyranids apiece as they bounced along. She examined one as they sped over it. The hex cage was intact, but the specimens inside were so much smashed meat. 'Ruined!' she spat.

'We may gather more, mistress,' said Khulo Khale. He instantly regretted trying to placate her when the muzzle of the venom rifle swivelled down to point straight at his head.

'If you were not flying this transport, I would hollow out your head with pain crystals. Be silent!'

Behind them, the gateway closed. No change came over the ancient wraithbone archway, all that was visible beyond it was a continuation of the conduit, but all of a sudden, there were no more aliens pouring through, as if someone had swept a brush across a line of ants.

A change came with it. As the webway portal closed, Hesperax was relieved of a part of the hive mind's pressure. The line of the creatures lost some of its organisation, and started to bunch up around the leader-beasts.

'How many came through?' said Soltarun. The horde of monsters stretched away to the next curve of the webway.

'Who knows? Hundreds, thousands maybe,' said Uriqa.

'Does it matter?' said Hesperax. 'A thousand or ten thousand, they all must die. I suggest starting at the rear.'

She indicated to Khulo Khale that he should drop low. In the confined space of the tunnel, the others followed.

Weapons blazing, the Cult of Strife smashed into the rearward portion of Hive Fleet Kraken.

The next four cycles went by in a blur for Iyanna. The light of the webway was unchanging. She walked the space between two worlds. She ceased to be aware of her body, and instead became aware of many bodies, all the same and marching in unison. The minds that glowed dully in their armoured heads all thought the same thoughts, their memories of themselves indistinct. She was a dreamer living the dreams of the dead. Her eyes unfocused, and she no longer saw those who walked in front of her. Her senses became innumerable impressions, half-formed, seen by a thousand eyeless dead. Althenian was her single fixed reference point, always there, ready to steady her should she stumble, ready to help her on when she faltered.

They did not sleep. Command of the living was taken up by the force's three autarchs. They paused twice a day to eat and drink, and in those times Althenian gently stayed Iyanna with his giant hand. She came back from the death-trance long enough to take nourishment, but the thoughts of the dead were never far from her. And when eating was done, on they walked again.

The webway tunnel narrowed as they left the nameless port city behind, becoming far too small for anything larger than the super-heavy tanks accompanying the army, and in places the column had to make space for the flying machines to come closer to the floor or they would not fit. The wraithknights went through these constrictions bent double, the wraithlords' helmet crests brushed the stuff of the webway.

A confusion of tunnels and branchings met them, and twice the Phoenix Host came to nexuses that were similar in form to the dead city but far lesser in scope. These were dangerous realms. Although they had been well-used, those days were long gone. As the rangers said, areas of the labyrinth had collapsed, and many tunnels led off to nowhere, or worse. The True Stars formed a ring around the Eye of Terror many light years across in real space, and so a number of the tunnels here would go directly to the crone worlds.

Parts of the network were shored up with wraithbone pylons, where the energies shackled aeons past by the Old Ones had given out or been deliberately sabotaged. In other places armoured gates sealed off tunnels, but not all dangers were thus captive. Disaster awaited them at every wrong turn. The rangers led them on unerringly, directing the scouting Vypers and war walkers down the correct conduits. Only the followers of the Laughing God knew the webway better than the outcasts.

A sense of urgency was over the living part of the host, and this helped drive the dead forward through their foggy perceptions.

At the close of the third cycle, Iyanna felt Althenian's massive hand once more close gently around her chest.

'We stop here, now time to sleep, spiritseer, time to rest.'

She looked up at him bleary-eyed, felt the other spiritseers withdraw from communion with her and the dead. The wraithguard stopped. Life left them again.

Iyanna blinked. Althenian was speaking to her.

'You must sleep, unceasing your labours are. Rest, great seer.'

She nodded. There was a roaring in her mind, distant, like far-off thunder or the rumble of the waterfalls of House Haladesh's Hidden Gorge heard from afar.

Althenian, sensitive to her thoughts as always, told her what it was. 'The hive mind. The call of the Devourer, even here We are close.'

Iyanna mumbled, weak and incoherent as a child. She half-fell against the wraithlord's arm. She was asleep before he caught her. When she awoke a few hours later, she was still in his grip, cradled like an infant.

The living members of the Phoenix Host ate and refreshed themselves before the army moved out again. In the face of the hive mind's roar, psychic communications were problematic, and the army switched to electromagnetic means of discourse.

'We near Dûriel,' said the rangers' leader. 'We will pass through a large hall wherein many conduits join. We will lead you through there into the tunnel to the surface. There are many exits – Dûriel was a jewel among the True Stars and the webway adjoining it is correspondingly complex. The safety of most ways we can vouch for, some few we cannot. Be wary, and do not chance a path unless we or your wayseers permit it.'

Once more Iyanna reached out to the dead, waking them gently from their dreams of life. She felt stale and sticky, her saliva thick in her mouth. Whether this was an effect of four cycles without washing or the proximity of the gigantic mind of the tyranids, she could not say for sure. She hoped to lose the feeling in joining with the dead, but the hive mind was as audible to the dead as the living, if not more so. There was a change in the ghost warriors, a quickening of their mood. They sensed that their vengeance was at hand and their minds became more focused on the here and now as a result.

Iyanna marched on. At some point Taec had joined her. When she noticed him walking by her side, she raised a hand in greeting, but the gesture drifted off halfway through. She was invested mind and soul in the world of the dead. Bound into individual spirit stones, through her the honoured ancestors found a rapport of a sort not dissimilar to that offered by the infinity circuit. The sense of it was intensely comforting to her. They felt no fear. The dead were aware that battle brought the risk of She Who Thirsts, but they did not care. What drives they had came from the past, not from fears for the future, for they had no future. There was solace in their company, and Iyanna had to fight to prevent herself from sinking too far into their embrace. Were she to go too deep, she might never find herself again, and be like the others of her house; minds separated from their forms without the interposition of bodily death. Form, mind and being – she had to remain alert to the qualities of each, or risk losing them all. It was exhausting work.

They came to the nexus the rangers had described, an elegant cavern carved from the boundary between real space and the Othersea. The cavern was far broader than it was tall, and roughly kidney-shaped. They emerged onto a sculpted platform ten paces high that filled a third of the cavern. Ramps descended to a lower level, and from there three major arterial routes exited, one opposite the tunnel the army came out from, the others to either side. Three-score smaller tunnels of lesser diameters went out at various other points. There was a pleasing asymmetry to the cavern, a place of smooth curves and ramps sculpted from glowing energy. There was evidence of vanished structures underfoot: wraithbone spars and time-worn psychoplastics.

Iyanna, her eyes attuned to the sight of the dead, saw the place as it once was. No settlement this, but a place of shrines, a small park. A rest stop for journeying eldar. There were half a dozen or so quays for small void-runners, but big ships could not come this way for whatever reason the beings that had built the webway had decreed. She had the sense that it had been a place of peace. How its modest structures came to be so eroded in the changeless labyrinth was a mystery, but then so much was within the infinite halls of the webway.

The rangers led them down one of the winding ramps and over the broad floor of the cavern, twelve thousand paces across, to the rightmost tunnel.

It was wide, and in her dream trance, she supposed it was once the main way to Dûriel from this particular nexus.

They went into it.

An uncertain period of time passed. Iyanna trudged on, her grace gone, as leaden in her movements as were the dead. The final corner was rounded, and they came to the top of a long, sweeping slope.

'Dûriel is beyond,' said the rangers. 'In one tenth-cycle we will come to the place where the wayseers might open their temporary paths to the surface. The main gate is just beyond. You will see a large tunnel to the left and behind you there – this is the road to Biel-Tan. My band will look for their coming.'

Taec said something to her, but she did not hear.

The army picked up speed.

Iyanna came into herself, her sense of being rushing to alertness.

The minds of the dead were waking. A sharpening of perception swept through the army, as ripples from a stone cast into water.

'Wait!' said Iyanna into her comm-bead. 'There is something wrong. The dead are stirring. Wait! We must stop.' No one responded, and Iyanna could not be sure whether she had spoken aloud or not. Her mind was weak. The strain of directing so many of the dead for such a long march had taken its toll. She forced herself to greater wakefulness.

'Wait!' she shouted.

'Halt!' shouted Taec by her side, and the army halted. 'What is it?' he said to her.

'Something is wrong.'

* * *

Taec shut his eyes, delving into the skein. They flew open, and he gasped at what he saw.

A terrible sound echoed up the corridor. Scout Vypers came speeding back from the front of the column, guns spitting. One impacted on the wall of the tunnel and spun out of control, crashing into a group of wraithkind.

The noise drew closer, a rattling sound, hollow stalks knocked together.

'No,' said Iyanna. 'It cannot be.'

'Voidspawn! Voidspawn in the webway!' The cry went up, alarm sweeping through the Phoenix Host. That the most sacred of grounds should be so invaded was abhorrent to them. Iyanna and Taec struggled with the eldar's dismay. The army's ranks fell into disarray, the dead and living alike paralysed by shock.

The noise burst upon them, the clacking noise of hard alien limbs, underpinned by hissed vocalisations. A wall of psychic pressure came next, a division of the hive mind, exhilarated at its discovery of the Phoenix Host.

The alien horde rounded the corner, filling it from side to side with hideous bio-constructs.

War walker pilots, momentarily stunned by the unexpected sight of Far Ranging Hunger within the webway, found their purpose and opened fire. Heavy weapons blazed as they stalked backwards from the threat. Aspect Warriors pushed their way to the front, forming firing lines.

Taec recovered his wits. 'We'll never prevail against them trapped like this,' he said. 'Fall back!' he called by voice and telepathy, his powerful psyche pushing back against the hive mind.

Quick response pulses clicked in his ears as the autarchs and exarchs responded to his command. He looked down the tunnel, the slight rise allowing him to see down onto the fight at the front of the column. Living tanks came to the fore of the horde. Working in packs, the beasts trapped war walkers, preventing them from fleeing, then butted the fragile machines with their massive heads, smashing them to pieces. Laser and shuriken fire streaked across the dwindling gap between the armies.

'I must go,' said Althenian. 'Forward I am needed now, remain here.'

Iyanna raised her hand, then faltered. The giant construct stalked off, forcing its way roughly through the throng. Other wraithlords went with him to join the rest of their kind at the front.

'Fall back now!' shouted Taec, empowering his words with a psychic pulse strong enough to be felt over the hive mind's racket. This woke the army from its collective shock. Grav-vehicles lifted into the air to fire over the host, Guardians streamed backwards. Taec dipped again into the skein, hunting over possibilities. 'Why did I not see this? Why?' he muttered to himself over and over. In his mind, and upon the skein, he found no answer.

He called up the images of the autarchs in his helm's viewing orb. 'The skein is clear, many futures end badly, the best threads bring delay. Hope comes from unexpected quarters.'

'We should go to the gate, hold them there at the tunnel mouth, and await the armies of Biel-Tan,' said Autarch Culthain.

'I concur,' said Autarch Jethlesar.

'And I,' finished Autarch Herinim.

'No,' said Taec. 'We cannot fight into them, we will lose all advantage of our ranged weaponry. We must fall back and bring them to battle across a wider front.'

A pause, and then Jethlesar spoke. 'We shall see to it, crystal father.'

Taec turned off his images of the others, but listened in to their chatter as they set their plans, checking them over in the skein and offering advice where needed.

'Come, Iyanna, we must go back.' He pulled at her robe. Now was not the time for social nicety; Iyanna was as one drugged, half in the world of the dead.

'I... The dead...' she said.

'They cannot operate here,' said Taec urgently. 'Imagine the calamity that would occur should their wraithcannons breach the webway. In this confined environment, they would slay us all. We would all be lost, and the labyrinth dimension damaged. No, this must be done with blade and fire, but with care! We must go.' He looked back towards the nexus. 'Perhaps there it will be safe enough to make use of our Phoenixes, but not here!'

He tried to call for a transport, but the way was choked with floating battle tanks shooting down the slope of the tunnel. The armies had met, and ferocious fighting marked the thin seam between blue and yellow, and red and bone.

A flight of jetbikes rushed overhead, dodging through the crammed airspace, Jethlesar at their head.

'Fighting withdrawal. Fall back by unit on my command,' the autarch said, his laser lance already blazing.

'Now, Iyanna! Now!' said Taec.

A group of Guardians formed up around them. Taec scanned the surrounding area for threats. As yet, the voidspawn were distant.

'Spiritseers! Bring the dead with you, bring them back into the nexus!' he called.

They went as fast as they could. Reports from the battle line were not encouraging to Taec's ears. How many eldar were dying he did not like to think. Despair lapped at the edges of his consciousness. To not foresee this... How much else had he not seen?

Within the tenth-cycle they had made it in good order back to the nexus. Culthain was dead, he heard, cleft in twain by a blow from a monster's claw. Jethlesar fought in the air still. Herinim greeted Taec in the nexus. Together they deployed their forces as best they could, ranging heavy weapons upon the platform, barrels pointing at the webway tunnels.

'Wraithblades upon the wings,' said Herinim. 'Place the wraithguard in the centre. They will be the breakwater that lessens the ocean's power. From above we will rain death upon them.'

Taec rode the skein, testing what threads he could see through the Dragon's shadow, seeing those that depicted the collapse of the line and the destruction of the host, others where they were victorious. All were ephemeral and uncertain.

'I cannot see,' he said. 'Either I am blinded by the tumult of the alien mind, or...' He was unwilling to voice his thoughts.

'Farseer? You have grave concerns.' Herinim's helm plate was impassive, white framed by dark red, his flight pack wings folded behind his head.

'Or I am being actively blocked, and that is why I did not see this incursion into the webway,' Taec said. 'We cannot rule anything out. This is a far more cunning foe than any of us could ever have guessed. Our arrogance once again trips us. That, or...' He let his fears of Slaanesh's involvement go unsaid.

'But now, what do you see?'

'Hold the wraithknights in reserve. Should the voidspawn break through the wraithguard, only they will hold them back.'

'We cannot hold for long, perhaps we should consider withdrawing from the webway?'

'And let Dûriel fall, and all I have seen come to pass, the voidspawn nesting in the webway into the bargain?' said Taec. 'No. Our undertaking is to prevent the merging and we must attempt to with all our will and might.' He looked off into the tunnels. The sounds of fighting were coming closer. 'Besides, we do not have to prevail, merely slow the tide. Help comes from unexpected quarters. From where is hidden to me, but it comes.'

'Farseer...'

'You echo my own reluctance, Herinim. Tell me, what troubles you?'

'If this foe is so mighty and so wise, strong enough perhaps to interfere with your vision, then is it not conceivable that your hopes are false? All we can do is trust in fate, as we have for a thousand arcs, but if we no longer can, what does the future hold for us?'

Taec frowned within his helm. He had had the same fear himself. 'Then we will have to wait and see, as all mortals ultimately must. Bladecraft and gunfire will see us through, or they will not. We have no choice but to try.'

They waited, as orders were sent out to the troops at the front to fall back in earnest. They trickled back in small groups. Transports, freer to operate in the nexus, swept down upon the shattered units and whisked as many as they could to safety. Others ran for their lives.

Wraithlords erupted from the tunnel, sprinting hard for the lines of silent wraithguard. Behind them were the wraithknights, moving easily backwards, ceaselessly scanning the tunnel mouths.

The horde flooded from the main tunnel to Dûriel, the last eldar firing desperately into them before they were overwhelmed.

'Do not commence firing! Wait until our warriors are clear!' shouted Herinim.

Iyanna and the other spiritseers, stationed back on the platform, drew themselves closer to the world of the living, dragging the minds of the dead with them.

The wraithguard raised their weapons in a single movement.

'You will wait,' said Taec, his eyes half-lidded, his mind half in the world of now, half upon the skein. 'You will wait, you will wait. You will not hit the fabric of the webway.'

The voidspawn were coming closer fast. Taec could feel Herinim's anxiety growing.

His eyes snapped open. 'You will fire now!'

A dreadful drone set up as the reactors of the wraithcannon activated. With a sickening psychic backwash, they opened fire.

Five hundred glittering points of light opened among the voidspawn's front line. The monsters carried on regardless as the lights grew into glowing spheres, then collapsed in on themselves to leave balls of glowing blackness crackling with purple lightning. Taec drew his breath sharply. Through the gaps in reality, malicious eyes burned, and they coveted his soul.

Alien monstrosities imploded and exploded, their shapes twisted out of true by the pull of the warp. By the hundred they were drawn into the howling maelstrom as miniature portals pierced the veil between the worlds. Wind blew over the host as the atmosphere of the labyrinth realm was sucked away.

The wraithcannon shut off. The warp breaches snapped shut with peals of thunder. Great bites had been taken from the alien army, but such were their numbers that the gaps were filled in an eyeblink, and the wall of bone and red surged onwards.

One more volley from the wraithcannon, one more volley where Taec felt his soul shrivel a little more, and the aliens were on them, a spearpoint of twelve towering assault beasts breaking into the line of wraithguard, bowling them aside like game pins. The psychic shockwave came with it, the ravening hunger of the hive mind, and Taec staggered under its onslaught.

'Destroy the leaders!' shouted Herinim. 'Bring then down and the rest will fall!'

The line of Guardians opened fire. Laser light, shuriken, plasma packets, clouds of monofilament wire – all the terrible arts of killing the eldar had perfected over the aeons – poured into the horde, picking out the larger creatures, those that, even to the non-seers, glowed with psychic power. Where they fell, Taec felt the densely woven synaptic network of the swarm ping apart like the strands of a spiderweb cut. But there were so many of them, thousands, and the directing will remained strong.

The voidspawn pushed deep into the ranks of wraithguard at the front of the army. The ghost warriors were tough, sung from the hardest wraithbone, and did not perish easily. Few of the great beasts fell, but so did few of the wraithguard, and all the while a great tally of lesser aliens was accounted for by the guns of the living and their armoured vehicles.

Taec saw opportunity. 'Now, Herinim, it must be now. We have them trapped, crush them!'

Herinim relayed a complex series of orders. Wraithblades swung in from the wings, attempting to isolate the initial assault.

At the same moment, the wraithguard parted. The wraithknights of Iyanden came forward, the Avatar at their head. Towering over even the great warrior beasts of Far Ranging Hunger, they smote all about them with crackling blades, their shields glimmering as they deflected return attacks. The Avatar howled with uncanny fury, the rage of the god-fragment invigorating all the eldar, making the sluggish dead quick and the living eager to spill blood. Its burning sword howled and whooped as it sliced through the ranks of the aliens.

Slowly but surely, they were pushing the horde back.

'Plug the tunnels! Keep them contained!' shouted Taec.

More tyranids were joining the fight, spilling from subsidiary tunnels that must link with the main way. Either that, or more than one gate on the planet had been compromised and that Taec could not countenance.

Battle raged on. By the middle of the cycle, as the eldar reckoned it in the timeless webway, the aliens' advance had been blunted. Wraithknights stooped to enter tunnels heaving with the beasts. Still the voidspawn appeared endless, and slowly the numbers of the Phoenix Host were being whittled away.

And then, a slow smile spread across Taec's weary face.

'Aid,' he said. 'Aid comes at last.'

'I see nothing,' said Herinim.

'Wait. Now. Look.' Taec pointed to a tunnel where several thousand smaller tyranids were throwing themselves madly against an implacable wall of wraithguard. For every wraithguard that died, a hundred or more of the leaping creatures were slain, but they had the numbers, and the time.

Herinim zoomed in with his helm lenses. 'I see nothing still, farseer,' he said doubtfully.

'Watch.'

A disturbance. Flashing light came from behind the tyranids. A glimpse of blue, a tall helm. Aliens fell dead, and then, suddenly, there were none. The voidspawn had been annihilated. Eldar warriors took their place.

The wraithguard parted. Asurmen himself stepped into the cavern, surrounded by his fabled Crystal Sons. The eldar spread out, the wraithguard following his lead with no aid from the spiritseers. The living and the dead formed lines, and opened fire.

'And there,' said Taec. 'And there.'

He pointed to other tunnels. From one, a dead serpentine creature fell. A tall warrior in black armour decorated by bones stepped onto its lip, levelled the scythed cannon in his hands at the milling creatures below and began to methodically cut them down. From another tunnel Jain Zar leapt, flipping through the air to land between a pair of hive tyrants. Baharroth soared into the air. Fuegan strode forwards from a dark tunnel, fusion lance blazing.

'The Phoenix Lords... Five of them...' said Herinim with awe in his voice.

'Six, I believe,' said Taec.

'Aid from an unexpected quarter,' said Herinim.

'Fate is with us,' said Taec.

Joined by their legendary heroes, the eldar fought harder. More and more of the tyranids' node creatures died, and the swarm lost cohesion. The Phoenix Lords leapt from tunnel edge to broken wraithbone to the backs of the enemy, always where they were needed most, destroying the largest and most ferocious creatures with contemptuous ease. The psychic shocks of shattered waystones diminished in frequency, and a fervency gripped the army. The eldar scented victory. But the battle was not done.

'There! Look!' A panicked voice – Taec never knew whose.

A boiling mass of tyranids came from the tunnel to the front of the cavern, piling into a weak point of the eldar line.

'An inconvenient happenstance,' said Herinim.

Before Taec could access the skein and attempt to find a counter-move, a flight of dark-finned attack craft came speeding from the tunnel, barbarically attired eldar riding them. Black light stabbed from ostentatiously decorated weapons.

A female voice spoke over their communications network, a derisory note to it. 'Cousins! We come to your aid in the nick of time, it seems. You are late for your battle.'

Explosions ripped through the cavern. The entire nexus was shaking. The webway here would not go unharmed by this melee.

'Let us finish this,' said Taec.

At Taec's command, Herinim ordered the Phoenix Host to fall upon the voidspawn.

They were utterly destroyed.

CHAPTER TWELVE
THE FATE OF DÛRIEL

Silent shapes slid across an ocean of stars, a mirror to the ocean of blood within Yriel's mind. The bridge of the *Flame of Asuryan* was alive with activity, but the admiral-autarch of Iyanden saw none of it.

Yriel gripped the Spear of Twilight hard in his right hand. His left elbow rested upon the arm of his command pod's chair. He chewed at the first knuckle of his forefinger, his eyes staring off into vistas no other could see.

The waves of blood beat harder. Iron spray filled the air. The unmoving sun had moved, sinking low to the horizon and raising sparks as bright as lance fire from the swell. All was blood red, the sky striated with clouds crimson as wounds. The fell presence of the spear was behind him, closer now than ever before, so close Yriel thought he might reach and touch it, if he were but fast enough.

The sun was hot on his face. The bubbles popped and churned in the foam on the sea, each one a short-lived screaming face.

The presence grew closer.

He turned.

'Admiral! My admiral!'

Yriel awoke from his vision with a start. Yaleanar stood by him, his face troubled.

'Are you well, my lord?' asked Yaleanar quietly.

Yriel nodded dumbly. He was staring at his lieutenant with wide eyes, his face slack. He noticed his hand, knuckles raw and slick with spittle, and hid it behind himself.

'Yes, yes.'

'The spear...' said Yaleanar.

Yriel nodded. Yaleanar understood. He composed himself. 'Do we approach Dûriel, my shadow?'

'Yes, my prince, only...' Yaleanar's face was worried.

'What?'

'See for yourself, Yriel.' He pointed at a viewing globe. It showed Dûriel, icons and runes denoting the position of the hive fleets. Far Ranging Hunger's was dark on the anti-solar side, Starving Dragon's ships an albedo twinkle.

It was not to the fleets that Yaleanar pointed, but the single moon of Dûriel,

Ulaniel. The satellite was small, distant from Dûriel; enwrapped itself by tendrils of Starving Dragon, feasting no doubt on the Imperial stations there. It shone with a ruddy light as red as the seas of Yriel's nightmares.

'A red moon, my prince,' said Yaleanar. 'The omen of the doom of Eldanesh.'

A rush of feverish energy gripped Yriel. This rush of unholy vitality had come before every battle where he had borne the spear. He despised it and welcomed it in equal measure. He rose, and came down from the command pod.

'Aye! And the sign of the first of the Triple Woes! We should fear, yes?' he said angrily. 'You believe this?'

Yaleanar shrugged. 'It makes no matter to me, my prince, I would follow you were you to cast open the gates to the crone worlds and make for them at full sail. But the others? They might fear.'

'Then let the others hear!' shouted Yriel. 'You look at a red moon, I hear, then hear this. An omen, ill-starred perhaps, but that is all it is.' Yriel walked around the bridge. 'Many of you are veterans of the Eldritch Raiders. Many of you fought by my side against Far Ranging Hunger when two-thirds of the fleet died. We triumphed then, did we not?'

His bridge crew looked to each other.

'We triumphed, prince,' said one.

'Aye, we did. And against Rekkfist, and against the humans who sought our home. Some few of you have been by my side since I defeated Kallorax, also in the shadow of a red moon, and the fateful day I broke the sceptre of command, cast it to the floor of the Chamber of Autarchs and took my leave of Iyanden.'

Yaleanar bowed.

'And do I bear a sceptre now?' No response. 'I asked, do I bear a sceptre now!?' he shouted. He looked about the bridge, his staring eyes stabbing into the viewing orbs of every one of the ships' captains, his words conveyed to all the fleet.

'No,' came the replies.

'No, I do not.' He held the spear above his head. 'I bear the Spear of Twilight, the weapon of Ulthanash himself! It too is an ill-starred omen, but I yet stand, and I do not intend to fall today. Who will stand with me?'

Shouts rang out over the ships' network, boosted by the spirit circuits of each ship and pushed past the psychic roar of the hive mind.

'Let it be known that I put no faith in omens, or the dead gods, but only in my skill, in your skill, in the right of the eldar race to tread the stars unopposed, not as refugees or skulking wretches, but as the masters of the galaxy!'

'Yriel! Yriel! Yriel!' came the chant.

'A most rousing little speech.' Lord Sarnak's silky voice cut over the shouts, his perpetually grinning face appearing in the principal of the *Flame of Asuryan*'s viewing orbs. 'You are absolutely wasted with these path-bound dullards. Come home with me to Commorragh. You'd be the season's darling in the corespur, I absolutely guarantee it. I am very moved, yes, positively overcome with positive feelings for our coming victory.'

'You care nothing for omens either then, Lord Sarnak?'

'Quite the contrary, Prince Yriel. I have lived far too long to foolishly dismiss superstition.' His grin moved closer in. 'But red is my most beloved colour.'

Yriel laughed. Pain throbbed up his arm, needles jabbing his flesh from the spear. 'Mine also, of late.' The laugh died on his lips, and he turned his sallow face from Sarnak. 'You are ready?'

'As we agreed, O princeling.'

'Then send out your signals to all the fleet! Make all speed! We will deliver the Fireheart to the surface of Dûriel, then rip the heart out of this splinter of Far Ranging Hunger as we ripped the heart from the one that came before it. This I swear upon the Spear of Twilight. To Dûriel! To Dûriel and glory!'

Sunspear's Wave Serpent exited the webway into extreme turbulence. Immediately the minds of all aboard were gripped by the ravening horror of the hive mind. Several of them gasped. Strong-willed as the eldar were, the insurmountable size and vile, alien nature of it was hard to bear. The clouds were thick and red, the atmosphere choked with spores. Tiny alien creatures blatted upon the hull by the thousands.

'Take us to the surface,' said Sunspear.

The craft dipped down low, Durantai-Bec's instruments blinking light-patterns of warning as he strayed close to the rock of the mountain.

'Shall I set us down, autarch?' asked the pilot. There was an edge to his voice, one of concentration rather than fear.

'Yes.'

The Wave Serpent swept low to the mountainside, bare stone visible through curling streamers of wind-driven spores. It set down near where Aloec had directed the earlier battle. The Inner Command disembarked swiftly.

They looked upon the world in horror.

The Valley of the Gods was unrecognisable. The forest had been stripped away to the bedrock. Massive creatures, little more than gaping maws on stout legs, bulldozed the land with shovel-like mandibles, scooping up the little remaining plant material, topsoil and voidspawn without discrimination. A vast digestion pool occupied the centre of the valley, steaming with noxious vapours, one of many that dotted the ravaged landscape. Young capillary towers composed of multiple stalks pushed upwards, the base of each stalk hundreds of paces across. The stalks writhed as they grew before the eldar's eyes, vying with each other in the race up to space. Hive ships, invisible through the murk, showed up on the eldar's helmet lenses as they descended from low orbit, their mouthparts waiting for the towers' tops to reach them.

There was shocked silence as images of wider Dûriel, relayed by scout craft, played for the Inner Command. The state of Dûriel before had been cause for woe enough, but now it bore as much resemblance to its former beauty as the flensed skull of a maiden does to her full flush of youth.

Warrior beasts roamed the land. Their purpose done and without foes to battle, they fought one another, creatures from both swarms intermingling and fighting freely. Ripper swarms clotted the exposed bedrock, scavenging for every last piece of biological matter. Where they encountered one of the warrior beasts, they swarmed over it, pulling it down by sheer weight of numbers and stripping it to the exoskeleton in short order. The rippers swept away from these downed fighters when done, leaving their gleaming bones to be broken up by slower-moving variants equipped with massive, crushing jaws. Similar beasts chewed upon rock, extracting mineral and microbial wealth.

Spore chimneys and bloated, barely mobile creatures belched endless clouds of micro-organisms into the sky. These drifted until they bonded with the desired chemical elements or free-floating native life, to be picked up by flying, insectoid creatures. These in their turn flew back to the pools once glutted, gathering in dense swarms like twisting smoke over the bubbling bile. A constant downward motion was visible in these shifting double-helix formations as the creatures flew into the acid pools, but there were always more to gather at the top.

That was not the worst of it. Tyranid corpses had been seen in some number in the atrium nexus of the webway opening out onto Dûriel. Sunspear, disquieted, had ordered an investigation. He did not have to wait long.

'Autarch,' a senior Guardian signalled Sunspear. 'We have had contact from one of the Dark Kin's gladiators. The wych–'

'I will speak myself!' said a second voice, heavily accented. A tattooed face appeared in the viewing orb. 'You did not shut the door when you fled,' the eldar said contemptuously. 'My mistress Hesperax has been forced to pursue the voidspawn into the labyrinth. She is most displeased.'

'This is a bad turn of events, Sunspear,' said Altariec quietly.

Sunspear's face burned with shame under his helmet. He could rail against the wayseers, but the responsibility was ultimately his. 'How many?'

'Many thousands,' said the wych. 'I was bidden to wait by the gate to inform you of your mistake. They breached the right-hand tunnel.'

'Iyanden comes that way,' said Kellian.

'Then Far Ranging Hunger will be destroyed,' said Sunspear with some relief. He dismissed the wych's image as he opened his mouth to speak again.

'Yes,' said Forlissiar. 'But how long will the Phoenix Host be delayed?'

Altariec clicked his staff upon the ground. 'No matter! What is done is done. The voidspawn no longer have this world to themselves, and they will not devour it uncontested,' he said. His body language was of support for the commander, but all could hear his disappointment.

As if in proof of Altariec's words, the clouds above flared with light as grav-vehicles broke through from the labyrinth dimension, a few at first, then a great many, so that the red clouds looked wracked with lightning from the webgates' flashing. Brightly painted Vypers, bearing warriors whose diamond-patterned wargear declared their allegiance to the Laughing God, flew to battlegrounds of their own choosing. Bladed skimmers carried the Dark Kin off to wait over the valley, where they would fight by prior agreement. Guardians and their support batteries came from the main gate on foot, arraying themselves in a defensive perimeter around the mountain peak to await the arrival of the Fireheart.

Elsewhere, as before, webway portals sung into being by wayseers cracked open, and eldar squads strode through, dispersing into the rocks all around the Valley of the Gods and the peak.

'What are they doing?' said Kellian, pointing out a pair of great assault beasts who fought as hard as ambull males at the rut. 'Why do they fight?'

'I have seen this from seized mon-keigh records,' said Sunspear. 'Their purpose is done. They await the command to abandon their form and return to their component matter. Our cousins were fortunate the invasion of Iyanden never reached this stage.'

'Fortunate?' said Kellian. 'I do not think so. I have experienced the destruction in a sensorium. Iyanden is in ruins.'

Sunspear fixed Kellian with a grim eye. 'Fortunate, for if the consumption of their craftworld had reached this pass, they would all have been dead. The malice of the Great Dragon knows no end. Iyanden is ruined, but it lives on.'

Kellian twisted his hands around his spear. 'That is a misinterpretation, noble autarch. There is no malice here. The Great Dragon is a force of nature, nothing more. It is not evil as the Doom of Souls is, but merely terrible in its endless hunger. A force of nature, nothing more, but awful for that. We are leaves before the hurricane.'

A chime in Sunspear's helmet broke off their conversation. 'Autarch, Irein Tardoen of Flight of Amberwings Over Water. I have something to report.'

'Go ahead, Irein.'

The Vyper squadron leader sent an image feed to the Inner Command. Aloec accepted it, and a shared viewing globe materialised.

'Something unusual, autarch.'

The Vypers transmitted multiple views of a trail of corpses leading to a massive mound of dead. The eater beasts did not approach this great heap. Rather, warriors of both hive fleets surrounded it.

'Fighting?' said Sunspear.

'Yes, autarch. Not each other. There is weapons discharge there, and a movement of large numbers of Far Ranging Hunger's beasts that way.'

'Quickly,' said Sunspear, hope tugging at him. 'Take me there.'

He left his Wave Serpent with the Inner Command. Hethaeliar and other autarchs he tasked with marshalling the stream of Dark Kin and Biel-Tanians flowing through from the webway. The seers awaited the Fireheart.

Sunspear took a Falcon grav-tank alone, with six more falling in behind him bearing his honour guard, and jetbikes and Vypers flanking those.

Many weapon tyranids were abroad below, their bio-signals crowding the Falcon's sensors so much they appeared as thickly as a glowing fungus on the displays. For the most part they wandered aimlessly, but their presence troubled him. Sunspear signalled the Inner Command. 'There are many more of Far Ranging Hunger than we hoped,' he said. 'Many to the north. They have been reinforced.'

'Low orbital passes by hive ships suggest so, autarch,' came Hethaeliar's perpetually distracted voice. Sunspear thought he heard the note of something else to it. She affected detachment, but he had heard whispers from his supporters that she sought to supplant him as Lord Autarch. His defeat must have been the cause of some joy to her. 'There is another wave approaching. Feedships follow in their wake. The consumption phase has begun. Dûriel has a matter of cycles remaining, no more.'

'Then we are back where we began,' he said. 'Far Ranging Hunger to the north, Starving Dragon to the south, the pair about to mate and the last of the Eldanar caught betwixt the jaws. It is almost as if they anticipate us!'

'It is possible, autarch.'

'Is there yet any sign of Prince Yriel?'

'The fleet has not entered the system as best we can tell,' said Hethaeliar. 'He may have arrived. He is operating cloaked and under silence. Such a vaunted steersman as he should have piloted his ship here by now, I would have thought.'

Sunspear grew irritated with Hethaeliar's tone. 'Keep me informed,' he said, and severed contact. Yriel's tardiness was indeed grave. They had discovered late that the Fireheart could not be brought through the webway. Sarnak's flagship was heavily shielded and had gone through the greatest conduits; those from Biel-Tan required smaller vessels, and the possibility of the Fireheart activating accidentally within such a delicate and constrained part of the labyrinth would have been disastrous. Thus Yriel escorted it along with his Titans, and every moment he was late brought the merging of the hive fleets closer.

'The die is cast, I must work within the situation,' he said to himself. He went back to studying his viewing globes until the pilot called him.

'We approach, autarch.'

Sunspear brought up an external view to replace his maps. The mound of Far Ranging Hunger's corpses appeared bigger close to. North of the Godpeak, three triads of Vypers zoomed around it high above, hidden from the void-spawn by their own spores and the eldar's technology.

A ring of creatures surrounded the mound, clambering over their dead to get to whatever had slain them. There was a flash of firelight, playing through the interlocked limbs of dead voidspawn.

'No, it can't be...' His heart quickened. Involuntarily, he leaned closer to the viewing globe. The globe responded to his movement by expanding and zooming in.

There was a flare of orange fire. A spear burst through the chest of a broad-mouthed serpent rearing atop the pile. A bloody fist pulled a warrior beast's feet from under it, then grabbed at the hissing creature and crushed its skull.

From the heap of dead, the god of war emerged.

'The Avatar! The Avatar of Khaine lives!' Sunspear said. He keyed his communications net to widecast, and shouted it again to all the eldar upon Dûriel. 'The Avatar is with us!'

The Avatar strode down the mound, into the heart of the horde surrounding him. His body leaked molten iron from a dozen wounds, but his fires were undimmed. He cast the Suin Daellae, sending it in a wide circle where it smashed through alien after alien. The Avatar punched its fist into the side of a living tank, and pulled out a handful of clotted matter that ignited in its furnace grip. The living statue held out its other hand and snatched the spear from the air as it returned, spinning on its heel to smash it through the face of a warrior beast that ran at him.

'Attack! Attack!' cried Sunspear. 'Aid our Avatar!'

The Falcons following in his wake split wide to either side, the jetbikes and Vypers peeling away. They dropped from the clouds, weapons firing. At the back of his mind, Sunspear felt the deadly intelligence of the hive mind shift, its attention drawn to this troublesome spot on the world. But it was of no matter to him, when some small part of his honour might be restored. 'Aid the Avatar! For the glory of Khaine!'

The tanks set up a complex fire pattern of interlocked laser blasts, felling voidspawn monstrosities by the score. 'Create a cordon! Set us down, set us down here! Hethaeliar, send immediate reinforcement!'

Sunspear's Falcon was first down, others following, swiftly deploying their cargoes of Aspect Warriors before zooming off to take up firing circuits in the air. The Aspect Warriors set about destroying the aliens near the mound, allowing the tanks to range further out.

'This is it,' said Sunspear, surveying the carnage wrought by the Avatar. The summit of the Godpeak reared over him to the south, where webway portals twinkled with new arrivals still. 'This is where we will make our stand!'

On the plain, surrounded by his defeated foes, the Avatar swung his head from side to side, seeking new victims. There were none near, and the autarch urged the idol to return to his side. In the crowded psychic space of Dûriel, where the hive mind choked all communication, still the god-fragment heard, and deigned to accept. It turned, and climbed back up the hill of woe, iron feet leaving smouldering prints on the hides of the vanquished. Sunspear's blood quickened, his nostrils flared, eager to drink in the stink of blood and hot metal. The Avatar stood by him, radiating fierce heat.

Drawn by the presence of their war god, the Biel-Tanians were already converging upon the place of death. Transports swooped down unbidden from the clouds. Aspect Warriors by the score disembarked, arraying themselves in disciplined ranks around the autarch. Sunspear let them come.

Sunspear took off his helm, and regarded them with eyes made fierce. The spore-heavy air burned his nose, but he did not care. 'The Guardian host will guard the peak! The Dark Kin will reave the valley, but we of the shrines, we of the Path of the Warrior, here we shall make our stand! This is the sign of our undying supremacy! This is the sign of our right to the stars, that no hunger, no matter how vile,' he clasped his hand around his waystone, 'will defeat us! Here we will fight, to buy with our lives the time the seers will need to activate the Fireheart and destroy this threat to us once and for all! Far Ranging Hunger will not pass! We will not allow it to join with Starving Dragon!'

A great shout went up from six hundred warriors. Aloec smiled with savage glee, but as he did so he glanced to the sky. A fresh wave of drop spores were streaking fiery trails through the air.

And still there was no sign of Prince Yriel.

* * *

Four hundred million paces astern of the *Flame of Asuryan*, the majority of Yriel's fleet engaged the tyranids in space as Yriel and five squadrons of escorts drove planetwards like a spear, forcing their way through a cordon of Kraken ships. The shelled monstrosities were fast for void ships, acting as a screen for those larger hive vessels descending to feast upon Dûriel. Yriel's task force rushed past them, leaving the creatures lumbering in their wake. High-velocity boarding worms shot across space. Most missed, the eyes of the hive fleet baffled by the holofield-shattered silhouettes of the ships, but in such great volume the torpedoes came that some hit home. A couple of vessels lagged behind as they were penetrated and warrior beasts disgorged into their interiors. Screams and the sounds of fighting echoed through the communications webs, those conveyed psychically distorted by the hive mind's crushing might.

The input from one hundred and ninety-seven ships would have been overwhelming for most commanders – tactical displays and bridge views, external images of close engagements, voice feeds, psy-feeds, all coming into the bridge of the *Flame of Asuryan* – but Yriel was no ordinary admiral. Burdened by the spear, he hunched like a crow, but he watched the displays with a hawk's eye.

Audio reports sounded from every quarter.

'Get those cruisers away from *Vaul's Caress*!'

'Under heavy fire, taking damage...'

'We shall draw away the thirteenth echelon from the rearguard...'

Every so often, the sober reports of Iyanden and Biel-Tan's captains were interrupted by the whooping shouts of some of the more free-spirited corsairs or Dark Kin, or the hysterical laughter of Lord Sarnak as another hive ship detonated, spilling its entrails into the void.

'Sarnak is bold,' said Yaleanar.

'He is reckless, my shadow,' said Yriel, watching as the Kabal of the Black Heart's void cutters sliced deep into the hive fleet's heart.

'Sounds like someone I know,' said Yaleanar.

'He seeks to kill the norn ship, the queen at the heart of the swarm, and garner glory for himself. He mocks us also for our supposed timidity. He should wait until we have delivered *Vaul's Caress* to the surface. Sarnak!' he said loudly. 'Do not penetrate too deeply. Pull your fleet back. You cannot hope to take the heart of the swarm yourself.'

Sarnak appeared in an image sphere. 'Oh, don't be so tiresome. Could you leave me be, I am a little occupied.' The picture broke up as his ship took a hit. The bridge juddered, and Sarnak and his crew were thrown from their feet. A scream followed. 'On the other hand, perhaps we should reconsider our tactics,' said Sarnak, more soberly than Yriel had ever heard him speak. 'Yes, I will do as you say.'

'Concentrate your efforts on drawing away their quicker vessels. Keep them off my fleet until the Fireheart is delivered. If you can destroy the swifter escorts, we will have a greater advantage when we attack.'

'You send me into danger to save yourself?' Sarnak raised an eyebrow. 'Are you sure you are not a Commorrite, Lord Yriel?'

The *Flame of Asuryan* jibbed sharply to starboard, the violence of the motion overcoming its dampening fields and causing Yriel to lean into it to keep his balance. 'I assure you, it is equally perilous here. If you do not do as I ask, breaking through to the core ships will be impossible and no matter what the result on the surface, we will have lost. Draw them off, destroy them piecemeal. If you dare the swarm entire, they will overwhelm and destroy you.'

'Aha! The death of a thousand cuts, I like it. A particular favourite.' Sarnak looked directly at Yriel, eyes alive with amusement over his preposterous grin. 'I ask you again, are you sure you are not a Commorrite, Lord Yriel?'

'Will you do it or not, Sarnak?'

Wrath kindled in the kabalite's eyes at being addressed so, but another massive detonation rocked his craft and he nodded. Yriel cut the feed, switching back to a remote view of the Dark Kin's impressive fleet. They sped through space alive with void-hardened organisms as they broke off from their attack run. One of their larger cruisers was not quite nimble enough, and was snared by the thousand-kilometre tentacles of a Kraken ship. Delicate spars were wrenched free from the vessel and it was brought to an abrupt halt. The ship opened up with its weapons batteries, blasting directly into the creature's shell aperture. The Dark Kin's vessels had been equipped with toxin cannons, and the tentacles blackened rapidly and the creature drifted away.

'Their weaponry is efficacious,' said Yaleanar. 'Next time, we should do the same.'

'There will be no next time. And they are not efficacious enough, my dear Yaleanar. Watch.'

Three more ships grabbed at the cruiser as it limped away. One made straight for the vessel, energy fields playing over its stubby tentacles. There was a flash as a massive discharge of bio-electricity shorted out the dark eldar ship's shields. It was rapidly torn apart.

'A costly loss,' said Yriel.

Yaleanar reached for his friend, placing a hand on his shoulder. 'Leave them to it, my prince. We have monsters of our own to slay.'

Yriel nodded, directing his attention to a frontal view. Dûriel rapidly approached, its atmosphere swirling with red cloud, lit from within by lightning. A swarm of ten space-borne leviathans, strange organs within them counteracting the pull of Dûriel's gravity, were descending into the upper reaches of the atmosphere, their feed tentacles probing down from their undersides. Their sides rippled as they ejected mycetic spores.

'In all my life, I have never seen anything like this,' said Yaleanar. 'At once I am astounded by what the galaxy has to offer, and surprised how the same forms are repeated endlessly. To look upon the voidspawn from above, like fish in a pond, I do not know whether to be amazed or bored.'

'These fish have a powerful bite,' murmured Yriel. His quick eyes darted over the image, tactical scenarios playing in his mind. He spied a weakness quickly enough; not a fatal one, but one that would allow *Vaul's Caress* through and that was all that was required of them at this stage. 'Squadrons Kurnous's Eye,

Isha's Grace, the Star Wraiths, target the creature on my mark. Honourable Way, The Third Imperative, drive its friends away.' Targeting runes locked on one of the beasts, slightly off the group's centre. 'In three, two, one. Now!'

Swift eldar vessels sped ahead of the *Flame of Asuryan*. At the same time, the *Flame* opened up with every forward-facing weapon it had, a barrage of lasers and torpedoes cutting across the void and slicing into the flesh of the beast.

The *Flame of Asuryan* sailed close to the planet, the last tenuous wisps of Dûriel's sheath of air dragging at the keel, *Vaul's Caress* and its escorts close behind.

'Come about, go for another pass!'

The *Flame* banked, broadsides raking across the group of creatures. To their stern, the Wraithborne acted as fleet rearguard. They turned side on, tempting the Krakens to snare them in their tentacles. The creatures on the boarding worms were quickly overpowered by the ghost warriors crewing the ships. The dead eldar then boarded the craft holding their own ships, blasting the Krakens apart from the inside with their distortion cannons.

'So far so good,' said Yaleanar.

'Let us not count our blessings yet, my shadow,' said Yriel as the *Flame* lined up again on the targeted bio-ship. Its fellows were being herded back by flights of fighters and bombers and the harrying actions of his other escorts. The bio-ships had anti-gravity, of a type, but their beast munitions did not, and Yriel had the advantage of being higher in the gravity well.

'Again!' he shouted. Another fusillade ripped along the voidspawn, and gaseous clouds of atomised body fluid billowed out. *Vaul's Caress* opened fire a second later, adding its lesser fire to that of the *Flame*. The bio-ship slid to one side, tentacles flailing feebly. 'Again!'

The *Flame* turned sharply, dodging a Kraken that had made it through the Wraithborne. Behind the flagship one of the wraithships exploded in a brief nova-flash. Below it, laser and plasma fire stitched bright lines of blue and red across the roiling mass of Dûriel's atmosphere.

'Admiral!' said Yaleanar excitedly. 'The ship is dying, it is dropping! A masterly stroke!'

'Again!' said Yriel through gritted teeth.

The *Flame* sent another broadside smashing into the wallowing bio-vessel. The port side of it split open entirely and it fell with sudden rapidity, its skin glowing hot with the stresses of atmospheric entry.

'Fighter wings, form up. *Vaul's Caress*, go now. May Asuryan guide you safely to the surface.'

The Naiad-class cruiser shot out from behind the *Flame*, sails folding as it drove into the atmosphere at great speed, friction fire streaking from its energy shield. Fighters flew either side as they punched through the hole in the feed-ships' swarm.

'Three-tenths until Starving Dragon makes contact with the fleet, admiral,' said the master of the ship's eye.

Yriel gave a dry laugh. He wore a rictus grin not dissimilar to Sarnak's. 'They are slow, we will be long gone by then. Destroy the rest of those wallowing below us, then we shall go and help our Dark Kin take their prize. Far Ranging Hunger will trouble the galaxy no more after this day, I swear. Charge all weapons! We engage at close quarters.'

In the thick air of Dûriel, *Vaul's Caress* burned bright, and then was swallowed by the cloud. In its wake, bio-ships died under Yriel's relentless barrage.

CHAPTER THIRTEEN

THE BATTLE FOR DÛRIEL

The eldar were an island of colour in a ravening sea of bone and blood. Sunspear stood at the peak of the island, a bold figure atop a promontory of the dead. Far Ranging Hunger's weapon creatures were ranged against them from one side of the plain to the other, an endless tide coming at the Aspect Warriors of Biel-Tan. Immense gun beasts carrying symbiotic cannon were crawling into range, their waddling gait sending their high backs rocking, so that they looked like bizarre, knobbled ships bobbing on a swell of claws. Sunspear directed his tanks and aircraft against these creatures, gunning them down before they could bring their own guns to bear. This still left his Aspect Warriors to deal with the heavier assault beasts. No matter how many his shrines of Fire Dragons brought low, there were always more. And yet more came in their wake; a steady rain of spores, heavy over the northern plains, each landing with a wet crack that could be heard over the racket of battle, disgorging yet more warrior creatures.

Hethaeliar the Fourth-Blooded's contemptuous purr sounded in his ears. 'Autarch, Starving Dragon attacks.' Images of the other hive fleet, the mass of its creatures writhing as if they were one organism surging up the valley, came into his viewing sphere. The roars of the beasts were clear through Hethaeliar's audio pick-up. 'We have no contact yet upon the peak. Our warrior-seers are ready, but the device and the rest of the council have yet to arrive.'

Sunspear looked heavenwards. The hive ships were invisible behind Dûriel's atmospheric death shroud, but his helmet lenses painted their outlines onto his retina. Fiery trails cut through high-altitude clouds, but from what the debris came, he could not tell; eldar or voidspawn, it could so easily have been either.

The meteor storm intensified. The rain of spores diminished, replaced by much larger chunks of burning matter. Several were of many megatonnes, and came rushing through the sky trailing smoke and fire. They came to ground tens of thousands of paces distant, their impacts shaking his position. His instinct was to tell his troops to take cover, but there was nowhere to hide. His heart lifted a moment as he saw a wreck that was identifiably voidspawn. The massive creature floundered in the sky, crumpling under the influence of gravity it was not bred for. Eldar cheered as it fell sideways towards the earth.

'We must fight on,' said Sunspear. 'Prince Yriel approaches.'

* * *

Vaul's Caress shook, a toy in the hand of a mad giant. Ariadien gritted his teeth. He was helpless in his cockpit, the *Sound of Sunlight* strapped fast into the hold of the cruiser. He was frightened, more frightened than he had ever been. The roar of gases against the hull was the roar of the Dragon, the fire its fire, the swiftly approaching ground its maw... He could see it in his imagination, coming up at them remorselessly, the jaws ready to snap shut.

The ship bucked, throwing him about in his steersman's chair. He bit his tongue, and tasted blood in his mouth.

+Brother.+ His sister's voice in his mind. +Be calm, brother. Do not be afraid.+

She was unafraid, her soul peaceful. Her calm enveloped him as surely as a caress, driving back the thunder of descent. He pictured her, cradling his head against her breast. Ariadien burned with shame at his cowardice. +It is I who should be brave for you. You never wanted this.+

She laughed sadly in his mind. +Can a poet not be brave? To write the heart's desires and present them, raw and bloody, to an uncaring audience is more terrifying than war!+ In his mind's eye she kissed his brow, a tender sending from her. +You are no coward, brother. All your life you have sickened yourself with worry for me, and I thank you, but it was needless. I am your twin, and am as strong as you. Together we are stronger than any other. Do not be frightened.+

+Neidaria...+

A psychic pulse rushed from the spirit core of *Vaul's Caress*. The *Sound of Sunlight*'s systems came to life, its own spirits stirring at the command of the ship. Ariadien came back to the present with a rush, his mind slipping from that of his sister and into abrupt communion with the souls of the Titan's core.

'The doors open, let Khaine set forth his bloody plans and take his tally of blood,' spoke the captain.

Immense g-forces tugged at Ariadien as the ship pulled up from its dive and levelled off, its inertial fields useless in the gravity well of the world. Another shift in gravity as it banked around, and a sudden, chest-crushing halt.

The restraints holding the *Sound of Sunlight* whipped free. Ariadien turned his – the *Sound of Sunlight*'s – head to the right, and watched as the *Curse of Yriel* stepped out from its throne, head bowed against the low ceiling. Its weapons appeared from the wall, and it took them up in huge hands. The rear doors of the cruiser swung open with haste, and red light flooded into the hold from outside.

The *Curse of Yriel* drew itself up to its full height, and strode off, framed against a boiling red sky.

The *Sound of Sunlight* looked to its sibling, the *Silent Scream*, seated opposite.

+After you, dear sister,+ it said.

Their souls bonded to each other and the spirits of their Titans' cores, now it was for Ariadien and Neidaria to be giants, and to take their turn at shaking the world.

Around Khaine's mound, voidspawn died in their hundreds, but each successive wave came closer to the lines of Aspect Warriors, and in two places assault beasts had broken through and were being destroyed only with much loss. In the centre of the worst of these conflicts, the Avatar of Khaine fought, his spear bringing death with every thrust. Confident that the god-shard would bring victory there, Sunspear turned his attention to the right, where four living tanks bellowed out the hive mind's anger, tossing their heads and sending brave warriors flying from their brow horns.

'Shrines Ninth Blackened Hearth and Words of Reason to the right flank. Destroy the breakthrough of Far Ranging Hunger.'

'Yes, autarch,' said the exarchs of the shrines together. Sunspear looked down the hill of corpses. The two shrines pulled back smoothly from the front line and moved the hundred paces to the breakthrough, traversing the treacherous, ichor-slick carapaces of the dead tyranids quickly. He waited for them to engage, watched Ninth Blackened Hearth melt half a living tank with concentrated fusion fire before turning away to find another target.

He was alone on the mound of the dead, the rest of the Inner Command remaining upon the Godpeak. He checked his multiple viewing orbs. He itched to join the fight, to hold his sword in his hand and spill blood by the side of Khaine, but his place was to oversee. His honour had been compromised by failures in command, not in combat. His direct involvement would have to wait.

A sonic boom shattered the sky, rolling across the battlefield. A few of his warriors looked up, and several were pulled down by their foe in doing so, for the Great Devourer's creatures were of more singular purpose.

Sunspear looked up himself, as a flight of twenty bright-yellow fighter craft came towards the ground, engines howling. They pulled up at the last moment, screeching scant dozens of paces from the ground over the horde besetting Biel-Tan's Aspect Warriors. Baleful energies crackled around their prows and were released, a crescent of howling, horrifying force that carried with it the cries of the dead. Sunspear felt a shadow upon his soul, a bitter taste on his tongue.

'They have made weapons of the souls of the dead,' he said unbelievingly. 'Now Iyanden goes too far...'

His outrage dissipated when he looked again to the horde of aliens. Broad swathes of them had been felled, as neatly as crop stalks fallen to a scythe. The aircraft came hurtling round, eldritch weapons charging again. He watched this time as the discharge rippled out over the heads of the voidspawn, and saw them collapse like puppets with their strings cut. The pressure on his lines abated. The assault beasts assailing the right lost their support, and were soon surrounded and shot down.

A second later, another peal of ship thunder, and a larger shape came tearing down from the heavens, as roaring and deadly as the rage of Asuryan himself.

Vaul's Caress plummeted earthwards, fire streaming from its fins and weapons blisters. To see a void-runner in atmosphere was a rare thing, for even the ships of the eldar struggled against the heavy embrace of a planet, and yet here one was. Sunspear gazed up at it, transfixed. It seemed as if it would crash down on his very head, but it too corrected course several thousand paces over the battlefield, its gravity generators halting its downward trajectory in short order. Its momentum redirected, the great craft swept on towards the Godpeak, weapons suited to the great destruction of space combat blasting huge holes in Far Ranging Hunger's endless hordes, sending spumes of earth high into the sky and eliciting a loud cheer from the Biel-Tanians.

'The Fireheart has arrived, my brave warriors!' he communicated to his men. 'Prince Yriel is winning the battle in space. We must fight on!'

A rain of fire began, the burning debris of dead hive ships, bringing with it the stench of burned meat.

Battle raged fiercely in the webway. The Iyandeni had advanced down the tunnel they had initially walked. Close to the webgate to Dûriel, tunnels branched in bewildering profusion. The swarm had been shattered, its intellect driven back into the shadows. Eldar in small groups fought with the splintered remnants in many of the tunnel mouths. 'Leave none alive!' shouted Taec. 'The stain of the Dragon must be removed from the sacred labyrinth!'

Jetbikes screeched overhead, blasting apart a group of warrior creatures advancing on a gang of wyches. The bikes barrel-rolled, dodging through their Commorrite counterparts coming the other way. One of the Dark Kin came within paces of Taec, laughing insanely. Where Herinim was, he had no idea.

Another laugh caught his ear. He ignored it, thinking it to be that of another half-mad Commorrite. He grabbed at the arm of a Guardian and sent his squad down another tunnel where a glimmer of the hive mind lurked.

The mind of the aliens was coming apart, he sensed it. There had been many come into the labyrinth, but their leaders had been hacked down by the Phoenix Lords. Although the roar of the hive mind was deafening, its influence in the realm of the webway was much reduced. Cut off from the warp and real space, the creatures of Far Ranging Hunger were adrift from the Dragon's psychic direction, and the small submind that had formed among the swarm was breaking down. The synaptic web of the aliens was close to folding in on itself completely.

'Victory is only a few deaths away!' he called.

Laughter again.

This time he turned to face it. He caught sight of bright cloth disappearing around a corner. On impulse, he followed.

An eldar in motley, her face hooded and masked in silver, waited for him. Taec stopped short of her in amazement.

'You must come with me. The battle is nearly over, and your doom is not here.'

'Who are you, Harlequin?' said Taec. 'I see from your garb that you are a Shadowseer.'

'That I am. Sylandri Veilwalker they call me.' She curtseyed deeply, lifting imaginary skirts.

He drew himself up, trying to capture an authority he had never truly felt. He was wary of Cegorach's dancers. 'And why are you here?'

'Why, to see what must be, is, and what must not be, isn't.' She giggled. 'If you see what I mean. To wit, in this instance, to guide you to Dûriel. Your thread has taken an inopportune kink. A friend of mine told me it should be pushed back in the correct direction and trimmed.'

'Only Morai-Heg can trim a thread.'

'Or another god,' she said with an equable shrug. 'Morai-Heg is dead, after all.'

'And if I do not come with you?'

She held thumb and forefinger together, making a circle. She held it up to her eye and made a show of peering through it.

'We have many dooms, which do you want? You're the farseer. You tell me. Look far!'

'How do we leave?' said Taec, avoiding her question. 'I see no door.'

'That is because you do not know where to look, Silvereye, far-seeing though you are. Now, choose. Come with me, or not. A useful death now, or a pointless one later?'

'And what of my other death?' he said, his mouth dry.

'There is no "other death", Taec Silvereye of House Delgari. Even eternity is a temporary affair. Only laughter lasts.'

She reached out a hand. Taec looked over his shoulder to the eldar behind him. They were intent on the battle. The screeches of dying aliens filled the webway.

'Will you come or not? The fate of a world turns on your head, and the fate of our kind turns upon that.'

The vision of him dying, his waystone cracking in the heat, the waiting caresses of She Who Thirsts, rose unbidden in his mind.

He hesitated only a moment.

He nodded reluctantly and took her hand. She wore a soft glove of light green. There was no reassurance in her touch, only destiny.

'My place is upon Dûriel,' he said.

'Then follow me, through a door where there is no door.'

She stepped towards the webway wall. The energy that defined it did not constrain her, and her foot slid through with barely a ripple. Taec went through, and disappeared once more from the host of Iyanden.

Taec and Sylandri traversed a tunnel so small that Taec had to stoop, his staff held out in front of him. The walls of the way touched his elbows as he went. When they did, shocks of power ran up the crystallised parts of his body, and he became uncomfortably aware of watching eyes on the other side.

'I have never seen such a tight passageway,' said Taec.

'Few have,' said Sylandri. 'No eldar remembers truly the full extent of the webway, nor how to correctly use it. The dark ones, the exodites, the craftworlders, corsairs – outcasts all, they squander the legacy of our kind and the Old Ones through fear and hubris. No one knows it well, no one, except we of the wandering folk, and the Guardians of the Black Library, perhaps. But Cegorach knows all the tricks, and he teaches us generously.'

'Why do you not share this knowledge? It would help bring us together again.'

'Or drive us apart. The shattered kindreds are incautious in their senescence, old old old!' she trilled, and laughed. 'We keep the knowledge, we guard it. Upon the advent of a new generation, a strong generation, mayhap we will share, but the time of renewal is not yet on us.'

The tunnel became steep, twisting as it climbed. Sylandri stepped lightly along its undulations.

'We are nearly there,' said Sylandri. 'Close to the peak of gods, where your efforts are most required.'

'My efforts and my demise. You are my executioner, Veilwalker.'

Sylandri shrugged. 'You are a seer as I am, you have seen what must be done for our kind to have a future. The end times approach, Taec Silvereye. You see that clearer than all. The great struggle of this age looms ever nearer.' She looked at him over her shoulder, the rippling energies of the webway reflecting in her silvered mask. 'Will you tell me it is not true?' she said. 'I will know whether you believe it yourself or not.'

He shook his head. 'I would not attempt to mock the mockers.'

She laughed. 'It matters not how skilfully the jest is woven, it is better to laugh in death's face. We laugh, we prosper, and so our souls are safe.'

'Mine is not.'

'No,' she said baldly. 'But that is your doom, as to wear this mask is mine. I laugh, but you will never know if I am crying or not, for none shall see my face. Aha!' she said brightly. 'We are here.'

The tunnel narrowed to nothing. Ordinarily, the tunnels of the labyrinth seemed endless, but here was a tapered end.

'This crevice?'

'A crack of doom,' she said gleefully. Somehow within the constrained space she managed a small dance that ended in a bow. She ushered him on. 'Please. Go with the graces of what few gods remain.'

Taec set his face and stepped forwards.

'I thank you, my executioner.'

A hand on the crook of his elbow stayed his progress. The silver-masked head shook. 'What executioner would let their charge go free?'

'And you would?'

'You are free to go, if that is your choice. Your own feet carry you to your death, not mine, farseer.'

Taec stared into the mask for a moment, at his distorted reflection. He made to go, but the hand gripped him tighter.

'I would apologise, but those who belong to the Laughing God do not sorrow for themselves or for others. Laughter is the best tonic, do you not think? Laughter will not come easily to you in the coming arcs, but one day, Silvereye, when all this is done and your torment is over, we will meet again under happier skies where we will laugh long and hard together. You can be sure of that. If you can hold on to that thought, think it often, and laugh in the face of our enemy. She really doesn't like that very much.'

Then with a movement so swift it took him completely by surprise, Sylandri turned and shoved him, sending him headfirst into the fissure of energy. He shouted in alarm.

A soft laugh answered him.

Taec did not fall. He found stone under his feet, and a bitter scent on the air even through his helm's filters. A stormy sky loomed over him, cliffs on many sides. He blinked, dislocated. He looked for Sylandri, but the Shadowseer had disappeared, and there was no sign of a webgate that he could detect with his mundane or uncanny senses.

He stepped out from behind a rock, and into the end of the world. The skies were red, as in his vision, choked with life alien to the place. Lightning flickered within them. A strong, hot wind scoured the surface, the scent of acid and vinegary putrefaction thick upon it. The very rock groaned with pain, what little was left of the world spirit gnawing in agony on itself. Flights of eldar vehicles sped through the tortured heavens. Screeches of alien nightmares sounded endlessly, along with the distant thunder of many weapons.

He looked upon the place of his doom. 'Dûriel,' he said.

He was on the Godpeak as promised, some way from the main webgate.

Vaul's Caress hung over the mountaintop, its gravity engines whining loudly against the pull of the planet. The Titans of Iyanden stalked from its holds; lesser doors had opened, and a stream of Guardians in blue and yellow were emerging to bolster those of Biel-Tan guarding the peak. Tall among them was the building-sized Fireheart, a tower floating on repulsor fields, shepherded by robed eldar who moved with final purpose.

As Taec walked down the hillside to the rocky plateau, *Vaul's Caress* finished its rapid deployment and shot off into the sky, guns vaporising airborne tyranids that dared its power. Clouds streamed over its sleek hull, and it disappeared.

He watched the hole it had punched in the sky for a moment, then walked to join the seer council of Biel-Tan.

'The Fireheart must be set here,' Kellian was saying. 'The signs are quite clear.'

'The geological survey is not, however,' Altariec replied. 'Our senses say here, our sensors say there, where the old volcano's principal vent was.' He pointed to a cave in a crag a few hundred paces away.

'There, brothers,' said Taec, walking into their midst. He pointed to another pinnacle of stone. The seer council started, because he had approached them unheard and unseen; shielded still by the glamours of Cegorach, perhaps. 'That outcrop there is close to the last active fault upon this mountain, and also to a crystal branching of the dead world spirit. Place it there, and the Fireheart will consume the planet and its dead soul. This is why the portents and mundane knowledge differ.'

Kellian nodded. Altariec went away to direct the technicians and seers bringing the great device into place.

'How came you here?' said Kellian. 'Where are the forces of Iyanden?'

Taec walked to his side with slow steps. His limbs were stiffer than they had ever been. 'I came by another path. The others will arrive soon. The webway was infested. Only by the efforts of the Dark Kin wych cult, our Phoenix Host and the Phoenix Lords was disaster averted.'

'The six…?' whispered Kellian.

Taec nodded. 'All of them, Asurmen at the fore.'

Kellian looked upwards, arms spread. 'So much is obscured. We are blind and deafened by the noise of the Great Dragon! Great things are happening here.'

'More I suspect than we shall ever know, Kellian of Biel-Tan,' said Taec.

There was a mighty bang as the Fireheart reached its position, and its repulsor field was shut off.

Kellian looked to the towering construct. 'I remain here. The Inner Command must direct the fight still, glean what little the skein can show us.'

'And I must go,' said Taec. 'I am needed for the activation.'

They exchanged a profound, wordless farewell, and walked their own paths away from each other.

Taec entered the circle of seers. Despite the clamour of battle ringing from the valley at the mountain's feet, a strange peace settled on them. Taec losoked up at the Fireheart. It was old, as old as the ancient empire. The architecture of it was neither that of Commorragh nor that of the craftworlds, but somewhere between the two – sharply fluted sides sweeping up to an angular parapet that resembled a crown. Held in the arms of the summit was a gem so large five eldar would be needed to link arms around its girth. This gem, and the many that ran up the fluting of the sides, were milky and without spark of life. Otherwise it was a deep, glossy green so dark as to be near black, and without other adornment.

The seers gathered around it, twenty-four of them in total, the greatest Biel-Tan had to offer. Taec was humbled by their sacrifice, one from which Biel-Tan might never recover. He was risking the eyes and ears of that worldship for the fulfilment of his plan, and he felt sick even though he was certain it must be done.

Without signal, the seers rested the butts of their staffs upon the ground, dipped their heads, and thrust the staffs forward, the runes dangling from them chiming. They stood a moment in silence, the wind soughing over them, stirring their robes in the dust.

Then they began to sing.

One by one, each added his voice to the choir, a complex song of interwoven melody that, when all the seers had begun voice, told twenty-four stories at once. Upon the skein, their minds reached for one another. They were fireflies in the face of the vast presence of the hive mind, glowing motes beneath its contempt. The attention of the Great Dragon, its two consciousnesses nearly blended, was elsewhere.

+The Great Dragon is a predator, and fights those who dare to fight back. Great it may be, and ancient, but it is also weak in its single-mindedness,+ thought Taec, and the others shared his thoughts.

+We are not weak,+ they thought back. +We will see the ancient days reborn.+

They bent their mental might to one point, interfacing with the psychic circuitry of the Fireheart. Gems lit, starting at the ground, the light rushing up all of them until the great gem at the top glowed from milky white to a dull red.

Responding to their mental touch, the Fireheart activated.

The machine directed their minds and amplified them, pushing their strength down, down into the rock. Taec and the seers went with the Fireheart as its semi-sentient core sought the fault that had once fed the eruptions of the Godpeak. It thrust down, past a domed magma chamber empty of heat, through plugged tubes that had once rushed with molten rock, down, down to the mantle, whose currents of molten stone were as yet unperturbed by the war on the surface.

And on, on to the core, a ball of iron as large as a moon, spinning quickly, the seat of life of all Dûriel, and the centre of the world's essence.

The Fireheart took the seers' minds, moulded them into a hand, reached for the liquid metal of the core and, as one might take the temperature of a bath, perturbed its tranquillity.

Under the seers' feet, a faint tremble troubled the rock. They sang louder.

CHAPTER FOURTEEN

THE FINAL BATTLE

Yriel's crew cheered as the last of the hive ships died, the matter of its body breaking up in a fiery end.

'Full power to all engines! Let full sail!' the admiral ordered.

Behind the flagship, the squadrons keeping the Kraken vessels at bay broke off their fight. Three remained. The low orbit of Dûriel was choked with shattered shell fragments and the bloody chunks of dead voidspawn. Amid the slaughter's aftermath floated delicate flinders of wraithbone.

'The attack has not been without cost, prince admiral,' said Yaleanar. 'Endless Glory has lost two-thirds of its number, and we have suffered five wrecks among the other squadrons.'

'A fair price,' said Yriel levelly.

'What of the remaining three tyranid ships?' Yaleanar said. He brought them up on a viewing orb with a thought. The holographic image showed them close, curved shells like those of sea beasts or ram's horns, their wide, fluted apertures alive with writhing tentacles tens of thousands of paces long.

Yriel gave the image a cursory glance. 'Leave them. They are slow. They are too close to Dûriel. They will not break free before the destruction of the planet.' He ran his hands over targeting jewels, selecting vessels of priority in the greater part of Far Ranging Hunger that Sarnak and the others kept at bay. 'Look at them,' he said. 'Weak, lumbering things. It is in space that the Great Dragon is at its weakest. These are vessels suited for long travel, not war. They may move quickly between systems, but once within sight of their prey they are vulnerable.'

'Yes, my prince,' agreed Yaleanar. 'But still, there are a great many of them.'

'That is their only advantage, my shadow,' said Yriel. 'Steersmen! Take us on around Dûriel!'

'Prince, is this wise?' said Yaleanar. 'That will take us right into Starving Dragon's fleet.'

'You are the only one who dares to question me, brave Yaleanar, but you will never make a voidsman.' System cartography blinked up, pushing the various bubbles of visual feed aside. 'We drive past them, not into them. They come for us. If we sweep under their noses, they will chase.'

'I see,' said Yaleanar, not seeing.

'Predators and fast targets, my friend,' explained Yriel. 'The hive mind will be unable to resist. But we are by far the quicker. We will be past them before they can close, and they will follow us around the planet, taking a longer road than the one they are currently upon. They will catch nothing, we will be gone.'

'You use the world to slingshot us.'

Yriel stabbed a finger at his friend. 'Exactly!' He flung his hands wide, and called out with theatricality, 'All ships, into formation!'

Behind the *Flame*, *Vaul's Caress* and the dozen or so remaining escorts fell into line, captains apprised of their admiral's plan. Sails filled with solar energy, pumping power into the vessels' stardrives. They sped on, outpacing the remaining Kraken ships of Far Ranging Hunger. Dûriel's bruised sky slid beneath their keels, and then they were over the terminator, from day into night.

'Steady at the helm, we come at them now,' said Yriel.

'Asuryan's grace,' said Yaleanar hoarsely.

Ahead was the vast fleet of Starving Dragon, that which the Imperium named Leviathan. It was a name well chosen. Starving Dragon attacked like Far Ranging Hunger, spreading itself as tendrils across a broad range of space. But the hive mind had learned, and the fleets of Starving Dragon, though divided, were far bigger than those of Far Ranging Hunger. There were so many voidspawn vessels in the Dûriel fleet they blotted out the stars, a long, snaking line of them a billion paces across stretching far back into space.

'Quickly now! Make all speed. We are seen,' said Yriel. He snarled. The shaking in his limbs subsided to nothing. A dry heat burned in him.

The small taskforce whipped around Dûriel. The hive mind saw them – they all felt it, its immense, alien psyche reaching across the stars to crush them – but they were too fast. The ships crashed through the picket line of Starving Dragon's Kraken ships – these of mottled purple and slightly different evolutionary form to those of Far Ranging Hunger – and went hurtling through the crowd of hive ships dipping their beaks to the feast below. A lucky volley of bony torpedoes clattered on the hull of the *Flame*, and they were through, outpacing the bio-ships before they could come around to face them. From night to day they went again, accelerating to a substantial fraction of the speed of light under the impetus of Dûriel's gravity. The wraithbone core of the *Flame* pulsed with the delight of its resident spirits, and they were away. Dûriel fell behind them until it was a coin of light and Sarnak's rearguard came speeding into view, heavily invested against the larger part of Far Ranging Hunger's void swarm.

'Drop sails! Prepare for immediate attack!'

The battle here had gone worse for the eldar. Far Ranging Hunger's hive fleet was vast, and the sons of Eldanesh had been forced to abandon some of their speed in order to tempt the voidspawn to stay in place and keep them clear of Prince Yriel and the Fireheart. The flotsam of broken eldar vessels spun everywhere. The *Flame* dodged past a dark eldar cruiser snared in the crushing embrace of a Kraken ship. Squadrons of escorts duelled with void-hardened fighter creatures propelled on daggers of bio-plasma.

'This,' said Yriel angrily, 'is an unforgivable mess. Sarnak! Lord Sarnak of the Kabal of the Black Heart! I call upon you! Answer me!'

An image, much disrupted by rainbows of interference, sprang into life. Sarnak was bloodied, his bridge even darker than before. Sparks showered in one corner. A dead eldar hung from a wrecked steering console behind him. Gunfire could be heard from some distant quarter. His ship, the *Poison Leer*, had taken a good deal of damage, but Sarnak, true to himself, was still smiling.

'Ah! Prince Yriel!' he said, as if they met upon a pleasant boulevard rather than in deadly battle. 'So good of you to join us. You were successful in your venture, I trust?'

'The Fireheart is delivered, we were successful. You less so.'

'This is no pleasant feast, my prince,' said Sarnak. 'You see their numbers. We have done what was asked of us, and might I add, only at the charitable intention of my Lord Vect.'

'You did not listen. You did not do what was asked of you. You are glory-mad. I told you to wait for my aid, and you did not.'

Sarnak's eyes narrowed. 'Nobody speaks to me like that, prince. I should blast you from the sky this very–'

'Cease your idiocy, Commorrite!' shouted Yriel. 'Your ship is coming apart at the seams. Are we to fall to blows while our common enemy waits to pick our flesh from the void? Truly you of Commorragh have become insane!' He slammed his spear shaft hard upon the deck, setting it ringing.

Sarnak's expression darkened further. Yriel sighed deeply, collecting himself. He spoke quickly before Sarnak could retort.

'Tell me, Sarnak, do you wish to survive this engagement?'

Sarnak looked at him with amazement, and his hostility turned to a laugh. 'Why, yes. That would be an agreeable outcome.'

'Then have your ships withdraw to this quadrant. This is our prize, the lair of their queen.' Bright lines delineated a huge, slug-like shape hidden at the heart of the fleet. 'Destroy the norn ship, and these three ships here – her consorts – and their defence will falter. Are you with me?'

'Yes, my prince!' shouted the crew.

'As you say, we have tried, with no success,' said Sarnak.

'I said, Lord Sarnak of the Black Heart, are you with me?' Yriel hissed the words, spittle flying from his mouth, the Spear of Twilight across his chest.

Sarnak's eyes flicked to the blade of the ancient spear. Slowly, he nodded. For a brief second, his eternal grin slipped from his face. 'So be it.' His smile returned. 'It is the prize I wished for anyway,' he said with forced breeziness, then, behind him: 'We are in the hands of the exile now, all ships follow the Prince Yriel's lead! This I, Lord Sarnak of the Black Heart, command!'

Upon the Godpeak the farseers sang. The subsonic pulses of the Fireheart grew stronger with every moment, resonating throughout the crust of Dûriel. Tremors erupted periodically, sending skittering avalanches down the flanks of the awakening volcano.

At the head of the valley, Ariadien and his sister flanked the *Curse of Yriel*, volleying fire into the swarming voidspawn of Starving Dragon. The eater beasts had retreated, and tens of thousands of warrior and weapons creatures had replaced them. Ariadien picked out the larger creatures as he had been instructed. He had not known which were the higher priority, but he had quickly identified which deaths had the most impact. The synaptic web of the hive mind was almost tangible to him in his heightened psychic state, and he felt it quiver with each of the leader creatures he killed.

His sister used her vibro-cannons to send shockwaves through the ground, ripping up linear plumes of rock dust across the valley floor, flattening aliens to paste. These tremors joined those of the Fireheart, creating complex earth music Ariadien found as pleasing as he did disconcerting.

As he rained fire on their enemies, he watched the other eldar forces. He and his sister were fortunate, as their guns far outranged those of the enemy. Although terrible in effect, the convulsive muscle mechanisms most of them utilised to propel their ammunition restricted them to closer quarters, and so far the twins had avoided any form of direct contact.

Others were deeper in the thick of it. Another Gemini squadron stalked the battlefield, these of Biel-Tan. More twins. One giant was all of white with a green helm, the other reversed, both with curling patterns of black thorns decorating their limbs. They stalked through the heaving swarm, crushing tyranids underfoot. He briefly wondered what it would be like to meet them, but the only communication they had shared was a brief dip of weapons by way of salute.

The sky was clotted with eldar grav and aircraft. Starving Dragon had begun the battle with a terrifying aerial force; but that had been dealt with, mainly thanks to the large number of sky-runners the Dark Kin had brought with them, and now speeding jetbikes of both kindreds strafed the seemingly endless ground horde. Hemlock fighters arriving with *Vaul's Caress* cut swathes through the masses, and the pulse of missile detonations launched by Crimson Hunters knocked hundreds of aliens flat. Ariadien zoomed in on different parts of the conflict; to the west, cult wyches of Commorragh leapt over giant creatures sporting huge symbiotic cannons, other wyches fought daring battles of speed with snake-like creatures that erupted from the ground. At the foot of the mountain the Great Troupe of Harlequins battled a horde of six-armed, bulbous-headed horrors that were possessed of reflexes almost to match their own. Almost. The motley-clad warriors were even more graceful in battle than they were in war.

At various points, Aspect Warriors guarded the way to the summit and the Fireheart, while around Ariadien and his sister was ranged a host of Guardians from both craftworlds, more of their own kind here than elsewhere. He heard occasional reports and orders coming from Sunspear's position to the north, but how they fared, and where the rest of the Phoenix Host were, remained unknown to him. Near their position debris burned as it fell from orbit, and it was possible it was falling on the autarch's force.

'Be alert! Starving Dragon attempts to force a passage,' said the triple voice of the *Curse of Yriel*.

Ariadien followed indicators to the disturbance. There, at the foot of the mountain. His Titan brought up a close-in image, partly obscured by a shoulder of rock. A thick formation of Starving Dragon was forcing its way upwards. A guard of heavily armoured creatures was at its front, many dozen of the large warrior beasts behind them. A number of the larger snake-creatures followed and, at the centre, three of the great generals of the Dragon, hive lords, whose minds focused the diffuse attention of the hive mind to needled immediacy. Shining Spears and the Reavers of the Dark Kin darted around them, shooting many down, but they came in such multitude, and with such ferocity at arms, that the eldar's valour made small mark upon the horde.

'Direct fire upon the leaders and their guard. They must not get through,' the haughty female Biel-Tanian autarch ordered them.

Ariadien dutifully swung his pulsar weapon arms around and opened up on the swarm. It was a poor angle, and many of his shots blasted red-hot scores into the rock between himself and the advancing aliens, but some got through. A blast of jets washed over him. He looked up to see his sister leap into the air, landing on a bluff where her vibro-cannons would have a better line of fire.

With foreboding in his heart, Ariadien followed.

The *Poison Leer* and the *Flame of Asuryan* flew side by side, their path cleared before them by the Wraithborne. On their flanks, eldar ships flew daring, jinking paths, drawing Kraken vessels away from the flagships. Dark eldar cruisers lured them close, before ravaging them with poisonous broadsides.

A wall of vessels, each tipped with a staggeringly scaled bone ram, was forming up in front of the speeding eldar craft, blocking their final attack run to the norn ship. Dazzling light poured from one of the many viewing orbs on the bridge as another of the Wraithborne's craft detonated. The five dark eldar destroyers that had been following it broke away in every direction in an attempt to dodge the debris cloud. One was too slow, or unlucky, and caught a chunk of wraithbone across its primary sail. Rolling out of control, it was easy prey for a darting shoal of attack annelids who latched onto it and, squirming obscenely, injected floods of acid into its hull.

'Hard to port!' shouted Yriel. The *Flame* heaved over violently, the remnants of the Wraithborne ship flaring up as they hit the flagship's energy shields. They were closing on the ram ships, who were accelerating towards Yriel and Sarnak's vessels. Long straight shells made up a third of their length, housing bio-plasmic drives. The remainder was taken up by their immense beaks. These were living missiles.

'Concentrate fire on my mark!' ordered Yriel. He selected three ships, painted them in the runes of firing, and sent his orders on.

The *Poison Leer* and the *Flame of Asuryan* blasted away at the ram ships accelerating towards them. At first, the laser blasts and torpedoes they flung at the tyranid vessels seemed to have little effect, exploding on the bone prows with no visible damage, or scoring deep gouges in shells intended to survive the worst the void could throw at them. But then one, and then a second, began to emit colourful clouds of burning gas from ruptures in their sides. The first detonated; the other drifted, propelled off course by the gas it vented, into the path of its brood mates.

'Now!' shouted Yriel. He wrenched control of the ship from his bridge crew. His fingers playing with supernatural speed over the control jewels of his command pod, he channelled power to the engines and adjusted the trim of the sails, sending the *Flame* leaping ahead of Sarnak's ship. The gap in the wall of ram ships was closing. Two smaller eldar vessels shot through; a third attempting a bold manoeuvre impacted against one of the larger voidspawn craft, sending flame roaring around the bio-ship as it exploded. Wings of fighters ran out ahead of the *Flame*, guns silent. The pilots were aware that they could not harm the horned hides of the ramming ships, and saved their energy and concentration for evasion.

'Sarnak! Follow!' said Yriel.

All weapons blazing, the *Flame of Asuryan* blasted through the wall of ram ships, the *Poison Leer* behind it. More of the vessels collapsed or exploded as eldar broadsides opened up all around.

Then they were clear, and the norn ship was ahead of them.

'And now the real test begins,' said Yriel.

Half a dozen ships had made it through, along with several wings of fighters and bombers. The rest of the fleet remained entangled with the wall of ram ships; although the bio-ships could not catch the swift eldar, they prevented them from proceeding to reinforce their admiral. To their rear Kraken vessels, tentacles waving, were closing.

'Guard our backs, save yourselves,' said Yriel. 'Lord Sarnak and I shall kill the brain, and then we shall dismantle this swarm from the inside out.'

'How delightful,' said Sarnak. 'I can't wait to tell my friends about this at home. They will be so envious.'

Dark eldar, Biel-Tanian and Iyandeni ships rushed towards the norn vessel, a gargantuan slug-like thing a hundred times the length of an eldar battleship. What could be described as a head was apparent at one end, an arachnid protuberance surrounded by a fringe of pseudopods. The body was massive behind this tick-like thing, covered in a sheath of bone and horn armour that was pockmarked by long passage through the void. As the eldar started their attack run, glittering puffs erupted from spiracles studded all over the ship's integument. The heavy presence of the hive mind grew thicker, muffling the eldar's minds, and dulling their senses as if they were underwater. A sense of incredible terror came with it.

'Ignore your fear, my Eldritch Raiders, it is a projection, intended to scare us away! Be more aware of the passive defensive systems,' said Yriel. 'Clouds of crystal and aggressive organisms. They will refract your laser fire and punch through your hull using your own velocity against you.'

'I have done this before, you know,' said Sarnak. 'You speak to me as if this is my first battle.' But his words lacked bite, his voice strained.

The two battleships, their escorts and attack craft sped on, running fast over the head of the norn ship and down its length. Laser banks set to a broad spread vaporised the clouds of living chaff, but one after another the smaller craft flew into unseen banks of the stuff. Their shields overloaded with sparkling flashes of light before their hulls were shredded, eaten through by suddenly active organisms whose instincts were triggered on contact, or the armour stripped away simply by dint of high-velocity collision.

'Be wary of the clouds!' screamed Yriel. 'We are losing too many,' he said to Yaleanar.

'Incoming fire!' shouted a bridge officer.

Banks of orifices along the flanks of the hive ship spasmed, shooting out larger munitions of bone and bio-crystal. Complex subsidiary creatures bedded into the norn ship convulsed, and balls of greenish plasma rushed at the oncoming vessels. More eldar craft were caught, wreathed in ghostly blue flames before exploding.

'Here! It is here we must attack,' said Yriel. He highlighted a portion of the hive ship's body that looked much like any other.

'Not the head?' asked Sarnak.

'Not the head,' said Yriel. 'That is only the sensory cluster of the vessel, and most probably a decoy. The seat of the hive mind dwells within the belly of the beast. Load vorpal torpedoes!'

The eldar ships yawed over, spiralling into the shadow of the creature. The underbelly of the bio-ship rushed over them, a strange landscape of wrinkled skin. Lesser tyranids scurried over it, closing its wounds with silk, while others toting weapons symbiotes headed to more advantageous firing positions. Eldar fire picked them off, smearing their juices over the body of their mother where they rapidly froze in the chill of space.

'There!' said Yriel. 'The ship-birthing canal.' A sphincter the size of an asteroid came into view, set into a ridged crater. Horn plates were closing over it as they approached.

'All ships, open fire! Torpedo banks, loose on my order...'

The entire fleet swarmed around the orifice, launching hundreds of volleys of missiles into its depths. The weapons, directed by their own sophisticated guidance systems – the psy-links the armsmen normally used were non-functional in the face of the hive mind – flew under the horn plates and exploded. The sphincter was caught by the concentrated blasts and twitched, exposing the innards of the vessel for just a second.

'Now!' screamed Yriel, leaping to his feet and brandishing the Spear of Twilight. Its dark power burned through him. Time slowed. He saw the spread of vorpal torpedoes flung out from the bow of his ship, twisting deftly through scattered debris and chaff clouds. One exploded, brought down by a spread of hyper-velocity interception grubs, but the other four flew on, through the gaps in the horn plates as they slid closed over the torpedoes.

'It is done!' said Yriel. 'All craft, break off or we will die with it.'

The eldar ships swooped around, tearing away from the massive norn ship as fast as they could. The flash of explosions was visible around the plates covering the birthing canal. Distortion warheads in the vorpal torpedoes activated, opening short-lived portals into the warp. The raw power of the Othersea seized at every eldar mind as the norn ship was torn apart from the inside, the rear section imploding with great violence. The front half of the vessel came away, leaving what was left of its rear end wreathed in flickering warp lightning.

And then the breaches collapsed, and the fury of the warp went from the eldar's mind sense.

The hive mind went with it.

Psy-links all over the fleet sprang into life. The battle leapt into sudden clarity for the eldar. At the same time, the tyranid fleet collapsed. Ships blundered into one another, or stopped moving. As on Iyanden, Yriel reckoned a quarter of them died on severance from their guiding intellect.

He snarled. 'Now, let us destroy them all. Let none live lest we must repeat this experience again!'

The hive lords of Starving Dragon and their horde continued their inexorable ascent of the mountain, defying all the attempts of the Guardian host to stop them. Bundles of monofilament wire landed in their path, pulse blasts hammered down on them, distortion cannons ripped open the walls of reality itself and spilled them into the warp, but on the aliens came. The smaller creatures died in their hundreds, but were constantly funnelled forward to take the brunt of the eldar's fire, and the leader-beasts at the attack's head remained unscathed. Elsewhere, the individual elements of the eldar army were being isolated, kept from counter-attacking against the alien push up the mountain.

Separated and bogged down, the eldar's efficiency as a fighting force was much reduced. They began to die in some numbers. Ariadien lent his support to others where he could, whenever the advancing prong of Starving Dragon's purple monsters went out of sight behind a shoulder of rock or cliff, but he and his sister were detailed to keep back the tyrants and their assault and when they reappeared he sent all the fire he could that way. The war in the air had ceased to be so one-sided, as creatures flocked to the last remaining point of conflict on the planet. Every eldar craft and warrior that flew was duelling in the clouds over the Godpeak. The battle was turning into one of attrition, and it was not one they could win.

By now, the mountain was pulsing as if to the beat of a mighty heart. The ground rumbled with tremors. The rock shifted under Ariadien's feet. Cracks were opening in the ground.

+All we need is a little more time!+ said Neidaria, catching her brother's thoughts, their birthlink and Titan relays allowing them to communicate mind to mind even over the howl of the hive mind.

A terrible screech split the air. Full of foreboding, Ariadien turned to the source of the noise.

Stalking from a side valley to the east came a bio-titan, the largest of the voidspawn's weapon-kinds. The Harlequins and wyches there had become bottled up by the swarm, leaving the way to the mountain clear. There were precious few defenders on the lower cliffs, the majority having been drawn off to stymie the attack of the hive tyrants to the south-west.

'Enemy titan!' said Ariadien.

The *Sound of Sunlight* spun on its heel gracefully, pulsars volleying shots at the monster. The titan was a hunchbacked horror supported on four long insectile legs, the forelimbs gene-tweaked to carry two enormous cannon symbiotes.

'They are seeking to exploit our weakened left flank,' said Hethaeliar. 'Titans of Iyanden, move to engage.'

They acknowledged reception of the order. The *Curse of Yriel* went first, tongues of sun-bright flame stabbing from its jump pack as it vaulted into the air. Neidaria and Ariadien followed close by. Leaping from crag to crag, they bounded down the lower reaches of the mountain into the valley proper, firing at stray knots of aliens or kicking them from the mountainside as they went.

They landed in the swarm, crushing voidspawn and incinerating them with their jets. Seeing this new threat, the tyranid monster shrieked and turned upon them, scuttling with surprising speed at them.

Neidaria ran forwards, sonic lances ripping her targets messily apart. The *Curse of Yriel* levelled its twin pulsars at the approaching bio-titan and let fire, stabbing beams of energy into it. The beast lowered its head, covering its face with crossed arms, and ran head on at the Titans. Ariadien leapt to one side, his jets carrying him out of the way. He landed easily, his own pulsars vaporising three serpentine monsters slithering after the *Curse of Yriel*.

The bio-titan slammed home, its high back connecting with the Phantom Titan's groin and staggering it backwards. Ariadien and Neidaria ran to its rescue, attacking from both sides at once, his beams of light and hers of sound intersecting at the creature's midriff. The monster roared, but did not stop its battery of the Phantom. It fired its wide-mouthed arm cannons at point-blank range into the Phantom's chest. Armour smoking with acid, the *Curse of Yriel* staggered backwards, kicking itself free from the bio-titan's pinning feet, smashing down with an elbow upon its back and cracking its armour.

The great creature raised its cannons again, pointing them at the weakened area on the *Curse of Yriel*'s chest.

'No!' shouted Neidaria. She ran at the side of the bio-titan, sonic lances singing. The air rippled with the passing of her sound beams. Armour shattered where they touched the creature, thick ichor spouting from its side. As she neared, she jumped into the air, lance arms up, feet before her. She engaged her jump pack at full blast, sending her Titan as a living missile at the cracked bio-titan's plating.

Ariadien felt her excitement at the battle, her fear for the fate of the Phantom, her need to act.

Her strike connected, staggering the bio-titan sideways. But her feet slipped on the creature's shell as it moved under her, and she fell backwards. Her Titan landed heavily on the scoured rock. Screeching horribly, the bio-titan rounded on her.

She made to get to her feet. The *Silent Scream* was halfway up and nearly out of the way when the bio-titan's cannons vomited a tide of thick, acidic gruel all over her.

The flood caught the *Silent Scream*'s left leg and arm. It ate through Neidaria's armour in heartbeats. Her pulsar dropped free and her knee joint gave way, sending her back to the ground. Pulsar fire from Ariadien and the *Curse of Yriel* hammered into the creature, filling it with holes, but so intent it was upon its prey, the bio-titan ignored its own death. With a final scream, it drove its pointed foot through the chest of the *Silent Scream*. The Titan twitched around the piercing limb, and lay still.

Firing madly at the enemy bio-titan, Ariadien felt his sister slip away, her mind overwhelmed by the psychic shock of the creature's death. 'Neidaria!' he screamed. He fired his weapons until they glowed red, ignoring the chiming alarms that filled his cockpit and his mind.

The creature toppled over, and was still.

'Neidaria,' he said. +*Neidaria!*+ The *Sound of Sunlight* shouldered the dead bio-titan aside with two hard pushes, and knelt by the corpse of its sister.

'Mourn her later,' came Hethaeliar's command. 'You must fight on or more will die.'

A shadow fell over him. Ariadien looked upwards. The Phantom stared down at him. Wordlessly, its triplet pilots and spirits reached out to him, and urged him to rise.

All around them, aliens were closing in.

Another wave of Far Ranging Hunger's creatures crashed against the mound of dead. Sunspear was weary now, and his weapons had been blooded. Twice the enemy had fought their way through the line and he had been forced into combat. His cordon was thinning; but there was hope. A vortex swirled high over the Godpeak. Another earthquake shook their position.

'Autarch, they retreat!'

Sunspear looked over the heads of the creatures attacking his force. Those beyond the front no longer came towards him, but moved off to the south-east.

'They do not retreat. They are moving on the mountain.' He looked upwards. No more spores were descending. 'Prince Yriel has been true to his word, it appears. Autarch Hethaeliar, what news from the peak?'

The other autarch responded instantly. 'We are assailed on two fronts, Autarch Sunspear. Forces are attacking from the south-east and south-west. We have them stalled for now, but I do not know how much longer we can hold out. All my own troops are committed and I have no reserves to bolster the lines or stop any breakthrough.' Her audio feed was full of screaming and the noise of weapons fire. 'I have dispatched the Iyandeni Titans to stop a bio-construct to the south-west, but a large number of Starving Dragon's creatures are attempting an ascent, and they are succeeding.'

Sunspear looked away to the peak, over the back of the remainder of Far Ranging Hunger's creatures making all haste there.

'That must be it. Far Ranging Hunger is moving off. They detect your weakness.

You will soon be attacked on three fronts, Hethaeliar. I am still engaged here, it will take some time to extricate myself.'

'Then we had better pray to the dead gods that Iyanden's Phoenix Host arrives soon.'

CHAPTER FIFTEEN

THE TIDE TURNS

Yriel's Wave Serpents deployed from drop-craft in the high atmosphere, and fell earthwards. The whole world was in turmoil; the clouds of spores were dissipating, either having served their purpose or being consumed by the death of the planet. Away from the Godpeak, the tectonic plates were coming apart. Lines of bright fire glowed through the murk. For the time being they were restricted to the ocean boundaries where the crust was thinnest, but it would not be long before the mountains became unstitched. Dûriel's surface was a roil of black and red. Yriel was put in mind of a burned head, the meat black and raw, the glowing faultlines the revealed sutures in the bone.

Away to the west, an ocean of lava glowed bright in the encroaching night.

'A red ocean,' he said to himself. 'Now all makes sense.' The spear shuddered in his hand.

'My prince?' asked Yaleanar.

'Nothing, my faithful shadow.' Yriel gave him a smile that he intended to be reassuring, but from Yaleanar's reaction it was a feral one. 'An image I had in mind, bad poetry from one never destined to tread that path. Taec's plan has worked.'

'Or almost so. There is still a large concentration of voidspawn around the Godpeak.'

'Tell the fleet wayseers to begin their door-songs,' he said. 'I have a feeling that we come not as avenging warriors, but to evacuate our kin.'

The Wave Serpents pierced the dispersing cloud deck, shrieking low over the cracking plains. Voidspawn were everywhere, many dead. Ash fell like snow, cutting visibility and interfering with their telemetry systems. The pilots adjusted their power fields, setting them to filter the air around their engines' intakes, in case fine ash should be drawn in and coat their workings with glass.

There was a knot of aliens fighting Aspect Warriors in the colours of Biel-Tan on the plain near the mountain. The enemy's numbers were few, and already transports were flocking to collect the eldar there. They banked around the scene.

'Sunspear needs no aid, onwards to the mountain!' ordered Yriel. He had trouble maintaining his outward calm, for the spear thirsted for blood.

They sped up the mountain flanks. Here were many more of Far Ranging

Hunger's creatures, making their way towards the summit in a broad spread, unperturbed by the rocks falling past them.

'See, Yaleanar, here is where the true battle is, perhaps we should put down... Ah.'

Yriel's eyes went to the towering Fireheart, an island of calm in a sea of war. Beyond that was revealed a much larger host of the aliens, these of the purple and white of Starving Dragon.

'Perhaps there instead,' he said.

'I do not see the Phoenix Host, my prince,' said Yaleanar.

'Some of Iyanden at least is here to fight. Come! To battle.'

The Wave Serpents swept in, depositing Yriel and fifty of his corsairs at a gap in between two rocks. Starving Dragon would have to pass them to attack the Fireheart. The vehicles drew off, turret weapons running hot.

The hive lords tore through the last line of Guardians.

'They swat them as easily as we would a fly, my prince,' said Yaleanar.

Yriel hefted the spear, and threw back his coat to free his legs. Under his helmet he looked terrible, he knew, pallid and beaded with sweat. Not the way he wished to appear in his final battle. He trusted to whatever artist would depict his fall to paint away such flaws. 'They will find these flies are not so easily crushed.'

'You speak truly,' said Yaleanar, unslinging his preferred weapon, a large lasblaster. 'Luckily for you, this is more my arena than space warfare.' He sighted down the barrel of his gun, and dropped a large alien warrior before it could smite a fleeing Guardian. 'You see?'

Yriel's soul was running out, the dreadful spirit of the Spear of Twilight taking its place. He could manage no more than a smile. It was all he could do not to hurl himself headlong at the aliens and bite at them.

'Aha, here they come!' said Yaleanar, either not noticing or choosing to ignore his lord's silence.

The hive lords charged.

Battle raged on the plateaus below the summit of the Godpeak. Taec licked his lips nervously. The hive lords and grand serpents of Starving Dragon clambered up the final slopes, their claws slick with eldar blood. The Guardians in their way put up a brave fight, but they could only slow the monstrous creatures, no matter that the numbers of warrior beasts had been whittled from thousands to a few dozen.

On the other side of the plateau, the red and bone creatures of Far Ranging Hunger approached, led by a single, immense swarmlord of dreadful aspect. Four swords of bone slashed before it, felling whoever sought to stop it. It was further away than the lords of Starving Dragon, but closing faster. There resistance was much lighter, and the aliens made headway fast even as the Guardian host to the south bowed under the assault of the lords of Starving Dragon. To make matters worse, fresh hordes of airborne monstrosities had flown in and the pressure of the hive mind was intolerable, squeezing the eldar's souls as the gestalt being's immense intelligence regarded them with its full malice.

All around the Godpeak and the valley below, the eldar fought. Isolated, embattled, unable to support each other; the way to the peak was open.

Time was running out.

A gale blew over the device, a vortex whirled in the clouds over the control gem, ringed with lightning. The tremors were constant. The machine was protected by a hard exclusion field, to ensure it functioned to the bitter end. Outside its limits the rocks shifted, opening up fissures all around the Fireheart's base, leaving only the circle of stone protected by the field unmarred.

Taec stared up at the pulsing gem at the top of the Fireheart. 'We must not falter! You must sing!' he called. 'The enemy is nearly at the gates, we must finish the ritual!'

A violent earthquake rocked the land around the Fireheart, but it did not move. The land groaned in pain. Taec felt the dead world's spirit matrix fizz with unnatural energy. The ground rumbled again, the tremor going on for several seconds. A great roar, and thousands of tonnes of rock slid down the mountainsides.

The Fireheart worked on mercilessly, multiplying the seers' psychic energies to agitate the core, sending it off its axis and perturbing the rotation of the whole world. The lava chamber beneath the mountain's feet would be filling for the first time in hundreds of thousands of years. Already the lands beyond the extinct volcano were coming apart.

The drone of the seers was swept up by the howl of the building wind. Psychic energies blazed from sky, earthing themselves in the gem atop the device. With it came the attentions of She Who Thirsts. The times Taec had experienced her gaze had been uncomfortable, there was a wildness and despair to her, but this cycle brought also curiosity. She watched this fragment of her parents' past glory in action with great interest.

A spark of hope lifted in Taec as he saw a flight of seven Wave Serpents come thundering down through the sky, bearing the colours of Prince Yriel.

It was a hope short-lived.

There was a tremendous bellowing, and a bow wave of terror coming thick on the warp. Taec fought his impulse to flee, and turned to face the source.

The swarmlord of Far Ranging Hunger had made it to the seer circle, and behind it came several hundred lesser beasts. Huge and ancient it was, with respiration chimneys on its back billowing red gases. Its armour was deep red, patterned with mottled black, darkened by age. This creature had lived a long time in this form; it was wise and dreadful, and yellow eyes glowed with fell intelligence beneath a horned brow. It hissed as it approached the farseers.

A squad of Guardians ran to intercept this leader, their shuriken catapults spitting razored death at it. The discs thunked into its armour without effect. Its swords moved in a blur, impossible to dodge, each blow severing a thread of destiny and leaving an eldar dead on the ground. Dozens of bolts of light hammered into it, fired off by the Guardians' support weapon platform. The swarmlord turned to it, smashing Guardians aside with its fists and tail. It ran at the weapon. One of the Guardians held his ground, and died under a bonesword for his bravery; the other ran screaming, clutching at his pointed helmet as the terror of the hive mind drove him mad. A second blade fell, cutting the cannon in two with a shower of sparks.

There was nothing to stop it.

Tail swishing, the swarmlord of Far Ranging Hunger strode towards Taec, as if it knew – as if it *knew* – what they were attempting, and who led them.

'Do not stop!' he cried without taking his eyes from the monster. 'We are almost done! The doom of the world is upon us!' The wind was a hurricane, the ground shook as if it were a blanket tossed by children.

Taec stepped from the group, actinic light blazing from his upraised staff.

The tyrant raised all four swords. Roaring, it charged at the farseer. It brought its weapons down. Light flared brightly around Taec. Swords hammered into his force dome one after another. Taec struggled to keep up his defences in the face of such aggression. He waited for the chance to retaliate, hoping to strike out at the beast with his mind, although it was almost certainly a futile gesture. None came. The swarmlord's swords blurred through the air, hitting his psychic shield repeatedly. The barrier of energy glowed brighter and brighter, and Taec fell to his knees with a cry.

He could endure no longer. With a sob, he fell, the protective dome winking out.

The swarmlord of Far Ranging Hunger reared over him, its head cocked on one side. Taec looked up into its alien eyes. Two minds looked back at him: the individual thread of the swarmlord was strong and readily apparent to the seer, but like all the creatures, it was but an extension of the hive mind. Its individuality was a useful illusion. Even in his terror, Taec found it somewhat fascinating.

Snorting, the swarmlord turned towards the seer council. It cut one down, then another. The psychic choir faltered, the song grew weak. The seers bravely kept up their ritual. The swarmlord's followers were finishing the remainder of the Guardians protecting the south passage. Only a tiny group of corsairs and Prince Yriel stood between the Fireheart and the lords of Starving Dragon on the southern side of the peak. The jaws of the Great Devourer were about to snap shut.

Yriel's veins burned with the power of the Spear of Twilight. His weak and aching body retreated from his consciousness, and he became only motion. One of the hive tyrants of Starving Dragon carried some secondary beast, a creature bent into the shape of a cannon: long-snouted, vestigial eyes at the root of an immense proboscis, tiny legs gripping the wrist of the creature that carried it. Ridged tubes led from its rear into the hive tyrant's elbow, joining them as one. A flaccid sac pulsed sickeningly beneath it. The palpitations of the sac became rapid, and the tyrant raised its weapon to fire.

Yriel ran past the foremost leader-beasts, dodging their blows. A scythe-like claw whistled through the air at him. Empowered by the spear, he leapt clean over it, spinning as he went. Pushing off a chitinous limb with his feet, he landed upon the back of the cannon-carrying tyrant. He gripped the respiration chimneys on its back, raised the Spear of Twilight one-handed, and drove it down, aiming for a join between the armour plates. The spear's tip blazed with heat as it penetrated. An almighty crack sounded, and the blade went through the outer armour layer. Slowed only a little by ablative cartilaginous layers under the exoskeleton, the spear passed right on into the soft meat beneath. Yriel let the spear take the merest sip of the creature's soul, then yanked it free. Denying his weapon its feast took all his effort.

The hive lord howled and reared backwards, stamping its feet. Yriel clung on for a moment, then used its motion to leap free, landing on his feet as it hit the ground.

He felt psychic impulses – orders, no, thoughts, thoughts that moved the lesser beasts as he might move his limbs. Creatures rushed at him from all sides, the hive lords pressed on into the mass of his corsairs, unwilling perhaps to attack him.

Yriel opened his eye.

Lightning spewed from the Eye of Wrath, stabbing at the creatures, burning holes in their bodies. They fell shrieking.

Yriel reeled a little; the Eye was not used lightly, and it taxed him further. He stepped forwards, leaving smoking bodies behind him.

He set the spear's butt on the ground, and whistled.

'I am not yet done, Starving Dragon!'

Another of the hive tyrants turned. A further was staggering, close to death, ichor leaking from a hundred small wounds inflicted by his corsairs.

Roaring a challenge, the hive tyrant moved to engage the prince.

Taec closed his eyes and awaited the deathblow. 'So it has all been for nothing,' he murmured.

A deafening scream hit him. He opened his eyes. The swarmlord was writhing, bright starpoints glowing from its body. More light shone behind it. With a wet crack, the creature collapsed in on itself, and Taec's soul was buffeted by the open warp.

Through the dying beast strode the Phoenix Host of Iyanden. Five silent wraithguard marched at their head, their wraithcannons smoking. Althenian Armourlost was behind them, Kelmon the wraithseer at his side. With them was Iyanna Arienal. The webgate flared wider and wider, and a stream of grav-tanks and bikes shot out into the storm-troubled skies of Dûriel. In their wake came Asurmen himself, leading his legendary Crystal Sons. Iyanden's Avatar of Khaine came behind them, its fury pouring into the heart of every eldar atop the mountain.

For the first time in a long time, Taec felt awe. Here was the glory of the elder days born anew.

The wraithguard deployed in a line, crashing into the tyranids following in the swarmlord's wake. Taec sensed the enemy's disorganisation; the last of their leader-beasts destroyed, the creatures of Far Ranging Hunger cried for Starving Dragon's guidance, but it was taking time to assert its dominance over them.

'Destroy all, let weapons sing songs of death, end them now,' said Althenian, his fusion guns turning warrior beasts to steam. He smashed one to a pulp with a blow from his fist. 'Drive them back, let the living do their work, dead make dead!'

Asurmen led his crystal warriors into the fray, their weapons slaying dozens of warrior beasts. In short order, the voidspawn were driven back from the Fireheart.

The seers recovered. The faltering song re-established itself. Iyanna and Kelmon joined Taec. Seven seers of Iyanden silently filed around the Fireheart, filling the spaces made by the dead seers of Biel-Tan.

'You took your time,' he said to Iyanna.

'We are here now,' she replied.

'Yriel is below.' He inclined his head. 'The three of us. It appears the High Council is gathered for the final battle.'

Iyanna looked about. 'The end comes. We will begin evacuation, the spirit stones of the fallen will be retrieved.' Already eldar spiritseers were plucking glowing jewels from the breasts of the dead. Others were taking to the air, borne away by swift transports or jetbikes to seek out others. The ritual collection bags they carried were empty. Taec knew they would come back filled with woe.

'I will join the song,' said Kelmon.

'I have business elsewhere,' said Iyanna. She looked from Taec to the statuesque Kelmon. They were both battle-worn; his armour was scratched in a dozen places, her face bloodied. 'We share the burden.'

Taec hurried back to the circle. Iyanden's warhost was deploying rapidly from webway gates crackling into life all over the peak. The remainder of Far Ranging Hunger's attack from the north-west was isolated and butchered. Hive node creatures were tackled first, and once the coherency of the synaptic web was disrupted, the creatures of both fleets became easy prey.

Taec joined the song close by Kelmon. Bolstered by the newly arrived seers of Iyanden, the chanting of the group grew in intensity. The Fireheart pulsed with renewed rapidity. Gems blinked in sequence. Subsonics vibrated the ground at their feet. The mountain rumbled. Fissures opened around the device, running away in all directions. Steam spouted from them.

Eldar craft were taking to the air all around the mountain, troops falling back to their transports. The forces of Iyanden left their webway gates open, wraithguard and Guardians providing covering fire as they beckoned warriors to retreat from the shaking earth. With an almighty crack, the valley floor split, draining digestion pools in an instant. Lava welled up through the fissure, making the Valley of the Gods a lake of fire. The voidspawn were consumed by the hundred, and eldar too, cooking in their armour. The psychic perturbations of waystones shattering rippled over the skein as eldar experienced the horrors of the true death, their souls falling into Slaanesh's waiting maw.

Still the seers sang.

A half-tenth cycle passed. The Fireheart stood on a tall column of rock, only its power fields maintaining its integrity. A vast pit had opened around the farseers, and they were lit by a fierce orange glow. The shields of the Fireheart rippled like oil on water as tephra pattered into them.

Still the seers sang.

Yriel plunged his spear deep into the rearing serpent. It keened terribly, and Yriel salivated as his weapon drank. Since the day he had lost his eye due to the spear feasting on the limitless hive mind, he had managed to control its fell power and its obscene appetites, but at this final pass he no longer had the strength, and the spear's murderous soul overwhelmed him. He could not stop it feeding, drawing upon the infinity of spirit the Great Devourer possessed. Yriel felt the hive mind, heard it howl. It thrashed about, and Yriel was battered by its anger. Its thoughts were utterly, unimaginably alien. But one thing came through strong and loud. Hatred, hatred for this creature that had for the first time in untold aeons wounded it.

The spear drank and drank. Yriel's spirit swelled with stolen soul-stuff, a tsunami of alien experiences drowning his mind. As it engulfed him, so it threatened to subsume him. Here was an ocean, an ocean of thought of a scale that was unimaginable. Only a god could drink an ocean. This ocean was pure poison, and Yriel no god.

For a moment his spirit flame flickered between two threads – that of Prince Yriel, and the immense cable of fate that was the hive mind, the Spear of Twilight black betwixt them.

The light of his being glowed low. With one last effort, Yriel plucked at the greedy sentience of the Spear of Twilight and dragged it free of its meal.

He staggered from the dead serpent, the spear rasping on the ground. The last moments of the battle raged around him, confusing and confused. All but a handful of the assault swarm were dead. His remaining warriors were snatching up the waystones of the dead, and calling the transports back to their position. The air was thick with grav-craft fleeing into the webway. As far as the eye could see, fountains of lava shot skywards, growing more violent with each tremor. The valley ran with molten rock. Screams of dying eldar sounded from everywhere, but they were brittle in Yriel's ears, and his vision was lined by shadow. He breathed hard, but no air seemed to fill his lungs. His head pounded, the veins in his temples throbbed like war-drums.

He was dying. His heart ran slow, slow as a human's. The spear pulsed with each beat, savouring the end of its meal.

He wavered at the edge of the precipice. A number of eldar bounded past him, driving back more of the creatures, breaking their assault. Yriel could not say from which kindred they hailed.

Slowly, he fell to his knees.

And then a hand, armoured and sure on his shoulder.

Yriel's head lolled on a neck gone weak as rope. He tumbled, and the other stooped low to catch him across his knees. 'Yaleanar? Is that you, my shadow?'

'My prince,' said his lieutenant, his voice clear despite being emitted by his helmet. 'We will take you from here, your battle is done.'

'No, not my battle.' He managed a smile. 'My time is done, loyal Yaleanar. Leave me, save yourself.'

Yaleanar unclasped his helm, and let it fall to the ground. His perfect face smiled down at the prince.

'The eldar need you, my prince. Iyanden needs you.' He set Yriel down gently, propping him against a fallen weapon-beast whose shattered cannon dribbled reeking fluids onto the rock. 'I will summon aid. I love you, my prince, I will not abandon you.' Yaleanar spoke aside, to others. 'They will be here soon,' he said when he had finished.

Yriel's mouth ran with the bitter precursor to vomit, soaking his cloak and armour, but no vomit came. 'Faithful, brave Yaleanar, there is nothing to be done,' said Yriel, 'it is the spear...' He looked about him, suddenly frantic. 'Where is it? Where is the Spear of Twilight?'

'It is in your hand, my dear prince.'

Yriel gasped and clutched it to his bosom. He coughed, the pain of it ripping at his lungs. He closed his eyes. 'I cannot give it up, even as it drinks the last of me.'

There was a surprised cry. Warmth came into him. 'I feel stronger, a little. Stay with me, Yaleanar, stay with me as I pass. I will pass on my regards to Iyanna's new god.'

There was no reply.

'Yaleanar?'

Yriel opened his eyes. He was not sitting as he thought, but standing in a steady combat stance, the spear held out before him.

Transfixed by the spear's tip was Yaleanar, his mouth round with shock.

Yriel's eyes widened in horror. 'Yaleanar!' he screamed. He tugged the spear free. Yaleanar fell forwards. The waystone in the centre of his chest was lightless. Yriel rushed to catch him, moving with the pure energy the spear had taken from his friend. Still he was weak, and staggered under the armoured weight of Yaleanar.

'No! No, no!' he howled. He knelt upon the lip of the cliff, his friend's corpse in his arms, as cries fuelled by the stolen soul of Yaleanar escaped his lips.

Below him, wide sheets of lava covered the lowlands of Dûriel. The ground roared and shook, and a plume of ejecta rained from the summit of the Godpeak.

Yriel wept before a red ocean.

A shadow fell over him, something in the sky blocking out the rain of rock and ash, but he was past noticing.

Yriel fell across Yaleanar's soulless corpse, and the oceans all were gone.

'Retreat! Retreat!' shouted Sunspear, sending out the order by every means at his disposal.

Falcons dropped from the sky, and Aspect Warriors ran into them. The world was dying around them, and the voidspawn had been driven into a frenzy. They came on at speed, leaping the fissures spreading over the ground. Sunspear's warriors fired as they fell back into their transports. A Falcon waited to evacuate him, together with four exarchs and their remaining warriors who had joined him at the peak, sniping from the summit of the dead, felling aliens so that more of the eldar could escape. He watched as the Avatar was guided into the hold of a Wave Serpent by a patient warlock. It bowed its plumed head, and entered.

He followed the craft with satisfaction. There was a stain removed from his honour.

'My autarch, you must go now, swiftly,' Oskirithil of the Sorrows, exarch of the Burning Rebuke, said to him urgently.

Sunspear shook his head. 'Not until every last eldar here is safely off the ground.'

Earthquakes rocked the plain furiously. To the north, where the bulk of Far Ranging Hunger had begun the short war, a lake of lava covered the ground. A fountain of molten rock spewed from its centre ceaselessly.

Black clouds of ash had replaced the red. Through them a fresh rain of tyranid drop spores came plummeting.

'They come too late,' he said with satisfaction.

Vaul's Caress came from the sky, descending over the Godpeak itself, four smaller ships in its wake. Their shields sparkled with the constant impact of volcanic debris.

'It is time for you to depart,' said Hethaeliar. 'Join us on the peak.'

Sunspear looked again at his men. There were few voidspawn near now. The last of the Falcons climbed skywards, heading for the webway gates over the mountain.

'Very well.'

He took one last look around the battlefield. How much the planet had changed, two transformations in the space of four cycles.

'It is the season of destruction,' he said. 'And the falling leaves have made their cuts. Away!'

The Falcon rose up from the heaped bodies. Lava was rushing towards it, the corpses it encountered bursting into brief pillars of fire. Before they had made it a thousand paces into the air, the lava was at the foot of the pile of dead.

Then they were up into the clouds, joining the streams of craft heading for the webway.

Sunspear brought up a viewing globe of the valley, and his heart turned to stone as he saw the many eldar of all kindreds falling into gaps in the rock, or being rent asunder by alien claws. Their souls would be forfeit to She Who Thirsts, for their spirit stones would surely be consumed by the fires of the world's death. Some were stranded. He saw one group of a dozen trapped on a lump of rock. They clasped hands and bowed their heads as their refuge split, the pieces dissolving, sending them tumbling to their true deaths. Many others were leaping from rocky island to rocky island, heading for webway portals springing up all around the valley. A number of these, opening over beacon sites set at the beginning of the war, were suspended now over burning stone.

He watched as grav-craft performed daring swoops to catch as many of the stranded as they could. He lingered for a moment on the image of a group of winged scourges carrying Biel-Tanians away from the fires, and he wondered at that.

He had the Falcon set him down not far from the Fireheart. It was here that the end would come last, consuming the device when it had fulfilled its purpose. The mountain shook around it, and splits gaped in the stone as hungry as tyranid mouths. He ran down the boarding ramp and sent the craft away.

All was pandemonium. Eldar fled the planet with little order or discipline, breaking from their units, stopping only to help one another or let off shots at pursuing weapon-beasts.

An explosion sounded. The mountain rocked, sending Sunspear reeling. A cloud of grey ash spewed from the volcano's side. His attention drawn to this, his eye caught movement beyond.

Out on the plains to the south, capillary towers stood tall. Most had collapsed or were collapsing, falling to burn in the planet's lifeblood. But this one cluster stood tall, and above them were the looming shapes of hive ships. Prow down, they lowered questing feeder tendrils from their mouthparts. They locked one by one onto the capillary towers. With mounting horror, he watched variegated tubes pulse with peristaltic motion, pumping the biogruel of Dûriel up to the waiting ships.

Within were the combined essences of Far Ranging Hunger and Starving Dragon, rich with the genetic codes of man, ork, and eldar.

Sunspear cried out in despair.

Once more, he had lost.

CHAPTER SIXTEEN
THE RED DEATH OF DŪRIEL

'Fly faster!' Hesperax ordered. Her Venom skimmed over the boiling lava, gobbets of it splattering on the hull with every convulsion of the planet. Several Raiders followed her.

'We have them ahead, my mistress,' said Khulo Khale. 'We shall have our prizes!'

On a large island of rock, wyches goaded large creatures into eight hex cages, hollow, polyhedral balls adorned with runes. Five of them were already full.

Eldar were everywhere fleeing to their transports, or hurling themselves into webway portals. In the chaos, no one noticed the wych cult trapping their beasts.

'Some of each, as I commanded, and the largest too. Very good,' she said. Khulo Khale smiled with pleasure at her praise. He banked the Venom around, bringing it to hover a safe distance over the island of rock. The others went lower, taking position over the cages, grappling arms latching onto those that were already occupied.

The last creatures were lured by leaping wyches into their cages, blasted with high-voltage goads where they strayed away. Hesperax laughed as one of the goaders was crushed by a crab-like claw. Lapilli rained on her warriors, burning unprotected skin. Their fear was quite delicious.

'Quickly now! I will have my prizes and I will have them intact! We do not have much time, this world is finished!'

Other eldar took the place of the dead wych. A stream of anaesthetic crystals were shot into the creature's vulnerable mouth, and finally it was herded into the cage. The runes on the bars flared, the spars of the door flowed, melding seamlessly with the cage.

The wyches looked at her expectantly. She nodded.

They leapt into action, running for their transports. No doubt they were relieved. They were weak. The Raiders picked up the last few cages with supple claws, then rose high.

'We are successful, my mistress,' came the voice of Uriqa in her ear-beads.

The skimmers retreated upwards from the unbearable heat of the lava.

'A good hunt, my mistress,' said Khulo Khale.

It had been a good hunt, but Hesperax did not answer her lover to agree. She was imagining what she was going to do to Khale by way of celebration. The anticipation of his screams made her smile. If his pain pleased her, she might resurrect him and do it all over again.

'Away to home! We return to the dark city in triumph!'

The wych craft rushed for the safety of the webway as red-hot rock fountained into the air behind them.

Giant winged creatures dived at the *Curse of Yriel*, scoring its armour with their diamond claws. They came in a line, each one attempting to hit the same mark and slice through to the wraithbone core beneath, but the *Curse of Yriel* was too quick for them and their blades bit all over, wounding the machine only superficially. A chance hit cut into the infinity conduit running down its left arm, and light leaked from it. It retaliated, blasting the creature's fragile wings to pieces as it flew by, sending it spinning into the magma.

Lava erupted into the air on three sides of the Titans. The land was cracked and hellish with red light. Only the mountain to their backs remained dark.

+We must depart, defend me!+ the triple voice of the Phantom pilots sounded in Ariadien's mind. The Phantom lifted its wounded arm. The clasps of its pulsar retracted, and it jettisoned the broken weapon.

Ariadien was numb from the soul outwards, and obeyed without thought. He sprayed rapid pulsar fire across the rupturing landscape, gunning down the few beasts left capable of hurting them. The greatest threat came from the sky, but the increasingly violent geysers of lava vomiting from the ground kept the airspace close by free of the enemy. Nevertheless, he could spare little attention for the Titan as it went to the fallen *Silent Scream*. It reached out one long finger to a panel in the downed Revenant's chest. A large gem rose up in a housing, and the Phantom plucked it free, then reached forward and wrenched the Titan's corroded head from its neck mounting.

+The dead are retrieved,+ the Titan said. The ground screamed. A fresh crevasse opened up between it and the *Sound of Sunlight* and sheets of steam whistled into the sky, lit orange from below. +We must depart.+

The Phantom Titan's jump jets flared, and it bounded up the mountainside. Sparing one final glance for the ruined form of his sister's mount, Ariadien followed.

They leapt up from rock to cliff. The entire mountain shook, boulders rolled free from their seats, and more than once Ariadien almost lost his footing. But the triplet exarchs of the *Curse of Yriel* were swift and sure, and he followed the larger Titan closely. By this way they came to the summit of the mountain. *Vaul's Caress* awaited them, struggling to maintain position in the hurricane of fire sweeping over the planet. The main webgate flashed over and again as eldar craft streamed into it.

They ran leaning into the wind, their long legs carrying them over the ground in few strides. The captain of *Vaul's Caress* saw them coming, and the ship rotated on the spot, opening its doors to them.

The *Curse of Yriel* was in first, jumping clean into the hold. The ship dipped as the Titan landed inside, then again as Ariadien jetted in after it. The ship began to rise even as they positioned themselves for restraint, their mounts struggling to maintain their balance.

Only when the *Sound of Sunlight* was strapped into its transit throne and deactivated, did Ariadien allow his tears to fall.

The world disintegrated around Aloec Sunspear. *Vaul's Caress* and the smaller ships hovered near to the Fireheart, its shields absorbing a punishing barrage of volcanic ejecta. The land as far as he could see to the north, west and east was covered in lava, that to the south riven with cracks, molten rock boiling from the mantle as the world began its final convulsions. The Fireheart pulsed, its subsonics shaking his bones, its psychic resonance his mind. Thunder cracked as lightning stabbed the melting surface of Dûriel.

Eldar fled. Those of the craftworlds went both ways, rushing in and out of the gates, trying to evacuate as many of the warriors as possible. The Dark Kin carried their more wholesome cousins from the field too, although they did not return once they had departed. Bravest of all were the spiritseers riding grav-vehicles, snatching up waystones before they could be consumed by the molten rock. The shrill psychic screams of those whose stones were breached came often, chilling shrieks against the ever-present mind-roar of the voidspawn.

Sunspear's Falcon came back down. The ramp opened. Warriors beckoned to him. 'My autarch, we must go! We have to leave now!'

Sunspear did not listen. Dûriel died in a tempest of fire, and yet the despair that filled his mind and heart was the greater storm. He sank to his knees.

'We must go now! They are about to seal the gates!' Hands reached out to him, humble Guardians and ancient exarch alike shouted his name. Beyond the tank, the gates to Dûriel winked out one by one, sealed forever against the death of the world. The forces at work here would gravely damage the webway, should the gates remain open.

'I cannot leave,' he whispered. His eyes dropped. 'I die here with my failure.'

A loud bang had his eyes searching the boiling clouds.

That was no thunder.

Nine Razorwings hurtled through the clouds, weaving their way through the globs of lava falling through the air. Their pilots' skill was breathtaking. They were heading for the capillary towers.

'They are too few, they cannot do it...' whispered Sunspear, tortured by hope. His warriors had ceased calling to him, they watched too. All held their breath. The ribbed tubes of the capillary towers pulsed, pushing the chyme of Dûriel's biomass towards the waiting stomachs of the hive craft.

The Dark Kin's fighter craft did not open fire. In perfect formation, they flew directly for the tubes and accelerated. Sunspear's hands clenched into fists.

With a supersonic scream, the Razorwings hit the tubes with their sharp, forward-swept wings. The flesh of the capillary towers' oesophagi parted easily, sending a shower of acidic gruel spurting out in all directions. In rains it fell upon the rising flood of molten stone, in steam it rose, obscuring the capillary towers.

The ground rocked mightily. Slabs of crust thrust upwards, tilted vertical, then slid under the seething orange sea of fire.

'Now, autarch!'

Sunspear nodded, and stood. The despair receded. They had won. He dashed for his Falcon grav-tank. The door eased shut, and the craft sped for the waiting holds of *Vaul's Caress*.

'Go! Go, my friends!' shouted Taec. He sent a powerful psychic impulse to wake the seers from their trance. 'Your work is done! Save yourselves,' he said.

Kelmon stared down at him. 'You remain.'

'I remain,' said Taec. 'The Fireheart will cease to operate if we all depart. One must stay to the end. It is my doom.' He tried a smile. It was a lie on his lips.

'We have both seen it,' agreed Kelmon. He said no more; there was nothing else to say, for destiny's will is inviolable in the end, no matter how hard one seeks to change it. 'Farewell, Taec Silvereye of House Delgari.'

Liquid stone fell brightly behind Taec, framing his ancient face.

'Farewell, Wraithseer Kelmon Firesight of House Haladesh. May we meet again when the gods return.'

Kelmon went, following the still-singing seers into the hold of a waiting void-runner. Taec watched them go, he felt their sorrow and horror at his fate as the ship departed. But most of all he felt their relief that it was he and not they that would face She Who Thirsts.

He began the song again. His voice faltered, and so he started over. Lifting his staff over his head, he forced every iota of psychic might he possessed into his voice. Runes whipped out of his pouch, orbiting his head in one final, complex pattern.

The void-runner shot off at speed, heading for the horizon like an arrow, then climbing vertically until suddenly it pierced the clouds. Scores of smaller craft followed in its wake. A thrum announced the departure of *Vaul's Caress*; it turned and presented its prow to the sky, then it too accelerated to enormous speed in the blink of an eye and vanished. The remaining ships followed slowly, holds still open, welcoming in the last of the fleeing eldar.

Mercifully, the ships departed without further loss, their shields and armour weathering the worst the planet had to throw at them. Taec felt the terrible despair of the last few eldar on the world, followed swiftly by their deaths, and the crack of their spirit stones.

The skein resounded to the triumphant laughter of She Who Thirsts. She was waiting for him now. Her presence pushed aside the limitless mind of the voidspawn. The horrors of the flesh had been displaced by that of the spirit.

He would die the true death, and know unending torment.

Still he sang.

The throbbing of the Fireheart beat quicker and quicker. The mountaintop shook as the device's voice became a single note, rising in pitch until it screamed like a dying god.

With a cataclysmic detonation, three pillars of fire erupted from the Godpeak, sending plumes of molten rock spuming thousands of paces into the air. The world shook violently, and this earthquake did not cease, but built in intensity as Dûriel's tectonic plates tore themselves one from the other in final convulsion.

The air ignited, billows of fire rocketed around the planet. Protected by the Fireheart's exclusion field, Taec saw this. He was still there when the core, influenced by the Fireheart's deadly harmonics, ruptured.

The Godpeak exploded. The Fireheart, its work done, finally succumbed to the fury it had unleashed, and toppled into ruin.

Taec lived outside the field for less than a second before his body was incinerated. His flesh turned black and then to ash in an eyeblink, his crystallising limbs melting like glass. His death was mercifully short and painless.

The same could not be said for the aftermath. His waystone glowed, then shattered. He was pulled from this world. Before Slaanesh dragged him to her embrace, he saw the skein as he never had before, free of form's material trammels. It stretched away in all directions, a multiplicity of universes and futures. There, ahead of him, he saw the future of his race.

Taec Silvereye's soul sparkled with joy before She Who Thirsts pulled him into her thrall.

Vaul's Caress rushed from the planet, its engines pushed to the limit by its steersmen. From the epicentre of the Godpeak, a blast of fire radiated around the planet as the atmosphere caught fire. Pillars of lava chased the eldar ships through the burning air into orbit.

The ships broke from the gravity well and accelerated, leaving the final death throes of Dûriel behind, heading towards the combined warfleet of the three kindreds. The hive ships of Starving Dragon were also breaking from the planet, but they were too slow to avoid the debris flung out when the planet's core detonated. Two-thirds of the planet disintegrated, cast out as continent-sized lumps into space. The leading edge of Starving Dragon was decimated, hive ships smashed to pieces by the thousand.

The eldar were quicker, and outpaced the asteroid storm that had been Dûriel.

For fourteen cycles after the war, the husk of Dûriel glowed dimly in the long night of space, becoming briefly the lambent flame of Taec Silvereye's cryptic prophecy, long enough to light the destruction of Dûriel's orphaned moon by the wreckage of its parent.

Only then did it burn out. Dûriel was no more.

Wherever he was met within *Vaul's Caress*, Aloec was formally but sincerely congratulated. Eldar of all kindreds crowded the corridors, soot-stained and weary. The craftworlders avoided conversation, centring themselves in private meditations to avoid the extremes of sorrow and triumph victory brought. The

Dark Kin and Aspect Warriors had no such qualms, and openly celebrated their victory. To see the followers of Khaine, still wearing their war masks, celebrate so was right and proper, but the Commorrites disgusted Sunspear. They gloated about their survival, laughing over the deaths of their unfortunate companions. Worst of all, they appeared rejuvenated, glowing eyes betraying souls fat and sleek on the suffering of those who had not survived. Sunspear could not look at them; his awareness was keen that but for them he would have failed. Such ignominy was too much for his pride to bear and he grew more withdrawn with every passing cycle.

Shame clawing him, he retreated to the quarters loaned him by the Iyandeni whenever he could. By day he attended council after council. Great good had come from the victory, no matter how it was bought; part of him saw that. The hive mind had retreated. The future of Taec's vision had been averted. New vistas of possibility were opening up on the skein, the renewed alliance between the craftworlds of Iyanden and Biel-Tan a fulcrum upon which fate could be swung in the eldar's favour. The Fireheart too could be replicated, much to the councils' surprise, and already there was talk of deploying it again, a bold scheme to present the approaching hive fleets with a desert of scorched worlds. Where once such grand strategy would have enthused Sunspear, appealing to his sense of manifest destiny, he felt instead a little sick; the eldar no longer had the power to bring life to worlds, but they once more had the power to inflict death upon them.

Those were conversations for the day. He did not sleep. At night he bade the others of the craftworlds' councils goodnight, and went to the ship's small shrine. The night was for him and him alone. The night was when Aloec Sunspear knelt before the idols of dead gods.

He could not shake the feeling of shame. It gnawed at him. He, the greatest general of the Swordwind, had demonstrated his limitations most publicly, once certainly, and twice as he saw it. This feeling of inadequacy grew from a seed to a tree of despair. He went to the shrine in an increasingly vain attempt to uproot its dark boughs from his soul, but the tree only grew under the sunlight of his anxiety.

On the night of the third cycle, he went into the shrine once more. He entered head down, long fingers worrying his chin as he brooded on his failures. It was not until he had walked the length of the chapel that he realised he was not alone.

A spiritseer in the robes of Iyanden, clean but marked with burns, stood facing away from him, her long braid falling the length of her back.

'I am sorry,' he said. 'I thought to find the chapel unoccupied.'

The spiritseer did not turn, but continued to regard the statuettes of the gods in their niches.

'It has been kept clear for you, Autarch Sunspear,' she said. 'Please, continue your meditations. I mean not to disturb you, but to help.' She turned her head.

'Iyanna Arienal?' Sunspear took a step back. She was as beautiful as they said – more so – and he almost blurted this out. A kernel of self-deprecatory humour surfaced through his shame, that he of all people should be struck this way. She had a burn on her chin, dark blisters on her cheek from the hot ash of Dûriel, but these imperfections highlighted her beauty rather than diminished it. It was a cold, hard beauty. There was nothing of joy in her features, it was as if they had ossified, and she were a memorial to herself. He was not surprised, knowing what he did of her family history.

She nodded. 'We have not been formally introduced.'

Sunspear recovered. 'Your efforts on the battlefield at the side of my warriors are all the introduction I need, my lady.'

She laughed at that, a sudden, bright sound as swift in passing as a breeze through leaves, gone as quick as it came, no less glorious for its brevity. 'You of Biel-Tan are so formal. Do you know this is what we think of you?'

He gave a little bow of acquiescence. 'Ours is a martial world, lady.'

She smiled, again quickly. There was a hint of mischief to it, and he wondered what kind of woman she had been before her family had been slain, laughter had left her and she had taken up with the dead. 'Please, autarch. My title or name will suffice.'

'As you wish... Spiritseer Iyanna.'

She gave a sharp nod, and turned back to the statues.

'We thought you were dead,' he said.

'I very nearly joined my charges, it is true. I was not evacuated with the seer councils, but returned with the other spiritseers. My duties and injuries prevented me from rejoining the High Council, until today.'

'Injuries that appear almost healed, I am glad to say.'

'Your healers are proficient.'

'They have much practice,' he said. 'You gathered many waystones?'

'Not enough. Over five hundred souls were lost to She Who Thirsts, and I do not know how many of the Dark Kin were consumed. They are black-hearted, scoundrels at the best, evil at the worst. But they are eldar nonetheless, and I mourn their spirits' loss.'

Sunspear sank to his knees with a heavy sigh, dropping his head in the ritual aspect of prayer. 'A high price to pay.'

'No price was too high to secure this victory, autarch. You speak as the loser. Recall, I beg of you, that it was your victory, not your defeat.' She paused. 'Is this why you pray, to expiate some secret shame? Prayer is a hollow action, autarch, all the gods are dead.'

'And yet you are here.'

'I honour their memory as we honour the memories of all our ancestors. I commit an act of remembrance, not worship.'

'Prayer calms me,' he said. Already, he could feel his self-control slipping; his shame called for his tears. He could weep an ocean.

'There are those who are worried about you, autarch.' She looked down at him. 'Do they worry without cause? I sense your shame. It is needless.'

Sunspear shook his head. His throat was closing with emotion. He could not keep his shame bottled any longer. It came close to overwhelming him.

'There are only two cycles before the fleet returns to Biel-Tan, where I will be greeted as a hero. But I am no hero. Only the blackest of villains assured our victory, not Aloec Sunspear of Biel-Tan. I do not deserve the approbation of my people, nor the honours I will be given.' He raised his face to the idol of Kurnous, father of the eldar. 'I failed. How can I bear that?'

Iyanna knelt beside him with a sudden movement, bowing her head in the same manner as he. Her arm came free from its sleeve. He saw through the clear dressing on it that it was badly burned.

'There are no heroes or villains, not now, autarch. In these black days, the two are one and the same. We must take aid from who we can, or we will perish. We succeeded, in greater part thanks to you. Do not turn from your path, autarch, if that is even possible.'

'It is possible,' he said. 'I do not have to abandon the path completely as did your Yriel. I can withdraw from the Path of the Leader. Although it is rare for one to do so, it is possible.'

'Then keep such occasion rare!' she admonished. 'We need leaders, Autarch Sunspear, not another wailing self-obsessive crawling the sharp-toothed path of shame. Only through the actions of the likes of you will Ynnead be born and our race free of the depredations that await us beyond the veil of this life. Put aside your pride, the eldar need you more than you need yourself.' She began the hand talk, her gestures stiff and ritualistic, adding supplementary meaning to her words that did him great honour.

'Perhaps that is so,' said Sunspear. 'But although I am greatly impressed by your armies of the willing dead, I do not trust your new god,' he said carefully. 'Kysaduras's idea is a fairytale, a dangerous one at that, because it distracts us from the only path that will lead to our reinstatement as rulers of this galaxy.'

Iyanna downcast her eyes. He feared she was mocking him, and looked at her quizzically. His worries evaporated as he watched her. She was quite possibly the most beautiful woman he had ever seen. Her lips were especially full when viewed from the side, and Sunspear found himself captivated by the space between them changing as she formed her words. Only belatedly did he remember that she was a powerful psychic, and his thoughts would be as an open book to her, and he dropped his gaze again.

If that were so, and he was certain it was, she made no acknowledgement of them. 'Your trust means nothing, your opinion on Kysaduras less. Ynnead already is, and Ynnead will be. How can something not be that is eternal? She is already there, Sunspear. Kysaduras was a visionary. Your thoughts on the matter are irrelevant. You pray to the old gods, but they are dead, autarch.'

'Like I said, it calms me.'

'You do not feel calm to me. Do they answer?'

Sunspear looked at the idols, all beautiful sculptures by Kereth Lorainareath of Iyanden, a sculptor famous even on Biel-Tan. It was a lifeless beauty, the faces and blank stone eyes as dead as the beings they represented; a deliberate choice on the sculptor's part.

'No,' he admitted. 'They do not answer.'

She looked at him until he returned her gaze. Her expression was still grave, but her eyes had come alive. She took his hand in her uninjured own. He flinched, almost withdrew from this unlooked-for intimacy, but let her cool fingers slip between his.

'I pray to a god that answers. I have the tools to bring her awakening soon. Tell me you are not intrigued? Surely every avenue must be explored, if there is but a chance of salvation to it?'

Aloec agreed reluctantly, by mien and gesture.

She relaxed, and he realised his favourable reaction meant something important to her. 'Come then,' she said, standing and pulling at his hand. 'Let me show you something wonderful.'

CHAPTER SEVENTEEN

THE DAY OF THE DEAD

The ships opened their doors, and sombre warriors came out. No celebration attended their victory. There were so many who would not be returning home.

The laying of the dead took over Iyanden. Too many caskets bearing freshly inhabited spirit stones came out of the ships' holds, only a few with corpses, for most material remains had been consumed by fire and that made the eldar's woe greater. Those on the Path of Mourning marched one to each lost soul: in groups by the waystone chests, singly by each coffin, others in long train behind the material remains of the dead, and one further for each eldar spirit lost to She Who Thirsts.

The mourners wept openly, a few rending their garments or pulling at their hair, crying not only for those whose loss they had been asked to remember, but for all eldar dead upon Dûriel. With so many killed, there was much grief. They pummelled themselves and wailed in place of all the others, for those who dared not grieve for fear that grief would overwhelm them. The families and kinsfolk of the dead stood in utter silence, faces set behind veils of white, as the funeral procession wound onwards towards the Dome of Final Contemplations. No songs were sung that day but those that addressed the true death, and the end of all things, and they were sung over and again.

But in the procession there was one who grieved openly in defiance of custom. Ariadien, cradling the waystone of his sister, his mind enwrapping her somnolent spirit as hard as his hand clutched the stone it dwelt within.

'They tried to take you from me, but I would not let them,' he whispered to it. 'They tried to take you, and I fought them. They look at me with contempt, for I grieve you myself. Let them look.'

Neidaria's spirit stone was warm in his hand, and when he spoke to it he thought it became warmer.

He staggered on only for a short way. As soon as the procession left the docks, he stumbled from the lines of dead and mourners. 'Let me through! Let me through!' he shouted. He was behaving without decorum, and worried looks were cast his way. Someone tried to stop him, Ariadien did not know his name. The eldar spoke words to calm him, but retreated when Ariadien snarled at him. He shoved his way out of the crowd, ducking through the wraithkind lining the route of the funeral. They had come to welcome the dead in their own way, and were unmoved by the crowd's reaction to Ariadien. Back in the procession, someone called out after him; other voices joined the first, but he was away, running with the waystone of his slaughtered sister clamped tight to his chest, his face a waterfall of tears.

Away from the crowds, Iyanden was eerily quiet. 'Death is everywhere,' he whispered. 'Oh my sister, my sister! I am sorry, if it were not for me, perhaps they would not have chosen us as a Geminiad. I am sorry, I am sorry!' He choked on his own words, barking out an ugly cough. Grief coiled in his gut, its hooked fangs buried deep in the tender places of his belly. It bit harder with each sob. His sorrow was a physical, unendurable pain.

He staggered home to the domes of House Haladesh. He came through a twisted forest of new wraithbone whose semi-sentient branches reached out to touch his pain, and the whispered voices of other dead murmured plaintively in his mind.

Through this way and others less canny, he came to those parts where the living yet ruled, and thence made his way to the apartments he shared with his sister, now his alone.

He stumbled into the door, so anguished that the mechanism at first did not recognise his psyche. He clawed at it with one weakening hand, beseeching it to open and let him pass. It did so, though whether by his design or its own, he never understood.

Once inside he blundered like a mad thing. Howling daemoniacally he upended furniture and smashed all that came to hand regardless of its beauty or value, Neidaria's hot waystone at his breast all the while. His sister's things in particular enraged his despair, and he treated them most cruelly of all, dashing her poetry crystals against the walls, ripping at her favoured garments with his fingernails.

Eventually, exhausted, he collapsed. He found the strength to crawl to his cabinet of best liqueurs, and pulled forth a potent darkvine spiked with dreamleaf and other, less acceptable narcotics. He put it to his lips and drank a great draught, hiccuping it so that it poured from his open mouth like the blood from his broken heart. Retching with misery, he drank the remainder down.

He fell into a fugue, losing himself deep in woe. He floated on a sea of cerise water. In the distance, his sister waved to him from a shore of grey sand, but he could not reach her, and as he paddled towards her she turned away and walked up towards the dunes, to where a figure in motley played a shrill and heartless tune upon a pipe carved from a thighbone. She did not look back.

In the end, blackness overtook him.

Ariadien awoke an unknown time later. He was enwrapped in velvet darkness, but he was awake. He was quite sure of that.

'Ariadien, can you hear me?' A voice spoke close by, stentorian and slow, the voice of an eldar drugged or lost to ennui. The voice of the dead.

'Wh-where am I?' he said. He did not feel his lips move, and the voice he heard was not his own. He realised then with mounting panic that he could not move at all, nor could he see. Reaching out with his mind he sought his sister, looking for her presence. He found it readily enough, close at hand. But it was the sluggish dead thing he had closed his mind around on the terrible journey back from Dûriel, and not the vibrant soul she had been. He wailed anew. 'Dead! Dead! She is dead!'

'Dead,' said the voice, 'but not yet gone. Calm yourself, Ariadien.'

Tranquillity was imposed upon his mind, not true relaxation, but more akin to the bars of a cage.

'A seer,' he said. 'You are a seer.'

'I am a seer. Wraithseer Kelmon, I for whom duty did not end when life ended. I fight on, to make reparation for the mistakes I made in life. Tell me, Ariadien, if you were given the choice, would you choose to serve Iyanden after your demise?'

'Why? Why should I? I have done all I can. I have fought for Iyanden, and if I did not do so unwillingly, having my sister appropriated to the same cause without her assent was worth two lifetimes of obedience. I watched my sister die, fighting a war she should not have fought. I have lost all I cared for! Let me be.'

'This war is the war of all eldar, willing or not. It is the Rhana Dandra begun, surely you can see this?'

'She wanted to be a poet!' he screamed. 'The path was to be of our own choosing, so said Asurmen himself, but she and I, we had no choice! Curse you and all the seers! You betray the Asurya!'

'And yet Asurmen was trapped on one branch. He is trapped still.'

'By his own connivance,' sobbed Ariadien. 'By his own doing.'

'By necessity,' said Kelmon out of the dark. 'A necessity he embraced. Necessity dogs our steps on the path closely, Ariadien. Whether we will a branch or it is thrust upon us, we must tread it as best we can.'

Icy calm descended on Ariadien. 'What have you done to me? What have you done to us? Why are you telling me this?'

'Iyanden is reliant upon the dead, Ariadien. The dead dwell within the Tears of Isha. They feed the new god, Ynnead, who will break the Dark Prince and free us all.'

'Fanaticism! The gods are dead, wraithseer, as dead as you.' Dread held fast to Ariadien's soul.

'The truth, and not the truth. Nothing ever dies. The gods never died. They live within our enemy, as all the souls she has consumed since the Fall dwell within her. They wait to break free. The time approaches. Ynnead will free them. Tell me, Ariadien, whence come the waystones, the spirit traps that guard our souls?'

'The crone worlds,' whispered Ariadien. Kelmon used part of a mnemonic chant, inculcated into him in his earliest schooling. Ariadien was compelled to answer.

'Who gathers the tears? Who risks the thirst? Who are our greatest heroes?'

Ariadien resisted. 'Vagabonds! Renegades! Pathfinders, rangers, sellswords and sell-souls!'

'Who are our greatest heroes?' repeated Kelmon patiently.

'The knights,' said Ariadien feebly, his strength spent. 'The wraithknights. They find the tears.'

A sense of satisfaction emanated from Kelmon. 'Open your eyes.'

Ariadien could see. He looked down upon Kelmon's head from some height. The displays of various instruments flickered in his field of view, not dissimilar to those of his Revenant. His body he felt too, but it was not his own.

'You will learn to use it all in time, fear not,' said Kelmon.

'Brother,' came an emotionless voice. 'We will fight again, you and I, an eternity together, until the Great Enemy is cast down and we may be reborn.'

'No!' shouted Ariadien. 'No! This was not what she wanted! This was her greatest fear! This is not fair!' He tried to lash out at Kelmon, but his arms would not move.

The wraithseer raised his arms and spoke. 'Arise, Ariadien-Neidaria, united in death which in life could not be parted. Arise, knight of Iyanden. You may despair of your fate for a while, but it will pass, and you will be a hero. You are the future of our race. That, or...' His arms dropped, and he paused. 'Or you, Ariadien, may walk away now. You may exit the knight and begone to whatever fate you feel you deserve. But let me tell you this, Ariadien of House Haladesh, if you choose this path, if you choose self over selflessness, you will never be in your sister's presence again.'

The wraithseer turned away.

'I leave you now to think on it. Discuss it between yourselves. On the morrow, I shall return to hear your answer.'

Kelmon went from Ariadien's perception. Either the lights went out or the vision of the knight was deactivated. Neidaria's presence was a candle beside him in the dark, the only warmth in an uncaring universe, and it was not lit with her consent.

Ariadien's screams went unheard.

Iyanna Arienal, last of her house, led a procession of spiritseers deep into the infinity core. They sang as they descended, complex melodies woven with the names of the newly dead. Fifteen of them, all of the most senior of their path, with four-score wraithguard following. Between the towering wraithbone warriors, forty caskets floated on anti-grav fields, each carrying twenty spirit stones. The procession went down the spiral ramp running around the shaft of the core. The shaft was the central node of the infinity circuit, brainstem of Iyanden. Three hundred paces across, its smooth walls glowed yellow, shot through with a tracery of veins which shone a brighter light. The circuit's capillaries were close to the surface here. This was the closest one could get to being in the circuit physically. It was the borderlands of death, a place for crossing over from one realm to the next.

The procession went slowly, their laments loud yet tinged with hope of rebirth in the distant futures yet to come, when the Great Enemy's thirst was quenched and the hurt to the world undone.

The spirits of the dead crowded curiously around the group. They had grown quieter, many of them sinking into lethargy and forgetfulness now that vengeance had been delivered and the threat of the Great Dragon's merging averted.

Iyanna and her seers reached the bottom of the shaft. They moved in ritual pattern, the wraithguard gathering the spirit stone caskets in the centre.

The song continued as the casket lids slid open.

'As we pass from spirit to flesh, this is the first passing,' said Iyanna. 'As we pass from flesh to spirit, this is the second passing. As we pass from spirit to wraithkind, this is the third passing,' she continued. 'As we pass back from wraithkind to spirit, this is the Fourth Passing. You have served again, O dead, now return to your rest.'

No other speech was made, all that needed to be said was sung. The spirit stones were lifted carefully, one at a time, from their resting places and set against the wall. 'This is the Fourth Passing,' the spiritseers sang as they placed the stones on the wall. Here, in this place of power, the process of wraithbone growth was swift, and the spirit stones were engulfed into the fabric of the walls. A flaring of lights speckled the walls around the embedded stones as the dead welcomed their own back to the infinity circuit. The light in each glowing waystone went out, the waystones reappeared as the wraithbone drew back, and the empty vessels were taken down and replaced into the caskets. No other eldar could use these emptied stones; they were retained against future necessity, should the spirit that once dwelled inside need to be called back to serve Iyanden anew. As those who had served in the Phoenix Host departed, the seers sent them back to their rest with songs of thanks.

Iyanna and the others wept behind their masks as they went through the ritual. These stones were of those ghost warriors who had expressed a strong desire to return to the circuit. A quarter of them all told. Many remained ambulant; still Iyanden was a city of the dead.

The seers wept not for these departed souls, for they were safe and home, but for the dead whose waystones had been lost in the volcanic tumult of Dûriel's red death, Taec Silvereye's among them. Iyanna could only hope that her plan would come to fruition, and the Dark Prince be defeated finally by the god of the dead. Iyanna could feel the presence of the new god, right on the edge of her psychic senses. A powerful presence, moving closer to wakefulness with each eldar spirit that was added to its aggregate soul.

The Ritual of the Fourth Passing went on for two cycles. There was no climax – it ended as simply as it had begun, the seers departing the way they had come and still in song, their dead honour guard marching after them.

Iyanna was tired when they returned to the Dome of Final Contemplations, the centre of her path's power. She underwent the rituals with her colleagues, and unmasked they embraced and wept all the harder for those they had not been able to save.

But Iyanna could not rest yet. There was still one spirit that needed to return home.

* * *

Althenian was waiting for Iyanna by the door to his shrine, patient as only the dead can be.

'You are here,' he said, his voice sepulchral as the rest of wraithkind. The fire that ordinarily set him apart from the others was absent. 'I am gladdened by this, I thank you.'

'I came,' she agreed sadly.

He nodded his great head, the runes and charms depending from it jingling. Iyanna could not read what that nod meant. Whether he was pleased or in agreement with himself on some matter was impossible to discern; his blank face was inscrutable as it ever was.

The door to the shrine slid open at his touch.

'We go in, both of us for the final time, not again. I reborn, this door closes to you always. No return. Do not come, the way will be perilous, this is truth.'

'I am aware of this,' she said. 'Khaine's wrath will scorch my soul.'

'Fear for form. New dragons are often wild. Dangerous. Do not come. Not all encountered within, will be tame.' He led the way, limping from damage to his wraithbone shell suffered in the battle.

The Shrine of the Fire's Heart had changed greatly since their last visit. The dome had been landscaped with sharp ridges of volcanic rock. Cliffs reared up in front of them, razor-edged and ominous, obscuring the view of the shrine's central temple. Basilisks grown from Iyanden's biological databanks basked on stones overlooking cracks in the ground. These had a ruddy effulgence, and steam shot from them in short-lived blasts. It was hot, volcanically so, reminding Iyanna uncomfortably of the Fireheart's activation.

'See you here, destiny is hard at work, new Fire's Heart,' said Althenian.

'All things are linked,' she said. 'No thread is spun in isolation of the others.'

'This is so. Please watch your step, my lady, stone is sharp.'

He caught her looking at the reptiles. 'Be at ease. Do not fear the basilisks, they are young. I guide you, I will protect you from them, they are weak.'

'As you have protected me for so long.'

'As always, and I will continue to, where I can. I swear this,' he said. 'Even after our bond is gone, I do so.'

They went through a maze of sharp formations of gneiss, black stone alight with the glitter of crystals. Althenian pointed out certain places where he would train his new followers, or particularly appealing formations. 'All is here, all is as I remember it, to the last,' he said.

'It is as Iyanden remembers it,' she said. Iyanna did not share his enthusiasm.

Boiling pools of mud surrounded the shrine temple, and Althenian mothered her along the correct path, much to her irritation. She was awhirl with emotion, close to snapping at him one moment, crying the next. She fought hard to regain her poise, knowing what she felt to be the foreshadowing of fresh grief.

The temple interior was cool after the broil outside its doors. Black sand coated its floors, and red light glowed from unseen sources. Grumbles and snapping sounds came from side passages, as if there were something living in hidden chambers, or perhaps the temple itself were alive. There was a strong, fiery presence to it that had been absent before. The Shrine of the Fire's Heart truly had been reborn.

They passed from the open areas of the shrine, where those newly grasped by the dragon aspect of Khaine would be trained, to its inner precincts. The shrine's long arming chambers had been filled with new battlesuits in the colours of the Fire's Heart. Armour of deep orange plating and high crimson helms were racked upon stands, gleaming golden fusion guns by their sides. Althenian's great head swung to and fro and he nodded appreciatively. 'Fine weapons, I am honoured by those, on Vaul's Path.'

When they reached the exarch's chamber, Althenian's pleasure increased. His sculpted body showed no sign of it, but Iyanna felt it, radiating off him in waves.

At the centre of the room was his armour, and by it a lengthy fusion pike.

The armour was exquisite, its plating most artfully made. Red light lit it from below. Sockets for spirit stones waited all over its breast and vambraces. Althenian walked over to it and looked down on it. She sensed his impatience.

'Now I lose you,' she said.

He turned back to where she stood in the chamber's doorway.

'Yes you do,' he replied. 'I have long been lost to Khaine, Iyanna. I change not, this is no transformation, this changing. I return, back to my rightwise being, Iyanna. I am sad. There is sadness for us both, Iyanna. Also joy, the phoenix risen again's promise. Do not weep. Iyanna, fair Iyanna not for me, it must be. You know it, my soul was forfeit to Khaine, for so long. It is now, five thousand passes since I fell, to the wrath. Iyanna, you offered me respite, it was good. For this boon, I can never repay you, to my shame. Remember, my war rages eternal, 'twas ever thus.'

'You need offer no repayment,' she said, and then turned from the wraith-lord so that he would not see her tears.

'Do not weep, if there were anything to give, Iyanna, only you, ever would I give it to, and gladly. Do not weep, Lady Arienal great seer, do not weep.' He took two limping steps across the floor. With surprising tenderness, he knelt and embraced her in his long arms, the mounts for his weapons snagging in her robes. She rested her cheek on the hard panels of his pauldron for a while, and then he withdrew.

'It is time,' he said. 'Do quickly what must be done, I beg you.' He bowed his head and a seam opened in the front of his smooth helmet, dividing it in two, the twin dragons in opposition turning from each other for the last time. The great head of the wraithlord swung open, revealing layers of armour of various kinds: hard plastics, ablative soft gels, cunningly woven composites in strata like those within rock.

Under it all was a compartment, crafted with care and beauty. Within it were seven spirit stones, each set in its own recess. Six lesser surrounding one greater; those eldar who had fallen to Khaine, become exarchs and joined their essence to that of the original Althenian. Iyanna reached out carefully and removed these smaller six, leaving the greatest till last. They offered no resistance, almost falling into her hands in the same manner ripe fruit is easily plucked from the tree. She placed the six into a velvet bag at her belt, then reached out and took

Althenian's greatest spirit stone, that which housed the soul of the eldar who had originally borne his name, into her hands.

Althenian was warm to her touch, the gem of his dwelling flawless, perhaps even more so than other waystones. The light within it was a fiery orange, and this brought a smile to her lips even as she cried.

She carried the stones carefully to the waiting armour. She sang the ritual song of the Fourth Passing, homecoming, the same one she had sung in the infinity core that same day, as she installed the waystones into their mountings, although the words were different, for Althenian went to no rest. She left Althenian's primary stone until last, holding it up in both hands, took one final look into its flickering depths, and slid it into position in the recess on his breastplate.

The stone clicked, and she stood back. Dancing orange light glowed bright in all seven spirit stones, then died back to the faintest glimmer as Althenian slipped back into dormancy, awaiting new life.

'Goodbye for now, dear Althenian,' she said.

She turned and walked past the kneeling wraithlord shell, and left the shrine as quickly as she could.

Once more Yriel was upon the beach of bones. It had finally become dusk, and he could not tell if the dark sea was still of blood or had become water. It tossed in front of him, white caps slapping noisily into one another with extravagant sprays of luminescent foam glowing white in the gathering dark. A stink of iron was on the air, and of fire, but the wind from the sea blew fresh and strong, carrying the scents of war away, and replacing them with the smell of salt oceans and of life.

He sank to his knees, absent-mindedly running the bone sand through his fingers. He was so tired, even in his dreams he was tired, deriving from sleep none of the refreshment that slumber should bring. With his nightmares came the revelation of another kind of tiredness, deeper and spiritual in nature, behind the petty weariness of the body. Prince Yriel suffered from an exhaustion of the spirit.

He waited disinterestedly for tonight's tableau of horror to assail his senses. The whole thing was boringly predictable to him. He was so weary he no longer had any care for his own soul. All he desired was an end.

Time passed, nothing happened. No presence came. The sound of the waves began to relax him. The smell of war gave way entirely to that of life. The evening was refreshingly cool, the beach warm from the day's sunlight. After a time, Yriel felt his eyelids grow heavy, and lay down on the sand, letting the heat of the powdered bone soothe his limbs. He filled his hand with the bone, let it run through his fingers close to his face. When he looked hard, trying to see the tiny skulls trapped in the eldritch beach, all he saw was rounded grains of sand.

Yriel slept, the rush and boom of the waves his lullaby.

Yriel awoke long before Iyanden's artificial dawn. For the first time since he had taken up the Spear of Twilight, he was calm. His palsy was stronger than ever; his pains clawed at his innards, competing with the horror at Yaleanar's death. But although his weariness remained, it was of that good, clean kind that is born of a worthy task finally done, that sort which purifies the soul, and Yriel felt at peace.

The spear called to him, and he answered, going to its cradle and staring at it. What emanated from it now was gentler.

'It is time, is it not?' Yriel said to it, crooning the words almost, as if he breathed them direct into his lover's ear. 'My last battle has been fought, our work together is over.'

He spent a portion of the night kneeling by the spear's cradle in his palace, eyes closed in silent contemplation.

At the conclusion of his vigil, Yriel dressed himself extravagantly, an attempt he supposed to recapture in funereal splendour the dash of his more carefree days. If he was to die tonight, he would die looking like the prince he was, not the walking corpse he had become. He did not call for his servants, but walked his extensive chambers alone, taking what he needed. He had always prized his freedom; dependency sickened him.

He painted his face, coloured his hair a deep blue. He put on a shimmering body suit patterned with interlocking flames of two dark blues. He donned high boots. Next he went to his armoury, and took out his armour, his life-support unit with its high pennants and his war-belt with its holsters and sheaths, and into this he put his weapons. From his rooms of armoires he took his finest chains from their boxes. Over it all went his high-collared admiral's coat. Finally, from its stand in the centre of the armoury, he took the Eye of Wrath and locked it into place over his blood-red eye.

He examined himself in his mirror hall, inspecting every angle of his body. 'Every inch the general,' he said wryly.

For the final time, he took up the spear, the tingling in his hand flaring up as he did so as if in acknowledgement of his tragic errand.

He left his chambers without word. There would be few abroad at this hour, and any who challenged him he would simply pass by, or such was his intention. He spoke no farewells, passing through his house without comment from the few of his servants about their work. Upon reaching the wide boulevards of House Ulthanash no other seemed to see him either. As he passed more and more of his fellows in his finery without a single one seeing him, he realised he moved through them as if in a dream, that he was invisible to them. Such things had long ago ceased to surprise him, and he was glad of his easy passage.

So it went as he traversed predawn Iyanden; none noticed him. Not revellers or lovers abroad, or friends walking. Not even a pair of seers who knew him well. He glanced at the spear, hot in his hand. Doubtless it was the cause. At Red Moon's New Birthing there were three eldar in private prayer at the shrines around the walls. They too were unaware, and he walked through the energy field to the Shrine of Ulthanash unseen.

Yriel trod the precincts of the shrine slowly this time. Iyanden was quiet, perpetually in mourning, the Shrine of Ulthanash as deathly still as it had been that fateful day ten passes ago when he had taken up the Spear of Twilight.

His journey had taxed him. He was so weak, his soul spent. Pain was his constant companion; that, and guilt. His bones were like ice in his flesh, snapping agonies chased up and down his nerve endings. It was all he could do not to use the spear as a walking stick, like some decrepit mon-keigh in the last cycles of its short life. He did not, but unknowingly he let the shaft droop behind him, so that his unsteady footprints were joined for short spaces by a wavering line in the dust of the halls.

His walk through the shrine seemed an age in duration, although the light of a new cycle had still yet to be born. He regained a little of his strength as he approached the heart of the shrine; the dais with its pedestal and empty rest, the weeping statues of Ulthanash's sisters either side.

He did not hesitate this time, but walked straight to the dais to replace the spear. The light came on as he approached, and he held the spear out crosswise in front of him, meaning to slot it back into place. He bowed his head in silent prayer to devoured Asuryan, trembling with the effort of holding out the weapon where before he had done so effortlessly.

'Mighty lord of us all,' he thought, 'I thank you for the use of this gift. I now return it.'

He felt the last few particles of his being slipping into the spear as the sands in a glass run out. His waystone was dull, no resonance from his spirit to make it shine, just like poor Yaleanar's. Soon he would pass – the moment he replaced the spear, he would die. He wondered what would become of him.

'There will be no rest in the infinity circuit for Prince Yriel,' he said. He closed his eyes as he lowered the spear to its cradle, anticipating his death not unhappily.

A hand on his shoulder stayed him. He looked up to find his face reflected in the smooth silver mask of a Shadowseer.

The Harlequin shook her head slowly before springing away and laughing. Coruscating patterns of diamonds followed her movements, filling the shrine with light.

'There will be no rest anywhere for the Prince Yriel of House Ulthanash, not yet, not for ever so long.'

'Veilwalker?' he said.

The Harlequin bowed. 'The very same! Come to tell you, O scion of the defeated one, that your labours are not yet done. Fire and night come upon us, the skein is quirked. You are needed yet, no night for the prince, no rest. Not yet.'

There was a hiss from the tubes on the Veilwalker's back, a fleeting perfume. Then the shrine flickered as if lit by a fire, sheets of light and shadowplay leaping into life all around the dais. They grew in clarity, taking on form, until the walls danced with images.

And such things he saw.

'What is this?' he breathed.

'The skein in living colour for you to see, no gnomic pronouncements from me, my friend. See the galaxy to come, see it burn. Would you leave it now, abashed, head bowed? Where is the proud son of Ulthanash when war calls?'

Gods walked the earth. Gods long thought dead. Legions of daemons fought the ranked majesty of dozens of craftworlds fighting side by side. He glimpsed exodites, the Dark Kin, a troupe of Harlequins of unprecedented size that filled a battlefield with their glittering fields and garish costumes; all branches of their shattered race reunited. The blue and yellow of Iyanden was prominent among them, and the green and white of Biel-Tan. Armies of mankind and other lesser creatures fought alongside them too. He could not see what was happening clearly; he would look at one image to have his attention snatched away to another.

'The Rhana Dandra,' he said. 'The final battle.'

Then he saw himself, swollen with power, the Eye of Wrath blazing with energies its mechanisms alone could not produce. Atop a pile of broken daemons, he whirled the Spear of Twilight over his head, a flaming sword in his other hand. The image faded, its place taken by another.

'This is the future?' he asked.

Sylandri stopped her prancing. Legs crossed at the ankle, she placed a finger against her mask, a caricature of thought. 'Maybe, maybe not. One future, a good one, a bad one. Who knows really, other than the Laughing God? Perhaps you would like to choose one? They are all here to see, if you but know where to look.'

'I am no seer,' he said. He spoke without venom, all his anger bled away. The calm he had felt when he awoke had grown; indeed, he was calmer than he had been for a long time. He simply stated a fact.

'One does not need to be a seer, O prince, to see an empire born anew. It waits in the dawn of possibility, on the other side of night's chaos. The stage is set, shall you provide the cue to call it from the wings?' She pointed to another image. Iyanna, bloodied, pulling a glowing stone from the hand of a necrontyr in the throes of terminal malfunction. 'She will find it, the last one of Morai-Heg's tears, and then we shall see who thirsts the most!' Sylandri laughed. 'See, O prince, that what has withered can grow strong again!'

She bowed, holding out her hand in extravagant gesture, pointing to his arm.

Yriel looked at his right hand. He still held the spear over its cradle, as he had been doing since Veilwalker had grasped him. He was astounded at the steadiness of his hand.

'How is this possible?'

'It simply is, why question? Do you accept, O prince? Once more a choice is laid before you, the cup is poured, now will you sup?'

Yriel withdrew the spear and set its butt upon the floor. The click of it, the audible acceptance of this new fate, acted as a trigger for rejuvenation, and his body flooded with new strength. He gasped as it filled him, the sound turning from surprise to one of genuine pleasure. He stood tall, taller than he had for many cycles. Warmth returned to him, his soul replenished. All his pains were swept away.

'Well done, once-exile, well done indeed! The sacrifice of your friend was not after all in vain. Come, come!' Sylandri backed away from him in a half bow, her pace a sinuous exaggeration of temptation. She kept one fist balled behind her back, while on the other hand she crooked her forefinger and beckoned. Shadow enveloped her as she left the cone of light fixed upon the empty cradle. Yriel glanced from it to the Harlequin.

'This way, O prince!' she said, now totally lost in the blackness. 'Come with me, and set your feet upon the path of a new destiny!'

Yriel did not pause to think. Images of glory filled him, and that would once have driven him to accept alone, to swell his pride if nothing more. But far greater an impulse came from what he had glimpsed. Not war or power influenced his decision, but instead a flash of peace, brief, but unmistakable nonetheless.

Grasping the spear of his ancestor more tightly, Yriel stepped into the shadows after the seer, and was gone from Iyanden for many long cycles.

EPILOGUE

Moisture ran down the rippled walls of the dungeon. The mass of it was sculpted from living bone, raw and pink where the thick black slime growing on it had been scraped off. Tumorous lumps set into the wall ticked with the minute twitches of residual nerve activity. Veined membranes, stretched taut across apertures that would in any saner environment be windows, pulsated with agony. The pain of the building was on the air, a heady taste that fizzed on Hesperax's senses. This lounge was intended for the relaxation and enjoyment of the Ebon Sting's favoured clients, a demonstration of their arts in flesh sculpting. And, no doubt, to induce a little fear. This kind of place was uncanny even for a true eldar.

Hesperax thought it none of these things. She found it trite. What the Great Harlequin who accompanied her thought was as impenetrable as his sculpted smile. He lounged against the slimed wall as if whiling away the hours in a corespur pleasure arcade, his pose not exactly insouciance, but perhaps an exact replica of it.

She ceased pacing the smooth floor, one giant sheet of skin that quivered with agony at her every step, and rounded upon the wrack left to attend her and the Great Harlequin.

'How long will this take?' she snapped. The wrack spread a selection of its many limbs and bowed in abject apology.

'This haemacolyte pleads for your forgiveness, mistress,' it said, its hands and instruments waving elaborately. 'One cannot hurry the work of my masters. They are artists, and true art is planned meticulously no matter how swift its execution might be. Their examination will be done when it is done, Mistress Hesperax, and not before. This one cautions that it is not wise to disturb them.'

Hesperax growled softly at the back of her throat, her eyes narrowing. She was gratified with a slight flinch from the wrack. The wrack was more self-possessed than most, and the thing's rebuff, no matter how servile, had her seething. She considered removing its head. In her mind's eye she could see the masked face arcing away from its deformed shoulder, spouting whatever it had for blood – she fancied some dark, sweet liquid, looking at the black patterning of blood vessels under the exposed skin of its chest – but she restrained herself. Slaying the servants of the haemonculi in their lair was not done, even for one as exalted as her.

'Very well,' she said. She continued to stalk around the antechamber, letting the play of her armour's fastening hooks in her flesh calm her with easy pain, and trying to ignore the milky eyes of the haemonculi's wrack on her body. After a time, she could no longer bear his lascivious gaze, and stared at him until he scurried from the antechamber. The door, two thick curtains of flesh, opened with an audible moan. Musky air billowed from them as they slapped shut behind the wrack.

Hesperax turned to the Harlequin King. Why in the fifteen worlds he had insisted on accompanying her was a mystery, and his mocking, motley-clad form, so at odds with the fleshy room, irritated her greatly. 'You told me this would be a simple matter.'

The Harlequin arched supplely from the wall and bowed. His extravagantly collared coat was of many colours, his mask pure white. The mouth was fixed in a grotesque smile that put her in mind of Sarnak, the brows sharply arched, as if it enjoyed a pitiless joke. A single sapphire tear adorned one cheek, a high crest of hair that shifted colours curled over his head. He performed a complex mime.

She gaped in exasperation. 'You said nothing, of course. Very well, you conveyed to me that that would be the case. Does that satisfy your pedantry?'

The Harlequin gave another bow, accompanied by a teasing wave of its hand. There were two eldar in the immediate vicinity besides herself, and she would gladly see them both dead. The wrack she wished to kill out of spite, but the Harlequin King... Hesperax ached to test her blades on him. There were few in all the Great Wheel, the Labyrinth Dimension or the Othersea who could best her in combat. She had a sneaking suspicion that this Great Harlequin might be one of those rare individuals. As she imagined him fighting for his life in the arenas of the Cult of Strife, his motley stripped from him, his mask nailed to his face, she stared a little too long into his gemstone eyes.

He cocked his head and waved a warning finger, shaking his head slowly. To her surprise, she experienced a small rush of fear. It only served to excite her. She wet suddenly dry lips, her tongue running over the stickiness of their reactive paints.

'One day, you and I will dance together, king of fools.'

He shrugged in exaggerated fashion. As usual, his gestures carried overt mockery.

A movement in the air. Hesperax whirled around, her ponytail whipping with near lethal force, her knife leaping with preternatural speed into her hand. She stayed it as it pricked a bead of dark blood from the wrack's throat. He held his arms up.

'Do not approach me without warning!' she shouted.

'This one is sorry!' the wrack babbled. 'This one comes only to say that my masters are ready, come, please, come now, mistress!'

She pulled back her knife. The wrack nodded encouragingly. 'This way, mistress, master, come!' It beckoned them to the door, which opened with the same moan of pain.

She followed, the Harlequin silent behind her.

Down corridors formed of fused ribs they went, the gurgling systems of the building and the soft sounds of its constant pain always with them. They came to a stairway made of iron hooked deep into the living wall, from whose wounds thick blood welled, creating rank stalactites of clotted matter. The wrack beckoned them down this, to a storey of the tower floored in more conventional means, although the marble was puddled with the building's excretions.

Here were the oubliettes of the Ebon Sting. Cries of pain competed with those of the building, emanating from tiny cells that were little more than blisters on the wall. Cages of ribs and thick cartilage contained larger specimens. Here was life taken from all over the galaxy, and all of it in pain. Horribly mutilated creatures of all kinds called to her, begging without exception for release from their suffering. Hesperax shuddered with pleasure; the intense nature of such distilled agony excited her deliciously.

The wrack took them to a portcullis of dark metal, retracted the grating into the ceiling with much irksome pantomime, then gestured for them to follow on.

They entered a cavern at the roots of the tower. There the living bone of the tortured edifice thrust deep into the spire it parasited. The floors and walls here were of more mundane materials, and crowded with the workstations of haemonculi. Shelters of skins held upon poles by scarred slaves kept the constant rain of effluvia off the haemonculi's work. There was space for several to work together at once, but there were only two within, attended by half a dozen wracks or so, and twice that many slave creatures.

They were working around two of Hesperax's prizes: a pair of living tanks, still within their hex cages, one with a red carapace, the other purple. The first was missing much of its face, the wounds that had carved it away surgical in nature. The other had had its giant crustacean's claw cut open, exposing the workings within. Neither seemed much concerned by their vivisection.

'What have you done to my trophies?' hissed Hesperax. 'How are they supposed to fight in the games?'

One of the haemonculi retreated behind the hex cages, pretending to be intent on its work. The other rose into the air, the thrum of its grafted gravorgans deliberately audible. It floated towards her, wizened feet trailing clawed nails.

'Ah, Mistress Hesperax, welcome. Do not alarm yourself. We have ascertained the structure of these creatures. The vivisection is a necessary stage, but we are sure we can replicate as many as you might require. Their gene-weavings are delightfully simple.'

Hesperax jabbed a finger at the haemonculus. 'That better be the case, Vral. I have paid you well for this work.'

'It is not wise to threaten a haemonculus in his lair, Mistress Hesperax. Especially Vral Dulgyre.'

'It is not wise to cheat the Cult of Strife,' she retorted.

He spread his hands and shrugged. 'Perhaps. But you will not be cheated. There are few cults of my brothers that could manage what you require, in the time you demand. But we shall. We work in concert, our coven. Art takes time, and many hands make light work.' He lifted three of his own by way of emphasis. 'Soon you will have your monsters, of that I assure you.'

She walked over to the cages and peered in. Vral followed after her, wringing his long fingers constantly together. The tyranids had a curious reek, almost oceanic, salt water and dimethyl sulphide, a savoury tang. She stared into their eyes. They watched back with bovine disinterest. Their eyes were animal, flat dead discs, devoid of the ferocious intelligence of the hive mind. She noticed racks of cylinders depending from booms over the cages, pipes leading from each to holes drilled into the creatures' armour. She pointed.

'You have drugged them?'

Vral nodded once. 'Yes. They do not suffer. Their reactions to pain stimulus are merely reflexive, but they are extreme. To caress them with our full art would bring us no dark energy, and carry a significant risk to our laboratories.'

'They are strong enough to break the cages?'

'Oh, mistress, yes. They are strong enough.'

Hesperax stared at them, ignoring the wracks bustling around their strange instruments. She gave a sudden laugh. 'Then they will gather me much glory.'

'And dark energy, mistress. Oh, not from them, but imagine the terror they will generate in our combatants! Imagine the thrill of the crowd!'

Hesperax nodded. She could imagine just that, taste the bloodlust, hear their shouts as she stood upon one of these dead creatures, the audience chanting her name!

'We can manipulate them, grow more.' Vral sank lower, closer to her, his thick breath washing over her face. 'Meld them with other creatures to create unheard-of exotica!'

Her head snapped round. 'Never mind that now, what of what I requested? Can it be done?'

'Oh, yes, mistress!' Vral smiled around pointed teeth and a black tongue. 'The two strains can be combined very easily.' He inspected his pointed nails. 'Child's play. The creatures' genetic strands are designed to be easily assimilated and altered. Our flesh vats are more than adequate for the task. The resulting menagerie will be the talk of the corespur!'

Musical laughter came from behind them. Taken aback by the sound, the succubus turned.

The Great Harlequin was chuckling, the first sound she had ever heard him make. Hesperax narrowed her eyes, went for her knives, but before her hands touched the hilts he performed a deep bow, blew her a kiss, then flipped backwards into the shadows. Hesperax was sure she could see a second figure waiting for him, its face a smooth, mirrored bowl. They vanished into the dark together.

She sprinted over to the far side of the cavern. When she got there, the shadows were empty.

Iyanna stood alone in the Shrine of Asuryan, lost in contemplation. The shrine was dark, still scarred by the attack of Kallorax at the start of the Triple Woe. Once it had been a beacon of hope for the eldar, not merely those of Iyanden.

Eldar from many worlds had come there to see the Fire of Creation. Lit from the shrine at the heart of the old empire, it had burned since the time of the Fall in the great malachite bowl in the temple. It was a symbol of Asuryan's endurance, and of the eventual rebirth of the eldar race. It was Iyanden's great shame that they had failed in its guardianship.

Now no one came. The dome was restored, but the scars of the attack remained. The architecture was blackened by the fires of cyclonic torpedoes, and the one fire that they wished to maintain had been blown out. The altar had been cold and inert since the battle all those passes ago. All attempts at rekindling it had failed, for nothing present in the material realms was sufficient to fuel it.

Iyanna looked at the broken floors, the shattered statues. The shrine's desolation was a metaphor for the fate of Iyanden's people. She came here when she felt doubt; looking at the dead shrine drove it out, making it clear to her that only Ynnead's embrace offered any hope of salvation. The old gods were dead. The coldness of the chamber was proof of that.

Thinking on the flame had her thoughts turn to Asuryan's chosen, Yriel. No one had seen Yriel for more than thirty cycles; he had vanished in the dead of night from his bedchamber, taking the Spear of Twilight with him. She was certain he still lived, but the threads of his fate were so tangled that not one of the craftworld's farseers could divine what had befallen him. Iyanna did not greatly regret Yriel's absence, for she had always found him aggressive, rude, and arrogant. He had opposed her plans as often as he had supported her. He was so obsessed with proving himself he did not see the real struggle, nor that it could not be won by force of arms. If he had ever perceived her true plans, doubtless his objections would have become difficult to surmount, especially now that Taec was gone. But Yriel's arrogance had blinded him more surely than the spear had, and he had thankfully remained ignorant to the last.

However, Iyanna could not deny that his loss had diminished Iyanden and their race. She reminded herself that it was in his nature to disappear and then return when needed, something of a double-edged blade.

With one last look around the shrine, Iyanna turned to leave. Only one tear of Morai-Heg yet remained unaccounted for, and a group of rangers in from the Winter Gulf insisted they had promising news of its location. There was much to be accomplished before Ynnead could be awoken and She Who Thirsts finally thwarted.

Iyanna's footsteps receded, her heels clicking on the shattered marble of the shrine's floor, leaving only echoes.

Silence persisted but briefly.

A disturbance swirled the air above the bowl of the altar. The hangings of the fane over the bowl wafted with it. A guttering sound came from within, made louder by the bowl's perfect acoustics.

There was no one to hear and no one to see as the Fire of Creation flared into sudden, brilliant life.

WRAITHFLIGHT

GUY HALEY

The wayseers sang their songs; songs that remembered days of glory and days of beauty. Sad songs that were never intended to be so, glad songs made sorrowful by their singing in these terrible times. The webway responded to these paeans of glory still, though the singers were of a diminished people. The membrane of reality split. The gold of the webway changed to the black of space. The Great Wheel's cold embrace awaited the Iyandeni.

Iyanna Arienal reached out to the dead around her. To those within the infinity core of her ship, *Ynnead's Herald*. To those in the Hemlock fighters, and in the cores of the battleships. To the ghost warriors crewing the ships of the Wraithborne squadron, to the spirits guiding the wraithbombers. There were many. In the fleet of Iyanden, the dead outnumbered the living.

+We go again to war,+ she told them.

The unliving shifted, their attentions turned from the things of the dead. The urge for revenge kindled in their slow thoughts. The escort of *Ynnead's Herald* formed up about the cruiser, awaiting further direction, the Aconites of the Wraithborne, House Haladesh's undying navy. Dozens of fighters waited behind.

The webway opened like a mouth and disgorged the fleet of Iyanden from its golden throat. On swift wings, craft after craft sped into real space, their yellow and blue livery bright against the black.

Before them was the world the humans called Krokengard, an ugly name for an ugly planet. An ash-grey atmosphere marbled with pollutant cloud obscured the surface. A dying world, infested with the human plague. And yet even this poisoned morsel appealed to the Great Dragon. The tyranids of Starving Dragon, that which the humans called Leviathan, attacked. Human ships fought them, desperate to keep their soiled den safe.

At the back of the bridge of *Ynnead's Herald*, Iyanna Arienal lay upon a couch. She was surrounded by other spiritseers. The Angel of Iyanden was curled at the centre, the other seven arrayed about her like petals around the heart of the most perfect of flowers. From the point of view of those piloting the ship, the spiritseers were arranged on the vertical plane, but gravity's constraints meant little to the eldar. Three living crew manned the *Ynnead's Herald*: two steersmen and their captain. Behind the spiritseers' station stood wraithguard. A crescent of a dozen of them, still as tombstones, watched over the Angel of

Iyanden. Many more of the dead passed as bright lights through the exposed infinity core of the ship, lending their power to the vessel, working its systems. Among them were mighty dead, those that had carried their strength and purpose with them through the gates of Morai-heg.

The helmets of the spiritseers were off. Their eyes were shut. Their breathing was steady. To an observer, Iyanna might appear to be a sleeper, albeit one with troubled dreams. A frown creased her perfect brow. Her eyes were agitated behind lids tinted a delicate blue.

She was not alone in her disquiet. The hive mind hurt the eldar. As the ships left the webway, a sudden weight that descended and threatened to crush their souls. Snared in the hive mind's psychic shadow, their minds became as sluggish as those of the dead. So far out from the tyranid ships, and yet dread insinuated itself into their hearts. The hive mind had adapted. The roar of its composite soul had increased twentyfold since the battle of Duriel. Where before it had brought pain and despair, to draw close now spelled death for sensitive eldar psyches.

Lesser eldar might quail and flee at this intimate violation, the Iyandeni did not. Bitter experience made them strong. Their anger outweighed their fear. The Great Dragon was not the only being capable of adaptation. The Great Dragon was not the only being that made use of the dead.

+Forwards,+ Iyanna sent.

The sails of the battlegroup filled, the engines of the attack craft flared blue. They picked up speed, and moved away from the main battlefleet of Iyanden.

The hive fleet of Starving Dragon stretched out in an elongated teardrop billions of lengths long. The vanguard was close to the planet. Beaked monstrosities and tentacled assault beasts were only several hundred thousand lengths from Krokengard. This front wave was being pounded by a line of human ships and orbital defences. A mist of organic detritus clouded the stars. But the humans could not win. Every living ship destroyed saw the Great Dragon gain on the human's position. Every one killed had a dozen replacements. More were coasting into the system with each passing cycle.

Iyanna had seen examples of artifice from many human cultures. At the height of their art, humanity had made ugly things, and in this age of the Corpse-Emperor they were far from their height. Their ships were an offence to the eye.

There were those philosophers who took grim delight in pointing out how the humans' fate was unfolding as a cruder version of the Fall. Iyanna did not agree. Their fate was an inverse of the eldar's. The humans' god had been alive, and was dying a slow death. He could not save them. Her goddess Ynnead was yet to be, and undergoing a long birth. Her advent would restore the eldar. Yet the humans thought themselves masters of the galaxy.

The time of humanity was ending. In future ages historians would look back upon this interruption of eldar dominance and note the passing of mankind with disinterested diligence. For sixty million arcs the eldar had ruled the stars. They would do so again, and soon. What was ten thousand arcs of despair in the face of sixty million? This was an era of renewal. Humans were vermin infesting a closed-up home, unaware that the true owners would soon return.

The human ships, though unlovely, were holding their own. Iyanna was forced to admit that. But their defiance would not last; the teardrop was flattening, growing denser. Soon, all the voidspawn would arrive at the battlefront and the human fleet would be smashed, the world they protected devoured.

That could not happen.

Ynnead's Herald rolled and swept from side to side, her steersmen making the ship dance for the joy of it. Behind her came dozens of eldar fighter craft. Nightwings and the Nightshade interceptors of Crimson Hunters, all piloted by living eldar, fanned out in three crescent-shaped attack wings. These split further into two squadrons of six each, each squadron guarding a similar number of Hemlock wraithfighters.

The ships of the living spun and jinked, surging ahead of one another as eager as dolphins in spray. In marked contrast, the craft directly behind *Ynnead's Herald* flew steady on courses so straight they did not appear to be moving at all. These were wraithbombers, piloted solely by the dead. Through the tumult of the warp, they looked to Iyanna, lidless eyes fixed upon the glimmer of her soul. She was the beacon guiding them to their duty. Her mind was joined to them via the infinity core of *Ynnead's Herald*; she was with them. A slender thread of fate separated her from them, and it could so easily be cut.

+Lord Admiral Kelemar, I am moving to engage.+ Her message was hard to send and harder to hear, a weak shout against the psychic roar of the hive mind. Only the large number of ghosts within her ship enabled it to be heard at all. Their energy impelled her thoughts, boosting the machines that conveyed her sendings. She considered switching to simpler technology, but the hive mind assaulted them on every level, and the electromagnetic interference was as bad as the psychic.

Kelemar responded. +The Great Dragon sees you through a billion eyes, and adjusts his coils. Be wary, spiritseer.+

Iyanna followed Kelemar's mental impulse. Parts of the fleet were breaking away from the main swarm, setting themselves a defensive perimeter.

+Sweep them from the stars. Allow us safe passage through.+

+Shatter the web, and we will follow,+ responded Kelemar.

For the moment, the main body of the Iyanden fleet hung back away from the tyranids, at the edge of the hive mind's well of pain. They could approach no closer. From this relatively safe distance, delicate war barques and sinuous battleships sent invisible blasts of energy into the tyranid vessels manoeuvring to block Iyanna's attack. Shattered shells leaked lakes' worth of fluid into the path of her battlegroup that froze or boiled away into clouds of icy gasses.

The strength of the hive mind grew and grew as *Ynnead's Herald* pressed on. The pressure was immense, even though Iyanna and her group were shielded from the worst of it. Her contact with Kelemar slipped away. She became apprehensive. Like all their encounters with the Great Dragon, there was an element of desperation to this gambit. Every battle brought new perils and new evolutions. Iyanna forced herself to relax. She must keep her mind clear so as not to confuse the wraithkind. They would win as they had won all their recent battles. It was preordained.

She pushed herself into deeper communion with the wraith pilots. The scales of mortality fell away from her second sense and she saw the world as the deceased did. The glittering shield projected by the multitudinous dead of *Ynnead's Herald* extended before the cruiser, sheltering her attack group from the full power of the hive mind. The dead protected the living.

Beyond the shield she saw the Great Dragon's true form. Not the hideous intrusions into the mortal realm that swam the black star sea, nor as a Farseer might see it, as a great and braided cable of malicious fate dominating all the skein. The first was merely a part of the whole, the second psychic abstraction. What Iyanna instead saw was the reality of its soul.

It was a great shadow when seen from afar, a wave of dread and psychic blindness that preceded the hive fleet's arrival. But the greatest shadows are cast by the brightest lights, and seen closely, the soul of the hive mind shone brighter than any sun.

She was so close now that she perceived the ridged topography of its mind, larger than star systems, an entity bigger than a god. It contemplated thoughts as large as continents, and spun plans more complex than worlds. It dreamed dreams that could not be fathomed. She felt small and afraid before it, but she did not let her fear cow her defiance.

Against this vista flickered the souls of eldar, their jewel-brightness dimmed by the incomparable glare of the Great Dragon. And this was but a tendril of the creature. The bulk of it stretched away, coils wrapped tight about the higher dimensions, joining in the distance to others, and then others again, until at a great confluence of the parts sat the terrible truth of the whole. She stared at its brilliance. Unlike her passionless dead warriors, who felt nought but the echoes of wrath at the sight, she was fascinated by the beauty on display. She thought, if only such a thing could be tamed it would drive out She Who Thirsts forever. If only its hunger was for things other than the meat and blood of worlds...

She ceased her speculation. Such an entity was entirely other, inimical to all life but its own, a giant animal intent only on its prey. There was no thought to its doings, no intellect. It was cunning. It exhibited signs of an emergent, mechanical intelligence, as evolution might appear to possess if sped to the rate of change the hive mind evinced. But there was no true intelligence to it. The hive mind was non-sentient.

As they came closer to the battle human psychic sendings, crude and ill-formed as their craft, teased at her higher senses. She doubted another human could have caught these missives, overwhelmed by the roar of the Great Dragon. But she felt them, although to extend herself past the ghost shield to find them exposed her to the raw power of the hive mind and seared her inner being. She read the messages' sense, and snatched herself back to safety.

They were inelegant poems, messages sketched in dull metaphor.

All were horrified pleas for help.

The infinity core of *Ynnead's Herald* pulsed. Her captain spoke.

'Lady Iyanna, the humans are attempting to hail us.'

+I know+ she sent. Her mind voice echoed from the fabric of the bridge. She thought a moment, wishing she had a Farseer's prescience. +Allow their transmission.+

A frantic human voice crackled into life. Their technology was no match for the fury of the swarm, and much fine tuning was required by *Ynnead's Herald* before the words became discernable. 'Eldar craft, please identify yourselves. Eldar craft, are you friend or foe?' Whether this made any material difference was doubtful – her ships were too distant and swift for the humans to draw firing solutions even had they not been battling the Great Dragon.

Iyanna found humans disgusting and fascinating. The words were little better than the grunts of animals, slopped out of skilless lips, but the emotions behind them were pure if weak, and they betrayed something higher. Iyanden remembered them from before their first fall, when they had been something better. She could not truly hate them because of that.

'Have you replied, Yethelminir?' She spoke aloud, an alien and uncomfortable sensation while she lay in communion. Half-wrenched from the perfect wrath of the dead, she was repulsed by her own flesh. Her body was a thing of clotted clay, her teeth rough stones set into it, her tongue a corpse-worm that writhed between the stones.

'No. The humans are still requesting an audience,' said Captain Yethelminir dreamily. He was also half-lost to the craft's infinity core, drowning in the comfort of the dead as she did. He was tall, beautiful, his robes as colourful as a rainbow, but his face was as grim and shaped by sorrow as that of any Iyandeni. 'Shall we speak with them? They may be useful.'

Iyanna considered. She agreed.

'I will speak with them.' A channel was opened, attuned to the crass technology of the mon-keigh.

'I am Iyanna Ariennal, spiritseer of Iyanden,' she said. Human speech was so limited, incapable of conveying subtlety other than at great length. She was thankful for that. They would take what she said at face value. 'We come to offer aid.'

There was a delay, messages restricted to the speed of light. A psychic impression came long before their reply. The sense of relief was palpable. These were creatures who would burn her alive simply for being what she was. How things were different when they were alone and afraid. The minds of the mon-keigh were blunt as pebbles.

Presently, a human male appeared in a vision bubble. The machines of *Ynnead's Herald* perfectly reproduced his ugliness. His face and voice betrayed his suspicion.

'I am Captain Hortense of the *Glorious Conquest*. We should consider coordinating our efforts. What are your intentions?'

Iyanna opened her eyes, and allowed her image to appear to him. 'We kill their mind ships, then their mother.'

Another pause.

'The great vessel at the heart of the fleet?'

Iyanna inclined her head slightly. To an eldar, this would have indicated an affirmative, although one layered with sarcastic approval at the other so obviously stating the correct option. Then she remembered with whom she was speaking. 'Yes,' she said.

'We are close. Your disruption of their flank will allow us to penetrate deep into the swarm. We will press forward and destroy them! We fight together?'

Iyanna winced at the rough barking of the human's speech. Spit flew when he spoke. Eldar children had more control of themselves. 'Yes. Together.' She said it slowly, lest the human not understand. 'Hold them from turning back, until we have disrupted their psychic network. Then you must press forwards without delay.'

He stared at her dumbly while her message winged itself on artless wave forms to his craft. Then he nodded, invigorated. She was help unlooked for. Relief ran with the sweat from his face.

'Perhaps we might...'

'I have spoken.'

She cut their chatter with a thought. The humans were tiring to listen to. She had deeds that must be done. Her attack group neared the outer limits of the swarm.

'We approach our target, Lady Iyanna,' said Yethelminir. 'The psychic shielding is holding. The dead perform their task and shield us well.'

Iyanna was sorrowful at this news. The wraithkind expended much of themselves to protect her. They would be lesser because of it. Some would fade away, consumed.

'In one half-tenth cycle we will be among their picket ships,' continued Yethelminir. His eyes flicked back and forward, viewing some machine-projected display only he could see.

In the eyes of the dead, their target resolved itself from the glare of the Great Dragon as a knot in its complex being-web. One of the great hive ships, not the largest, but important nonetheless. The oppression of the hive mind was great so close to such a thing, and would grow worse the nearer they went. The dead had no such issues. There was no physical form their souls could be driven from. Iyanna led the ghosts of Iyanden to their vengeance so that the living might follow.

The shattered bodies of tyranid ships floated by. More were moving up to plug the gap. Already Nightwings and Crimson Hunters were engaged in quick battles with vermicular torpedoes and serpentine hunter-killer creatures that chased them on tails of bright green bio-plasma.

First the way must be cleared.

+Cut the crone's cord,+ sent Iyanna.

At her command the Hemlocks raced forward, the escorts blasting away the anti-ship spines and grubs that came at them. They tore towards their targets, bringing their weapons to near range. Grappling tentacles on closing kraken ships waved in anticipation. Anti-laser ice fields puffed from spiracules. Flesh chaff belched from subsidiary mouths.

This kind of defence was useless against the weapons of the Hemlocks.

A howl built in the othersea, the outraged wailing and pain of the dead. It set Iyanna's teeth on edge to hear it, and she was one well accustomed. She felt the anguish of the warlock pilots as they guided the fury of the dead into the weapons pods of their craft. These fashioned the essence of the dead into a scythe whose screaming edge cut the soul. Pain spiked every eldar mind within range, followed instantly by relief as the psychic weapon swept through the warp, severing the souls of the hive ships from the hive mind. Their pseudopods and chelae ceased to writhe, and their propulsion systems' emissions puttered out. Bioluminescence flickered.

Dead shells were all that remained.

The minds of the ships guarding the psychic node vessel were gone. They floated lifeless upon the tides of battle. The oppressive pressure of the hive mind lessened a little. Iyanna grinned savagely.

+On! On!+ she sent, her triumph goading the dead further. They drew closer to the hive ship.

The firing tubes of unaffected tyranid craft spasmed, bursts of gas venting from their weapons exhausts. A shoal of anti-aircraft worms sped towards the Hemlocks.

The hemlocks peeled aside in perfect formation. One was hit by a worm that ripped into its wing as straight as a spear. With the target reached, the worm lost its stiffness. It flailed loose then wrapped itself around the ship and squeezed hard. The fighter exploded in shards of glittering wraithbone. The psychic screams of its warlock pilot and wraith co-pilots were keen against the dull roar of the hive mind. Even there, in this space of light and shadow dominated by the fires of the dragon, Iyanna heard the distant, insane laughter of She Who Thirsts.

Another craft exploded, smashed by a missile of bloody raw bone. A third ran foul of a cloud of tiny beetles who came alive upon its skin and chewed their way down in a frenzy. A fourth then a fifth exploded, consumed in plumes of plasma.

'The Dragon is targeting the Hemlocks,' said Yethelminir.

+Of course it is,+ sent Iyanna.

But the others were past, the Crimson Hunters escorting them weaving through the worms and serpents and tentacled things. They rendered them to pieces with their bright lances. Others performed high speed flicks of their wings to cast the worms off for their following squadron mates to eviscerate with laser fire.

It was done. An empty funnel of space lined by the soulless husks of defence creatures led directly to the node ship. Iyanna focused her witchsight upon it, imparting urgency to the wraithbombers that flew in her wake. She dwelt upon her own memories of the Triple Woe, recalling the invasion of Iyanden by the tyranids. Domes shattered by organic weapons, gardens consumed by mindless beasts to make more mindless beasts with no thought for the sublimity of being. Eldar, quick and beguiling in life, ground to paste under the hooves of living tanks. Her own anger burned hot as a flame.

+Now,+ she thought to them.

The minds of the spirits were quickened by Iyanna's memories. Their lust for vengeance dragged them out of their dreamworld and back, for a time, into the material realm. Howling with grief, the eldar wraithcraft sped at the hive ship, curving elegantly around the drifting bodies of its dead escorts.

Iyanna watched through the eyes of *Ynnead's Herald*, temporal and psychic. In the Great Wheel, the ships cut across the blackness strewn with flesh chunks towards the slug-like hive ship. The size of it was impressive, as big as a large world dome upon Iyanden. It was too strongly linked to the greater part of the hive mind to be excised from it by the disruption scythes of the Hemlocks, and too invested with the Dragon's might for the living to come close to. Physical destruction was the only option. Frost sparkled on gnarled skin pockmarked by aeons of void travel. A tentacled head, tiny in comparison to the astronomical bulk of its thorax and abdomen, writhed at the front. The other end terminated in a flat leech-like tail. Lesser creatures scuttled over its body, seeking firing positions for the enormous cannons grafted into their backs. Shell-plaques slipped open over firing orifices along the lateral line of the ship.

Glistening weapons ports emptied munitions into space. The hive ship quivered as it opened fire. The weapons beasts dwelling upon its carapace trained their parasitic cannons on the wraithbombers and vomited glowing plasmas.

Iyanna gritted her teeth. The wraiths were too slow to avoid the fusillade on their own. The ghost ships of the wraithborne supported their smaller brethren. Pulsar and plasma cannon fire annihilated swathes of the living missiles, but there were so many. Iyanna and her fellow spiritseers guided the wraithcraft as best they could. An agony of choices. There were too few spiritseers to guide them all, too many souls to save. Which vessel would it be that had their guidance? Which vessel would then be unguided, and blindly crash into the anti-ship fire? Iyanna chose which souls would return to the infinity circuit of Iyanden and which would suffer the worst of all fates without thinking. After the battle, she would be horrified by her choices, whatever they were. She had no time for that now. She put the anticipation of grief from her mind.

The wraithbombers closed on the head and the flank, those going aft seeking out the great ship-birthing canals on the underside. The wraithborne raked the hive ship with punishing pulsar fire.

+Release your revenge, dead of Iyanden,+ Iyanna thought. Her mind-sending was repeated seven times by her servants.

Missiles streaked from swept-forward wings. They swam the void sea as things born to it, swerving elegantly past anti-ordnance spines spat from the hive ship.

The missiles had been adapted, taking inspiration from the burrowing creatures of the hive fleet. They plunged into the surface of the vessel, fusion generators at their tips melting deep into the creature's body. Seconds later, unlight bloomed. Iyanna looked away. She made the dead look away. Perfect globes opened a way into the warp, and for the briefest fraction of time, Slaanesh looked at them directly with ravenous eyes. How terrible, to be caught between two insatiable appetites.

The portals shut. The hive ship's flesh was riddled with vast spherical spaces. It writhed in agony, its death scream horrible. As it faded, another built. The Great Dragon roared with fury as a part of its limitless spirit was obliterated. A black space appeared in the light of the Dragon's soulfire. The pressure in the minds of the eldar lessened further.

Outside the cordon of living ships, Admiral Kelemar continued his bombardment. The hive fleet, still stretched thin as it entered the system, was engaged on three fronts. It bulged outwards towards the main body of the Iyanden fleet. They flitted away, pulsars sounding their invisible, soundless songs of death.

To the front, the Imperial fleet pushed forward towards the chief vessel of the Dragon, the norn ship. Several of their ships drifted, the beaks of tentacled kraken ships buried deep in their hulls. The remainder attempted to lumber into advantageous firing positions. They were heavily beset, but Iyanna's strike near the core of the hive fleet was drawing away reinforcements from the front, and they were coming close to their prize.

Iyanna selected another vessel, a bloated thing like a leathery jellyfish surrounded by darting shoals of fighter craft. This was much smaller, not a main-line hive vessel, but a potent node nonetheless.

+Target the second,+ she sent.

Again the hemlocks cleared the way, and again the wraithbombers delivered their deadly cargo. As the synapses were severed and the hive mind dwindled in potency, Kelemar brought his fleet in closer, sweeping over the swarm and raking it with deadly fire.

So it went, again and again, until a seventh great ship died under Iyanna's attack.

The humans had penetrated into the heart of the swarm, where they pounded the great norn ship, where the tyranids' terrible queen dwelt. The battle was won for the eldar.

+That is the last of them. Withdraw,+ Iyanna ordered. Instantly, her ships came about, and headed through the debris field they had created, back towards clear space.

+Casualties are light in the living and the dead. You are to be congratulated, my lady,+ sent Kelemar. With the synapses of the swarm destroyed, the hive mind was reduced to a background hiss, and they could communicate freely again.

+It is fated,+ sent Iyanna.

She began to ease her mind from the world of the dead. Before she was done, she sat up and stretched, letting her soul sit in two worlds. The sensation of her own body went from disgusting to glorious as she slid back fully into her physical being. The stretch of her muscles delighted her, and she smiled.

'The humans signal us again,' said Yethelminir.

Iyanna shrugged. Allow them to speak, the shrug said, but I do not care what they will say.

Captain Hortense's face appeared again. It was clouded, his lumpen human features exhibited dismay, or some simple human feeling kin to it. 'What are you doing?'

'We have accomplished our task,' said Iyanna. 'The skein has shifted in our favour. The future conforms to our design.'

The pressure of the hive mind, already broken by their extermination of the hive ships, diminished further as *Ynnead's Herald* sped back towards the webway gate.

'You are leaving us to die! You are leaving our world to be consumed.'

'Not so,' said Iyanna. 'Look.'

Upon the grey marble of Krokengard a flame was lit.

Hortense was distracted for a moment, his crew delivering information. Iyanna knew what it must be. Hortense's face hardened.

'This, it was all a ruse. You came to attack us!' His mouth twisted. 'Exterminatus! You have destroyed our world. "Perfidious are the eldar, trust them not!"' He quoted some human religious text. 'I should have known no kindness would come from you.'

Iyanna could have cut the feed, but she did not. Some feeling crept into her for this lesser creature. He had fought bravely. 'A Fireheart,' she explained. 'A device to destroy this world so that the Great Dragon may not feast upon it. We kill you, yes, but it is better we do than the Great Dragon draw sustenance from your world.' She paused. 'You have my apologies.'

She surveyed the battle. The hive fleet remnants fought on, disunited but deadly still.

'To attack these creatures and aid you further would result in unacceptable losses to my people,' she said. 'There are times coming when we will fight by your side. Today is not one of those occasions. The ship of their swarm-queen is dying. This world is dead. There is nothing for them to feed on but their own dead, and nothing to reconstitute them if consumed. This tendril is destroyed, and the way through here will offer no sustenance should the Great Dragon choose to force it in future. Surely this is worth your sacrifice? One world for many?'

She blinked, examined the human curiously. She pitied him. His own kind did the same elsewhere, and yet he was still appalled. How many others had he thoughtlessly condemned himself? One's own extinction always seemed to matter more.

'If you withdraw now you might save some of your ships,' she continued. 'You have, after all, nothing left to defend here.'

Hortense spluttered. She hoped he would heed her.

'This is an ou–'

Her psychic impulse ended their conversation.

'Take us home, Captain Yethelminir,' she said. The captain bowed.

'Yes, my lady.'

The webway gaped wide, and *Ynnead's Herald* accelerated towards it. Behind them, the pyre of Krokengard's destruction shone brightly.

Iyanna was triumphant again. Fifteen worlds had been denied the ravening hunger of the Starving Dragon by the deployment of the Firehearts, funnelling it away from the eldar towards...

Something was wrong. A sensation at the back of her mind. The sensation grew teeth, became pain.

Her soul was gripped by agony.

Iyanna screamed, falling from the edge of the couch. The pain abated, then squeezed her anew. She vomited.

The dead were dismayed. The blow against her raced out across her attack group, leaping from mind to mind. Wraithbomber engines guttered out. The Wraithborne's sleek cruisers turned viciously, wallowing in psychic swell.

Bright light burned at Iyanna's soul. A long tunnel telescoped away, encompassing infinite distance. A tube stabbed through the fabric of the world. She felt its ripples in the warp. She felt its ripples in the webway.

She had the sense of an eye, slave to a great power. An intellect that dwarfed the Great Wheel of the galaxy. She opened her second sense, to find the Dragon looking at her with terrible regard.

For aeons it seemed it held her in its gaze. And there was fury in that examination.

The Dragon was angry, and it was angry with her. Not with the galaxy, or this sector, or her species. But with her *personally*. The promise of endless torment came from it, her very being enslaved to its ends and used against others, her body rebuilt over and again so that it might suffer the Dragon's revenge.

Terror of a kind she could not have conceived of flooded her mind. She screamed again, and this time every eldar in the fleet screamed with her.

When she awoke later, *Ynnead's Herald* was dark. She exhaled brokenly. Her legs were weak. She hauled herself to her feet by grabbing at a couch's cocoon. Her fingers had no strength to them. The other spiritseers lay limp in their cots. Two, she was sure, were dead.

The steersmen were slumped over their control jewels and the captain was a crumpled peacock on the floor. The main viewing bubble glowed still. Through it she saw the eldar fleet was in disarray, drifting powerless. The humans fought on however. The norn ship burned fiercely. Was this what had severed the connection between her and the Great Dragon?

Thinking of the contact made her nauseous.

As her mind reached out to the ship, the dead of *Ynnead's Herald* woke too, creeping from their hiding places in the infinity core, shocked and timorous.

The lights came back on. A dull glow from the walls that grew until the ship looked as it should. Yethelminir groaned and rolled over. He stood shakily, struggling with his iridescent cape to free his arms. The steersmen and other crew came to groggily.

'My lady?'

'I am well, Yethelminir,' she said. Her eyes were fixed on the desperate battle. The hive fleet was shattered. Even bereft of direction, the individual ship-beasts were still deadly, and the humans were outnumbered twenty times to one.

She watched as one of their light cruisers was snagged by a trio of kraken ships. It broke apart, its reactor dying with a bright plasma flare.

She came to a decision.

'Lord Admiral?' She spoke aloud.

There was a long pause before Kelemar answered.

'My lady?' His voice was weak.

'What is the status of your ship? Your fleet?'

'They are undamaged. My crew are distressed. Some are dead.'

'Rouse them.'

'What was that?'

'The Great Dragon,' she said. She kept her voice cold, frightened her fear would creep into her voice. If it did, she was sure she would lose her mind. 'Bring your ships back into battle order.'

'We do not return to Iyanden?'

'We do not return to Iyanden. We remain to help the mon-keigh.'

'That was not in the plan.'

'Plans change,' she said. 'Every weapon will be needed in the coming fight.'

Slowly, the eldar fleet regained its prior order, and drove on back at the tyranids.

'Tell the humans we are coming,' she said.

Yethelminir nodded. His face bore lines it had not had before.

Iyanna slipped back into her couch and reconnected with the dead pilots of the wraithbombers, informing them of their new task.

They welcomed it gladly, for the vengeance of the dead knows no bounds.

THE LAST DAYS OF ECTOR

GUY HALEY

CHAPTER ONE

THE CHOOSING

Stubber fire raked the metal plating of Euphoria sublevel 18. Kal Groston ducked behind a pillar of rusting steel as sparks ran in quick lines towards him, nearly tripping backwards over Tunny. His own gun was heavy in his sweat-slick hands. He never sweated, not like this, but this was no territory grab or revenge raid. Today they were being watched. Today was a day for great deeds. Kal scanned the ruined walls of the chasm, looking for signs of movement. They had to be watching, didn't they? He couldn't see anything. Maybe this was all for nothing. He took his irritation out on Tunny.

'Stop slinking down there. Get some covering fire out.' Kal nodded to a broken machine twenty metres ahead. 'I'm going for that.'

'Are you broken? They got a big barker up there. Foundry Boys'm crash you down for sure.' Tunny peeked out from behind the pillar to look up at the fort. He pulled his head back in quickly when a bullet buzzed past his ear. The Foundry Boys' heavy stubber rat-a-tat-tatted.

'I sabby I be head-broke, but we're double-crashed if we're on the skulk. Face forward, Tunny.'

'Where're our blockies?'

'How the depths should I know? Point that piece like you do so well and give it hard snap when I say. Ready?'

Tunny swallowed and blinked. Kal took that for a yes.

'Now!'

Kal burst from cover. Bullets raced after him in a deadly game of tag. The Foundry Boys had the better weapons, but they lacked a certain finesse. Tunny's gun rattled away. Tunny was a bundle of nerves, but always a good shot, even when you thought he was about to soil himself. There was a squawk from the fort, and incoming fire slackened. Kal grinned.

A bullet spanged from the dead machine's housing as he threw himself behind it. Looked like one of the Foundry Boys was a bit brighter than the others.

The fort was thirty metres away, that was all: a ragged, two-storey construction of plates stolen from the hive walls. Not that anyone cared about these levels; they hadn't for hundreds of years.

The fort perched on the crumbling lip of the Basement Gap, the yawning chasm at the base of the hive. Rainbow Falls thundered off somewhere deep,

deep down. Far upaways, the planetary transit tube buzzed with never-ending traffic.

Deadaways down here, nothing but juveniles and no-marries living off the scraps. Kal had a dim awareness all this had been built, but what the Gap was for he had not a clue, and he cared even less. Prime territory, usually. But he had bigger things on his mind than prising good scrounging grounds out of the hands of the Foundry Boys.

A low whistle came from his right. Marny was there, with Jimmo and Haradd. No bullets went their way, so the Foundry Boys hadn't seen them yet. Kal leaned right back so he was sure the Foundry Boys couldn't get a bead on him, and frowned a question at Marny. He held up his fingers, eight. She shook her head. Held up three, drew a finger across her throat.

Pondo, Moop and Darl – dead. Their bad, Kal thought. He dragged his filthy sleeve across his nose. Bump and bump my damn hands, he thought, suddenly angry. Sweaty sweaty.

He passed his gun from hand to hand as he wiped them down his trousers. Home-made, cobbled together from cast-offs, like all their weapons. Most of them didn't even shoot straight.

His did.

Marny scowled at him pointedly, thrusting her head forwards. Impatient bitch.

He nodded, set his gun on his thigh to take the weight while he signalled with his free hand. He gestured that Marny split her team: she to go with Jimmo, Haradd to break right for a pile of debris. Marny's frown deepened. She'd be annoyed with him that he wasn't sending her out on her own. She was as good a fighter as any of them, so why wasn't he? He pushed the reason why aside. She was a girl. That was all.

He looked back. Tunny was peering round the pillar. He was clever too, Tunny. Hadn't looked at Marny's blockies the once.

Kal gestured to him that he should break left. Jimmo was going to get in there, Marny behind him. There was a lot of sparky flak coming from the fort, but Kal was pretty sure they were down to three. They'd killed six of them at least, and two more had run off screaming. Emperor bless Tunny and his pipe bombs! He reckoned one was wounded, perhaps badly. That left just the two. Only that heavy stubber was their equaliser. Far as he could see it was bolted in place. If his blockies got in there under it and through the door, the Foundry Boys'd not be able to spin it round and they'd fold quicker than quick.

He held up his hand, three fingers. He counted them down. Three, two, one. He clenched his fist.

He stuck his head out, drawing immediate fire. He shot back wildly, spraying bullets with no thought. Tunny took his opportunity, as did Marny, Haradd and Jimmo. The stubber on the roof swung to catch some of them. A sweep of bullets sprayed across the machine cave, rattling hard on broken engines. Haradd swore loudly, but he ran on, head down.

Haradd and Marny kicked hard and were through the ramshackle door to the fort. Kal and Jimmo covered the Foundry Boys' supposedly hidden escape hole, a flap-hatch behind a spur of the fort's rusty wall. Shouting came from inside. The shooting stopped. The hatch flipped open. A surprised, grubby face came level with Kal's gun.

'Don't you twitch, little rat,' Kal said.

The Foundry Boy cursed and slammed a fist down on the buckled plating of the floor. As per the rules, he put his hands on his head. He wasn't happy.

Kal had been wrong. There were four Foundry Boys in the fort, including the rat. But they'd won, so what did missing one matter? They sat on the Gap, catching their breath before they began the long climb upaways. The thought of it made Kal more nervous than the trial had; none of them had ever been up the stair so high.

'How deep is it?' asked Tunny.

Kal spat over the edge, and watched his glob of phlegm plummet downwards, glinting in stray light before being swallowed by the dark.

'Deep. They say it goes down, right down to the rock. Ocean of muck down there, all off of Rainbow Falls, or so they say. Listen and you can hear it rumble.'

'I don't gunny it.'

'Me either, not all. I seen the pretty river, but the rest? Load of old sparl. Get down that far mutants'll have you, or worse. You never see no rock, there or not.'

'Are they on the eyes out, Kal? You codging they see what we did?'

Kal looked up into the void. The far side was several hundred metres away, a wall of dark, broken windows and fallen bridges. He still did not see movement. He covered his worry with bravado.

'Oh, they're watching all right. I codge that certain. Even if they ain't, we take these flags back, right as right. They see we're the winners. Jimmo, you carry their flag. Haradd, you still got ours?'

'Yeah, Kal, I got it.'

'Eyes out, Haradd. See nothing happens to it, you sabby?'

'Yeah, Kal, I'm grabbing it. Eyes out.'

'Marny, sharp there on the prisoners.'

'Don't see why I should do the do,' said Marny sullenly. 'They won't take me, no matter. I'm not going stairways.'

'It's a team effort,' said Kal.

'Yeah, and what for me when my "team" gets the off and off? Rot here like eff spill, stinking in the dark, that's what.' She was rarely emotional, but today Marny was close to tears. 'Bump and bump you, Kal.'

Kal scowled at her. 'You're always squeezing the joy. We won!'

'Ain't no victory for me,' she said. 'Ain't no victory at all.'

Upon the Landing of the XIV Ascension, the Space Marines of the Crimson Castellans Chapter waited. Chaplain Gorth had chosen the place of selection. It was most fitting, he thought. What else would the successful aspirants do but ascend? Despite its apposite name and vast size, the Landing of the XIV Ascension's glory days were past. This was poor man's territory at the heart of the industrial middle hive. The ancient artwork adorning the walls was obscured by cascading pipework, or had been carelessly bored through to make way for vents and waste conduits. Soot furred the statuary clinging to the sides of the shaft. The poorly filtered air was soupy with the scent of others' breath.

Gorth was a grim character, short-tempered and dour, but possessed of a hidden love of coincidence and portent that could, on occasion, verge on the ironic. For those who knew him well, and they were few, his humour was on display in his selection of this landing.

At Governor Hiro Hoyel's order an ostentatious dais had been erected there, heavy with bas relief and swags of bright cloth. Set far back from the single approaching staircase, it sat at the centre of the space between the two stairways sweeping up from the left and right sides of the landing. These twinned stairs took many quarter turns before they opened onto the next landing, some six hundred metres above. In this way – a landing approached by two stairways and then a landing approached by one – did the Infinite Stair crawl doggedly up the central shaft, from the very lowest level to the very highest.

The shaft itself, built to carry the great tubes bringing warmth from beneath the planet's crust, tapered gradually from base to top, making the hive a hollow needle. Here it was four hundred metres across. Here, as elsewhere, the Stair occupied much of it, the single flights two hundred metres wide, the double pairs seventy-eight apiece. The geothermal pipes were the only thing besides the Stair that went the height of Luggenhard, from sump to spire. In the fog of popular consciousness, the Stair had become the more important. In reality, the pipes were vital, the stairway only symbolic.

The Stair was referenced so often by the priests as a metaphor for the Emperor's ascension that their parables had taken on the mantle of fact. A man might set out from the bottom of the shaft and never reach the top, whether from meeting a violent death, or merely owing to the myriad distractions that greeted him at every landing. Not that many ever saw the extreme ends. The top was accessible only to the most privileged, the bottom was a myth. No man could live long enough for his feet to touch every step, it was said. A few had tried, none succeeded. To walk even a quarter of it was a great feat of devotion. In the Imperium the simplest truths were often obscure. Such were the stairs of Luggenhard.

The traffic that crowded the steps had, for three hours only, been halted. Planetary defence troopers formed human cordons, keeping the central hundred metres of the steps clear. Enforcers kept a careful watch on the hivers from justice stations. The Castellans own hundred men-at-arms guarded the approach to the landing in both directions, their crimson uniforms forming a wall of simple colour that held back the garish crowd.

All were silent as the Crimson Castellans demanded; no congratulation or cheer would be offered until the final selection was made, on pain of death. The people of Luggenhard waited breathlessly, their eyes flicking back and forth between the living gods upon the Stair and the viewscreen picts of those who sought to join them.

With Gorth upon the dais were Brother-Sergeant Yoth, commander of the Crimson Castle of Ector, and Brother-Captain Raankin, Master of Recruits, Captain of the Tenth Company and Holder of the Key of the Ebon Tower. Of them all, Raankin bore the most responsibility for the choosing. He ceaselessly watched the screens hanging from brackets around the Stair and puttering jerkily overhead; not even now, with all the drama over and the aspirants making a slow ascent, did he take his stern eyes from them.

Five of the Space Marines of the garrison stood behind the three officers, the much-decorated Veteran Senior Brother Karsikon at their head. Fourteen more lined the landing. The twentieth of the standing garrison, Brother-Sergeant Philodon, stood at the top of the approaching stairs bearing the garrison banner. Unlike his brethren, his crimson armour was mostly hidden beneath a white and gold surplice and hood. Tradition demanded it be so, and so it was.

A score of crimson servo-skulls tracked the aspirants. Via the skull feeds projected onto the screens, Yoth watched the youths climb through the silent crowds. They had ascended three kilometres, far from their home. The gangers looked at the gaudy crowds of richer folk nervously.

Yoth had come to know the world well over the six years of his garrison duty. Probably none of the gangers had ever had the cause, or the nerve, to climb the Stair this far, excepting perhaps their leader. Kal Groston was his name. His swagger was either the result of experience, or a clever play. If the latter, he was a good actor. His gang, dirty urchins all, eyed their surroundings with suspicion, looking upon each crumbling frieze and statue as if it might suddenly spring to life.

The youths' eyes grew wider when they laid sight upon the Crimson Castellans. Yoth's mind went back to his own trial, seventy years gone on a very different world. The expression on his face was probably the same when he saw the Angels of Death for the first time, when he had come to stand in front of them. A moment that, for its wonder, he had wished would never end. He was terrified that he would be rejected at that last hurdle.

He had not been rejected. It had not been the last hurdle.

Many more trials had to be passed before his acceptance into full brotherhood. All but one of the six aspirants who joined with him had died or failed on the way – Perelith during the second implantation, Jothel during psychscreening, Matherath during the third implantation, and two more in battle as Scouts. For a select few of these Ectorian youths, similar fates awaited.

The Crimson Castellans were recruited from many different worlds, ever since the Grey Phage had laid waste to their home world of Vorl Secunda and forced the Chapter into space. Each bore the look of his planet, but each was also in likeness to his brothers: tall and powerful, a giant among ordinary men. But it was in the eyes that their kinship was most apparent. These brothers born of a dozen systems had eyes that were all the same: yellow, the colour of morning sunlight streaming through good, pale wine.

Gorth, bald-headed and grey-skinned, forehead adorned with seven service studs. Captain Raankin, nut-brown and craggy with age, yet ageless as an oak, his hair a single grey strip across his head. Pale-skinned Yoth with light hair. Yoth doubted the Ectorians noticed these differences. The eyes were what people remembered of the Crimson Castellans.

The gangs clumped naturally into their opposing camps, both groups glancing with open hostility at their rivals. Brothers Meklenholm and Bost left their station to make sure the candidates were in their correct places. Philodon turned to present the garrison banner to the dais and the garrison stamped their feet and tilted their boltguns upwards to rest. The noise sent murmurs through the crowd. Gorth stared around sternly until the whispers died. Then he began.

'Aspirants to the battleplate of the Crimson Castellans, you have done well. Seven gangs were chosen. Only two remain. As is our custom, I, Chaplain Gorth, will pronounce the selection made by Brother-Captain Raankin of those who will join us in servitude among the stars.

'Our way is thus. Not for our Chapter the picking of an individual here, another there. We consider the quality of brotherhood above all others, and look for it among our chosen. He who stops to save a comrade is serving himself. Men who fight as one so that none fall serve all. We prize loyalty and solidarity above all other qualities.

'You have fought alongside your comrades, you have accomplished the task we demanded of you. You have made the journey here bearing your prizes.' He paused, looked at each of them in turn. They stared defiantly back – underhivers were not easily cowed. 'And now we will make our choices from amongst the gang we deem to have functioned optimally.

'Iron Rats, you vanquished your foe. You took their flag and kept your own. But you have not been selected. There is a lack of coordination in your group, pronounced rivalries that, carried over into our Chapter, may prove toxic. You must return whence you came. Carry the honour that you came this far with you for the remainder of your lives. It is no small thing that you have done.'

The four surviving Iron Rats shrank in on themselves. The youngest was on the verge of tears. The two oldest glared blame at one another when, Yoth thought, they should blame only themselves. Here was evidence of their disunity for all to see.

The other gang puffed up with pride in direct proportion to the other's misery. Their eyes gleamed. They grinned foolishly at one another. Boys still with boyish ways. They would learn quickly to forget them.

'Spire Hounds, step forward.'

They came to the foot of the dais, and Gorth addressed them.

'You worked together well, a functioning unit where your peers were in disarray. You are all bold, and I see signs of intelligence in you. We asked you to defend and attack fortresses, for we are the Crimson Castellans. Our skill is in garrisoning, defending, and in the toppling of enemy strongholds. I see the beginnings of such expertise.' Gorth turned his attention first to Tunny. 'You are small and mocked for your cowardice. You have none. You are merely cautious, and a fine shot. You have been selected.'

Brother Osko came to the boy and led him away to the side, where he was draped in the crimson robes of the accepted aspirant. Brother Kervony shouldered his bolter, and placed both hands on the youth's shoulders, pulling him in close. 'Welcome, novitiate,' he said.

'The boy known as Jimmo, step forward.'

Jimmo smiled at his friends. They smiled back.

'You obeyed orders from your leader even when unsure. You showed no hesitation when afraid. From these characteristics unshakable courage will grow. You have been chosen.'

Jimmo was taken aside, and welcomed as Tunny had been. They grinned stupidly. If only they knew what awaited them, thought Yoth, they would not smile so.

'The girl named Marny,' said Gorth. Marny stepped up, expression sullen. 'I have watched you. You are valiant and have the makings of a fine warrior. But we are the sons of the Emperor's sons. There are no women among us. There are those who deem themselves daughters of the Lord of Men, but they are not present here.' For a moment, Gorth's manner softened. 'I am sorry.'

'What do I do?' said Marny in a small voice.

Gorth was momentarily surprised she addressed him at all. Kindness fled his voice as he answered. 'You must remain.'

Yoth watched the leader, saw his face colour. Don't do it, boy, he thought. Don't throw it all away.

It came out anyway. 'You can't do this!' blurted Kal. The outburst surprised the boy as much as it affronted Gorth, for he stopped with a sudden look of horror. Gorth glared at him. Committed, the boy continued. 'She's the best shot among us,' he said more quietly. 'She's better even than Tunny, and four times as brave.'

'The process that makes us what we are would destroy her, should we be cruel enough to begin it. It is the way of things. She must serve the Emperor another way, if she serves at all.'

'You have servants, serfs, yeah, uh, lord? Can't she be one of those?'

'There are no women among us,' repeated Gorth.

'That's just not fair,' said Kal. Yoth admired his persistence, if not his wisdom.

'Fairness is not a criterion for selection. Utility is.' Gorth stared the boy down. 'I will not approve Raankin's selection of you,' said Gorth, gesturing at the boy. 'Signs of insubordination at this early stage are prime markers for rejection of psycho-conditioning. Your loyalty to your companion is commendable, but displays signs of attachment. You cannot be husband to one, you must be brother to all. Remain here and get children by her. This is what you wish.'

Kal's face went white as he realised what he had done. 'But...'

Gorth stared at him. Kal's mouth shut with a click. Then he looked at Marny and flushed bright red again.

'Aspirant Haradd, step forward...'

Another welcome. The final acceptance was voiced by Gorth, a brief speech, to the point as was his way. The crowd was permitted to cheer.

Somewhere above, a band struck up.

CHAPTER TWO

HIVE FLEET LEVIATHAN

On every world the Crimson Castellans deigned to garrison there was a Crimson Castle. For long stretches of years the castles were mostly empty, as the Crimson Castellans were wont to spread their brothers and their men-at-arms across the worlds they protected. On Ector, Yoth dwelled in the castle alone with his servants. Tonight there was an air of sombre conviviality. The twenty garrison members were together to honour their visiting superiors. They sat to meat in the great hall, which for once did not seem so lonely. Higher ranking serfs ate with the brethren, at the same table, for such was the way of the Chapter. All endured simple fare as the rule of the Crimson Castellans demanded, protein-laced mulch of high nutritious value and little taste. Their singular luxury was their wine, which they drank from plain granite goblets. Many Chapters sought perfection outside of war in one art or another; however, the Crimson Castellans chose to be vintners, viticulturists and oenologists. They did little else.

'A fine vintage, Brother Yoth,' said Chaplain Gorth.

'This world is cold, but its soil is rich. The sacred vine fares well here.'

'It is sweet. Pleasantly so.'

'The grapes are exposed to the cold to freeze, my Lord Chaplain. It intensifies the sugars.'

Gorth made appreciative noises and signalled to a serf for more.

Yoth saw his chance. 'Three candidates,' he said cautiously. 'It is not many. Fifty years ago we took a dozen from this hive alone.'

Gorth ate another spoonful of mush and swilled it down with Yoth's wine. 'The selection gets harder every visit,' replied Gorth. 'We can only accept those suitable. Another Chapter may be happy with lesser candidates, but not the Crimson Castellans.'

'Ector is getting too civilised, lord,' said Yoth. 'Governor Hoyel is a good man. I would say unusually efficient. Perhaps we should move on to less peaceful pastures and do our hunting there in future?'

Gorth stared at the rim of his goblet, and Yoth knew then that he had overstepped the mark.

'Garrison duty is no shameful thing, Brother-Sergeant Yoth,' said Gorth. 'Your desire for action is a discredit to your oaths. This world is strategically vital to our efforts in this sector, and your station here a personal favour from Chapter Master Caroman to Governor Hoyel, a man you profess to admire.'

'You misunderstand my intent...' began Yoth.

'This world has proved, and still proves, to be a ground of good recruitment. Tradition and obligation demand we continue our five decennial selections. If we fail to find what we require here, we shall move on to the next world, and then the next, until we have sufficient aspirants, but only when I or Brother-Captain Raankin decree,' said Gorth tersely. 'Your motives are suspect, brother. Do you seek personal satisfaction at the expense of your brothers?'

Yoth became deferential. 'I mean no offence, Lord Chaplain. I simply seek to make conversation. This is a matter that concerns us all. My brothers and I have had little news from the Chapter these last six years.'

'Idle chatter is the enemy of diligence, Brother-Sergeant Yoth. Your record is exemplary. I am disappointed by your frivolity.'

The castle chamberlain, Meretricion, a young serf of good repute, inclined his head.

'My lords, I beg your forgiveness but invoke the right of all to speak, full brother or not. I say, let us keep the peace at this time of celebration. Surely now is the time to feast together in gladness?'

Gorth looked at him appraisingly. 'Perhaps, chamberlain. You do not misspeak, but nor do I.' He drained his goblet again. 'Brother-Sergeant Yoth, loose talk is the key by which many a fortress gate is opened. You risk handing entrance freely to the enemy by questioning the wisdom of your superiors. Taciturn and vigilant upon the wall, that is the way of the Crimson Castellans, not this chatter. I will consult with your captain upon my return to the fleet. Perhaps you have remained too long amid others, and it is time for you to go home and reacquaint yourself with our ways.'

'Thank you, my Lord Chaplain.'

'It is no boon I give you. Your weakness, not your desire, informs my decision.'

Gorth called to the astropath attached to the Tenth Company, an ancient man who sat some way down the trestle. 'Hostor Mazurn, astropath prime.'

'Yes, my lord?'

'Finish your meal, then be away to inform the *Redoubt* that we have made our selection. The number of aspirants is eleven in total. We leave tomorrow.'

'Eleven, my lord?'

'Eleven. Now be about your duties, astropath prime.'

'As you wish, Lord Chaplain.'

'Now, let us heed the words of our wise chamberlain and eat and drink with gladness. The aspirants have spent six hours in meditation. Let us bring them in and allow them their first taste of the grapes of the sacred vine. Their barrel is prepared. Let the initiation begin!'

The Crimson Castellans, dour as they were, cheered and drank another draught.

* * *

Hostor Mazurn left the great hall as the ritual got under way. The vile food of the Chapter had been cleared. The aspirants would be fed gallons of wine laced with pseudo-hormones that would initialise their transformation into Space Marines. As a younger man, Mazurn would have regretted missing the celebration, but he was old now, and neither his head nor his stomach – or his bladder, for that matter – were as strong as they used to be.

With relief, then, he headed out from the Crimson Castle and through Hive Luggenhard. Here, the mass of humanity, in such close proximity, made telepathic communication over interstellar ranges nigh on impossible. The density of habitation on all hive worlds necessitated that astropathic stations be isolated as much as possible from the populace, and the regulations of the Adeptus Astra Telepathica stipulated this be so. But the regulations were not always obeyed, and even when they were, the shielding employed was often inadequate. A muddying of message content, and a headache for Mazurn, was the usual outcome. Ector's planetary governor was diligent in all matters though, and his astropaths had access to several dozen stations of the highest specification. Mazurn set out to the nearest.

The Crimson Castellans were honoured guests, and so Mazurn's route took him through the loftier parts of the hive. In these places the richer Ectorians lived, although not the richest. Still crammed cheek by jowl, the inhabitants of the upper levels were sleek and well fed, their concerns far removed from mere survival. The hour was late, but hives were round-the-clock societies, and Ector was no different. The snatches of thoughts Mazurn caught as he walked were of conspiracy and intrigue, revolving around the acquisition and display of wealth. He was tired. Being on such a densely populated world was wearing. It had not always been so for him, but age weakened his power even as his skill in using it became more refined.

He felt many fearful eyes on him as he passed. Now and then he sensed the unfocused thoughts of a latent psyker, one not so latent; the fear of discovery was uppermost in their minds. They need not have been afraid, for Mazurn's gifts did not lie in that direction. He was no sniffer dog for the Inquisition. It was difficult for him to tease the glowing strands of a psyker's mind from the undifferentiated mess of human souls around him. The crowds parted for him. Not only was he an astropath – and interference with such brought swift death – but he was also a servant of the Space Marines, and so doubly interdicted. A man would have to be insane to harry him.

Mazurn left the core of the hive, where habitats crowded around the geothermal conduits like undersea creatures around volcanic vents, and passed into its middling parts. Here service modules and servants' quarters were crammed one against the other, oftentimes indistinguishable. The temperature dropped as he went further out. By the time he reached the outer edge of the hive and neared the entrance to the Bridge of Sighs, the air was chill in his lungs, and his flesh goose-bumped.

Two soldiers in gilded armour stood watch either side of the doorway to the bridge. The doors were embossed deeply with the serene face of an astropath, rendered in the geometric styling of the world.

Mazurn was blind, as most astropaths were. He saw none of this directly. He perceived the world through his own precognitive visions, seeing where he would be, rather than seeing where he was. To a lesser degree he could see through the eyes of others. On the one hand, his vision was that of memory, on the other, it was distorted by subjectivity. The picture that came to him was fragmentary at best, but a lifetime's experience enabled him to stitch together an impression of his surroundings, at once more revealing and yet more dreamlike than true sight.

The guards snapped to attention, laser pikes clicking as they were set upright. Mazurn dipped his head to them. A third man appeared from a hidden closet, although not so hidden to Mazurn's mind's eye. With a fur coat draped over his arm, he helped the astropath prime into it, placed a breathing mask over his face and withdrew with a bow.

Mazurn passed into an airlock. When the outer door opened, a cold wind whistled in on whisper-thin air. Mazurn pulled the neck of his robe tight.

A slender pier arched gracefully from the edge of Luggenhard to the station, suspended two hundred metres from the hive's skin, four thousand metres in the air. At this altitude, Mazurn was high enough to avoid the broil of hydrocarbons that clung to the planet's equatorial regions. The temperature was astonishing after the warm fug of the hive interior. Ector was a tundra world, on the edge of Valedan's habitable zone. Even this far south it was cold all year round at ground level, and up this high the thin air was forty below. The coat, issued to him by the Crimson Castellans quartermasters in expectation of such extremity, was extremely warm. Nevertheless, his exposed face chilled rapidly, and he hurried on to the astropathic station as fast as he dared, panting pressurised air through his mask.

The wind buffeted at him. Emptiness surrounded him. The railing and its skull-topped posts were an insubstantial blur in his mind, all that stood between him and certain death. The lack of true sight was something of an advantage here, for he could not see the drop, but a dangerous disadvantage also. His feet slipped every other step. The placing of his staff brought the crunch of ice as much as the dull ring of metal. His ancient joints ached with the cold. The bridge reached its peak, and swept down. Here it passed through the centre of circular psychic baffles arrayed in sequence. The constant pressure of one hundred million people's thoughts lessened. When he passed through the fourteenth baffle, it cut out altogether.

Two burly men flanked the entrance to the station, clad in cold-weather gear. Their psychic presence was minimal, both having been selected precisely for their lack of talent. By the time the door had responded to Mazurn's psychic impulse and opened, his lips were blue and he was shivering hard.

It was warm within, the wind's keening muted but not entirely absent. Occasional stronger gusts shook the station upon its mounts, metal thrumming with the strain.

Mazurn shuddered violently as his coat slipped from his shoulders into the hands of an attentive servant. He ignored the man and stamped his feet, sighing in vibrato as the warmth reclaimed his extremities.

Eager to be about his task and thence to bed, he mounted the stairs to the sending chamber.

There were five couches in the chamber. One was occupied. The astropath mind-sent a short greeting that was barely cordial, Mazurn's superiority of rank notwithstanding. This other's business was only beginning, and he left in mind soon after Mazurn had taken his place on a couch.

Mazurn lay back gratefully. Not all sending stations were so comfortable, physically or psychically. He chuckled to himself. When he was undergoing the agony of soul binding, his eyes scorched from his head by the terrifying might of the Emperor, growing old had been the last thing on his mind.

'And yet here I am,' he muttered to himself. 'Here I am.' He half expected every message he sent to be his last, that his frail body would give out under the demands placed upon it. This conviction grew stronger every day. 'I have my duty,' he said. 'Soon may it be over.'

His private grumble done, he focused, diverting his mind in upon itself. The infinity of worlds that were within every man opened before his eyes.

Mazurn had constructed the bulk of the message on the way. He put his finishing touches to it as he lay upon the couch.

His senses expanded exponentially, rushing out from icy Ector and its Girdle of Steel. The sensation was a close-knit blending of ecstasy and pain, an echo of his long-ago soul binding on Holy Terra. He had learned to bear it. His soul's own feeble powers shone with greater light thanks to the Lord Emperor, a proud privilege. He absorbed fleeting impressions of the cosmos, chance message fragments coming into the world from other astropaths, the burning tear that was the Vortex of Despair at the edge of the Valedan system, beautiful and deadly, and the echoes of the past and future that issued from it. The raiment of heaven unrolled for him and he thought, for the thousandth time in his long life, that this was a gift worth paying his sight for.

The message bloomed, the mind-sequence he had made. He held in the gaze of his third eye a chequered board of steel and stone, life-size statues carved from red granite upon it. Chaplain Gorth, Master of Recruits Raankin and the twenty Space Marines of the Crimson Castellans garrison ranged behind. In front of them were eleven pawns: identical, faceless boys peeking over the ramparts of miniature castles. Snow drifted onto the metal game board, his own modestly poetic imagining for Ector. His mind played the message, pushing the pieces one at a time away from the board into a metal box cast in the likeness of the *Redoubt*. The board faded to black, leaving the box to become a living image of the ship, hanging against the steady stars.

He set the message free. He relived being a young boy releasing a bird into the air, this being his message-sending trigger. He watched it go. Satisfied, he began to bring himself from his trance.

Something gave him pause; what exactly, he struggled to define in later years.

The rational side of him suggested the highly tuned senses of his subconscious picked up what the upper layers of his mind did not perceive. The mystic in Mazurn, the greater part, perhaps, held that the Emperor Himself worked through him that day – an opinion Chaplain Gorth favoured.

He halted his withdrawal and cast his mind to below the galactic plane. Here, out in the southern reaches of the galaxy, the depth of the galaxy's wheel was lesser. It was a hard thing for him to see the galaxy as a three-dimensional object; most messages traversed the long laterals across the Imperium. Of course, there was no such thing as direction in the empyrean, where all his messages were cast, but his mind imposed such order. No man can escape his own mind.

The number of messages coming from below the plane and that part of the galaxy referred to as the 'south' by men was necessarily fewer than those coming from elsewhere. They were a long way from Terra, but messages there should be. And yet he sensed none.

Mazurn looked further out, grasping for any notice of communication. What he found instead – indeed, what he half suspected he would find – was a great, black wall. Through it he could sense neither the empyrean nor the firefly souls of his fellow psykers shouting their missives into the night. The burning glare of the Astronomican, into which he ordinarily dared not look, was a fitful glow, a fearsome sun with a shroud cast over it.

With a growing sense of dread, Mazurn looked into the dark.

Terror wracked him, an alien horror that tore at the fabric of his being. Mazurn was not to be deterred. He was of a high grade, optimo astropath prime, selected to serve the Adeptus Astartes in the direst of passes. Here was one now.

Defiantly, he dared the horror as long as he could.

Beyond the black wall was something immense and ancient, an out-thrusting of a vast being greater in scope than time itself. It clove the warp as a giant ship cleaves the swell of a sea, imperturbable and sure upon its course. All psychic emanations, of whatever source, were shattered to glints upon its bow wave. A terrible, alien voice smote the heavens, piercing to the core of Mazurn's psyche. He cast up his mightiest psychic shields, but they were as sandcastles in the tempest.

Before he was overwhelmed, Mazurn's only instinct was to flee.

And then the wall smothered him, and for a time all was black.

Mazurn came to an hour later. Sticky blood from his nose coated his lips. His head throbbed. With sudden urgency, he pulled himself upright and vomited upon the floor. He gasped as he fought to bring his stomach back under control. At the sound of his retching, the servants came heavy-footed up the stairs. Their exclamations of shock alerted him to the death of the other astropath; he was lolling from the couch, his face contorted with horror.

'How many adepts in the Chamber of Receiving?' asked one. Mazurn could not tell the servants apart – his third eye was dazzled. Their identities ran into one another like spilled paints.

'I... I...' said a second. Even in his fuddled state, the man's fear was clear enough to Mazurn.

'How many?' shouted the first.

'Two, two, master,' said the second. 'Adepts Fidelius and Tastrac.'

'What are you waiting for? Check it. Check the Chamber of Receiving now!'

'Yes, sir, sorry, master.' Footsteps receded at speed.

Hands took Mazurn's arms, a soft cloth was pressed to his mouth, wiping his lips, cleaning the blood from his face. The first voice spoke to him softly. 'Adept? Adept, are you well?'

'I live, that is enough,' he managed.

'What happened, my lord?'

Mazurn ignored the question. 'Give me a vox,' he croaked, then, with as much force as he could muster, 'Give me a vox!'

A heavy handset was pressed into his grasp. With palsied hands Mazurn keyed it on. He accessed the Crimson Castellans more public channels.

'Lord Chaplain,' he requested.

Shortly, Gorth responded.

'Astropath prime? You have sent the message?'

'Lord...'

'Have you done your duty?' Gorth was, as ever, short with him.

'Of course, my lord. The *Redoubt* should be en route as we speak. But there is something else we must discuss. There are... complications of a most disturbing nature.'

Gorth caught the tone of Mazurn's voice. 'You have company?'

'Yes, my lord.'

'Come to me.'

'My lord, I cannot. Do not command me, I beg of you. I am afflicted.'

There came a pause.

'You are in an astropathic station?'

'Station Five, my lord, the closest to our last meeting. I made all haste to deliver your message.'

'Wait there.'

Gorth's voice cut out. Spent, Mazurn lay back and allowed the servants to fuss over him. His strength gradually returned, but his soul remained chilled with fear.

CHAPTER THREE

COUNCIL OF WAR

Governor Hoyel's audience chamber occupied the very tip of Hive Luggenhard. Beyond its point was nothing but the wisps of Ector's upper atmosphere. His throne was in the centre of the single vast room, under the highest part of the conical ceiling. This pinnacle soared two hundred metres above the floor, every inch of its metal incised with intricate designs. Its magnificence was mirrored in the floor, where interlocking wheels of exotic alloys, each sporting time-worn friezes round their rims, spread as wide as fields from wall to wall. At the edges, statues of past governors stared sternly with blank marble eyes. Great windows between them gave view to the skyscapes of Ector. The governor's own guard stood at attention in alcoves set into the window's grand mullions: a thousand of them, garbed in purple cloaks and gleaming golden armour.

The filth of the lower levels was absent. All was light, gleaming metal, brilliant blue skies and white clouds. Yoth felt as if he had stepped through a portal and fetched up on some other world entirely, far from the hellish mountain-cities. It was as if he had chanced upon the realm of the god-saints of his childhood. He had to remind himself that beneath his feet, stretching down for kilometres, was layer after layer of humanity, pressed one atop the other in various degrees of desperation.

Hoyel sat in full pomp, robed priests in files either side of him singing of his Emperor-sanctioned right to rule. Servo-skulls and cyber organisms buzzed overhead. Counsellors stood silent by him: Lord Seneschal Hobin Majar, General Rovor of the Ector militia, Astropath Primary Annelia Battrell, Episcopant Myrrdin of the Adeptus Ministorum, Lord Kyrax of the Adeptus Administratum and others of similarly high rank. Besides these worthies, the entire court was there – perhaps two hundred nobles and innumerable flunkies.

Hoyel wore his robes of office, a stiff, high-necked military uniform of dark purple, decorated with medals that Yoth had heard he had actually earned in his younger days. A feathered cloak, pinned with a giant brooch, hung from his shoulders and pooled upon the steps to his throne.

Hiro Hoyel and his spire-dwelling elite were not of the same stock as the rest of the hive population. That they had bred true for so long spoke of deep-rooted sociological divisions upon Ector. The causes of this unusual layering of ethnicity were lost to the mists of time, but however it had come about, Gorth approved.

'Such stratification is a living reminder of the divisions within the Imperium, such as those of rank and merit within our own Chapter, that allow the realm of the Emperor to function,' he had told Yoth not long after the recruiting mission had arrived. 'Divide and rule. Imperfect and inhumane it might be, but these are imperfect years.'

'Lords of the Adeptus Astartes, I bid thee welcome,' said Hoyel.

Gorth, Raankin and Yoth stepped before him and bowed their heads briefly. They did not kneel as others did. Stars do not defer to planets.

'Your choosing goes well? I trust you have found boys of sufficient talent to join your ranks?'

'Yes, lord governor,' said Gorth. 'Eleven. Three from this hive in our final choosing today.'

'Eleven from billions,' the governor said. 'That you have found so many of exceptional quality gladdens me.'

'They will strengthen us. We thank you again for the service they will provide.'

'It is gladly given, Lord Chaplain, a source of pride to this world.'

'There is another matter. One of grave import. We are sorry to impose upon you in this manner, Lord Governor Hoyel,' said Raankin.

Hoyel leaned forwards. 'When the Adeptus Astartes request an audience with any man, that man would be a fool to decline, no matter his rank. Your sergeant, Yoth, has provided good service to me. Whatever you wish, you have but to ask.'

'Then we ask that we speak with you alone,' said Gorth.

The court was scandalised into action. Heavy robes rustled as whispers were exchanged behind hands.

'There is reason for this?'

'Just reason, my lord,' said Yoth.

Hoyel nodded equanimously. 'Very well.'

The guards stepped forth from their alcoves.

'Wait!' Hoyel held up his hand. 'General Rovor, Seneschal Majar, Astropath Primary Annelia Battrell and Lord Kyrax of the Adeptus Administratum will remain,' he said. 'I trust these are military matters you come to me with, yours being a military order. If so, you will not begrudge me my military advisors.'

'No, my lord, of course not,' said Raankin.

The rest were ushered from the hall, including the protesting Episcopant Myrrdin. 'Military matters,' was Hoyel's response, and the ecclesiarch was shut out with all the rest.

When the gargantuan doors to the chamber were closed, and the Great Brass Elevator of Audience was squealing its way down from the tip of the spire, Hoyel stood, shucked off his cloak and walked down from his throne. He groaned with pleasure and rotated his shoulders.

'The cloak drags at me so, but one must stand on ceremony,' he said.

Close up, Hoyel appeared surprisingly young. He was a slight man with a carefully trimmed goatee and soulful brown eyes. He had the paleness of any hiver, but there was a yellowish cast to his skin that spoke of his highborn ancestry, as the Ectorians reckoned it.

'You may speak when you will, my lords. Do not wait on my account.' Hoyel walked around, stretching his legs.

'It is simply this,' said Raankin. 'A tyranid hive fleet is en route to the Valedan system. We suspect it to be a branching of Leviathan. It will enter the system periphery within a week. We have plotted its course as best we can, and believe it will fall first upon Daea, then Megus, Valedor and then upon your world, my lord.'

Hoyel stopped his perambulation and came swiftly around to the Space Marine's front. He waved his counsellors to silence, for they had all begun to talk one over the other. 'You are sure of this? I have heard nothing.'

'The hive fleet travels rapidly through the void, my lord. It moves upon a narrow front. Any shipping it encounters will have been destroyed. Our astropath prime felt the presence of its shadow upon the warp. Without that, we would have no warning at all. Messages sent by the Adeptus Astra Telepathica are blocked by it.'

'Annelia?' asked Hoyel.

'It could be the truth, my lord. I have not detected anything,' the astropath said.

'I regret to inform you that one of your own astropaths was caught and slain by its psychic roar, my lady,' said Raankin.

'I have heard nothing of this!' Battrell said.

'Our men-at-arms guard those who know. We thought it prudent to keep the matter secret until we had spoken with Lord Governor Hoyel. News of Leviathan's coming will encourage mass panic. It is best to be prepared.'

'Quite right, quite right,' said Hoyel. His face had become paler, but Yoth thought he was taking the news remarkably well. 'Can we stop them?'

'Regrettably, no. We cannot hope to hold them in space. There are too few warships in this system to mount a workable counter-offensive. They will be here within two weeks,' said Raankin. 'No time to gather sufficient reinforcements to repel them.'

'Can we not hope to blunt the attack, to give our men time on the ground to drive them off?' said Rovor. 'We have succeeded in driving xenos off in the past. This system is attacked frequently.'

'To do so would achieve little. The tyranids are not like any other xenos you have faced,' said Gorth. 'They cannot be discouraged. They have no morale to break, their numbers an infinitude. As long as the fleet remains intact, the tyranids are capable of raining an endless tide of monsters down upon your world. To defeat this foe, their fleets must be crushed in orbit. Only then is there any chance of destroying their ground forces and saving the planet. So it was in Ultramar, and at Piscina IV. All else serves to delay the inevitable.'

'The inevitable being?' asked Hoyel.

'The destruction of all life and consumption of the planet's biomass.'

'Surely not?' said Rovor. 'This world is well fortified. We are close to the Vortex of Despair, we are no strangers to war. Your Chapter has some renown at siegecraft. Together we can stand!'

'No, my lord,' said Raankin. 'Not even we, the Crimson Castellans, can hope to hold this tide. Not if all our brothers were gathered here together and stood shoulder to shoulder could we do this. Too many of our brother Chapters have been destroyed in attempting to contain an entire hive fleet alone. Even the mighty Ultramarines were sorely taxed by Behemoth, and they had all of Ultramar to support them.'

'Destruction? You speak of the Scythes of the Emperor?' said Annelia.

'Among others, my lady. This foe is beyond us.'

'Ultramar, you say?' Rovor pointed a finger at Raankin. 'This is a densely populated system. We have four million men under arms on this world alone. Valedor three and a half. There are twelve regiments of Imperial Guard stationed upon Megus. Not to mention the multitude of hands into which weapons might be pressed. We can stand, I am sure of it,' he said.

'It will not be enough,' said Raankin. 'Perhaps with half a segmentum warfleet the system could be saved, but we have no such support, and we Crimson Castellans are only twenty-two in number. Send out messages for reinforcement or aid. None will come in time, even were it permitted. The strategic index of this system is insufficient to guarantee its saving. I am most sorry to bring you this news, lord governor, but this world is lost. All the worlds of this system are lost.'

'There is nothing to be done?' said Hoyel.

'You must leave. That is your only realistic course of action,' said Gorth.

Hoyel paced up and down the metal interlocking rings of the floor, studying the ideograms that described the deeds of his ancestors. For a moment he was lost in thought, and the Crimson Castellans feared he had abandoned hope. It was not unheard of, in the face of so terrible an enemy, for mortal men to succumb to their fear.

Hoyel was forged of harder iron. He was sombre when he spoke next, but his voice was steady.

'If I leave, what of my people? Are we to abandon them to their fate? No, I say. It is given unto me the charge of those beneath me. I will not flee while they die. I command you, as is my right, use your skills to hold back the swarm, so a portion of the population might be saved.'

The Space Marines looked to one another.

'It can be done, can it not, brother-captain?' said Gorth.

'My men will fight to the last, though they be but few,' said Yoth.

Raankin thought for a moment. 'If you commandeer all craft in orbit around Ector, and issue an emergency petition to the Imperial Navy Segmentum Command at Hydraphur, we might be able to save seven hundred thousand souls. More, if the governors of Valedor and Megus pledge their aid. It is unlikely that the Naval authorities will send further craft piecemeal to this system to be destroyed, but I can see no good reason why they would deny you the use of those that are already here. They will be running before the storm in any case.'

'Megus especially has many craft in its service,' said Yoth.

'They will not come,' said Hoyel. 'And who can blame them? We are all in the same corner.' He rubbed at his face. 'We share the same sun, yet relations between the worlds of Valedan are fractious. Valedor and Megus are bound tightly, and so Governor Mothrein of Megus is dependent upon Governor Torka of Valedor's goodwill, and will follow his lead. There has been rivalry for untold generations between the houses of Hoyel and Torka. The present Lord Torka would not put out a fire that would consume him, if he thought I would burn also. Commodore Justarin, who commands the Navy here, will jump whichever way Mothrein says. His remit in this system is to guard the ore shipments from Megus and it is unlikely he will do more. He is an inflexible man.'

'You propose evacuation, my lord. There are forty billion people resident on Ector,' said Annelia. 'Seven hundred thousand is nothing.'

'Better those seven hundred thousand than none at all,' said Gorth.

'Who do we save?' said Rovor. 'And how do we choose?'

'I have a solution,' said Kyrax, breaking his silence. 'We shall hold a lottery.'

'That will cause much strife,' said Raankin.

Kyrax smiled bleakly. 'Unless you have a better suggestion, lord, I do not see an alternative.'

Hoyel agreed. 'See that it is done,' he said. 'All Imperial servants of the higher orders are to be saved. The remainder will be drawn from the women and children only, no exceptions,' he said sternly. 'Everyone is to have an equal chance, or we will be killing each other before the xenos arrive. Make it known that anyone who attempts to fix the lottery will be executed, and any of the nobility especially caught cheating will be delivered to the Adeptus Arbites precinct house. Annelia, send messages to the other planetary governors by vox and astrotelepathy. I call upon my rights to assemble a system-wide council of war.'

'No, no, no!' said Governor Torka emphatically. He was a large, bearish man with a huge beard and an augmetic skullcap under his tall shako. His wrath was expressed obviously and often. This behaviour doubtless terrified his servants, but had no effect upon the Space Marines. 'I can spare no aid. We prepare to defeat the aliens ourselves! I require my men to defend Valedor. I thank my lord Space Marines for their intelligence on this matter, but I cannot in all good conscience follow your advice. Abandon my world? Never!'

It was four days after Mazurn's vision, and preparations were in train. The governors of the three populated worlds of Valedan were all present upon Ector in person, an unusual happening in itself. Still, Torka was intransigent as expected, Mothrein followed his lead, also as expected, and the council had made little progress.

The banqueting hall that they held their meeting in echoed with their disputes. A host of generals and Naval officers were there, as were major officials of Valedan's Imperial adepta. The air was cloudy with narcotic smokes and plates of half-eaten food held down unfurled charts. Servants whispered past, trying to keep the disorder to a minimum. Data-slates were scattered about. Archive-savants mumbled in dirty robes, repeating the words of every man present and so committing them permanently to their damaged minds – scriveners scribbled, pict-artists documented. Even when the delegates were silent, the room was noisy, a hushed dissonance of droning machines and voices.

A holographic map of Ector rotated over the banqueting table. Habitable regions were in the tight band of the tropics. All twenty of the planet's hives were in this zone, some a little further to the north or to the south, but none beyond twenty degrees either side of the equator. A metal tube, elevated high from the surface and broad enough to be seen from orbit, carried multitudinous roads, rail links and other infrastructure right around the planet. Each hive either stood directly over this artery, or was linked to it via short spurs. Habs and facilities clung to it like barnacles. The result was, in effect, a long, continuous hive studded with twenty spires – Ector's Girdle of Steel. Where the hives gave out, a narrow industrial wasteland blended into the steppes and tundra that covered the rest of the planet's ice-free surface. A large polar ice cap crowned the arctic region, a lesser one the antarctic. Still large enough to swallow two-thirds of the hemisphere, it extended far into the tropics. Ector was a dirty ball of snow and drab grey plains, a ring of metal and light about its middle.

'You would be advised to evacuate, governor. The hive fleet will make planetfall upon Valedor first. Your population is smaller – flee now and send what aid you may so that we might save more of the people of Ector.'

Governor Torka snorted. 'Abandon my post? Leave my world? Is that your response, Governor Hoyel, flight? What of Megus? Will you request that the Imperial Guard regiments stationed there withdraw to aid you too?'

'These creatures have stripped a thousand worlds bare. If we remain, we will all perish. The best outcome is the removal of the people of Ector. It is the moral action, and will deprive the tyranids of much prey,' said Hoyel.

'You have no right to command me! Should I run and become a beggar king? Never! A lord with no domain is no lord at all. I stay to defend my birthright. You will be held to account for leaving yours.'

'He will not,' said Gorth coldly. 'The High Lords have decreed themselves that evacuation of all planets below aestimare G279 is to be undertaken in the face of tyranid invasion, should insufficient Astra Militarum assets be present. This system is wealthy, but strategically unimportant.'

'I say sufficient assets are present!' said Torka.

'You have not fought this foe before,' said Raankin.

'Nor have you, I have heard,' countered Torka. Mothrein nodded nervously, a slim, anxious man drowning under a weight of jewels and responsibility.

'We know those who have. We have studied the Tyrannic Wars in great detail. Scorched earth is the only viable strategy. We must evacuate,' said Gorth.

'Scorched earth? You would destroy our worlds too, as well as divesting us of them? Outrage!' Torka's large fist slammed down.

'If we had my way, I would have each and every one of the worlds of this system subjected to Exterminatus,' said Raankin. 'Be glad we do not possess the means. To remove your people is to deprive the aliens of what they seek. You, my lord, are their food. Do you not see? We must concentrate our efforts, defend one world, and evacuate as many men, women and children as we might.'

'I will not abandon my command. Perhaps your efforts on Ector will preserve we of Valedor?'

'I remind you that they will come to you first, my lord,' said Gorth.

Torka threw up his hands. 'The boldness of the Space Marines is much overrated if you rout at the first sight of an enemy. We remain,' he barked.

'You are ill-advised to call the Adeptus Astartes cowards, my lord,' said Yoth, half rising.

'Sergeant Yoth!' barked Gorth. Yoth glared at Torka and sat again. 'And you, Lord Mothrein,' said Gorth, addressing the other governor directly. 'What is your response?'

Mothrein licked his lips, looking at Torka as he spoke. 'My world will be struck before Lord Governor Hoyel's and before Lord Governor Torka's. Perhaps they will pass us by? We are few in number, the world is poor in biologic resources and we are well defended.'

'In these circumstances, every fortress is a trap,' said Gorth.

'I have twelve Imperial Guard regiments to aid me,' said Mothrein.

'And they will perish. We cannot let ourselves be divided,' said Hoyel.

'Ever has the House of Hoyel tried to further its own interests at the expense of the House Torka!' bellowed Torka. 'This is madness, selfish madness!'

The chamber erupted into shouting. The exalted rank of the three Imperial governors was forgotten as generals, astropaths, officials and others hurled accusations and threats at each other.

'Silence!' shouted Gorth. He stood to his full height. His muscles were huge beneath his loose crimson robe. He glared down at the men beneath him. Several flinched. 'Call yourselves masters of the Imperium? You are children! Master yourselves and your fear before it destroys you all.'

Shocked silence. Torka's face was as crimson as Gorth's vestments with outrage.

'I will send no aid to Ector. If you wish for a united front, we make our stand on Valedor,' he said quietly, anger barely checked. 'You are welcome to join us. Mothrein, what say you send your regiments and planetary defence forces to my world – we have time to fortify. We shall prevail.'

'I... I... My lord, I cannot stand by and let my people be slaughtered. Remove my men? The tithe for Megus is the highest in the system. It is there we should fight, surely, where the wealth of Valedan is concentrated? We are all liable – you, I, Hoyel – for the preservation of our worlds.' Finding no approval for his words in Torka, Mothrein now looked to Hoyel.

Torka's face darkened.

'I see in my hour of need, my ally deserts me. So be it,' Torka said. He gestured for his delegation to stand. A dozen officers and officials rose to the scraping of chairs.

'My lord, where do you go?' said Hoyel.

Torka cleared his throat, and spoke quietly again, this time with less anger.

'The time for talking is done. I return to Valedor, there to prepare my own world for invasion. Let Ector look to its own defence. Emperor preserve us all.'

Mothrein stood hesitantly. His own men looked to him for leadership. Yoth thought they would find little there.

'My Lord Mothrein, please!' said Hoyel.

'I am sorry, Hiro,' he said. He ducked a quick bow and followed Torka. His officers made courteous farewells and went after him.

Some others remained, Commodore Justarin and a number of the officials whose responsibilities were supra-planetary within the system.

'And so the plenum is dissolved,' said Hoyel wearily. His savants murmured his words back at him.

'My lord,' said Justarin. 'If Lords Torka and Mothrein give no order for evacuation, then I shall pledge the Navy's vessels to your service. Our friends of the Crimson Castellans are correct – to stand divided before the swarm is to fall. I do not have sufficient ships to oppose the tyranids, but I will send every bulk carrier under my command to this world, and see that they are escorted as safely as possible out of the Valedan system. I have been ordered by Hydraphur to withdraw. It is my discretion to execute my orders as a fighting withdrawal.'

Justarin is not so inflexible as suspected, thought Yoth. He stood, and looked at a long-range scoptic capture of the swarm in space: a fuzzy mass against the stars, terrifying in its magnitude.

'We must plan our defence,' said Yoth. 'The better prepared we are, the longer we shall hold out. How go the preparations?'

'Fear is rife,' said Rovor. 'But the lottery has given my men heart. They are frightened, but aware that they are fighting for the survival of their families, their children. They will not run. They will stand. The planetary governors of the Gospar system have agreed to take us in.'

'That is rare good news,' said Raankin. 'I expected no less. The people of Ector are stout-hearted. As for we of the Crimson Castellans, we will despatch each of our brothers back to their hives. They will organise the defence batteries. We must be quick to work. We have little time.'

'You will not lead from the front?' said Rovor.

'Not at first,' said Raankin. 'That is not our way. We might inspire your troops and your people, but only for a short space before we fall. Our efforts are best placed in Fire Control. We will devise killing patterns far superior to any that could be conceived by your men. This way, we will slaughter many times more than if we were to meet the alien face to face. Greater kill ratio efficiency is assured.'

'My men may think you cowards if you hide,' warned General Rovor.

'Your men would be as foolish as Torka to do so. And they will not think so, once they see the devastation we shall wreak upon the foe. The Crimson Castellans are masters of defensive warfare, General Rovor. We play to our strengths, as all wise warriors must. Your men will live longer if we do. The time for melee will come, but not before we have rebalanced the scales a little in our favour,' said Raankin.

'What of the fences? If they land to the north, can the fences be used against them?' Rovor spoke of the two lines of watchtowers upon the plains, linked by sections of high, electrified fencing. 'The outer is strong enough to keep the megamamut and icesharks from our herds on the tundra, but will it stop the tyranids? I have never encountered such creatures, but I am guessing, my lords, that it will not.'

'Your assumption is correct,' said Raankin. 'There is much harvestable material in the north – these creatures of yours. This is attractive to the Great Devourer, and the tyranids will likely land at least a part of their forces on the far side of the fences. If the fences slow them, then so much the better – but it will only slow them, and only if we are lucky. To focus our efforts on either fence would be a grave error. And I doubt the lesser, inner fence will provide any barrier to them at all. In any case, they are as likely to attack the hives directly.'

'With your permission, lords, I will lay minefields where I might, close by the Girdle,' said Yoth.

'Of course,' said Raankin.

'I will not have time to cover much ground, and will require much manpower.'

Hoyel nodded. 'See that Sergeant Yoth has everything he needs.'

'At my Lord Governor Hoyel's request, I have ordered the withdrawal of every man, woman and child upon the surface into the safety of the hives,' said Seneschal Majar. 'They may well perish here, but whatever chance at survival we have must be taken. The ice trains are making their way south. All personnel have been instructed to abandon unnecessary material and make all haste. I have seized all transportation assets from every noble house and cartel to ensure that Lord Hoyel's orders are obeyed.'

'And the lottery?' said Gorth. 'I have heard reports of disturbances in the lower hives.'

'It goes well, lord,' said Majar. 'Things are quieter than we expected.'

'My priests will give sermons,' said the Episcopant. 'The Emperor will call them to fight.'

'Be warned, some will refuse,' said Raankin.

Hoyel was irritated by this. 'Of course, lord captain. We are masters of a hive world, not ingénues abroad. We are aware of what might happen.'

'You might be, Lord Governor Hoyel. Others have a less realistic view of the true hearts and minds of men,' said Raankin. 'If it offends you by my saying, I am sorry, but it is better to speak a truth if it leads to betterment than not say it for fear of offence.'

'Lord Hoyel has shown prudence in ordering the nobility to fight,' said Majar. 'To show all men that in the face of this threat they are equal.'

'To a tyranid swarm it does not matter if you are high or lowborn, all are prey,' said Raankin approvingly. 'There will be riots and general disturbance. Better to keep your people's minds on the real foe, or they will turn upon each other. You rule wisely, lord governor.'

'Thank you,' said Hoyel tightly. 'Is there any chance that we might weather this and survive?' he said. 'I pray daily that it might be so. Tell me the truth again so that I will be prepared. To abandon a throne is no small thing, my lords.'

Raankin played with a crystal glass half full of wine. It was toy-like in his giant hands. 'If the tyranids are driven off once, they will attempt a larger assault, then a larger one still, until the hives are overwhelmed. And they will be overwhelmed. Their resources are greater than ours. They have no fear, no remorse, and will not tire. They cannot be bought or bargained with. They reproduce as fast as they are slain.'

'Very good,' said Hoyel grimly. 'Just so that we all know what we face. Now what?'

'Lord governor,' said Raankin, 'now we prepare, and then we wait.'

Their discussions went on long into the night, and were but the first of many.

CHAPTER FOUR

XENOS IN THE UNDERHIVE

A few days before the war council, when the invasion was but one wild rumour among a million more, Senior Enforcer Schreck paid a visit to the middle hive. He keyed open the express lift with his officer's badge and he and his two men went into the heaving industrial guts of Luggenhard.

'This way,' he said, gesturing to his men. They set off down an arterial path that skirted a hundred manufactoria of prodigious size. It opened up after half a kilometre, giving them a view down to a roadway where haulers laden with raw materials crawled. The route was thick with people, more crowded than the upper levels. Out and out poverty was not much in evidence, but the shadow of it was never far away. Clothes were threadbare, faces pinched with hunger and overwork. From side corridors came the sounds of babies crying and couples squabbling in tiny, windowless quarters. The fabric of the hive thrummed with the pounding of sleepless industries, the noise rising so loud at times that Schreck had to shout to speak to his men over their helmet voxes. To Schreck this was normal. He had been born down there, after all, and he shoved his way remorselessly through the crowds as all those who were born to them did.

Passing a row of peeling posters – 'The Hand protects' each read, below a white hand on a black background – they reached a plaza: a round, low-domed room, the sides of which were covered with hissing pipes. Five major manufactoria opened up off this place, their entrances grandiose and topped with motivational slogans cast in metal. Tolliver often used it for his meetings.

'There he is,' said Schreck. 'Take it easy, all right? We don't want to spark a riot. We're here to kick down the fire before it catches light, not douse it in promethium. Got that?'

'Yes, sir,' his men said.

People stood around in knots, the rearguard of a large mob crowded around a man – the demagogue Tolliver – who stood upon an oil barrel. Crudely printed placards framed him. The image they depicted was also of a hand, this one shielding a stylised family of four. 'The Hand protects' was printed beneath. Similar images were posted to the piping of the hall, while other placards bobbed among the crowd.

'Look at this place,' Schreck muttered to his men. 'No one's working. Again!

Lord Condirion will have my hide for this. Make way, make way for the enforcers of Hive Luggenhard!' he cried out. 'Official business. Clear the way!'

The crowd moved grudgingly, but were wary of the black carapaces and weapons borne by the enforcers. They were not rebellious, yet. Not even if Schreck brought down his entire station would he ever be able to stand against so many, but he was not expecting a riot. A light hand for light misdemeanours, he always said.

'...come into the protection of the Hand. Join with us! He brings food, he brings medicine, he brings news of the terrors in the dark below and the dark up there. Information is power! Know thy enemies, it is said, to better defy them!' Tolliver pointed upwards. 'The Hand shows us the way, the way to weather the storm that approaches. We have no creed, no message of disobedience. We desire only safety, and safety the Hand may provide...'

'All right, Tolliver, the speech is over. Everyone get back to work.'

Tolliver searched the crowd until he lit upon Schreck, stood in the middle of a widening circle. 'Senior Enforcer Schreck, a pleasure to see you!' he shouted. Tolliver was a wiry, shock-headed individual whose thin limbs were all at play at once, except when he spoke of the Hand. Only then was he still.

'Get down off that barrel. Come on, everyone back to work!' Schreck clapped his gauntleted hands together. His two men moved off and began to push people gently away.

Tolliver didn't so much jump as collapse off the barrel, arms waving. He landed awkwardly but the jumble of elbows and knees somehow reassembled themselves into the shape of a man.

'We don't often see you down here, Daen.'

'Senior Enforcer Schreck, Tolliver.'

'You know I find that hard,' Tolliver smiled. He bobbed about as he spoke. 'I'm just glad you haven't forgotten us, now you're an officer of the law and all.'

'I'm down here a lot more often than I'd like. There's been too much stoppage, Tolliver. They've not got anything against social groups up top, provided you keep the politics out of it.'

'We are apolitical,' protested Tolliver. 'We do exactly as I say. We are a charity. So what if our benefactor is a little mysterious, he—'

'Save it.' Schreck held up his hand. 'No more stoppages, Tolliver, do you understand? Any more of this and the arbitrators will start to get interested. You don't want the judges poking about in your business. They might just think a pre-emptive strike is in order, just in case your lot get a little too above themselves. Keep your meetings to shift changeover and rec time. No more speaking during shifts. Do you understand? I go light on you because of the old days. My men haven't even broken out their mauls. I want it quiet, do you hear? You keep things quiet and the workforce working, I don't care. I'm a ranking enforcer now, Tolliver. I keep coming down here to remind you of this, and people are going to ask a lot of questions. The answers will be more uncomfortable for you than for me. Emperor knows neither of us want that, do we?'

Tolliver stopped his constant movement for a moment and nodded his head. 'Yes.' He hesitated.

'Something on your mind? Spit it out, I'm a busy man.'

The plaza was almost clear again. Tolliver glanced about nervously. 'Daen... Daen, there's something up.'

'Emperor save us, Tolliver. Don't tell me you did this deliberately to drag me down here? You want to speak to me, use the system – don't throw a meet to coax me down.'

'No, no. I didn't do that. Really. But you're here now. I was going to send a message upaways, even though you are so hard to get hold of. You've no time for your old friends.'

'Didn't I say that I'm a busy man, Tolliver? I have a lot of responsibility.'

'Well, you're here now.'

Schreck looked about. Business was returning to normal. One of his men was reaching for a poster to rip it down. Schreck shook his head slightly. The enforcer dropped his hand.

Tolliver was unusually still, something had got to him. When he spoke, Schreck listened.

'In the underworld. There's something.'

'Yeah yeah, Papa Bones, King Silence and the Mother of Rock. They're bogeymen, as in not true. Stories to scare kids. The only things down there are muties, scum, break-in ice vermin and giant rats, if they aren't bad enough.'

'This is worse.'

'Now you're wasting my time, Tolliver.'

'Wait!' Tolliver grabbed Schreck's shoulder as he made to go. 'This way, please. I have evidence.'

Schreck stared at the offending hand until Tolliver dropped it. 'This better be good.'

'Oh, oh. No, it's not good. In fact,' said Tolliver, coming in so close Schreck could smell the metaelph bone mould on his breath. 'It's very, very bad.'

Schreck thought little of what Tolliver had to show him. There were things in the underhive that no man could name. That is, until a few days later, when the news of the invasion broke, broadcast from every screen and address system and private entertainment unit.

Then he became very concerned indeed.

After planning out the deployment of minefields in concert with General Rovor's staff, Yoth spent much of the following week in Hive Luggenhard. It was the capital, the planet's largest space ports were situated there, and so it was determined that there the last stand would be. The situation was tense, the lottery nearly over. There had been no outright sign of unrest yet, but Yoth was sure it would come. Much against the wishes of the rich, Governor Hoyel's decree that, after valued Imperial servants, women and children would be given priority had been rigidly adhered to. It was a weakness, this humanitarianism. Yoth would rather fighting men were removed to fight again, but it was admirable, in its way.

Captain Raankin was to direct the hive's outer defence, and so Yoth spent his days supervising the lockdown of the space ports under the Castellans men-at-arms, then organising the civilian population of the city. As in the other hives, those facilities that could be repurposed to the manufacture of weaponry were. Yoth oversaw the construction of strong points all through Luggenhard. Sections were sealed or, in some cases, collapsed. The transit tube around the planet was rigged for demolition. The high walls around the city were provisioned, repaired and fully garrisoned. All known entrances into the hive, excepting a handful, were blocked. For those left open Yoth devised a staggered series of defence lines. Yoth was diligent here, but concerned in case attack came from below once the walls fell. The underhive was an unknown quantity, for the foot of the hive was a mess of ancient metal crags and ice caverns that opened on many secret places. He had as many as he could find stopped up. He was sure there were ten thousand more.

He worked for day after day, grabbing a little sleep here or there. Where his duties were light, he made use of his catalepsean node, but even his altered metabolism struggled with the demands placed upon him.

The fateful fortnight went by. The lottery was accomplished, seven hundred thousand refugees, selected by the Emperor Himself, it was said. A rebellion by Hive Joteun's nobles was brutally suppressed, in part thanks to their own servants turning on them. The hive fleet reached the system and psychic communication became unreliable, then impossible. Vox frequencies were wracked by weird interference. News was scant. Refugees fleeing the van of the fleet told of the fall of Megus to the tyranids after a mere six days of fighting. Valedor kept contact longer, until Leviathan opened its maw and swallowed it whole. Fragments of comms traffic suggested it held out better than Megus had; their dwindling over time told of man's slow extirpation from the planet.

Dread became the default emotion for the Ectorians. The population worked hard, but at rest it was mute. After the public execution of Joteun's ruling caste, disturbances were minimal. When they occurred Yoth found himself dragged into them as often as not. The Adeptus Arbites had come out of their precinct house to bolster the local enforcers. Whereas these agents of Imperial justice inspired fear, the Space Marines inspired awe, and consequently Yoth and his brothers were frequently petitioned to bring a peaceful end to one dispute or another.

It was a request of this nature that he expected when Enforcer Schreck came to call.

Yoth had returned to the Crimson Castle, spoken with Raankin and was preparing to grab a few hours rest when Chamberlain Meretricion knocked upon the door of his cell.

'My lord, I am sorry, there is an enforcer requesting an audience.'

Yoth groaned. 'Now?'

'He says it is urgent, my lord.'

Yoth looked at his pallet longingly. 'Who is it?'

'Senior Enforcer Schreck. He has news of some import. Events in the underhive that demand attention, or so he insists.'

'Can it wait?' said Yoth.

'He says not, my lord.'

'Show him into the Chamber of Hospitality Minoris. I will be there in a few moments.'

Yoth dragged his robes back on, and made his way down cold metal stairs into the public areas of the castle.

Within the small, comfortably appointed room, he found the enforcer, looking at paper plans scattered about.

'This is all bad, isn't it?' said the enforcer as Yoth came in.

'My answer depends on how you will react,' said Yoth.

'Me? Oh, I expect we will all be exterminated like rats in a trap. Everyone's got to go sometime. At least I'll have company.'

'In that case, yes, it is very bad.' Yoth sat down heavily in a chair. 'We will keep the gravity of the situation secret as long as we may, but Ector will fall.'

The enforcer was a tall man by the standards of non-Space Marines. His bulk was enhanced by his armour, a light carapace patterned after that worn by the arbitrators. He held his helmet in the crook of his arm. He had a square, stolid face marked with scars. He bowed to Yoth.

'My lord,' he said. 'I'm sorry. I forget myself. Sign of the times, I suppose.'

Yoth pulled a face. 'I really don't care. My vocation is the preservation of mankind, not to seek reverence. I'm a warrior, not an idol, although people often forget that. What news have you for me?'

'I've been trying to bring this to someone's attention for a couple of days. It's got very difficult to get anyone to listen. You're all busy, my lord, as are my men.'

Yoth nodded. 'Tell me, will you take some wine?' He rang a bell. A serf entered. 'Two bottles, two goblets,' Yoth said. The serf departed. 'Now, what is it you have for me? I must sleep or I will fall onto my face.'

'I have this.'

Schreck pulled a roll of flimsy prints from his belt.

'What is it?'

'Normally, my lord, I would not bother you with this. But with the invasion, well, I put two and two together. I hope I haven't made five. Although it might be better if I were mistaken. There are images there, from the edge of middle hive.'

He unrolled the flimsies and handed them over.

'This was taken by pict-augurs operated by the Hand organisation.'

'Should I have heard of it?' said Yoth.

'No, my lord. It is a charitable affair, taking care of the sick, orphans and the like. There's probably a spire lord who feels a bit guilty behind it. Who, I do not know. They cause no trouble, other than their spokesman, Tolliver, who sometimes preaches the cause in shift hours.'

'You have not acted against them?'

'I have advised Tolliver myself to cease his meets in the hours of activity, but no, I have not moved to stop him. They're proving their worth in the current crisis. Without such groups, the middle hives would crumble into anarchy. They might not be strictly legal, but it's best to police them carefully, I find.'

'Your judiciousness is commendable.'

Schreck was relieved. 'Thank you, my lord.' He pointed at the images. 'These picts are from augur eyes around the Decimus Nine district, Foundry 87-34. They were taken several days before the news broke. I admit only then did I properly check them, because Tolliver is... Well, he's a little crazy. The next picture, that one. It shows a service tunnel that runs under the workers' quarters. They had some problems with ice vermin coming up from a rent in one of the tubes a few years back. The problem was resolved, but the augur eyes remain. The foundry allows the Hand to use them to guarantee the peace.'

'That is generous,' said Yoth.

'The Condirion family are no fools. Low crime and reasonable freedom from want makes their workers happier, and happier workers work harder. It does not cost them anything. And it makes my job easier.'

'There is nothing here.' Yoth leafed through the grainy images. The print quality was appalling. 'I... Ah, I see.'

'My lord, you know what you see? Before the news broke, I thought it could be something from the deeps. I have never seen its like before, and it resembles none of the creatures of the outside world. I bring no shadow play.'

Yoth nodded. 'I believe I know its type. You have this in motion?'

'My lord,' said Schreck. He unclipped a small data-slate from his belt. He fiddled with it, and brought up multiple augur images presented as a standard, surveillance grid pattern. 'The sequence is less clear than the enlargements, but it is in this image here.'

Yoth leaned in closer. When the clip was done, he said, 'Bring up that sequence again, from forty-five-zero-eight. Isolate the relevant feed alone.'

'Of course.' The enforcer played the segment again, enlarging it. It was not much clearer. They watched in silence. A blurred shape moved past the augur. It was hard to see what it was, but it was large. A long tail whipped back and forth as it slipped into a gap that looked too small to take it.

'Who knows of this?' asked Yoth.

'Tolliver told me that none but he had seen it, but I do not see how that can be so, my lord. It is difficult to keep any kind of secret in the hive. Too many ears, and too many tongues. Is it... well, is it what I think it is?'

'Yes. Yes it is. This puts a different cast on the situation. It is worse than I feared,' said Yoth. 'The tyranids are already here. Has it killed yet?'

Schreck shook his head. 'Not that I know. Should we leave it?' he asked. 'I'm assuming it's not harmless, but one can't make a difference, can it?' He sounded hopeful. Yoth disappointed him.

'It can. This is a scout.'

'Do they have a way of communicating intelligence, should they even gather it?'

'Almost certainly.' Yoth levered himself up from his chair. The enforcer took a step backwards as the Space Marine loomed over him. 'If it has not killed yet, it will begin to soon. They have another use, as terror weapons. One alone can cause much panic.'

Yoth touched a vox-pendant at his neck. 'Brother-Captain Raankin, this is Sergeant Yoth.'

'Brother-sergeant, how goes it?'

'Badly, my lord. I have evidence of tyranid vanguard organisms already present within the hive.'

'These are poor tidings.'

'The creature will be cataloguing all the weaknesses in our defences. I ask your leave to investigate.'

'Of course. Go swiftly, and may the Emperor's favour find you. Shall I send support?'

'No, my lord. Our brothers and men-at-arms are needed at their stations. But I will not go alone. I will take the enforcer who brought me this news.'

'Now just wait a minute–' began Schreck.

Yoth silenced him with a glance.

'Very well. Report back when you may.'

'Yes, captain. Yoth out.'

The serf returned with the drinks, left them on the table and withdrew. Yoth poured.

'I never said I'd come with you,' said Schreck. 'I have duties and responsibilities...'

'We all have,' said Yoth. 'Who says you have a choice in what they are?'

'Down there in the underhive, it's not pretty, my lord. We enforcers don't venture below the six hundredth level unless we have to.'

'I have waged war in some of the worst places in the galaxy. Warriors of the stars we may be, but I have fought in the grandest palace, and the grimmest sewer. I need aid. You are to provide it. Is that clear?'

'Of course, my lord,' Schreck said. 'I'll do what I can, but... I was a middle-hiver, I used to run in the underhive as a boy. But not deep. There's all kinds of danger down there. Ice vermin get in from outside sometimes, and it gets cold where there are breaches. But most of the danger is of the human kind. The scum down there are ungovernable.'

Yoth became thoughtful. 'The children... The dispossessed, they are there also?'

'Yeah, sure, a crying shame, but what are we to do?'

'That is not what I meant, enforcer. We shall seek our guides among them. Now drink. We leave immediately.'

The Spire Hounds' bunkhouse was a pile of scavenged junk on Euphoria sublevel 12. It lurked in a corner on the edge of a rust-coloured lake, a sheer wall of plates rearing right out of the water. Not easy in, not too easy out, a good position. Kal thought he'd never see it again, but there he was, rattling about it with Marny like they were knucklebones in a box. With the rest of the gang dead or gone, it was too big. No life to it. He remembered the good old days when there was a ring of dirty faces crowded round the fire, roasting rats on the griddle. Tunny made that. Tunny had made everything, but he was gone now, and the fire lit only the pair of them. Kal squatted at the edge, poking it needlessly, arm on his knees, face half hidden behind it. Marny stayed back from the warmth; it was freezing down there, but she wouldn't come close. It was like he was contagious or something. Diseased.

Didn't stop her talking, though.

'You're head-broke, Kal. I don't gunny it. What were you thinking, speaking uppity like that?'

'I don't sabby,' he said quietly, although he knew only too well. The big one in the red and black, the Chaplain – he knew how he felt about Marny. Now she knew too. He was burning with embarrassment.

'You tossed it, like it was nothing. You and your lip. They were going to choose you!'

'Drop it, Marny, would you? I'm a-thinking.'

She made a strangled noise of annoyance. He feared for a moment that she'd bring up what the Chaplain had said or, worse, walk away, but she didn't.

'What you a-thinking on?'

'We'm gotta get aways from here,' he said, glancing around. 'No ways we can defend this on our own. We either get gangers, new gangers, or we'm get out. Mebbe join with some other blockies, make a new place with them. Two of us here? Someone come and take this offa us so easy, we'm better giving it away before we'm killed for it.'

'You trust anyone? Who you got in thinking, for new blockies, I mean?'

'I dunno,' he said, and poked his fire again. 'That's why I need the quiet. Give me thinking space. We can't stay.'

'The boy is right.'

A voice from the dark, soft yet commanding. Marny squealed. Kal near jumped out of his skin, but had presence of mind enough to grab his gun.

'Who there?' he shouted. The shadows danced in the fire.

A huge figure stepped forward. For the briefest second, Kal thought Papa Bones had come for him, and his legs nearly gave way. He fired reflexively and his bullet spanked off armour. The whistle of the ricochet died slowly. A Space Marine stepped into the firelight. He spread his hands in a gesture of peace. He wore no helmet.

'Brother-Sergeant Yoth of the Crimson Castellans is here. I require your services. I need a guide.'

'A guide, for what?' Kal asked.

'Have you not heard? There is an invasion en route to your world.'

'Yeah, I'm hearing. I don't sabby how that's my problem, yeah?'

'Underhivers works for themselves, is true,' said Marny, finding her voice again. 'There's another here, Kal. Enforcer.'

'What you'm want? I ain't going to the pokey! I ain't been doing none bad.' He jabbed his gun barrel at the Space Marine's face.

'This is no trap. I speak the truth. We have no interest in whatever crimes you may or may not have committed. The time for that has passed. All the hive must fight. This is your problem, boy, as much as it is mine. Do you know the tyranids?'

Kal shook his head mutely.

'They are devourers of worlds. They come unannounced from the depths of space. After slaughtering every sentient being of a world, they take everything, leaving nought but barren rock behind. They will come through here. They will kill you and consume your body. They are, in fact, already here. That is why I need your help.'

Kal shrugged as if the end of the world meant nothing to him. Hivers like him were insular; the outside world was a myth, never mind things from the stars. Was this naivety or bravery, thought Yoth, or has he simply given up?

'No seen nothing,' the boy said.

'The beast is cunning. You would not see it unless it wished you to, and then you would be dead. I need you to take me here.' Brother Yoth held out an auspex. A map was displayed upon its small screen. Kal looked at it uncomprehendingly.

'Foundry 87-34, Level of Ambitions Realised, sublevel 6 of that. You know a way in and out of the ducts below?' asked Schreck.

Kal glanced at Schreck.

'No sabby,' he said.

'Bottom Iron, last factory on Burnt Zone upside,' said Schreck.

'Yeah, yeah. I know it,' said the boy.

'You will take us?' asked Yoth.

'I will if you'm feed us.'

Yoth laughed. 'Agreed. See, Enforcer Schreck, we have one of the most cunning guides you could wish for.'

Kal nodded at Marny.

'I ain't going without my blocky.'

'You are in the service of the Crimson Castellans now, boy.'

Kal shook his head. 'Down there, hunting offies? Just me and you'm and the lawman? We need her, need her to be eyes out.'

'Very well.'

'And I'm bringing my gun. Take it everywhere. Made it myself.'

Yoth glanced at it. 'Impressive work. I would advise you to arm yourself in any case. You will need it.'

CHAPTER FIVE

RAINBOW FALLS

'This be the place,' said Kal, pointing at a ragged cleft in the metal.

Through the small spaces the boy had taken them, where it was hard for Yoth to go. He did not wish to remove his armour. The way would have been easier for him, but the risk outweighed the benefit and so he forced himself through every narrow passage they came to.

The A-shaped conduit under Foundry 87-34 was broad enough to take him, if low. His head brushed the cabling running along the apex, forcing him to hunch. His shoulder pads scraped at the metal of the walls. Lack of space caused him to keep his bolter tight into himself.

Kal looked back up at him. Not once had the boy bemoaned his fate. He had accepted the Chaplain's judgement. He had stood up for what he believed in and taken his punishment as just, and soberly. Yoth respected his stoicism. He and Gorth had never been close; Gorth's high-handed manner was alienating. The Chaplain was Yoth's superior, and so Yoth respected his decisions utterly, but in this instance he increasingly felt Gorth had made a mistake.

He motioned to the boy. 'Get behind me, stand with the girl.' Kal ducked between his legs. 'Is all clear, Enforcer Schreck?'

'Yes,' said the enforcer from the back of their line. 'I'm not getting anything from my men at the entrance either, my lord.'

Yoth went down on one knee. He stared into the hole. The blackness within was complete; no artifice of his helm could penetrate it. The beam from a luminator, borrowed from Schreck and shone within, vanished. Residue was upon the sharp edges of the hole. Scrapings from some hard substance.

'The augur eye must've distorted it,' said Schreck, peering over his shoulder. 'Made it look bigger than it is. There's no way it could have squeezed in there.'

'The creature is as big as it looked, and it did go in.' Yoth paused, weighing their options. 'But we cannot follow.'

'Lemme through, er, my lord,' said Kal. He still was not at ease addressing Yoth so. Yoth thought it important that he learn. 'I can squirm in, easy as.'

'You broken?' piped up Marny.

'I agree,' said Yoth. He barred Kal's path into the hole with a mighty arm, as immovable as a mountain's ridge. 'It would be folly.'

'What we do then, lord?' said Kal.

'Do you know where this crevice emerges?'

'No,' said Kal. 'But I can guess.'

They went a tortuous route that finally brought them to a level only twenty metres below. Another corridor, this one rarely trod. Foundry 87-34 was on the edge of the Burnt Zone. That area of the hive had suffered a catastrophic fire some generations past, and had been abandoned. As a result, the underhive intruded far into the middle hive in those places. Yoth looked constantly to his auspex.

'No signs of life, no movement,' he said.

'I don't expect much,' said Schreck. 'No one and nothing here, except dregs, lawless dregs. Not many. Life's too hard in the Burnt Zone. We're only a couple of hundred metres above the true underhive. Better down there, even if it's nearer the surface.'

'Ain't no such place,' muttered Marny.

'There is, girl, and an outside,' said Schreck absently.

'Should be someone here. Should be gangs, scavs, orphan-babes. Too high for muties, but should be someone. It ain't gone crashed'm all down, this beasty-beast from the black?' Kal looked to the Space Marine. Yoth gazed impassively back.

Kal shivered. He pointed forwards to a hole in the ceiling. 'I reckon that's it. That where that hole come out. Right here. Trust me.'

The hole might have been an access hatch, but it had been forcibly enlarged. Blows from within had shattered the frame, and it lay with other fresh debris upon the floor: wires, sections of pipe and bent ceiling panels. Water dribbled down a jag of metal, falling from it in slow drips to puddle beneath the tangle.

Yoth checked the edges of the hole: more of the residue. Around the corridor were fresh scuffs and scratches. 'The creature has passed this way many times.'

'Well, duh,' said Kal. Yoth stared at him sternly. The boy coloured. 'Sorry. I mean, my lord, I can see that.'

'Can you track it?'

'I gunny it. Need to go frontwise, though. You hop along behind us, yeah? My lord,' he added hurriedly.

'Lord Sergeant Yoth,' said Schreck, laying a hand on his arm. 'Down yonder is the underhive proper. We don't want to go down there if we can help it.'

'Do we not now?' Yoth surveyed the corridor disapprovingly. 'This place is riddled with holes. How are we to cover every way to the middle hive from below? Truly hives are the worst fortresses of all, but that is no excuse to allow the enemy free range. We go on.'

Kal nodded, and went forwards. 'Don't you'm shine too many lights on this, yeah? Need to pick it out with me hive eyes. And stop when I say stop. Righty?'

'As you wish,' said Yoth.

Kal set off slowly, examining the floor.

'There's loads of holes, I know. But that's why we have walls, yeah?' said Marny in a frightened voice. 'They'll keep the xenos out, won't they?'

'A wall can be circumvented, passed over, or undermined. At the last they can be stormed. They will slow the enemy, that is all.' Yoth walked on.

Schreck gave Marny a squeeze on the shoulder and an understanding look. 'Cheery, these Space Marines. You stick with me, and I'll see you right.'

Marny bit her lip, and smiled.

'You just keep that gun up.'

'You don't need to tell me that,' she said, and her face hardened again.

Onwards and downwards they proceeded, through the charred precincts of the Burnt Zone. The stink of fire still clung to the place a hundred years on. They said the fires had burned so hot there that the bones of the inhabitants had turned to ash, and the metal in the walls had run. Kal saw the truth of it as they passed pooled slicks of metal, hardened like old lava flows. Nothing had lived there since.

'The creature is hiding out of sight, coming up only to scout,' said Yoth. 'This is its pathway.'

'Yep, something or so,' said Kal. 'Nearly down in our zone now, out of the burn, down in Euphoria. Home sweet home.'

Only it wasn't, not without his blockies and monsters running about and all, but he dared not say that.

They passed out of the Burnt Zone into the underhive proper. Charred service corridors gave way to rusting halls, manufactoria and habzones abandoned so long ago. There was little of worth in them, as all had been stripped out and recycled. The ceiling was frequently buckled by the weight of the hive above. Wide pillars of gleaming adamantium braced these sections, incorruptible wonders shining amid the decay. The further they went, the fouler the air became. The walls were streaked with moisture. Pools of contaminated water gathered on floors, running away in dirty rivulets. Filth dripped from stalactites of effluvia to join them. The rivulets became brooks, then stinking streams, hurrying off to join an underground torrent whose voice came and went, becoming louder with each return.

'Rainbow Falls,' said Kal. 'Not been much deeper than this. Hey, mebbe we'm catch a flicker of them, Marny? Won't that be grand? Went down once, saw the river, never made it to the falls. Always wanted a vez.'

Marny scowled back.

'Another weakness in the defences,' said Yoth.

They came upon the river four hours later, a coloured rapid whose steams reeked of poison and glowed with chemical light. Unspeakable muds formed its banks, thick with rubbish and bones. Yoth's suit indicators went wild, screaming the danger of toxins. Schreck coughed, eyes streaming from the fumes, and clipped his helmet respirator across his face. The children pulled rags from their clothes and tied them across their noses.

'This'm big bad river, not nice. Bad to drink, bad to smell. Whatever's doing, don't fall in, you sabby? That very bad. Even you, mister lord, melt you through even that.' He pointed at Yoth's battleplate.

'Do not concern yourself with me. I am a Space Marine of the Emperor. You look to your own safety.'

'Just saying. Thing went this way, along the banks.' Sharp-clawed footprints showed up in the muck. 'Kiddy could follow this, it's just not trying now.'

The caustic river had burned its way through the hive, linking room after room into one long watercourse running through a canyon of layered metals. Strata of crushed floors were revealed by this erosion, while those uncompressed formed darkling caves into which the party looked warily. Narrow where it ran deep, spread wide into wetlands sheened with oily, rainbow scum where it did not, the river flowed rapidly, its acid spray etching the walls into disturbing patterns.

They followed the river. Yoth estimated that now they were nearing the planet's original surface. Schreck confirmed this to him.

'We never come here,' he said. 'This is mutie country.'

Mutant signs were everywhere. There were paths beaten hard into the filth, bridges of metal over tributaries to the reeking flood. Of their makers, there was no sign. Signs of habitation increased, but no inhabitants presented themselves. Kal, initially buoyant and cocky, grew nervous, Marny too.

A vast space opened before them, forested with columns of adamantium bearing up the hive. The river meandered between them in garish loops, its acids unable to harm the columns but eating the floor around them, so that they took on a strange, half-natural aspect. They skirted the cliffs, now drawn two hundred metres apart, passing under a dark-eyed fort atop the precipice. Yoth saw no sign of life within and they moved on.

And so they came then to the edge of the abyss.

The Basement Gap, the boy called it. The cliffs of the river's canyon bent back around it, the river pouring through a deep cleft in the floor and thundering over the edge in a choking spume. The river's luminescence could not save it from the blackness, and it disappeared into a night that would never break.

This 'Gap' was the bottom of the hive's central shaft, its round shape distorted by the river's action. It was over three-quarters of a kilometre across at that point. The ancient walls were ribbed by geothermal conduits and, in their midst, the Infinite Stair. The Stair was the same dimensions as above, and so seemed isolated in the shaft's wide centre. It came down through the hive-sky. Black and unknowable as the abyss's depths, only a faint shine in the dark hinted at the bursting city high above. Shortly after it came clearly into view, a hundred-metre section was missing entirely. Spars and dangling girders traced its path, the steps corroded to nothing. Then, fifty metres down from the lip of the chasm, it was suddenly whole again, and plunged downwards after the river. One landing, two stairs, one landing, one stair, one landing, two stairs and on and on, up and down, the same pattern here as in the hive's upper reaches.

'We are above the bottom of the hive,' Yoth said, checking his helm displays. 'My cogitator suggests we are only three hundred and twenty-nine metres from the planet's surface.'

'Really? You gunny it? It don't be so,' said the boy. 'Long ways down, for sure, but no matter how far you is, the Stair is always going further downaways. Down and down, it don't never stop.' He said this with quiet fear and awe. 'I been down here once, only once. Never did see the falls, and swore never try again.' He looked about. 'But ain't no muties, not now. I don't gunny it, Emperor and all, I just don't gunny it.'

There came a soft slap and splash behind them, just audible over the thunder of the water, and then only to Yoth. The Space Marine was instantly alert.

'We are being watched,' he said. 'Stay close. Do not run. Do not seek cover. Death waits in the shadows.'

He raised his gun.

A blur in the gloaming. Something huge moving fast. Yoth stepped back in time to save his life, but not his weapon. A claw as tall as a man sheared through the barrel, jarring it from his fingers.

Kal, Marny and Schreck all opened fire.

The shadows shrieked and shivered. Camouflage rippled, and before them a lictor was revealed, its body taking on the bone and purple colouring of the Leviathan strain. Three metres tall, mantis claws arched up from its shoulders to add half again to that height. Multiple eyes glinted in deep-set sockets above a mouth massed with tentacles. Hooved, backward-jointed legs supported a chitinous torso. Beneath the giant scythed claws were two arms ending in grasping hands.

'Stay back!' shouted Yoth. Marny and Kal scattered. Schreck stood his ground, firing methodically with his pistol. Claw-tipped sinews sped from the beast's body, hooking themselves into Schreck's flesh. The lines convulsed and Schreck was dragged from his feet. The creature embraced him, bent its head to his and bit down with a crunch.

The beast sucked at the enforcer's cranium as his legs kicked frantically. A final spasm, and Schreck was still.

The beast dropped his corpse, blood and cranial fluid dribbling from its tentacles. It rounded on the children.

Yoth pulled free his bolt pistol and fired a pair of swift rounds at the beast's side, aiming for the intercostal spaces of its thorax.

One was deflected. With the other he achieved a partial embedding. The bolt detonated too close to the surface, lifting a section of bony chitin free. The lictor screeched in annoyance. The thing was tough, practically unharmed. Yoth's goal was partly achieved, however, for it turned from the underhivers and leapt at him in their stead.

The xenos creature was unbelievably swift, almost too quick for him. His shots went wide as it closed the gap. Great hands closed themselves around his body. Tentacles slobbered against his faceplate, probing at his helmet and seeking to wrench it free. Yoth's right hand was pinned. He could not raise his pistol. With his left hand he reached for his combat knife. His helmet display fizzed as the tentacles in the creature's mouth tugged. He swung up and out, severing a number of them. The lictor reeled back. Gunfire from the hivers smacked into it, but their autoguns were too weak to harm it, and barely distracted its attentions from Yoth.

Yoth hacked again and again. He spun his knife around in his hand and drove it upwards, directly into the creature's mouth, towards its brain. His hand jarred as the knife bit into bone, and the lictor flung its head back, tearing his blade from his grasp.

The beast's grip weakened. Yoth kicked and twisted free, landing on his back. His arm freed, he slammed four rounds into the creature's chest before the gun was knocked out of his hand. The lictor stared down at him, eyes cold and unknowable. Then it reared backwards, stretched its scythe claws to their greatest extent, and prepared for the killing blow. Yoth scrambled away, but he knew he could not escape. The scythe-arms of the beast would pin him to the floor, and then it would devour his mind.

A burst of projectiles came hissing through the air, spinning discs glinting in the half-light. They buried themselves in the xenos beast. It roared loudly and swung about in time to receive another volley to its face. For a moment it swayed, and then crashed down with an awful shriek.

Yoth was up and had retrieved his weapon before the creature was dead. He took cover behind the body and tracked the pistol around the cavern, searching for his saviour.

'Come out!' he shouted, his voice brutal through his vox-grille. 'Show yourself.'

A grey figure emerged briefly from the edge of one of the columns, before disappearing into the shadows again.

'I see you,' called Yoth.

'I show myself because I wish to be seen, and I would have you know I am not your foe.' It was not a human voice.

'Who are you?'

The figure re-emerged, then disappeared with a laugh. Yoth could not keep his bolt pistol trained upon the figure. Despite his helm's image enhancers, Yoth struggled to see him; his form was inconstant, some kind of cloaking device or cameleoline.

'I am a friend, Space Marine.'

'You are xenos, and not welcome here!'

'We desire no harm to you, none at all. The contrary in fact. I am Isarion the Dispossessed, an agent of the Hand, he who protects the people of Ector!'

The figure was as stealthy as the lictor. Now here, now there, its voice thrown to further Yoth's confusion. 'We have no quarrel, you and I. Our goals are the same. We eldar do not wish to see the Valedan system fall.'

'You are eldar? You cannot be trusted!'

'Always the same songs your kind sings. You are the ones not to be trusted, I say. We know much, but trust you only with what you can be trusted with – that is why we appear untrustworthy. You cry foul when the crime is yours alone. Now, push the body of the beast into the river. Let the foulness of the water dissolve it. If you do not, others of its kind will follow its death-scent. There are several here. You cannot find them all. Beware – should they devour its brain-stem, they will know you and your ersatz brothers are present, adept of the stars. They might already know and they might not, for their psychic network is but weak in such small numbers. Stay away from the depths, they cannot be held. Let your presence here be an unpleasant surprise to the void spawn, if it can. The less the enemy knows of either you or I the better, Brother-Sergeant Yoth of the Crimson Castellans!'

The figure reappeared. Yoth opened fire. The muzzle flash of his bolt pistol lit up his surroundings, its bark mingling with the thunder of the falls. Bolts exploded off a column. A flash of movement, then nothing. He stopped when he'd shot off half a clip.

He waited. There was no further communication, no further movement.

He ran forward, hugging levees left by flood and heaps of metal roof-fall.

When he reached the last place he had seen the eldar, there was nobody there.

CHAPTER SIX

HIVE FLEET KRAKEN

Mazurn slept often. The hive mind troubled him. Sleep offered some respite, although the dreams of astropaths were not lightly endured. With a sleeping mind open to the warp, an astropath's nights are parades of horror and temptation. Mazurn's own will was lacking. Only the gifted soul-shine of the Emperor kept him safe as he slumbered. Yet awful as his dreams were, they were better than the waking presence of the hive mind.

Mazurn's dreams were coloured by his recollections of his sighted days. Faces long gone but untarnished by time, locked safely in his memory. His mother, his father, his brother and cousins; those to whom he had been close before the Black Ships came. Too often these precious memories were tainted by nightmare. So it was that his mother's face ran like wax in a fire as she told him a bedtime story, and the expanse of the void opened up in its place. Where his childhood room was safe and warm, instead he hung unprotected in the full and pitiless gaze of the stars.

Space rippled, the blackness convulsed. Stars do not shimmer in the void, for there is no air to distort their glow. These wobbled frantically. A tear appeared, twisted as a cruel mouth, and parted. A lipless maw that held terror in its gorge. Unclean light blazed, unnameable colours that entranced and repulsed equally.

The sleeping mind of Mazurn stared into the throat of hell as the Vortex of Despair yawned, the transient warp rift of the Valedan system.

Something emerged. There was a flash, a crack of thunder in the noiselessness of the void. The rift closed. Empty space was empty no more. The vortex had spat a fleet into real space, thousands upon thousands of ships. Mazurn's ethereal being rippled with horror as he took in the endless vessels. Bio-constructs of the tyranids, blasphemous in form and awful in their multitude. For a moment, they seemed dead, adrift without direction, and Mazurn prayed they would remain so.

It was not to be. There were signs of movement. Small twitches, the shuddering of drive-palps. The sealed-over aperture of one curled shell cracked and fell away. A tentacle unfolded from within to taste the nothingness of space, and then dozens followed suit. The fleet shook the unreality of the warp from itself. Mazurn's psychically sensitive mind picked up the rolling motion of a vast intellect awakening. It looked about itself with alien malice. A trip through the howling madness of the empyrean would drive any sentient creature insane, but the tyranids' hive mind was unshaken. It had passed through the inferno, and emerged merely hungry.

Mazurn observed the flare of bio-plasma from retrosphincters as the fleet drew closer together, and arrayed its vessels according to its predatory plan. Innumerable psychic tendrils, part of the hive mind and yet separate, reached out. One brushed him, and once more Mazurn felt the soul-numbing terror he had experienced in the sending chamber.

Shocked from sleep, he sat bolt upright in bed.

'Emperor preserve us,' he said. 'Emperor preserve us!'

He leapt from under his coverlet, running madly at his door. He grappled with the handle, but in the depths of his fear he could not work it. He pounded upon the rough plasteel until his fists were bruised. His servants, used to his nocturnal voyaging, were quick to react.

'Call Chaplain Gorth, call Tenth Captain Raankin, call them all!' Mazurn wailed as the door was shoved open and his men grappled with his flailing limbs.

'Calm yourself, my lord. Calm yourself!'

'No, no, no!' he wailed, and collapsed into the arms of his serfs. 'There is another hive fleet coming. Tell our masters, there is another hive fleet coming. Oh, Emperor save us all!'

Yoth spent a fruitless hour combing the deeps for the eldar.

'Aren't we going back to the surface?' asked Marny. Neither she nor Kal could keep their eyes from the hollowed skull of Schreck. They had seen horror in their lifetimes, but this awful sight was too much for them.

'No, we are not. The eldar are devious xenos. Who knows what their purpose is in your underhive. I have heard tell of them aiding the warriors of mankind, but they are just as likely to open the gates to our enemy or foment rebellion. He must be found.'

A chime in his helmet. An incoming message. The vox tracked over the frequencies, but could not get a lock.

Yoth's attempt to snag the signal refocused his attention on his helm's displays. Ghostlight, all of it, intensifying the claustrophobia of the underhive.

'Brother-Captain Raankin, this is Sergeant Yoth. Brother-captain?'

Squeals and pops in his ears; the weight of the hive crushed vox-waves as well as the human spirit. When Raankin replied, Yoth was relieved.

'Brother-Sergeant Yoth. I am glad to reach you. How goes your hunt?'

'With complication. The tyranid is slain. If there are more, I cannot say. But I have encountered an eldar.'

'They are tricksters, deceivers. We must be wary. They laid claim to this system once, perhaps they seek to profit from our destruction.'

'I will hunt him, my lord, and wring the answers from him myself.'

'You will return. Whatever the purpose of this intruder, it must wait. We have a greater problem. A second hive fleet is inbound and will arrive within hours.'

Yoth froze. His mind fell back on his conditioning. The defences, all he could think of were his defences. 'The walls, the minefields, they are incomplete,' said Yoth.

'Just so, my brother. Now is the time to test our mettle against the Great Devourer. We shall stand shoulder to shoulder, and let them break upon the walls of our armour.'

Yoth stood for a moment, digesting the news. Two hive fleets attacking one system was unheard of, and eldar in the underhive... Yoth was not the sort to think on what this all meant. His kind were the builders of walls, and so he would build more.

'We must go,' he said to the underhivers. He holstered his gun. Grunting with effort he heaved at the dead lictor, pushing it towards the falls. The weight of the thing was phenomenal; only when the children of Ector found metal poles and levered at it alongside him did the corpse tumble into the river. Colourful effluent snatched it away.

'What about him – the lawman? We'm can't just leave him crashed and out like this. I got no love for the law, but he was okay. We all sabby him well,' said Marny.

Kal nodded. 'Yeah, wouldn't be...' He searched for a word, little used in his day-to-day argot. 'Honourable.'

Yoth nodded reluctantly. 'It would not, but I cannot carry him back.'

'You plenty mighty!' said Kal accusingly.

'I am. But I need my hands upon my weapons.' He glanced at his shattered boltgun as he said this. 'Let us put him into the water. It is a vile grave, but better that than the creatures of the enemy devour his flesh and make it part of their own.'

Kal and Marny said a childish prayer to the Emperor as Yoth dropped Schreck as gently as he could into the torrent. No matter Yoth's care, it was an undignified funeral.

'So passes a bold servant of the Emperor,' said Yoth. He left the riverside. 'We are done here. We must go.'

There was little time to redeploy the defence grid. Much of the planet's orbital weaponry had been moved to the sunward side of the planet, the expected approach vector of Hive Fleet Leviathan. Against Kraken, coming from the other side, Ector's depleted network of defensive stations and war satellites held but briefly before collapsing. Those heavy lasers and mass casters in range took their toll, but the tyranids came in such numbers that the orbitals were swiftly overwhelmed, and the vox frequencies were alive with the screams of dying men. Blasted to glittering clouds of junk by living torpedoes, or bodily grappled by tentacled Kraken ships into the atmosphere, one by one the orbitals died.

Kraken enveloped Ector like a hand, multiple tendrils encircling the globe. Imperial ships, the *Redoubt* among them, played games of cat and mouse with the fleet, turning aside a handful of Kraken's probings before losses forced the ships to fall back to the evacuation corridor, where they fought tooth and nail to keep the way open. Commodore Justarin's orders ceased around noon, his ship overwhelmed by Leviathan further in-system. Thereafter, Tenth Captain Raankin gave the order that the remaining ships follow the lead of Sergeant Tularis, acting as captain of the *Redoubt*. The danger offered by the Girdle's defence lasers kept the Kraken back from the equator, but only through Tularis's quick thinking and rapidly shifting tactics was the space lane kept completely clear for the evacuees.

Imperial ships of all sizes came in as close as they could to the planet. An endless stream of shuttles roared between hive and orbit, gathering up those lucky few whose numbers had been drawn in the grand lottery.

For a time, Raankin feared that Tularis's efforts would be insufficient, and indeed it appeared to be that way, for three of his frigates fell to the invaders in quick succession and the cordon was stretched thin. But the swarm appeared content to have extracted the Imperial fleet's fangs, and formed a wall of their own, away from the fire arcs of Ector's terrestrial defence lasers. To the north polar region they went instead, where few weapons were to be found, and Ector's autochthonous beasts dwelt aplenty.

Behind multiple screens of escorts, the hive ships came in close to the planet. These immense living vessels were the size of void whales, their long slug-like abdomens sheathed in layers of bone and ablative keratins, tipped at the prow with a tiny head and thorax. The craft shoaled high over the pole, their flanks shuddering as they spat out their cargoes. Thousands of seed-like pods accelerated towards Ector. The night sky lit up with fiery trails as they rained down.

Shortly after this landfall, the first of the polar stations went dead. Scoptic capture showed giant tyranid combat beasts battling the ferocious polar fauna of Ector. These were worthy first targets for the hive fleet's hunger.

The scouring of the pole took five hours. After this time there was no living thing larger than a snow hyrax above the planet's fiftieth parallel. The few human installations were overrun, the fires of their burning glittering upon the carapaces of a billion tyranid creatures.

With one purpose, the Great Devourer turned south.

The beasts of Kraken came to Hive Valentis shortly after the fall of the ninth evening. The Ice Spire, they called it, the most northerly of all Ector's city-peaks, and the smallest. It terminated a branching line of the planet's massive transit system, far out past the limits of the Brown Wastes in the steppe proper. A centre for the herders and meatmen of Ector, here the cryodons and metaelphs were brought for slaughter. Their meat fed the rich, their by-products the poor. Potent extracts from their cold-adapted bodies were sent off-world to the laboratories of the Adeptus Biologis of Kaidar VII. Here too was the Huntsmens' Guild of Daea, those men who once braved the hellstorms of Valedan's innermost world to snatch similar prizes from creatures born to fire, but nevermore. Man's time in the Valedan System was done.

The lottery was over. Those not chosen were ready to fight. Propaganda broadcasts were constant. Priests in every major thoroughfare exhorted all inhabitants of the hives to repel the aliens. Stern officers and commissars gave speeches on floating screens carried by pseudo-cherubim. Servo-skulls and less venerable constructs blared dire threats amid motivational paeans. 'All must fight, all must fight, all must fight,' they chanted as they swooped over the bastions on the skirts of the hives. 'To fight is to honour the Emperor,' they said to hive gangers crouched in the dark reaches of the underhive. 'Abhor the alien, crush the alien, slay the alien. Fight, and live. Embrace cowardice, and die,' they said to citizens in the richer districts, grasping weapons in unsure hands. Everywhere, Adeptus Arbites, commissars of the planetary defence regiments, officers, brute squads, foundry foremen, enforcers, factory martinets, dormitory arbitresses and every other keeper of order stalked the city, keeping a watchful eye on the people of Ector lest they break and hide, or turn on each other through fear.

At the Fire Control Centre of Valentis Hive, Brother Karsikon was ready.

'Firing solutions present themselves, Lord Karsikon. The xenos approach the inner fence.'

Brother Karsikon looked over the shoulder of the gunnery officer. There were innumerable augur eyes all over the hive, showing the outer shell, ramparts and wasteland from a dizzying array of angles. His attention, however, was fully given to a bank of semi-holo projectors depicting a mass of tyranids running fast over the steppe. Ector was seldom truly dark; so much snow and ice gave the planet a high albedo, and the sky glowed with reflected light. The tyranids came through this unsure twilight, so many it appeared that the steppe was covered in spiny, writhing grasses. They were as yet many kilometres distant, and the silence of their advance on the screens was eerie.

With image enhancement, Karsikon could clearly see the make-up of the horde. Hundreds of thousands of hormagaunts ran in front of a secondary line of tyranid warriors. These creatures had been unfamiliar to him, but Raankin's briefing had been thorough. The warriors, which Raankin described as the aliens' officer cadre, were accompanied by greater creatures: living tanks who tossed their heads and snorted plumes of gas through the chimneys on their backs. Beyond this line were greater shapes, some as large as Titans.

'Let them come,' he said, his voice carrying to the artillery officers' implanted vox-units. 'We are ready.'

Sixty-nine per cent of Ector's heavy weaponry emplacements had been redirected from orbital scouring to ground target annihilation. As Raankin had promised, a wall of fire awaited the tyranid invasion force.

'Hold fire until my command,' said the Crimson Castellan. 'We shall wait until the first ranks of their horde are well within our maximum ranges, only then shall we open fire. I wish to destroy as many as we can, and will not risk their turning back at our first volley. Is that clear, men of Ector?'

'Aye!' came their replies.

Karsikon watched power read outs flicker as the tyranids overran the inner fence. Already they had crushed the outer to negligible effect on their numbers. Energy that would deter the greatest of Ector's snowbeasts did nothing to them. The inner fence, intended only to ward the hives' hinterland from the hivers' own giant livestock, was lesser in stature and quickly cast down.

Karsikon paced up and down the lines of gunners sat intent over their read outs. Every man commanded a dozen artillery pieces slaved to an incorporated servitor. There were five hundred men in the gunnery station, buried deep in the most heavily armoured part of Hive Valentis. Six thousand large guns pointed at the onrushing horde, and there were many thousands of others of lesser potency, directly manned, in emplacements and studding the ramparts of the bastions hugging the base of the hive exterior. All the men, at General Rovor's order, hung on the word of Brother Karsikon.

Tension built in the room, fingers hovered over firing icons. Feeder lines linking cybernetic rangefinders to the brains of the men assembled and their servitor slaves hummed with building energy.

Karsikon made sure to cover as many of the galleries as possible. He was aware that his presence was an inspiration. His armour whirring behind the men as he passed emboldened them. 'I am an Angel of Death, and under me, you shall be my messengers!' he said. He checked in his helm display, mirroring in miniature the larger read outs of the hive's holobanks. He waited until the lead elements of the swarm were just outside the reach of the shorter-ranged weapons at his disposal.

'Open fire!' he cried. 'For the Emperor, for your homes, for your very lives, fire, fire, fire!'

The men of Ector obeyed. Following firing patterns set by the Crimson Castellans, the heaviest weapons – defence lasers, macro cannons, medusae and others – sought out the biggest creatures of the alien swarm, slamming shells and las-beams into them. The lesser guns took for their targets the medium-sized beasts. The least of them, should any survive, would be left to the men manning the walls.

The steppe boiled with fire. Explosions were so numerous they blended into a continuous wall of earth and flame. The tyranids were entirely obscured. The firestorm whited out most of the displays, and the men fired blindly, on and on, shell after shell. The hive shook with anger as millions of tonnes of munitions exited the muzzles that bedecked its every level.

Still the tyranids came on. For two hours the barrage proceeded, until the ground shook and Karsikon's metahuman eyes were wearied by the screen burn of atomic detonations. Reports came in to Karsikon from his brethren as the main belt was assailed. The same situation there as at Valentis: endless slaughter.

Three hours passed by, and the guns ran hot in the freezing winds of Ector.

'Colonel Chorstroff, what news from the walls?' asked Karsikon.

Chorstroff's voice, tinny on inferior vox equipment, spoke over the quiet chatter of men about the business of shattering a world.

'No creature seen for a full half hour, my lord.'

Karsikon stopped pacing.

'Cease firing, all weapons,' he breathed. 'Let us see what we can see.'

He waited for the earth to settle, then recalibrated the displays, keying his helm's tactical read outs into the hive's external augur eyes. The images clear once more, he scanned rapidly over the field. Smoke blew over a broken landscape in ethereal flags of surrender. Fires guttered in the shells of dead aliens. The permafrost had melted under the barrage, and the ground had become a quagmire of mud and alien blood. The steppe was no more. A lone alien bounded sideways across the view, parallel to the hive line. There was no other movement.

Hours passed. The smoke blew away from the wounded steppe. The heat of weapons' discharge dissipated, and frost rimed the raw earth. Night deepened.

Karsikon was satisfied. 'Brother Karsikon reporting. All tyranids in Valentis sector destroyed.'

Similar replies came from other hives. Men sat back. Some dared smile.

'Be vigilant. This is but the first of it,' came Brother-Captain Raankin's command. 'There will be more waves. Reload your guns, tend to your malfunctions and your bodily needs, and ask that the Emperor turn His gaze upon you. It will be a long night.'

CHAPTER SEVEN

THE FALL OF HIVE VALENTIS

Seven weeks passed. The Crimson Castellans vigilance did not cease. In Hive Valentis's Fire Control, Karsikon took an incoming message from one of the Chapter men-at-arms at Luggenhard.

'The eighty-ninth transport group is away, my lords.'

'Acknowledged,' said Karsikon. His brothers followed similarly. Karsikon needed sleep less than the unaltered men, but they were being fed a constant drip of stimulant via their hard-wiring. It was likely none of them would ever know the pleasure of a full four hours sleep cycle again. The men were encouraged by the news, and Karsikon allowed them ten seconds of jubilation before silencing their cheers. One hundred and six more transport runs were planned, then the cargo ships in orbit would be full, whereupon the fleet would run for Gospar. These warriors would be left to die.

'Riots continue in three of the hives.' Captain Raankin's voice replaced that of the man-at-arms. All communications between them were now secretive, conveyed over the Space Marines own vox-net.

'I will keep this from my men,' responded Karsikon.

'I command that all will,' ordered Raankin. 'The fewer distractions the better.'

'Is the rioting within expected parameters, brother-captain?' said Brother Philodon.

'As we anticipated, the worst riots are occurring around the evacuation ports. They are, however, less serious than I expected. They are an annoyance, diverting resources away from the outer defences, nothing more,' said Raankin. 'These people of Ector have backbone. Remain vigilant, brothers.'

'Acknowledged, brother-captain,' Karsikon said, as did the others.

The tyranids will come again, thought Karsikon, but when? After the first attack they had been expecting them to mass immediately for a second, larger assault. None had come. From what Raankin said, their tactics were unsubtle but brutal. Karsikon was disturbed.

Later that day, Karsikon discovered the reason for the delay.

'My lord, we have multiple contacts approaching our position,' his augur array officer said.

'Put them on the general screens. Give me holo.'

Multiple viewscreens in the room displayed the hive's auspex readings. A glowing mass of pulsing contacts filled each one from side to side. Like the first swarm, it was coming at them from the dropzones to the north.

'Prepare weapons!' shouted the gunnery officers.

'Wait!' said Karsikon. 'This is different.' He scrutinised the read outs. The blobs were moving fast.

'The enemy is at elevation, lord.'

'Air swarm,' said Karsikon. 'All guns, maximum elevation! Pick your targets by section. Prioritise the larger creatures. Imperator victorius!'

This new wave was on them in minutes, streaking through the cold dawn of Ector. A horde of creatures all with wings. Some were truly exceptional in size, harridans with broods of gargoyles clustered all over their bellies like a litter of pups at the teats of their mother.

They were testing our defences, as Raankin said they would, thought Karsikon. And now they have adapted.

'This is the true attack. Stand fast. Keep your focus. Open fire!' he shouted.

Once again, thousands of weapons spoke. Defence lasers lit the swarm ruby red, scores of searing energy beams that struck lines of tyranids burning from the sky. Airburst shells exploded in their midst, consuming hundreds in fire, shockwaves blasting more to the ground.

But this horde was faster, far faster than the terrestrial creatures – faster than anything with wings had any right to be. Tens of thousands were slaughtered, but the creatures did not falter. They closed range quickly. Many of the guns were too big to target them. Anti-starship projectile cannons made for effective ground weapons, but were ineffective in countering the aerial assault. Vox chatter increased enormously as the aliens came within range of the ramparts, beneath it the sounds of weapons fire. First the smaller artillery, then man-portable heavy weaponry, then the crack of lasguns, so many discharging at once that the noise was like water dropped into boiling fat.

Shortly after, the screams started. The hideous chittering of the aliens made its own war on shouted orders and gunfire.

On the screens, Karsikon watched the tyranids assail the ramparts. Biological guns, bonded to their wearers, spat streams of grubs at the men on the walls. As they neared, the creatures vomited searing venom that melted through the cold-weather scarves and goggles of the Ectorians. Many fell to the ground, clawing at their faces.

'Concentrate support on sector fifteen,' Karsikon ordered. 'Sector twelve, sector three, sector two!' Heavy bolters emplaced in the walls swivelled down, gunning for the tyranids crawling all over the walls.

'Ground forces approaching!' shouted an ops officer.

Augur eyes up to the height of the bottom third of the hive were obscured by knots of flapping wings and teeth. The augurs were failing en masse, smashed to pieces by the creatures, who appeared to know all too well what they were. The higher imagers were safe, for now, and looked down on a boiling cloud of beasts swarming all over the hive's lower reaches. Further out, a fresh line of tyranids was advancing over the steppe.

'Heavy artillery, elevate and engage. Direct line fire weaponry only on the aerial swarm! Engage flamers. Burn them from the sky.'

'We will hit our own men.'

'It is inevitable. They are lost already. Fire!'

Flames billowed out from the flanks of the hive over the ramparts, incinerating tyranids and men alike. But Karsikon was right. There were few men left to die this way.

'My lord, they have taken the lower rampart – east section seventeen!'

So quickly, thought Karsikon. 'Colonel Chorstroff's concern. Keep up fire,' he said. 'Slaughter as many as you can. We will–'

A resounding boom shook the hive.

'What was that?' called someone.

'Concentrate!' said Karsikon, as disquiet ran through the stacked tiers of his gunners. 'Sounded like an impact. Something solid. Get me an auspex feed.'

The auspex was uninterpretable. There were so many contacts that whichever device Karsikon viewed the input on, he could make no sense of it. The vox crackled into uselessness. They were being jammed, somehow. Perhaps by the clouds the larger creatures emitted from their carapace chimneys. Perhaps by some more uncanny means.

Another bang, then another. More followed. Alarms clamoured.

'Get me a fix on those impacts.'

'Augurs are out all over the upper reach now also, lord.'

'Find me one that works!'

A crackling image from a damaged eye came on. Dark shapes, as large as gunships, were plummeting in line from the sky, their wings folded. The first fell past the augur. Shortly after there came another loud bang, and the squeal of metal.

'They are striking the hive!' someone shouted.

More alarms. 'Breaches are reported in fifteen, seventeen, twenty areas.' The calls of Karsikon's men were getting ever more panicked.

'The tyranids have entered the lower halls, the tyranids have entered the lower halls.' Colonel Chorstroff's voice overrode the dying vox-net. 'All citizens, prepare to fight!'

The banging continued with more frequency. Other augurs showed more of the plummeting creatures coming in multiple trains. Images tumbled away as the weapons the eyes were attached to were shorn off by razor-sharp wings, and always came the endless banging as the creatures raked their pinions down the side of the city-mountain. Debris tumbled onto the ramparts, crushing the few men still battling there. The walls were lost. A few bastions held out, but their remaining time could be numbered in minutes.

Gargoyles and harpies flew in thick streamers to the ruptures made in the hive's skin. More and more of these opened up, and after a time power feed indicators began to fall as the creatures attacked the hive's power lines. Karsikon was unconcerned; the energy feed for the defensive weapons' banks came from generatoria beneath Fire Control itself, but it showed an alarming amount of intelligence on the part of the aliens.

Karsikon was barking orders and redirecting his dwindling banks of weapons when he stopped dead.

'Lord?'

'Shhh!' He held up a gauntleted hand. The frantic chatter of the men died away. Karsikon dialled his vox volume down and listened intently. He dropped his hand. 'Gunfire. Close by. They're coming for us,' he said. 'Door guard, stand ready.'

'You are sure, my lord?'

'These are not animals. Something sinister is at play here,' said the Space Marine.

'I have movement,' said the officer watching over the approach to Fire Control. 'I can't see much, but they have something big with them.'

Karsikon spared a swift glance for the display. It was poor quality and the image juddered as the hormagaunts went by. In the smoke behind, a hulking shape loomed. He had the impression of a giant claw, then the feed cut out.

'They have disabled the corridor augurs.'

Karsikon unhitched his bolter. 'Lieutenant Gord, you have command. It is time for me to bring my other skills into play.' He communicated his intentions to Captain Raankin.

'Go with honour, Crimson Castellan,' came Raankin's abrupt reply, shattered to near unintelligibility by the disrupted vox.

His brothers began the litany of ending for him. Their static-broken eulogies filled his helmet with music, and his heart with resolve.

Karsikon stepped through the armoured doors of Fire Control onto the arching bridge that linked it to the rest of the hive. A metal canyon separated the control room from the main body of Valentis, its sheer-sided walls – windowless and streaked with moisture – disappearing into darkness above and below. Fire Control was a thin sliver of metal and technology delicately poised in the dark. Karsikon imagined the weight of the hive slamming the gap closed. He shook away the image.

A bunker was set either side of the bridge, bristling with weapons, five elite Ectorian Guard in each.

'Men, stand ready,' he said to them. Four heavy bolters held in cupolas above the bunkers whirred to life.

The sounds of fighting came from the far side of the bridge. Beyond mighty blast doors, a full platoon held more bunkers commanding the corridor approach. As thick as the doors were, Karsikon heard weapons at play through them, muffled by half a metre of plasteel but apparent to his sensitive hearing nonetheless. Alien screeches and human screams mingled.

They stopped.

Regular banging came upon the door, plangent booms that echoed over the chasm.

Guns clicked and powered up behind the Crimson Castellan as he strode forwards onto the narrow span.

'You shall not enter,' said Karsikon. 'I bar the way.' He prepared himself, setting his stance, thumbing the safety catch on his bolter, checking the chamber.

Thoom, thoom, thoom, the door vibrated.

'I am the walls, I am the tower,' he said. His gun clicked as a bolt slid into place in the chamber. He touched each of his oath papers. Some of these papers were fresh applications of old oaths made as a neophyte, some newly taken for this engagement. He knew they would be his last.

Thoom, thoom, thoom.

The tabard between his legs, white, emblazoned with a crimson tower, fluttered in a sudden draught. Screeching sounded from somewhere very high above him.

Thoom, thoom, thoom. The door shivered visibly. Incredibly, bulges appeared in it.

'I am the bastion, the moat. I am the ward, I am the keep!' He levelled his gun at the door.

Thoom, thoom, thoom! The door bent inwards and gaps appeared at the top left corner, then all around it, the housing twisted out of shape.

'I am the gate.'

The door burst, flying from its mounts and banging from the bridge railings with force. Clangs rolled out as it smashed into the side of the chasm and fell.

Smoke and tongues of fire billowed through the doorway. Sparks of electricity lit it like lightning in the clouds. Dark shapes moved.

Tyranids came screaming out of the smoke.

'I am the gatekeeper. This way is shut.'

Karsikon opened fire, as did the men behind him. Bolt-rounds and las-bolts streaked across the bridge, blowing the first wave of attackers apart. Their body parts spun away into the dark. Fountains of blood burst sideways, then fell like rain into the hive's never-ending night. More came, then more still. Shattered alien corpses piled on the span, providing a degree of cover. A scythe-armed monster the size of a large dog made it through, clearing the gap between the bridge end and Karsikon with one bound. The Crimson Castellan tracked the creature through the air with his gun. He fired a round into its throat, exploding it in midair and showering him with gore.

A terrible roar. A great weapon beast, three times the height of a man, forced its way through the doorway. Plasteel grated on chitin, crab-like claws, each the size of Karsikon, buckling and scoring the metal as the creature pulled itself through onto the bridge.

The men behind him behaved commendably, firing with precision. They targeted its weak spots, the eyes, the mouth, the gaps between its armour, but their weapons were ineffective. A heavy bolt-round found a soft spot, bringing forth gouts of blood. The lower left of the creature's four arms went limp and it roared. It hunched down, lowering its head and presenting the thick armour of its back to them. It crossed the giant claws of its forearms across its face. Its vulnerable parts thus shielded, the carnifex walked across the bridge.

'Intensify fire!' shouted Karsikon. The heavy bolters chattered louder. Their miniature missiles bounced from the beast's armour in all directions. Chitin blackened where las-bolts scored it, but on the beast came.

A rattling from behind told Karsikon that one heavy bolter was dry of rounds. A second followed shortly after. He snatched out his combat blade, firing his bolter one-handed.

The creature halted in the centre of the bridge. An awful scream built. Suddenly, it dropped its claws, lifted its head and vomited a ball of incandescent energy from its pulsating throat. Karsikon dived aside, sliding on the metal of the bridge. There was a sickening sensation as he felt it give out underneath him. He dropped his knife and grabbed at a railing post, stopping himself just before he fell from the side.

The bunker burst apart as ammunition within detonated, taking two of the door heavy bolters with it. Karsikon dangled from the post as the carnifex stomped past, the bridge vibrating. Gunfire battered into the xenos as harmlessly as rain against a roof.

Karsikon tried to haul himself up one-handed, but even with the aid of his armour, it was too arduous a task. With a shout of frustration, he dropped his boltgun into the darkness below. He slapped his other hand onto the bridge, and heaved. His chestplate scraped and he was onto the span again. With difficulty he got his backpack under the railing.

He stood in time to hear the carnifex scream once more, right against the second bunker's viewing slit. The vile energies these harmonics generated filled the fortification with brilliant light. The firing from within stopped.

There was but a single heavy bolter still active. The carnifex reached up, closed an immense claw around it and pulled it free from its housing in a shower of sparks.

The creature turned its attentions then upon the door into Fire Control.

More tyranids were coming to the edge of the bridge. Karsikon pulled his pistol from its holster and snapped off three shots, killing two. The others withdrew, hissing. They were waiting, he was sure, for the door to come down, then they would be upon him and his service to the Emperor would be done.

He cast about, attention flicking to the far end of the bridge and back again. The carnifex ignored him, intent upon breaking through the armoured door into the complex. Karsikon found his knife. He grabbed it up, and came to a quick decision. He put away his pistol.

Karsikon ran at the carnifex. Winding up his arm as he came, he put all his strength and momentum into the knife, slamming it into the poorly armoured joint at the back of the carnifex's left knee. The creature roared and lumbered about. Karsikon held fast. He levered the blade upwards, creating a gap in the ribbed cartilage there. Ripping a krak grenade from his belt, he jammed it into the gap, and let go.

The carnifex towered over him, roaring. The grenade exploded. The leg remained attached, but buckled under the creature's weight. The carnifex flailed with its three functioning arms as it toppled sideways. Doomed by its own top-heavy anatomy, it tumbled off the bridge. One of the great claws closed around the full depth of the bridge's metal, scissoring it partway through. Karsikon walked over to it, pistol out again. Taking careful aim, he pumped a full magazine into the elbow joint. Bolt after bolt exploded there until, with a wet tear, the arm gave way. The carnifex fell roaring into the dark, bright plasma trailing it. The claw remained, bitten deep into the metal.

Immediately, Karsikon was facing the bridge end again, pistol reloaded. Creatures were coming through the far door unhindered. He fired once, twice, then five times. Twelve shots and his gun was empty, all his ammunition spent.

He looked back to the door. It was so badly buckled that he could not retreat within.

Casting his pistol away, he held his combat knife reversed in front of him, palm flat on the pommel.

A winged tyranid warrior, paired crackling symbiote swords held in its upper hands, came through the door and advanced upon him.

'I am the gatekeeper,' Karsikon intoned.

The fleshy weapon in the warrior's lower limbs spasmed, the gills along its length rippling obscenely as it pumped a stream of acids and grubs at him. Searing pain stabbed him as it ate into his armour.

Against the warrior with the swords, Karsikon stood little chance. He was still staggered by the effects of its gun when it charged at him. He dodged one swipe, then a second. The third bit into his left arm. The weapon was of sharpened bone, but the disruption field around it was every bit as deadly as that of an Imperial powerblade. It sheared through his armour with ease. He grunted as his arm was severed. A second blow cracked his chestplate and brought him to his knees.

He was coughing up blood into his helmet as the tyranids swarmed past. They ignored him; his time as a threat to them had passed. He lived long enough to see the tyranid leader beast shatter the weakened door, and then he died.

In a similar manner, all the hives of Ector would fall.

CHAPTER EIGHT

THE LAST DAYS OF ECTOR

'They are coming again, make ready!' Yoth called. His small army manned the barricades. They were a motley band – gangers, underhive scum, factorymen, upper hivers, nobles, soldiers, children, matrons, wives and mothers. They fought side by side, no matter their age, sex or origin. They were all dirty now, whatever finery an individual might have had left tattered by weeks of war. For once, the citizens of Ector were equal.

'Sergeant,' said one, 'I see movement!'

Yoth scanned the darkness down the Infinite Stair. There was little power at this level any longer. His helm lenses glowed as image intensification picked up the unified movement of a number of tyranids. They ran together, switching direction like birds in flight, flitting from cover to cover. The hive had taken much damage and debris blocked the stairways in many places. This only made it easier for the tyranids to assault them.

'Steady,' shouted Yoth. 'Hold your fire!'

Ammunition was scarce. The last of the factory levels had fallen three days before. They would be getting no more.

Something was wrong. There were too few tyranids in evidence, and the approach of this group was too obvious. Yoth was holding one of those landings approached by two stairs coming together, to its left and right sides. Behind him, the next rise went up alone. He marched to the other end of the landing, Kal in tow. They peered down the second stair. Yoth took an improvised flare offered him by Kal, magnesium scavenged from the lost manufactoria. He flicked the switch on its ignition source and hurled it as far down the left-hand stairway as he could. It trailed sparks as it flew, clattering loudly in the emptiness of the ravaged hive as it bounced.

With a sputter it caught, revealing a second swarm of xenos creatures creeping forward. They shrieked at their discovery and broke into a run. An answering chorus of screeches came from the opposite stair, and the two groups attacked at once.

'Fire!' bellowed Yoth.

Guns spoke together. A mix of improvised slug-throwers, sanctioned civilian sidearms and Astra Militarum-issue lasguns, their individual sounds coalescing into a symphony of death. The rounds smacked into the onrushing creatures, killing many. Their corpses tripped those coming behind, but it served to slow them only a little.

Yoth's bolter boomed, the propellant of each bolt streaking the darkness. The light trails vanished as the rounds hit home. Gaunts exploded, showering the stairs with blood. He shouldered it as the aliens came closer, drew out his pistol and lobbed a grenade down into the horde, bringing short-lived illumination to the scene. Before it had died away, he had drawn his combat knife.

The aliens neared. The light fleshpistols they had bonded in pairs to their fists crackled and spat their poisoned darts. A man cried in pain near Yoth, sliding down and convulsing as the toxins did their work. Another volley, and the creatures were upon them, scrabbling over the barricades. Yoth laid about him with his combat knife, chopping creatures down left and right, hewing their limbs from their bodies.

Men and women wrestled with the beasts, rifles held crosswise in front of them to keep snapping jaws from their faces. Yoth helped where he could, firing shots from his pistol or stabbing with his blade. His blows shattered the aliens' armour with ease, but the unenhanced struggled. Clumsy strikes from kitchen implements and sharpened metal slivers skidded from chitin. Yoth saw one man impale his own leg in this manner, then die screaming as his opponent leapt up and savaged him.

The situation was hopeless. These were among the enemy's weakest creatures, and they were too much. Yoth caught sight of larger shadows moving up to engage.

'Fall back,' he cried. 'Fall back to the next line!'

Many of his militiamen were torn down screaming as they ran. Kal and Marny kept pace with him; he'd never been able to shake them. The ones who survived longest tended to be the underhive gangers. In perverse circumstances, they were finally ascending to the better parts of their city.

They wove a path through a debris field up the single flight. The pursuing tyranids did not see the mines secreted within. Explosions boomed behind Yoth as he made it to the barricades fronting the next landing. Waiting hands pulled them through its narrow gate. Yoth looked back. Two or three stragglers, no more, a horde of xenos on their heels.

'Open fire! Shut the gate!'

A heavy stubber raked the stairs, setting off unexploded mines and slaughtering tyranids by the dozen. Small arms joined it, dropping more of the creatures until there were none left to see. The stragglers were cut down along with the enemy.

So had the battle of Luggenhard gone on for a fortnight.

One by one the hives had fallen, Valentis first, Uxtar soon after. There were gaps of many days between the losses, then a handful would go at once. The last before Luggenhard was Kirithia. In their desperation to escape, its population had attacked the space ports there en masse, leaving the city wide open. Panic was the deadliest of all foes.

Once the city walls had fallen, the Great Devourer had found its way into

Luggenhard through the porous lower levels, as Yoth predicted. His battle had gone on in a similar vein ever since: he'd hold a landing for a day or two, then retreat to the next. All the while the population shrank until the great city's middle portions were empty. There were so few left, barely enough to hold the Infinite Stair and the corridors around it.

'They're coming!' yelled the landing lookout. 'Ware below!'

Huge creatures lumbered out of the grey, perpetual twilight of the hive.

Yoth cursed fluently. 'Remember, aim for the eyes, aim for the joints. Do not waste your ammunition on their shells!'

Five creatures, carnifexes, living tanks equipped for heavy assault. 'So it ends,' whispered somebody.

'It's not over until he says it's over!' shouted Kal. Marny was next to him. He released the grip on his gun and squeezed her arm.

The militia levelled their weapons. Defiance was more important than survival now. On the landings above, others were waiting, no doubt in fear at the sound of the battle coming closer. Yoth was proud of how these men and women had held their ground. Knowing that there was no escape for them, they fought on anyway.

Before Yoth could order them to fire, the shaft was filled with shards of glittering light. Through the gaps between the tank-beasts, Yoth and his men saw glowing alien warriors, clad in bright armour. A nimbus surrounded them, as of light shone through crystal. The sounds of shrieking alien weaponry rang up the stairs. The creatures turned to face them.

'The Hand! The Hand! He is here again!'

'The Hand!'

Others took up the cry, until all were chanting the name. There was relief, and tears.

'Silence!' roared Yoth. 'We do not know the true purpose of this aid. The alien is to be feared. None are as devious as the eldar.'

Yoth hated to admit it, but he had come to rely on the mysterious eldar. He caught a glimpse of the one called the Hand, a slender being decked with shimmering banners, a tall helm upon his head. He danced around the carnifexes' clumsy swipes, slashing at them with a long sword. Discs from the device mounted on the back of his other hand joined the merciless hail of projectiles shot by his followers, a hail that hissed into the tyranids, slicing through their armour and severing their tendons. Like the men of Luggenhard, the eldar interlopers targeted the weaker points of the creatures, only their weapons were far more effective. A living tank fell to the floor as its knees gave out. It dragged itself forwards on its other four limbs, roaring in outrage. Yoth and his men watched as a glimmering warrior leapt onto its head, put the fluted barrel of its weapon against the creature's neck and slew it.

The Hand accounted for two himself. Yoth was entranced by his skill at arms. Relief vied with hatred in his heart. The Crimson Castellans were a xenophobic breed. Yoth defiled himself by his acceptance – gladness, even – of this filth's intervention, and yet... And yet as he watched the alien weave his way through the blows of the carnifexes, felling them with pinpoint strikes to the few vulnerable parts of their anatomy, he could not help but feel the respect one warrior holds for another.

The Hand's men, if men was a fit word for them, were not invulnerable. One was caught despite his agility. Crushed in a claw, his screams mingled with the shattering of glass.

'Chaplain Gorth,' Yoth signalled. 'Sergeant Yoth. The alien fights here again on our side.'

Gorth replied. His voice was hoarse. Many long days of command had taken their toll. Raankin was dead, slain by the sky swarm, as were all but four of their brothers. Once their commands had fallen, these few had made their way back to Hive Luggenhard, the last redoubt of Ector. Their adventures would fill whole tomes of the Chapter's history. Their deeds would go unrecorded.

'By your side?'

'No, my lord. He is yet distant. We look on and he slaughters the enemy in our stead.'

'That is a great shame, for proximity brings opportunity. Should you get such opportunity, Sergeant Yoth, I expect you to take it. Strike him down. We have lost. Felling such a warrior as he will cause the eldar some discomfort. A trifle in recompense for this world, but a stone to be built into the walls of the Imperium nonetheless.'

'Yes, my lord,' said Yoth, hoping the hesitation did not show in his voice. 'We have been driven back to the nine hundred and fifty-first landing. We are nigh to the middle hive wall and the upper spire.'

'Hold them as long as you can. Withdraw fighting. The last of the evacuation fleet is preparing to depart the system. They are as yet unmolested. The *Redoubt* holds position. There is little to remain here for. Kill as many as you can, and then we shall leave this world to its fate. These are the last days of Ector.'

'There are men here who have fought bravely, my lord.'

'And we will honour them when we return to the fleet. Their families, at least, had their chance in the lottery. Their deaths may serve the Emperor here – yours will not. You are worth ten thousand lesser men. Do not sacrifice yourself. We have lost too many brothers already. Do you understand, sergeant?'

'Yes, my lord,' said Yoth.

Gorth's voice cut out.

The last of the carnifexes were dying artful deaths. A pair fell simultaneously, and the fight was over. The eldar came to a halt. From somewhere deep in the hive, Yoth heard the crackle of weapons. Distant alien screeches troubled the air, followed by a brief hush. This silence was ill, unnatural in a city such as Luggenhard. It was the quiet of Death himself; his breath stirred Yoth's tabard.

The glittering warriors gathered behind their leader. The Hand was taller than they, with broad armoured shoulders, a red helm with a white war mask inset, and a black and white crest curling over its height.

'A tempting shot,' said Yoth in the privacy of his helm. He looked from right to left at the men beside him, their faces showing wonder at the glimmering apparitions. He wondered what they would do should he gun the Hand down. Would they turn upon him?

Perhaps they would be right to, he thought. Such a course of action seemed deeply dishonourable, no matter Gorth's edict.

The aliens, forty or so, moved as one up the stairs. They did not advance as physical beings, but flickered like phantoms from place to place, although their weapons were solid enough.

'Stand ready,' said Yoth. 'This may well be a trick.'

His men blinked at one another as if they had woken from some enchantment. Those with their wits about them jostled their fellows and gestured at the eldar. Reluctantly, the hivers aimed their guns at their saviours.

Yoth's finger tightened on his bolter's trigger. The aliens came to a halt well within range. Still Yoth did not give the order to open fire.

The warriors were silent. They stared at the humans from behind blank faceplates. Prismatic light shifted around them. For all the beauty of the aliens, and the aid they had brought, the men behind the wall became uneasy. There was something coldly sinister about them.

'Is this the manner in which the sons of Terra greet their saviours, with blade and bullet? Shame on you and yours. Put up your weapons!'

A musical voice Yoth recognised: the eldar Isarion he had encountered in the underhive. A shadowy figure came from within the midst of his shining comrades. Remarkable for his mundanity, he gave off no glow. Instead, his cloak was the stuff of shadow.

Talk went down the line of the defences. Fingers relaxed, guns were pointed elsewhere.

'Stand firm!' bellowed Yoth, the harshness of his vox-grille making his men flinch.

'We would speak with your leader, the altered mon-keigh named Yoth. We stand here under the oath of truce. Let no one draw aim upon us nor loose shot, or there shall be dire consequences.'

'You see me,' said Yoth. 'Why do you not address me directly?'

'I seek no offence and you find it, even though it is you who offer it. I would not address you without your permission lest you take it as insolence.' Isarion swept back his arm to encompass his ghostly comrades. 'Here are the heroes of the eldar. It is a great honour they do you in fighting for your cause, and you would slay them! Mankind has fallen far into folly.'

Yoth stared at the Hand. The eldar stared back. Yoth's will was great, armoured by catechism against the influence of others, and yet he felt small under the dread eldar lord's gaze. He was acutely aware of his own filthy state, the battered and streaked nature of his armour and tabard.

'The Hand desires you to know that the end is upon you. Ector will fall soon. A great host of void spawn makes its way hither. The beasts you saw us slaughter are but its vanguard. If you wish for the remainder of your chosen people to depart, you must join forces with us. Let us fight side by side. We have no quarrel with you, only common cause.'

'Today, perhaps,' said Yoth. 'But oftentimes the words of the eldar prove hollow.'

'It is because you do not listen, and assume the speakers are all the same. Are you the same as these men? Is your word not worth more than theirs? The might you have to effect your promises is greater, and so your word is greater, is it not?'

Yoth glanced at the tired and dirty men beside him.

'So it is with us. We are among the mighty of our people. We give you our word we seek no advantage here, at least none to your detriment,' said Isarion. 'Our threads run together for a time. Do not question it.'

A roar rumbled up from far below, then many more. Isarion looked back into the dark beyond the lambency of the silent warriors. 'Be quick about your choices, Sergeant Yoth. We gain little from this debate. If you decline then tell us so, and we will depart.'

Gorth's words came back to Yoth. 'Proximity brings opportunity.'

'Let them in,' Yoth shouted, holding his hand aloft. 'For now, we fight as allies.'

'Here is where we will make our stand,' said Isarion. A holomap flashed crystal-perfect from his hand in the dark, the interior of Luggenhard depicted in breathtaking clarity. 'This grander landing, twelve levels up. Pull your men from the intervening stations. With their and our arms en masse, we will stay the void spawn long enough for your last transport to depart.'

Yoth thought on the eldar plan. It went against his own strategy, but the time for this constant, attritional retreat was coming to an end.

'Bring your men in from the galleries and chambers around the Stair also,' Isarion was saying. 'It is the biological mass of this world the tyranids desire. Concentrate it in one place, and they will come all at once and be hindered by their own numbers. Upon the narrower front, they can afflict us less. The presence of the wall will give them only one avenue of attack, even should they break through into the upper reaches.'

Yoth nodded. 'Very well. Whatever the merits of your suggestion one thing is true – the endgame approaches.'

'This ultimate stairway,' Isarion's map scrolled upwards, 'below the wall that separates the poor from the rich. This has been prepared for demolition?'

'It has,' said Yoth, not liking that this alien knew so much.

'Then when the situation is hopeless, go from this place, destroy the Stair and seal the wall.'

'We have refrained from doing so thus far, for fear it would concentrate the attention of the aliens upon the upper spire directly.'

'And wise you were to do so. Now is the moment to enact your final plan. It is a delaying tactic.'

'That was our intention.'

'Well now is the time for delay.'

Yoth sent out his orders. Two of his brothers responded. Bost and Meklenholm.

Bost had been organising the defenders on the far side of the spire wall dividing the upper realms of the city from the lower reaches. Meklenholm had been leading search and destroy missions within the hive shell. They discussed the situation, and agreed. Meklenholm would withdraw to Bost's position, and await Yoth.

'What of Philodon and Osko?' asked Meklenholm.

'Let them remain in the spire space port,' said Yoth. 'Their efforts are needed there. The air swarm harries it. I will inform them of my retreat once I am on my way.'

He was relieved his brothers did not insist on descending to his level of the Stair. The presence of the Hand and his followers added too many complications.

'I am ready,' he said to the eldar, trying hard to keep his voice neutral.

'Then lead on,' said Isarion.

'No. You and yours will go first. I will fight beside you, but I do not trust you at my back, eldar.'

CHAPTER NINE

THE BATTLE OF HEAVEN'S WELCOME

They went upwards many landings. The darkness above solidified as they drew closer to the hive wall. There the Infinite Stair went through twin gates: round, extravagantly decorated holes in the horizontal spire wall. The gates could be closed, and with them all fresh air and water to the lower hive cut off. They were a standing defence against the threat of rebellion; it was to Governor Hoyel's credit that they had remained open throughout his reign.

An hour into Yoth's trek he received notice from Bost that Meklenholm had come through the wall.

As they passed the intervening landings, Yoth gathered his warriors band by band. Soon a stream of humanity was heading upwards to the final landing of the middle hive – the Landing of Heaven's Welcome.

They reached it shortly after noon. The constant darkness of the powerless city made a nonsense of the term.

Heaven's Welcome was the largest landing in all the hive, and the site of a great deal of official business before the invasion. Now its five hectares of heavily decorated floor were as silent and lifeless as everywhere else. The toll booths and document offices were empty, papers scattered all over the floor. Queue dividers were heaped high in the centre, the queues long fled or devoured. A grandiose place once, but in the light of its few remaining lumoglobes and lamps, it seemed a mausoleum before the last candles of burial burned themselves out.

The people of the hive had fortified the landing as best they thought, barricading right the way across the top of the single stair approaching the landing. But the stairway was very wide here, filling the full three hundred metres of the shaft's diameter, and with so much ground to cover the barricade was somewhat scrappier than those below.

'Not good this, is it, my lord?' said Kal. 'I don't sabby this be way defensible.'

'You have a good eye. It is not. Let us do something about it,' Yoth said. 'We will strengthen these walls,' he said, shouting to the weary men, women and youths coming up the stairs. There were ten thousand or so people on their way. A great many it seemed, but a tiny fraction of the hive's original population of one hundred million. Yoth, a native of a backward, sparsely settled world, still found such numbers hard to comprehend.

The defenders of Heaven's Welcome greeted their fellows warmly, but at the sight of the eldar making their way up the centre of the stairway they became restive, half afraid, half awed. Yoth shouted at them, chivvying them to greater efforts. He gathered his more trusted lieutenants and sent them off into the hive, ordered to scavenge materials.

Four hours he gave them. A quarter of them did not return.

When the four hours had passed, he had the towering doors into the hive proper sealed. That left only the stairway and the shaft as avenues of attack – and the twin gates six hundred metres above him, should the tyranids break into the spire. He trusted his brothers would prevent that from happening.

The dark clamoured with the noise of tools as the last men of Ector worked to remain alive a little longer.

Under Yoth's direction, a maze of defences sprang up to await the creatures. Two walls, one upon the lip of the Stair, the other one hundred and seventy metres to the rear. Obstacles dangled from the Stair's supports and the catwalks that criss-crossed the central shaft. The stairways were mined. Snares of razor wire coiled across the steps.

It was as good as he could manage, this ad hoc fortress. Once it was completed and the noise of construction ceased, there was quiet for an hour. The humans rested while the eldar stayed aloof. Yoth wished that the enemy would come. The wait was sapping the hivers' morale. Yoth suspected the tyranids delayed deliberately.

The first shriek of the approaching creatures brought more relief than fear. The landing came alive, people rousing themselves from sleep or terror's trance. Gun bolts slid and clicked, orders were spoken quietly. In the earlier days there had been bravado from the gangers and cowardice from those from more peaceful levels. Neither were apparent now. The war had winnowed out the terrified and the boastful, leaving a hardcore of the courageous, the clever and the lucky. How rapidly they have become warriors, thought Yoth.

'Look out below,' called one lookout, then another, then a third. A scream above and one of the sentries was torn from his perch amid a flurry of leathery wings. His body thumped hard onto the landing.

'Eyes up!' shouted Yoth. Heavy stubbers, emplaced behind the main barricades for the purpose of air defence, opened up.

So were the first shots fired in the battle of Heaven's Welcome.

Five times the swarms of tyranids came up the stairs. The first wave was annihilated by the mines and razor wire traps. The second broke in a fury of claws upon the defences. Scavenged fabrics and chains channelled gargoyles into the heavy stubbers' fields of fire. Their bodies rained down, taking a toll on the defenders equal to that reaped by the bio-weapons. For four hours this opening skirmish raged, until there were no more tyranids in the air or upon the ground.

A short time passed. The remaining lights failed, then another wave came. Yoth ordered more defenders forward as their fellows were killed. They skidded on the blood of the slain as they rushed to man the battered walls. The aliens were repulsed at great cost.

Having exhausted the defenders' energy and depleted the larger part of their number, the Great Devourer set upon the walls of Heaven's Welcome a fourth wave of larger creatures. A phalanx of warriors were in the lead, twelve of them, tall and hideous, heading with purpose to a point in the barricade that had been much weakened. A carpet of leaping beasts, like giant lice, swarmed about the warriors' feet.

The Hand was there at the broken wall, his shining warriors with him, pouring shuriken fire into the horde. Their hissing discs dismembered half the warriors. The remaining six slammed into the wall nevertheless.

The towering tyranids were imposing, and men fled from them as the eldar braced for their assault, but the true danger came from the tiny rippers. No matter that the defenders fired into them, bursting hundreds like ripe fruit, there were tens of thousands and not even a fraction could be stopped. They bounded up the rough barricades on scrabbling legs, then poured over the top. Men were pulled down, disappearing under the writhing mass of the creatures. Their screams were bloodcurdling, high shrieks turning wet and bubbly as the flesh was stripped from their bones.

Giants came next, crushing the ripper swarm underfoot. Gunfire clattered from their armoured shells. They barged into the metal plates that made up the wall, smashing them wide. The rippers poured in through the gap in great swarms, and the defenders fled.

'Fall back!' shouted Yoth. 'Fall back!'

Then he was away, pushing terrified hivers towards the gate of the second wall. Improvised flamers scoured the ground of the rippers, burning them by the thousand until there were but scattered groups of them, and these were finally gunned down.

Fire and the glimmer-glow of the crystal warriors were the sole sources of illumination upon the landing. As he reached the second wall, Yoth glanced to the upper hive. Lozenges of bright light marked the entrances, shining hard upon the grand stairs leading up to them. Sanctuary.

He turned from it.

The eldar slaughtered the tyranid warriors to the last. They duelled with carnifexes. They felled several, but there were many and the eldar retreated.

In the eldar came, rushing past Yoth. He was bathed in their cold light. Isarion then, thanks flying from his lips. Finally, the Hand.

The lead carnifex following bellowed, yellow saliva dripping from long tusks. Yoth withdrew through the gate.

'Close the gates,' he said. Three men pushed a great sheet of metal across the entryway. Girders were hurriedly welded into place.

Corpses were thick upon the landing outside the wall. Only five hundred hivers were left alive, and fear had taken the majority of them.

They were given no respite. The gate shook with claw blows. Men shot wildly into the mass of giant creatures at the wall. Yoth had bade them build it as high as they could, yet still the uppermost parts of the carnifexes overtopped it.

There was a terrible wail and greenish plasma lit up the landing. A section of wall was engulfed. It glowed red-hot, the men standing there turned to ash.

More clanging began. Yoth looked frantically for its source. He stared down at the floor as it heaved upwards. He was thrown sideways as a multi-limbed, snakelike monstrosity pulled itself through the hole and slithered onto the landing. A rush of smaller, similar beasts came with it. The monster reared high. Its torso shook and a dozen quills the length of spears shot from its chest, impaling men all along the wall. Its cohorts spat black grubs from their own chest-weapons, killing many more. One went for Yoth and he parried desperately, avoiding a spray of mucous and ammunition beetles. It stabbed hard at him with long, bony fingers, penetrating the weaker, flexible part of his armour around the stomach. He ground his teeth in pain, and ended the creature with a blow from his knife.

'Trygon!' shouted Yoth. 'A trygon!' How it had come there amazed him. There were multiple skins over the underside of the stairs, covering a maze of ducts and service ways, but the full depth of them was not great. For it to squeeze its way through such confines was something he had thought impossible.

Squeeze through it had. With the trygon's arrival, the defence was effectively over. The gateway was barged in. A triad of carnifexes lumbered through. One of its number began the cry that would unleash another burst of plasma. A second roared and fell, shell shattered by shuriken fire. Yoth recovered his feet, clutching at his wound. He shot repeatedly into the glowing maw of the screaming carnifex to no effect, his rounds detonated by the heat of its gathering plasmas.

Something hit him hard from the side. It was not enough to knock him down, but he fell sideways, teetering near to the edge of the hole created by the trygon. Nothing but darkness and the howls of alien horrors was below.

A slender hand grabbed him, pulled him back from the brink.

Isarion nodded to him. Yoth raised his bolt pistol. Isarion's eyes widened in shock. The Space Marine pulled the trigger, exploding the head of the ravener rearing up behind the eldar prince.

Another ravener came at them. Yoth wounded it, narrowly deflecting its response. Isarion pushed himself away from the ravener's arm blades. He sidestepped adroitly as Yoth brought his blade around in a whistling arc. Strength Yoth had in great excess, but he felt as agile as a tree compared to the prancing eldar. He growled in frustration. Isarion laughed and dropped the ravener with a blast of fire from his weapon. The ravener's tail jerked with the violence of its death throes. It swung at Isarion, catching him unawares, and sent him to the ground. The laughter was knocked out of him along with his breath.

Yoth stood over the eldar. Isarion reached out a hand.

In reply, Yoth pointed his bolt pistol down at Isarion's head.

'Proximity brings opportunity.' Gorth's words rang in his mind again.

His finger hovered over the trigger. Kill Isarion, he thought, and the way to the Hand is open. The eldar hero was fully engaged fighting the trygon, wheeling and spinning between its jabbing arms. One shot, perhaps two, thought Yoth.

Isarion looked up at him. A profound stillness had come over the eldar prince.

'Why do you pause? Slay me. You have your wish – destroy the enemy of man. That is what you are, what you are made for. Do it!' he shouted.

Yoth stared down. He hated this creature, hated it for what it was not. And yet it had saved his life twice. Yoth stood at a fork in the road. Dishonour lay down each branch of the path. He chose the lesser shame.

'No,' he said. He stood back, bolt pistol pointing to the ground. He offered no hand to aid the eldar. With a fluid movement Isarion was back on his feet.

'You hesitate, my friend, and it reflects well upon you. Perhaps there is wisdom and honour left within the race of mankind, if in small measure. Now, I will tell you something. Fifty-three of your years hence, Brother Yoth, on the world known as Malefix, do not hesitate. You will know the time. Farewell!'

Isarion ran to the aid of his leader, joining his master in his duel with the trygon.

Yoth wobbled, light-headed. He'd lost a lot of blood, despite his gifts. It ran down the inside of his armour, pooling hotly in his boot.

'What are you waiting for?' shouted Isarion, as he leapt in between the creature's swiping arms. 'Your time here is done. Run!'

'Fall back,' Yoth ordered. 'The middle hive is lost. To the spire, to the spire!'

His men were all dead bar two score. They ran back to the stairs, frantically dodging swooping gargoyles. The surviving eldar warriors were fully invested. The trygon bled from a dozen wounds, its snake-bodied brethren all dead. An awful rumble came up the stairs, the clatter of sharp hooves on metal. Shrieks preceded them.

Kal was by him, and the girl.

'My lord, we gotta go,' said Kal.

'I...' said Yoth.

'Marny, get his arm!'

Their attempts to help him were laughable. Neither adolescent had their full height, and the circumstances of their birth meant that would never be great. Their heads came only to his chestplate eagle. They could not shoulder his weight, and yet their desire to aid him stirred something in Yoth. They tugged at his unmoving, ceramite-clad arms, and he went with them, limping to the stairs, snapping off shots when aerial tyranids came too close.

Later, Yoth would recall the climb into the spire as a shattered mess of terrible images. Somehow, he and the youths made it to the top along with a handful of others.

They passed through the yawning gates at the top. On the marble floor of the upper hive's entrance hall, Yoth turned back. Far below, a glittering arc of eldar warriors stood on the landing around the base of the stairs, facing an onrushing horde of creatures.

He watched a moment, Kal and Marny clutching at his sides. Then he unclipped his auspex from his belt and depressed a button.

A string of explosions leapt up and down the length of the stairs like fireworks, as far as the Landing of Heaven's Welcome, obscuring Yoth's view of the eldar with smoke. For all the violence of the charges, the stairways seemed untroubled, and his twin hearts skipped a beat.

Time stilled for an instant, until with a tortured groan the ornate structures folded in on themselves, one crashing from its mounts into the other as they fell. Together embraced, they plummeted into the depths, the booming of their fall echoing around the hive's cavity. The screams of tyranids came after it. Yoth had hoped that the weight of the stairs would bring down other flights. He was satisfied that it was so.

Some vile creature flapped towards them. An emplaced weapon shot it down. Here there was power and warriors still. 'Come, let us get away from this place,' he said. He keyed his vox on. 'This is Brother Yoth. I return. Close the spire wall.' The massive doors of the upper hive started their slow closure. For the moment, nothing else dared approach them.

The smoke had cleared by the time the gates were nearly shut. The lower landing boiled with alien monsters. Of the eldar, there was no sign.

With the two children by his side, Yoth made his way upwards once more.

CHAPTER TEN

FAREWELL TO ECTOR

The grand hall beyond the gates was deserted. The hive shaft continued upwards, rising all the way to the palace wall, which divided the House of Hoyel finally from its subjects. The Stair was the same: two flights, one flight; the world Yoth and his companions passed through, utterly different.

This had also been a place of official business, for those who made it through the month-long queues on Heaven's Welcome faced another ordeal on this side of the wall. But no longer. No scribes wrote in the dusty tomes left upon lecterns. No enforcers turned rejected petitioners aside. The Infinite Stair was empty. The hivers looked about with wonder. The hall, with its endless ranks of gleaming galleries, rows of luxurious shops and eateries, and parklands gazing down from on high were like nothing they had ever seen. There were tears among them, and anger at such inequality.

Yoth was increasingly pained. His wound was deep, the functions of his armour compromised. Slowly, he made it across the hall and up a flight of marble stairs to some barricades. The hall, as huge as it was, was a perfect killing ground. The corridors around it were full of armed hivers waiting to take their small measures of revenge.

Brother Meklenholm and Brother Bost awaited him.

'You have returned, and mostly intact,' said Meklenholm. They all embraced, awkward in their battleplate. Meklenholm switched to a private vox-channel. 'Come, brother. We depart in an hour. This world is lost.' He spoke through his vox-grille again, this time to the hivers around him. 'My brother is injured. We must take him to our Apothecary. Hold the hall if the enemy breaks through. Do not advance. Sell yourselves dearly if you need to. Repay the alien with fire doubly for what they have taken from you!'

A weak cheer went up. Meklenholm looked at Kal and Marny.

'They're coming with me,' Yoth said.

Meklenholm said nothing. Yoth's tone made it clear that there was no room for disagreement.

'Yes, brother-sergeant, of course,' said Bost.

Away from the hall the upper hive was crowded with people. Millions remained. Hysteria reigned. Drinking, fighting, fornication and prayer were the order of the day. The Space Marines passed crammed cathedrals, crowds surrounding wild-eyed preachers, lines of wailing flagellants, orgies and brawls. This was the end of the world.

'We must go quickly,' said Meklenholm. 'Our Thunderhawk is prepared. The situation here has deteriorated. The populace is quiet for the moment, but should the people realise we are departing, then I believe everything will come apart quickly. Make way,' he shouted aloud. 'Make way for the Crimson Castellans!'

People stared at them. Some cheered. Others muttered darkly. Kal and Marny were terrified by the opulence around them, and shrank into Yoth's sides at the crowd's attention.

'How goes the outer defence?' asked Yoth.

'The aerial swarm has retreated, brother-sergeant,' said Bost. 'The tyranids have won now, and they know it. We should be able to depart. If not, we shall fight our way free. It is after all but a short boost to orbit, and their aerial creatures cannot pursue us beyond the atmosphere. The evacuation has been unmolested. The last three shuttle loads bound for the *Lady Karomay* gather. As we planned, the third will not be leaving. A distasteful deception, but necessary if we are to extricate ourselves from this place and not die with it.'

'The majority of our serfs are evacuated,' added Bost. 'Gorth kept the neophytes here, but them aside, only ten of our men-at-arms remain. All others await us on the *Redoubt*.'

They took deserted corridors guarded by these last crimson-clad men. Osko and Philodon joined them. As they passed through each intersection, the men-at-arms fell in with them, casting wary looks behind.

'How fare you, brother?' said Philodon wryly, taking in Yoth's sorry state.

'Badly,' he said. He did not have energy for anything else.

They went through multiple doors to the outer bounds of the hive. A final set opened, leading them onto a flower-like landing pad cantilevered out from the side of the hive. Its armoured petals were closed, but as soon as the Space Marines set foot upon the pad, they ground open. Air roared out through the widening gaps. Gunfire sounded outside.

Awaiting them, its bold red and white colour scheme striking amidst the chrome and soft golds of Luggenhard, was their transport.

Gorth and the neophytes were already aboard. The survivors ran to the Thunderhawk as best they could before the air was all sucked away.

'My lord,' said Yoth before Gorth could speak. 'I bring these two with me, as the boy has been of much service. If it pleases you, I beg that you reconsider his induction into our Chapter. He passed the trial. His genetic coding is a match. Brother-Captain Raankin approved him. He has atoned for his insolence with his service to me. Whether he survives the process is down to him and him alone, but I will vouch for him as he strives. As long as he is with us, I will stand in responsibility for his actions.'

The Thunderhawk's ramp whirred shut. Marny stared open-mouthed around her.

Gorth frowned. They took their seats. The neophytes who knew Marny and Kal nodded at them, but there was already distance between them.

The gunship's engines rumbled into life and it took off at great acceleration, pushing them so hard into their seats that Marny blacked out momentarily and Yoth nearly broke his teeth grinding them against the pain. Weapons thumped away on the outside of the hull, but soon they were away. Ten minutes later they passed into space. An apothecarion serf attended to Yoth, checking the state of his wound via his armour.

As they flew to rendezvous with the *Redoubt*, Yoth summoned enough energy to explain Kal's actions in the hive. Gorth listened silently. When Yoth was done, he spoke directly to Kal. 'Perhaps I was wrong about you,' he said. 'According to my brother, you showed great mettle in the face of the enemy.'

'But... but... I failed. You said I was insubbled or something,' said Kal.

'Insubordinate, boy. The word is insubordinate,' said Yoth.

Kal looked at the floor. 'I didn't sabby the meaning.'

'Blind obedience is not the sole test of who we are. You passed one far greater,' continued Gorth. 'No trial I could set is the equal of what you did. Our way is of duty to the Imperium, and of sacrifice. You were willing to lay down your life to aid Brother-Sergeant Yoth. No doubt you regard that as the natural thing to do. It is not. The urge to survive, or only to flee, in the face of such alien horror often triumphs over human altruism, strong though that is. The question is, boy, can you learn to obey?'

Kal looked at Marny.

'Do it, Kal. Do it. I'll be okay. I never was the one for you.' She shot a sad look at Jimmo. He stared forwards, and did not acknowledge her.

Kal hesitated, suddenly grasping what Marny meant to tell him but could not. He looked up into Gorth's expressionless yellow eyes. 'I think I can, lord.'

'As do I. Not all men would agree with you, however.' Gorth looked to the remaining brothers. All gave barely perceptible nods.

'It is agreed, then. I retract my prior judgement. You are hereby offered a place among our neophytes. But I warn you, I shall set especial vigilance over you. I have violated one of my own principles in altering my ruling. Any deviation from our ways, any dereliction of duty or inability to master the warcraft of our Chapter will reflect doubly poorly on Yoth and myself as it will on you. For in this opportunity and its acceptance, you have taken upon yourself a bond of honour. We will not be dishonoured. Do you understand?'

Kal sat up straight. 'I give the noddy... I mean, I swear, that I will do my best to do right by you. I won't let you down, my lord.'

'The correct appellation is "Lord Chaplain".'

'Then I will not let you down, Lord Chaplain.'

Gorth gave him a long, hard look. 'See that you do not.'

'What about Marny, Lord Chaplain? She did right by Brother-Sergeant Yoth too...'

'I approve of your attempts at proper etiquette, but the correct term is "Lord Yoth",' said Gorth.

'She is a bold warrior,' said Yoth thickly. He was exhausted and the drugs pumped into his system by suit and serf dragged at his mind.

'We will see to it that the girl is housed and fed. But she cannot remain with us. If the Emperor wills it, we will find a place for her with some adepta or other, where she shall be trained to some useful service.' Gorth glowered at them all. 'I cannot and will not offer any more than that.'

Satisfied, Yoth let himself fall asleep, lulled by the rumble of the Thunderhawk's engines. He was grateful that Gorth did not interrogate him about the eldar just yet, although that was surely coming.

EPILOGUE

TO DÛRIEL

In the bosom of the webway, the Crystal Sons of Asuryan gathered around their leader. No song did they sing, nor talk make. They were silent and grim. They were at peace for the moment and it weighed upon them. Such warriors have no desire for peace.

Isarion was agitated. He addressed the Hand, the Phoenix Lord Asurmen. 'Great one, you must not risk yourself in such a manner. If you were to fall on a world like Ector, your body might prove irrecoverable. What then for the eldar, without the lord of all Phoenix Lords?'

'You presume much to tell me my business, prince of no world,' said Asurmen. 'This war is just beginning. The die is cast, and forces move upon this system that have not been seen since the days of glory. Here a beacon of hope will be kindled. Would you rather I stand by so that I fall not, while in my stead our race shall? There are no sacrifices too great to make, Isarion. You of all people know this. Do not forget it.'

Isarion bowed his head. 'It sorrows me to speak thusly, but I feel that I must. Why else did you bring me into your service, if I must remain as mute as your warriors?'

'They speak, young one, if they must. They have no need, and you do. Your advice is noted. I appreciate your timely deployment of our webway portal. Without it your dire warning may have come to pass, but no more! I am the Hand of Asuryan, and master of my own destiny.'

'Great one, I–'

'Hush now, another comes. What she has to say has greater import than our discussion here.'

From some fold in time and space, the slender form of Shadowseer Sylandri Veilwalker stepped into view. Isarion blinked. Already his mind was convinced she had always been there, listening quietly. The wonder of her appearance diminished. Since the loss of his throne, he had experienced a surfeit of marvels.

Sylandri cocked her head, her face hidden behind her mirrored mask. Isarion wondered what beauty was trapped within the polished bowl. A part of him whispered unbidden in his mind, 'Only shadow.' A tremor of horror afflicted him.

'Something troubles you, Isarion the Dispossessed?' she asked sweetly.

'N-no, my lady,' he stammered.

Sylandri laughed, a tinkling noise as beautiful as the shattering of mirrors. 'You lie badly. Tell me, quaking princeling, did the one named Yoth survive the battle?'

'Yes,' Isarion managed.

She clapped gloved hands together. Silver bells rang, although she wore none. 'That is good! Many threads converge here. It is a delicate time for our people in the present and the future. Yoth has his part to play when time demands. That he lives bodes well.

'But now, to matters imminent. All the pieces are set upon the board of Dûriel. It is time to make the play of ages. Should the initial stratagem succeed, the skein will quake and the restoration of our people go from unattainable dream to wild hope.

'The first move is complete,' she said. 'Now I say, to Dûriel without delay. The god of war calls, and he will not be denied.'

DEATHSTORM

JOSH REYNOLDS

PROLOGUE

ASPHODEX, CRYPTUS SYSTEM,
RED SCAR SECTOR, ULTIMA SEGMENTUM

The black flesh of the void was torn asunder by a sudden eruption of red as *Blade of Vengeance*, flagship of the Blood Angels fleet, thundered into real space, weapons batteries roaring out a brutal announcement of arrival. More ships followed, plunging out of the warp like coursing hounds. The massed batteries of the fleet joined those of the flagship in a dull, pulsing war-hymn. The burning remains of the Cryptus System's defence monitors were swept aside by the song, the detritus of their final heroic stand against the enemy washed away by volley after volley of high-powered energy beams.

The audience for whom this sudden performance was intended was not appreciative. The vast shapes of the outlying bio-ships of the tyranid hive fleet, their bloated, shimmering forms faintly reflecting the deadly red light of Cryptus's twin suns, reeled and shuddered like wounded animals as the fusillade cracked their shells and ruptured the soft contents.

The Blood Angels fleet swept forwards with slow deliberation, bombardment cannons sweeping aside the swarms of escort drones which leapt from the flanks of the massive bio-ships and spiralled into death with unseemly eagerness.

Such was the considered opinion of Captain Karlaen, as he watched the performance unfold through the massive vista-port of the flagship. Ships moved across his vision, pummelling one another in a grand dance of life and death, duty and instinct, honour and abomination. The arched, cathedral-like space of the vessel's tacticum-vaults echoed with the relentless song of war. Karlaen could feel the roar of every cannonade through the deck-plates beneath his feet and in the flicker of every hololith display as enemy volleys spattered across the battle-barge's void shields.

This battle was merely a microcosm of a greater engagement which now spread across the Cryptus System and the Red Scar Sector. The monstrous shadow of Hive Fleet Leviathan, as the Ordo Xenos had classified this particular xenos incursion, stretched across countless worlds, being enveloping Segmentums Ultima, Tempestus and Solar. Worlds were being scoured clean by the Great Devourer, and even the most sacred sites of the Imperium were under threat, including Baal, home world of the Blood Angels.

When the bow-wave of Hive Fleet Leviathan washed across the Cryptus

System, the Imperium had met it with all of the strength that the Astra Militarum, Adepta Sororitas and the household troops of the ruling Flaxian Dynasty could muster. But orbital defences and massed gun-lines had proven unequal to the task. Within a cycle, tyrannic spores were darkening the skies of every major world within the Cryptus System. And now, at last, the Blood Angels and Flesh Tearers Space Marine Chapters had arrived to deprive the monster of its feast. Though the system was lost, they could at least diminish the biomass that the hive fleet might recycle and use against Baal.

All of this passed across Karlaen's mind as he watched the Blood Angels fleet engage the enemy. Battle was a thing of vivid colour and riotous fury, even in the cold, airless void of space, and he felt something in him stir as he considered it – like a persistent, red hum deep below the surface of his thoughts. It had been with him since the day of his Sanguination, but familiarity did not breed affection. His reflection stared back at him from within the slightly shimmering surface of the vista-port. A battered face, blunt and square and lacking all but a trace of its former good looks – acid scars pitted his cheeks and jaw; his hair was a grizzled golden stubble that clung stubbornly to his scalp and his nose had been shattered and rebuilt more than once. A bionic eye occupied one ruined socket, and the magna-lens of the prosthetic orb whirred to life as he examined his reflection, seeking out some niggling imperfection that he could not name.

He was clad, as was his right and honour as commander of the First Company, in the blessed plate of Terminator armour. It was the toughest and most powerful form of personal armour ever developed by the Imperium of Man: a heavy blood-red shell of ceramite-bonded plates, chased with gilding and brass, reinforced by sections of plasteel and adamantium and all of it powered by thick bundles of electrical fibres and internal suspensor-plates.

It had taken twenty red-robed Chapter serfs and dull, cog-brained servitors to encase him within it, hours earlier, when the prospect of a boarding action first reared its head – they had worked feverishly, connecting fibre bundles to nodes using spidery, mechanical limbs which possessed the inhuman dexterity required for such a precise task. Others had cleared air and build-up from the pistons and pneumatic servo-muscles that enabled him to move, while the senior serfs, their gilded masks betraying no emotion, polished the ceramite with sweet smelling unguents and blessed oils, awakening the primitive soul of the ancient relic, stirring it to wrathful waking. The armour was heavy and powerful, and, in those moments when he succumbed to the lure of poetry, Karlaen thought that it might be the closest thing going to the Word of the God-Emperor made harsh reality.

Karlaen raised a hand, his fingers tracing the outline of the Crux Terminatus on his left shoulder plate. It was said that the symbol contained a shard of the Emperor's own Terminator armour, which had been shattered in that final, catastrophic duel with the Arch-Traitor in ages past. At the thought, Karlaen's breath hitched in his throat, and his vision blurred, as the red hum grew louder, now pounding where it had pulsed, as if a thousand hammers were beating on the walls of his skull, fighting to be free. For a moment, his vision blurred, and he saw a different face, not his own familiar battered features, but *a handsome and radiant face which he recognised but could not name, twisted in loss and pain the likes of which no mortal could bear, and he heard the snap of great wings, and felt the rush of heat and pain and* his fingers touched the surface of the void-hardened glass.

He closed his eyes. Swallowed thickly. Opened his eyes. He looked up at the stained glass which marked the circumference of the vista-port. It showed scenes from Imperial history – the discovery of Sanguinius on Baal Secundus by the Emperor; Sanguinius, angel-winged and radiant, taking command of the Ninth Legion; other scenes, dozens, hundreds, all depicting the glorious history of the Blood Angels, a history which had shaped Karlaen, and made him who he was today. *I am Karlaen,* he thought. *I am Captain of the First, the Shield of Baal, and I am true to myself. I am not flesh, to be swept up in the blood-dimmed tide, but stone. And stone does not move or yield to those red waters, no matter how they crash.* The hum faded, hammer blows becoming taps, and the pressure retreated as it always had. Irritated with himself, he concentrated on the world beyond the curtain of void war.

Asphodex – it was an inelegant word for an inelegant world. Beyond the shifting, shimmering distortion of the battle-barge's void shield, behind the bloated shapes of the bio-ships which clustered about its atmosphere like feeding ticks, Asphodex roiled in its death throes. The magna-lens of Karlaen's bionic eye whirred to its next setting, bringing the world into stark relief. The heavy grey clouds which shrouded the atmosphere were shot through with infected-looking strands of purple, each one squirming with billions of tiny shapes. The lens clicked again, focusing on the bio-ships clustered about the world's poles. As they moved across the atmosphere, he could see corresponding disturbances in the clouds. Someone joined him at the vista-port. 'They are feeding,' Karlaen said, out loud.

'Yes,' Sanguinary High Priest Corbulo said softly. Clad in crimson power armour edged with white, he was the spitting image of the face which haunted the black dreams and red memories of Karlaen and every Space Marine of the Blood Angels Chapter. His voice, too, throbbed at the roots of Karlaen's mind, stirring to life ancient thoughts which were not his own. Corbulo was a ghost, though whether of the Chapter's past or its future, none could say. 'That is what they do, captain.'

'They will strip the planet of all life soon,' Karlaen continued. He had seen planets caught in the grip of the Great Devourer before, and had calculated Asphodex's chances of survival on an idle whim. The planet was doomed. He looked at Corbulo. 'Why am I here, Master Corbulo? I should be making ready to–'

'To what, Captain Karlaen?' Corbulo asked. His voice was gentle, but resonant, like the crash of waves against a distant shore. He looked at Karlaen, and his eyes caught and held Karlaen's own. They were deep and pale and powerful, and Karlaen felt the red hum in his head grow in strength. He looked away. 'You are exactly where you should be, captain.' Corbulo spoke with such surety that Karlaen could not help but feel an atavistic thrill course through him.

'As you say, master,' Karlaen said. He kept his face stiff and still.

Corbulo smiled, as if he could sense Karlaen's reluctance. 'I cannot help but feel as if you doubt me, brother,' he said.

'Detecting doubt – or worry, anger, or any other emotion for that matter – on Karlaen's face is a skill akin to the detection of geological shifts on Baal, Corbulo. One must know where to look for cracks in the stone. Isn't that right, brother?'

Both Karlaen and Corbulo turned as Commander Dante, Chapter Master of the Blood Angels, strode towards them, his golden artificer armour gleaming in the reflected light of the hololiths that studded the tacticum-vaults. His features were hidden, as ever, behind the golden mask which was said to have been modelled on the features of Sanguinius himself.

Karlaen inclined his head. 'As you say, commander.'

Dante looked at Corbulo. He gestured to Karlaen. 'You see? Stone,' he said. 'Karlaen is the rock upon which the First Company stands.' He looked at Karlaen, his gaze taking in everything and missing nothing. Karlaen, for his part, could only hold his superior's stare for a few moments before it became unbearable. Dante was the oldest living Space Marine in the Imperium who could still function outside of the sarcophagus of a Dreadnought, and he carried with him the weight of history wherever he went. Like Corbulo, his very presence stirred the red hum in Karlaen's head to fretful agitation.

Karlaen made to sink to one knee, but Dante gestured irritably. 'No,' he said. 'No, I am in no mood for such gestures today, captain.'

Stung, Karlaen straightened, the joints of his armour wheezing and hissing in protest. Dante crossed his arms and gazed up at the vista-port. The flagship shivered slightly around them, and the void shield writhed as it was struck. Dante said, 'Report, captain.'

On firmer ground now, Karlaen cleared his throat. 'The first wave of the assault is preparing for their descent to Phodia,' he said, referring to the principal city of Asphodex. He did not think it tactful to mention that, as Captain of the First Company, he should have been overseeing those preparations.

'You are wondering why you are here, rather than there,' Dante said. It was not a question. Karlaen looked at Corbulo.

'You see, he is too disciplined to ask, though I have no doubt that curiosity is eating at him.'

'Discipline is the armour of a man's soul,' Corbulo said.

Karlaen looked back and forth between them, vaguely concerned. When the summons had come, he had not known what to expect. Was the honour of leading the vanguard to be taken from him? The question would not have occurred to him, once upon a time. But now, after... His mind shied away from the thought. Shadows clustered at the edges of his memory, and voices demanded to be heard. He closed his eye and shook his head, banishing shadows and voices both. When he looked up, he realised that both Dante and Corbulo were watching him. Corbulo reached out and clapped a hand to his arm.

'I hear them as well, brother. Do you wish to know what they say?' he asked, his voice barely above a whisper, and his eyes full of quiet contemplation.

Karlaen ignored the Sanguinary Priest and looked at Dante. 'I wish only to know what is required of me, my lord. I am the Shield of Baal, and I would serve as you see fit.'

Dante was silent for a moment. Then, he said, 'You are still leading the assault, captain. And Phodia is still your target. But I require more than simple battlefield logistics from you this time.' He looked at Corbulo.

The Sanguinary High Priest said, 'Augustus Flax.'

Karlaen blinked. 'The Governor of Asphodex.' Part of his responsibilities as Captain of the First was to know everything there was to know about potential battlefields – everything from weather patterns to cultural dialects was of potential importance when planning for war, and Karlaen had studied and synthesised all of it.

He knew everything there was to know about the Flaxian Dynasty, and its current head. Augustus Flax had assumed the gubernatorial seat at the tender age of seventeen standard Terran years, after his father, the previous office holder, had been murdered by separatists in a civil war which had briefly, though bloodily, rocked the Cryptus System. Flax was an old man now, and his reign had been an unmitigated success, as far as these things were concerned. Karlaen felt a small stab of pity for the man – the system he had reportedly fought so hard to retain control of and hold together was now being devoured out from under him.

'Yes. I – we – need him found, brother.' Corbulo looked towards the vista-port. Silent explosions cascaded across the face of the void, as ships continued their duel. Karlaen cocked his head. Questions filled his mind, but he clamped down on them. His was not to question, merely to serve.

'Then I will find him, Master Corbulo,' he said.

'He or his children will do,' Corbulo said. 'Failing that, a sample of their blood.'

More questions arose, but Karlaen ignored them. If Corbulo was here, and this mission was being undertaken at his counsel, then there could be only one reason for it. Corbulo's overriding passion was no secret. The Sanguinary High Priest had one desire above all others: the elimination of the twin plagues which afflicted the sons of Sanguinius, whether they were Blood Angels, Flesh Tearers or Angels Encarmine. Corbulo had dedicated his life to unravelling the secrets of the Red Thirst and the Black Rage, and had spent centuries on the hunt for anything which might alleviate the suffering of Sanguinius's children.

Karlaen bowed. 'It will be done, on my honour and the honour of the First Company. Or else I shall die in the attempt.' He straightened. 'I will need to requisition a gunship, or a drop pod...'

'Speed is of the essence, brother,' Dante said. 'Time grows short, and Asphodex dies even as we speak. This world will be consumed by the beast, and we do not have time for you and your Archangels to attempt an entry from orbit,' he said. 'Report to the teleportarium. Your men will be waiting for you there.'

'Teleportation,' Karlaen said. He grimaced. There were few things that could stir the embers of fear in Karlaen's heart, but teleportation was one of them. There was something wrong with it, with how it worked. There was no control, no precision, only blind luck. He shook himself slightly. He knew that Dante would not have authorised it if it were not necessary. Countless battles had been won with just such a strategy, and Karlaen reassured himself that this time would be no different.

He looked at Dante. 'As you command, my lord. I will not fail you.'

'You never have, captain,' Dante said.

Karlaen turned away and took one last look at the war-torn heavens and the dying world. There was nothing but blood and death lurking beneath those grey clouds. If Augustus Flax, or any of his kin, still lived, it would not be for long. Yet his orders were clear.

It was his duty to find Augustus Flax, and the Shield of Baal would see it done.

CHAPTER ONE

PHODIA, ASPHODEX

The air of the continent-sized city had been thick with black toxicity, even before the arrival of the tyranids. Beneath the choking darkness and roiling clouds, billions had slaved and died in manufactorums and vapour-farms at the behest of the city's overlords. Now, where man's industry had once claimed and poisoned the air and ground, new masters set their mark. Alien growths coiled and crawled about the battle-scarred ruins of the Planetary Governor's palace, and hundreds of fume-spewing spore-chimneys had thrust up through the cracked and broken surface of the ground, masking the faded grandeur of the city skyline in a forest of monstrous growth.

Among the rubble, clicking feeder-beasts feasted upon the hillocks of corpses which lay like a thick carpet throughout the structure. Many-limbed shadows moved through the upper reaches of the ruins, and alien voices stuttered and warbled in a song of ending. The song ceased abruptly, as the air became greasy and metallic. There was a sound like thunder, and arcing lighting of an unnatural hue sparked and snapped to sudden life. The feeder-beasts scattered with frustrated squeals and protests as the lightning swirled, flashed and faded, revealing heavy, crimson figures. The Archangels had arrived.

Twenty carmine-armoured Terminators stood on a patch of scorched stone. They were among the greatest warriors of a Chapter replete with such, and each of them had participated in dozens of gruelling defences and surgical strikes, against tyranids as well as orks and every other enemy that had dared test the might of the Imperium. Karlaen had chosen from among the most battle-tested for this mission, and each of them had stood with him at Balor's Hope, as well as participating in the destruction of the space hulks *Divine Purgatory* and *Twilight Aegis*.

'Well, isn't this pleasant?' one of the Terminators said, the vox-amplifiers of his helmet transforming his voice into a crackling growl. Brother Aphrae, Karlaen knew, recognised the Terminator by his vox-signature and the delicate coiling script flowing across the scroll stretched across the front of his chestplate. Aphrae had a passion for calligraphy, as well as an inability to properly observe vox protocols.

'No,' Karlaen said. 'Fan out and establish a perimeter – I want detailed augur scans and vox-channel analysis before we move out.' Long-range auspex echoes taken by the fleet had proven disappointingly vague, and teleportation was not an exact science. He needed to be certain that they were where they were supposed to be in the Tribune District, and that meant triangulating their exact position via vox signals and augur readings. 'Alphaeus – you know what to do,' he said, looking to the closest Terminator.

'When has it ever been otherwise?' Alphaeus rumbled, dropping one gauntlet to the pommel of the power sword sheathed on his hip. The Terminator sergeant had served with Karlaen longer than any other Space Marine, and familiarity had bred a congenial deference that Karlaen still found slightly disconcerting.

He had chosen Alphaeus as his second-in-command for good reason. Among the warriors of the First Company, there were none, save himself, with greater experience in battling the scuttling minions of the Great Devourer than Alphaeus and his squad – jocular Aphrae, taciturn Bartelo, and the twins, Damaris and Leonos. The latter pair snapped to attention as Alphaeus ordered them to scout ahead, and then turned to relay orders to the other squads. Satisfied that Alphaeus would see to things, Karlaen scanned their surroundings.

The city was already being consumed; the presence of the feeder-beasts and the spore-chimneys were proof enough of that. He had seen similar sights often enough, but it never failed to awaken a thrill of revulsion in him to see humanity and all of its artifice reduced to a slurry of protein and bio-matter. Death was one thing, but the tyranids took even what little dignity remained afterwards.

His fingers tightened on the reinforced haft of the master-crafted thunder hammer he carried. The Hammer of Baal was one of the most exquisite relics possessed by the Blood Angels Chapter; it had been forged by master artisans millennia ago, and entrusted into Karlaen's care by Dante himself, upon his ascension to the rank of Captain of the First Company. The weapon hummed with barely restrained power. It was much like its wielder in that regard. Karlaen lifted the ancient weapon and rested it against his shoulder plate.

He turned, his bionic eye whirring and magnifying the landscape. Rotting corpses and the burning wreckage of battle tanks stretched as far as the eye could see. For a few brief days the world had been a battlefront, and the soldiers of the Imperium had made the tyranids pay a bloody toll for every patch of ground. He checked his suit's augurs, searching for any life signs among the carnage.

'They died well,' Alphaeus said.

Karlaen turned. 'Report,' he said.

'We're probably in the right place.' The sergeant had removed his helmet, revealing a shorn scalp and a permanently determined expression. A service stud gleamed over his right eye. As Karlaen watched, he sucked in a great lungful of toxic air. 'Paaaah,' Alphaeus grunted. 'Smells like home. If home was an overgrown sludge pit.'

'Which it is,' Aphrae called out, from where he stood examining a spore-chimney. He lifted his chainfist in considering fashion. The weapon groaned to life, and the teeth rotated with a snarl that echoed across the plaza.

Before Karlaen could move to stop Aphrae, Alphaeus barked, 'Aphrae, please refrain from whatever it is you're planning to do.' He looked back at Karlaen. 'We were able to scrape the recordings from the orbital vox-arrays, but that information is days old at best. This looks like a palace forecourt, if that helps.' He gestured towards the immense, battle-blasted archway that dominated the other side of the plaza. Great steps, each one a hundred metres wide, rose up towards what he suspected were the remains of the Phodian Gates, the entrance to the palace. 'Those steps are definitely palatial, in my considered opinion.'

'You know a lot about steps, then?' Karlaen asked, examining the archway.

'I know about architecture. You can tell a lot about a people from their architecture.'

Karlaen glanced at Alphaeus, who ran his palm over his bare scalp in a gesture of contemplation.

'I could be wrong, of course. Who knows what sort of upheaval the planet has gone through since those vox-arrays were functional? Remember Fulcrum Six? The whole southern continent folded up like a leaf caught in a blast of heat,' said Alphaeus.

'This isn't Fulcrum Six,' Karlaen replied, smiling slightly.

'No, and thank the Emperor for that.' Alphaeus stamped the ground. 'I don't approve of continental land masses shifting unexpectedly.' He looked around suspiciously. 'I don't approve of this either.'

'This place is an abomination unto the eyes of the Emperor,' Bartelo said glumly, gesturing at the spore-chimney with the barrel of the heavy flamer he carried. It took a special sort of warrior to go into battle equipped with what was a highly volatile amount of promethium mixture strapped to them – one ruptured hose, or clogged mechanism, and Bartelo would be cooked inside his armour quicker than he could scream. But he seemed to take pride in his position as fire-bearer for Alphaeus's squad, and he was skilled at employing the cleansing flames to greatest effect.

'So is wasting valuable promethium. Stay alert,' Alphaeus said. He shook his head and cocked an eye up at the dark sky. 'Gargoyles,' he murmured.

Karlaen looked up. The magna-lens of his bionic eye spun, focusing in on the innumerable swarms of winged bio-beasts swirling across the horizon like a vast tornado of fangs and talons. 'Where are they going?' he murmured.

'East,' Alphaeus said.

'What's east of here?'

'Organic–' Damaris began.

'–matter,' Leonos finished.

Karlaen looked at the two Terminators as they trudged towards him and the sergeant. Some quirk of the Sanguination process had taken two unrelated men and made them replicas of one another, as if they had been cast from the same mould. Even through the vox-link, their mellifluous voices sounded identical, down to the slightly strained intonation. With their helmets off, they reminded him of Corbulo, with too-perfect features that belonged on the ivy-shrouded statues of long-forgotten deities rather than on men.

'There's fighting to the east, in the area around the manufactorums,' Leonos said. 'This whole district looks as if it's been left to the feeder-beasts.'

Karlaen quickly flicked through the vox-channels. Most were clouded with interference from the hive fleet, but he quickly hit upon cries for aid and pleas for reinforcement. Just as he found them, something exploded in the distance. The front had moved east, the Imperial battle lines battered back by the ravenous hordes of bio-beasts.

'The fabricae districts,' Alphaeus said. He frowned. 'It's a last stand.'

Karlaen said nothing. The vox crackled, as the screams of the soldiers of the Astra Militarum filled his ears. Part of him yearned to take his men and strike out for the manufactorums where the last defenders of Phodia were selling their lives in the mistaken assumption that help was coming. But those were not his orders, and that was not what the Sons of Sanguinius were here for this day.

Asphodex was a firebreak and nothing more. The war against Hive Fleet Leviathan would not be decided here, or indeed anywhere in the Cryptus System. But this tendril of it would be annihilated. Within a few standard hours, the remainder of the Blood Angels First Company and the full strength of the Second – supported by elements of their successors, the Flesh Tearers – would be making planetfall. Then the true war would begin. A war of annihilation, a war to taint the wells and break the supply lines of the enemy. A war that the chosen of Baal knew well how to fight.

But that was still in the future. For now, Karlaen had his mission. 'Form up and fan out. We will proceed,' he said, shutting off the transmissions. Alphaeus nodded and pinged the vox, alerting the other squads that it was time to move out, even as Leonos and Aphrae joined them.

In moments, a line of crimson-armoured giants was on the move, marching across the plaza towards the great archway that was the Phodian Gates. As they climbed the steps, Karlaen took in the carnage which stretched up the steps to the entry plateau. The corpses of Imperial Guardsmen were piled in messy heaps among tumbled sandbag emplacements. The stink of alien ichor was strong here, and dead tyranid weapon-beasts lay where they had fallen, brought down by the guns of the Astra Militarum.

At the top of the steps, the broken corpse of an Imperial Guard officer bore silent witness to the approach of the Blood Angels, his dead gaze staring out at the battlefield defiantly. He still clutched a bolt pistol in one bloodied fist.

Karlaen sank down to one knee beside the corpse, which lay propped up against the scorched and shattered archway. He studied the slack features, memorising them as he had done a thousand times before. His warriors stood silently, understanding that this was a sacred moment, and one that they themselves might have to perform one day.

This man, Karlaen thought, had been a hero, though they did not know his name. He had died unsung, and would not be remembered by any save themselves. But they would remember him. The Blood Angels always remembered, even when the memory proved burdensome. 'Sleep, soldier,' Karlaen murmured, the familiar words escaping him with ease. 'Lay down your burden, and return to the Emperor's light. Your fight is now ours. And we will make them pay, measure for measure.' He reached out and closed the staring eyes.

He stood. 'Come,' he said. 'We have a governor to find.'

Across the plaza from the armoured giants, hidden by the fallen bulk of a statue of the Emperor, a pair of alien eyes watched the Blood Angels enter the governing palace of the Flaxian Dynasty. White, vestigial lips peeled back from a wall of clenched fangs as the flat, crimson eyes of the creature once called the Spawn of Cryptus narrowed in baleful interest.

As the Blood Angels vanished into the interior of the palace, the broodlord pushed itself upright, its four arms clutching at the statue. It rose to its full height, tasting the air. The fires of distant battle were reflected in its pale, shiny carapace. It cocked its bulbous skull, listening to the distant drumbeat of battle. Hundreds of kilometres away, the defenders of Phodia were waging their final battle against the forces of the Hive Mind, and the Spawn of Cryptus could feel the ebb and flow of that conflict in every fibre of its grotesque being.

It longed to join that distant fray and wet its talons in the blood of its enemies. That was what the Hive Mind asked of it, whispered to it, deep in its skull. The song of the Hive Mind filled its head, driving out all other thoughts save those which moved in time to the cosmic rhapsody of aeons. It was a song of consumption and survival, of grand design and joining. The song filled it and warmed it, driving out fear and anger and leaving behind only iron purpose.

The broodlord shook its large head and gave a snort. There were yet things to be done – important things, more important even than the all-consuming song of the forces that had guided it up out of the darkness and into the light.

It had lived on Asphodex for years, long before the coming of the Leviathan whose shadow even now lay over its monstrous soul. The people of Phodia had given it its name, and the raconteurs among them had claimed that it was a child of their solar god, sent to punish them for their transgressions. The creature found some small amusement in that, for the storytellers were not far wrong.

That amusement was not in evidence now, as it watched the red giants disturb and disperse the feeder-beasts as they tromped into the demesne that it had claimed as its own. It had never seen such beings before in all the years of its long life, but it knew them for enemies even so. It could taste the harsh violence of their thoughts, even at this distance, and its long, crimson tongue flicked out from within its thicket of teeth to lash and curl momentarily, before retreating back into its maw.

It did not know what they were after, and annoyance burned across the surface of its brain like a black comet. Their minds were open to it, and it could smell their intent to enter the palace as if it were the scent of prey carried upon the night wind. Its talons dug frustrated grooves into the stones around it, and it hissed in growing anger.

For a brief instant, the song of the Hive Mind grew ragged and weak, and the old pain came back, thundering to the fore of its mind. It saw faces, fleshy and soft, but familiar, and a whine of agony escaped it. A single quavering note of loss, swiftly borne under and erased by the snarl that followed. The Spawn of Cryptus shook itself, sending the fragments of memory fleeing. With a single fluid movement, the beast leapt down from its perch and crept into the ruins, claws clicking. Lesser creatures fled before it, and in return for such obeisance, it duly ignored them.

It would gather its brood. It was past time for the Children of Cryptus to have their due.

CHAPTER TWO

TRIBUNE CHAMBER, FLAXIAN PALACE, PHODIA

The interior of the palace was just as much a scene of horror as the plaza outside. The stab-lights mounted on the Terminators' armour illuminated signs of a ferocious running battle as they moved through the immense, shadowy corridors. The exquisite artworks which had once covered the high walls were torn and pitted by acidic bile, lasgun fire and the heavy craters left behind by shellfire. The floor was carpeted in the dead, both human and otherwise. And everywhere, clicking, clattering ripper swarms worked to render the mangled heaps of blood and bone down into something more palatable.

The signs of the Hive Mind's consumption were everywhere. Whole side corridors and cathedral-like foyers had been given over to the bubbling, noxious digestion pools of the feeder-beasts. As the Terminators pushed deeper into the depths of the palace, grisly shapes flapped, crawled and scuttled just out of sensor range.

When they reached the entrance to what Karlaen though must be the governor's Tribune Chamber, he raised his hammer, signalling a halt.

'We go our separate ways from here, brothers,' he said. He swept the hammer out, indicating the corridors diverging from the central hall they now stood in. 'Four squads can search more swiftly than one, and time is not on our side in this place.' As if to punctuate this statement, the dull boom of distant explosions rolled through the corridors, echoing and re-echoing throughout the wide, vaulted spaces.

'Melos, you and your squad take the western sector,' Karlaen continued, gesturing to the Terminator in question. Melos stroked the gilded skull set into his gorget and nodded. Melos's relic armour had a reputation, Karlaen recalled. He hoped that it would serve Melos better than it had all its other owners. 'Joses, the east,' he continued, pushing the thought aside. Joses grunted, and hefted his storm bolter. Like Alphaeus, he was bareheaded, and he had battle-scarred features. Karlaen looked at the last of his subordinates. 'Zachreal...'

'Up,' Zachreal rumbled, pointing a finger towards the upper levels of the palace. His crimson armour was scored by hundreds of gouges, battle scars earned over the course of a hundred-odd boarding actions, and a trio of silently fuming, golden censers hung from his chestplate, filling the air around him with a vermilion mist. 'Always send somebody to clear the upper decks, captain.'

'Then that honour falls to you,' Karlaen said. He looked at Alphaeus. "I'll accompany your squad, Alphaeus, if you'll have me. We'll keep moving forwards, through the Tribune Chamber, and sweep the heart of the palace.'

'If we must,' Alphaeus said, smiling slightly.

Karlaen ignored the Terminator's attempt at humour, and said, 'Observe vox protocol. This is no different than any floating hulk we've boarded in the past.'

'Except that it's a building, won't lose gravity, and we damn well know it's full of tyranids, rather than merely suspecting that such is the case,' Aphrae piped up. Bartelo gave a snort of sour laughter, and the twins chuckled.

'Quiet,' Alphaeus snapped.

Karlaen ignored the by-play. He had fought beside Alphaeus and his squad often enough to know that Aphrae's jocularity, misplaced as it was, was as necessary to the unit's survival as the promethium in Bartelo's tanks. Laughter was the gates of the soul, as discipline was its walls. 'If you find any sign of the governor, you are to retrieve him, dead or alive, and fall back to the Plaza of the Emperor Ascendant for extraction. The plaza will be rallying-point alpha in the event of overwhelming resistance. Do not hesitate to fall back, should it be necessary. Pride is merely the seed of hubris, and death without victory is wasted,' he said, quoting a line from the *Philosophies of Raldoron*. He looked about him as he spoke, trying to impress the gravity of the situation upon his men. 'Eyes open, sensors on, my brothers. May the wings of our father shield you from the rains of bad fortune.'

He turned back to Alphaeus and his squad as the others slowly moved off, each to their designated sector of search. The dark of the chamber swallowed the bobbing stab-lights of the others, until only the six remained, standing before the Tribune Chamber. Karlaen hesitated for a moment, and then said, 'I will take point.'

'Captain–' Alphaeus began.

Karlaen ignored him, and moved towards the beckoning gloom of the entryway. The passage was blocked by the piled sandbags of a heavy bolter emplacement. Without pausing, he shoved his way through it. The servos in his armour hummed softly as he toppled the heavy gun platform and sent the headless body of the gunner slumping to the ground. A moment later, his stab-lights illuminated the interior of the Tribune Chamber.

In better times, the governor would have held audience with his district lords here. It was large enough to land a squadron of the Chapter's Stormravens. He let his stab-lights play across the curve of the vast, domed ceiling, but they could only pierce the edges of the darkness that marked it. It was simply too high and wide.

He looked around as he moved forwards. The chamber was marked by twisted debris and toppled statues. Whole sections of the upper floors had collapsed down, puncturing the floor, and amidst the structural devastation, the bodies of hundreds of Imperial citizens lay, heaped in great, gory mounds of mutilated meat and shattered bone. Karlaen had seen far worse butchery in his time, but it never failed to give him pause.

There was a stark contrast between the slaughter that had taken place in the plaza and what he saw before him. The red hum pulsed along the underside of his mind, and he felt a wash of anger. They had been innocents, not soldiers – civilians seeking sanctuary from the horrors that stalked their world. The soldiers outside had died trying to protect them, and it had all been for nothing.

No, not nothing, said a small voice inside him. *Some good may yet come of this, if you succeed.* That was what Corbulo would have said, had he been here; Karlaen gripped the thought as if it were a holy relic, and drew what strength he could from it. 'Necessity is the shield of faith,' he murmured. It was another line from the *Philosophies of Raldoron*. The text was a comfort to him in moments of doubt. Such moments had become far too common for Karlaen, but the words of the Equerry to the Primarch and first Chapter Master of the Blood Angels had ever brought him back to certainty.

While he spoke, the red hum faded, replaced by another sensation – that of a prickling on the back of his neck. Swiftly, he swept the chamber with his bionic eye, flicking through the different settings, hunting something he could not name. He was being watched, though he could detect no life in the chamber. Their enemies were close.

He waved Alphaeus and the others forward. The Terminators fanned out, scanning the mounds of corpses with augurs and eyes alike. 'Search the dead,' Karlaen ordered. 'If Flax and his men fell here, his body may still be salvageable.'

'And if not?' Aphrae asked.

'Then we keep looking,' Karlaen said.

'What if he's not here?' Aphrae pressed. 'What if he's in the manufactorums or in the Agrarian District? What do we do then?'

'I suppose we'll just give up, Aphrae. Is that what you'd like to hear?' Alphaeus said harshly. 'Would you like to inform Commander Dante that we failed, or shall I do it?'

'I was just asking, sergeant,' Aphrae said jovially. 'Just trying to establish mission parameters.'

'It could be worse,' Bartelo said morosely.

'And how, pray tell, oh sour one, could it be worse?' Aphrae said.

'We could be waist-deep in corpses, rather than just knee-deep,' Bartelo said, pushing over a pile of bodies with the barrel of his heavy flamer.

'Quiet, all of you,' Karlaen said. He shoved the broken corpse of a man aside with a gentle tap from his hammer and activated the bionic augur-lens in his prosthetic eye, seeking any sign of human life or of the specific genetic code which he had been tasked to retrieve. *It always comes back to blood, with us,* he thought. With Corbulo, especially, of late. There was a flaw in the Sons of Sanguinius, a flaw which spread down through their successors like a crack in marble, growing wider and more obvious the further down it spread. And Corbulo was determined to repair that flaw by any means necessary. Even if it meant sending warriors to dig through a world turned charnel pit.

He tossed aside another body, and paused. Through a haze of auspex data, he had caught a glimmer of something – a ghost-reading, snaking through the lines of code and readouts, slithering towards him beneath the blanket of corpses. Even as he registered this, he caught a whiff of a familiar, acrid odour – almost insect-like, but not quite. He turned his head slowly, letting the bio-augur play across his immediate area. More ghost-signals, sliding hidden beneath the charnel detritus, zeroing in on him and his men with deadly surety.

The sound of him readying his storm bolter was loud in the stultifying silence of the chamber. Alphaeus looked at him. Karlaen nodded, once, tersely. Alphaeus lifted his own storm bolter. Karlaen turned back to the pile of corpses before him. The dead shifted, slightly. He took one step back, narrowly avoiding a spray of gore as the bodies exploded outwards as something large, with far too many arms and teeth, lunged for him out of concealment.

The storm bolter in his hand thundered, and the genestealer was reduced to purple mist and ragged tatters of alien flesh. But there were more where it had come from, and they made themselves known a microsecond later. All around him, throughout the vast chamber, the heaps of the dead burst like foul seed pods, disgorging multi-limbed monstrosities. Genestealers scuttled towards the Terminators from every shadowed recess and hillock of rotting remains, jaws agape and claws clicking.

The broodlord hung suspended far above the heads of its chosen prey, clinging to a fire-blasted shank of support girder with four of its six limbs. It rotated its head, following the massive, red forms of the invaders as they entered the Tribune Chamber. There were only six of them now – the others had split, forming smaller packs.

This pleased the Spawn of Cryptus. Divided prey was easy prey, as it had learned in its infancy down in the bowels of Phodia's substructure. It had hunted gangers and slaves in those dark, cramped tunnels, growing strong on their flesh and fear. It had only taken what was its by right of blood, as it had when it had overseen the taking of this palace – its palace. Its flat, red eyes narrowed and its head throbbed as it reached out with its singular will and touched the gestalt mind of its fellow tyranids, scattered throughout the palace.

It inhaled sharply, suddenly able to see... everything. Through the eyes of its kin, it watched as the other armoured giants made their ponderous way through the eastern sector of the palace, and the western, and the high gardens which marked the upper levels. It saw them all, from dozens of angles, heights and positions, and it shook itself slightly as it fought to control the sheer flow of sensory information that flooded its mind.

The broodlord had always had the power to cloud the minds of its prey, and to feel the thoughts of its children as they went about its business. But since the coming of the Leviathan, those powers had grown exponentially, so much so that their use now pained it slightly. Sending out its thoughts to lance through the minds of the nearby tyranids was akin to stretching a limb to the breaking point and holding it there until just on the cusp of agony. But where once it had only been able to influence, it could now compel.

It shuddered on its perch as it felt the wet scraping of movement from its children and their kin, who had come to Asphodex in the belly of the beast but whose minds tasted of familiar things. Its thoughts pulsed outward, spreading like ripples in a puddle, touching hundreds of bestial minds. Silently, it stirred them to wakefulness, and then into a killing fury, filling their primitive skulls with its own boiling rage.

The giants had come to interfere in the Hive Mind's plans somehow and it would not allow that. After everything it had done, after everything it had endured, it was *owed* this moment. A gurgling hiss escaped it, as it leapt from its perch and dropped towards the shadows below.

Phodia belonged to it. The city and everything in it was its by right. And no red-shelled invader would prevent it from taking its fair due in the time Asphodex had left.

CHAPTER THREE

'Back to back, brothers. Don't let them isolate us,' Alphaeus roared, shouting to be heard over the noise of the storm bolters. Karlaen backed away, still firing. For every beast he put down, two more seemed to take its place, bounding out of the dark.

The genestealers came at the embattled Terminators from every direction, flinging themselves into battle. Normally, genestealers were canny, crafty beings, but these seemed to have been goaded into a fury. Karlaen knew from experience that such berserk tactics were nothing less than the influence of the Hive Mind at work. He twisted, avoiding a slashing claw. Genestealers could peel open battle tanks with ease; Terminator armour, while tough, was little obstacle to them. A genestealer came at him, darting in and out of his reach, trying to find a weak point. He stepped back, and something squelched beneath him. Servos whined as he fought the momentary imbalance. The genestealer lunged. Karlaen spun his hammer and caught the creature on the upswing, smashing its bottom jaw up through the top of its skull and sending its twitching carcass flipping backwards.

'Somehow, I get the impression they were waiting for us, brothers,' Aphrae said. His chainfist licked out, and the rotating teeth bit into the carapace of a squealing genestealer. He lifted the squalling xenos, and its weight caused it to split in two along either side of the whirring blade. 'How thoughtful of them to send us a welcoming committee. It is considerations like that which truly denotes a civilised race, don't you agree, Bartelo?'

'I'm sorry brother – what? You'll forgive me for not listening to you prattle. I was busy doing the Emperor's work,' Bartelo said, sweeping the barrel of his heavy flamer across a row of charging genestealers. 'Burn, filth. Burn and die, in His name,' he spat, as the xenos turned into shrieking pillars of fire, the light of their demise reflected in the optic lenses of his helmet.

Karlaen pulped the head of a leaping genestealer as he reached the others. Leonos and Damaris fought side by side, moving like mirror images. Their storm bolters thundered in unison and their power fists shot out like pistons, each gauntlet wreathed in a nimbus of crackling azure energy which caused alien flesh to sizzle and burst like overripe fruit where they touched. The twins turned in a slow circle, covering one another with an inhuman precision that Karlaen could not help but envy.

Nearby, Alphaeus's sword flickered out and a genestealer fell, grotesque skull split. He pivoted and cut the legs out from one that sought to dodge past him. As the beast fell, he trod on it, reducing its head to a messy residue. 'Back to back,' he roared out again. 'Just like that time aboard the *Charnel Horizon*.'

'There's rather more of them this time, sergeant,' Aphrae said. A genestealer sprang for him, and he extended his chainfist, ramming the blade down the creature's gullet. He hefted the twitching bulk and slung it at another xenos, knocking it out of the air as it dove towards Leonos.

'More alien filth just means more targets,' Bartelo rasped. Smoke curled from the nozzle of his heavy flamer as he stroked the trigger. Fire spurted in quick bursts, driving back genestealers.

'More targets means–' Damaris began.

'–more ammunition expended,' Leonos finished. As if to lend emphasis to his words, he ejected the clip from his storm bolter as Damaris covered him. He was firing as soon as another clip was in place, covering Damaris, as the latter reloaded his own weapon.

'The twins are right, sergeant,' Karlaen said. He whirled as a proximity alarm blared in his ear and shoved his hammer forward like a spear, using the flat of its head to pin a genestealer against a shattered statue. The creature hissed and spat, clawing at him. He pressed the hammer forward, cracked the monster's sternum and squashed its heart. 'They're trying to overwhelm us. At this rate, we'll use up our ammunition in a few minutes. Time to adapt our tactics.' Karlaen scanned the chamber, and caught sight of one of the many ornately decorated entrances to the side corridors that he thought must run parallel to the Tribune Chamber. He gestured with his hammer. 'There, we'll narrow the field a bit. Give them less room to run about in. Fall back,' he said. 'Bartelo, Aphrae, covering fire.'

'Our pleasure,' Aphrae said. Bartelo grunted and stepped forwards, flamer roaring. As the two Terminators laid down covering fire, Karlaen led the others towards the archway he had indicated. He cycled through vox frequencies, trying to contact Zachreal and the others, but his scans found only the disturbing hum of white noise.

'The others?' Alphaeus muttered.

'We're on our own for now,' Karlaen said.

The squad continued to fall back, their retreat harried by hissing genestealers, who darted in and out of reach, attacking and scuttling away before a blow could be struck in return. Though many fell to the covering fire of Aphrae and Bartelo, or were caught by a lucky blow from a hammer, power fist or sword, they continued to attack.

The squad had almost reached the dubious safety of the side corridor when a genestealer slipped beneath Aphrae's guard and tore open the back of his leg in a spray of blood and machine oil. Aphrae sank down to one knee with a grunt. Karlaen realised that the Terminator was not with them when Bartelo made to go to his aid. The others had reached the entryway and were firing at the horde that closed in on them from all sides. Karlaen knew that in mere moments there would be no reaching Aphrae. 'No,' he said, decision made. 'We need your flamer to clear us a path. I will get him.' Bartelo looked at him, and nodded once. Then he took aim and sprayed the hissing genestealers that stood between the Blood Angels and their fallen comrade, burning a corridor for the captain to move along.

Karlaen started forwards. Aphrae swung his chainfist out and decapitated his attacker. More moved to take its place. Aphrae fired his storm bolter at the oncoming wave of chitin, ichor and fangs, emptying the weapon. He tried to lever himself to his feet, but his wounded leg was unable to bear his weight. Karlaen fired his weapon and laid about him with his hammer, trying to clear himself a path to go to the other Blood Angel's aid. Bartelo and the others lent their own firepower to his efforts, and soon he was bulling through the enemy towards Aphrae as the xenos fell to scything bolter fire and curling flames.

Genestealers crawled over Aphrae, attempting to pry him out of his armour. He was unable to regain enough balance to throw them off, and it was all he could do to catch hold of those who got within reach and crush their limbs or behead them with his still whirring chainfist. Hoses and bundles of fibre were torn loose from their housings and he sagged forwards, slapping his free hand down to catch himself. One of the xenos clambered up onto Aphrae's shoulders and began to twist and fumble at his helmet.

Karlaen reached the embattled Terminator and swatted the genestealer from its perch, sending it careening through the air, over the heads of its fellows.

'Can you walk?' Karlaen said, trying to haul Aphrae to his feet. The Blood Angel's armour responded sluggishly to his movements, and Karlaen suspected that its internal workings had been damaged.

'No, leg's a mess. I'm fairly certain it's only still attached by a ligament – singular – at this point,' Aphrae grunted. He could barely stand, even with Karlaen's help, and Karlaen could hear the pain in the other Blood Angel's voice. As novices, they were taught how to block and channel pain, even for grievous injuries. Where a normal human would already have died of blood loss, if not shock, Aphrae was still capable of fighting. Unfortunately, he did not appear to be capable of moving.

'Lean on me, I can…' Karlaen began, but his words died in his throat as the air came alive with a cacophony of hissing. His eyes were drawn upwards, towards the great domed roof of the chamber, where the shadows had suddenly become alive with hundreds of writhing shapes. 'By the blood of the Angel,' he muttered, as what he had taken for the shadowed reaches of a solid dome was suddenly revealed to be a mass of genestealers pressed close to the underside of the chamber's glass ceiling.

'I take it back,' Aphrae mumbled, following Karlaen's gaze. '*That's* the welcoming committee.' Above them, the genestealers began to fall. The creatures hurtled down towards the two Terminators, with obvious and deadly intent. 'Get clear, captain,' Aphrae rasped, lurching forwards to smash Karlaen out of the way of the plummeting genestealers.

Off balance, Karlaen staggered back as the tide of alien killers swarmed over

Aphrae, biting and tearing. Aphrae tore the head from a genestealer and sent it spinning away with a backhanded blow and, for a moment, the way was clear. Karlaen met the other Blood Angel's eyes, and said, 'Aphrae–'

'Go, captain. I would only slow you down, and you said it yourself – we're running low on time. I'll make them bleed, and buy you a bit of it back.' Aphrae turned and caught a creature by the throat with his free hand; at the same time, he swept his whirring chainfist out in a wide arc, filling the air with stinking ichor. He staggered as genestealers slammed into him and swarmed over him. 'Go! In Sanguinius's name – go!'

Karlaen hesitated, but then turned and pressed back towards the others, cursing himself while he did so. He heard Aphrae's chainfist stutter and growl as the warrior fought on, but all too soon it fell silent, and all he could hear was a cacophony of screeches, hisses and clicks. As he cleared the archway and joined Alphaeus and the others, he looked back, but saw only a seething tide of xenos horrors hurrying towards him. Aphrae was gone.

And if they did not move fast, Karlaen knew that the rest of the squad would share his fate.

The broodlord stalked through the mounds of human corpses and the bodies of its fallen children. Those bodies gave it pause, though it could not say why. There was no room for sentimentality in the gestalt mechanism of the Hive Mind – all were one and one was all. Nonetheless, the broodlord had been the leader of a pack long before it had been subsumed by the great, calming song of the Hive Mind's singular will, and it sank down beside the body of one of its children. It hesitated, then reached out towards the ruined carcass with a claw. Gently, it stroked the body.

All things died. All things were matter to be consumed, mass to be added to the whole, reshaped, reforged and repurposed. It knew this and it accepted it, for it could not do otherwise. But still, there lingered in its blighted soul some shard of something it could not name, a memory of another time, and of other dead which were not repurposed but were instead taken away to be interred in silence and darkness. Memories rose slowly over the gestalt hum, flowering and spreading and quickly fading, before it could fully examine them. It saw faces, and heard names, but no longer truly understood. Nor did it care to.

It rose to its feet and stepped over the body. The wave of death which had accompanied the attack on the invaders had only served to stoke the rage that bubbled within the creature. This ambush had not gone as well as the others, and its quarry were escaping deeper into the ruins of the palace, bloodied but unbowed. Its massive claws clenched and relaxed constantly as it paced towards the struggling knot of genestealers.

The red-armoured warrior who fought them did so even though his situation was hopeless. His weapons were gone or useless, and his armour had been rent and torn, its power cables severed and the exoskeleton twisted out of shape. Still he struggled against the churning mass of multi-limbed horrors that swarmed about him. The broodlord could not conceive of such an emotion as admiration, but it felt some faint stirring of something akin to it nonetheless as it hunkered down across from the stricken invader.

It scraped the ground gently as it studied its enemy; a flurry of images from the other ambushes flowed through its mind, and it closed its eyes for a moment, indulging in the pleasure those images brought. A roaring, black-haired giant fired his weapon until it ran dry, and then was swarmed under; another, wreathed in pungent smoke emanating from gilded censers, was attacked from all sides. On and on the tide of images rolled, and when the broodlord at last opened its eyes, it did so with a hiss of fulfilment. The ambushes it had organised were going well, and though many of its children had died, the enemy was scattered and bloodied.

Its children had managed to wrest the warrior's helmet off, and ruined hoses spurted recycled air as the hunk of metal was tossed aside. It caught up the helm as it rolled past and held it, turning it over in its claws. It looked at the warrior, and crushed the helmet with a single flex of its segmented limbs. The metal buckled and popped with a shrill cry.

The warrior spat and said something. The broodlord did not bother to listen to his words. Instead, it focused on his thoughts, plucking them out to examine one by one, as if they were the petals of some colourful flower. It needed to know why they had come. What did they seek, here, in its territory?

Every thought tasted different, and as it consumed them, names swam through its mind... Bartelo... Alphaeus... *Karlaen*. The names of the surviving invaders. Names were useful, it knew. Names were like keys to the locks of the mind. With a name, it could pry away the will and strength of its enemy and render them helpless before the strength of the Hive Mind.

That was how it had made Asphodex ready for consumption, though it had not been aware of the true reason for its actions at the time. It had weeded out the strongest minds from among the planetary aristocracy, and used the name it had been given by the fearful under-dwellers to strike terror into the very heart of Phodia. And it had done so gladly, for they were traitors, one and all.

Yes, betrayal. That was the word for what it had felt, so many cycles ago, before it had heard the song of the Leviathan and found its true purpose. It had been betrayed, and now, it would exact the blood-price for that treachery. Asphodex would burn, as would every world that the Flaxian Dynasty had presumed to control. They would burn and be consumed.

It hissed in growing frustration. The warrior's mind refused to give up the one thing it needed to know above all others. It lunged forwards and grasped the struggling man's head between its claws. The other genestealers released their grip on the captive and scuttled back as the broodlord loomed over its wounded foe. It stared down into his eyes, searching, as he pounded useless fists against its carapace. There was another name there, beneath the surface of its captive's thoughts. It could taste his defiance, his blood-lust and... something else. Some strong desire... No, not a desire. *Hope*. Hope which was attached to one last name.

Its eyes bulged in fury as it caught a whiff of that name. Alien muscle twitched and swelled, and genetically augmented bone cracked and shattered beneath a sudden, inexorable pressure. The dead man slid out of its grip, and his armour clanked loudly as it struck the ground. The broodlord's throat sacs bulged and twitched as barely used vocal cords swelled, and a sound that might have been a name slipped from between its jaws as it threw back its head and screamed its anger to the dying sky.

CHAPTER FOUR

Karlaen heard the scream as it echoed through the palace. He knew no human throat had made that sound, and something in him could not help but shudder. It was a raw, animal cry, of something driven far beyond the limits of frustration. Whatever it was, part of him hoped that Aphrae had died before coming face to face with it.

'Whatever it is–' Leonos began.

'–it sounds angry,' Damaris finished.

Karlaen looked back at the twins. Like them all their crimson armour was caked in gore, and many of the heavy ceramite plates had been cracked and scored by the claws of the genestealers. The barrels of their storm bolters still glowed hot. Neither appeared to be wounded however, which was a relief.

As they moved down the corridor he looked around, taking stock of their surroundings as they put distance between themselves and the Tribune Chamber. The genestealers had not followed them directly into the spacious processional corridors beyond the chamber, but Karlaen could make out their shapes moving through the inky darkness of the ruins around them, and his sensors pinged relentlessly, alerting him to the presence of unseen foes. Occasionally, they would make as if to rush the slowly moving squad of Terminators, but would dart back into the darkness as the Blood Angels levelled their weapons.

The corridors were wider than he had anticipated, shattered by the battle that had gutted the palace hours earlier. Whole sections of the dividing wall were missing, torn out by alien acids or heavy weapons fire. Ancient artworks, created by generations of Phodian craftsmen, and now reduced to scattered debris, crunched beneath the steady tread of Squad Alphaeus.

'Aphrae is dead,' Bartelo said, softly. It was the first thing he had said since they'd left the Tribune Chamber behind. Karlaen glanced at him in surprise. Bartelo was taciturn at the best of times, unless Aphrae was prodding him.

'He died as the Emperor willed,' Karlaen said. The words did not sound as comforting aloud as they had in his head, and he fell silent. Death was the companion of every Space Marine, for were they not the Emperor's Angels of Death? Yet, even so, the Chapter was diminished by every death, and the loss of even one of their own cast a pall over the survivors.

For Karlaen, particularly, that feeling was like an old companion, and one whose company he did not welcome. For a moment, he was somewhere else, not on a world, but within the vibrating innards of a space-going hulk, and he could hear the screams of the men who had followed him into the darkness as they died.

He closed his organic eye and tried to banish the memories. But instead of fading, they clamoured more loudly, and his ears filled with a red hum. He wanted to return to the Tribune Chamber and kill and kill and kill until there was nothing left alive. For a moment, the desire overwhelmed him. Then, Bartelo's voice pierced the haze and he was once more himself.

'We were inducted together, he and I,' Bartelo said. He spoke steadily, as if in eulogy. 'We journeyed to the Palace of Challenge together, across the desert, and fought back to back in the gladiatorial contests which awaited us there. He was uncouth, even then. There was too much laughter in him.' He looked at Karlaen. 'Captain, was he laughing as he died? I was not close enough to hear.'

'No,' Karlaen said. 'He was not.'

Bartelo was silent for a moment. Then he nodded. 'Good. It is meet that a man should die with dignity. Laughter would only sully the moment.' He sounded quietly pleased.

Karlaen looked at the other Terminator for a moment, and then away. There were many in the Chapter like Bartelo – grim, unswerving and lacking in mirth. That he and Aphrae had been friends, of a sort, was obvious, but even so, almost inexplicable. Karlaen knew as much about the warriors under his command as a proper leader ought, but even so, some subtleties escaped him. He wanted to speak words of comfort to Bartelo, but was uncertain as to how to go about it. What was there to say?

'Orders, captain?' Alphaeus said, interrupting his train of thought.

'We keep moving. According to the augur scans, there should be a security hub somewhere ahead of us,' Karlaen said, grateful to turn his thoughts to his duty. 'When we reach it, we might be able to use the security logs to track down our quarry.'

'Good,' Alphaeus said. 'The sooner we're out of here, the better. Listen to that racket – this ruin is crawling with tyranids.' He smiled humourlessly. 'If I wanted to wade into that sort of mess, I'd have joined the main assault.'

'I did not force you to come, brother,' Karlaen said.

'No, but who'll keep you out of trouble if not me?' Alphaeus said.

Karlaen snorted. Though he would not say it out loud, he found the sergeant's humour reassuring. 'Keep moving, and keep an eye on your sensors. They've had a taste of our blood and I intend to see that they get no more than that.'

He led them on, following the whispers of the augur readings towards the security hub. More than once they were forced to stop and form up as lean, monstrous shapes flooded towards them from out of side corridors, or plunged through the gaping holes in the close-set corridor walls. But as before, the genestealers would always retreat just before initiating contact, as if their harrying of the Blood Angels were no more than some demented child's game. Then they would stalk above and below the squad, testing the limits of the Terminators' patience before attacking again.

In truth, Karlaen suspected that the beasts were attempting to entice them into wasting ammunition. Twice, he was forced to hold Bartelo back from simply filling a side passage with fire. While the promethium reserves of a heavy flamer were substantial, they were not limitless, and the genestealers seemed to know that. So they attacked again and again, heedless of casualties, trying to force the Terminators to expend valuable resources. A suicidal stratagem, but one that worked all too well.

To Karlaen, that meant only one thing: there was a synapse creature close by – a commander of bugs and bio-beasts, a central node of the abominable will that guided Hive Fleet Leviathan. Tyranids were like any other feral animal, acting on instinct. But a synapse creature could turn those mindless beasts into a dedicated army with but a thought. That was what they were now facing – an enemy that would sacrifice a hundred for one without blinking, and seemed fully committed to doing so.

That, in the end, was the greatest weapon at the Hive Mind's disposal. Every world consumed only added to the incalculable number of bio-organisms that the hive fleet could employ in battle. Every fallen warrior was simply a bit more mass to be added to the bio-vats. And as the hive fleet swelled, more worlds fell beneath its expanding shadow.

As that bleak thought hung heavy in his mind, he cycled once more through the vox signals, hoping to contact one of the other squads, or even elements of the forward invasion force. He knew, with an unerring instinct honed in a thousand confrontations with the tyranids, that he and the others would not be able to complete their mission without significant reinforcement. To think otherwise was hubris. Unfortunately, the only thing he could hear over the transmitter was the hiss of static and alien whispers.

They pressed on, moving more quickly now. The palace occasionally shook, as if in sympathy with distant explosions, and the sound of talons scratching on walls and floors was omnipresent. The bio-sensors screamed warnings about foes that the Terminators could not see. Time was growing short.

'Sounds like every beast in this part of the city is flooding into these ruins,' Alphaeus murmured.

'Good,' Bartelo said. He hefted his heavy flamer. 'More bodies for the pyre.'

'Save your fuel,' Karlaen said. He pointed at the reinforced security portcullis that blocked the corridor ahead with his hammer. 'We're here.' He didn't stop, but bulled into the portcullis, which was covered in hundreds of talon marks. The metal squealed as he peeled it open with his hands. When he had created enough of a gap, he used his hammer as a lever and forced it fully open. His sensors showed that the chamber beyond contained only one life form, if it could be called that. It was weak and thready, but Karlaen was determined to find it.

'Survivors?' Alphaeus asked.

'I don't think so. At least, not the kind you're thinking of,' Karlaen said. 'Come.' He forced his way through the damaged door and into the security hub, followed by the others. The space beyond the door was wide and filled with debris. It had seen hard fighting, despite the reinforced door. The walls and ceiling were badly damaged, and Karlaen took note of the toppled piles of sandbags and hastily erected barricades that marked portions of the chamber. Two parallel rows of statues marked the main drag of the chamber, and almost all had been knocked from their pedestals and shattered into unrecognisable lumps of marble.

'They made a stand here,' Alphaeus said, indicating the spent lasgun power cells and blood stains. He kicked at a crawling feeder-beast and sent it scuttling through a hole in the wall. He wrinkled his nose in disgust. 'These blasted beasts have already broken down the corpses. I can smell one of those digestive pools nearby.'

'Not all of the corpses.' Karlaen heaved a heavy chunk of fallen debris aside to reveal the twitching form of a servitor. The mindless drone of meat and metal flopped and sparked, its body broken beyond repair. Karlaen saw immediately what had befallen it. It had been caught by the debris and smashed to the ground, its limbs and spine pulped.

He sank down beside it. There was something pitiable about the dull-eyed thing, and for a moment, he allowed himself to wonder who or what it had been before it had been converted to the mindless husk it now was. The ruined mouth tried to speak, and sparks flared from its burst larynx, spattering the front of Karlaen's armour.

'It's not a combat servitor,' Alphaeus said.

'It is a holomat,' Karlaen said. 'A messenger. And it was likely on its way to deliver a message when it was caught in the attack.' He tapped a finger against the curved mark that had been etched into the servitor's pale expanse of forehead.

He took the damaged servitor's head in both hands and tore it loose from the damaged chassis with an effortless twist. Holding up the head by its cables, he examined it for a moment to make sure it was undamaged. Then he attached it to his belt. 'I'll extract the data when we have found a more defensible location. For now, we should–'

He broke off as a lean, alien shape leapt over the gap above him, and Karlaen looked up. The others followed his gaze. Proximity sensors began to blare warnings to every Terminator in the chamber. He readied himself for an attack from above.

Instead, the attack came from a section of acid-chewed wall, and targeted not himself, but Bartelo, who turned as Damaris, the closest to him, shouted a warning. Something crystalline streaked out of the darkness and caught Bartelo as he turned, knocking him from his feet with a bright burst of heat and light that momentarily illuminated the area, revealing fallen statues and shattered debris. Karlaen and the others moved to aid their downed comrade as his attackers moved into the glare of the stab-lights.

Three long-legged shapes, taller than any Terminator and just as broad, loped into view in a rattle of chitin plates and bio-armour. The trio of tyranid warriors were monstrous parodies of the human form, stretched and distorted into something nightmarish. The beasts charged towards the Terminators on flat, heavy hooves, smashing through the rubble as they came. They wielded bio-whips and bone blades with a precise, inhuman grace and filled the air with sub-sonic hunting calls as they lunged to the attack.

CHAPTER FIVE

Karlaen levelled his storm bolter and pumped shot after shot into the charging monstrosities. Alphaeus and the others did the same, as Bartelo began to struggle to his feet, a smoking rent in his armour. The tyranid warriors split up, moving swiftly. They were big beasts, with broad, wedge-shaped skulls and four arms. Powerful, jointed legs propelled them forwards and acidic bile streamed from their toothy maws as they exposed their fangs in anticipation.

Karlaen shouted, 'Get Bartelo on his feet.' Then, hammer in hand, he moved to intercept the closest of their attackers. The creatures were the synaptic foot soldiers of the hive fleet, and Karlaen wondered if these were the source of the malign will behind the suicidal attacks of the genestealers. They were powerful and deadly creatures, and a match for any Space Marine, even one clad in Terminator armour. There would be more on the way, as well. Where there was one brood, there were many.

The closest of the tyranids leapt from the ground onto a statue toppled on its side, scaling it swiftly. It clashed its bone blades together in what might have been a challenge as it dived from its perch to meet Karlaen. Four deadly lengths of sharpened bone swept down towards him. He twisted aside, letting the edges glance off his armour with a sound like a scream. He jabbed his hammer forward like a spear, catching the creature in its segmented gut. It bent double with a coughing roar, and he smoothly altered the hammer's course to meet its descending skull.

There was a crackle of energy, and the tyranid warrior staggered back, jaw burned and broken. Its blades scissored for him wildly. He stepped back and smashed the bone swords aside, before striking his opponent in the chest. Chitin cracked and burst, and a thick ichor ran down the armour plates as the thing screeched. Before it could attack again, he shoved the barrel of his storm bolter against the shattered area of its thorax and pulled the trigger. The creature jerked wildly and toppled towards him, its swords and claws seeking to pull him down into the darkness with it even as it died. He forced it away, wincing as the tip of a bone sword skidded off his cheek. It hit the ground and lay still.

With the higher castes of tyranid warrior-beasts, it was best to kill them as quickly as possible. They could fight on despite incredible wounds, easily withstanding the sort of damage which would test even an ork's vigour. Luckily,

Karlaen had more than a century of experience in killing such creatures, whether on the battlefield or in the close confines of a space hulk.

He turned, narrowly avoiding the stinging lash of a bio-whip. The second beast was duelling with Damaris and Leonos, keeping their power fists at bay with wide sweeps of its bone sword and a snap of the other bio-whip it wielded.

Karlaen fired his storm bolter, distracting the beast. It twisted towards him instinctively and opened itself up for Leonos, who clamped one arm around two of its own, pinning blade and whip. The tyranid shrilled in rage and tried to fling the Terminator off. Its strength was so great that it jerked Leonos from his feet and swung him about as easily as it did its whips. Damaris rushed in and caught one of its two remaining free hands in his power fist. He shoved his storm bolter against the spot where the limb met its body and fired.

The limb, and the bio-whip it clutched, came free with a wet, tearing sound, as acidic ichor spattered the floor. Its remaining bone sword flashed out and caught Damaris on the side, carving a long gouge in his armour. He staggered, and Karlaen stepped past him, hammer descending on the side of the tyranid's skull. Chitin crumpled and the xenos sank to one knee. Karlaen struck it again, with more force this time, and his blow crushed its skull. Even so, it continued to struggle. Leonos set himself and lifted a boot to brace against the uncrushed side of the alien warrior's skull. With a grunt, he tore its arms free of their sockets. The tyranid made a wailing squeal and flopped onto the ground. Damaris finished it off quickly, crushing what was left of its head beneath his boot.

Even as the creature writhed in its death throes, Karlaen was striding past, towards where Alphaeus sought to haul Bartelo to his feet, while fending off the remaining tyranid's blistering fury of attacks. Alphaeus parried blow after blow, wielding his power sword with an elegance and speed befitting one of the Chapter's foremost swordsmen.

The tyranid slammed its four blades down on the length of Alphaeus's one and loomed over him, trying to drive him to his knees. It threw back its head and a powerful scream ripped from its throat sacs, nearly deafening Karlaen. The scream echoed, redoubling in strength, and Karlaen winced as he felt something scrabble along the underside of his mind. The creature's scream had not been merely a cry of frustration, but a summons to war.

As the echoes faded, a new sound took their place – claws, scrabbling on stone and steel. Karlaen staggered as the ground beneath him shifted and then erupted in a tangled thicket of flailing claws and snapping jaws. Momentarily off balance, he swung his storm bolter down and fired until it was dry. He fell heavily, but managed to drag himself forwards, away from the growing hole. Through the smoke and dust, genestealers clambered after him. He rolled onto his back and lashed out with his hammer, pulverising the first to leap. Damaris and Leonos moved to his aid.

He heard a shrill cry, and saw a flood of xenos squirming through the shattered portcullis. The twins turned their weapons on these new foes, but not for long. As their weapons stuttered to silence, they were forced to defend themselves without the benefit of bolter fire. Karlaen pushed himself awkwardly to his feet, backhanding a genestealer with his storm bolter in the process. There was no time to reload. He laid about him with the ancient relic of his Chapter, splitting skulls and cracking carapaces.

Then came a roar of heat and incandescent light as Bartelo, still on one knee, fired his heavy flamer, consuming the whole, scrabbling pack of creatures climbing through the portcullis. 'Step aside, captain. Let me light their way to the Emperor's judgement,' Bartelo rasped.

Karlaen fought his way clear of his enemies as Bartelo directed his flames towards the hole in the floor. Genestealers screamed as they burned, their screams echoed by the final tyranid warrior. Too late, Karlaen saw that Alphaeus had been sent sprawling by the beast. It lunged over the sergeant, and its blades smashed home, erupting from Bartelo's chest in a gory spray. Bartelo slid off the blades and smashed to the ground, unmoving.

Alphaeus was on his feet a moment later, his face contorted in an expression that Karlaen recognised all too well. His power sword hummed as it caught the tyranid in the neck, beheading it as it turned to confront him. It fell and Alphaeus drove his blade down into its body again and again, until Karlaen's hand on his shoulder shook him from his rage.

Karlaen looked at Leonos, who crouched beside Bartelo. 'Status?' he asked softly, even though he knew. There was too much blood, and Bartelo was too still.

Leonos stood. That was answer enough. Karlaen closed his eyes. The inside of his head itched with red, creeping thoughts that he pushed aside with difficulty. Twice they had made contact with the enemy, and twice they had lost a brother. There would be no third time, not if he could help it. But he could see their situation plainly: if they stayed where they were, or tried to press forward, they would be overwhelmed. Already, the proximity sensors in his armour were alerting him to movement in the corridors beyond them. And without Bartelo's heavy flamer, they would be at even more of a disadvantage than before.

'Adapt and persevere,' he muttered, eyeing the chamber walls. His bionic eye clicked and whirred as he scanned through settings and lenses until he came to the geo-imager. Before his eyes, a holographic grid map of the palace formed. Outside the chamber, the sound of clattering claws grew louder. Alphaeus fired his storm bolter down into the hole in the floor. Bartelo had only given the horde outside momentary pause.

'Orders, captain?' Alphaeus asked. He sounded deceptively calm, and his face might as well have belonged to one of the toppled statues.

'How much promethium is left in Bartelo's tanks?' Karlaen said, studying the grid.

'Not much,' Leonos said. 'A single, concentrated burst.'

'Enough to clear the passage,' Damaris added.

'Pierce them,' Karlaen said. 'And get ready to move.'

He plotted the quickest alternate route to the Plaza of the Emperor Ascendant. While part of him was disgusted with the idea of retreat so soon after making contact, this mission was not about battle. They had a duty, and it was up to him to see that it was fulfilled. If that meant swallowing a bit of pride and falling back to a position where they could make more effective use of their remaining firepower, so be it. Also, it was possible that once clear of the palace walls, his vox signals would reach Zachreal and the others. Reinforced, they could make a concentrated push.

'What? But–' Alphaeus began. Then, remembering his place, he nodded crisply. He looked at the twins. 'Do it. His armour will survive the fire, but whatever is coming for us won't.' He looked at Karlaen. 'Whatever you're planning, brother, I'd make it quick – I'm picking up massed bio-readings in all directions. They're closing in on us.'

'That's the idea, Alphaeus,' Karlaen said. He strode towards the closest wall. 'I want as many of them in here as possible, before we leave.'

'What are you thinking?' Alphaeus said, following him.

'Do you remember that time aboard the *Seraglio of Abomination*?' Karlaen said. He raised his hammer. 'They're expecting us to press forwards, or try and escape back the way we came. So let's surprise them, eh?' He took a leisurely practice swing, his bionic eye gauging the wall's weakest point.

'If you're thinking of doing what I think, I feel it is my duty to remind you that it didn't work as well as you hoped that time,' Alphaeus said.

'You act as if you didn't enjoy seeing all those genestealers go spilling out into the void, sergeant.'

'Given that we were spilling out into said void alongside them, you'll forgive me for being somewhat distracted at the time,' Alphaeus said. The sound of claws grew louder, filling the chamber with a relentless clicking of talons on metal.

'Well, there's no void to worry you this time,' Karlaen said. The tang of promethium fumes reached him. He glanced back at the twins. 'Status, brothers,' he called out, over his shoulder.

'Promethium tanks–' Damaris began.

'–punctured, captain,' Leonos finished.

'Good. Fall back, and take up flanking positions,' Karlaen said. As he spoke, genestealers spilled into the chamber, heralded by a cacophony of screeching. As before, they charged with reckless abandon, driven berserk by whatever synaptic impulse commanded them. Alphaeus barked an order, and three storm bolters were readied to roar out in reply to the alien shrieking. But they would not fire yet. Not until the last possible moment.

Karlaen swung the Hammer of Baal in a wide arc. The wall burst outward at the point of impact, filling the promethium-laden air with dust. Karlaen bulled through, picking up speed as he raced through towards the next wall opposite him. Behind him, he heard the roar of storm bolters followed by a crackling thunder and then his armour's sensors screamed at him as a wave of heat washed over him, flooding through the hole he had made.

He heard the heavy tread of the others following him and smiled in satisfaction as he tore through the next wall. The fumes from the spilled promethium had turned the security hub into an inferno, and whatever had been inside at the moment of the explosion was no longer something they had to worry about.

Room by room, corridor by corridor, the four Terminators smashed and fought their way through the ruins. Never stopping, pausing only to kill any tyranid unlucky enough to get in their way. The Blood Angels left behind them a trail of shattered wreckage and broken xenos bodies. Then, with one final blow of his hammer, Karlaen led his men out into the Plaza of the Emperor Ascendant.

As he stepped out into the red Asphodex light, his vox came alive, free of interference. He heard Zachreal's voice, and Joses's roar, as loudly and as clearly as if they had been beside him. He heard the bark of storm bolter fire, and alien screams as well, and knew then what he had only suspected before. The ambush had not been by random chance; rather it was the work of an overarching will. The others had not yet found any sign of Flax. Alphaeus met his gaze, and Karlaen knew he had heard the signals as well.

'We're on our own, brothers,' Karlaen said. He turned and saw the fallen statue after which the plaza was named, depicting the Emperor in all of his glory, wings wide, face uplifted towards the boiling red sky. The statue had been seared by fire, burned by ichor and smothered in creeping strands of fleshy bio-matter, but there was no indication as to what had felled it in the end. Karlaen stared down into the marble face of the Master of Mankind and felt something stir within him. Not the hum this time, but a black, brooding anger that brought with it the images of Aphrae going down beneath the enemy, and Bartelo being ripped open, and others, from a greater distance – faces, names, dying screams from that one red moment.

The Sons of Sanguinius had always been better at dying than their brother Space Marines. Martyrdom was in their blood, and for a Blood Angel, there was no greater glory than death in a good cause. But that fierce sense of selflessness which sent them rushing headlong into the jaws of death all too often flowered into obsession. He could feel them pressing in from all around him, the ghosts of all of those who had followed him and died. For a moment, barely the blink of an eye, the plaza was *full of pale, carmine shapes, facing the enemy, and he could hear a voice like fire and smooth stone and the* crack *of great wings as his Father spoke and* then the genestealers were boiling out of the hole he had created in the wall like ants out of an anthill.

He tore his gaze from the statue and shoved down the tide of rage and black memories. He raised his storm bolter. 'I want interlocking fields of fire. Go to pattern epsilon,' he grated. 'Combat protocol sigma.' The others fanned out around him as the genestealers scuttled towards them through the ruins and debris that dotted the open plaza. Karlaen glanced at the statue one last time. Then, he turned to face the enemy. 'The Emperor watches, brothers. Do not fail him.'

Then, with a roar of storm bolters, the battle commenced.

CHAPTER SIX

PLAZA OF THE EMPEROR ASCENDANT, FLAXIAN PALACE, PHODIA

Interlocking fire patterns and close combat protocols were the mortar of victory, or so Karlaen's teachers had always claimed. Now, several centuries on from his days as an aspirant, eager to sup on the accumulated knowledge of his masters, he was willing to admit that there was some truth to the saying.

The storm bolter bucked in his hand, the reverberation of its voice causing his exoskeleton to tremble slightly. The barrel glowed white-hot, and his head ached from the targeting information fed into it by his bionic eye. But pain was the price paid for victory.

The tyranids made assault after assault, coming in waves as they had before, but now they were charging directly into the teeth of an organised gun-line. Before, the Terminators had been scattered or cramped, unable to take full advantage of their firepower due to their surroundings and each other. Now, out in the open, the battle was theirs before the first genestealer darted from cover. That had ever been the way of it, in Karlaen's experience. One of the more successful strategies the First Company had learned in centuries of gruelling warfare was that an enemy that relied on numbers could be drawn into a situation where those numbers rapidly became a disadvantage.

Such was the case now. Each assault was repelled, and at significant range. Only once did a tyranid warrior get close enough to engage the Terminators, and Alphaeus swiftly put it down with two hard sweeps of his power sword.

Finally, the attacks ebbed away, until there was only the soft ping of cooling gun barrels and the dripping of tyranid ichor to be heard in the plaza. A haze of smoke hung heavy in the air over the mounds of xenos corpses as an eerie quiet descended. Karlaen waited, counting moments in his head. Then, with a grunt of satisfaction, he lowered his storm bolter.

'They've fallen back, likely to plan their next move,' he said.

'And like as not, we're being watched,' Alphaeus said, as he reloaded his storm bolter. 'I can feel it, scurrying around in my head.'

'Then we'd best take advantage of the time we've bought for ourselves,' Karlaen said. He unhooked the head of the servitor from his belt and held it up. 'We'll start with this.' Deftly, he extracted the contact nodes of several power cables from his armour and plugged them into the nodes hidden within the dripping stump of the head. Almost immediately, the servitor's mouth opened, and its eyes widened as the influx of raw power jump-started its functions.

A deluge of meaningless code burst from the servitor's bloody lips, followed by a hollow, mechanical voice. '*Warning. Warning. Plaza defences compromised. Warning. Security hub J-7 compromised. Warning. Tribune Chamber compromised. Warning. Security hub J-8 compromised. Warning. Unit to report ongoing situation to Governor Flax. Warning.*' More warnings followed, a veritable roll call of failed defences and counter-attacks.

Connected to the servitor's memory banks via his armour's systems, he slowly peeled back the layers of its programming, and found that the drone had been heading to deliver its report to Flax in person when it had been caught in the rubble. He looked at Alphaeus. 'It was Flax's envoy. He sent it out to take stock of the palace defences and then report back to him, wherever he's hiding.'

'Do you think it can lead us to him?' Alphaeus asked. He sat down on a toppled pillar and sank his sword into the ground, point first, before him.

Karlaen did not reply. Instead, he continued his exploration of the servitor's memory banks, taking note of the various routes and passages it held maps of. The servitor had a signal-lock on Flax's bio-signature, as well as all relevant security information – ID codes, crypto-keys and system overrides – to reach him. Karlaen blinked. He looked at Alphaeus. 'There's an undercity. That's where Flax is.'

Alphaeus grimaced. 'That means tunnels. And we've no heavy flamer to clean them out.'

'According to our friend here, the tunnels are still sealed. The tyranids haven't found them yet,' Karlaen said. He frowned. 'Or they hadn't, according to the drone's last sensor sweep.' He unhooked the head from his armour, and its eyes glazed over as its mouth went slack. If it was attached to his armour's power source for too long, there was a chance the fragile mechanisms in the head would burn out, and he still had use for it.

'Was that before or after it was pinned under the rubble?' Alphaeus asked. When Karlaen did not reply, he sighed and nodded. 'It always comes back to the cramped and the dark, doesn't it? What I wouldn't give for another stand-up fight.'

'We do what we must, brother, for the good of the Chapter,' Karlaen said, placing the now-silent servitor head back on his belt. He looked up, gauging the time. The chronometer in his eye ticked over. It was just past midnight. It had taken him longer to filter the information contained in the head than he had thought.

The dull crump of distant explosions told him that the battle for Phodia was not yet over. A tendril of guilt squirmed through him, as he turned his thoughts to those embattled survivors. Their fight would soon be over, and not for the better. They were chaff before the scythe, left to dull the enemy's blade with their meat and bone. Asphodex would be erased, and her people with it.

You have no heart, only fire, he thought, trying to banish such thoughts. Guilt, doubt, fear – all fuel for the fires of determination. All men died, whether hero or coward, mortal or Space Marine. But if their death meant something, then it was no kind of death at all, but transcendence. The road to a better world was paved with the bones of brave men. Had the Angel's death not provided the Emperor with a chance for victory against the Arch-Traitor? So too would it be here. The dead of Phodia, of Asphodex, of the Cryptus System, were the foundation on which Baal's survival would be built.

He turned and watched the fires on the horizon. Karlaen knew it was true, that all of this was necessary. But that did not mean he had to like it. He closed his eyes, feeling bands of red and black tighten about his mind and heart. He opened them and met the calm, blank gaze of the statue of the Emperor, and let out the breath he had not even realised that he had been holding. 'It is time, brothers. We must move out. If the others were going to reach us, they would have by now.' He looked towards the palace. 'It is time to find our quarry. And this time, we will not stop until we achieve victory, or death.'

'Let's hope it's the one, rather than the other,' Alphaeus said, uprooting his sword from where he had driven it into the cracked ground.

The squad began to move back towards the palace, across the blasted landscape of broken alien bodies. They moved slowly, picking their way forwards with care, senses straining to catch any sign of the enemy that they all knew was not far away. As they moved, Karlaen could feel eyes on them, peering out from the gloom that surrounded them. Alphaeus had been correct – they were being watched. He could feel it himself now, scratching gently at his mind. The augur-lens of his bionic eye scanned the darkness that crept across the ruined plaza, but nothing revealed itself. That didn't mean that it wasn't there, simply that it was very good at hiding.

The broodlord had always been good at hiding. It had an instinct for dark, cramped places and wide shadows that had kept it alive for those first few weeks after... It hissed and squeezed its eyes shut.

When it opened them, it glared at the invaders, gauging their numbers and strength. It could feel the gathered minds of its children massing around it in the shadows of the ruins. It would sacrifice them all, in the name of victory, though it loved them. Yes, that was the word... *love*. It loved its children, even as the Hive Mind loved it, and it would send a hundred of them to their deaths without hesitation if it meant pulling down just one of the red-armoured giants striding through the plaza.

Its plaza.

Its sudden spurt of anger was passed to its children through the synaptic link that they shared, and it heard a ripple of soft snarls and creaking chitin. It forced itself to remain calm, and allowed the song of the Leviathan to dull the edges of its anger. It opened up the link between itself and its children, allowing them to glimpse the unfettered glory of the force they now served. Snatches of words fluttered through its mind, carried by the voices of those long dead: elegant, descriptive phrases which might describe the heaving, coiling presence that rose over it and its children and spread from horizon to horizon like a hungry sun.

It felt its mind and will fray at the edges as the song swept through it and around it. Some part of it longed to be one with the Leviathan, after being alone for so long. And it would be, soon enough. That was the fate of every living thing in Phodia – to be meat for the great beast that slithered through the void, following the light of a distant star.

But not yet. Its mind slammed shut to the voice of the Hive Mind, cutting off the song, and disturbing its children. The closest genestealer snuffled and clicked interrogatively, and the broodlord grunted in a placatory fashion. It focused on the invaders again. It could sense the rest of their number drawing near, just as the ones below moved towards the palace steps. Soon, there would be more of them. Far too many, in one place. It sat back on its haunches, considering.

No, it could not risk it. It would kill as many as it could now and thin their numbers before it considered its next move. It slouched forwards, reaching out with its mind, feeling for the burning sparks of the invaders' consciousness. Willing as it was to sacrifice its children in pursuit of its goals, it saw no reason not to employ every advantage it possessed.

It would show them the beautiful thing which awaited them all.

'Contact, grid twelve,' Alphaeus said. Karlaen checked his sensors, and saw the flare of red that meant an approaching bio-signature.

'Contact, grid eight, nine, eleven–' Leonos began, only to be interrupted by his twin.

'–contact on multiple grids,' Damaris said urgently.

'They've decided to stop hiding,' Karlaen said, as his targeting lens whirred and focused in on the shapes scuttling through the darkness all around them. There was more subtlety to the genestealers' actions now, as they crept through the darkness, staying close to cover at all times. In the gleam of his stab-lights he caught sight of a rounded skull or a flash of chitin, but that was it. 'Form up. If they rush us, we will drive them back. Whatever else happens, we will not be driven back again. We will go forward.'

He checked his sensors again, noting the positioning of the enemy. They were cut off in all directions, as if whatever mind was directing the xenos had seen and learned from his earlier strategy, and was now attempting to block off any avenues of escape. And yet, they did not attack. Karlaen stared out into the darkness and tried to discern the motivations of his unseen enemy. What was it waiting for?

The answer came a moment later, when his mind suddenly convulsed, wracked with stinging webs of malign thought. Karlaen grunted and bent forwards, clutching at his head. The others made similar motions, twitching as an unheralded pain tore through their thoughts, savaging them from within.

A haze of red descended over his eyes, but not the one with which he was all too familiar. This was a sickly haze, such as might overcome a dying animal's last moments. He groaned as alien thoughts wormed into his own, boring through the walls of discipline and hypno-conditioning to hook into the kernel of humanity within. Old memories, long buried under new, were uprooted from the murk and brought forth screaming into the light. He could recall the darkness of the sarcophagus he had been entombed in as an aspirant, only barely aware of the passage of time as the blood of the primarch changed him into something other than the youth he had been. The dark had squeezed and crushed him, and even in his almost comatose state he had screamed himself raw for those first few weeks.

More memories came, dragged up by the inhuman will which assaulted him – he felt the heat of weapons which had almost claimed his life, and felt the sour shadow which threatened to rise up in him in his darkest moments. His mind shuddered and squirmed in the grip of his enemy, and the memories began to change, becoming more horrible and utterly alien. He felt the discordant song of the Hive Mind as it thundered through him, washing what was *him* away and leaving only smooth purpose – to consume. These were not his thoughts, but those of the enemy. He had fought tyranids often enough to know that where most attacked with claws, poison and acidic bile, some could use a man's own thoughts against him.

And yet, there was something else. Something that, even in his agony, Karlaen could see… A flaw in that smooth, remorseless wall of gestalt hunger that threatened to overwhelm him. A hunger that was not merely for bio-matter, but for something else. Something more human in scope. Whatever it was, it was a weakness, and he knew what to do with an enemy's weakness, physical or otherwise. He focused on it, bringing every iota of his will onto it, as if his thoughts were the hammer which hung, forgotten, in his hand. He saw unfamiliar faces – a man and woman, a boy – and felt a surge of anger that was at once bestial and all too human, tinged as it was with grief, or perhaps madness. He felt the quiver of surprise go through the invader, a startled roar echoing in his head and from the darkness, as his mind bucked in its grip.

The haze which afflicted his vision began to clear, and he could see the savage shapes of genestealers rushing towards them. Teeth gritted against the whips of pain which still lashed his mind, he swung his storm bolter up and fired. A genestealer pitched forwards, its head a wet ruin. As if the sound of his shot had been a signal, Alphaeus and the others joined him. The dark was lit up by flashes of bolter fire, and genestealers fell in their dozens. But there were still more behind them, hundreds perhaps.

The ache in his mind began to lessen and he scanned the darkness behind the leaping, shrieking shapes of the enemy, searching for the thing which commanded them. It was here, somewhere, scrabbling in their minds to make them easy prey for the others. The augur-lens on his bionic eye flashed as it focused in on a shape crouched atop one of the few still-standing statues which dotted the plaza.

It was a broodlord, and larger than any he had ever had the misfortune to encounter before. A genestealer almost three times the size of those now assaulting him and his men, with talons that would put even the largest tyranid bio-beast to shame.

Red eyes met his, and he felt the creature's hideous thoughts begin to reassert themselves in his mind. It took every ounce of will and psycho-conditioning he possessed to hold it back. It had surprised him once; it would not do so again. He raised his storm bolter and a flash of pain, like acid on flesh, ripped through him. He ignored the pain and his finger tightened on the trigger as his targeting sigil flashed red. The creature reared up on its perch, spreading its four upper limbs as if in invitation, and he could sense its amusement.

Then, it was gone. The targeting lock ceased to flash, and he cursed. The creature had not moved; it had simply vanished as if had never been. *Another psyker's trick,* he thought angrily. Wherever it was, it hadn't gone far. He could still feel its thoughts, lurking on the underside of his consciousness. It was almost as if it was speaking to him, not in words, but in impressions. Though its first attack had been parried, the duel was not yet done.

'Captain, to your left,' Alphaeus roared suddenly, shocking Karlaen back to attention. He turned and saw the gaping, fang-studded maw of a genestealer closing in on him. Karlaen swept the genestealer aside with a thrust of his hammer and started towards the spot where he had last seen the broodlord. If he could catch it and kill it, he and the others might yet survive this mission. If not, well, better death than the ignominy of failure. He activated the vox and said, 'Alphaeus, hold the line until I return. If I don't, attempt to contact the others and request extraction.'

'Where are you going?' Alphaeus demanded, shouting to be heard over the din.

'Hunting,' Karlaen said, as he charged into the darkness.

CHAPTER SEVEN

Karlaen knew that rushing off alone, out of the line, was not a particularly sound decision, strategically. Tactically, however, it made perfect sense. Behind him, his brothers were waging a desperate battle against overwhelming odds, a battle in which, under different circumstances, he had no doubt that they would triumph. But now, they were not fighting the scuttling hordes of the Hive Mind alone, but the brutal psychic domination of the broodlord as well. And that was a battle they could not hope to win. Not unless he could find it, and kill it.

He used his bulk to push through the horde, smashing genestealers with his hammer, shoulders and feet. The xenos did not swarm him, as he expected, but instead broke and flowed around him, as if given orders to avoid him at all costs. He killed those that came within reach, but took advantage of the lull to press forwards, towards the statue he had seen the broodlord perched on. If the creature wanted to meet him, he would oblige it. While the broodlord was occupied with him, it would have no attention to spare for Alphaeus and the others, or for commanding the other genestealers. Alphaeus and the others could break their enemy, while Karlaen hunted his.

And it was his enemy. What he now stalked through the shadow-haunted plaza, away from the bellicose fury of the battle behind him, was the central intelligence which had dogged them since they had arrived on Phodia several hours before. He felt it in his gut. It had harried them and slain two of them, and he was determined to see that its tally grew no larger.

Despite his determination, he felt a flicker of disquiet. His bionic eye clicked and shifted in its socket of steel, trying to pinpoint the creature as the hiss of alien whispers filled his head anew. But it was nowhere to be seen. It was as if it had been erased from his perceptions. He could not smell it, taste it on the smoke-clogged air or see it. It might as well have been a figment of his imagination.

You can hide from me, but not the machine-spirits, beast, he thought as he activated the data-capture spirits within his augur-lens. Almost immediately, a haze of blinking after-images on a one-second delay showed him the brood-lord still crouched on the statue, then its leap, and the arc of its trajectory as it hurtled towards him. As the first image registered with him, he rerouted the data from his augur-lens to his storm bolter's opti-scope, allowing his armour's targeting system to lock onto the descending shape of the broodlord.

He fired a long burst, hoping to cut the creature in two before it reached him. Through the augur-lens, he saw it twist out of the way in mid-air and crash down into the rubble separating them. The broodlord rolled to its feet in a cloud of dust and rose up over him. It towered above his not inconsiderable height, and was easily of a size with the tyranid warriors he had faced earlier.

For an instant, they stared at one another. Then they came together with a crash of chitin on ceramite. Talons tore jagged grooves in armoured plates, and pale flesh darkened where the hammer's energy field touched. They broke apart, but only for a moment. Karlaen spun his hammer in a tight circle, parrying a series of blinding claw strikes as the broodlord came at him again. Such was its speed, the creature caught him more than once, leaving ragged furrows in his armour. Even his genhanced reflexes were no match for the sheer, unnatural speed of the beast. It would wear him down, one vicious strike at a time.

He swung the hammer out in a wide, looping blow. The broodlord flipped backwards, avoiding the blow and landing on all fours out of reach. Karlaen snarled and fired his storm bolter. The beast began to run, and he tracked it, firing all the while. It leapt from fallen statue to wreckage pile, staying just ahead of the explosive rounds until he was forced to turn, and it leapt onto him. He staggered, his armour's stabilisers and servos whining as they compensated for the additional weight.

It scrambled up onto him, one foot planted on his shoulder plate as it hooked its claws into the armour around his head in a splash of sparks. A hose was torn loose, spitting a hiss of air. He rolled with it, and smashed both his side and the creature into a fire-blackened column. Chips of marble spattered his face as the broodlord was sent flying. It hit the ground and slid until its claws thudded down, anchoring it in place.

The broodlord shoved itself upright as he charged towards it, roaring out an oath to Sanguinius and the Emperor both. It leapt straight up as his hammer slammed down, cracking the ground. Its feet struck the top of his armour and then it was lost in the shadows again, circling him just out of sight. He whirled, trying to catch a glimpse of it. But it was not relying on mental trickery this time, just its own speed and stealth.

Karlaen turned in a slow circle. His vox-link was still open, and he could hear the voices of his men as they fought on. He could hear other voices as well, those of Zachreal and the others as they met their own enemies in battle. The scene in which he found himself was being played out across the vast stretch of palatial ruins, in one form or another.

The genestealers and the tyranid warriors were but pieces on a board for the beast he now confronted – it could move them into position with an errant thought, and drive them berserk with equal ease. It could flood the palace with feeder-beasts and ripper swarms, or drown them in bio-beasts, if it wished.

But it did not. He knew it and could feel it. It wanted something, and it was delaying the consumption of this place until it got it. What abominable purpose was it seeking to fulfil? The question lodged itself in his mind like a splinter.

Overhead, the roiling, red sky was split by spores streaking to the planet's surface from the tyranid vessels far above. They moved almost gracefully, like sentient creatures rather than obscene tumours of bio-matter. His armour's sensors tracked them, recording their descent and relaying it to the Chapter fleet above automatically. More and more spores fell to earth, and the ground shook beneath him. Asphodex was dying; time was running out, both for his mission and the beast which glared at him from the shadows. He could feel its frustration boil across the surface of his thoughts, and he smiled.

'I know you can hear me, beast,' he said aloud. 'I know that you understand me, though I do not know how. I will speak slowly, regardless, for your benefit.' Karlaen could not say why he bothered to speak, save that in that instant when his mind had touched that of his enemy, he had felt something human... or something that had once been human. The thought was not a pleasant one, and he felt a chill, deep in his bones, as it occurred to him.

'You cannot win. We will come for you, with fire and sword, and we will overturn your nests and scour every trace of your vile species from this world, even if we must crack its crust and drown it in magma to do so. Asphodex will not fall to you. We will burn it to ash before we allow you to claim dominion.'

At first, he did not think that his words had had any effect on the beast. Then came a bubbling, liquid snarl of pure malice, and with it, a torturous flood of mental imagery. This stabbed into his mind, again and again, and he took a step back, almost overwhelmed by the sheer malignancy of it.

The broodlord darted from concealment and pounced on him as he reeled. Its lower set of claws dug into his cheeks as it bent over him, its feet digging into his belly, its larger talons sunk into his armour like anchor-hooks. He staggered beneath its weight, as before, and as it lunged to sink its fangs into his face, he rammed the haft of his hammer between its teeth.

Burning driblets of saliva hissed and smoked where they touched his armour as the beast struggled to bite through the weapon. Its eyes bulged obscenely in their sockets as it flung its thoughts at him. He closed his mind, throwing up mental walls, as he had been taught during his days as an aspirant. But as fast as he raised them, the beast knocked them down. It was more powerful than any such creature he had had the misfortune to encounter.

'What *are* you?' he grunted.

Images flapped against his mind like the wings of insects against the bulb of a stab-light. He saw the Tribune Chamber, full of life and sound, and on the throne that had once stood at the far end, a man sat. No, not a man... something else. Disgust welled in him, as he began to understand. As if sensing his revulsion, the broodlord uttered a muffled shriek of rage around the haft of his weapon. A claw slid between the plates of his armour and he felt a stab of pain.

His mind wavered as the creature's thoughts rode the pain into the depths of him. But the discordant pulse of the Hive Mind was met by the red hum that crouched sealed away in his subconscious. It rose, like a crimson tide, filling him and driving all other thought before it. Anger flared in him, and more than anger. He wanted to smash this thing, to strike it until it was no more than pulp and memory.

With a groan of servos, Karlaen forced the beast up, until it was barely holding onto him. Then, with a roar, he hurled the creature towards the statue it had been crouched upon. It struck the base of the plinth with a *crack* and tumbled down, limp and unmoving. The agony in his mind began to fade and he shook his head, trying to clear it. The world had gone red around him, and all he could see was the thing – his enemy – lying there, helpless.

Karlaen swung his hammer up and charged. He would end it here and now. He would see his mission accomplished. No more of his brothers would die. The red hum filled his mind, carrying him forward. The Hammer of Baal snapped out, wreathed in snapping strands of blue lightning. The broodlord–

–moved.

At the last moment, just before his hammer struck home, the creature opened one eye and flung itself aside. Whether it had been playing dead, or had actually been stunned, he could not say. It rolled away from the blow, which continued on to strike the statue. The hammer smashed through the lower section of the statue in an explosion of dust and stone splinters, and Karlaen allowed the force of the blow to spin him around.

He swung his storm bolter up as his targeting array locked onto the broodlord where it crouched, as if waiting for him. Karlaen heard the sound of stone grinding. His armour's proximity sensors blared a warning, and he looked up, the fury draining from him as he realised his mistake. The statue crashed down atop him. Its immense weight knocked him flat and pinned him to the ground.

Sensors blared warnings into his ears as his exoskeleton groaned and creaked. The plaza cracked beneath his hands as he tried to shove himself upright. Armour plates buckled at the point of impact, and the ancient suit of armour seemed to sag about him in defeat as he tried and failed to heave the statue off himself.

A slow hiss of satisfaction escaped his opponent. The broodlord watched his struggles with a flat, red gaze, its long, sinuous tongue flickering out to taste the air. Then, when it was certain that he was not going to escape, it began to crawl towards him. Its eyes never left his as it drew closer and closer, and he knew it was taking pleasure from his predicament.

Trapped, barely able to move, Karlaen could only watch as the broodlord crept towards him, its hideous face split into what could only be a leer of triumph.

CHAPTER EIGHT

The broodlord moved slowly, savouring its moment. Karlaen struggled against the statue's weight, trying to pull his arm free. If he could just extricate his storm bolter, he might stand a chance. But he did not think the creature was going to give him the time to do so. The rage that had held him, the red fury that had driven him to rashness, had been snuffed out like a fire doused in water. Now he was left with only cold certainty – he had been foolhardy, and now he was paying the price.

'Come on then, beast,' he spat. 'Come on.' He shifted, trying one last time to heave the statue aside. 'Take your due, if you would, but it will be the last time, I swear to you.'

The broodlord paused and examined him, as if in amusement. Then it started forwards again, eyes locked on his face. Karlaen continued to struggle. Even if it were hopeless, even if he died here, pinned beneath a statue, he would not give up. He would not resign himself to the monster that crawled ever closer. That, in the end, was what it meant to be of the blood of Sanguinius – even if your fate were woven into the universal skein, even if your doom was in your very blood, you would not surrender. Death in the name of duty was not defeat.

'Come on,' he rasped. 'Come and have your taste, vermin. Come, hurry!' If it got close enough, he might be able to blind it, with the help of the poison created by the Betcher's gland implanted in his hard palate. It would not be much of a victory, but it would be satisfying.

As if sensing his thoughts, it paused and eyed him suspiciously. It extended a claw, but hesitated. He felt its thoughts brush across his own, though without the urgency or ferocity of its earlier attempts. It was as if it were... curious.

His gaze caught something over the creature's hunched form. Beyond it, high in the red sky, which was beginning to lighten as dawn approached, dark shapes fell towards the city. At first, he thought that they were more spores, then he realised that they were drop pods. The warriors of the Chapter had arrived at last, beginning the final cleansing of Asphodex. As the drop pods drew closer, he could see that mingled among them were black-armoured warriors, riding on wings of flame. A chill coursed through him as he realised what had been unleashed upon the world.

The Death Company had been loosed upon Phodia, and no tyranid would be able to stay their wrath. As if plucking the thought from his head, the broodlord tensed and twisted about to watch the invasion force descend through the roiling clouds. Orbital bombardment from the fleet above Asphodex struck the continent-spanning city, covering the Blood Angels in their descent. The newcomers hurtled closer, so close now that he could make out the red marks on their ebony power armour, and Karlaen winced as his vox spat a mangled flurry of gibberish. He glared defiantly at the broodlord. 'Your death is coming, beast. If not by my hands, then by theirs. Scuttle back to whatever hole you crawled out of, if you would see another dawn.'

It was a desperate gambit, but it worked all the same. The broodlord turned back to him, cocked its head, and then snorted. It had apparently understood him. It turned away, as if to leave. Karlaen seized the moment. He had been rerouting power to his exoskeleton for one last gamble, and now was the time. With a grinding roar, he forced himself up. Dust and debris cascaded over him as he forced his armour to the utter limits of its load capacity and shifted the statue just enough to cause it to roll aside. Servos whining, he lunged for the beast, even as it whirled to meet him.

It avoided his awkward blow and slashed at him, driving him back against the statue. Before he could push away from it, the broodlord shot forwards, faster than his eyes, organic and bionic alike, could follow. A claw sank into his chest, puncturing an armour plate and digging into the meat within. Karlaen grunted in pain. The broodlord jerked its claw free and leapt back, out of range of any retaliatory strike. It eyed him as its long tongue flickered out to lick the blood from its claw. Then it was gone, vanished into the pre-dawn gloom.

Karlaen staggered forward, pressing a hand to his wound, as he vainly sought some sign of the beast. His superhuman enhancements were already stemming the flow of blood and sealing the wound. The vox popped and crackled in his ear. He could hear the others, and knew from the tenor of their voices that they were on the cusp of being overrun. His gambit had failed, but disaster could still be averted.

He pushed aside his pain and began to move back towards the battle, picking up speed as he went. 'I am coming, brothers,' he said, over the vox.

'Did you kill it?' Alphaeus asked over the crackling link.

'No,' Karlaen said, reluctantly. He did not elaborate, and Alphaeus did not press him. He caught sight of the squad as he made his way through the rubble. They had fallen back to the statue of the Emperor once more, putting their backs to it as the swarm of alien horrors sought to drag them down through sheer weight of numbers.

The vox popped and he heard familiar voices. He turned, and saw Zachreal on the steps that led into the palace, the storm bolters of his surviving squad-mates opening a path in the horde. Karlaen saw Melos and Joses as well, though they, like Zachreal, were leading the depleted remnants of their squads to the aid of Alphaeus and the others. Of the twenty Terminators who had teleported to the surface, barely half that number remained, and the survivors looked as if they had waded through the rivers of damnation. Karlaen's gut twisted at the thought. *Just like last time,* he thought. He forced the memory aside and kept moving. There would be time for self-recrimination later.

A tyranid warrior rose up before him, its bone swords swinging down towards him. The creature was riddled with wounds, leaking ichor from every joint, but even half-dead it was dangerous. He blocked the blow, grimacing as the movement caused his wound to pull painfully, and shot one of its legs off. The creature fell with a scream, which he cut short with a swift blow from his hammer.

The plaza was full of hissing, clawed shapes. There were genestealers clinging to every surface, perched on every statue and tumbled column. They swarmed up the fallen length of the statue of the Emperor Ascendant, surrounding the embattled remnants of Squad Alphaeus on all sides. Fire discipline had kept the horde at bay for a brief time, but now it was the wet work of sword and fists. Karlaen heard the crackle of Zachreal's voice in his ear and he said, 'All units, converge on Squad Alphaeus's transponder signal. We must push the creatures back. We must not fail–'

'–the Emperor!' A new voice, harsh and raw, intruded on the vox-link. The air was filled with the sound of thrusters and the grinding howl of chainswords. Black shapes, daubed in red, hurtled through the air over the plaza on wings of flame. 'Take heart, brothers. We shall show these traitors how the Sons of Sanguinius deal with those who would defile Terra.'

A genestealer's head was sent spinning from its neck to bounce off Karlaen's armour with a wet thump as the Death Company sped past. Where the black-armoured berserkers passed, xenos died. Karlaen was frozen with shock, and some revulsion, as he watched the newcomers descend on the plaza with eager cries. They spoke gibberish, challenging invisible foes and calling out to friends who lived only in memory. They were the Death Company, and they were irretrievably mad – victims of the Black Rage that lurked in the heart of each and every Blood Angel. Karlaen had felt it himself more than once, riding the edge of his anger, though he had never succumbed.

The Death Company was the doom of their Chapter made manifest. It was the savagery of the Red Thirst, mingled with the inescapable madness that came upon some warriors when they were consumed by the fires of an ancient struggle and became lost in the shadow of great wings, only to be reborn in a world of rage, hatred and nothing else.

Karlaen had heard that those who were so consumed were overcome by visions and ancient memories, and could not tell the past from the present. They fought the shadows of enemies past, and believed themselves to be on Holy Terra, fighting the forces of the Arch-Traitor. Despite this, they were warriors without equal; it was as if, in their madness, they had been gifted with some small part of Sanguinius's own strength. The warriors of the Death Company would fight until they died, and only death could quiet their rage.

Corbulo wished to eradicate the scourge of the Black Rage from the Chapter, and Karlaen knew that his mission here was tied in to that desire. But seeing the enraged Space Marines in action only pushed home the importance of finding Augustus Flax as soon as possible. More and more brothers fell to the Black

Rage with every passing century, and if it were not checked, the Blood Angels might vanish into madness and despair, leaving only the echoes of what might have been to mark their passing.

Karlaen caught sight of the leader of the Death Company squad – or so he guessed by the markings on the warrior's armour – wielding a wide-headed thunder hammer. The newcomer banked and circled the fallen statue of the Emperor. The Space Marine's body shuddered and twitched as he dropped from the air. The paving stones of the plaza cracked beneath him as he landed, and the head of his hammer was surrounded by a nimbus of crackling energy as he swept it out, driving the genestealers back.

The rest of the Death Company followed suit, dropping from the air to crash down among the genestealers like the wrath of the Emperor given form. Even as they landed, they attacked, filling the air with gore wherever they moved. The adamantium teeth of chainswords gnawed apart chitin as fists and hammers pulverised the alien bone. The brutality of the genestealers paled in comparison to the fury of the battle-maddened Blood Angels.

The Death Company fought without discipline, each warrior a whirlwind of death, but despite this, the genestealers began to waver before them. With the absence of the broodlord, Karlaen knew the genestealers were prey to their own instincts. They were not creatures of open battle, like the tyranid warrior-broods, but beasts of shadows and cramped spaces. It was in their nature to retreat in such situations.

Karlaen whirled as his vox crackled in warning, and he smashed a leaping genestealer out of the air. He saw Zachreal and the others hurrying towards him. The Terminators were like a blood-red wedge driven into the mass of alien bodies, Zachreal, Melos and Joses in the lead. The black-haired Joses was bloody faced, the left side of his jaw bare of flesh, bone showing through. One eye was a red ruin, but he still fought on, his storm bolter hammering. Melos's armour was blackened and stained, with only the skull set into its front free of charring, and Zachreal's armour was covered in hundreds of deep score marks.

'Captain, I have made a successful investigation of the upper decks,' Zachreal rumbled as he blew a hole in the centre of a genestealer's torso.

'And your report?' Karlaen said, smashing a xenos to the ground.

'Full of genestealers,' Zachreal said. He laughed, a great booming noise that echoed over the tumult of battle.

Joses ignored his fellow sergeant's mirth. A genestealer leapt towards him, and he caught the creature around the chest. As it snapped at him, Joses's head snapped forwards, catching the creature full in the face. Bone crunched, and Joses let the dead creature fall. Ichor stained his features, but Karlaen could see that he was grinning mirthlessly. Joses had always been something of a savage, he recalled. While most Blood Angels sought to distance themselves from their brute origins by refining their aesthetic senses, a few remained true to the primitive codes of the pure-blooded tribes of Baal and its moons.

'Zachreal's dubious attempts at jocularity aside, captain, we are at a disadvantage,' Melos said. 'We are facing nothing less than an army.' He pivoted, firing at the genestealers that sought to pull him down. Slowly but surely, the Terminators were pushing their way to Squad Alphaeus's side.

'Yes, but that army is, for the moment, leaderless and disorganised,' Karlaen said. He made no mention of how he knew this, and to their credit, they did not ask him. 'We must reach the others. Together, we can drive them back.'

He joined them, taking the point of the wedge. Together, they moved towards the fallen statue of the Emperor. Alphaeus and the twins were like an island chain in a swirling sea, just barely holding themselves above the waterline. As Karlaen and the others drew closer, however, the genestealers began to scuttle away, fleeing the plaza.

Alphaeus hacked down one of the slower xenos, and his seamed face twisted in a smile as he caught sight of Karlaen. He extended his arm, and Karlaen caught his forearm in a warrior's clasp. 'I was worried you weren't coming back. I would hate to have to explain to Commander Dante how I let you get yourself killed,' he said.

'You might still have to. This mission isn't over yet,' Karlaen said.

'At least we've got reinforcements,' Alphaeus said, gesturing with his sword. Karlaen turned, and saw that the Death Company had formed up around their nominal leader in a rough approximation of unit formation. They bounded across the plaza, hurdling piles of dead xenos, their chainswords licking out to lop off limbs and snarling heads as bolt pistols barked.

The black-armoured warriors were driving the bulk of the genestealers before them. The scuttling beasts scrambled up the steps and into the palace, seemingly fleeing before the Death Company. The hammer-wielding sergeant leapt over a dying genestealer, activating his jump pack as he did so, and careened towards a shrieking tyranid warrior. The beast spread its arms wide, as if in invitation, and the Space Marine smashed into it – then on through it, tearing the creature in half at the point of impact.

'Very effective reinforcements,' Karlaen murmured. He marvelled at the sudden change in their situation. Only a short time ago, the Blood Angels had been set to make a final stand. Now it was the tyranids who were being pushed back into the ruins.

'But uncontrollable,' Melos murmured gravely. 'Why would Dante send them here, unless…' He fell silent. Karlaen knew what he meant, but said nothing. If Dante had sent the Death Company to reinforce them, it had been because they were expendable. Only death could end their torment, and the ruins of the palace held plenty of that.

'It doesn't matter,' Karlaen said harshly. 'They are here, and we must employ every weapon remaining to us to achieve our goal. The tyranids want to keep us out, brothers, so we must go in, if only to teach them the folly of such hubris.'

Before anyone could reply, a deafening bellow echoed across the plaza, and Karlaen realised that the genestealers had, perhaps, had other reasons for retreating than just the arrival of the Death Company. One of the ruined structures on the other side of the plaza from the palace steps exploded outward, as if struck by a mortar. Chunks of stone and shrapnel filled the air for a moment, heralding the arrival of a hulking shape. A second bellow, louder than the first, echoed out across the plaza.

Armed with razor-sharp talons easily the size of a man and a massive bio-cannon beneath its heavy amethyst carapace, the carnifex strode into the plaza. Bits of rubble slid from it as it stomped forwards. Its heavy, wedge-shaped skull oscillated slowly as if taking stock of the armoured figures before it. Then it reared up to its full impressive height, and let loose a cry of challenge, before it thundered forwards, the ground trembling with every step it took.

CHAPTER NINE

The carnifex stamped forwards, its enormous claws swatting aside broken statues, its weight causing the stone squares of the plaza to crack and buckle. The immense bio-beast levelled its bio-cannon at the closest members of the Death Company, who spiralled towards it on tails of flame, roaring out challenges in the name of the Emperor. The organic artillery piece tensed and spat a living round, its barrel venting gas from the gill slits which opened in its length as it did so.

The projectile exploded into a constricting tangle of thorny vines that lashed out and caught the Space Marines, dragging them to the ground. They hacked at the vines to no avail, and the carnifex ignored their struggles as it stormed past, intent on getting to grips with the rest of its enemies. Its tiny eyes fixed on the heavy shapes of the Terminators, and it emitted another roar of challenge.

'Well, now it's a party,' Joses grunted. 'Look at the size of him.' He raised his power sword in readiness. 'He'll take some work to bring down.'

'Work and time,' Karlaen said. 'And we don't have enough of the latter.' He raised his hammer. 'Form up, phalanx-pattern sigma. Overlapping fields of fire, hold nothing back. If it gets to us...'

'I'll handle it,' Joses said, swinging his sword experimentally.

'See that you do,' Karlaen said. There was no time to argue. The beast was charging towards them faster than any creature that size ought to have been able to move. Another Death Company warrior charged to intercept the creature, his chainsword held in both hands. The carnifex swung its monstrous head towards him, and the air around its jaws began to shimmer with a greasy light. There came a roar of boiling plasma, and in a flash of superheated bile, the black-armoured warrior was vaporised in mid-leap.

The carnifex continued on, lumbering through the smoke of the warrior's passing. Its bio-cannon swung about, vomiting more strangling thorns across the plaza, and its scything talons swung out in deadly arcs, sending Death Company berserkers crashing to the ground in clouds of blood and entrails, their power armour cracked open and their torment ended. It spat plasma, incinerating anything that dared stay its progress. And when none of those weapons sufficed, it simply crashed through the opposition, be it a living warrior or an unfeeling statue. It was unstoppable, and it was heading right for Karlaen and the others.

As one, the Terminators fired. The carnifex shrugged off the explosive shells and continued to bull forwards. It would not stop, Karlaen knew, until it was dead, or until something even bigger decided to get in its way. Nevertheless, he continued to fire, his targeting array trying to find some weak point in its carapace. The ground shook beneath his feet as the carnifex closed in. Joses readied himself to meet it, his face split by a wide, feral grin. Karlaen could smell the incipient blood-lust in the other Blood Angel's sweat, and see it building in his eyes. He hesitated, wondering if he should order the sergeant to step back. Would that stop him? Would he listen? Or was he already too far gone?

Before the question could be answered, something black smashed into the charging carnifex from the side and sent it slewing through a column. The carnifex rolled to its feet in a cloud of dust, but its attacker was on it before it could move. Metal talons, each as long as a sword blade, flashed out, carving bloody tracks in the carnifex's flesh. The alien reared back, screaming in rage. Its cry was answered by its opponent.

'Come, traitor. Come to Cassor. Come and fight, come and die, but come all the same,' the vox-speakers mounted in the Dreadnought's hull crackled. 'Come and meet thy doom, dogs of abomination. Come and feel the angel's wrath, curs of Angron. Come screaming or in silence, but come so that Cassor might lay thy hearts at Sanguinius's feet. The walls of the Palace stand, the Eternity Gate remains barred and Cassor will break thy crooked spines across his knee.'

The Dreadnought, hull painted black and daubed in red, set itself as the carnifex charged towards it. The talons mounted on the ends of the piston-like arms rotated and flexed. Then one rose, revealing a storm bolter mounted beneath the claw. The storm bolter spat, and the carnifex shuddered as its already abused flesh received new punishment. It crashed into the Dreadnought and drove it back into a statue. The Dreadnought shrugged off the blow and rammed itself into the carnifex's gut, lifting the beast into the air momentarily before smashing it down onto the ground.

'By the wings of the Angel, it's Cassor,' Alphaeus breathed as he watched the battle unfold before them. Karlaen did not ask him how he recognised the Dreadnought, for there was only one Cassor.

Cassor the Chained, Cassor the Mad, Cassor the Damned – whatever name he was known by, he had been one of the greatest warriors ever produced by the Blood Angels, even before he had been interred in a Dreadnought sarcophagus, to rise and fight again after his death on some far-flung battlefield.

He was also a warning, a testament to the dark truth that even the dead were not truly safe from the curse which afflicted the Sons of Sanguinius. For almost three centuries after his death, Cassor had served the Blood Angels from the war machine's sarcophagus, until that final, fateful day at Lowfang. In the early hours of the battle, his mind had shattered, though no one could say why. Some swore that it was the shadows of the wings of the Sanguinary Guard falling on him as they passed overhead. Karlaen suspected that there was more to it than that. Whatever the reason, however, Cassor now belonged to the Death Company and was far too dangerous to be unleashed without cause.

He could barely tell friend from foe, and he was, in his own way, as monstrous as the tyranid creature he was now fighting.

'The Damned One,' Zachreal murmured, as he watched the battle. He looked at Karlaen. 'Truly, our mission must be important if Commander Dante has unleashed him to aid us, captain.'

'Were you ever in any doubt?' Karlaen said, watching as the black-hulled Dreadnought crashed into the carnifex again. The two maddened beasts, one metal, one flesh, came together like rival bovids. The stones of the plaza were crushed and churned to rubble as they strove against one another.

'Ho, traitor, strive and strain all you wish, you will never conquer Cassor. While Cassor stands before the gates of Holy Terra, none shall pass. Shriek, daemon. Scream out your prayers to the gods of wrong angles and shattered skies. Summon them. They shall not defeat Cassor. It cannot be done.'

Cassor's emotionless, rasping monotone echoed across the plaza, drowning out the shrieks of the carnifex. The carnifex ripped at the Dreadnought with its huge claws, scoring the ancient armour but failing to pierce it. Cassor slashed at the beast with his own talons.

Xenos and Dreadnought reeled across the plaza, brawling through the ruins, the carnifex howling out bestial challenges as Cassor roared out gibberish in reply. Suddenly, a ceramite plate buckled, and one of the carnifex's claws lanced down into the nest of grav-plates and fibre bundles that made up the Dreadnought's innards. The claw crashed down through the war machine and on into the ground, pinning Cassor in place.

'Pinned. Inconceivable. Cassor shall not stand for this, puppet of false gods. Release me, so that I might wipe thy stain from the earth,' Cassor rumbled.

In reply, the carnifex opened its maw wide. A greasy ball of plasma began to form between its jaws.

'Sorcery. You dare? Suffer not the witch to live, so says Cassor.' One heavy mechanical claw closed around the carnifex's throat, holding it in place. The beast, as if understanding what Cassor had planned, began to struggle, but to no avail. As surely as it had the Dreadnought pinned, Cassor had it held fast. Before the monster could release the burst of bile it had prepared, the Dreadnought brought up his wrist-mounted meltagun and shoved the barrel between the creature's jaws. With a dull hiss, the back of the beast's skull vanished in a cloud of superheated gas.

The carnifex toppled sideways, freeing Cassor in the process. The war machine shoved himself upright. His chassis rotated, as the optic augurs mounted in the hull scanned the plaza for more enemies. 'Listen, traitors. Hear Cassor's words: I still stand. The Emperor's hand is upon my shoulder. I am death incarnate!' The words echoed out over the area. But no new challengers appeared. Then, with a grinding of unseen gears and a whine of servos, Cassor the Damned stalked towards the palace, in search of new foes to slay.

In the aftermath of the carnifex's death, silence descended on the plaza. The gore-spattered survivors of the Death Company had cleared the plaza and entered the ruins of the palace, followed by Cassor. Karlaen could hear the sounds of battle echoing from the gaping doors of the palace, and knew that some of the genestealers, at least, had not made a clean escape. He looked about, taking stock.

Alphaeus and the others joined him. Karlaen clasped the sergeant on the shoulder for a brief moment, and then turned to look at the others. 'We still have a mission to complete, brothers. Our enemy will soon turn its gaze here, and the full might of the Hive Mind will fall on us. If we are to succeed, we must move and swiftly.'

'We don't even know where they are. Our searches revealed nothing,' Melos said, his fingers playing across the curve of the skull set into his armour.

'Yours, perhaps, but ours was more successful,' Karlaen said. He patted the servitor head dangling from his belt. 'I know where Flax is, and I know how to get to him.' He smiled slightly. 'We were right on top of him the whole time.'

'What?' Melos asked.

'Easier to show you than explain,' Karlaen said. He started towards the palace. 'Come. Let us go claim Corbulo's prize.'

CHAPTER TEN

As they entered the ruins of the palace, they could see the handiwork of the Death Company all about them. The broken, ruined corpses of genestealers and tyranid warriors lay everywhere, reeking in the dust and gloom. Karlaen led his men back to the Tribune Chamber, past the fire-blackened ruins that marked Bartelo's final passing.

Silence descended on them as they followed the trail of carnage. The vox popped and hummed, but no voices broke the stream of static. Outside the palace, the consumption of Asphodex had entered its final stages. Parts of the planet's crust were already being scoured of every trace of organic matter, from cowering human survivors to the mould clinging to the rocks in the deepest caves. Soon, the oceans would be drained, and the air made toxic. But the warriors of the Blood Angels and Flesh Tearers would tear up the roots of the hive fleet before then, if all went according to plan.

An eerie sight was waiting for them in the chamber. The remains of Aphrae lay broken in the centre of the Tribune Chamber, arms flung out to either side, his ruined features staring upwards towards the shattered glass of the dome above. The survivors of the Death Company surrounded the corpse, staring down at it in complete silence with something that might have been reverence. Their silence was eerie after the brutal, snarling cries that had filled the air upon their arrival. The Death Company sergeant knelt beside Aphrae, one hand on his chest, head bowed. His helmet sat on the ground beside him, and Karlaen stopped as he caught sight of the other Space Marine's tortured features.

'Raphen,' he murmured. Sadness filled him, dousing his momentary sense of triumph. Raphen's head turned, as if he had heard Karlaen, and he rose slowly to his feet. The other members of the Death Company turned, weapons raised. Madness and violence bled off them, and Karlaen felt pity and disgust in equal measure as he gazed at their twitching, shuddering forms. This, then, was what awaited him – what awaited them all – if he failed here. He could not bear to look at them, at his brothers, so distorted by rage that they were no longer proud sons of the Imperium, but instead battle-frenzied beasts.

'Raphen,' Alphaeus whispered. 'You were aspirants together, were you not?'

'We were,' Karlaen said softly. Memories of another young aspirant, the scars of battle fresh on his body, sitting across from him in the three-day vigil that followed their selection. He remembered fighting beside Raphen on a hundred worlds, battling the Chapter's enemies. But he had taken one path, and Raphen another and now... here they were.

There was a crash from behind them, and Karlaen, shocked from his reverie, spun, raising his weapon. The others followed suit, only a half-second more slowly. Cassor lumbered towards them from the other side of the chamber, hull painted with steaming ichor. The Dreadnought raised his storm bolter talon. 'Who comes? Friend or foe? Announce yourselves or taste my fury.'

'Hold, gentle Cassor,' Raphen croaked. His voice had the raw tinge of one who had screamed himself hoarse. 'Can you not see that these are our brothers? They wear the colours of the Legion. What word, brothers? Does the Eternity Gate still stand? What of the primarch?' There was a terrible desperation in his words, like those of a tormented child seeking comfort. Raphen shoved past the other black-armoured warriors in his haste to meet them. 'Has the Khan come to relieve us, as he promised? Speak, brothers.'

Karlaen hesitated, uncertain how to answer. The things of which Raphen spoke had taken place millennia ago, when Sanguinius still walked among them. He was possessed by ancient memories which were not his own, reliving battles he had never fought. He was mad and broken and Karlaen, for the life of him, could not think what to say.

He stared into the cold, blue eyes of the man he had once called a friend and said, 'Do you know me, sergeant?'

'I... cannot say,' Raphen said. Insanity danced behind his eyes, and his face contorted as if he were seeking to wrestle his memories into some semblance of coherency. 'Did we fight on the walls of the Palace together? Did we... Are we embarking for the *Vengeful Spirit*, brother? Has the Emperor assembled his strike force? Is it time to smite the Arch-Traitor, cowering aboard his battle-barge?' He reached out, as if to touch Karlaen's armour. His fingers curled into a fist before they reached Karlaen, and fell. 'Say yes, brother. Say that the Angels are to be the point of the spear,' he growled, half-pleadingly.

Karlaen stared at Raphen, pity wrestling against necessity within him. Then he closed his eyes and said, 'Yes.' He heard a soft, communal sigh rise from the Death Company. He looked at Raphen. 'The honour of leading the advance is yours, brother. You and your men will form the tip of our spear, as we seek out the one we have come to find.'

'And what of Cassor, brother? Is there honour here for me as well?' Cassor rumbled. His great claws snapped together in eagerness. 'Are there traitors to be slain? If so, Cassor will slay them.'

'There are traitors here, mighty Cassor,' Karlaen said. 'You will accompany us, and rain down your wrath on those who would seek to block our way.' He pulled the servitor's head from his belt. 'But first, we must find them.'

He directed Alphaeus and the others to the centre of the chamber, where they swiftly cleared away many of the bodies from a circular area. It was a seemingly innocuous patch of floor, but the information he had gleaned from the servitor's memory showed him that this was the entrance to the undercity of

Phodia. He sank to his haunches and uprooted the stone that hid the crypt-lock. He lowered the servitor head, tilting it so that its eye was in line with the lock's sensors. There was a click, then, with a whirr, a section of the floor irised open. Bodies tumbled into the gap in a sudden avalanche.

Damaris examined the aperture. The Terminator glanced at his twin, and then said, 'Tunnels, captain.' He stepped back as the Death Company moved quickly past him and into the darkness. Raphen, his helmet in place once more, led them. Cassor followed, mechanisms wheezing. Karlaen watched them descend, the servitor head dangling from his grip.

Alphaeus came up beside him. 'That is what they are here for, captain,' he said.

'And how long until someone says the same of us, Alphaeus?' Karlaen said, bitterly.

'Hopefully never,' Alphaeus said.

Karlaen shook his head. 'Sometimes I wonder if that is our true curse – hope. Hope that we can escape the fate that befell our brothers. Hope that we can change the inevitable.' He looked at Alphaeus. 'I hear it, brother. It's like a melody I can't help but hear, a song from an unremembered past. I heard it when I woke for the first time, after my Sanguination, and I'll hear it when I close my eyes for the last,' Karlaen said softly.

'We all hear it, captain... brother,' Alphaeus said. He raised a hand, as if to place it on Karlaen's arm. But instead, he dropped it. 'All that matters is whether you choose to follow it.'

Karlaen jerked his chin towards the loping, black-armoured shapes of the Death Company. 'I don't think they had a choice, Alphaeus. I don't think any of us do.'

Alphaeus said nothing. Karlaen did not look at him. 'Come. We still have a governor to find,' he said, placing the head back on his belt and hefting the Hammer of Baal. Then, weapon in hand, he led his brothers down into the dark.

The Spawn of Cryptus watched its enemies descend into the depths of the undercity. It clung to the dome of the Tribune Chamber's roof, hidden by the shadows and its psychic abilities. The enemy ranks had swelled, but its carefully laid out ambushes had thinned the herd, as it hoped. It did not wish them dead. Not yet.

Not until they had found its quarry for it.

The broodlord crawled along the curve of the dome, its eyes on the open access hatch. It had known of its existence, but had been unable to breach it, even with the aid of the larger bio-beasts the Hive Mind had provided. A lesser creature, one whose will was completely subsumed in the shadow of the Leviathan, would simply have allowed the ripper swarms and feeder-beasts to ferret out what openings they could find, and left the cowering remnants of the Flaxian Dynasty to a stifling death in the depths of their self-made tomb.

But its will was not a lesser one. It never had been, and though the broodlord could not defy the Leviathan, it could subvert and distract it. It had kept back the swarms of tunnelling horrors and crushing beasts, shielding the palace with its will as it set its children the task of ferreting out a way into the depths.

It had been enraged, at first, when it learned the reason for the presence of the invaders. That they had come to take that which it had sought for so long had driven it into a murderous frenzy. But when the frenzy abated, its mind had begun to work. It was not a beast, and it had once had teachers who had tutored it to the limits of their ability. It knew so many things that its mind sometimes ached with the weight of that knowledge.

It paused in its descent, waiting patiently for the last glimmer of light from its enemies to fade into the darkness. That there were depths which even it had not known of was frustrating, to say the least. But then, its quarry had always been more cunning than it seemed; cunning and treacherous. A stab of anger elicited a gurgling snarl, and its muscles tensed. Rockcrete crumbled beneath its talons as it pushed away from the wall and dropped to the floor of the chamber.

It rose to its full height, arms dangling, and looked around the chamber. Its eyes scanned the great murals – now ruined by blood, ash and impact craters – which covered the walls. It could remember them, how they had been before. On more than one night, its belly bloated with the meat of its prey, it had come here, creeping through the shadows, to sit and study them. They were its history, as much as that of its quarry. The history of Phodia, of Asphodex, of Cryptus and the Flaxian Dynasty.

The broodlord went to the closest wall, talons extended, and traced the faces painted there. It had been told the names that went with those faces, once upon a time, but it could not recall them. It could not recall many things now. The weight of the Leviathan's shadow pressed down on its mind more each day, erasing those things which the Hive Mind had no use for. Soon, it would not be what it was, save in form. Its mind would be smoother and less complex. It would be at peace.

It traced the faces on the mural and tried to remember just one name. Just one, to satisfy itself that it was still what it had been. Its claws dug deeper and deeper into the painted, blood-spattered surface, destroying what remained as it tried to remember.

It did not fear the song of the Leviathan, or the complete sublimation of its will and individual impulses into the gestalt of the Hive Mind. But it did fear that it would occur too soon, and take with it the dreams which had driven it for so many years. The desire which had kept it alive in the dank, dark access tunnels below Phodia, after it had been betrayed and after...

The broodlord's eyes closed. Faces, voices, scents all rose up in its mind, like ashes stirred from a dying fire. It heard snatches of music, and felt the comforting touch of one who had adored it. It heard the echo of booming laughter, and the stroke of a cloth across its muzzle, as blood and offal were wiped from jaws not yet dextrous enough to chew unaided. The fire in its head was no longer dying, and the song of the Leviathan faded into a comforting background hum as its rage was stoked.

It swung back from the wall, spreading its claws, and screamed. The scream was at once a summons and a warning, full of heat and demand. Its claws looped forwards, striking the wall, striking the faces it would soon forget, and tore great gouges in them, obliterating them.

It turned, as it heard and felt the arrival of its surviving children. They swarmed down the walls or loped across the floor, surrounding it. It felt their minds rise up below its own and it tilted its head, letting out a slow hiss of satisfaction. The way was open. Its quarry, trapped. There was nothing now, save the end.

And then, it could forget, and lose itself forever in the shadow of something greater.

CHAPTER ELEVEN

THE UNDERCITY, FLAXIAN PALACE, PHODIA

Karlaen held up the servitor's head. The drone's mouth twitched into motion, and a babble of binary whispers fled its vox-unit. The heavy plasteel blast door before Karlaen ground open with a groan of tortured metal. The turreted auto-cannons mounted to either side of the door lowered their barrels and slid back into their security-niches.

It was the seventh such door the Blood Angels had come to since descending into the darkness of the undercity well over an hour before. The undercity was a mass of ruins, canals and tunnels beneath a roof of gridwork and pipes. Water dripped down constantly, somewhere out in the dark, striking metal. The sound of it echoed through the vast stretch of the undercity, bouncing from one hard surface to the next, until the point of origin was impossible to determine, even for one with the enhanced senses of a Space Marine.

When the blast door had fully opened, Karlaen stepped aside, allowing the Death Company to enter beyond first. It galled him to do so, but Alphaeus was right. The black-armoured warriors were here for one reason and one reason only – so that by their death his mission might prove successful. Nonetheless, the thought of it tore at him, even as it drove him on. If he were successful, then Raphen and his warriors might be among the last such doomed berserkers. It was too late for them, and for Cassor, lurching in their wake, but not for the rest of the Chapter.

He followed the Death Company through the blast door, along with the other Terminators. The vox was silent; noise discipline was being enforced now. Helmets had been retrieved and no flesh was visible, to guard against possible chemical attacks. The Terminators moved without speaking, their attentions fixed firmly on their sensors.

The undercity was the sort of battlefield with which they were all painfully familiar – cramped and crowded, full of shadows and noise. The ground vibrated with the hum of the hidden generators which powered the undercity and kept the air circulating, and ruptured pipes spat steam into the damp air. Alien mould was already growing in the nooks and crannies, and in places the floor had buckled, allowing the first, pale shoots of newborn spore-chimneys to peek through into the dim, artificial light.

The Death Company were waiting on the other side of the blast door when

Karlaen passed over the threshold. They murmured to one another unintelligibly or stared ahead with fixed intensity, their powerful frames twitching with impatience. The reason for this was readily apparent – their path forward was blocked by a vast vacuum-lock portcullis, its cog-toothed blast door marked by the seal of the Flaxian Dynasty.

There were no sentry-weapons on display or combat-servitors standing guard. Karlaen hesitated, considering. His armour's sensors scanned the door and the immediate area, trying to discern some trap or pitfall. When none was forthcoming, he hefted the servitor's head and stepped forwards as he had before. The servitor twitched in his grip, its jaws unhinging to a disturbing degree as multiple vox-units mounted in its throat sprang to life and spat duelling glossolalia of what might have been code, prayers or something else entirely.

With a hiss of escaping air, the massive portcullis cycled open. After the gloom of the sub-city, it took Karlaen's senses time to adjust to the splendour which was revealed behind the secondary blast door. Outside and above, the city of Phodia was a rain-soaked ruin, hunched beneath spore clouds, the streets thick with signs of alien infestation. The undercity was not much better – long-neglected areas collapsed in on themselves, while overhead, the dull glow of illuminators flickered and grew weaker with every passing hour.

But here there was no sign of power failure or tyranid infestation. Empty buildings lined broken streets, beneath a humming solar illuminator that cast its radiance across the vaulted reaches of this protected enclave. Karlaen took in the faded grandeur of the city-within-a-city at a glance. The servitor head squawked and fell silent. Through his armour's connection to the decapitated head, he could see that they had found the object of their search at last. He quickly unhooked the servitor and re-attached it to his belt. It still had some use left in it – specifically, plotting the quickest course out of the undercity.

'What is this place?' Alphaeus muttered.

'A hideaway,' Karlaen said. 'A home away from home, in the event of a planetary disaster. Or so our friend told me.' He patted the servitor's head.

'Big for a hideaway,' Alphaeus said.

'It's meant to house a significant portion of Phodia's necessary population. I wondered why so many of them sought sanctuary in the Tribune Chamber.' Karlaen looked around. 'The tyranids breached the palace's defences before they had a chance to evacuate, I expect.'

'Or he left them to die,' Alphaeus said.

Karlaen made to reply, but fell silent. That was all too likely. Different men reacted differently in moments of danger and loss. Some found wellsprings of courage undreamt of, while others cowered beneath the bodies of braver men and hoped to ride out the storm. Was Flax hidden away down here, he wondered, while above, his people fought to the last against an indefatigable enemy? Whatever the answer was, Karlaen did not intend to leave until he found out. He made to order the advance, but was beaten to the punch.

'The city is silent, brothers. The traitors await. Let us hunt,' Cassor rumbled, and started forwards, claws snapping together in barely restrained fury. The Death Company fell in around the Dreadnought, loping through the winding streets, their rasping mutters and unintelligible cries spreading through the stale air. Karlaen held the Terminators back, just for a moment. In the open now, some of the Death Company had begun to hack and hew at imaginary enemies. He knew, with sickening certainty, it would not do to get too close to them, not now.

'Eyes open, brothers. Sensors to full extension, with geosynchronous positioning. I want this hideaway of Flax's mapped and recorded, just in case a hasty exit is called for.' Karlaen started forwards, Alphaeus, Leonos and Damaris fanning out around him. The other squads did the same, until a rough line of crimson-armoured giants was moving steadily through the seemingly abandoned city.

Before they had moved very far, however, Karlaen saw Raphen stop. The Death Company sergeant trembled like a dog catching a scent, his head cocked. Then, with a shout, he began to bound through the ruins. His warriors followed, and Cassor lumbered in their wake, pistons wheezing as he picked up speed.

'What did they–' Alphaeus began.

Karlaen held up a hand.

'Listen,' he said. 'Music.' He recognised the haunting melody which had attracted the attention of the Death Company. It had been part of the initial briefing on Asphodex and the Cryptus System. The Blood Angels always included such items of cultural relevance in briefings; a people's culture was a window into the way they thought. The song was an ode to the glories of the Flaxian Dynasty, a hymn to their wisdom, forbearance and courage. Karlaen did not find it strange that it should be playing here and now; humans often sought comfort in the past when the future proved too frightening. Indeed, the music gave him heart – if it were still playing, there was a good chance that Flax, or one of his family, still lived.

He moved quickly, following the Death Company. If the maddened Space Marines reached the source of the music first, there was no telling what might happen. Alphaeus and the others followed. The Terminators trudged through the tight, winding streets until they reached a central plaza, wider than the Plaza of the Emperor Ascendant, and filled with life and sound. The plaza was occupied by a massive garden. Wilted alien flowers gave off a riot of strange, cloying scents which did little to mask the odour of excess rising from the occupants of the plaza.

Everywhere, noble men and women, the scions of Asphodex's greatest noble houses, lay senseless, or as good as, in the grass. Bottles of rare intoxicants, some banned by Imperial law, lay strewn about, and billowing obscura censers pumped hazy vapours into the perfumed air. In the centre of this scene of decadence, surrounded by attentive slave-servitors, an ancient man reclined feebly on a floating bed of silks and cushions. As Karlaen looked at the old man, a warning light flashed in his helmet, alerting him to the proximity of the genetic sequence he had been sent to claim.

Before he could act, however, there was a creak from the network of pipes, grates and illuminators above. Proximity warnings flashed and he looked up, expecting to see genestealers crawling along the roof of the hidden city. Instead, he caught a flash of metal, as a number of combat-servitors dropped from the roof to interpose themselves between the newcomers and the aristocratic loungers.

The servitors were repulsive things, made to order, and shaped more like the tyranids they were on guard against than the humans they were protecting. Jointed limbs stuck out from serpentine bodies composed of segmented, armoured sections, and human faces glared out from within cobra-hoods of ceramite. Karlaen snatched the servitor head from his belt, hoping that it could get them past the combat-servitors without violence.

They were little threat to the Blood Angels, but there was every chance that the man they had come to find might be caught in the crossfire. Luckily, the drones did not seem to be armed with anything more than blades. They were a last line of defence, rather than proper weapons-servitors; bodyguards whose only goal was to see that their masters remained undisturbed in the final hours of their existence.

Before he could present the head, Raphen gave a shout and the Death Company bounded forwards, weapons ready. The combat-servitors moved forward to meet them with eerie grace, bladed limbs whirring. Raphen ducked under the lunge of the lead servitor and rose up beneath it, catching it with his shoulder and flipping it over his back. As the servitor tried to right itself, Raphen snapped around and drove his hammer into the drone's head, crushing it with one blow. The serpentine body spasmed and then fell still.

The Death Company swarmed over the rest of the marble-fleshed drones like ants, hacking and shooting. The servitors fought with single-minded intensity, but they were no match for their attackers. The last of the brass-limbed monstrosities fell to Cassor, who crushed its skull in his claw and slung the twitching remains aside. They crashed down at Karlaen's feet as he increased the volume of his vox-unit and roared out, 'Hold!'

Raphen, thunder hammer raised, ready to spill the brains of a prostrate noble, turned. Karlaen met his gaze and several tense moments passed before the sergeant lowered his weapon. His warriors followed suit, albeit reluctantly. The combat-servitors had raised the ire of the Death Company, and they were eager to shed blood in the name of the Emperor.

'Why are we not killing these degenerate sybarites, brothers? What purpose do they serve? Cassor can smell the Phoenician's stench on this place, and he would cleanse it.' Cassor turned slowly, blades clicking impatiently.

'Stay thy wrath, mighty Cassor. There will be time enough for killing before we are done here, I fear,' Karlaen said calmly.

The Dreadnought twisted to face him, and Karlaen forced himself to remain where he was. The blood-red optic lenses mounted on the black hull whirred and focused in on him. Cassor extended a talon towards him. The tip of one of the blades touched his chestplate with a soft *ting*.

'I know you.'

Despite the emotionless basso rumble the words were delivered in, Karlaen could hear the uncertainty there. He steeled himself and said, 'And I know you, mighty Cassor, hero of Lowfang and Demeter's Fall. I know that you are a true son of Sanguinius.'

'I... I am a true son. I hear the Angel's voice, brother. I see his face, in yours. I... I will stay my wrath, brother. For now.' Cassor lowered his claw and turned away. Karlaen let out a slow breath. He turned back to Alphaeus and motioned for his second-in-command to follow him.

The intoxicated nobles had not reacted to the brief melee, and they did not react when Karlaen and Alphaeus moved through them towards Flax. The old man remained as insensate as his followers until Karlaen was looming over him. When Flax registered first the shadow and then the grizzled, golden-haired giant who cast it, his rheumy eyes widened in sudden panic. He began to babble in fear as Karlaen drew close.

'Governor Flax, I presume,' Karlaen said. 'I am Captain Karlaen of the Blood Angels Chapter and the Baal Expeditionary Force. I have been ordered to see to your immediate evacuation. If you will come with us, we will get you to safety.'

Flax's eyes narrowed. The fear was gone, replaced by something else. Resignation, perhaps, or exhaustion. The old man shook his head and slumped back into his cushions. 'I am Flax, aye. And your orders mean nothing to me, captain.' The old man smiled mirthlessly. 'You see, if you are here, then I am already damned.'

CHAPTER TWELVE

'Damned?' Karlaen said, slightly startled by the old man's matter-of-fact dismissal. Humans, even politically powerful ones, were wont to be slightly in awe of the warriors of the Adeptus Astartes. They were the Emperor's word given form, and few were the men brave enough to match their gaze and not quail back from them. Flax did not seem to be a brave man. Perhaps it was simply that fear had been burned out of him.

'Oh yes, and not a moment too soon,' Flax said, lolling among his cushions. 'I half feared you were him, at first. Now I see that his game has been interrupted. He will blame me, of course, as he always has, and he will have no choice but to bring an end to it.' He smiled. 'For that, I must thank you, captain.'

'Who is "he"? Who are you talking about?' Karlaen asked, knowing the answer even as the words left his mouth.

'The beast, captain. You've seen it – fought it. I can tell.' Flax reached out with a withered, liver-spotted hand as if to trace one of the many long gouges in Karlaen's armour. His fingers stopped short, however, and he pulled his hand back to clutch it against his chest. He smiled wearily. 'As telling as a signature, those marks. I've seen their like more times than I care to admit in my life. On doors and walls and, aye, on the bodies of my people.'

Karlaen touched the mark as he gazed at Flax. 'The broodlord has been on Asphodex for some time, then.' It was not unheard of – creatures like the broodlord had been reported on many worlds just before those planets came under threat from one tendril or another of a hive fleet. The creatures seemed to act as a beacon for the hive ships. They would lurk unseen for years, decades even, waiting for the right time to summon their hungry kin across the bleak stars to feast on the bio-matter of their chosen hunting ground.

'Broodlord – is that what you call it?' Flax chuckled. 'My people called it the Spawn of Cryptus, as if it were a curse on the whole system rather than just this world.' His smile faded. 'Maybe it was – a sign of the Emperor's displeasure with us if there ever was one.'

'The Emperor had nothing to do with that creature,' Karlaen said.

Flax gestured morosely. 'Oh, to be sure. I know full well where the fault lies, captain.' He grinned crookedly and patted his sunken chest. 'With us, with the dynasty of Flax. We are damned, captain, and rightly so, for that thing, that beast, is our burden. It is our sin made manifest.' The old man jerked forwards to cough into a clenched fist. Karlaen, alarmed, immediately ran a sensor scan of the old man. Humans were astonishingly fragile, and if Flax were broken or ill, it would hamper the extraction effort.

Flax's coughing faded into a wet wheeze, and he shook his head. 'Our sin,' he said again. 'Mine and my parents', captain. A sin I allowed to stay buried, hoping that the shadows and years would swallow it. That it would crawl into the depths and die. But not everything dies in the dark... Some things take root and flourish.' He looked up towards the pipes and grating that made up the roof. 'And now here I am, cowering underground. Full circle,' he muttered.

'What are you talking about?' Karlaen said. Something about the old man's words had pricked his curiosity. He was afraid, but his fear was not of the tyranids, Karlaen thought. Flax looked at him.

'My brother,' the old man said, simply. 'My brother, Captain Karlaen. You met him, briefly.' He gestured to the claw mark on Karlaen's armour. 'And he made quite the impression.' Flax's eyes closed and he hunched forwards again, fists pressed to his eyes. 'My Emperor-be-damned thrice-cursed brother, whose throne I took for the benefit of my people, much good as it has done them.' He stiffened, and looked up again, eyes bulging. 'Do you hear me Tiberius, you gangling monstrosity?' he snarled, shaking his fist aimlessly. 'I know you're listening, little brother. I took your throne and I'd do it again, a thousand times over, no matter the consequences.'

Karlaen reached out to steady the old man. As Flax was overcome by another coughing fit, Karlaen shared a look with Alphaeus, who frowned and tapped the side of his head. Karlaen looked down at Flax again, then shook his head. No, Flax was not insane. Karlaen suspected there was a horrid truth to the old man's ranting; he had seen it before, though only rarely. It was as abominable a heresy as any which existed.

Wheezing, Flax said, 'Satys, captain, that's where it began. I was a boy at the time, learning my limits here in the centre of our power, when my parents left on a trade mission.' Flax's face contorted. 'When they finally returned, they weren't my parents anymore. Everyone knew, everyone could see... something had changed. My mother was... pregnant, and the child was to be the new heir.' He spat the words like bullets. 'I was set aside as if I were nothing more than a placeholder.' Wrinkled hands curled into trembling fists. 'Set aside for a child yet unborn.'

Far above, something clanged hard – metal striking metal. Karlaen looked up. His bionic eye scanned the roof of the undercity, but there was nothing to see. He glanced at Alphaeus, who nodded and gestured to Zachreal, who stood some distance away with the others. The Terminator made his way towards them, gently shooing drunken nobles from his path. Alphaeus moved to meet him. Karlaen turned back to Flax, confident that Alphaeus would know what to do. 'And when it was born?' he asked.

'It was not human,' Flax hissed. His eyes were glassy, as his mind wandered back into memory. 'He was a monster from the first, a mutant, I thought, but he – it – was something far worse. Oh, they doted on him, though. They loved him as they had once loved *me*.' His voice became a savage rasp. 'After the first assassination attempt, they hid Tiberius away, below the palace... Here, in fact. This was his world for so many years,' Flax said, raising his skinny arms to indicate their surroundings. 'His playmates were servitors, and his few visitors... Well, they never left.'

Flax dropped his hands into his lap and stared at them. 'Dissidents and criminals, mostly. Though I know father, in his infinite foolishness, tried to arrange a marriage for him. They found the girl's body floating in a sump pipe some months later.' Flax smirked. 'That was the moment the nobility rallied around me. I was old enough then to know which way the wind was blowing, and since my parents had seen fit to abandon me, well... It was easy to reciprocate.' His smirk faded and he twitched nervously, as something rang hollowly, far above among the pipes. Karlaen saw Zachreal and two others moving off, away from the group, weapons ready. They would investigate and report back any sign of the enemy.

Karlaen could feel their presence, though the sensors showed no sign of them. There were thousands of kilometres of tunnels, ducts and pipes between where they now stood and the palace above. It was inconceivable to him that the genestealers had not found a route down here at some point and time, regardless of Flax's assumption that his defences had kept them at bay. He looked back at the old man. 'You became governor,' he prompted.

It was not curiosity now which drove his line of questioning, but the need for information. It was on Satys that Corbulo had discovered the secrets of the Flaxian bloodline, and developed his theory that they might hold the key to freeing the Blood Angels of their twin curses. And it was on Satys that this monstrosity who now dogged his steps had originated. It was possible that it was a coincidence. It was also possible that whatever factor made the Flaxian genetic structure so valuable to Corbulo had also played a part in the corruption of Flax's parents. And before he escorted Flax from the ashes of his kingdom, Karlaen intended to find out which it was.

'Yessss,' Flax said, drawing the word out. 'An orderly transition of power, backed by the nobility, whose sons and daughters now loll insensate here with me in my final hours. It is the least I could do for them, for services rendered.' He coughed again and then laughed. 'Make no mistake, captain, they did not help me out of the goodness of their shrivelled, ambitious hearts – no, they were frightened. Can you imagine the nightmare that would have followed Tiberius's coronation? The people would have risen up, there would have been a civil war, and all the good the Flaxian Dynasty had done would have been unmade in an eye blink.'

There was a certain amount of sense there, Karlaen knew. Genestealers undermined societies from within, damaging the social and political structure as well as corrupting the bodies and souls of the populace. They were a virus, unleashed on worlds and sectors in order to make them ripe for the coming of the hive fleet.

'You killed your own parents,' Alphaeus said, speaking up for the first time. There was a hint of revulsion in his voice. Flax noticed it, and his lips peeled back from his teeth in a feral grimace.

'Not willingly, I assure you,' he rasped. His eyes closed and he leaned back, his hands flexing uselessly, as if they yearned to grip someone's throat. 'I still loved them, even then. You should have known them in their prime, captain. My father with his booming voice and hearty laugh. My mother, quiet and stern – the perfect match for him, the blade to his bludgeon. Between them, they brought this sector to heel in a way no other Flax had ever managed. And in the end, they were reduced to ruin by their love for a foul, unfeeling beast.' He grunted and shifted his weight on his bed. 'I had to kill them – there was no other way. It was Tiberius. They were protecting him, protecting him from me, their true son.' His words came fast now, tripping over each other.

Flax pounded his chest. 'I was their son. Me! I was the heir, not him. Not that squalling, shrieking *thing*.' He glared at Karlaen. 'Imagine it, captain. Imagine sharing your life, your parents, your world, with a parasite... with a thing that creeps into your chamber at night, and strokes your face in a parody of brotherly affection. A thing that follows you through the vents of the palace, always watching you, always snuffling at your heels, as if it were a real child and not some star-born abomination come to steal everything. Do you hear me, Tiberius? Are you listening, Spawn of Cryptus? It was mine. All of it, and our parents – *my parents* – deserved death for what they allowed you to make of them,' he shrieked.

He sagged back into his cushions. 'And I deserve it too. For what you made of me, brother,' he muttered. He looked at Karlaen. 'When I had... When it was done, I found that he was gone. Escaped into the undercity of Phodia.'

The illuminators overhead flickered. The vox clicked and crackled. Karlaen turned and saw Zachreal and the others he had left with hurrying back towards the group. Somewhere, pipes rattled.

Alphaeus drew his power sword. 'We must go, captain. It is past time, and the rest of his story can wait for later.'

A flicker of a smile crossed Flax's age-ravaged features. 'He will not let me go, captain. He has spent decades reminding me of my crime, haunting my capital and breeding more of his filthy kind in the dark places. He was ever just out of the corner of my eye, one turn behind, trailing me down through the years. My father taught him how to hunt, and my mother taught him patience. And now, at the end of all things, he wants to enjoy the kill.'

The slave-servitors arranged around Flax's bed suddenly stiffened. As one, their mouths opened and a hollow, mechanical monotone said, '*Void-gate epsilon open – void-gate gamma open – western defence grid offline.*'

Then, with a harsh crackle, the lights went out across the undercity.

CHAPTER THIRTEEN

The stab-lights on the Terminators' armour immediately hummed to life, as did the spotlights mounted on Cassor's hull. The darkness was pierced by dozens of shafts of light, and in that light, familiar, bestial shapes raced forward.

'Contact, grids seven, ten, twelve, fifteen,' Zachreal rumbled. Similar statements followed as the Terminators formed themselves into a wedge. Storm bolters roared, and the genestealers retreated, fading away into the dark like ghosts.

Alphaeus looked at Karlaen. 'Time to go, captain. Gather our prize.'

Karlaen plucked Flax from his bed without ceremony.

The old man squawked, but did not resist. 'No, don't you understand,' he babbled. 'He's coming. There's no escape.'

'Let him come,' Karlaen said. He felt the heat of his rage building in him. He remembered Aphrae vanishing beneath a tide of chitin, and Bartelo toppling forwards, his flame extinguished. He remembered others, more than he cared to count, warriors who had followed him into the dark, against the enemy he now faced here on Asphodex, and had died because of him. He had thought to carry the light of the Chapter into the darkest recesses of the galaxy, and he had paid the price for his hubris. *Come beast,* he thought, with savage longing. *Come and pay your debt, for Aphrae and Bartelo and all of the others whose blood stains your claws.*

'Cowards! The dark shall not hide you from the Emperor's light. Come out and fight, or die in the dark. Make your choice,' Cassor roared, as if echoing his thoughts. The Dreadnought hurled his words into the dark like artillery fire and clashed his claws together. 'Come, dogs of Chemos. Come vermin of Nostramo. Fight Cassor the mighty or be damned for your timidity.'

Raphen and the rest of the Death Company shared the Dreadnought's eagerness. They fanned out, weapons at the ready, forming a barrier between the Terminators and the enemy that lurked in the dark. Soon the air was full of the growling of chainswords and the bark of bolt pistols as the Death Company fired at darting shadows.

The intoxicated nobles were beginning to sober up, Karlaen saw. He felt a flash of regret as he pressed forward, shoving some of them aside with force. They could not be allowed to detain him or his battle-brothers. Men and women screamed as he trod on them, or swatted them from his path. Flax railed at him, pounding withered fists on his armour. Karlaen ignored the screams and curses both as, holding Flax to his chest, he moved towards the other Terminators, Alphaeus following close behind. 'Brothers, we must withdraw to the entrance,' Karlaen said as he moved. 'Formation beta-ten, squad by squad. Covering fire, concentrate on the flanks. Let Raphen and the Death Company handle the rest. Joses, take point. We make for the Plaza of the Emperor Ascendant.'

'Gladly, captain,' Joses growled. Blade in hand, the dark-haired Blood Angel moved to the tip of the wedge and began to stride towards the entrance. Genestealers came out of the dark, and fell to Joses's blade or the storm bolters of the others. Above it all, Karlaen noticed that the grinding metal sound he had noted earlier growing in volume. The air grew damp, and his armour's sensors flashed in warning. He looked up, his bionic eye focusing in at last on the source of the noise and water.

Far above, the great sewer sluice gates which ran from the city above ground open, unleashing both alien invaders and a torrent of filthy water onto the streets below. Waterfalls of rain slammed down hard enough to rupture the street and sweep several Death Company warriors from their feet. Weak red light filtered down from above, illuminating the dark all around them, as the undercity began to slowly flood. Heavy shapes descended, dropping down from the sluice gates to crash onto the street, causing it to crack and shudder. Karlaen felt a tremor of alarm as he saw the familiar, hulking shape of a carnifex rise to its full height amidst the unceasing downpour.

The lenses of his eye cycled and clicked, bringing the lumbering monster into clear focus. Its skull was discoloured by a ruinous, newly healed wound, but it moved as quickly as he recalled.

'Is that...?' Alphaeus asked.

'It doesn't matter,' Karlaen grunted. 'We'll kill it again, if we have to. We'll kill them as many times as it takes.'

As water thundered down around them, the Blood Angels made ready to receive their enemy. Genestealers sprinted through the ranks of the Death Company as tyranid warriors and the newly arrived carnifex crashed into the berserkers. The multi-limbed aliens slewed through the rising water, bounding to the attack and, in some cases, on past the Terminators towards easier prey. Karlaen heard the screams behind him. He hesitated, tempted to turn back, to try and save someone, anyone.

Alphaeus caught his shoulder. 'You can't, captain. We have our orders. Flax brought them down here to die, and that's what they're doing. The longer the genestealers are occupied chewing on Phodia's upper crust, the longer we've got to get Flax to the plaza and off this dying hunk of rock.' His words were harsh, but not unfeeling. Karlaen knew that Alphaeus and the others were wrestling with the same urge to go back, to protect those men and women they had left behind. But to do so would be to condemn their mission to failure. They had what they had come for, and now it was time to leave.

Karlaen trudged on, ignoring the screams of the dying and the damned.

Ahead of him, he saw Raphen spiral through the air, propelled by his jump pack, his crackling thunder hammer lashing out to crush and maim the enemy. Several of his men followed suit, hurtling over their fellows to land amidst the genestealers briefly, killing and then moving on.

The Blood Angels pressed on, creating a bloody path through any genestealer or tyranid that tried to stop them. But the creatures came on regardless of how many fell. Karlaen could feel the itch in his brain that said Flax's abominable sibling was nearby, driving its servants to the attack. Between the darkness and the water pouring down from above it would be next to impossible to pinpoint the beast, even if he had been tempted to do so.

The wound in his chest ached at the thought. It had already sealed itself, but the memory of the claw punching into him was hard to shake. He had been wounded before, and many times, over the course of his service to the Chapter, but this one was different. It was almost personal, as if the broodlord had wanted to leave him something to remember it by. He touched the punctured spot on his armour with the tip of his hammer, and felt a tugging at his mind.

Then Flax was screaming in his ear and he came back to himself, knee-deep in water, as genestealers exploded upwards, claws reaching for him. Karlaen swung his hammer with a roar, bashing one of his attackers off its feet, but the others slammed into him, grabbing his legs and his arm, trying to pull him down.

'Captain,' Alphaeus shouted, turning towards him. The sergeant hammered his power sword down on the back of one beast's skull, killing it instantly.

The others swarmed over Karlaen, dragging him to one knee through sheer weight of numbers. Flax screamed as talons sought his withered flesh. Thinking quickly, Karlaen hefted the old man and tossed him towards Alphaeus. The sergeant caught him as he beheaded a leaping genestealer with a sweep of his blade.

'Keep going,' Karlaen snarled, trying to fight his way to his feet. He tore the servitor head from his belt and sent it sailing after Flax. 'Take this – go, brother. I will join you when I can.'

Alphaeus did not protest. He caught the head and shoved it into Flax's trembling hands. Then, with a grimace of frustration, he turned and began making for the exit. Karlaen saw the closest Terminators form up around him like a phalanx, cordoning him off. Then they were lost from sight as genestealers closed in around him. Karlaen rammed the haft of his hammer into one's gut and flung it off him. He surged to his feet as the others closed in, his storm bolter rising. The weapon roared, and alien bodies burst like overripe fruit as he swept the storm bolter in a line.

Suddenly, there was a shriek, and a bulky form slid through the water, smashing aside genestealers. Karlaen sidestepped the bleeding, reeking hulk as it slowed and came to a stop. The carnifex whined deep in its mangled throat as it sought to heave itself upright to continue the fray, but its limbs were nothing but dead weight now, broken and pulled out of shape. A heavy shape stomped towards it, and with a grumbling hiss, Cassor's meltagun carved a blackened tunnel through the beast's head for a second time.

The Dreadnought was covered in ichor and battle scars. Hoses flapped free as Cassor spun back and forth, firing his weapons in a wide arc. Something sparked inside his chassis, and Karlaen could smell burning promethium and scorched metal. The Dreadnought's limbs groaned and wheezed, but he fought on. 'Come, come and meet death, traitors. Come and feel the bite of my blade.'

Cassor twisted, backhanding a genestealer in mid-leap and sending it flying into a nearby building with enough force to pulverise the beast. More leapt and clawed at the Dreadnought, scrambling over him in a wave of talons and teeth. Cassor roared and slashed at the living wave, killing genestealers with every flick of his talons. But there were always more, and soon the Dreadnought was lost to sight, enveloped in a tide of chitin.

Karlaen swept his hammer out in a wide arc, sending the closest of the Dreadnought's attackers flying. He fired his storm bolter at those that got past him, and almost paid the price for his inattentiveness. Only the screech of his armour's sensors and his own combat-honed instincts warned him in time to avoid having his skull split like a melon. A tyranid warrior sprang out of the streaming water, its bone swords slicing at him. He avoided the first blow, but the second caught him high on the shoulder. The force of it staggered him, and he nearly fell. The tyranid seized the opportunity and came at him, all four blades hammering down in a cruel rhythm.

He stumbled back, caught off balance and unable to retaliate. The tyranid continued its attack, driving him steadily back. Genestealers scuttled out of reach, like wolves waiting for their prey to tire itself out. The tyranid shrieked and blocked his awkward attempt to push it away. Karlaen cursed himself for a fool and tried to regain his footing. A genestealer darted in, and he felt a slash of pain crawl up the back of his leg. Momentarily weakened, he sank down to one knee. The tyranid kicked out with one bony hoof and caught him in the side, knocking him onto his back in the rising water.

Karlaen floundered for a moment which seemed to stretch for an eternity. Better warriors than him had died in worse ways, and more foolish, but that was small comfort. If he died, the failure of his mission was almost certain. Rage built in him, and his thoughts were drowned in a persistent hum of red. The tyranid stabbed down at him, four blades angled to pierce two hearts. It had seemed so fast before, but now, in the red, it was slow. He could see the droplets of water crawling along the length of the blades, and hear the sound they made as they pierced the air in their descent.

The Hammer of Baal rose from the water and whipped out. Four bone blades shattered. The tyranid warrior, over-extended, leaned forward. Karlaen's hand shot up, catching its lower mandible. Servos hissed and he wrenched the creature's jaw from its skull. It reared back in pain and surprise, and he shoved himself to his feet, clasping his hammer in both hands as he brought it around for another blow. There was no thought of tactics or strategy now, only a boiling need to see the ichor of his foe spill into the murky waters that rose around them.

Karlaen battered the creature, knocking it one way and then the next, until finally it sank to its knees, its carapace covered in scorched craters and spider-webbed cracks. He raised his hammer and brought it down with a snarl, caving in the tyranid's skull. As it fell, he turned, rage not yet sated, to look for new enemies.

The genestealers which had been harrying him were only too happy to oblige. They came in a rush, darting in at him from all sides, moving too fast for him to follow, distracted as he was. Claws punctured his armour in places, opening fresh wounds, and he roared. As he fought, he struggled to swim free of the crimson murk which had settled over his mind. He was not yet lost to the Red Thirst, and he forced himself to concentrate on the pain, using it to centre himself once more. To lose himself now would be to lose everything.

As if sensing his new focus, the genestealers redoubled their attack, piling onto him without heed to casualties. For every one he swatted from him, two more clawed at him, trying to pull him down off his feet again, where he would be easy prey.

Through the haze of battle and the spray of murky water, he saw that Alphaeus had reached the gate at last, Damaris and Leonos to either side of him. The barrels of the twins' storm bolters glowed white-hot as they held back the tide. The rest of the Terminators were equally beset, fighting for their lives against tyranids and genestealers alike. Nonetheless, Alphaeus had reached the gate. Relief flooded through him, only to be stolen in a moment.

As Alphaeus lifted the servitor head to open the blast doors, a shape darted down the great stone wall which housed the exit. Karlaen voxed a warning and raised his storm bolter. He fired, his targeting array fighting to keep a lock on the shape. Bolter rounds chewed the wall around the beast as it moved. A band of light caught it and Karlaen felt a chill as he recognised the broodlord. It had been waiting for them. It had allowed its kin to harry them, drive them to distraction, so that it might claim its prize.

As he watched, the broodlord dropped down among the Terminators, its claws flashing out to vivisect one unlucky warrior. Ancient armour, a relic of a golden age, tore like paper beneath its claws, and blood filled the air. The Terminator fell, and the broodlord vaulted over the tumbling body to reach Alphaeus.

Karlaen charged forwards, bowling over a hissing genestealer, knowing that as he did so he would not be in time. Joses moved to intercept the creature, his blade flashing out, carving sparks from the wall as the broodlord weaved beneath the blow. Four talons shot forwards and punched through the Terminator's chestplate. Joses coughed blood and sagged against his killer. The broodlord heaved the dying Blood Angel backwards, slamming his dead weight into Alphaeus.

The sergeant staggered, and the broodlord was on him a moment later. The creature plucked a screaming Flax from Alphaeus's grip and bounded into the darkness on the other side of the blast doors as they cycled open at last. Even as the broodlord vanished, its children took its place, boiling through the open blast doors and washing over the Terminators. Storm bolters fired and power weapons hummed, but the Blood Angels were pinned in place by their attackers, unable to follow the broodlord.

Karlaen, still charging towards the exit, paid no heed to the creatures which pursued him, and he was knocked to the ground by them just before he reached the others. The genestealers swarmed over him, pinning his arms and tearing at his armour. He thrashed, trying to hurl them off, but there were too many. One raised a claw over his head, ready to end him. The Red Thirst pounded in his skull, and his thoughts jangled incoherently as he faced his death.

'No, brother. Thy doom is not writ this day. No son of Baal shall perish so ingloriously, not as long as Cassor stands.'

Cassor loomed over him, scattering genestealers with a gesture. The Dreadnought's claws snapped out and sank into a genestealer's body. The creature screeched in agony as Cassor plucked it from Karlaen's chest and lifted it into the air. 'Heed my words, ye traitors. Thy cause is dust and Cassor shall cast down thy champions.'

The Dreadnought spun, hurling the genestealer at a knot of its fellows and bowling them over. The storm bolter mounted beneath Cassor's claw roared, and the stunned xenos were reduced to bloody tatters. Cassor turned back to Karlaen. 'Up, brother. Cassor shall hold the enemy. Finish thy mission. Cassor shall see to the slaughter here.'

Karlaen pushed himself to his feet, his rage fading. He picked up his hammer and, with one last glance at the Dreadnought, charged towards the gate. He had cleared himself a path in moments, as his brothers formed a cordon around him, holding back snarling, hissing would-be obstacles. The blast doors had begun to cycle closed as he reached them, but he plunged through the steadily shrinking gap without hesitation.

As the blast doors clanged shut behind him, Karlaen followed his enemy into the dark.

CHAPTER FOURTEEN

Karlaen marched alone through the labyrinthine tunnels under the palace. The shadowy foundations rose up around him like a second city. It was a damp, dark reflection of the one above, and a fitting place for a beast such as the Spawn of Cryptus. He could hear water rushing all about him, through pipes and culverts, through the sewers of Phodia. Even now, this close to the end, the city's servitors kept the water running, as they had been programmed to do. They would do their duty until the end. Karlaen smiled grimly. In some ways, there was no difference between himself and those mindless drones.

They were merely differently shaped cogs in the same great machine, programmed to fulfil a necessary function – theirs, to see to the sanitation network of Phodia, and his, to kill the enemies of mankind. It was a core truth, and one it had taken him decades to accept – decades of arrogance and hubris, of fiery war and bloody slaughter. Once he had thought himself special. A prince of war, bestowed with divine gifts to bring the galaxy to heel on behalf of his Chapter and the Emperor. But age had worn that purpose to a lethal, killing edge. Now, he knew that he was but one warrior among billions, all of them striving against the same hungry darkness.

As that darkness closed around him, one thought filled Karlaen's mind, one repeated hammer blow of memory which he could neither escape nor bury any longer beneath thoughts of duty and necessity. He could hear them as he moved, like a ghost signal on an open vox-link – the voices of his dead brothers, murmuring softly to him in the dark.

He had failed them again. Alphaeus and the others would pay the price for his failure to consider all of the angles and to prepare for all possibilities. Once before, he had led his brothers into the dark, and they had died because his pragmatism and practicality had failed them. Now it was happening all over again. The memory of that last, doomed stand rose up in him again, through the red.

They had gone to meet the enemy, and they had triumphed, but at great cost. It had been a necessary thing, a thing which had to be done, but the doing of it had tarnished him. In his quiet moments of contemplation, which were thankfully few and far between, he knew that he was not worthy of the title Dante had bestowed on him – for what sort of shield could not protect those who stood behind it?

Karlaen saw faces swirl about him in the dark, and heard voices in the drip of water, or the scrape of chitin on stone. He heard the thunder of guns and the cries of the dying in his ears, as loudly as he had that day. Even now, the dead did not curse him. Even now, their understanding was more painful than any wound he had yet sustained. They had trusted him to lead them out of the dark, and he had allowed their light to be snuffed out.

He wondered whether Alphaeus still lived. Joses was dead, like Bartelo and the others. That they had died doing their duty was small comfort to him now, in this moment. Here, in the dark, he was alone with the weight of their lives pressing him down. He tried to recall some snippet of wisdom from leaders past of the Chapter, from Raldoron, Thoros and others that might alleviate that weight, but the words that came seemed hollow and unfitting.

Karlaen had done as he thought best, for the good of the Chapter, and men had died. *Like Flax*, he thought. Grim amusement flashed through him. Now both he and Flax were paying the price for bloody necessities past. Men had died under his aegis, and now he would make certain that their deaths were not in vain.

He keyed off his stab-lights. As the dark rushed in, he activated the augur-lens of his bionic eye. The lights would be of little use, save to mark his position for the enemy even now creeping about him. He was approaching the next in the line of blast doors, his armour's sensors locked on Flax's bio-signature. Wherever the broodlord took his captive, Karlaen would follow, even if it meant descending into the bowels of Asphodex. Somehow, he did not think that would be the case – no, the beast wanted a reckoning. Both with its brother, and with Karlaen himself.

He brushed his hand against the hole in his armour. He knew it was no idle theory on his part. The broodlord had as good as challenged him, and Karlaen thought he understood why. The creature wanted what it could never have, yet it was determined to best any who challenged its right to the throne of this dying world. Why else had the full might of the Hive Mind not yet descended on the palace? Why else would the creature endanger itself to get at Flax? It had a mission, just as Karlaen did.

Through the haze of the augur-lens, he saw ghostly shapes dancing and squirming at the edge of his vision. No guilt-bred figments these, but enemies. He paused, scanning his surroundings. The shapes seemed to flow across the foundations, staying just out of sight. He checked his storm bolter. Less than half a clip of ammunition remained, and he had no more replacements. He frowned and lowered the weapon. He hefted his hammer and swung it experimentally. It had seen him through thus far. He hoped it would not fail him now.

He started forwards again, water splashing across his armour as he walked. The whole sub-section would soon be flooded. When he reached the blast doors, he realised that they were not going to open. Gene-locked as they had been, he needed a sample of Flaxian DNA or a suitable substitute, like the servitor's head, to open them. He cursed. He had not thought to grab the head, nor had the foresight to take a blood sample from Flax. Karlaen closed his eye and pushed through the tide of self-recrimination.

His eye opened, and fixed on the door's control panel. His bionic eye whirred, focusing in. The blast doors had been old when Phodia was young. They were simple things. The genetic signature activated the electro-pneumatic impulses which controlled the door's functions. He stepped back, and readied his hammer. If he could identify a weak point, he might be able to open a hole. It was not much of a plan, but it was all he had.

Before he could so much as swing his weapon, however, he heard a hiss from his left. He turned, and saw the shapes which had kept pace with him down the corridor spring into motion. There were two of them, he saw now, moving to either side of him. Karlaen smiled as a thought occurred to him. The creatures were the broodlord's children, created by it; an army raised in secret. There was a reason that the broodlord could pass through the blast doors without help – it was as much a part of the Flaxian Dynasty as the governor himself, though it was a monstrous, degenerate part. And that meant that its children were as well.

The genestealers reached him a moment later, coursing down the length of the wall with inhuman speed. He set his storm bolter onto its grav-clamp holster on his hip, and stretched the fingers of his free hand. He would need to be quick.

He sent his hammer shooting out, letting the haft slide through his grip with a precision honed in hundreds of close-set, cramped corridors. The head smashed into the skull of the first of the genestealers, dropping the stunned creature to the ground. The second lunged for him, and he flung up his free hand, catching it by the throat. It struggled in his grip, its claws drawing sparks from his armour. He swung it around and slammed it head first into the door's gene-lock. The lock flashed as it read the struggling alien's genetic code, and the door began to cycle open. Karlaen grunted in satisfaction. Behind him, he heard the first creature scramble to its feet.

He spun, smashing its fellow into it, knocking it down again. Before it could rise for a second time, he brought his hammer down on its chest, pulverising it in a wet crackle of energy. Karlaen looked at the genestealer he still held. The creature's thrashing became more agitated as his servo-assisted grip on its throat slowly tightened. Then, with a wet crunch, it went limp. Carefully, he twisted its head off. He would need a key, in case of further blast doors.

As the door opened, he heard the telltale clatter of chitin echoing from the other side. He glanced at the bloody head in his hand and dropped it. It appeared as if he would not need it after all. There would be plenty more where it came from.

Hammer in hand, the Shield of Baal stepped through, into the dark.

Augustus Flax looked around, bleary-eyed, and then gave a bitter laugh. 'Oh, Tiberius – really? Is this the sort of thing that whatever passes for your mind thinks is meaningful?' He lay prone on the surface of the intersection of the four great bridges which met above the main artery of the Phodian sewers, just beneath the palace gardens. Below him, water roared into the dark, converging on the great drain from dozens of sluice gates. Above him loomed the towering foundations of the palace he had claimed in blood and deceit.

That was the legacy of the Flaxian Dynasty, was it not? He almost smiled at the thought. He had won his throne with plenty of both, to be sure. He had turned his people over to criminal overlords and brutal manufactorum bosses, and enriched himself at their expense – all in an effort to stymie a hidden foe. It had been necessary. Or so he had convinced himself. Much good as it had done him, in the end.

The creature had dragged him through the dark, ignoring his screams, only to deposit him here. Now it sat, seemingly content merely to – what? Flax looked up at his brother, where it crouched on one of the shattered statues which lined the four bridges. Very big on statues, the Flaxian Dynasty. Even now, Flax was unable to name who half of them represented. *Statues in a sewer. Excess, thy name is Flax,* he thought bitterly. Even the creature could not escape that particular familial flaw. 'A crossroads, Tiberius. A turning point, meant to be symbolic of our situation, perhaps? I thought you ate your literary theory tutor,' he spat, glaring up at the creature.

It was a monstrous thing, all alien muscle and seething malice. He could feel its thoughts in his, like wriggling worms of doubt and dread, at once familiar and repugnant. How many times had he felt those same sharp thoughts clawing at his mind as a boy? Flax pushed himself upright, his arms and legs trembling with the effort. It watched his movements with evident curiosity. He wondered if it were savouring his broken-down state, or if, perhaps, it were disappointed in him. Did it dream of him, of this moment?

'We're not children any more, though, are we Tiberius?' he croaked. 'I am a decrepit sack of flesh, and you have sloughed off whatever frail shell of humanity you might have possessed to become the monster we always knew you to be.'

The broodlord leaned down over the statue, twisting its head so that it could meet his gaze. It hissed softly. Flax bent double, his body wracked by a coughing fit. The broodlord drew back, nostrils flaring.

Flax looked up and smiled a bloody smile. 'Have no fear, brother. I am not sick. Merely old and feeble, and broken on the altar of time.' He forced himself to straighten and spread his arms. 'Well? What have you to say to me, hmm? The moment is here, Tiberius. The moment I knew was coming the instant I put down the beasts you'd made of my parents...'

The broodlord snarled. The sound echoed across the width of the chasm below, rising above the thunder of falling water, and Flax could not help but quail back. The sound had never failed to strike fear in him. But a surge of anger stiffened his spine. 'Yes, snarl at me, I deserve it,' he snapped. 'I took the only creatures who ever showed you love and killed them. But while my finger might have been the one which pulled the trigger, you were as guilty as I. You ruined them – you almost destroyed everything that we had.' He shook his head. 'I say almost, as if the worst hasn't come to pass.' He looked at the broodlord. 'Are you satisfied, brother? How long do you think your new masters will let you rule the ash heap you've made of our kingdom, hmm? How long before you're rendered down the way my people have been?'

The broodlord leapt gracefully from the statue and landed in a crouch at Flax's feet. The old man stumbled back, tripping on the hem of his robes. He fell back, scraping his elbows and back on the hard stone. The broodlord scuttled towards him, eyes glinting.

'That's right, Tiberius – get it over with,' Flax hissed. Fear raced through him, paralysing everything but his mouth. He hurled words at the creature for lack of any other defence. 'Open me up and feast on my heart. It won't satisfy you, you know. *It won't bring them back.*'

The broodlord froze. It stared at him, unblinking. Flax smiled weakly. He had not expected the beast to react so obviously. Maybe it was more human than he had suspected. 'Oh. Oh my, how ridiculous you are, beast. To think, I have been frightened of you all this time.' His smile faded. 'Do you even know why you're doing this? Is it just some primitive impulse, or is there actually a mind in there? What are you, Tiberius? Man or monster?'

The broodlord shrieked. Flax stared into its maw, full of jagged fangs and lashing tongue, and saw his answer. The creature lunged, grabbing his shoulders and slamming him backwards. He felt his head crack against the stone and nausea flowed through him. Part of him prayed that the Blood Angels would find him in time, but it was a vain hope at best.

When they had first arrived in their battle-scorched crimson armour, he had experienced a moment of hope. But that too, he knew, was part of the creature's demented game. It had allowed him to survive, to escape, just as it had allowed him a moment of hope, so that it could snatch it all away. Even as he had snatched away its life, so long ago.

Flax did not struggle. There was no reason to do so. He wanted it to end, wanted the beast to finish what it had begun. Decades of slow torment, dwindling to these last bare moments. 'Go ahead, brother... kill me, the way you killed our world. Kill me, and be damned.' As he spoke, he fumbled in his robes for the hard shape of the knife he had secreted on his person. He had intended to cut his own throat, when the time came. Oh, how he'd gleefully imagined the frustrated look on the beast's face as he claimed his own life.

But that plan was ashes now. Besides, he was a Flax, and such a death was not for him. No, better to bury the blade in the creature's side and see what sort of death it bought him. Let it know one more moment of pain at his hands, before it finished this sad drama. The broodlord stared at him, as if trying to understand his lack of fear.

As it hunched over him, he drew the knife and rammed it home. The broodlord reared back and screamed. He didn't think the wound was mortal, or even debilitating, but that wasn't the point. The creature tore the knife from its side and glared down at him, talons poised to strike, every abhorrent muscle quivering with repressed need.

Flax smiled. 'They might have loved you at the end, brother, but they loved me first and best.'

With a howl, the broodlord struck.

CHAPTER FIFTEEN

Karlaen stomped down on the last squealing bio-beast, squashing it. The ripper swarm had attacked moments ago, drawn out of bore holes in the ruined foundations by the scent of him. He had dissuaded them with proper application of boot and hammer, but they had left him much to remember them by. He could feel blood leaking into the crevices of his suit, and a pall of fatigue muffled his senses. The creatures had swarmed over him, biting and burrowing, and it was only thanks to the armour he wore that he had survived.

The rippers were not the only threat he had faced. Genestealers had attacked him more than once as he hunted his quarry through the tomb-like foundations of the palace. They came at him in twos and threes, dropping down from the darkness above, or lunging out of crannies and side tunnels. Each time, his bionic eye had tracked their approach, and each time, he had put them down. But the attacks were constant, and even the superhuman physiology of a Space Marine could be worn down under such conditions. The bio-sensors in his armour mewled warnings about increasing fatigue-poisons and torn muscles. His breath rasped hot and harsh in his lungs. Blood and sweat stung his eyes. But still he pressed on, moving through slanted shadows, following Flax's genetic signature through the depths of Phodia.

The vox crackled intermittently, assuring him that at least some of the others still lived. Bereft of any other orders, they would make for the surface and the rallying-point as quickly as possible. Karlaen could not say what would be waiting for them when they got there. The signs of the planet's consumption had spread even to these depths.

Sewer channels that had once carried filthy rainwater from the streets far above were now choked with strange, barbed vegetation and the still waters were occupied by hideous, half-seen creatures. The foundations of the city were being strangled by new, poisonous growths which gaped and whined like hungry animals as he tore them from his path or crushed them underfoot. Karlaen had encountered these often enough to recognise the flesh-tubes of the hive fleet when he saw them. They were digging deep, to feed on the life-blood of Asphodex and drain even the soil of nutrients.

The tyranids were efficient, in their way, monstrous as it was. They broke worlds down, squeezing every grain of sustenance from them, one molecule at a time. They wasted nothing. Even the air itself was stripped of life. That was to be Asphodex's fate – the fate of every world in the Cryptus System: to be squeezed and drained and left barren. And once they were finished here, Hive Fleet Leviathan would move on to the next course in its galaxy-spanning meal – Baal.

The thought stirred the embers of his rage to life once more. He fought down the instinct to charge forwards into whatever waited ahead. He extended a hand and leaned against a wall covered in swelling, breathing growths of alien matter, trying to bring his red-tinged thoughts back under control. Anger swelled in him, and he tried to channel it into his desire to find Flax. His mind was filled with images of his enemy, and he could hear its screams as he pulled it apart, limb by limb. His teeth scissored into his bottom lip, releasing a spurt of blood into his mouth, and he swallowed without thinking. The shock of it startled him back to awareness.

His discipline was eroding the harder he pushed himself, but he could not afford to stop. This was the razor's edge which every Son of Sanguinius walked. To push themselves to the limit of discipline and hypno-conditioning without tipping over into the madness that crept about the edges of their psyche. To utilise the rage and the strength that came with it, without being swallowed by it. But that was easier said than done, and the fire could only be stoked for so long before it raged out of control.

Karlaen shoved himself away from the wall and stumbled. He felt the walls of his discipline crumbling, brick by brick. The world lurched around him and he felt his gut *twist in loss and pain the likes of which no mortal could bear, and he heard the sound of great wings flapping brokenly, and felt the rush of heat and pain and saw the face of god twisted into something beyond redemption and he* screamed as something snagged his arm and sank cruel barbs through the armour plates.

Karlaen jerked his arm back, uprooting the strangling creepers from the stone of the wall. They had slithered about him so noiselessly, so quickly, that he had been taken unawares. Pain flooded his nervous system, driving back the madness. He whispered a quiet prayer of thanks as he tore the whole mass of alien vegetation from the wall and extricated his arm from its tendrils. He flexed his hand, and, satisfied that he could still use it, he turned and pressed on, trying to ignore the ghostly feathers that fluttered at the edges of his vision.

The corridor ended in a square of dull light. As he stepped through, the omnipresent roar of water, muted until now, suddenly flowered into its full glory. He stopped just past the aperture and took in the scene before him – the four intersecting bridges, the great sluice gates set high above the bridges, water pouring down from them into the chasm below. And at the centre of the bridges, the Spawn of Cryptus crouched over a limp form.

Flax was not dead. Karlaen's sensors told him that much. But he was fading. The governor was too old and too feeble to handle the sort of stressors he had been exposed to. Karlaen could hear the erratic hammering of the old man's heart. He took a step forward, and the broodlord looked up. The alien met his gaze without reaction. It reached down and gently stroked Flax's hair. The gesture was almost affectionate.

Warnings flashed and Karlaen scanned the area. There were other shapes lurking in the ruined foundations that surrounded the bridges, or hanging from the support struts and railings of the bridges. He wondered how many of the creatures remained. How many children did the Spawn of Cryptus have left to throw at him? Karlaen took another step forwards. He considered trying for a shot with his storm bolter, but there was a chance he might hit Flax. Even targeting arrays had their limits, and between his fatigue, the damp haze that obscured the air and the broodlord's mind-tricks, he did not want to risk it. He left the weapon where it was, and raised his hammer. As he gripped it, the broodlord leaned forwards, as if scenting the air.

Karlaen started forwards. The broodlord screamed. Karlaen staggered as his mind suddenly rippled with pain. He stumbled and lowered his hammer, using its haft to keep himself upright as the broodlord assailed him psychically. Waves of pain rolled over him. Shards of memory, weaponised and honed to lethality by an alien psyche, tore at his defences as they had before. But this time, Karlaen was ready. He stoked the flames of his rage to a new intensity, welcoming the flush of clarity it brought. The broodlord was a thing of nurtured hate and bestial rage, but that was as nothing compared to the fury of one who lived with the dying scream of a demigod lodged in his mind. Alien whispers were shredded like smoke by the beating of great, unseen wings.

The Shield of Baal locked eyes with the Spawn of Cryptus and pushed himself to his feet. The broodlord's expression of animal serenity wavered. Its eyes widened in shock, then narrowed in consternation as it found its greatest weapon undone and useless. In the span of half a dozen heartbeats, the contest was decided. The creature blinked, breaking contact. It reared to its full height and let loose a shrill cry of command.

As the echoes of that cry rode across the thunder of the water and bounced from statue to foundation stone, the genestealers launched themselves into motion. The creatures raced forward from all directions. Karlaen met them with focused violence. The power field of his hammer crackled and sparked as he swung it in wide, precise arcs, driving the creatures back, or killing them in mid-lunge. Here in the open, he could employ the weapon to its fullest, and the Hammer of Baal hummed in his hands.

Through it all, he continued his advance towards the broodlord, neither slowing nor stopping. He had come too far and endured too much to allow himself to be stymied here and now. The last two genestealers between him and his quarry scrambled along the edge of the bridge, racing towards him.

Karlaen swatted the first out of the air with his hammer, driving it into the surface of the bridge with a resounding crack. The creature barely had time to squall before its carapace split and burst, and it was reduced to a wet stain. As the second genestealer sprang towards him, Karlaen turned, firing his storm bolter. The beast was plucked from the air by the explosive bolts and reduced to a dark mist.

He pivoted, ready to fire at the others that were closing in on him from behind, but the storm bolter clicked empty. Karlaen cursed and slammed it back onto its grav-clamp. He took a two-handed grip on his hammer and met the first of the creatures with a blow that sent its body rolling bonelessly across the bridge. The second joined it, and the third. Then, just as suddenly as the attack had started, it was done.

Karlaen turned back to see the broodlord step past the prone body of Flax, its features twisted in what might have been a sneer of contempt. Then, with a roar, it was upon him. They duelled for a moment, hammer against claw. As before, Karlaen was slower, but he was prepared for the beast's agility now, and he fought conservatively, blocking and parrying its blows rather than simply absorbing them. He knew his enemy now, and it knew him.

The broodlord ducked and weaved, avoiding blows that would have ended their conflict for good. It gave him no room to manoeuvre, circling and attacking from all directions as swiftly as possible. Karlaen had no opportunity to deliver the killing blow he needed. Finally, the beast leapt on him, and four arms strained against two as they grappled.

Whatever strength his rage had given him was flagging now. The creature was far stronger than him, built for this sort of battle. He was pressed back, and soon, the flat of one knee touched the surface of the bridge. His hammer was interposed horizontally between them, the haft caught between the creature's jaws. Centimetres away from his own, the broodlord's flat, red eyes showed nothing of what lurked in its alien brain.

Karlaen took a chance; he dropped his hand to his storm bolter and snatched it up. Empty as it was, it still had heft and weight. He smashed it across the side of the beast's skull, packing every bit of force he could muster into the blow. Stunned, the broodlord released him and jerked away. He shoved it back, away from him. It scrambled to its feet as he swung his hammer up.

But rather than striking the beast, he aimed his blow at the stretch of bridge beneath its claws. Metal and stone came apart with a scream of tortured steel as the hammer struck home. A whole section of the bridge gave way, carrying the beast with it. The broodlord tumbled into the darkness below, its limbs grasping in vain for anything that might arrest its fall. Its glare never wavered as it vanished into the dark, swirling waters below.

Karlaen stared down after it, breathing heavily, his hearts hammering in his chest. He shook himself and made his way around the edge of the hole he had created to retrieve Flax.

They had a rendezvous to make.

CHAPTER SIXTEEN

PLAZA OF THE EMPEROR UNCHAINED, FLAXIAN PALACE, PHODIA

Karlaen reared back and kicked the sluice gate out of its frame. The steel grate flew into the space beyond, crashing down with a resounding clang. As he stepped out into the open air, Flax's comatose form slung over his shoulder, he beheld a vision of carnage which was horribly familiar to one who had made war against the servants of the Hive Mind before. Asphodex had entered its final death throes – the air was thick with smoke and noise, and buildings had begun to collapse, adding to both.

The city had become an inferno – towers of dancing flame rose from the ruins and waves of billowing smoke filled the streets and choked the air. Tyranid organisms screamed and shrieked throughout the city as they were caught up in the raging fires. Bio-beasts fled, trampling one another in their haste to escape obliteration.

In the distance, Karlaen could see shuddering mushroom clouds rising above the tops of those buildings which still stood. The red sky flashed and quivered like a thing alive, and the great clouds which marked the upper atmosphere were shredded and reformed by unseen forces. The ground shook beneath his feet, not with the trembling of seismic activity, but as if some vast titan were smashing his fist down on Asphodex. The Blood Angels fleet had begun its preliminary orbital bombardment of the planet, in preparation for the first landings of Dante's main force. Time had almost run out.

Karlaen quickly triangulated his position. He stood in the eastern plaza – the Plaza of the Emperor Unchained. He calculated a route to the Plaza of the Emperor Ascendant. If Alphaeus or any of the others had survived the battle in the undercity, that was where they would be. Cradling Flax against his chest in order to protect him from the flames, he moved through the plaza, forging a path to the rallying-point.

The vox-net crackled to life as he left the sluice gate behind. Voices hammered at his ears: commands, warnings, oaths – the roar of a Chapter, roused to fury. He heard the red hum rise behind his thoughts. It was always this way when the Chapter went to war; the black tide of emotions which every warrior fought to control became stronger and stronger as the vibrations of Thunderhawk engines shook their bones and the heat of weapons-fire washed over them.

Between battles, in the cold stretch of the void or on Baal's blistered sands, the thirst for battle could be ignored, sublimated into more noble pursuits. Karlaen knew many battle-brothers who were as adept with a sculptor's chisel or a painter's brush as they were with bolter and blade. But here, now, on the sharp edge, the rage was given full flower. And if they were not careful, it could sweep them under and into damnation.

Heat washed across the plaza, withering the alien vegetation that had briefly claimed dominion. Without men or automated systems to control the fires they raged out of control, incinerating tyranids and any surviving Imperial defenders that were caught in the path of the flames. More than once, disorientated tyranids burst from the burning ruins and spilled through the plaza. Some attacked Karlaen, and he was forced to defend himself. He left a trail of crushed carcasses behind him as he trudged towards the Plaza of the Emperor Ascendant.

As yet, the tyranids were uncoordinated – they were little better than ravenous animals. But soon the Hive Mind would bring its incomprehensible attentions to bear on the invaders, and it would exert its will on the swarms, uniting them in terrible purpose.

By the time he reached the Plaza of the Emperor Ascendant, the air above him was full of the grotesque shapes of gargoyles. The flapping nightmares spiralled above the city like a living cloud of teeth and claws. Broods of gaunts crept through the haze that lay over the plaza, and Karlaen could just make out larger shapes behind them. But there was no sign of the others. He scanned through the pre-arranged vox frequencies, but only static greeted his ears. He moved towards the fallen statue of the Emperor.

Flax was still unconscious, and he barely stirred as Karlaen hid him in a cranny beneath the statue. It was a small mercy; no man should have to witness the death of his world and people, Karlaen thought. When he was satisfied that the governor was safe, he straightened and began cycling through the vox frequencies until he found the main Adeptus Astartes signal. The channel crackled with static. 'This is Captain Karlaen, of the First, requesting extraction from the planet's surface,' Karlaen said, raising his voice to be heard through the static.

Moments passed. The signal phased in and out, and he repeated himself. He looked up, trying to imagine the battle raging far above the planet. Void warfare was a thing of vast distances and acute angles. Up and down had no meaning; there was no high ground to capture, and precise calculations were required to even come close to striking the enemy. Servitors slaved to battle-stations – one part analytical engine and one part gunner – manned targeting computers as specially trained Chapter serfs followed their instructions, firing at enemies they could not see.

Karlaen had only experienced void warfare a few times. He had participated in boarding actions and repelled the same, when the enemy drew close across the incalculable gulf that normally separated the combatants. Even now he could recall the crushing cold and inescapable silence that accompanied such conflicts as one moved across the outer hull of a vessel. The way the maddening spiral of stars which stretched into infinity in every direction imprinted itself on the mind's eye, never to fade.

Making planetfall amidst such madness was even more nerve-wracking. Men died without ever seeing the surface of the world they had been brought to conquer. The upper reaches of the stratosphere would be a hellstorm of fire and fury.

As he tried to make contact with the fleet, he scanned the smoke and haze for the enemy. Behind the veil of grey and black, shapes moved, some large, some small, and he could hear the telltale click of chitin on stone. He clasped his hammer in both hands and waited. The vox crackled in his ear.

'Say again?' a voice asked. The line hissed and spat with static.

Karlaen grunted in satisfaction. 'This is Captain Karlaen, requesting extraction,' he barked. 'Rallying-point alpha.'

'Acknowledged captain. Extraction in process. Hold position until arrival.'

'Acknowledged,' Karlaen said, staring out at the ill-defined shapes slouching through the haze. He swung his hammer slowly, stirring the smoke. 'Come then, if you will. Here I stand, and I shall not move,' he murmured. Despite his words, he hoped that they would keep their distance. He was not afraid of them. Rather, he was afraid of himself. He could feel his control slipping with every confrontation. The Red Thirst scraped at the back of his throat and memories that were not his pressed down on him. He knew the signs as well as any, for he had seen men afflicted with them often enough.

He thought of Raphen. He closed his eyes, trying not to imagine how it would feel to be claimed by the same madness that had taken the other Space Marine, or Cassor. To be lost and damned by a curse in his very blood. Karlaen's eyes opened and his gaze flickered to Flax, where the old man lay, breathing shallowly. *Does the answer rest with you?* he thought. *Are you our salvation, as Corbulo thinks, or was this all for nothing?*

He heard a scrape of talons on stone and whirled, his hammer chopping out to catch a leaping genestealer. The brutal blow drove the genestealer to the ground, leaving it in a gore-stained heap. Karlaen scanned the plaza, sighting more multi-armed shapes creeping towards him through the ruins. The vox crackled with static as he tried one last time to contact the others. A second genestealer lunged at him from over the fallen statue of the Emperor.

Karlaen pivoted and his blow caught the creature in the side, smashing it against the statue. Ichor stained the scorched features of the Emperor as the body slid to the ground. Karlaen turned back to see more of the beasts bounding towards him through the smoke.

The next few moments passed in a blur of blood and death. With his ammunition depleted, and an unconscious man to protect, Karlaen was forced onto the defensive. His hammer was as much shield as weapon. He turned, twisted, stomped and slid, never slowing, always staying in motion, forcing his enemies to come to him.

Finally, he stood alone, surrounded by the mangled corpses of tyranids. His hammer was heavy in his hand; the Chapter symbols that marked the ancient relic-weapon were hidden beneath a sticky shroud of splattered meat and alien juices. Smoke had filled the plaza, and he was pressed to see anything. He backed towards the statue as embers drifted down from the sky. His eyes stung from the heat of the flames which drew ever closer on either side of the palace. The air was thick with poison and ash.

Karlaen squinted. What little sunlight there had been was now hidden behind a thickening veil of smoke. He could see nothing, hear nothing. Weariness crept into him, one muscle at a time, and with it came the red hum, which became louder and louder the more tired he grew. Soon he would not be able to resist it, or to channel it. He would only be able to sink beneath it. And then...

He shied away from the thought, and tried to marshal what strength remained to him. Through the downpour of embers, he saw the genestealers massing once more among the shattered statues which marked the plaza. And then a malign shape, larger than the rest, leapt up from the horde and onto a headless statue.

The Spawn of Cryptus looked the worse for wear after its tumble into the depths. Its carapace was cracked and befouled; filth dripped from it, drying and flaking away in the heat of the fire. Yet it still moved with the same eerie grace as always, and it did not seem to have lost any of its terrible strength. As it crouched on the statue's shoulders, its glare was one of hateful promise.

Karlaen shook his head. 'Determination is not the province of the Emperor's chosen alone,' he murmured. Another line from the *Philosophies of Raldoron*. Raldoron had been referring to orks, but the statement held true for the broodlord as well, he thought. He spat a mouthful of blood onto the ground before him and raised his chin.

'Well, beast. What are you waiting for?'

The broodlord watched its prey ready himself for what was to come, and felt a flicker of disquiet. Never before had it fought prey like this. Never before had it matched wills with a creature that could resist it.

It did not like this game.

It crouched on the statue and examined the red-armoured giant with distaste. The invader had ruined everything, and there was no more time. The broodlord could feel the weight of the Hive Mind's attentions turning towards it now, as the ground shook and the sky bled fire. Something was riding the charnel wind down from the pitiless stars, and every swarm would be mustered to counter it.

But not yet. Not... *yet*. Not while its brother was yet unpunished. Not while the usurper yet breathed. Its claws sank into the surface of the statue, as it imagined doing the same to his fragile flesh. It had waited years, decades, for this moment. This last revenge. To show him the full price for his treachery.

It could feel its brother's mind, dim and clouded by pain. That pain gave it no satisfaction, though it could not say why. His features flashed through its mind, and it wondered why it had not killed him when it had had the chance. It had wanted to so badly, but something had stayed its hand – other faces, other voices, memories it did not understand, a woman's voice whispering: *This is your brother Augustus. He will protect you, Tiberius.*

But he had not. And then, it was too late.

It closed its eyes, ignoring the sounds of its children below, of the death of the world it had sought to claim. It focused on the memories that swirled through its mind the way embers swirled through the air above the plaza. It remembered a man and a woman, and then Flax, raising a pistol. It remembered the man shouting, and the blood that followed a rumble of thunder. The plaza shook around it. The broodlord opened its eyes and clutched at itself as pain shot through it.

The fall had hurt it. The waters had seared its lungs, but it had hauled itself out and up into the light, its strength bolstered by rage. Rage at the thought that it might not taste the blood of the usurper. Rage that its long-delayed vengeance might never take place. Rage that its brother would survive while it was subsumed into the Hive Mind.

Rage that he might never understand what he had taken from it.

Only he did, didn't he? He had made that clear enough on the bridge. The broodlord touched the spot where Flax's knife had bitten into its side, still wet with ichor. No, Augustus Flax understood all too well.

And the Spawn of Cryptus would make him pay. No matter how many red giants stood between them, no matter how much fire fell from the sky, or how many cracks opened in the earth. The Spawn of Cryptus ruled Asphodex now. The old order would be swept away, and the song and shadow of the Leviathan would rise in its place, stretching from star to star.

The broodlord stretched to its full height on its perch and spread its arms. It threw back its head and for a moment it gazed up at the fiery rain that had begun to fall from the roiling clouds above. Then its head snapped down and it roared.

Its children echoed its cry, then loped towards their prey.

The final battle for the fate of the Flaxian Dynasty had begun.

CHAPTER SEVENTEEN

Karlaen raised his hammer and prepared to sell his life dearly. The broodlord's scream rippled out over the plaza, and the genestealers echoed its cry as they lunged forward as one. There were too many of them, coming too fast, for him to overcome. He made the calculation instinctively, and it brought him no shame to realise the inevitability of his position.

Indeed, part of him longed for it. Part of him longed to give in to the madness and drink deep of the red waters that rose behind his eyes, to simply give in to the Red Thirst as so many others had, and to shed the burden of duty in his final moments. He thought of Raphen and the Death Company, and wondered what it must be like to fight as they did, lost in the past. What would it be like, to battle alongside heroes long dead and gone to dust? Was it worth it? Was giving in to madness worth seeing the face of Sanguinius himself, as the dark closed in around you for the last time? He could almost feel the primarch's presence beside him, his great wings shielding Karlaen from the falling embers. He could almost...

The thud of his hearts drowned out all other sound. Shadows moved through the rain of fire; the flickering, ghostly outline of memories struggling to the surface. In the pulse of his hearts he heard the dim din of voices, and felt the reverberations of battle. But not this battle. He opened his eyes. The world might as well have been a painting. He could make out the gleam of the firelight reflected in the talons of his enemies, and smell the acrid stink of them. And among them he could see warriors who were not there – shades clad in armour of brass or amethyst, reeking of incense and spoiled blood. He blinked. The warriors rippled and vanished, as if they were no more than motes on the surface of his eye.

Karlaen steeled himself. He ignored the red hum and what it had stirred to the surface of him as the genestealers bounded towards him through the ruins, springing from statue to statue or simply scuttling across the open plaza. If he was to die, it would not be as a maddened beast. He would not give in. He would do his duty, and he would die here and now, at the talons of these beasts, rather than beneath the blades of enemies past, if die he must.

He let the head of the hammer dip. His mind began to calculate the best way to use their numbers against them, and to utilise his combat capabilities to the fullest. Tyranids were not men, and wounds that did not kill them outright rarely stopped them. But the swarms could be shaken free of the Hive Mind's control through sustained violence. Kill enough of them, and quickly, and the broodlord's synaptic control might slip as the remainder gave in to their feral nature and fled. The encroaching flames would make that easier. Like all animals, the bio-beasts instinctively feared fire.

The closest genestealer leapt, and time seemed to slow, the moment drawing taut like the string of a bow. Karlaen pinpointed the best place to land his blow for maximum effect, and the haft of his hammer spun in his grip as he brought it up. Even as the blow connected, his armour's sensors screamed a warning. The genestealer's head burst like an overripe fruit and, as it flipped through the air, bolter fire licked across the horde.

The vox crackled to life and Karlaen could not stifle a triumphant laugh as a familiar voice said, 'One would think you'd learned your lesson about haring off alone, captain.'

'Feel free to report me to Commander Dante once we're off-planet, sergeant,' Karlaen said, as genestealers fell. Terminators tromped into the plaza from out of the palace ruins, bolters thundering. Alphaeus, Zachreal and Melos were in the lead. 'Joses?' Karlaen asked, quietly.

Alphaeus's voice was sombre. 'He bought us time to retreat. The creature spilled his guts, and he was in no mood to fall back. We – I – thought it best to abide by his decision.' There was much left unsaid in that terse statement. Karlaen could think of nothing to say. Joses had always been close to the red edge of things. The taciturn black-haired warrior had never fully shed himself of the lessons of the desert and the mountain.

Karlaen shook his head and smashed a genestealer aside as it clawed at him. He would mourn later. 'I have signalled for extraction. They are on their way.' He jammed the end of his hammer into a genestealer's spine, shattering it. 'Where are–' Before he could finish the question, the whine of turbines filled the air and black-armoured shapes dropped through the smoke. The Death Company had arrived. Or at least what was left of it. There were only a handful of the berserkers remaining, though their enthusiasm seemed undimmed.

A genestealer that had been about to leap on him was crushed by a thunder hammer. Raphen landed a moment later and jerked the head of his hammer free from the ruin of the xenos's twitching form. The crazed warrior turned to Karlaen and nodded tersely. 'Thought to have them all to yourself, eh brother? For shame. The traitors owe us all a debt of blood, not just you,' he rasped, shivering in eagerness. He clapped a trembling hand to Karlaen's shoulder and said, 'We shall stand together. Holy Terra shall not fall. Not today.'

'No, not today,' Karlaen said. He hesitated, but then clasped Raphen's forearm in a warrior's grip. The sergeant jerked once, as if in surprise. His twitching subsided. He looked at Karlaen, and the eyes behind the lenses of his helmet were lucid. But the clarity lasted only for a moment.

'Can you hear him, brother? Can you feel the heat of his passage? We are in the shadow of his wings, and he calls the Ninth Legion to his side,' Raphen snarled. He spun, crushing a genestealer, then putting a bolt-round into the belly of another. The wounded beast charged on. Raphen made to fire again, but his bolt pistol clicked uselessly. He tossed the weapon aside. Karlaen moved to finish off the wounded genestealer, but Raphen beat him to it.

He caught the creature by its jaw and jerked its head forwards against his own. He smashed his head against the genestealer's own again and again, until the xenos stopped thrashing. He let the body fall and turned back to Karlaen, ichor dripping down the contours of his faceplate. 'The primarch calls us to battle, brother,' he whispered hoarsely.

Before Karlaen could reply, Raphen whipped back around, lifted his hammer and activated his jump pack, hurling himself into the seething ranks of the foe. As Karlaen watched him, the ground shook beneath his feet, and a loud voice roared, 'Faith is what fans the guttering spark of my rage. Witches and heretics shall be consumed in my fire. One side, brother – this plaza shall be their tomb.' Cassor stomped past the statue, storm bolter firing. Genestealers exploded in mid-leap or were slapped from the air by the Dreadnought's claws.

Karlaen felt a surge of relief as he watched the Dreadnought smash into the enemy. His earlier calculations fractured and came apart as he watched his brothers enter the fray. They were still outnumbered a hundred to one, but there was a chance now, where before there had only been inevitability. He swung his hammer with renewed strength. Alphaeus and the others joined him, marching steadily across the plaza to take up formation around the statue of the Emperor.

There was no need for orders. Not now. With the extraction called for, every battle-brother knew what was required of him, and they would fight until they fell. There would be no falling back, no formations, only the slow, steady grind of a slugging match. Terminator armour and storm bolters against claws, fangs and poison sacs. Karlaen found himself fighting side by side with Leonos and Damaris, the twins protecting his flanks as he put his hammer to use. He was glad to see that they had survived.

Bio-horrors poured into the plaza from the ruins surrounding it. They did not come in waves as before, but as a single, unceasing flood, attacking as one. Terminators were dragged away from their fellows, separated by the sheer press of the enemy, then pulled down. The Death Company smashed in and out of the horde like black comets, but they too were dragged down one by one, selling their lives to buy breathing room for the warriors of the First Company. As the battle raged on, Karlaen tried to spot the broodlord, but the creature was nowhere to be seen. For a moment, he hoped that it had abandoned the fight. But he dismissed the thought as fast as it occurred to him. No, it was still out there somewhere, waiting for its moment to strike.

Tyranid warrior-broods bounded through the swirling mass of genestealers, scattering their lesser kin as they sought to reach the Blood Angels. They trampled the smaller bio-beasts in their haste, scattering others with wide slashes from bone swords or snaps of bio-whips. The Terminators focused on the newcomers, pouring firepower into the synapse beasts, but some got through the gauntlet of explosive rounds and reached the Blood Angels lines.

Karlaen felt something splash against his armour and turned to see one of the tyranids pelting towards him, its grotesque bio-cannon raised for another shot.

'Look out–' Damaris began.

'–captain,' Leonos finished.

Both Terminators turned their storm bolters on the monstrosity as it bounded out of the smoke. The tyranid warrior contorted and flew apart as the explosive rounds pierced its carapace. Karlaen turned to thank them, but his words turned to ash in his throat as Leonos staggered, a bio-whip wrapped around his throat. A tyranid perched on top of him, hauling back on the whip. As the Terminator struggled to free himself, the tyranid plunged a pair of bone swords down through the top of his helm. His death was so swift that neither his twin nor Karlaen could prevent it.

Leonos sagged as the tyranid extricated its blades. It dropped from the slumping body, but had no time to seek out new prey, as Damaris uttered a roar of fury and slammed into it, driving it back against the statue with a booming crack. The tyranid squealed and writhed for a moment before Damaris's groping powerfist found its jaw and forced its head back past the breaking point. There was a second crack, louder than the first, and the beast was still.

Damaris staggered back, the broken blades of the tyranid's swords sticking from his chest. He spun awkwardly as a third tyranid tried to dart past him, bringing his fist down on the creature's back, snapping its spine. As it fell, he began to slump. Karlaen realised that the blades had not merely slipped through his armour, but had pierced something vital in the process. Karlaen reached Damaris as he sank down beside his twin's corpse. 'I have you, brother. I...' Karlaen trailed off. Damaris was not listening to him.

He said something unintelligible as Karlaen laid him down. He coughed wetly, and Karlaen knew that the blades had reached his hearts and lungs. Damaris reached out towards Leonos, but his life ebbed before his hand found that of his comrade. Karlaen rose unsteadily to his feet, all rational thought burning to ash in a sudden swell of rage. The world slowed and stretched, and he could see everything all at once through a muddy red haze.

He saw Zachreal and Alphaeus fighting back to back. He saw Melos catching a bio-whip in his powerfist and wrenching its wielder off balance long enough to get a bead on it with his storm bolter. He saw the survivors of the other squads gathered about the statue in a ragged formation, pouring their remaining ammunition into the horde that surged and swirled around them, selling their lives on behalf of him, and on behalf of his mission. He saw red- and black-armoured bodies scattered among piles of dead alien filth.

All of this he saw, but not the tyranid warrior that crept up behind him, bio-cannon levelled. He heard the hiss of dribbling acid and spun, but not quickly enough. The shot knocked him off his feet and he crashed down, a sizzling patch on his armour marking where the shot had struck home.

He rolled onto his back and groped blindly for his hammer. The tyranid advanced on him, eyes glittering with inhuman malice. Before it could fire its weapon again, however, a black form hurtled past and there was a sound like stone striking meat. The tyranid lurched backwards as one of its legs was smashed out from under it. Off balance, it toppled backwards and smashed down onto the ground. Raphen landed on it a moment later, the soles of his boots pulping its screeching features.

Raphen spun, his hammer lashing out to catch a genestealer. He reached out, as if to pull Karlaen to his feet.

Karlaen saw a shadow hurtle towards him. He opened his mouth to shout a warning, but was too late as something heavy pounced onto the other Blood Angel and bore him to the ground. Black armour tore beneath rending claws as the broodlord smashed Raphen against the stones of the plaza. His jump pack was torn from his back and sent hurtling aside, where it exploded. The beast hefted him over its head. Raphen, dazed, bellowed uselessly as the broodlord held him.

It met Karlaen's gaze, and he saw a question there. No, a demand. He felt the thing's thoughts claw at his own, stronger than before. It was angry now, and that anger gave it strength. He met its glare with his own, feeling his own anger press hard against his fraying discipline. Whatever it saw in his eyes seemed to answer its question, and it screeched.

Then it brought Raphen down across its upraised knee.

'No!' Karlaen rose to his feet and, weaponless, threw himself at the beast as it let Raphen drop. It leapt back, avoiding him, then sprang for a statue, slithering around it and out of sight. Karlaen turned back to Raphen, but there was nothing to be done. Like Bartelo, he had died instantly, his spine shattered and his neck crushed. Like too many others, he had died on Karlaen's behalf, at the claws of a creature that should not exist.

Karlaen scooped up his hammer and turned to seek his brother's killer.

CHAPTER EIGHTEEN

Karlaen's vox crackled with an unfamiliar voice as he stalked through the smoky melee. Some small part of him not yet claimed by the rage that drove him recognised it as the voice of the pilot sent to extract them. Almost against his will, he looked up, scanning the red sky. His bionic eye caught sight of it almost immediately, whirring and shifting to focus in on one of the Chapter's Stormraven gunships as it tore down through the swirling clouds of harpies and gargoyles that sought to bar its passage. The gunship's twin-linked assault cannons roared, clearing a path. As Karlaen watched, the vessel dipped its blunt nose towards the plaza and screamed down towards them, guns blazing.

As he turned to continue seeking out his prey, he felt its jagged claws sink into his mind. The world turned upside down, and he clutched at his head. The pain was far greater than before, and all the more intrusive for catching him unawares. Faces, memories, voices, pounded at him from all sides... He saw Aphrae's death at the hands of the broodlord, and tasted the coppery tang of his brother's blood. He felt Raphen's spine break on his knee, and a scream ripped free of his throat.

Something slammed into him from the side, rocking him on his feet. He lashed out blindly, and was rewarded with a shriek as the crackling head of his hammer struck home. He saw the broodlord roll to its feet. Rather than darting away into the smoke, however, it charged right for him. He snarled and lunged to meet it. But, within a few seconds, he found himself driven back. His armour barely warded off its powerful blows as it tore into him, body and mind. He could feel his control, already tenuous, slipping as he fought to stay focused against its mental attacks while simultaneously fending off its claws. It was not just the creature he was fighting; it was creeping fatigue as well. He dug down, trying to find what reserves of energy remained to him, but he knew his opponent was not going to give him time to recover.

Before, he had merely been an impediment. Now, it wanted him dead. He could see it in its eyes, those mad not-quite-human orbs which sparked with an all too familiar rage. He was fighting a losing battle against the Red Thirst, but this creature had already surrendered to its own form of madness. Whatever drove it, it was not planning on stopping until one of them was dead. A claw pierced his guard and opened his cheek to the bone. He tasted blood. The

Red Thirst surged up in him, and he felt his reason slip. He uttered an inarticulate cry and smashed the broodlord back, trading blow for blow as the battle rolled on around them.

They grappled through the drifts and piles of corpses, tearing at one another. Karlaen could barely focus. He heard the whine of the Stormraven's turbines growing louder and felt the ground shudder as more and more tyranids forced their way into the plaza, driven by the will of the Hive Mind. All he could see was the snarling maw of his enemy; all he could feel was the urge to smash the beast down and erase it from sight.

Man and beast strained against one another, the stones cracking beneath their feet. Gradually, he was being pushed back, but he refused to yield. It would die here, now, or he would. The broodlord leaned in close, jaws snapping. Its barbed tongue caressed his face, and he caught it between his teeth, champing down, ripping the hard flesh. The broodlord reeled, shrieking, and he shoved it back, breaking them apart. As it staggered, he spat out the chunk of wriggling flesh still caught between his teeth and crashed into it, knocking it to the ground. It went down hard, but rolled aside before his hammer could strike home.

He lifted his weapon for another strike, but the Spawn leapt on him, bowling him over. His armour struck sparks from the stone as it rode him to the ground. His hammer was torn from his grip. Human-like hands sought his throat as he made to rise and he found himself pinned. Its grip tightened, while its bladed upper arms rose over him. Its eyes flashed, and in his head an image of his death formed.

Behind the beast, he saw great wings unfurl amidst a bloody radiance. He felt strangely calm. This, then, was a good death. He would die with his men, as he should have done before. He had failed his men, Flax, Corbulo and himself, but he would not avoid the consequences. He stared up at the creature, willing it to strike. It paused, as if uncertain, its wounded tongue lashing, its features crinkled in confusion. Then, it hissed and readied itself to strike. The shadow behind spread, growing larger.

'No beast. Thy claws shall not find his heart. So says Cassor.' The Dreadnought's talons raked down across the broodlord's back. The creature turned, and found itself caught fast by a second claw. With a grinding of gears, Cassor hurled the broodlord aside, sending its body bouncing across the rubble. Karlaen stared up at the Dreadnought in incomprehension. 'You make this a habit, brother. Twice has Cassor saved you.' The Dreadnought turned, scanning the plaza. 'Where are my brothers? The enemy approaches.'

Despite the haze which clouded his thoughts, Karlaen could see that there was not a single black-armoured form left standing. The Death Company had earned their name, and their redemption. Cassor stared at the scuttling horde that clambered over the bodies of his fellows and rumbled, 'Cassor stands alone. So be it. Vengeance must take place and Cassor shall deal it in red increments. Come traitors. Cassor is waiting. He has waited all of his life for this moment.' The Dreadnought's optic sensors rotated down, to meet Karlaen's still stunned gaze. 'I know that I am no longer sane. But I still serve. You shall not fall here, brother. Not while one flicker of rage remains in Cassor's heart. Up, commander. Glory awaits.'

The enemy swept forwards just as Karlaen began to push himself to his feet. And though Cassor stood alone, as wave after wave of bio-horrors smashed into him, not one reached Karlaen. The Dreadnought burned, trampled and crushed the aliens until the stones were slick with ichor.

Cassor fought with all of the fury that had earned him the honour of being entombed in the sarcophagus of a Dreadnought. His storm bolter roared until its ammunition cylinders were depleted and his meltagun turned the air black with char. When both weapons were spent, he continued to slash and crush the tyranids. Karlaen surged to his feet, giving in to the red hum that quivered through his brain. He smashed his hammer down on snarling maws and bashed aside scratching talons.

The ground trembled beneath his feet as he fought, and he saw a familiar shape plough through its lesser kin with a bellicose roar. The carnifex, its hide pockmarked with death-scars, charged towards Cassor with undeniable eagerness. The Dreadnought turned. 'Again you seek to match me, hound of carnage. But thy end is come.'

The carnifex crashed into the Dreadnought with a roar, lifting him up and driving him back into the statue of the Emperor, shattering it and sending Terminators scrambling aside as a cloud of dust swept across the plaza. The Dreadnought, off balance, toppled back as the carnifex continued to bulldoze forward. Its great hooves and claws crushed and pierced the black hull plates and a strangled scream exploded from Cassor's vox.

Karlaen, without thinking, hurled himself at the carnifex. His hammer slammed down against its carapace, cracking it. The carnifex twisted around, jaws snapping. He staggered back as its blade-like claws tore through the air towards him. It stopped short of reaching him, and turned. Karlaen looked past it and saw that Cassor was not finished yet. He had reached out to catch the beast's leg in an unyielding grip.

'You shall not touch my brother, abomination. I shall endure a thousand deaths before I yield.' Cassor hauled back on the carnifex's hind limb. The carnifex twisted around and drove one of its scything claws through the Dreadnought as it had in their first encounter. But Cassor refused to let go. The carnifex flailed and snapped, its shrieks rising above the battlefield. It slammed its claws down again and again, until at last they became lodged in the ruptured hull. The carnifex's struggles became more desperate as it strove to free itself. The fallen Dreadnought rocked beneath the blows, but did not release it.

Karlaen, mind full of red, stalked towards the creature. It was the living manifestation of the enemy that was consuming this world and threatening his own. In that moment, he hated it more than any foe he had ever faced. He swung his hammer up. The creature wailed, as if it knew what was coming.

His first blow stunned it. His second split its scarred skull. His third and fourth opened that split further, and mangled the throbbing organ within. His fifth and sixth shattered its jaw and crushed its staring eyes. His seventh nearly tore its head from its neck. He smashed the Hammer of Baal down again and again until he could no longer lift the relic-weapon without trembling from the effort. Then, rage fading, he used his hammer to lever the corpse off Cassor's inert form.

'Brother, do you yet function?' he demanded, sinking down beside the great war machine. 'Cassor? *Cassor!*'

Gears whined and servos grated as the hull shifted. Optic sensors flickered and swivelled blindly. Karlaen froze as Cassor's claw rose. The tip of the talons brushed against the crimson teardrop set into the centre of his chestplate.

'I swore to serve in life or death. But I feel his hand upon me. I cannot move. My armour... is breached. I hear his wings, brother. I... see...' Cassor's rumble slurred into silence without revealing what it was he had seen. The lights on his hull blinked and faded. Karlaen laid his hand on the shattered hull. The rage had drained from him with his final blow, and he could feel his strength ebbing.

He pushed himself to his feet and looked around. The Stormraven had scoured the plaza of alien life as it landed, but there were always more tyranids. Something hissed, and he turned to see the broodlord limping back towards the ruins of the palace. It had been badly hurt by Cassor's attack. As he watched it, he knew he would never get a better chance to end the danger it posed. But there was no time. Not if he wanted to see his mission through.

With the death of the carnifex, the tyranid horde was drawing close again: a roiling sea of chitin and claws closing in on the survivors. Already, the remaining Terminators were fighting their way towards the waiting Stormraven, which covered their approach with the hurricane bolters mounted on its sponsons. He could hear Alphaeus calling to him, and he saw with some relief that Zachreal had Flax cradled in his arms as he tromped up the boarding ramp into the Stormraven's hold.

He hesitated, considering. It was worth his life, wasn't it? The broodlord could not be allowed to survive, even if it meant his death. He looked for it, trying to spot it in the smoke, but it was gone, lost in the haze and in the roiling tide of frenzied tyranid beasts now flooding into the plaza. He heard Alphaeus call for him again, and he turned.

Karlaen fought a path to them, his motions mechanical. He was tired, in body and soul. But he had done his duty. And he was not returning alone, as he had before. The Shield of Baal had not failed, not this time. Gusts of superheated air washed across the plaza as he reached the boarding ramp. The vessel was already starting to lift off as Alphaeus reached out to him. Karlaen gratefully accepted his help in clambering aboard.

Below them, tyranids leapt uselessly at the Stormraven as it rose into the air. Stormstrike missiles streaked from launch bays to hammer into the ruins, collapsing them, and sending tongues of flames licking across the plaza. The Plaza of the Emperor Ascendant would soon be a cauldron, and anything left in it would be consumed by the fires now ravaging Phodia. He hoped that their number would include the Spawn of Cryptus, but somehow he knew that would not be the case. The universe was not that kind.

The ramp began to close. Karlaen stood, watching until the last moment, hoping to see the beast lurch from hiding, wreathed in flame. Hoping that it would make a final, futile assault, and give him leave to finish it off for good. Instead, it remained hidden. He could feel it watching him, watching the Stormraven, calculating the distance and the odds, and he knew that it was not so foolish. 'Next time, beast,' he said.

The last thing he saw before the ramp clanged shut and the Stormraven took flight were two red eyes glaring at him through the smoke.

EPILOGUE

PORT HELOS, ASPHODEX

The Stormraven reached Port Helos, the largest of Phodia's many space ports and the only one currently in Imperial hands, just as the twin suns reached their height, bathing the embattled world in deadly radiation.

The desperate Imperial defenders had built a makeshift moat between the port and the city, flooding the streets with millions of litres of promethium and lighting it. Now a barrier of crackling flame, almost a hundred metres high, rose above the streets.

Dante himself had led the Blood Angels in securing the port after a savage battle in which Mephiston, the Chapter's Chief Librarian, had contested with the Hive Mind itself and survived. Though the enemy had been driven back, swarms of tyranids massed outside the flames, waiting for them to die down.

The Stormraven touched down with a heavy thump that was muffled by the roar of artillery. As the boarding ramp descended, the stink of burning promethium and the omnipresent odour of the bio-swarms washed over the passengers.

Karlaen stepped down from the ramp and onto the landing platform, a fog of exhaust fumes coiling about him. He said nothing as the others began to disembark behind him. He carried his hammer loosely in one hand and, as he stepped onto the softly vibrating surface of the platform, it slid through his grip. The head crashed against the ground as he closed his eyes.

The rage had dwindled to embers, but he could still feel its heat within him. Once stoked, such fires never truly died. He had come far closer to the edge than he cared to consider, but the thought lingered. He longed for the peace of the Chapter's fortress-monastery, and his pursuits there. Some place where he could go to find a new centre, and douse the fires that had been stirred within him.

He heard an intake of breath, along with the rattle of armour, and opened his eyes. A golden figure was approaching through the fog of exhaust, and the others had all dropped to their knees. Karlaen began to do the same in reflex, instinct taking over for his too-weary mind.

'Rise and report, Captain of the First,' Commander Dante said. Corbulo stood behind him, a flock of Chapter serfs and white-armoured Sanguinary Priests gathered about him. Karlaen briefly met the Sanguinary High Priest's calm gaze as he rose and removed his helm, but said nothing to him. He looked at Dante.

'Mission accomplished, commander,' he rasped, his throat raw. In short, precise sentences, he explained what had befallen him and his men in the ruins from the time of their arrival to their extraction. He said nothing of his unease, or of how close he had come to not coming back at all. Dante could tell regardless. Karlaen knew that his Chapter Master could read it in his face and hear it in his voice, but he said nothing.

'The creature,' Dante asked, when Karlaen had finished, 'is it dead?'

'I do not know.' The words rankled. He wanted to demand leave to hunt the aberrant beast down, and finish it for good. But he held his tongue.

Dante gazed at him for a moment. Then the golden helm twitched, and he said, 'You have done well, Shield of Baal. As I knew you would.' He reached out and clasped Karlaen's shoulder, startling him. 'You have never failed me, brother. I have said that you are the rock upon which the First is built, but you are more than that.' He gestured to the hammer that Karlaen held. 'You are the aegis that defends us, and you are the hammer blow which crushes our enemies. Though I would give you the respite I know you crave, I have need of you still.'

Karlaen bowed his head. 'Speak your will, my lord, and I will see it done.'

Dante lowered his hand. 'I will, but not yet. Rest, regain your strength. This war has only just begun, I fear.' He turned to look at Corbulo, who was watching as the Chapter serfs led a bewildered and groggy Augustus Flax away. 'Well, Corbulo?'

'He will live. And may prove as useful as I hoped,' Corbulo said, turning to look at them. Karlaen wanted to ask about Flax's relationship to the beast, but said nothing. He had told them everything that Flax had shared. If Corbulo was dismayed by such revelations, he did not show it. Indeed, he seemed satisfied with his prize.

Dante nodded brusquely. He looked at Karlaen. 'You will attend me, when you have rested.' He hesitated, as if there were something else he wanted to say. But instead, he turned and departed. As the Chapter Master left the landing platform, Alphaeus and the others rose to their feet. Karlaen waved them away. Let them rest while they could. The First's part in this war was not yet over.

Soon only he and Corbulo remained on the platform. Crimson clouds rolled past, eddying and billowing around the port. Karlaen did his best to ignore the other Space Marine. Corbulo stood quietly, as if waiting for an invitation to speak. They stood in silence for some time. Finally, Corbulo cleared his throat. 'Discipline is the armour of a man's soul, it is true. But armour must occasionally be removed, so that it might be tended and made strong again. So too with discipline. It must be tested, and then strengthened where it is found lacking.'

Karlaen grunted. He did not wish to speak about it, and especially not with Corbulo. He stared at the clouds and tried not to see the faces of his fallen brothers there. More names added to the tally of his debt. More men dead because they had followed him into battle. His grip on the hammer's haft tightened. Corbulo waited. Whether he was waiting for a reply, or simply waiting, Karlaen couldn't say. Eventually, the Sanguinary High Priest made to depart.

'I asked you before if you wanted to know what those whispers in your mind said of you, brother,' Corbulo said, as he turned away. Karlaen said nothing. Corbulo stopped, then smiled sadly, his face half-turned away. 'They said that they forgive you. But that you cannot forgive yourself,' he said. 'And that it will be the death of you.'

Karlaen did not reply. He turned away, and looked out beyond the port walls, towards the burning city below. He heard Corbulo leave, but said nothing.

He simply stared at the conflagration far below, and thought of two red eyes, glaring at him from the smoke.

SHADOW OF THE LEVIATHAN

JOSH REYNOLDS

The enemy burst out of the smoky darkness with a raucous, insectile clatter. The swarm of hormagaunts loped towards their prey, talons gleaming in the light of fading luminal panels, driven forward by the pulsing will of monstrous overseers. There were hundreds of them, a seething mass of ravenous jaws and twitching limbs, determined to devour every scrap of bio-matter in the hive-city.

Ghaurkal Hive was the last of the great Kantipuran Hollow Mountains, and soon it, like the others, would be claimed by the ravenous servants of Hive Fleet Leviathan. The work of centuries and generations without number would be undone in hours, as the once-prosperous world of Kantipur was stripped barren and rendered down to lifeless rock by the star-borne abominations – the hive-ships of the Leviathan – which even now hung bloated and foul in the upper reaches of the world's atmosphere.

The tyranids pelted through the battle-scarred streets of the hab-block, towards the curved rings of the broad marble steps, many metres across, which led from the cavernous hive to the broad, statue-lined avenue, then out of the mountain-hive and into the open air plateau occupied by the Rana Space port. In better times, hundreds of thousands of travellers would have moved up and down those vast steps, coming and going. Now, they were pockmarked by craters and stained by the blood of humans and monsters alike.

They were crowded with the shattered remnants of a once proud people making all haste for the dubious safety of the stars. It was these bloodied refugees that had drawn the tyranids, but as the creatures swarmed out of the darkness with ravenous intent, other, larger shapes moved out of the mass of panicked humanity to interpose themselves between predator and prey.

'As per the established stratagem, brothers,' Varro Tigurius, Chief Librarian of the Ultramarines, said to the blue-armoured shapes of his battle-brothers as they spread out in formation around him, moving to protect the screaming evacuees. 'Kill the synapse creatures first. We must be quick. Time is not on our side in this endeavour.'

'*Thank you for the reminder, Chief Librarian. In the heat of battle I might have forgotten standing orders,*' the vox crackled in response.

Tigurius smiled thinly. 'Merely doing my duty, sergeant. As are we all. Proceed at your leisure.' Clad in azure power armour, his bald, scarred head covered by the ornately engraved psychic hood that was both a sign of his office as well as protection for his body and mind, Tigurius made for an imposing figure, even amongst the finest warriors of his Chapter. Scrolls, parchments of incalculable age and purity seals hung from his battleplate, and he clutched an ornate force staff in one hand as his other rested on the butt of the master-crafted bolt pistol holstered on his hip.

'*Proceeding.*'

The response was curt, but then he hadn't expected it to be otherwise. The Sternguard were not men to waste words, and their sergeant, Ricimer, was taciturn even for one of that elite group. He was stolid, efficient and unmoveable – in other words, the perfect choice to command the Sternguard. The sons of Dorn would have been proud to call him one of their own had he the fortune to wear the colours of the Imperial Fists rather than the Ultramarines.

A moment later, bolters began to fire in a staccato rhythm, one after the other. Hellfire rounds thudded into the wide, armour-plated skulls of the tyranid warriors, delivering their deadly payload. The creatures staggered, slewing awkwardly through the swarm of their lesser brethren. One toppled backwards, yellowish smoke rising from its crumpled skull. Another stumbled forward a few paces, the tips of its bone swords dragging along the street, before it sank down and flopped over, twitching. The last ploughed on, ignoring the oozing craters that pockmarked its skull.

'*Reinforced cranial structure,*' Ricimer said.

'Yes,' Tigurius said. He stalked down the steps. 'I shall deal with it. Hold position.' He focused his attentions on the tyranid warrior and formed a killing thought in his mind – a thought of sharp edges and deadly speed, honed to a murderous point in the fires of his righteous anger. He sent it hurtling out with a gesture and felt it strike home as if it had been a physical blow. The tyranid swayed, reared back and shrieked.

He extended his hand as if to gather the tangled strands of the thought and made a swift, twisting motion. The tyranid's bestial frame gave a spasm, and a gout of superheated steam burst from its jaws. It sank down with a shrill wail, limbs twitching. The tide of hormagaunts stampeded around and over it, following its last command with mindless ferocity.

'*Fall back, Chief Librarian.*'

'No, I think not,' Tigurius said, facing the tide. 'I have fought these beasts before and I know how to send them scurrying for their holes. Hold position. Deal with any that get past me. I shall break them here.' He spread his arms and exhaled slowly. The sutras of strength and endurance unspooled in his mind. He brought his hands together, catching his staff between them. The air seemed to congeal about him as he lifted the staff, ramming the end of it down. The pavement cracked and split, venting steam and dust. A ripple of destruction spread outwards, tearing the street apart. A building, weakened by alien growths, collapsed atop the rear of the swarm, burying many of the skittering hormagaunts. The rest continued on, undeterred, plunging through the dust cloud to surge towards him.

'Come then,' he murmured. 'Come and die, little bugs.' Even as he spoke, he could feel the acidic heat of the hive mind bearing down on him from behind the eyes of every scuttling shape. It was an abominable weight on his mind and soul, but he bore it gladly.

Once, perhaps, his soul might have shrunk from that great, black shadow in the warp, but now he knew its secrets. And in knowing them, he could exploit them. Through such contact, he had come to know its wants, its drives and, more importantly, its weaknesses. He could sense the patterns of control and instinct which drove the servants of the hive mind, and disrupt them with ease.

In moments he was surrounded on all sides, the hormagaunts bounding towards him and talons scything through the air. Tigurius drew his bolt pistol. He fired swiftly, placing the shots where the leaping gaunts would be, rather than where they were. The creatures fell, skulls shattered. He pivoted, sweeping his staff out in a wide arc, to smash a third xenos from the air. The reinforced length of the staff, powered by genetically enhanced muscle, pulverised the creature's spiny shell, and dropped it to the ground in a twitching heap.

As the rest of the brood boiled towards him, Tigurius set his staff as if it were a standard, and let his fury flower to its fullest. The air before him ionised and, with a whip-crack of sound loud enough to shatter those few windows remaining in the closest buildings, his will slipped its leash. Leaping 'gaunts were obliterated, their bodies crushed beyond recognition as the cannonade of pure force hammered into their ranks. Ichor soon drenched the walls of the hab-units and street, and those who escaped the carnage scuttled back the way they had come.

Tigurius could feel the frayed pulse of primal fear that overwhelmed the creatures' natural ravenous inclinations. Without any of the larger synapse creatures to force them on, the broods were reduced to mere animals, with an animal's instinct towards self-preservation. He smiled in satisfaction. It was no longer a challenge to break the back of such swarms. He watched the last of them vanish into the darkness and turned back towards the steps.

'They're regrouping,' he said.

Ricimer didn't reply. The Sternguard sergeant began to issue orders, and Ultramarines moved to obey with crisp precision. Ten of the thirty who had accompanied Tigurius into Ghaurkal Hive moved to aid the evacuees in their efforts to reach safety. The rest split up into combat squads and moved out into the hab-block which extended out around the entryway to the space port. They would fan out and report any contact with the enemy.

Tigurius heard a rumble and looked up, through the shattered remnants of the immense stained-glass canopy that had covered the avenue to the space port. He watched as one of the vessels pressed into service for the evacuation lunged skyward on oscillating columns of flame. *Fly swiftly, fly true,* he thought.

Overhead, swirling clouds of tyranid gargoyles swooped and eddied. From a distance, the aliens looked like birds, moving with an instinctive synchronicity that eluded bipeds. They flew through the heavy, grey clouds and shot through with strands of sickly purple that obscured the sky. The vessel plunged into clouds and gargoyle swarms, rising steadily upwards and leaving the doomed world behind.

Outside of the hive, the air was thick with the black toxicity spewing from the thousands of fuming spore chimneys which had sprouted from the ground. The very stuff of the once-vibrant world was being broken down and reduced to its component parts for ease of alien digestion. Fuel for a fire that might yet claim Ultima Segmentum, unless some stroke of fortune snuffed it out.

Even here, in the last stronghold of humanity on this world, monstrous alien growths had begun to creep in and coil about the battle-scarred ruins. Many-limbed shadows moved through the upper reaches of the hive, scuttling amongst the networks of pipes and cabling which carried power, air and water to every hab-block and Administratum zone. The warble of the tyranid feeder-beasts slithered down from the upper spires, and the ululation of hormagaunts and still worse things rose from the underhive, combining to create a monstrous background cacophony.

And through it all, he felt the grotesque, singular pulse of the hive mind, watching, in hungry anticipation.

That was all it was, Tigurius knew. There was no true intelligence to be found there, only the avid hunger of an insect colony, bloated into something vast and far-reaching. The hive fleets were not enemies so much as storms to be weathered, or infestations to be exterminated. And such would be his pleasure, when the time came.

A number of other detachments of the same size and composition as the one he had led to Kantipur were engaged in similar evacuation efforts across the Gohla sub-sector. Indeed, the stratagem had been of his devising, after examining the skeins of fate and chance, and sifting through the premonitions which were his burden and his gift in equal measure. The Leviathan grew stronger with every world it devoured, and so, the Ultramarines had set out to deny this tendril of the hive fleet its provender, if possible. Starve the beast, rob it of strength and make it easy prey for the slaughter.

Exterminatus would have been easier, and had been suggested by others, with the Master of Sanctity, Ortan Cassius, among them. Burn the targeted worlds to cinders and let the swarm starve or devour itself. He knew the Blood Angels and their successor chapters were employing similar tactics in the Cryptus System. Tigurius doubted the long-term viability of such a strategy, however, and not simply because his premonitions had shown him glimpses of its ultimate futility. No, the Leviathan could be beaten, even as the Kraken had been, and the Behemoth. And if they sacrificed the very people whom they were sworn to protect, then what was the point?

Tigurius could feel the heat of every human soul still in Ghaurkal Hive in his mind. Each and every human – young or old, man, woman or child – had a tiny ember of flame within the chambers of their single heart... a flame which could burn as brightly as a sun. They were changeable things, humans, and capable of greatness, if given the opportunity. And for that reason, more than any other, Tigurius intended to make his stand and deny the Leviathan.

The Emperor made us to defend his chosen people, he thought, *and that is what the sons of Guilliman will do, or we will die in the attempt.*

He turned suddenly, looking out into the dark of the hab-block, and the hive-city beyond. He'd felt... something. It stirred in the dark, like an unseen shape sliding through black waters. A ripple of psychic disturbance which leeched his certainties away.

He had fought the mind-predators of the hive fleets before, and recognised their psychic spoor when he sensed it. Mind and body tense, he set his thoughts flying out over the cramped quarters of the hab-block, searching, hunting for any sign of it. The hive-city was full of swarms, mostly feeder-beasts, but worse things as well. Brute-simple warrior-broods and cunning infiltrator-species prowled the access tunnels and lower levels, in search of bio-matter to devour.

Tigurius stiffened as a lance of pain stabbed into his cerebral cortex. Even as he had been searching, so had something else – and it had found him first. He staggered, one hand pressed to his temple. A sound filled his head, swelling as if to drive out all thought and sanity. It was a scream, shrill and inhuman, and he dug his fingers into his skull, trying to marshal some defence against it. It was stronger than anything he'd yet encountered in his struggles with the hive mind.

'*Contact,*' the vox-feed crackled abruptly, and Tigurius stiffened. He recognised the voice of Geta, one of Ricimer's subordinates. He heard the stolid *crack-crack-crack* of bolter fire as well. Tigurius heard Ricimer speaking swiftly into the vox, making contact with the other squads.

'Estimate?' Tigurius asked into the vox.

'*Many,*' came the terse reply.

'Care to elaborate, brother?' Tigurius asked.

'*Too many.*'

'Thank you,' Tigurius said. 'Break contact and withdraw.' Geta didn't reply. Tigurius hoped that meant he was already falling back with the other members of his squad. Given the situation, he might not be able to.

Tigurius frowned and looked at Ricimer, who'd joined him before the steps. Ricimer was a bullet-headed veteran of the Ultramarines First Company. He held his helmet beneath his arm, and the majority of his blunt, chiselled features were hidden beneath the rim of the armoured collar of his Mark VIII armour. The pale furrows of old scars rose across his scalp from his cheek, a reminder of a previous conflict with the scuttling hordes of the hive mind.

'How long do we have, brother?' Tigurius asked, without preamble.

'There are still a few hundred left in the avenue. They're beginning to panic,' Ricimer said. He hefted his helmet and set it over his head, locking it in place with a hiss of pneumatic seals. 'We need to buy time, so the crew can finish getting them aboard.'

'Suggestions?'

'Offhand, I'd suggest shooting the tyranids,' Ricimer said. 'I've taken the liberty of ordering Metellus and the others to fall back. Stormravens are already en route. As soon as the last human is aboard and the transports are away, we can leave as well. We just need to hold until then.'

'And can we?' Tigurius asked.

'Emperor willing,' Ricimer said. He glanced at the shattered gates that marked the entrance to the avenue. 'Ten of us can hold that entry point, if they come in force. Less, if Metellus and Oriches get back here with the heavy flamers.' He turned and pointed through the gates, towards the avenue. 'Three possible strongpoints there, there and there, giving overlapping fields of fire for the gateway, allowing for withdrawal. Two more potential strongpoints at the avenue's mid-point. Even factoring in heavy losses, a fighting withdrawal should be possible.'

Tigurius smiled. Ricimer had his faults, but a lack of tactical acumen was not one of them. 'I'll defer to you then, brother. Arrange our withdrawal as you see fit.' The vox crackled again, loudly, in his ear. A garbled voice floundered in a wash of interference and then fell silent. The sound of bolter fire echoed up from the hab-block.

Ricimer cocked his head. 'Geta... report,' he said, hesitating. 'Metellus, Oriches, sound off.' Voices crackled over the vox, and Tigurius turned to see one of the combat squads hurrying towards them. 'Metellus,' Ricimer said.

'There's Oriches,' Tigurius said, gesturing with his staff. The second of the three squads came into view, firing behind them as they moved. One of the Space Marines, clutching the bulky shape of a heavy bolter, stopped and turned, levelling the weapon at some unseen enemy. The heavy bolter roared, and Tigurius heard the high-pitched cries of dying tyranid beasts.

'They're massing. Something's driving them forward again,' Oriches shouted, as he climbed the steps. His armour, as well as that of his men, was scorched and scored by blistering venom and alien claws. 'It's big, whatever it is.'

'One of the command-caste, perhaps,' Ricimer said.

'No,' Tigurius said. The echo of the scream was still in his head like an ache. 'It's something else. I can feel it.' He looked out into the dark. 'Geta?' he asked, looking up at Ricimer. Ricimer said nothing. He stared out into the ruins of the block. Tigurius could tell from the sudden flickering of his aura that the other Ultramarine was concerned. Geta should have fallen back with the others. If he hadn't, that meant his squad had engaged the enemy. The sound of bolter fire ratcheted through the still air.

Tigurius looked at Ricimer. 'Fall back into the space port, as planned. If I have not returned by the time of extraction, you are to follow standing orders. Evacuate and turn this planet to ashes from orbit.'

'Where are you going?' Ricimer asked.

'I shall meet the enemy in the field, as is my right and privilege,' Tigurius said. 'Someone must remind them that the sons of Guilliman are not a meal that agrees with them.' *And I want to know what that was that I felt*, he thought. If the hive fleets had given birth to some new monstrosity, he wanted to know about it and test its might if possible. Knowledge was power.

'One of us should come with you,' Ricimer said.

'Geta will serve in that capacity,' Tigurius said, over his shoulder. 'When you see us, know that the enemy will not be far behind.'

'I don't need to be Chief Librarian to know that, brother,' Ricimer called.

Tigurius chuckled, but didn't reply. He moved quickly, gathering his strength as he did so. Something, some flicker of foresight, told him he would need it. He broke into a run, sprinting into the labyrinthine confines of the hab-block. He trusted in his senses, physical and otherwise, to lead him to Geta and the others.

As he continued on, the sound of bolter fire grew steadily louder, drawing closer. Geta and his brothers were hard-pressed, Tigurius suspected. Then, if what he'd felt were any indication, they might soon be a good deal worse than that. He'd never felt such raw power, not from any alien psyker he'd ever encountered. He hurtled along a broad avenue, moving smoothly, until a flash of movement caught his attention. He smelled the acrid tang of fear, mingled with blood, as he slid to a stop.

A group of ragged figures stumbled out of a side-street. He raised his staff, then lowered it as two of his battle-brothers came into view just behind them. He recognised them both – Valens and Appius – as members of Geta's squad.

'Chief Librarian,' Valens said, smashing a fist against his chestplate in a hasty salute.

Several of the humans wore the battle-tattered remnants of the uniform of the local defence forces. The rest were clad in Administratum robes. All were wounded, some worse than others. They looked at Tigurius dully, exhausted and drained of emotion.

'We found them holed up in a signatorium,' Valens said. 'We almost missed them, but one of them managed to signal us.' He gestured back the way they had come. 'Geta and Castus stayed behind, to give us time to get the humans clear. The enemy were right behind us – swarms of them, 'gaunts and more besides.'

'Forgive me, brother, but I am more concerned about what might be behind the chaff,' Tigurius said. He could feel something coming closer, like the rumble of distant thunder. He tapped Valens on the shoulder-plate with his staff. 'I need you to follow your orders. Go. I will find the others.'

Valens hesitated. 'But...'

Tigurius reeled as a sudden flare of pain seared his mind. The humans screamed and staggered, one falling to the ground, her eyes rolling to the whites, and blood pouring from her nose and mouth. Valens and Appius felt it as well, the former shaking his head like a stunned bovid. 'What in Guilliman's name...?' he croaked.

Tigurius didn't reply. A bolter roared close by, and he saw Geta stumble out into view from the same side-street that Valens and the others had come from, shoving another battle-brother ahead of him. Their armour was scorched black where the bare ceramite wasn't showing, and it was wreathed in smoke. As the wounded Space Marine stumbled, Geta whirled about, his bolter rising. Something pale and radiating a sickly luminescence stretched out towards him. The wriggling ectoplasmic tendrils briefly fluttered over the Space Marine's head. His helmet burst asunder in a welter of blood, bone and brain-matter.

Tigurius's eyes widened as Geta's body sank to its knees, and slowly toppled over, covering the form of his wounded brother.

'Castus,' Valens began, starting forward. Tigurius caught his arm. He could feel a cold scrabbling at the edges of his mind, as if something were trying to pry back his thoughts, in the wake of that searing scream. Whatever had killed Geta was more dangerous than any mind-beast he'd encountered before.

'I'll go. Withdraw, get the humans to safety,' he said.

Valens hesitated, but only for the briefest of moments. Then he and Appius were moving swiftly, following orders, falling in around the small group of bedraggled soldiers and civilians. Quickly, the Ultramarines scooped up those humans who were too injured to walk by themselves, or bent so that the latter could climb onto their backs. Valens held a small child cradled to his chest, the girl's mother clinging to his neck. Tigurius felt a flicker of pride at the sight. *Let them bestride the galaxy like the gods of old, sheltering mankind from destruction at the hands of an uncaring universe,* he thought. A line from the Codex Astartes, and a good one.

That was what it meant to be a Space Marine. That was what it meant to bear the colours of the Chapter into war. Theirs was not merely to bring death to the enemies of mankind, but to preserve life, where they could. They were the shield, as well as the sword, of humanity, and Tigurius did not intend to falter in that duty. *Emperor guide my hand,* he thought, letting his mind reach out towards the distant, flickering star that was the holy Astronomican.

As he did so, however, he recoiled in disgust. An intrusive, creeping miasma spread across his thoughts, plucking at his senses. It felt like acid splashed on flesh, and he staggered, his hand flying to his head. Pain flooded his nerves, and he fought to regain control of himself. It was worse even than the scream had been. He turned, teeth gritted, and saw Geta's killer stride into sight.

It was a centaur of sorts, moving forward on four thick limbs, but possessing a barrel torso, topped by a heavy, pulsing braincase and two long, deadly looking talons. Cruel spikes rose from its segmented carapace, and the squirming meat of its mind pulsed wetly, filling the air with a diseased radiance. The world turned soft around it, and he could feel the terrible weight of its regard as it turned its eyeless skull towards him. Its fang-studded jaws champed eagerly as it stalked towards him.

Tigurius did not recognise the beast, but he knew what it was, regardless. It was all the horror and fear that flowed in the wake of the hive fleets made manifest, and its servants bounded past it, screeching in predatory anticipation.

Tigurius tore his eyes from the larger creature and sent a killing thought smashing into the scuttling hormagaunts. Even as they died, he wrenched his gaze back to the thing that had killed Geta. Whatever it was, it would die, as easily as all the rest. He sent a bolt of shimmering psychic force thundering towards it.

The sixfold mind-nodes which clustered on its skull flexed unpleasantly, and the bolt washed harmlessly across the shimmering barrier that had suddenly formed about the beast. Tigurius stepped back, readying another bolt, but his enemy was quick to take advantage of his moment of hesitation.

Its jaws opened soundlessly, as energy speared from its sightless cranium.

The psychic scream carved through his defences, obliterating the sutras that guarded his thoughts from the vast, alien mindscape that pressed down on his psyche. His skull felt as if it were swelling within the envelope of his flesh, and he clutched at his head. Streamers of vibrant agony ran up and down his spine, and he could taste blood and bile. The alien mind bore down on him, like a wrestler pressing an opponent to the ground. He sank down beneath its pressure until one knee touched the ground.

Tigurius drove the end of his staff into the broken pavement, as if it might anchor him in place. His thoughts clung to the intricate designs, finding strength in the millennia-old patterns. He had found it beneath the Great Bastion on Andraxas, and it was said, by the artificer-scribes of Corinth, that the staff might once have belonged to Malcador the Sigillite, First Lord of Terra. Sometimes, in moments of great stress, moments like this, he thought he could hear the rasp of a voice out of antiquity. A ghost of a memory of the man who had once fought to defend the Imperium, even as Tigurius himself now did.

He focused on that dry, rustling murmur, and strove to block out the pain that sought to drown his mind. He reached up and clamped his free hand around the staff. Grasping it in both hands, he hauled himself to his feet.

The creature loped towards him, its four legs pumping like pistons. Its great talons swept out, and he only narrowly dodged aside. He rolled away, drawing his bolt pistol as he came to his feet, and fired. The tyranid shrieked as bilious ichor spurted from its flesh. It turned swiftly, and the tip of one talon scored a line across his chestplate, sending bits of ancient parchment fluttering to the ground. He fired again, ignoring the growing ache in his head, trusting in his mental shields to hold against the creature as its mind-nodes pulsed. That trust, however, was in vain. Smoke boiled from the circuitry that lined the interior of his psychic hood as its synaptic connectors burned out one by one.

Tigurius staggered. His staff and bolt pistol slipped from numb fingers. The creature hissed and slunk around him. He could feel it prying at the gates of his mind, scrabbling about in the shadows of his consciousness. His limbs felt heavy and awkward, and he sank down once more, borne under by the enormity of its will. The world gave a spasm, like a faulty pict-feed. He smelled rancid meat, and heard a riotous murmur that overwhelmed his thoughts, smashing them aside. He felt heat, and hunger... a terrible hunger.

That hunger tore through Tigurius, smashing aside his certainties and assurances, his confidence and surety, in a way it had never done before. All of it, all of his training, his skill, his power as Chief Librarian, was as nothing before that inhuman ache, and he realised with a growing horror that he had never truly faced the hive mind before – that this hunger was a roaring inferno compared to the flickering spark he had touched previously.

It was a hunger such as a fire might feel, enormous and unending. A hunger which would never know appeasement and would never abate, not even when the last sun had flickered and died, leaving the galaxy a cold, barren void at last. Even then, the hunger would not end, even then the hive mind would hunt, feeding on itself until, at last, the surviving shard of its intelligence withered and starved, alone in the dark and quiet.

But before that, it would feed on every world. It would batten on every star, and strip every system and sector of life. The Imperium would fall to it. There would be no salvation, no last minute reprieve. The murmurs grew in volume, and he clutched uselessly at his head, trying to block them out.

As Tigurius fought, trying to shutter the gates of his mind, scraps of sound and memory burned across the horizon of his thoughts. He saw flickering images, as if he were seeing through the eyes of the hive mind as it spread out to consume Ultima Segmentum. He heard the slow scrape of the monster's claws as it advanced towards him, across the street. But he could not rise to confront it, could not stifle the images which overwhelmed his mind with thoughts and memories not his own.

They were flashes only, brief moments of time, crystallised and vivid.

He saw Sisters of Battle fighting back-to-back with Militarum Tempestus Scions as a tidal wave of chitin and talons loomed over them, ready to sweep them aside. He felt their fear and pain as the image burst like a bubble, parting to reveal a Terminator, clad in the crimson heraldry of the Blood Angels Chapter, grappling with a multi-limbed broodlord in the burning ruins of an Imperial palace. As the broodlord swiped its cruel claws across his brother Space Marine's chestplate, Tigurius clutched at his own chest, feeling the pain of the blow as if he'd taken it himself.

His mind reeled as the scene wavered and tore, revealing the sleek void-craft of the Eldar, locked in battle with a swarm of flying horrors birthed by the hive fleet. He felt the ground tremble beneath him as the beast drew closer. The alien stink of it was thick in his nostrils, but he could not focus, could not even see it.

The images came faster and faster, overwhelming him with their intensity. Some small part of his mind knew that the creature was using them to batter him, to weaken him, even as Tigurius himself had used his powers so many times to weaken the tyranid swarms – to make them easy prey. His head felt full to bursting. He saw a warrior of the Grey Knights, trapped between the gibbering filth of the warp and a horde of hormagaunts. Even as the Grey Knight moved to confront his foes, the image came apart like sand in the tide, and suddenly, Tigurius was caught in stultifying darkness. He saw green lights, and heard the squeal of ancient machinery coming to life, but too late. The steel-limbed necron warriors awoke from the slumber of ages as the tyranids flooded the tomb, smashing the automatons down as they rose.

He smelled and tasted blood. Blood Angels and Flesh Tearers fought against overwhelming hordes beneath a blood-red star, and he felt their rage and madness as if it were his own. It threatened to overwhelm him, and he cried out. The image shattered and he was smashed to the ground by a heavy blow. Another blow caught him across the back and he felt his armour rupture. He rolled over with a groan, mind sluggish, body barely responding. Hoses popped and seals burst in his armour as its weight settled on him, driving his wounded back against the street.

Its featureless skull loomed over him as he struggled uselessly against it. Blossoms of ectoplasm sprouted on its head, unfurling and growing, becoming tendrils like the ones which had been the cause of Geta's death. The tendrils quivered, and then stiffened and shot towards him. Something cold touched him and darkness invaded him. It was stronger than the scream, impossible to resist.

His thoughts were ground under the relentless clamour of an alien intelligence far older and crueller than he had ever suspected – this intelligence was nothing like the others; the Leviathan was stronger than the Behemoth, and more dangerous than the Kraken. Worse, he'd been wrong. There was a mind there, amidst the hunger, a true mind, a fierce self-awareness that put the torch to every assumption and scrap of knowledge about the tyranids that he'd possessed.

And that mind hated him. It wanted vengeance. It wanted him. For the first time, Varro Tigurius felt the first stirrings of fear. Such a thing could not be defeated. His will was as nothing next to that of the hive mind. It would devour him, and then Kantipur, and after that, the sub-sector. It could not be stopped. Even Holy Terra would fall.

No!

Even as the thought filled his mind, he refused it. Terra would not – *could not* – fall. He focused, looking past the horror that held him, and up into the darkness beyond it. He could still hear the voice of the staff, even though it was out of reach. It whispered to him and he closed his eyes, trying to focus on it rather than the horror reaching out to engulf him. He could feel the heat and light of the Astronomican, he could hear its song, swelling in his mind, dimly at first, and then more loudly.

Tigurius reached out, even as he drowned in that cold, hungry darkness, and felt the light of the Emperor's grace, just at the tips of his fingers. Was it the same light that Malcador had felt, the day he took the Emperor's place on the Golden Throne? Had the Sigillite felt the light of the Astronomican on him, the day he'd sacrificed his life for the good of the Imperium? The whispers grew in strength, filling his mind, driving out doubt and hesitation. Malcador had died for the Imperium – could he do any less?

He grabbed hold of the light with all of his strength, and sent it pulsing outward, against the dark. There was a scream, like that of a startled animal, as the shadow in the warp met the blinding light of humanity's guiding star, and then the weight was gone and he could breathe again. His eyes popped open and he saw the xenos monster stumble away, shaking its head. Greasy smoke rose from its brain-case, and could smell the stench of rancid, burning meat. He lunged to his feet.

Acting on instinct, he snatched up his bolt pistol and flung himself at the monster. He caught hold of its carapace and swung himself up. It heaved, trying to buck him off, but to no avail. He shoved the barrel of his bolt pistol against the meat of its mind, and emptied the clip. The great body convulsed, and it took a faltering step. Then, with a sibilant whine, it toppled, slamming into the street hard enough to crack the pavement. Tigurius rolled clear.

He came to his feet and retrieved his staff. As his fingers tightened about it, he spun and extended it towards the twitching hulk, ready for it to spring to life once more. Thankfully, it did not. It sagged, and the acidic bile that passed for its blood began to eat its way free of the armoured shell.

Weary, his mind awash in pain, Tigurius turned towards Geta's body. He could hear the sound of tyranids scuttling in the dark, and knew that they would come again, and again and again, until Kantipur was theirs. They knew neither defeat nor victory, only hunger. And when this world had fallen, they would hurtle into the void, in search of another. Unless they were stopped, once and for all. Emperor willing, Tigurius would be there when it was accomplished. Even if it meant his death.

But for now, his fight was done, and it was time to leave. He dragged Geta's body up, and slung it awkwardly over his shoulder. He would not let the hive fleet have it.

The other Ultramarine, Castus, groaned. Tigurius bent low and hooked his arm. 'Up, brother,' Tigurius said, dragging Castus to his feet. 'It is time to go. Kantipur is lost. But there are worlds yet that might be saved.'

TEMPESTUS

BRADEN CAMPBELL

'Oh, Ixoi, Ixoi. How cruel is our fate, to be denied by distance! You pull from above, I swell from below, but never, it seems, may we embrace. Must we only be content to gaze at one another; you, my fattened warrior, and I, your Goddess of the Brine?'
– *Cantos Continuous*, M41

CHAPTER ONE

The Shelsists had done well to hide themselves. They held their profane gathering in the deep recesses of a ruined librarium, where the thick walls would muffle their chants and hymns. They had draped a thick curtain of dried seaweed across the only entrance so as to hide the light from their torches. They had spread algae flowers in the dirt to conceal their footprints. To the casual observer, there was nothing amiss in the dead and silent city.

The Canoness knew better. She stood atop a shattered column, scanning the area before her. Lysios's moon hung, as ever, huge in the sky. It wasn't even at its fullest yet, but so plentiful was the dull red light it cast over the land that she could have read from the *Prime Edicts*. But there was no need; she had memorised the words of the Holy Synod decades ago.

'When the people forget their duty,' she recited in a whisper, 'they are no longer human and become something less than beasts. They have no place in the bosom of humanity nor in the heart of the Emperor. Let them die and be forgotten.'

She raised her right hand and made a flicking motion. The rest of the Sisters moved up to join her, silent except for the rustling of heavy robes and the creaking of powered armour. When they reached the base of the column, they knelt.

The Canoness turned and surveyed them. They would do their duty, as they had so many times before on this forsaken, deluged world. But these worshippers of the Brine Goddess were unusual for heretics. They bore none of the four traditional evil marks. They did not flagellate themselves or sever their digits. Rather, they were all but indistinguishable from the bulk of the planet's citizenry. She worried that because of this, her charges might harbour regrets towards their duty. The Sisters of Battle were defenders of the faith, after all, not wanton murderers. She decided that a rousing homily was needed.

'The Emperor gave up His life as a ransom so that humanity might live, so great is His love for mankind. The faithful repay Him with daily thanks and prayer, and they serve Him with all their heart, soul, and strength.'

Bowed heads nodded in agreement.

'But there are those on this world who renounce the Emperor's love, who cheapen His gift by offering their allegiance and devotion to false deities. What should He then do? Ignore this insult? Condone such behaviour? Or rather, should He administer punishment and correction, as a loving father would to his wayward children?'

She paused dramatically, just long enough to let her listeners consider the question and reach a unified conclusion.

'The worshippers of Shelse are devious, yes. They hide their heresy well, but the Emperor sees the wickedness within their hearts. He is not fooled by outward appearances and neither, dear Sisters, must we be. We are His chosen; He tasks us to purge the unclean so that the faithful may thrive. With bolt and blade and flame, we must make examples of all who would spurn Him.

'Superior Tarsha!'

One head among eight snapped up. 'Yes, Canoness Grace?'

'Can you vouch for the dedication of those who serve beneath you?'

The young woman smiled. 'Yes, of course. We are ready to tread the path of righteousness.'

'Then prepare your Sisters.'

Tarsha stood and spread her arms wide. As she began to recite the Adepta Sororitas battle-prayer, Canoness Grace turned back towards the librarium entrance.

For months now, she had led a continuing series of pogroms against the native religions of Lysios. The Shelsists, however, were the worst. No sooner had she put down one enclave of them, than another would establish itself. Their refusal to be eradicated was maddening enough, but what Grace truly hated was the romanticism of their sect.

The litanies of the Shelsists were an unending series of crude poems. Each was purported to come from the goddess of the sea, and none of them, the Canoness thought, was particularly well-written. She had come across hundreds of them in her quest, and each one contained the same awful, wistful tone. The author might as well have been a besotted teenage girl as an ocean deity. Still, something in the unrequited love story between the sea and the moon struck a chord with certain people on Lysios. The worship and veneration of Shelse had penetrated every level of society, from the lowest kelp harvester to the highest nobility. Even the planetary governor, it was said, had submitted himself to their heresy. Why else would he have gone into hiding as soon as the Canoness had begun putting the unfaithful to the fire?

Superior Tarsha completed the prayer by asking the Emperor to condemn His enemies to eternal death and damnation. 'That Thou wouldst bring them only death, that Thou shouldst spare none, that Thou shouldst pardon none, we beseech Thee, destroy them.'

In unison, the Sisters touched their foreheads, their chests and finally their weapons, signifying faith in mind, heart, and deed. Then they rose silently, and waited for their leader.

The Canoness jumped down from the column, her feet making deep impressions in the pebbly, seashell-littered ground. She pulled a bulky pistol from the holster on her hip. 'I shall lead. Flamer and heavy bolter on my flanks.'

While the Sisters assembled themselves into formation, Superior Tarsha dashed forward and tore down the seaweed curtain. Beyond was a long and partially collapsed passageway. The light from Ixoi illuminated only the archway. The interior was very dark.

'Braziers,' Grace ordered.

Mounted on each of the Canoness's shoulders was a metal cage filled with coals soaked in consecrated oil. Tarsha reached up from behind her and lit them. The coals burst into flame, and a wavering yellow light surrounded the Canoness. Eerie shadows danced all around.

They had proceeded only a short distance when they came to a curving stairway that descended into the catacombs. The stone walls were encrusted with white residue and glistened in the firelight. Grace touched them as she went. The fingers of her glove came away wet. Raising them to her lips, she was unsurprised to taste salt.

She ignored the several side passages they came to. The chambers beyond were lifeless and filled with damp, rotting wooden shelves and heaps of mush that had once been books and scrolls.

There was a faint echoing of voices from below. The Canoness signalled for the others to freeze, and peered around the curving wall. Eight men, large and bulky across the shoulders, were standing at the base of the stairs. Their armour appeared to be made of weighty iron plates fastened to a rubber undersuit with rivets and pieces of thick rope. Half of them were armed with a type of large, cartridge-fed speargun commonly used by the local fisherman. Two of them had shock nets. A low fire burned in an empty fuel drum and the remaining two men were warming themselves by it. Their backs were to the Canoness.

Grace frowned. Thus far, the Shelsists had been poorly organised and almost pathetically armed. The presence of these men seemed to mark a change in all that. They were wearing modified diving suits, she realised; heavy and potentially bulletproof. Additionally, she had seen the kinds of creatures the mariners of Lysios went to sea for. Their spearguns were designed to puncture blubbery hides and bulletproof shells. Their nets were made of metal cabling and could be electrified before being thrown.

The Canoness glanced at the Sisters on her flanks. Cairista, the flame wielder, was on her right. Sister Fayhew, she who wielded the blessed heavy bolter, waited on the left. When each of them signalled their readiness, Canoness Grace swept around the curved wall with bolt and fire on her wings.

When fired on an open battlefield, a heavy bolter was loud. In the confines of the librarium basement, it was truly deafening. Two of the guards were hit by shells as large as a closed fist. The iron plates of their suits could provide no protection. They were thrown backwards into the fire barrel, which tumbled over on to its side. Grace sent a bolt of white-hot plasma through the chest of one of the speargun carriers. He collapsed, and portions of his chestplate formed molten pools on the floor. Cairista covered the remaining five men in a wave of flames. Two more of the guards went down screaming. The stairway was filled with acrid smoke that stank of burning rubber and charred flesh.

The three remaining men were engulfed in fire, but to the Canoness's surprise they seemed to take no heed. Two of them raised their spear guns and fired. Grace was hit in the upper chest. Her armour held firm, but the sheer force of the impact was enough to send her staggering. The spear that struck Sister Fayhew rebounded off her pauldron hard enough to leave a dent. The third guard tossed his net at Cairista, who ducked swiftly out of the way.

Sister Fayhew bared her teeth, and squeezed the heavy bolter's firing lever. The men were knocked about like ragdolls as the shells tore them apart. When they were nothing but broken corpses, she released the trigger.

The other Sisters were now racing down the stairs with heavy footfalls. The Canoness raised a hand, and they slowed.

'We are unhurt,' she reassured them. She indicated the dent on Sister Fayhew's shoulder armour. 'But it would seem that the Shelsists have become more dangerous than ever before.'

'Canoness, over here!' Cairista called. She had moved past the dead guards and to the back of the small cellar. There was a gaping hole in the floor, wide enough to fit two grown adults.

The other Sisters gathered around. The Canoness leaned over the hole. By the light of her braziers, she could just barely see the base of the ladder.

'They were guarding this?' Superior Tarsha asked.

'It would seem so,' Grace replied.

'Where does it lead?' Cairista asked.

'Canoness,' Tarsha said, 'I volunteer to find out.'

Grace considered for a moment, and then consented.

Tarsha grasped her boltgun tightly, and jumped through the hole. With a loud splash, she landed in black liquid up to her knees. The air reeked of brine.

She peered about her. She was in a cavern that might have been able to hold, at most, ten people. The rock walls were rough and wet. As her eyes adjusted to the gloom, she was able to make out a doorway, covered with a curtain or heavy blanket of some kind. Around its edges leaked a dim light.

She waited for several seconds. The only sounds were the trickle of water on rock, and the crackling fires above her. She sloshed forward, and tore down the covering with her left hand. It was indeed a blanket, woollen and wet. Before her was a tunnel carved out of the rock. Lumens had been strung along one wall in a drooping chain.

She threw the blanket down. As she entered the mouth of the tunnel, she called up to the Canoness. 'The base of the ladder is clear. I'm moving–'

Something snapped beneath her boot. Tarsha froze and looked down to see tiny bubbles rising around her legs. She had just enough time to realise that she had triggered some kind of trap, and then there was a gurgling *boom*. Tarsha was hurled up into the air in a spray of sea water. She felt herself strike the roof of the cavern, and then fall back into the pool. She tried to stand up, but found that she could not. She flailed her arms, but couldn't break above the surface of the water. Seconds ticked by like hours. Then, at last, she felt the strong hands of her sisters grabbing hold of her and lifting her up.

Tarsha blinked and strained to hear. Sister Lygia and Sister Karyn had set her on a rock. The others were talking excitedly and pointing at her, but their voices were muffled. The light from the Canoness's shoulders made the chamber seem surreal. Her calves felt hot and itchy. That was strange, she thought, because her power armour was internally cooled. She reached a hand down to scratch them, and felt nothing but air. Confused, she looked down to see that her legs were missing from the knees down. Blood was spurting from the mangled stumps in hot streams.

She shook her head in disbelief. Dimly, she remembered stepping on something hidden beneath the water at the mouth of the tunnel. She tried to speak, to warn the others that the Shelsists had laid traps for them, but her tongue could no longer form words. She felt very thirsty, which struck her as funny, since Lysios was a world dominated by its singular ocean. She laughed at the irony.

Her sisters all turned to look at her, their faces etched with worry. The Canoness had knelt down in front of her and was saying something, but Tarsha couldn't hear properly. A piece of ancient rhyme, something about water everywhere and shrinking boards, drifted through her head. She laughed once more, and died.

The Canoness touched Tarsha's forehead and finished speaking the Martyr's Rites. 'Be favourable and gracious to Your fallen daughter, mighty Emperor, and be pleased with her sacrifice of righteousness.'

The other Sisters murmured an affirmation. Grace rose and wiped a fist beneath her nose. As a Canoness, she was more than just a military leader to the women serving under her. She was a teacher, a shepherd, a mother. Tarsha had been like a daughter to her, strong in faith and very capable. Grace had been certain that someday she would become a Canoness in her own right. But no longer.

The air was stifled and wet, and for a terrible moment, Grace was reminded of dead Sisters in the sewers beneath the capital city of Dessecran. On that far-away world, five decades past, she had stalked monsters, even as they, in turn, had stalked her. She shook her head. There were no tyranid monstrosities in these tunnels; no beings from the void come to harvest her for foodstuffs. There were only humans, and false doctrine.

'We have inflicted great damage upon this cult,' she said, 'and it is obvious that they now know and fear us. This is good, my Sisters. The people should know when they have done evil in the Emperor's sight, and they should rightly fear His wrath.' The Canoness drew her sword from its scabbard. Its blade was highly polished silver, the crossguard fashioned to look like a wreath of black flowers.

They followed the lumens and moved down the tunnel at a brisk pace. The Canoness took the lead, carefully watching for additional traps or explosives. It had been no homespun bomb that had killed Tarsha. It had been a military-grade landmine. Where the Shelsists had found such a thing, or who had provided it to them, she knew not. But she vowed never to let it happen again.

They turned sharply to the right, and emerged into a large cave. To their right was a pool of water that lapped against the rock. Stalactites hung like giant fangs from the ceiling. Parts of the ground had been covered with rusted grating. Piles of rubble were heaped up along the walls. At the back of the cavern was a raised area piled high with storage crates. On the rock face above it was a fresco showing Lysios's moon hovering over a tidal wave. Bizarre creatures were emerging from the wave. A small army of stick figures welcomed them with open arms.

The Shelsists were waiting for them. They had flipped over rusted metal tables and chairs, and were taking cover behind them. They were armed not only with harpoons, nets, and spearguns, but also with a collection of clumsy-looking kinetic rifles: a crude technology, but one resilient to Lysios's cyclical flooding.

There was a hooded figure atop the rock ledge. He carried a torch in one hand, and a strange staff in the other. He cried out, and a hail of small-calibre projectiles pummelled the Sisters. They ricocheted off their power armour and tore gaping holes in their vestments. The stone walls behind them shattered into fragments.

The Canoness threw her arm across her face, and felt at least one of the bullets mushroom off her vambrace. Spears whistled past her, or clattered around her feet. Somewhere to her left, there was a wet *smack* and a gurgling sound. She glanced over to see Sister Karyn slump to the ground. She had been pierced through the chest by a harpoon the size of her arm.

'Abominable traitors!' Grace cried. She charged forward, firing her pistol as she went. The chest of one of the nearest Shelsists vaporised as she found her mark.

The other women covered their leader's charge. Bolts crashed into the cultists and punched through their makeshift barricades. Cairista painted the room with white-hot promethium flames.

The cultists directly blocking the Canoness's path were consumed in fire. Their weapons discharged aimlessly as they screamed and flailed. Two of the bullets struck Grace's chestplate and bounced harmlessly away. She vaulted over the table behind which the cultists were cowering, and mercifully drove her sword through the heart of the man writhing at her feet. The others she left to their sins.

Beneath the fresco, the hooded figure was pointing towards the Canoness and screaming. Grace couldn't make the words out over the cacophony of the heavy bolter, but she could easily guess that he was calling for her murder. Half a dozen Shelsists surrounded him. Two of them were reloading a harpoon launcher ripped from the bow of a whaling ship. The others carried the clumsy autoguns of their forefathers. Grace was fairly certain that the rifles posed little danger to her, but the ballista had felled poor Karyn; it was obviously strong enough to puncture powered armour, and therefore had to be destroyed.

She had taken only a few steps towards their position when they fired upon her. There was nowhere for her to hide, and nothing nearby to take cover behind. So, she simply wheeled around and lowered her head. Bullets fruitlessly struck her back and legs. The harpoon let fly with a sharp *twang*. It impacted her spine with enough force to knock the breath from her lungs, but otherwise, her armour held true.

As they peppered her with bullets, the Canoness holstered her pistol. From her belt, she pulled a golden sphere crowned with a double-headed eagle. She tore the eagle off with her teeth, whirled around, and lobbed the sphere into the cultists' midst.

It detonated among them in a cloud of smoke and biting metal fragments. The Shelsists jerked backwards and ducked. Their armoured suits protected them for the most part, but the Canoness seized upon their confusion. She crossed the distance between them in a few long strides and leapt up to the ledge. She grasped her sword with both hands and swung, forever separating one cultist and his left arm.

Then the others were upon her, beating with the butts of their rifles and stabbing with bayonets. She managed to parry most of them. The rest skittered across her armour harmlessly.

'For the Emperor!' the Canoness screamed. She carved another wide arc, and two of her attackers were sliced clean through. She whirled around and thrust at the man behind her. The sword buried itself through his chest until the garland crosspiece touched his ribs.

The remaining two Shelsists continued to strike at her, but whatever blows they managed to land seemed to have no effect on Grace. The Canoness withdrew her sword as she slammed a spiked elbow plate into one of their faces. The last of her attackers had his head separated from his neck in a single, deft stroke. She faced the robed figure.

No, she saw, it wasn't a robe. Not as such. It was a sheet of waterproof tarpaulin tied around the waist with rope. The sleeves were long and the cowl left his face as a pit of black. He threw down his torch and grasped his staff in both hands. It was thick and knotted, and looked to be made of alabaster stone.

'Murderess!' he cried. His voice was deep and strange, as if his throat was filled with phlegm. 'Look what you have done.'

The Canoness cast a quick glance over her shoulder. She saw that the remaining cultists were either dead or dying. Charred husks that had once been heretics lay scattered everywhere. The crisping of their flesh and tightening of their muscles had drawn each of them up into the foetal position. Sister Fayhew stood before a considerable number of fallen men and women who lay in a wide crescent, limbs twisted and broken. Each had some kind of improvised weapon in their hands. They had tried to charge the Sisters' position, Grace saw, and had failed miserably. Some of the other Sisters were cut or bleeding, but they stood together, boltguns pointed towards the rocky ledge.

'It is no less than you deserve for rejecting the Emperor,' the Canoness said fiercely. She levelled the tip of her sword at the black abyss of his cowl. 'Now, foulness, tell me where you found these weapons. Tell me why your damned cult refuses to die.'

'Do not ask us anything,' the man groaned. 'The answers will be beyond you.'

In High Gothic, and using her best pulpit voice Grace roared, 'I will demand of thee, and answer thou me. If you channel a spirit, I would confront it.'

'What need have we for spirits?' the man said. 'We have a goddess.'

With a speed that surprised the Canoness, the man in the robe struck her with the end of his staff. Although her amour was unaffected, she felt the reverberations of the impact. She thrust at him, but the man easily avoided her. She slashed at him twice. Again, he ducked beyond the edge of her blade.

He jabbed the end of his staff into the centre of her chest. Her armour continued to hold, but he twisted it upwards, catching her beneath the chin. She brought her sword downward in a tight curve, and cut deeply into the flesh above his knee. Before he could react, she lunged and drove an elbow into his face.

The man stumbled slightly. His hood fell away, and his robe parted enough for her to see some of what was hidden beneath. Grace drew a sharp intake of breath.

The man's exposed skin was pale green and had the texture of scales. His nose had either vanished or fallen off, leaving only two thin vertical slits. His left eye was huge and sickly yellow. Small tentacles sprouted from his upper lip and jawline. Most disturbing, however, was the set of additional arms that unstuck themselves from his ribcage. They were thin, but wiry, and ended not in hands but with wickedly tapered claws.

'Mutation!' Grace cried.

'Not mutation,' the man said, his mouth tentacles twitching, 'bestowments.' His secondary claws slashed at her, tearing through the plates protecting her forearms. His strength had become something otherworldly. A line from the Catechism of Leadership raced through her mind: *Since the Emperor suffers to shield us, it is a blessing to suffer for Him in return.*

She impaled him through his lower abdomen. A great stink, like dead fish, erupted from his guts. Still, he did not attempt to flee the fight. Instead, he wrapped his claws around her neck.

'Hard-hearted, you are, Murderess. Loveless. Chaste by choice.'

The Canoness felt her heart and lungs begin to crumple within her. She fell to her knees, nearly dropping her sword. She couldn't breathe. The very life was being squeezed out of her. An image flashed through her mind of crushing tentacles, ghostly white, dredged up from the blackest depths of the sea where light had never shone. It felt like drowning. Her vision darkened.

With the last of her strength, she brought her sword up, and cut off his right leg. The man howled as he fell to the ground. Dark ichor splashed everywhere. Coughing, the Canoness dragged herself to her feet.

The man was muttering in his death throes, repeating the same thing over and over.

'What is that you say?' Grace demanded.

He smiled up at the Canoness with a look of deranged joy. Blood seeped through the spaces between his teeth.

'They are coming,' he said. 'They are coming at last. They are coming. They are coming at last.'

'Who? Who is coming?'

The man spasmed once, and said nothing more. His facial tentacles continued to twitch for several seconds after his death.

The Canoness tilted her head thoughtfully as the Sisters moved to join her on the rock ledge. The stakes had suddenly risen here on Lysios. The cult of the Brine Goddess was no longer a collection of malcontents playing at religion and making up stories as they went along. They were gaining in power. They had considerable weapons now. They also had... bestowments. Yes, Grace thought, that was the word the mutant had used. Bestowments. But from whom?

'Sister,' she said to Cairista, 'this man's flesh has become corrupted. Deliver him from it.'

Cairista brought her weapon up and bathed the man in promethium. The room filled with acrid smoke and the stench of melted plastek.

Later, after Grace had prayed for the souls of Tarsha and Karyn, she would compile a report of this latest encounter with the Shelsists and send it to Terra. For the moment though, she simply stood and watched the Brine Goddess's favoured burn until there was nothing left of him but ashes.

'I have loved you since the day this world was destroyed. All my life, it seems, I have chased after you. Will you never descend from your abode in the sky? How I long to join you. How I long to touch you...'
– *Cantos Continuous*, M41

CHAPTER TWO

The inquisitor began the day with his regular regimen: one hour of intensive physical exercise, followed by thirty minutes of sword practice. Breakfast consisted of a conglomeration of proteins and amino acids which he drank greedily from a tall glass. It was as thick as glue and utterly tasteless, but he refused to let the rigours of space travel weaken him in any way. The safety of the Sol System was parsecs behind him now. A new world awaited him, and he would not fall victim to it on account of being too frail or a fraction of a second too slow.

Sweat-covered and dressed only in a loose robe, he pulled down the viewport covering and looked out into space. The ship had emerged from the warp two days ago, and had been steadily decelerating ever since. Yesterday he had ordered a series of torpedo probes launched into the ocean, and their signals had confirmed his hopes. Within the hour, he and his team would be landing on the surface. Then the hunt would begin. Everything was proceeding smoothly. His only regret was that he would be achieving greatness on such an ugly-looking world.

Lysios had to be the most depressing place he had ever seen. Its only natural satellite, Ixoi, was so huge, and orbited so closely, that its gravitational field had distorted the planet into a permanent egg shape. The hemisphere opposite the moon was riddled with tectonic instabilities and fissures. The side closest to the moon was comprised entirely of ocean. It rose like a mountain made of water, kilometres tall. The crests of its waves scraped the stratosphere, and formed icebergs that tumbled down the leeside. Moreover, this vertical ocean moved. It took Ixoi a decade to complete a single revolution around Lysios, but as it travelled, it dragged the sea along with it. Thus, there was no place that was not subjected to regular flooding or even total submersion. It was impossible to think that it had once been considered one of the Ninety-Nine Wonders of the Segmentum Solar.

I bet it stinks down there, he thought. *Like fish and muck.*

He changed into a fresh set of clothes, and surveyed himself in the mirror. When he was satisfied, he opened the antique trunk in which he stored his weapons and equipment. His combat armour, although light, was exquisitely made. He secured his sword belt around his waist, and holstered a pistol beneath his left arm. He double checked to make certain that his refractor field generator was fully charged and operational.

There was a knocking on the bulkhead behind him. Through the door he heard a voice call his name.

'Inquisitor Ulrich?'

He knew who it was, of course. There was only one woman on board. He strode across the room and opened the door.

In the corridor stood a young woman as tall as he. Her hair was naturally platinum and longer than that of any Sororitas the inquisitor had previously dealt with: a testament to the fact that she spent her life ensconced in scriptoria rather than rolling around on filthy battlefields. Her skin was pale. Her eyes were the colour of jade. Of the rest of her he could make no judgement, as she was covered from neck to ankle by a thick, red scribe's robe.

'Sister Margene,' he said. His nose twitched. She smelled of parchment and ink, which he did not particularly care for.

She held out a thin stack of papers. 'Inquisitor, I have a readiness report from Tempestor Chavis. He and his men are prepping the two ground transports they brought with them, and await your presence in the loading bay.'

Ulrich left her standing in the corridor while he crossed to his desk. From a fruit bowl, he selected a poperin. It was small and round, and its skin was mottled red and green. He chewed it slowly as he flipped through the report. 'Would you like to look at it?'

'I'm sorry?'

He gestured to the window. 'Lysios. I thought you might like to see it, especially after all the time you've spent reading about it.'

'I would, yes,' she replied. 'My quarters have no viewports.'

'Well, we can't all travel in first class, now can we?' Ulrich took another bite of his exotic fruit, and watched closely as Margene crossed over to the window.

'I have never seen anything like it,' she said in a near whisper.

'I would think not,' Ulrich said. 'This is your first time away from Terra, yes?'

She dipped her head in reverence at the mention of humanity's sacred home world, but her eyes never left the strange planet before her. 'Very true,' she said. 'This is not only my first trip to another star system, but my first time beyond the Convent Prioris since my training began as a child.' She turned her head to look at him. 'Thank you once again for the opportunity, inquisitor. I will not fail you.'

'I am a man who remembers his friends. Serve me well on this little outing, and I promise that you will be suitably taken care of.' He tossed the report down. 'If I have one regret, it's that your first journey had to be to such an ugly waste of a world.'

He had hoped that they would share a jest at the planet's expense, but she frowned.

'I find nothing wasteful about it, inquisitor,' she said tartly. 'In fact, the native Lysites are, if anything, masters of recycling and ingenuity. They've been forced to become so, you see, because of the ocean. The "worldwave", as they call it.

The fact that, at any given time, half of the planet is submerged beneath kilometres of salt water has led to the development of a very unique culture.

'Everything here is tied to the ocean. It's the source of nearly ninety-five per cent of all foodstuffs. It is also used as a power source, both via various types of tidal generators and as a coolant for nuclear fission reactors. It makes the atmosphere so damp and saline that all machinery demands constant upkeep. Mobility and retrofitting are everything. They must always stay either just ahead or just behind the worldwave, never settling in one place.

'Take the hab-crawlers, for example. There aren't really any cities on Lysios any more. Not as you or I might understand it. There are ruins, of course, dating back to the onset of the environmental collapse three millennia ago, but no one lives there. No, instead they move about as I said in massive, tracked machines, each holding thousands of people. Our drop-craft, in fact, will be landing at–'

Ulrich tossed the core of his poperin into the bowl, turned on his heel, and promptly exited into the hallway. The raised soles of his boots made sharp clacking sounds on the metal deck plates. Behind him, Margene rushed to keep pace. Silence stretched out until they neared their destination.

'The Scion leader... What's his name again?'

'Chavis, sir,' Margene answered. She was unsure if this was a test of some kind, or if he had genuinely forgotten. 'Tempestor Chavis.'

'Yes. He and his men have been told little about the reason behind our coming here until now. They're a very "need to know basis" sort.'

'But now they need to know.'

'Correct.'

'You would like me to tell them about the creature, then?'

'No. I'll do that. Just run them through the basic facts.'

They entered into a cavernous space crammed with storage containers and fuel drums. Along the walls were racks where missiles and other armaments were safely stored. The centre of the room was dominated by a pair of oversized ground vehicles. Their armour plating was blocky and angular. Each had a large turret weapon mounted on its roof, and slablike, massively reinforced side hatches. Instead of tyres, the vehicles sat on quad track units. Exhaust pipes jutted out on either side of a frontal engine.

Eighteen men bustled around them. They were all dressed alike, with heavy, pale blue combat armour over beige uniforms. They were tall and fit, with sharply defined features and steely eyes. One of them wore a black beret atop his head, and when Ulrich stood in the doorframe and cleared his throat, it was he who called the others to attention.

'Thank you, tempestor,' Ulrich said. 'Before we begin, gentlemen, there is one formality to get out of the way.' He pulled a silver cylinder from the inside of his coat, deftly opened the top, and shook out a rolled-up parchment. This he handed to Margene before folding his hands behind his back.

Margene unrolled the scroll, and read aloud in her clearest voice.

'By the authority of the Immortal Emperor of Mankind, you, the selected members of the Tempestus Scions 55th regiment, also known as the Kappic

Eagles, are hereby required to submit yourselves wholly and unquestioningly to His servant, Inquisitor Damien Ulrich for a mission to be determined by the inquisitor and whose objectives and implementation will be divulged by the inquisitor at a time and place of the inquisitor's choosing.

'Failure of any man to comply constitutes heresy against the Ecclesiarchy, and will render said heretic *persona non grata excommunicatus* in the eyes of the Emperor.

'Here follows the signature of Inquisitor Damien Ulrich, dated 0712999.M41.'

Margene turned the scroll around so that the soldiers could clearly see for themselves the elaborate scrawl across the bottom. A purity seal of red wax, stamped with the symbol of the Inquisition, rested next to it. When they had nodded their acceptance, she rolled it back up and glanced at Ulrich.

'You have been given a wonderful opportunity,' he said, rocking slightly on his heels. 'Very shortly, we will descend to the planet Lysios. The mission is quite straightforward. It's the environment that may complicate things.'

Taking her cue, Margene stepped forward.

'Until M38, Lysios was a populous and productive Imperial world. Then, for reasons unknown, the binary stars at the heart of this system began a period of increased activity. The environment on Lysios changed radically, and within a year, the planet suffered a class-5 environmental collapse. Both of its ice caps melted and created a new ocean, which was pulled into a central location thanks to the gravitational influence of Lysios's single natural satellite, Ixoi. The ocean now trails behind the moon as it orbits, completing one revolution every ten local years. The surviving native populations have, over the past three millennia, developed a trio of heretical pagan belief-systems stemming from this catastrophe.

'First are the followers of Cryptus. Cryptus is an angry sky god, and according to those who believe in him, the twin suns are his hate-filled eyes. Cryptus burns everything he gazes upon, and smites those who disrespect him with various cancers.'

Behind her, Ulrich snorted.

'In actuality,' Margene continued, 'Lysios does boast both a very high UV rating, and an abundance of gamma particles at ground level. Everyone involved in this mission has been issued a supply of satyx, an anti-rad elixir. Take it daily, or face the consequences.

'Secondly, there is the moon. Ixoi, as he is known to the locals, is a warrior. He also loves to eat, as evidenced by his great size. His worshippers are few on Lysios, but are very dangerous. They spend their lives as nomadic raiders, attacking hab-crawlers and making off with all the food supplies they can lay their hands on.

'Third is the so-called "Goddess of the Brine", Shelse. According to the mythos, the ocean goddess is in love with the moon, and follows him everywhere. She reaches up as high as she can towards Ixoi, but is never able to touch him. This makes her angry, and so she causes storms and floods.

'In 998.M41, the Ecclesiarchy began a mission of repatriation on Lysios, under the command of–'

Ulrich cut her off with a clap of his hands. 'It's the third of these so-called deities that concerns us. The records are spotty, but it would seem that when the moon is at perigee, a creature of unknown origin can be seen rising up out of the worldwave.'

'What do we know of its capabilities?' Tempestor Chavis asked.

'Almost nothing. There are no known picts of it, nor any vid-pict recordings. What there are in plenty, however, are paintings and drawings. It seems the people who worship this thing find a particular joy in depicting it.'

'I have several examples on file,' Margene offered. 'I will of course provide them to you.'

Chavis paid her no heed. 'How would you like to proceed, inquisitor?'

'My plan is this: the worldwave is currently passing through the Kephorous mountain range. We will ascend to the top of Mount Loraz, whose plateau should put us near the upper third of the wave. We will establish a base camp, and when the tidal swell is greatest, we will lure the creature to shore.'

'How?' Chavis asked.

The inquisitor smiled slyly. 'Leave that to me.'

The tempestor rubbed his chin in thought. 'These worshippers you speak of, are they numerous? Dangerous?'

Margene answered before Ulrich could. 'There has been a concentrated effort to put them down for nearly a year now,' she said. 'It is still ongoing.'

Ulrich put his hands in his coat pockets. 'I wouldn't worry too much about the Shelsists. I doubt they're any match for trained and properly equipped soldiers.'

'What I mean to say, sir, is do you expect them to attempt to stop us?'

'Stop you from doing what?'

'From destroying the thing they revere.'

Shaking his head, Ulrich walked slowly up to Chavis. 'Although I appreciate your enthusiasm, tempestor, you and your men are not here to destroy the creature. You are here to capture it.'

CHAPTER THREE

The inquisitor and his retinue descended to the planet's surface in a boxy landing craft. Margene and the Scions were crammed into the cargo hold along with the pair of armoured vehicles. Chavis and Ulrich occupied the cockpit. As they passed through the cloud layer, the inquisitor drew an undecorated black handkerchief from the inside pocket of his coat. Carefully, he unfolded the corners. Wrapped inside was a stack of seventy-eight crystalline wafers that resembled a deck of cards etched in glowing glass. Ulrich shifted the deck to his other hand, and began to shuffle it.

Ulrich had always aspired to be someone of great import. He had worked ferociously to gain the attention of the Inquisition, and once he had it, he pushed himself even harder to gain entrance into their ranks. The authority he now held was vast. Still, it did not entirely satisfy, for within the Inquisition itself, there were hierarchies. For years, he had tried everything he could think of to promote himself, to win favour, to be inducted into the ranks of the Inquisitor Lords. He had failed.

Then he discovered the reports.

It had happened quite by accident. Ulrich had been in a vault of the Ordo Xenos, the Imperial agency tasked with identifying and countering the threat of the alien, desperately searching for a hint, a clue, anything that might let him discover an entirely new xenos life form. He envisioned dragging the carcass of some titanic beast back to Terra, throwing it down in triumph before his masters, and defying them to discount him any longer. Unfortunately, it seemed that everything had already been discovered or exterminated. He was close to despair, when he happened to come across a series of data-slates. To a casual observer, they were nothing: a series of field reports from a Battle Sister Canoness on the planet Lysios who was apparently having trouble eliminating a cult of heretics. Printed into the margins, however, were annotations written in a perfect, almost dainty hand. It was the excellence of the penmanship which caught his attention, and their content which held it.

The side notes proposed that the heretics might be influenced by an actual creature of unknown or alien origin. Ulrich tracked down the commentator, and discovered Sister Margene. She was alone and working by candlelight in a vault filled to overflowing with books and files. She was only too happy to expound upon her theories, and showed the inquisitor legends and observations dating back three thousand years. Ulrich became convinced that he had finally found a means to promotion.

He stopped shuffling and held the crystal cards face down. His fingers hovered over the deck.

'Will I find what I am searching for here on Lysios?' he whispered.

He flipped the topmost wafer, and smiled. Depicted on the reverse side was the Emperor, seated like a mummified corpse upon His Golden Throne, screaming silently for all the galaxy to hear.

'Warp travel, discovery, and hope amongst the stars,' Ulrich said, taking it to be a good omen. He placed the card back, flipped the entire deck over, and began to wrap it back up in its protective cloth.

He paused for a moment. The card on the bottom showed a planet, cracked apart like an egg. Chunks of it were tumbling off into the void of space. It was number fifty-two in the Emperor's Tarot: the Shattered World. It signified monumental events, conflict on an enormous scale.

Is this a portent? he wondered.

Tempestor Chavis's voice crackled through vox-speakers throughout the lander. 'Stand by, Scions, we are on final approach.'

The lander began banking in a long curve. Ulrich craned his head. They were through the clouds now. The land stretched away barren and brown in nearly every direction. To the west, the horizon lurched vertically in a wall of dark blue. Directly below was what appeared to be a large town. It was square and flat, with low buildings the colour of rust.

When Ulrich had finished wrapping up his cards, he returned the bundle to its resting place above his heart. If the tarot was trying to warn him of something, he decided, it was to beware the ugliness of the world outside the window.

He pushed up his left sleeve. Wrapped around his arm was a data display of exquisite quality. A series of numbers flashed on its emerald screen. He nodded in approval. The data from the torpedo probes hadn't changed. They had delivered their radioactive payload into the worldwave, and it had been absorbed by something big. The creature was real all right, and now, he would be able to find her with ease.

Ulrich pushed his sleeve back down. He checked his faded reflection in the window, adjusted his cravat, and then made his way down to the lander's main deck.

The shuttlecraft lurched and came to rest. Ulrich was the first to exit, followed closely by Margene. Behind them, the inquisitor could hear Chavis barking orders for his men to begin deploying themselves.

The first thing that struck him was not the smell, as he had thought, but the light. It was early afternoon on this part of Lysios. Everything was bathed in oversaturated, crimson hues. He squinted and made a shade with his right hand. Purple and yellow spots formed in his vision, and he blinked to clear them. The lander sat in the centre of a square area barely large enough to contain it.

Three sides were hedged in by storage buildings with only the vaguest memories of having once been painted. In one corner was a four-storey tower with large glass windows on the top floor and a satellite dish mounted on the roof. A chain-link fence cordoned off the remaining side. Through the haze, Ulrich could make out the silhouettes of people there.

'Angry sun god indeed, yes?' he quipped, turning to Margene.

'Sir?' The young woman was unaffected by the blinding double suns. She'd had the forethought to bring a pair of tinted goggles.

'Nothing.' Ulrich sighed. He looked down at his boots. 'Is the ground vibrating?'

'It's the crawler treads, inquisitor. This entire settlement is moving, if you recall.'

'And it does this all the time?'

'Constantly, albeit very slowly. It takes each crawler ten years to circumnavigate the planet. If it stayed still, it would eventually be swept away by the worldwave.'

'How annoying.' He looked about. 'Where is our reception?'

He dropped his hand and began to walk towards the fence. His sword banged against his leg. His coat tails ruffled behind him. He was halfway to his destination when a section of the fence drew back. He stopped. Marching towards him was a group of Battle Sisters. They wore white power armour and black cloaks. They were led by an intimidating middle-aged woman whose most distinguishing feature was the scar that ran down one side of her face.

Pursing his lips and frowning, he muttered, 'And what have we here?'

'Inquisitor?' the woman called out. Her voice was as loud and as clear as a chapel bell.

Margene gave an audible intake of breath.

'I am,' Ulrich said. He rested his hands on the pommel of his sword, and shifted his weight onto one leg. 'Who might you be?'

The Battle Sisters came to halt. 'I am Magda Grace, a Canoness for the Sisters of the Sacred Rose.'

'You may address me as Inquisitor Ulrich. This is Sister Margene. She'll be acting as my dialogus.'

Margene nodded curtly.

'Very good,' the Canoness said approvingly. 'Inquisitor Ulrich, it falls to me to bid you welcome to Lysios.'

'Falls to you? Why? Where is the planetary governor?'

'Governor Strachman has abandoned his post,' the Canoness said.

'Are you certain?' Ulrich asked. 'I wasn't aware of any such problems when I left Terra.'

Canoness Grace was steadfast. 'I can assure you, sir, that Governor Strachman and everyone attached to him have been *in absentia* for quite some time. Not long after we began our campaign against the Shelsists, he vanished and has not been seen since. The only conclusion can be that he is a heretic, and that he chose to flee our wrath.'

'I see. Well then, where is the commander of the local military forces?'

Margene leaned forward again. 'Inquisitor, Lysios has no indigenous regiment.'

'What?'

'There hasn't been an Imperial Guard unit on this world in three thousand years, inquisitor. Not since the environmental collapse.'

'Governor Strachman had a few units of professional soldiers who acted as his personal guard,' Canoness Grace offered, 'but they went into hiding with him. Until such time as he and his people are found and dealt with, you may consider Lysios to be under my control.'

Ulrich stared at her. 'So, you and a dozen Sororitas are the only Imperial authority on this world?'

'Myself and several thousand Battle Sisters, yes,' the canoness said, emphasising the true number.

For a moment, the only sounds on the landing field were the whistling of the wind and the distant sounds of the Scions' transports rumbling slowly out of the belly of the lander. Ulrich squeezed his eyes tightly, but when he opened them again, he still felt blinded.

'You will get used to the light here,' Canoness Grace offered.

'Thank you, but I won't be staying that long. In fact, I must be about my business.'

'You should be made aware, then, that my Sororitas are heavily involved in combating the three local heretical cults. If you plan to conscript some of them under the authority of the Immortal Emperor of Mankind, then our overall efforts to restore this planet will suffer.'

'I have no intention of taking your Sisters away from their duties. I have Tempestus Scions to assist me in my mission.'

'Scions? Is it not a waste of their particular skillsets to use them only to ferret out and destroy heretical cultists?'

'What are you talking about?'

'The Shelsists, of course.'

'What of them?'

The Canoness frowned. 'I presumed that as an officer of the Ordo Hereticus, you were here to offer us your assistance in purging them.'

'No, not at all,' Ulrich said.

'The inquisitor is of the Ordo Xenos, Canoness,' Margene said quietly.

'Xenos?'

Tempestor Chavis had made his way towards the group. He stopped behind the inquisitor, stamped the ground, and saluted.

'Sir, all men and materiel are safely groundside. Taurox transports are armed and ready, and awaiting your orders.'

'Very well. Sister Margene and I will travel with you in the lead vehicle. I'll decode our destination coordinates once we are under way,' Ulrich said. He gave a slight bow at the waist. 'Canoness, I'll take my leave.'

'One cannot take what is so freely given,' the Canoness said.

Ulrich narrowed his eyes. Her words sounded like a quotation of some kind. Uncertain as to whether or not he had actually been insulted by the woman, he simply gave her a slight bow. He took four steps towards the landing craft, and then spun back around. 'Oh, actually, there is one area in which you and your charges might be of assistance to me.'

'Yes, inquisitor?'

Ulrich pointed towards the fence, where a number of curious onlookers were gathering. 'Keep the local riff-raff away from this ship. Set up a perimeter, or some such.'

Canoness Grace's eyes went wide with incredulity. 'Guard duty? You want to use my Battle Sisters for guard duty?'

'The Emperor's Inquisition is tasking you with securing a valuable location,' Ulrich said. He watched her clench her jaw. It could be a dangerous thing, he knew, trumping someone's personal pride with Inquisitorial power. But damn if it wasn't satisfying.

'Your lander will be accorded the same level of security as that of any Imperial visitor to this world,' the Canoness growled.

The inquisitor returned to the Scions with Chavis. Margene bowed to Canoness Grace in a gesture of respect mingled with awe. 'It was an honour to meet you at last, Canoness.'

The Canoness gave her a quizzical look.

'I am stationed at the Convent Prioris, on Holy Terra. I have been the recipient of your progress reports. I know all about your struggles here on Lysios, particularly against the Shelsists.'

'But it's not them that brought you here.'

Margene seemed torn. 'I... I cannot speak of the inquisitor's mission. I am bound by an oath of servitude and secrecy. We all are.'

'Of course. I understand.'

'But I can say that I think our efforts will aid you greatly. If we are successful, that is.'

Margene backed away, and then ran to catch up with Ulrich and Chavis. Canoness Grace returned to the other Sisters.

'Superior Cairista, we have new orders. This field is to be secured and guarded until the inquisitor returns. No one goes near that landing craft, and we are to keep any and all citizens away from the entryway. See to it.'

'At once, Canoness,' Cairista replied. As part of her promotion, she had traded in her flamer for a boltgun with a small fire launcher mounted beneath it. She hoisted it up over her shoulder and began to issue commands to the other women.

Grace watched from a distance as the Scions, Ulrich and Sister Margene climbed into the two transports and rumbled away from the tiny space port. Overhead, the blazing eyes of Cryptus became obscured by wisps of blue cloud. A cool breeze ruffled her cloak.

Canoness Grace ran her fingers along the beads of the rosarius that hung around her neck, praying as she did so. 'Emperor, if it be Your will, watch over our sister, Margene. Grant her strength, and courage, and the conviction to do Your will in all things.' She touched her forehead, chest, and sword hilt, and then moved to supervise the establishment of the security perimeter.

She and Margene would never see each other in person again.

'I am the Brine. Everything that lives within me, I have made a part of me. Since you spurn me, Ixoi, the creatures of Lysios will suffer my wrath. I will devour them, and greatly. The things that live in me will feast upon the things that live outside of me, because without you, I am craven.'

– Cantos Continuous, M41

CHAPTER FOUR

Chavis was not his original name. It had been given to him twenty years previously, by a drill abbot who selected it from a long list of possibilities. He had been twelve years old at the time, the victim of a disaster he couldn't recall which had taken place on a home world he could no longer remember. One of a hundred boys brought before the Schola Progenium that day, he had been sprayed with a hose, deloused, and told to forget everything about his past. This included his name. His name was Chavis now.

'You should be proud,' they had told him. 'Each of the names on this list once belonged to a great hero of the Imperium. This man, Chavis, was known for his wisdom and commitment to success. Now, it's up to you to carry on his legacy.'

He did his best to comply, and he did feel proud to have been awarded such a name. He even enjoyed the brutal rigours of training, remaining stoically silent through aching muscles and the occasional snapped bone. Suffering became the price to be paid for the honour of bearing the name of Chavis.

He did not, however, enjoy the Correction Throne.

It was a standard phase in the development of a Tempestus Scion. All of them would go through it. He accepted that much. What he would never understand was why such a terrible thing was given such an elegant name. He had imagined a magnificent chair, like the one the Emperor sat in, but when he was at last brought before it, he found it to be nothing of the kind. The Correction Throne was a metal frame with leather straps around the arms and legs. Suspended above was what appeared to be a bowl filled with spikes. He was forced into the seat. Rough hands cinched the belts tightly around his limbs. The bowl was placed over his head. A block of wood was inserted into his mouth to ensure that he didn't bite through his tongue. Adepts in hooded robes, lurking in the dark corners of the room, muttered as they flipped switches and turned dials.

Then, like a billion young lads before him, he was mindscaped. The needles drove themselves through the back of his skull. The soft pathways of his brain were flooded with a neurochemical designed to wipe them clean. When he was at last allowed to rise from the Throne, his mind would be an empty vessel, fit to be filled with all the terrible doctrines of war. And fill it they did.

Two decades later, Chavis knew how to achieve any mission given to him. He knew when to take ground, and when to hold it; when to act with caution, and when to risk it all. And thus, despite the inquisitor's unparalleled power and authority over him, Chavis was unafraid to question his decisions.

From the hab-crawler, the two transports sped easily over kilometres of barren and empty country. Above them, the skies darkened. Thunder could be heard even through the thick hull. By the time they entered the foothills of the Kephorous mountains, a deluge was coming down around them. Rain beat against the roof and firing ports, and the Taurox rocked from side to side as the independent tracks scrabbled over rocks and crevasses.

'Is there a problem, tempestor?' Margene asked.

Chavis's head snapped up. 'Why do you ask?'

The interior of the Taurox was divided into two sections. There was a piloting compartment up front, with room enough for two people. The remainder was a rectangular space large enough to hold eight. Chavis and Margene were seated directly across from one another.

'The way you were staring down at the floor,' Margene said. Her face was hard. A boltgun rested in her lap, and she drummed her fingers on its engraved frame.

'The rain sounds very heavy,' Chavis said. 'I'm concerned that it may affect our timetable.'

'Storms are common on Lysios, especially as one moves closer to the worldwave. They tend not to last long, but can be intense. It's actually a bit ironic, because right now, on the other side of the planet, there's a terrible drought.'

Abruptly, the vehicle came to a halt. Chavis leaned forward in his seat and called up to the piloting compartment.

'Scion Cato, report!'

'Tempestor,' Cato replied calmly, 'we have a potential problem.'

Chavis unbuckled his safety restraints and leaned in between the driver and forward passenger seats.

'What is it?' Chavis asked.

Cato pointed through the narrow window slot before him. 'There are environmental concerns that should be evaluated before we proceed, sir.'

'All right. Let's have a look.' Chavis activated his personal vox-unit and called to the driver of the second Taurox. 'Erdon, join us up front.'

He returned to the rear section, shoved one of the side doors open, and jumped down into water that rose to his ankles. Behind him, he heard Cato and the inquisitor do likewise. Rain pelted his face. It tasted vaguely of salt.

They were half way up the slope of Mount Loraz, following a winding track barely wide enough to accommodate their transports. On the left rose a wall of rock and mud. To the right was a sharp drop-off that plunged hundreds of metres into the churning greenish waves of Lysios's ocean. To fall over the edge was to fall into oblivion.

From behind them came the sound of sloshing footsteps.

'Scion Erdon, reporting as ordered.'

Chavis adjusted his beret and the four of them made their way to the front of the lead Taurox. They stood in the glare of the vehicle's floodlights and surveyed the path ahead of them.

'Damn,' Ulrich said. He began fishing about inside his coat.

A river of rainwater, a hundred metres wide, was gushing from a crevasse in the mountainside. It fell in a torrent across the road before spilling over the drop-off.

'No way to know what condition the road is in under all that,' Erdon said to Cato.

'That's the concern.'

Chavis moved forward slowly, testing the ground with every step.

'Can you tell how deep it gets, sir?' Erdon called out. The water was now swirling around the tempestor's knees.

'Deep. But I shouldn't think that it'll come up over the roof.'

Behind him, Ulrich had produced a square of paper laminated in plastek. He began to unfold it. 'We can't go through this,' he said. 'We'll be swept over the edge for certain.'

'I've been through wider water hazards,' Chavis said. He looked out at the drop-off. 'We'll be fine.'

Ulrich lowered the sheet of paper. Chavis could see that it was a map of some kind, possibly part of an orbital survey. 'I beg to differ. Look here, this shows another way to the plateau.'

The tempestor returned to Ulrich's side and grasped one edge of the waterproofed sheet. After a moment's consideration, he said, 'No. That won't work.'

Ulrich looked as if he'd been slapped, and Chavis wondered distantly how often the inquisitor, or any inquisitor for that matter, found himself being contradicted. 'I beg your pardon?'

'Respectfully, sir, it won't work. Not given our time considerations.' He traced a line over the map with a thick finger, leaving a trail of condensation. 'The other route is kilometres to the west. True, it's not as steep, but it would take us half a day to get there. By that time, we will have missed our opportunity.'

Ulrich looked unhappy. He pointed to the water pouring down across the trail. 'You're telling me that you can get us through that?'

'Sir, I have twenty years of service to my name. I've yet to encounter the terrain that could best a Taurox.'

'But if the road gives way beneath it...'

'Sir,' Chavis repeated. 'If we want to capture the alien specimen, we need to stick to our timetable.' He held up his right forearm, into which was built a small, glowing display screen. He wiped the beads of rainwater from it, and tilted it towards Ulrich. In the upper corner of the display, a string of numbers counted steadily down towards zero. 'According to the information provided to me by the dialogus, we have just under four hours remaining. After that, the tidal swell of the worldwave will have moved past the mountain.'

Ulrich looked at Cato and Erdon, as if seeking a second opinion. He found none.

'I also have many years of experience, tempestor,' Ulrich said, 'in a profession that rewards carelessness with death.'

Chavis gave no reply. Twice he had stated his belief that the two Taurox would be able to make it across the raging water, and that was one time more than he was used to. Finally, Ulrich relented. He shook the water from the map, and began to fold it back up. 'If you have so much faith in this machine of yours, then you won't mind driving.'

'Not at all, sir. However, I'll need Scion Cato to sit next to me.'

'Why?'

'This could be dangerous, sir. Not only should there be a Scion ready to take over immediately should something happen to me, but you will be safer in the rear section.'

'Fine, fine,' Ulrich muttered. His shoulders were hunched and his arms were wrapped tightly around his body. His hair was plastered to his head by the rain. He climbed up into the passenger compartment.

Chavis and Cato made their way to the front. As Chavis fastened his safety restraints, Cato secured his helmet and faceplate.

'Scion Erdon?' Chavis said over the vox.

'Ready here, tempestor. We'll follow your lead.'

Chavis sent the Taurox forwards. Four status lights blinked on the panel in front of him, one for each of the machine's quad tracks. The moment they entered the torrent, the lights changed from reassuring green to cautionary amber. Water surged against the left side of the vehicle. The Taurox began to lurch up and down as it manoeuvred over submerged boulders, but its grip on the flooded road was steady.

As they neared the midpoint, the front of the transport suddenly pitched down sharply. Chavis's viewing slits became completely submerged.

'What was that?' Cato said.

Chavis bared his teeth, angry with himself for not having foreseen this. 'A trench,' he said. The constant rush of water had carved a deep fault in the mountain path, and they were falling into it, nose-first.

Erdon was shouting over the vox. 'Tempestor, I've lost you!'

'Erdon, exercise extreme caution. The middle section here is far worse than I thought.'

Chavis flicked a series of switches on the panel beside him, and the interior lights in the Taurox went out as power was transferred to the tractors. He pulled back hard on the controls. From somewhere underfoot came the noise of metal grinding. The Taurox shook violently and groaned before bursting up to the surface again, spraying mud everywhere. The water levels dropped back down below the firing slots. They were nearly to the other side.

As Chavis looked again at the track indicators, something heavy struck the side of the Taurox and rolled away. The passenger compartment reverberated with the sound of it. The tempestor's head snapped up.

'Rock, sir,' Cato said. 'Fell down from the mountainside after we passed through. I think maybe we–'

Through the vox, Chavis could suddenly hear a series of pings and bangs. At first, he took it to be gunfire of some kind.

'Tempestor, I have a situation,' Erdon said. 'We're being pushed over the drop-off.'

Cato let out a short, sharp expletive.

'Transfer additional power to your tracks,' Chavis ordered.

'They're at one hundred and twenty per cent, sir. It's not a question of power. There's nothing left to grip.'

Ulrich leaned into the compartment and demanded to know what was happening.

Chavis cut him off with a raised hand. 'Erdon,' he said, 'prep your recovery gear. Cato, get outside, grab that line and secure it.'

'Yes, sir,' Cato said. Mounted into his left shoulder plate was a compact vid-lens. When he activated it, the lens glowed dark red. Chavis looked down at his own forearm display, which now showed the view from Cato's vid-link. 'Your monoscope data is coming in fine. Go.'

'I asked you to tell me what's happening,' Ulrich said. 'All of our equipment is in that other transport. If it's lost–'

'Not now!' Chavis raised his arm.

Beside him, Cato reached up and unlocked a small round hatch. Rain and muddy water poured into his lap. He reached down beside his seat and pulled hard on the lever there, and with a sudden jerk, his chair rose up through the open hatch. The water coming into the front compartment slowed to only a few drops. On his monitor, Chavis could now see the road ahead, as well as the barrels of the battle cannon mounted on the roof of the Taurox. The picture inched around as Cato climbed up from out of the turret and made his way on hands and knees to the back of the roof.

'Erdon,' Chavis called, 'fire your cable.'

A moment later, there was a scraping sound on the roof, and Cato said, 'They're latched on to us. We're good to go, tempestor.'

Chavis pushed down on the accelerator, and the transport lurched forwards. Over the vox, Chavis could hear Cato grunting. After several tense moments, Erdon spoke.

'That's it. All of my track indicators are back on solid ground.'

The two vehicles ploughed through the last of the water and emerged safely on the other side. The seat next to Chavis dropped back down into place. Cato, covered in mud and soaking wet, removed his helmet and facemask. He exhaled loudly. 'The cable's released, sir.'

Ulrich was staring at him. 'Your hands,' he said.

Cato had left a pair of bloody imprints on either side of his helmet. He turned his gloves over to discover that several thick metal splinters had embedded themselves in his palms. 'Oh. Must have gotten them from the recovery cable.' He looked up at Chavis. 'It gave me a bit of trouble, sir.'

'Good work, Scion,' Chavis said. 'Get in the back and get those cleaned up.'

Cato nodded and squeezed past the inquisitor.

'I thought you said that we wouldn't have any problems?' Ulrich said.

Chavis switched off the vid-feed to his monitor. The tiny clock reappeared and continued its countdown. 'No, sir, I said that we would make it, and we did.'

'But I was right. The road washed out.'

'The road didn't wash out. The mountain came down.'

Ulrich's mouth twisted. 'Just get us up to the plateau,' he said quietly. He turned and went back into the rear compartment.

CHAPTER FIVE

By the time they reached the top of the mountain, the rain had stopped. The clouds were beginning to thin. The suns had set and the moon, Ixoi, was already visible in the sky as a massive, round, red disc. Nearby, the waves of Lysios's vertical ocean washed up on the tumbled rocks. Their sound was like thunder, and the spray they sent up plumed high overhead. The two Taurox had stopped near a large slab of flat rock. Ulrich had insisted on being the first to exit. He stood gazing out at the ocean with a strange look on his face. Margene and the eighteen Scions climbed down from the transports and began to gather near him.

The bulk of the worldwave was to the south of them, a dark wall reaching up into the clouds. The dusky moonlight only made it seem more surreal. The entire horizon appeared to bend at a ninety-degree angle.

Ulrich turned and faced them all. His eyes were alight with excitement. The wind whipped his coat around his calves. He had to shout to be heard over the pounding surf.

'I told you men before we landed that I had a plan to make our target come to us. Sister Margene, according to local legend, how often does the Brine Goddess come to the surface?'

'Monthly, sir. She reaches out towards the moon, and when she finds that she can't touch him, she despairs and causes tidal waves and storms.'

'Nonsense, obviously, but it did get me to thinking. If there really was a Shelse living in the blackness of the ocean, why would it come forth with such regularity? I believe that the answer is the moon. Well, moonlight, to be more exact. I mean, look around you.'

Ulrich swept his arm in a half circle. Ixoi dominated the sky, casting everything in the reflection of the two suns. No stars could be seen. Night-time on Lysios was the equivalent of dusk on most other Imperial worlds.

'You believe the creature is attracted to light?' Margene asked.

'Light and gravity, but I'm willing to wager that light will be enough. Tempestor, I want your men to begin setting up the searchlight immediately. How long will it take?'

'It's a standard Sabre platform, sir. Routine assembly time twenty-five to thirty minutes. We'll have it ready in fifteen.'

'Excellent. In the meantime, I will prepare the containment chamber. Margene, you're with me.' Ulrich began to walk towards the Taurox that Erdon had driven. Margene hurried to match his long strides. Chavis barked to the Scions. 'You heard the inquisitor. Unpack that platform. Get the light up and running.'

The Scions saluted, and hurried to their work. From the rear section of the second Taurox, they brought out four metal struts and a series of round floor plates. These were followed by a square bracket, and finally, a light that was nearly as wide around as Chavis was tall. Margene had seen such things before. The light they produced was blinding, and they were usually mounted onto buildings or used for signalling aircraft at night. Once the pieces of the searchlight were offloaded, the Taurox was empty save for her, Ulrich, and a tall cylinder.

It appeared to be made of sheet metal. The front contained a single narrow door with a round pane of glass in the centre.

'You're going to put it... in this?' Margene asked.

'It's stronger than it looks, I assure you. Heavier, as well. Take one side.'

She shouldered her boltgun and helped Ulrich lift the container out of the Taurox and down onto the ground. The Scions had nearly finished assembling the platform and the massive light. She had thought perhaps the tempestor had been bragging when he said that he and his men could build it in half the time of regular soldiers. Now, she conceded that he hadn't.

The waves were growing in intensity as the tidal swell approached. Their breaking on the rocks was deafening, and when the waves retreated, they seemed to suck the very air out to sea with them. Margene looked in awe at the approaching worldwave, when something farther down the shoreline caught her attention. In the distance was a procession of people. They were carrying torches.

'Inquisitor?' she said. 'We're not alone.'

Ulrich looked down the strand. 'Who are they?'

'Locals, I would presume, sir. Should we do something about them?'

Before he could answer, Chavis approached. 'We're ready, inquisitor,' he said.

'Turn it on, then.'

Chavis gave a signal to one of his men, and the searchlight flared to life. Its blinding beam cut a wide swath down the beach and far out into the ocean. Another wave crashed over the rocks, dousing everyone with droplets of freezing water. The searchlight crackled and hissed.

Chavis frowned. 'Sir,' he asked Ulrich, 'are you certain that we're high enough above the water line?'

'Of course.'

Margene did not share the inquisitor's confidence, especially not after yet another wave crested the rocks and travelled far enough up the shore to wet their boots. Green tendrils like fine seaweed, embedded with flecks of silver, glittered on the ground. Droplets popped loudly as they landed on the light and then vaporised.

Scion Cato was the first to notice that the torch bearers had altered their course and were now moving towards them. 'Tempestor!' he shouted.

'Byrdgon, Savdra!' Chavis ordered. The two Scions quickly left the searchlight to stand by Erdon. From their backs, the three men unhooked bulky lasguns with top-mounted scopes and thick barrels.

The group of torch bearers came to a halt a short distance from the Scions. They were led by a woman in her late thirties. She wore a blue, patchwork robe and tall boots. She carried a staff that seemed to be made from some kind of white stone. Her skin was burnt and wrinkled from a lifetime under the twin suns of Lysios.

'You shouldn't be here!' she shouted. 'Whoever you are, you must leave.'

Ulrich put his hands on his hips. 'Do you have any idea who I am?'

The woman stopped and planted the end of her staff in the rocky soil. Something about the gnarled white pole stuck a familiar chord with Margene. It wasn't stone, she realised, but a huge rod of coral.

'This night is sacred, off-worlder. You will not defile it.'

'What did you call me?'

'Off-worlder,' she drawled in a thick accent. 'Like the Murderess.'

The crowd behind her murmured.

Ulrich seemed slightly amused. 'I'm sorry, who is the Murderess?'

'The one who leads the women in white.'

'You mean the Canoness? Does she know you call her that?'

The ocean roared. The Lysites turned, to see the crest of an enormous wave rolling towards them in a spray of water and foam. Strange creatures began to tumble out of it. Fish the size of small children flopped about. More of the glittering seaweed covered the shore. Margene unslung her bolter.

'You must douse this light!' cried the woman in the blue robe. 'Only Ixoi may shine this night!'

Ulrich neither knew nor cared what she was talking about. He was about to order the Scions to chase the Lysites off with a volley of las-fire, when another wave pounded the nearby rocks. A large boulder rolled up onto the shore, and sprouted four pairs of stocky, segmented legs. A head shaped like a hammer uncurled from somewhere beneath it. Two antennae emerged from its neck and twitched as they took in the night-time air.

One of the old Lysite men broke from the group and ran towards it with all the speed he could muster. 'Me first, take me!' he shouted as he went.

'Orders, sir?' Chavis asked.

The boulder-thing pounced forward. Margene caught a glimpse of a fanged mouth on its underside.

Ulrich dug furiously into his coat pocket, and whipped out a hand-held auspex. He pointed it towards the creature. When it made a short, sharp buzz, he scowled. 'It's not what we're after. Kill it.'

Chavis barked to two of his men. 'Thieus, Brandt, directed firestorm.'

The pair's hot-shot lasguns lit up the stony beach with searing beams. The creature was struck, and a section of its rocky shell melted inward. It gave a high pitched squeal, and fell over dead. Its insides were on fire.

The old man who had been running skidded to a halt and fell to his knees before the carcass. He stared in disbelief. There was no sound for a moment except the pounding of the surf. The Lysites were slack-jawed and silent. Then the old man lifted his arms out towards the worldwave and began to wail.

'I was prepared!' he cried.

As if taking a cue from his outburst, the body of the dead creature shuddered. From somewhere inside it there came a tearing sound. A swarm of tiny things flooded out from underneath its burning shell, each a copy of the parent creature in miniature. They surged over the wailing man and began biting into his flesh. He collapsed beneath them.

Margene could have sworn that his cries had changed from sorrow to gratitude.

Ulrich took a step back in disgust. Another titanic wave arched over the boulders and came crashing down, soaking everyone and leaving more creatures in its wake. They dragged themselves up the shore on a pair of rubbery fins, while behind them a flat tail wagged. Their backs were covered in long spines that faced forward. They shook themselves off, sending a cloud of quills into the crowd.

One of the darts caught Ulrich in the temple, leaving a long scratch that oozed dark ichor. He drew his pistol with impressive speed and sent a bolt of energy into the thing that had dared to wound him.

Two more of the boulder-spiders dropped into the mass of Lysites, sending bodies flying in all directions. With terrible grunts, they disgorged their young, who began to bite and gnaw on everything around them. Down the beach, a varied collection of creatures were being cast ashore. A ball of gelatinous material rolled a short distance, and then collapsed into a pile of seaweed and fleshy slugs with ridged fins. They began crawling with alarming speed towards the searchlight and everyone who was gathered around it.

A memory flashed through Margene's mind of a time years ago when a moth had somehow found its way into the scriptorium. Again and again, it flew into her candelabra, until it had finally caught fire and died. It had been heedless of pain or any wounds it suffered, because it had been driven mad; mad by the bright light of her candles.

'Inquisitor, I think your beacon is working a little too well,' she said.

Chavis pointed to the two Taurox. 'Cato, Erdon, get in the turrets and prepare to give us fire support.'

As the two men ran for the transports, the pack of quilled beasts turned their attention to the Scions' firing line. Their faces were covered with the blood and gore of the Lysites they had just finished feasting on. The monsters shook violently as they ran forward. Byrdgon's right arm became covered in quills. He fired his weapon and one of the creatures exploded into flaming chunks. The other Scions followed suit, lighting up the stony beach with las-fire.

'Keep them back,' Chavis yelled. 'Don't let them get close enough to fire those barbs at you.' He glanced at his monitor. The countdown timer was almost at zero. 'Inquisitor, we're nearing peak tide. Which of these is the specimen?'

Ulrich waved his auspex back and forth. 'I'm not... it's not any of these,' he shouted.

Byrdgon stumbled backwards, and fell face first to the ground. On either side of him, the Scions continued pouring las-fire into the quill creatures, but it seemed that every one they killed was replaced by two more.

Chavis dashed to Byrdgon and rolled him over. His right arm was swelling visibly. Black gel was seeping out from the base of every quill. He tried to say something, but could only produce choking sounds.

The tide came upon them with a deafening crash. Water flooded around the base of the searchlight and the treads of the nearest Taurox. The pack of quill creatures seemed to be invigorated by it, and surged ahead. They leapt upon the Scions and unleashed a flurry of biting, scratching attacks.

Chavis pulled a serrated combat knife from his belt and filled the hole in the line. To his left and right, the Scions were beating at the monsters with their rifles until they went down, and then stamping their heads flat to ensure they stayed that way. There were a lot of them, he admitted, but their main threat seemed to be their poisonous quills, which were rendered useless in close quarters. He was quite confident that, so long as they weren't allowed to get *too* close, he and his men would quickly emerge as the victors in this fight.

Then, by the searchlight's glare, Chavis saw that larger creatures were emerging from the surf. They were slightly taller than a man, and dragged themselves forward on a pair of fat, chitin-plated claws. Their bodies were vaguely serpentine. Small bolts of electricity crackled around them.

They charged in an odd, scrabbling motion, bowling through the remaining quill creatures and impacting against the Scions. Chavis felt his whole body shiver uncontrollably as the things discharged a massive electrical shock. His muscles refused to obey him for a moment, and he dropped his knife. The next thing he knew he was on his back, claws trying to tear away his armour. There was a sharp and terrible pain in his thigh.

With great effort, Chavis dug his fingers into the thing's side, grabbed a fistful of blubber, and pulled. A gristly hole opened up, dumping reeking fluids all over him. The creature gave a high squeal and collapsed.

Chavis shoved its dead weight off him and scrambled back to his feet, ignoring the pain in his upper leg where he'd been wounded. His monitor started flashing a variety of telltales; yellow for Scions who were injured but recoverable, red for those who were beyond saving. He also noted that Margene had thrown herself into the fray. She had attached an oversized bayonet to the end of her boltgun, and was using it to chop through the bodies of the attacking creatures.

Ulrich fired his pistol into yet another group of aquatic horrors that were shambling and slithering their way towards the searchlight. It seemed as if every living thing in the worldwave were coming ashore with the intent to feast on them.

'Fire support on the water line!' Chavis yelled into his vox.

Atop both of the Taurox were cannons designed to blow apart light vehicles and heavily armoured infantry. Erdon and Cato began to shell the beach with them. With each explosion, a cone of gravel and water rocketed upwards. Chunks of shell and fatty tissue rained down.

Another of the clawed creatures leapt towards Chavis. He drew his pistol and shot the thing dead before it could shock him. The ocean was all around them now, completely covering the fallen and drenching those still standing almost to their waists. Sparks shot from the searchlight, and in an instant, it went out. The ruddy light of Ixoi came flooding back.

Ulrich's sword glinted in the moonlight as he slashed and thrust. His coat was torn at the shoulder and one side of his face was distorted. The bodies of dead things floated all around him.

Margene was the first to see it. She had just finished chopping one of the quill creatures in half, and was standing back to back with one of the Scions. His helmet was gone and one of his hands had been badly mangled. A shadow fell across them, and she looked up to see where it had come from.

Out of the worldwave, rose a tree. At least, that was her initial impression: a tree whose vast trunk was sheathed in bark the colour of dried scabs. Its hundreds of cream-coloured branches curled and twitched as they stretched across the face of the moon. Some of them were tipped with claws as large as the Taurox.

Her body shook involuntarily as the truth dawned on her. It wasn't a tree. It was an enormous tentacle. In fact, it was a tentacle that was sprouting a myriad of other tentacles.

One by one, Chavis, Ulrich and the remaining Scions caught a glimpse of it, and despite their varied backgrounds, all of them were struck dumb. The Scions paused for only a fraction of a second before regaining their focus and continuing to fight off their attackers.

Ulrich however, despite his training and experience, found himself standing slack-jawed and speechless. *This is Shelse,* he thought dimly. *No, worse: this is only a portion of Shelse.* His preconceptions crumbled within him, and were supplanted by sheer terror. Gone was any notion he might have once held that the creature would be captured in its entirety. All he cared about for the moment was surviving.

A rushing sound filled the air, and the full extent of the tidal swell came upon them. A wave, larger than any that had come before it, was curling up from the body of Lysios's ocean. The water looked purple in Ixoi's red glare. White caps glinted along its edge.

'Emperor, save us,' Margene whispered.

The wave reached its peak, and began to crumble. It struck the boulders along the shoreline with hurricane force, submerging them easily. A wall of water rolled towards them, and from its foaming crest came a monster. It was a thing dragged up from the deepest depths, with rubbery, ghostly-white skin. Its head was shaped like that of some gigantic fish. Its mouth was filled with teeth the size of swords. Its eyes glowed bright yellow, and a ridge of spines ran down the length of its back. Where it ended, no one could tell; the thing's body trailed back into the churning ocean.

'All Scions,' Chavis yelled into his vox, 'elimination protocol!'

Erdon and Cato continued to rain shells upon the shoreline. The giant thing bellowed as it was struck. One of its eyes exploded, showering the landscape in jelly. Wriggling the spines on its back, it swam forwards with the force of a runaway train. It swallowed two Scions whole, and knocked the searchlight into the water before it finally rammed its bulbous head into the side of Cato's Taurox. The side door caved in completely. The vehicle rocked, but did not tip over.

Margene, Ulrich, and Chavis began shooting at it, but none of the weapons they carried seemed to have any effect. Erdon hit it with another shell from his battle cannon. A hole opened halfway down the length of its body, and greasy blood gushed out.

In response, the monster raised itself up like a cobra preparing to strike, and then slammed its entire weight down onto the roof of Chavis's transport. The driver's section crumpled and the front tracks sagged in on themselves. Over the vox, the Scions could hear Cato screaming in agony.

The monster raised itself up again. It clamped the entire front half of the transport in its mouth, and shook it wildly. Metal plating and bits of machinery flew in all directions. Then the monster, satisfied with its catch, began to retract itself back into the ocean, taking the flattened Taurox with it.

'Kill it! Kill it!' Chavis was screaming.

In response, Erdon fired three more shells at the monster as it retreated. Two of them found their mark, and opened yet more gaping wounds in its hide. With a splash, it vanished back into the ocean.

Scion Cato's incoherent cries became the terrible sounds of a man drowning. Thankfully for all who could hear, his struggles were short lived.

Margene and Chavis kicked aside a myriad of dead creatures. Four Scions got to their feet. The rest were either dead or gone, the bodies washed out to sea.

Now that the beacon was destroyed, the number of creatures tumbling out of the ocean became greatly reduced. Waves continued to crest over the boulders, but these too were shrinking in magnitude. Still, it was not yet over.

The remaining quill beasts launched another volley of poisoned barbs, which bounced harmlessly off the Scions' armour. Chavis shot three of them. His last four men joined him at his side, and began firing their lasguns into the pack.

Margene quickly inserted a fresh clip into her bolter, and fired. Two more of the clawed things blew apart into rubbery pieces. When a half-dead quill beast attempted to bite her leg, she stamped it to death beneath her heel.

Erdon's cannon shells had transformed the water line into a pockmarked moonscape. The craters filled with seawater and mangled pieces of meat. At last, he ceased firing, for there was nothing left on the beach to shoot at.

Chavis watched his men torch the last of the quill creatures with las-fire. He holstered his bolt pistol and spoke into his vox. 'Erdon, the area is clear. Grab a medi-kit and get out here.'

Ulrich was standing farther down the shore, where the water was still knee-high. He was staring out past the boulders. No more creatures were coming ashore. The cut on his face burned with a mixture of poison and salt. By his quick estimation, ten or eleven men had been killed, leaving him with only half a dozen Scions and the dialogus. They were down to one transport, and his equipment was all damaged, or utterly destroyed. But worse than all this, Shelse was nowhere to be seen. The worldwave was moving on, passing the plateau in its unstoppable circumnavigation of Lysios.

Ulrich began to shake. His knuckles turned white as he gripped his sword. He let loose a scream that echoed off the rocks. 'Ten years!'

The tempestor trudged up behind the inquisitor. A wave broke over the rocks.

'The worldwave won't pass this plateau again for ten years. All my planning... this whole trip... It's all been a waste!' He stumbled a few steps towards the ocean.

'A waste,' Chavis repeated.

Ulrich spun around. 'This is not my fault!'

'I never implied that it was, sir,' Chavis said, 'but what are your orders now?'

Ulrich's face twisted as he furiously tried to think of some means to salvage this operation. Nothing came. He sighed. 'Return to the space port, and go home.'

He gave the worldwave one final, longing look, and then started walking back up the beach.

Chavis left to see to his men without saying another word.

They heard Margene yelling. 'Inquisitor! Tempestor! Over here!'

The two men broke into a run, passing Erdon as he opened a medi-kit and began tending to the surviving Scions. They found Margene near the place where the Lysites had tried to confront them. One of the Taurox cannon shells had fallen here, littering the area with human body parts and dead sea creatures. In the middle of the scene was a wide, but shallow crater. At the bottom, submerged in salt water and pinned beneath the half-corpse of one of the boulder-spiders, lay the woman with the blue robe.

'I heard someone calling,' Margene said, 'and I found this.' She leapt down into the crater, and yanked back the woman's tattered robe.

Below her neck, the woman's skin was dark purple and covered in overlapping plates. A secondary set of arms sprouted from the middle of her ribcage.

Margene levelled her boltgun at the woman. 'You. Mutant. Confess your sins, and I will consider them. Who are you? What were you doing out here?'

The woman coughed up blood and said, 'It's Ixoi's Night...'

'When Lysios's moon is at perigee,' Margene clarified.

'Yes... We escort those who... offer themselves as tribute.'

'To the Brine Goddess?'

'Yes. To Shelse. She... she sends the Things That Live Within Her... to satisfy her hunger.' Her head flopped back and her breathing became ragged. '*I will devour them, and greatly.*'

'Enough!' Reciting from her own litany Margene said, '*From the scourge of the Kraken, Our Emperor, deliver us. From the blasphemy of the Fallen, Our Emperor, deliver us.*'

Margene pulled the trigger and the woman's entire upper half flew apart. She looked up, but Ulrich was gone. She climbed up from out of the crater, and found him kneeling nearby.

He pulled a pair of long gloves from his belt and began to don them hurriedly. 'Get the containment chamber, Chavis,' he yelled, 'and bring it here. Now!'

Margene called to Ulrich, and received no response. She peered over his shoulder to see what was holding his attention so raptly. A segmented piece of tentacle was lying in a shallow depression in the ground. It was roughly the size of her arm. Ten or more smaller cilia sprouted from it like elongated fingers tipped with black talons, and there were bits of red shell near the bottom of it. It rolled and twisted, madly trying to escape from the hole.

'Is that–' Margene began.

She was interrupted by Chavis and Erdon rushing past her, carrying the heavy cylinder. They set it down next to Ulrich. Chavis opened the door and waited.

Ulrich finished putting on his gloves. He set his jaw, and then wrapped both hands around the tentacle piece. It immediately began thrashing about. The inquisitor had to fight to maintain his grip on it. With a grunt, he threw it into the cylinder. Chavis slammed the door shut.

The tentacle hammered at the inside of the container.

Ulrich was slightly short of breath as he said, 'Get it aboard the transport immediately.'

Chavis and Erdon lifted the containment chamber up, and started back to the remaining Taurox. Ulrich peeled off his gloves and put them back into his coat. He looked at her, his face beaming, and followed after the two Scions.

'Inquisitor,' Margene said as she came alongside him. 'There is obviously more transpiring on Lysios than meets the eye. We should send a message to the Canoness.'

'No, I think not.'

Margene pointed back to the crater. 'There is heresy here.'

'There is heresy everywhere, but I will not have that woman rampaging all around and getting in my way. No, I'm afraid that the Canoness's righteous fury will have to wait until my work here is complete.'

'Inquisitor, I have a duty to report religious sedition. I promise you, I will make no mention of that... *thing* in the storage container.'

'Communications blackout,' Ulrich spat. 'That means you don't talk to anyone, about anything, unless I say so.'

'I understand, inquisitor, but surely–'

'This conversation is over. For your sake, we should never have to repeat it.'

He climbed up into the Taurox.

Margene stood alone for a moment, trying to dampen her fury. Somehow, she knew, she had to contact the Canoness. Something on this world was coming to a head, and it had to be stopped before it was too late.

She climbed aboard, slamming the hatch shut behind her. The Taurox's engine roared to life, and the transport sped away.

The beach was deserted. Only the dead were present to witness the titanic shape that once again broke through the surface of the worldwave. It clawed at the moon, pining for its unreachable love and calling curses down on all of those who opposed it.

'What will our lives be like, my love, when we are at last united? Will you descend forever and join me, or will you scoop me up in your arms, and carry me back to your abode in the sky? Promise me, O, promise me, we'll be together soon. The stars begin to fall, and this era draws to a close...'

– *Cantos Continuous*, M41

CHAPTER SIX

The moon was beginning to set. It was as dark as night-time got on Lysios. To one side, the mountain was a wall of soaking wet rock. On the other was the receding swell of the worldwave. Erdon watched the road carefully as he drove. It was far rougher than it had been when they had used it to ascend the mountain earlier. The passing tide had heaved up rocks and covered it with a thick carpet of weeds and mud. On at least three occasions, warning indicators flashed on the dashboard display telling him that the Taurox was losing traction. That alone spoke to the treacherousness of their route.

Chavis sat in the command seat next to him, also keeping a watchful eye on the road conditions. Both men saw the problem at the same time. Erdon brought the Taurox to a stop.

'Stay here,' Chavis said. 'I'll take a closer look.' He got out of his seat, grabbed his helmet from a compartment on the bulkhead, and made his way to a side hatch. In the rear of the Taurox, Margene sat with her head down. Ulrich was sitting on the floor next to the containment cylinder. The tiny observation window was fogged over, and drops of condensation ran down the sides. The tentacle creature had stopped its mad convulsing within the first hour of the trip.

Besides Erdon, he had four other Scions remaining. Five if he included Byrdgon, who was lying in a near comatose state across three seats. His arm was clearly infected beyond the capability of any field medicine. Dark lines had begun to spread across his neck and chest. The others, Brandt, Thieus, Savdra, and Devries, had been patched up with supplies from the Scion's 'Martyr's Gift' medi-kit, including protein healing salves, suture tape, and in Thieus's case, a temporary bionic hand.

As he opened the hatch, Margene's head snapped up. 'What's wrong?' she asked.

'The road ahead of us looks very bad. I'm going out to see if it's passable.'

She was on her feet at once. 'I'll come with you.'

Chavis jumped down. His wounded leg gave a distant cry of pain that he stoically ignored. The air was cool and wet. Thick mud and weeds made sucking sounds beneath his feet as he walked around to the front of the Taurox. The night became as bright as day thanks to the amplifying lenses in his helmet and his suspicions were confirmed.

They had come to the place where, earlier, the mountainside had crumbled and nearly swept Erdon's Taurox over the edge and into the sea below. The road was now completely gone. Walls of rock and mud had come sliding down from somewhere above, and the trench they had fought to traverse was now a yawning abyss.

'Erdon?' he said into his vox.

'Here, tempestor.'

'This is no good. Not even a Taurox could get across a chasm this wide. We'll have to find another way back to the hab-crawler.'

'The secondary route to the west?'

'My thoughts exactly.'

Chavis turned around to go back to the Taurox, only to find Margene blocking his way.

'Tempestor, I need to ask you something.'

'Yes?'

Margene considered him for a moment. *'He who allows the alien to live shares in the crime of its existence,'* she said at last. 'Would you agree with that statement?'

Chavis's answer was immediate. 'Yes.'

'Of course you do. Any sane person would. But if that is so, then why is the inquisitor bringing that thing back? Why are we letting him?'

'We aren't letting him do anything. He does not answer to us.'

'Doesn't it bother you to have that thing on board?' Margene jerked a thumb towards the rear compartment.

Chavis considered the question for a moment. 'It's irrelevant. My mission is to ensure the inquisitor's safety, and return him to that landing ship.' With that, he walked past her and back into the transport.

'What if I told you that it's still alive? Would that change your opinion?'

Chavis stopped.

'I managed to steal a glance over the inquisitor's shoulder a while ago, and I'm almost certain that I could see it moving around inside that cylinder.'

'Almost certain?'

'Well... it was hard to tell, but–'

'Do you believe the creature represents an immediate danger to either yourself or any member of the team?'

'No,' she said hesitantly. 'I don't... I don't know.'

'Then we cannot take any action that would contradict our orders.'

Margene scowled. 'When it tries to kill me, though, you will make certain to avenge me?'

'Of course,' Chavis replied. He climbed back into the Taurox.

'Sir,' he called to Ulrich, 'I need to inform you that the route we used to get to the plateau has become totally impassable. However, there is another way back that should see us arrive by late afternoon.'

Ulrich shook his head, but did not turn his attention away from the containment chamber. 'It's simply one delay after another.'

'I could use that map of yours.'

'Fine. Just get me back to the lander and off this planet.' He pulled the waterproofed paper from his belt and tossed it over his shoulder. Chavis caught it in one hand.

'As quickly as possible, sir.' Chavis returned to the seat beside Erdon.

Margene climbed up and slammed the hatch shut. Wordlessly, she dropped into the nearest seat and stared into space. It took some time to get the transport turned around. By the time they were under way, the suns were beginning to crest the horizon, and the dialogus had fallen into an exhausted sleep.

The moth was fluttering against the candelabrum. She looked up from her desk where she had been steadfastly copying *Onward, Emperor's Daughters*, one of her favourite hymns, to see the little insect's wings catch fire.

'Why did you do that?' she asked it. 'You should know better. Now you're going to die.'

She dipped her quill in the inkpot, and returned to her calligraphy. Somewhere in the convent above her, she could hear the choir singing each stanza as she wrote it out, which was odd, because the walls in the scriptorium were so thick that normally she couldn't hear anything at all.

The moth continued to beat its wings furiously against the candles, even though it was now nothing but a burnt little husk. She did her best to ignore it, and dipped her quill again. However, now her lovely feather had become one of the sharp, poisoned spines that she had helped pull out of Scion Byrdgon. The inkwell was filled with water. It began to bubble up, spilling all over her parchment. The beautiful lines smeared and ran down the page.

The dead moth finally succeeded in blowing out the candles. She stood up to find a taper and relight them. The floor was covered in water. Stumbling about in the dark, she was unable to find either light or the door. The water continued to rise.

Something wrapped itself around her legs. There was an explosion of pain. She could not see it, but somehow she knew that beneath the rising water, cream-coloured tentacles were burrowing into her flesh. As she floated up to the rafters, more and more tentacles reached up from the depths to devour her. She struggled against them, but they were immensely strong. The water covered her face, and she discovered that it was salty. Above her the choir was still singing, but the lyrics had changed.

'*Promise me, O, promise me, we'll be together soon...*' they sang.

Her lungs burned as she tried to prolong her final breath. The tentacles had now produced razor-sharp claws, and were beginning to slice her legs open. Tiny, unseen mouths were taking bites out of her abdomen and neck. At last, she could stand the agony no more. Her dying scream came out as a stream of muffled bubbles, and then the room shook violently.

Margene startled awake and stared about her. Thieus, the Scion with the replacement hand, was sitting across from her. 'What happened?' she gasped.

'We just drove over something large, that's all.'

She ran a hand through her hair, and looked down the length of the compartment. No one appeared to have moved very much. Ulrich was still seated by his precious specimen, although his head wobbled as if he were on the edge of sleep. Scion Byrdgon's breath came in ragged gasps. His body had begun to emit a rank odour.

There was a sudden *boom*. The Taurox shook as if some giant, petulant hand had picked it up and then thrown it back down. Margene tumbled to the floor. She heard the containment cylinder topple over and strike something. Everything skewed to the left, and she realised that they were spinning. When the Taurox finally came to rest, the air was filled with pungent smoke. Margene held her hands to her nose. Blood was pouring out from between her fingers.

Ulrich was clambering to his feet, cursing loudly. He worked desperately to set the specimen container upright again.

'Another rock?' Margene asked.

Thieus shook his head.

Chavis wheeled around in his chair. 'It sounded like a mine. Scions, gear up and disembark.'

Moments later, Chavis, Erdon, and the others stood outside beneath the blistering twin suns. Erdon had donned a pair of insulated gloves that came up to his shoulders and brought out a large metal case filled with tools. The others had their lasguns at the ready.

The Taurox had come to rest along the perimeter of a circular plaza. A dark blast pattern radiated from the rear left tread assembly. Otherwise, the ground was covered with a dense bed of dried seaweed and fish bones. Patches of lichen bloomed in every nook and cranny. Everything was stained with the powdery white residue of dried salt. The streets were choked with weeds and tumbled blocks of masonry.

They had come down from Mount Loraz and wound their way through a series of wide canyons. The rock walls had been etched with chalky white horizontal stripes, evidence of past water levels. Chavis had been cautious at first. The walls of rock made for short sight-lines, and danger could be around any turn. By mid-morning, however, they had yet to encounter a single soul, and his alertness level decreased. This part of Lysios was apparently uninhabited.

Perhaps abandoned was a better word. They had begun to encounter ancient buildings: a few at first, but then growing in number and density. Chavis checked the inquisitor's map. They were passing along the edge of a small city. Whatever name it might have once gone by had been drowned and lost three thousand years ago. Its once mighty rockcrete towers and walls were now just a series of crumbling foundations and rubble piles, worn smooth by so many passing floods.

Erdon squatted down next to the Taurox. With one hand, he groped behind the damaged section. 'Pressure-sensitive mine, all right.'

'Home built?' Chavis asked.

Erdon shook his head. 'No. This was military.'

'Who would plant explosives out in the middle of nowhere like this?' Devries asked.

'An excellent question,' Chavis said.

'One we don't have time to answer,' Ulrich said. He was standing at the top of the rear boarding ramp. 'Let's move on.'

Erdon withdrew his hand. His glove was stained with some dark liquid. He sniffed it, and then held it aloft. 'Tempestor, that's fuel.'

Chavis lowered his head and exhaled slowly. 'Repairable?'

Erdon stood up. 'Patchable, yes, sir. Enough to get us back to the hab-crawler. But if we've lost too much fuel...'

'I know. Get to it.'

Ulrich threw his hands in the air, and returned to the inside of the transport. Erdon crawled beneath the Taurox while the others kept watch. He worked for nearly half an hour before finally emerging.

'I've managed to patch it, sir,' he told Chavis, 'but there's a fair amount of shrapnel damage underneath.'

'Do we have enough fuel to make it back?'

Erdon shook his head.

'We'll need to consult the inquisitor, then.'

'Consult him about what, exactly?' Ulrich called. He had been sitting just inside the rear ramp.

'About our next move, sir. I would recommend, since our transport no longer has enough fuel to make it back to the lander, that we contact the Battle Sisters and request an evacuation.'

Ulrich stood up and marched down the ramp. 'Absolutely not.'

'Sir, the alternatives are–'

'Tempestor!' Brandt cried. He had perched himself on top of a high mound of moss-covered bricks. He waved a hand in the air, signalling that something was approaching their position.

'Scions,' Chavis barked.

Devries, Savdra, and Thieus hoisted their guns to their shoulders. Erdon quickly dropped his insulated gloves and grabbed his volley gun.

The sound of engines drifted on the wind. With squealing tyres, a trio of groundcars came tearing around the corner of a ruined building. Each one had six wheels and no roof. They were packed with men in uniforms the colour of faded sandstone, with dark blue piping along the seams of their trousers. Their boots and armour were scuffed and weathered. The majority of their weapons appeared to be large-calibre projectile rifles, but Chavis counted at least three serviceable-looking grenade launchers. None of them wore any kind of hat or helmet. Their hands and faces were sunburnt and blistered, and each of them looked as if it had been months since their last good meal.

'Autonomous fire sanctioned!' Chavis yelled.

The groundcars spun wildly, and the men aboard them opened fire. Bullets ricocheted off piles of rock and the armour of the Scions. Two of the uniformed men hoisted a portable rocket launcher between them. The missile they let loose slammed into the side of the Taurox in a thundering ball of fire.

Chavis and the Scions returned fire with everything they had. The four soldiers in the lead groundcar were all struck in the centre of their torsos. The heat of the las-bolts melted their body armour and set their clothing on fire. Erdon had finished readying the volley gun. He struck their car with a howling salvo of las-fire that tore clean through the armour plating around the engine. The vehicle went up in a pillar of smoke and flame.

The soldiers in the other two vehicles sprayed the Scions with bullets. Savdra and Brandt killed two of them for their efforts. Devries jerked and fell onto his back. He clutched at his left arm where a bullet had pierced him through a gap in his armour.

'I'm all right,' he shouted.

The groundcars wheeled around, and began to flee down another street. Erdon fired the volley gun again. Steam began to rise from its heavy casing. Most of the shots struck the street and walls, leaving pools of glass in their wake. One of the groundcars, however, took a direct hit to its rear and exploded. The bodies of its occupants flew up into the air and crashed on the weed-covered pavement.

The third groundcar roared away.

Chavis cut the air with a flattened hand. 'Hold your fire. Move up and hold your fire.'

The Scions sprinted to where the first wreck sat smouldering, and took up a position against a crumbling wall. Chavis grabbed a dead man's boot and pulled him inside a doorway. The tempestor rolled the man's face from side to side, and considered his apparel.

'Professional-grade cloth,' he said. 'And this flak armour isn't something that the average Lysite has access to.'

'His weapon's in decent shape too.' Erdon pointed to a large patch on the corpse's left shoulder. It depicted several bright white stars against a field of dark blue. The number '99' was emblazoned across it in faded yellow. 'What about this?'

'A unit insignia of some kind. I don't recognise it.'

A shadow fell across them and a voice said, 'That's because it hasn't been used for quite some time.'

Erdon and Chavis looked up to Ulrich standing in the doorway. Margene was behind him.

'Only ninety-nine worlds received such emblems for their soldiers, and believe it or not, at one time, Lysios was among them. This man was a member of the Lysios Home Guard.'

Behind him, Margene gave a slight gasp.

'Inquisitor,' Chavis said, getting to his feet, 'you should remain in the Taurox. This is still an active zone.'

Ulrich waved a hand dismissively. 'Those men were driving groundcars. That means they must have some kind of fuel, yes? Fuel we can take and use?'

Chavis nodded. 'Yes, sir. I had the same thought.'

'Inquisitor,' Margene said, 'There was only one unit of trained soldiers on Lysios, and they were all attached to the planetary governor. If these men are here, then the governor must be somewhere nearby. We have to find him.'

'You'd think so,' Ulrich said, 'but in point of fact, we don't.'

'Then let me contact Canoness Grace, and give her the coordinates for this place. The Sisters have been searching for the governor–'

Ulrich cut her off sharply. 'I told you before: we are under a communications blackout. We will speak to no one, because no one is to be informed of our mission here.'

Margene glared at the inquisitor. 'Why?'

Ulrich gave her no answer. 'Tempestor, let's go find where these men have gotten themselves to.'

'Very good, sir. Devries?'

'Yes, tempestor?'

'I want you to stay behind. Seal up the Taurox, and man the cannon. If any more of these men show up...'

'I understand.'

'The rest of you, prepare to move out. This is a search-and-destroy scenario, sigma delta.'

'Sigma delta?' Margene asked quietly. Her eyes remained fixed on the inquisitor.

Chavis removed the ammo clip on his bolt pistol and inspected the first round. 'Urban combat environment, multiple targets.'

CHAPTER SEVEN

Chavis led the way down the ruined street. The tyre tracks were simple enough to follow among the seaweed and algae drifts, and it took them only a few minutes to encounter another attack group. Chavis could hear them fussing with something that sounded large and heavy. He motioned for everyone to stop, and carefully peered around the corner.

Beyond was a small square, hedged in on all sides by tall ruins. Chavis saw a group of soldiers gathered around the cracked base of an ancient fountain.

'Must be a checkpoint. I count two men with rifles, one with a grenade launcher, and what looks like a commanding officer,' he whispered over his vox. 'The last two have set up a crew-served heavy weapon. Looks like an Agrippina-pattern autocannon.'

'Only six of them?' Ulrich scoffed. 'This should be easy.'

Chavis was no stranger to the perils of urban combat. Years of experience had taught him that, within the confines of a city, nothing was easy. And if it appeared to be so, it was usually a trap.

'No,' he said, 'we should bypass this.'

'What?'

'A set-up like this is designed to draw us into any number of hazards. That square could be mined. Could be targeted by snipers. There could be sentry guns hidden on the perimeter. Trust me, sir, when I tell you that there's something amiss here.'

Chavis expected an argument from the inquisitor, and was surprised when he got none. 'All right then, we'll go around.'

Chavis led the group across a shattered cross street and into a low building, gesturing everyone to keep down. Through the empty windows and the holes in the walls, they could catch glimpses of the square and the checkpoint.

The tempestor picked up the groundcar tracks again one block to the north. They turned sharply and vanished down an access tunnel below the street. The tunnel entrance was heavily guarded. Chavis counted three platoons of solders, and at least as many heavy lascannons. All told, there were nearly forty men blocking their path.

'There's no avoiding this one, I take it?' Ulrich asked knowingly.

'That depends, sir. Are you still adamant that you will not contact anyone to come and evacuate us?'

Ulrich stared at the tempestor.

'Then, no, there's no going around this.' Chavis wished briefly that he had more men. But he did not. These four would have to suffice. He moved in between Savdra and Margene. 'A direct charge will see us all killed,' he said. 'We have to hit them on a flank, so that they won't be able to turn their total firepower on us. Erdon, when we get into range, your job is to slag those lascannons.

'Savdra, I want you to stay here with Sister Margene. Your job is to provide distraction fire. Make a lot of noise. Keep them focused here. If they try to get too close to you, give them some grenades.

'Thieus and Brandt, you're with me. We cover Erdon until he gets the volley gun in range, then we close the distance and finish them off.'

Chavis looked at Ulrich and remembered which of them was actually in charge of the mission. 'Is that acceptable, sir?'

'With one exception. I'm coming with you.'

Minutes later, Chavis, Ulrich, and the others had made their way around to the side of the underground entrance. The sound of Margene's boltgun could not be missed and the guards began to return fire, the lascannons blowing holes through the rockcrete around her and Savdra.

Ulrich and Chavis broke from their cover, followed by Brandt and Thieus. Erdon, in the rear with the volley gun, fired a quartet of searing las-beams into the nearest platoon. Three men were blown apart instantly. Brandt and Thieus, as they sprinted forwards, each managed to down two more before the element of surprise was exhausted. Three of the remaining five men wheeled around and fired their rifles. Most of the bullets impacted in the street or ricocheted off into the ruins. One mushroomed off Ulrich's refractor field, millimetres in front of his neck. The two men manning the platoon's lascannon desperately tried to turn it, but by the time they did so, Chavis was lobbing a grenade into their midst. It bounced far past its intended target, and detonated in a cloud of burning shrapnel.

Ulrich was the first to leap into the melee. His sword cleaved the air above the soldiers' heads as they ducked to avoid his blows. Chavis closed to point-blank range and shot the closest man through the heart with his bolt pistol. Brandt, Thieus, and Erdon rushed up behind their tempestor and began savagely beating whoever got in their way.

Margene and Savdra kept up their fire from across the street, but the second platoon of men were no longer fooled. They came charging forward to help their comrades.

Ulrich swept his blade downward, and cut clean through the two men who had avoided him seconds before. Chavis put another bolt through the armour of a soldier, while beside him, Thieus smashed the butt of his lasgun into an opponent's face.

The group that had rushed to reinforce their fellows punched and kicked at

Chavis's tiny assault group for all they were worth. The inquisitor absorbed the majority of their blows, letting them bounce harmlessly off either his refractor field or his ornate armour.

The third lascannon missed striking Margene by only the slimmest of margins. She ducked back down behind the wall she and Savdra were using for cover as the beam punched clean through. Savdra was hit twice in the chest by bullets, but his armour held firm.

Margene and Savdra thinned the remaining platoon while Ulrich continued his murderous spree. Two more soldiers died on his blade. Then three more. Before long, the dead and severely wounded were piling up around him. When the last of the governor's guards attempted to fall back into the tunnel, Ulrich led the charge that cut them down.

Silence swept back into the ruined city. Margene and Savdra emerged from the shattered building covered with a multitude of small cuts and the dust of vaporised rockcrete. Brandt had lost his helmet and was bleeding from a deep gash on his chin. Chavis's leg wound had opened up again. He tore a blue sash from one of the dead soldiers, and tied it tightly over his thigh.

The inquisitor seemed completely unharmed. More than that, Chavis thought, he seemed invigorated. He looked down into the tunnel entrance. 'We should keep moving. Who knows what might be waiting for us?'

Chavis took the lead once again. The group moved underground, past a long-abandoned rail platform. They were forced to stop at four separate junctions where additional tunnels stretched off into the gloom. At each one, Chavis scoured the floor for signs of the groundcar. Eventually, they emerged into a titanic space filled with trains.

At some point in the distant past, this place had been a depot of some kind. Now, it was a museum to decay. High overhead was an arched glass roof, covered in centuries of sediment. The light that filtered through was dim and buttery yellow. The locomotives and rail cars were massive, ornate affairs that had once impressed all who witnessed them. Now they were rusted and encased in salty residue. Everything stank of brine and rot. No fires burned in the trains' reactors, and no lights shone in their carriages.

No, Chavis saw. That wasn't entirely true. He could make out lights near the centre of the space. There was still life to be found here, below the dead cities of Lysios.

In the middle of the train yard was a squat, round building three storeys tall. Guards were posted on either side of the single entryway.

Ulrich surveyed the structure. 'Is this where they're holed up?' he asked. Then, without waiting for an answer, he walked towards the doorway. 'Well, come on then.'

Ulrich shot the two guards before they had time to react. As the Scions pressed in behind him, he kicked the door open. The ground floor of the building was set up as a single large room. Along one wall were a series of empty ticket kiosks. Tables and couches were scattered about. A pair of large signboards that had once hung from the ceiling now lay broken on the floor.

In the centre of the room was a wide spiral staircase. Thudding down it came twenty more soldiers.

Margene, Chavis, and the Scions burst through the door and fanned out to either side of the inquisitor. He charged forward, firing his pistol as he went. The soldiers on the staircase welcomed him with bullets. Ulrich's entourage returned the overture with las-fire and bolts. Heat poured off Erdon's volley gun as it fired.

Ulrich reached the bottom of the stairs and slashed the throats of two men. Then the rest were leaping down at him, hoping to knock him back under the press of their bodies. He twisted and turned. His sword tore through protective plates. Bodies began to fall off the sides of the staircase.

Chavis called his men into close assault, and the five of them pressed in beside Ulrich. Ulrich began to bleed from a cut above his eye, but the initiative remained with the inquisitor. The soldiers tried to retreat back to the second floor. Ulrich and Chavis swept their legs out from under them, and killed them.

Ulrich sheathed his sword. 'We need to search this entire building,' he said. 'Margene and I will start down here, the rest of you secure the upper floors.'

Chavis saluted with his fist over his heart, and led his men to the upstairs. They had only been gone a minute or two when Thieus came charging back down. He pointed at Margene. 'You need to see this.'

Margene glanced toward Ulrich, but the inquisitor was occupied within one of the abandoned kiosks.

She followed him to the third floor. The ceiling was a filthy dome of stained glass. The rest of the room was dominated by a carved metal desk large enough to accommodate half a dozen men. Seated behind it in a high-backed chair was what she at first glance took to be a mummified corpse. There was a single hole, the size of a bolt, in the centre of its chest. It was a man, or had been at some point. His skin was like vellum. There were strange machines all around him, connected to him by transparent tubes, coloured cables, and suction pads.

Everywhere, there was paper. Reams and reams, piled in stacks and rolled up into scrolls. Boxes upon boxes were filled to overflowing with sheaves. It was more than Margene had seen in her entire life.

All the Scions, save Chavis, had their weapons levelled at the man behind the desk. The tempestor gestured to the machinery and paper mountains. 'What is all this?'

Margene plucked a handful of sheets from the box nearest her. Each page was densely packed with words written in a tiny, perfect script.

'This was done by machine,' she said. 'I would say that all of this has been dictated into a transcriber.'

'But what is it?'

Margene flipped through the pages she had in her hand. Along the top of each one were the same two words in bold print: '*Cantos Continuous.*'

'What?'

'It's High Gothic. It means "everlasting song". It seems to be the title for all of this.' She read on a bit more. It quickly became obvious to her that these writings were supposed to have come from the Brine Goddess. It could hardly be called poetry. It was more like a series of incoherent ramblings. 'This is Shelsist literature. All of it. Emperor save us.' She dropped the pages to the floor, and crossed to the desk. She noted that the tall chair had obscured two additional rooms. One contained a large bed covered in mouldy sheets. The other held two smaller chairs and what appeared to be some kind of very old communications array.

She picked up another sheaf and riffled through them. 'These seem to be more recent,' she said, 'but they're just as nonsensical.'

Chavis seemed satisfied. 'As long as there's no danger here, we need to see about finding a drum or two of fuel.'

Margene nodded absently. 'I'll be fine. I just want to sort through some of this before we go.'

Chavis, Erdon, and Thieus left. Margene barely noticed.

Her eyes were fixed on the parchment sheet in her hand. Printed near the top, just below the title bar, was yet another paragraph wherein Shelse called out to Ixoi. What frightened Margene, however, was that she had heard it before.

'Promise me, O, promise me,' she read, 'we'll be together soon. The stars begin to fall, and this era draws to a close...'

It wasn't possible. There was no way that she could have dreamed these exact words. Yet here they were. The Shelsist leaders had received them and transcribed them, and she too had received them somehow. She thought about the Brine Prophet that the Canoness had encountered months before. Canoness Grace had said the man was possessed, that he was channelling an evil presence, and speaking as if on behalf of the Brine Goddess.

Was that what had been happening here, she wondered? Had the former Governor allowed Shelse to speak through him? Had he set down every awful word, and then passed it on to the cult at large? Very likely. But it still didn't explain how the words had come into her mind.

She looked into the comms room again.

Chavis, Erdon, and Thieus found a garage one level below the ground floor. Only one of the Governor's converted groundcars was there, although Thieus was the one who pointed out that there was room enough for twenty more such vehicles. In one corner, beneath a sheet of waterproof canvas, they found three crates filled with spearguns, and two empty cases for explosives. They also found a cache of fuel drums. They hefted one of the barrels into the back of the car, and Erdon started the engine and drove it up into the darkened railway tunnels. Brandt and Savdra met them outside the main depot building.

'Where's Ulrich?' Chavis asked them.

'He went to get the dialogus,' Savdra replied. 'Told us to come out here and cover you.'

There was an explosion from inside the main depot building and a shattering of glass. The five men raced inside. The ground floor was empty, but the smell of smoke and burnt flesh wafted down to them from above.

They emerged at the top of the stairs to find the room on fire. Part of the stained-glass ceiling had been smashed in. The gigantic desk was turned over on its side, and everywhere the *Cantos Continuous* burned. The bodies of five more Lysios Home Guard lay in heaps among the blaze. Chavis found the inquisitor on the floor near the bed. He seemed dazed.

'Inquisitor,' he shouted, 'are you wounded?'

'I'm all right.' Ulrich refused help as he returned to standing. 'They came in through there. Took us by surprise.'

'Where's the dialogus?'

Thieus ran into one of the adjacent rooms, and emerged dragging Margene beneath the arms. Her skin was blackened and cracked, and jagged pieces of shrapnel jutted out of her arms and legs. She left a trail of blood as Thieus dragged her.

She wheezed loudly, turned her blind, lidless eyes towards Ulrich, and died.

Thieus lowered his head.

Ulrich kicked something heavy across the floor.

Chavis saw that it was a man-portable grenade launcher, and a likely picture of events formed in his mind. Another unit of the governor's guards had come in through the roof. They had surprised the inquisitor and Sister Margene. In the ensuing fight, someone had used explosives in a confined space. The end result couldn't be anything less than death. It was all very neat.

He reminded himself once again that there was almost always something misleading about things which appeared to be simple.

'Her body,' Ulrich said. 'Perhaps we should take it with us, and return it to her sisters.'

Chavis blinked. This mission had so far cost the lives of eleven Tempestus Scions, and not once had Ulrich suggested that their corpses be recovered.

'Why would we do that, sir? Sentiment is a waste of time and resources. We need to focus all our resources on getting you back to the hab-crawler.'

Ulrich said nothing further. He simply walked past the burning stacks of the *Cantos* and down the stairs to the waiting groundcar.

Before they arrived back at the Taurox, Chavis's monitor informed him that Byrdgon had died. While Erdon and Thieus filled the tank with the pilfered fuel, Chavis took a moment to peer into the containment cylinder. The tentacle segment was lying very still, the cilia flaccid. He did not know why, but he felt certain it, in its own way, was staring back at him.

'Let's be on our way, tempestor,' Ulrich said. 'Leave the xenology to the experts.'

'Yes, sir.'

The hatches closed, the engine started, and the transport rumbled away from the nameless city. Above them, in the clear sky, a flaming object fell, trailing black smoke behind it. It was followed shortly by another.

Then another.

Then another.

'The time has come, the sky descends! The Murderess and her agents must be destroyed, so that a new world may be born. Your Goddess commands it...'

– Cantos Continuous, M41

CHAPTER EIGHT

Erdon's right eye was black and swollen, his hands red and blistered from handling the volley gun. Chavis had smeared his upper leg with an autocauterising thermic gel, sealing his wound with a thick layer of scar tissue. It itched beneath its dressing. Neither man complained. In fact, neither man had said anything since leaving the ruined city.

Behind them, the other passengers were quiet as well. Ulrich had gone back to his place beside the containment chamber. Devries had the Martyr's Gift medi-kit open on the seat next to him as he dug the bullet out of his arm and covered the hole with suture tape. Savdra and Thieus sat across from one another, helmets off and heads down.

The silence was broken when the air outside was filled with a high-pitched screaming that grew in volume. Everyone in the Taurox heard it. The Scions snapped to a state of alertness, for it sounded exactly like a bomb falling from a great height.

The sound grew into a roar. Brandt, Thieus, Devries, and Savdra each looked out of one of the viewing slots above their heads. They saw no sign of any missile coming towards them, but they did see a fireball. The nucleus was a large, dark mass, wreathed in orange flames. It trailed sonic booms as it passed overhead, and the Taurox rocked from side to side. The fireball landed several kilometres to the south of them, sending up a titanic cone of dirt and shaking the ground.

'Just a meteor,' Devries said as he sat back down.

'That was actually fairly close,' Erdon said.

'It was,' Chavis agreed. 'I'm going up to the turret to take a look.' He opened the hatch above his head and raised his chair.

The wind that battered Chavis's face was hot and smelled of ash. The impact crater to the south sent a pillar of grey smoke into the air. Aside from that, however, the land stretched out dead and flat from horizon to horizon. Centuries of oceanic flooding had erased any hills or valleys that might have once been here, and left the land so salted that not even the hardiest of weeds could survive. The sky above was pale blue and cloudless, but stained by multiple smoky black lines.

Chavis tried to recall if Lysios was known for particularly violent or spectacular meteor storms. The dialogus would have known, he thought. If only she hadn't died.

Behind him, the Taurox sent up a tall plume of dust as it sped across the wasteland. It made them an easy potential target. While he considered ordering Erdon to slow down, he noticed that theirs was not the only dust cloud being generated. He retracted the seat back down inside the Taurox and sealed the hatch.

'It's possible that we're being followed,' he said.

Ulrich suddenly looked worried. 'We're being followed?'

'Possibly, I said.'

'By whom?'

'I can't tell. They're quite some distance behind us.'

'Threat level?' Erdon asked.

Chavis shook his head. 'Minimal, if any at all. They won't catch up. Whatever it is they're travelling in isn't nearly fast enough.'

The meteors continued to streak across the sky, growing in frequency with every passing hour. Chavis checked behind them regularly and the other vehicles, whomever they belonged to, continued to follow along. Shortly after noon, the hab-crawler came into view. From the ground, it appeared as a gigantic block of machinery that rumbled along slowly on mammoth treads. The settlement proper rode on top like a collection of low buildings built on the back of a turtle. Access ramps trailed behind it. When they had left the crawler the previous day, these ramps had been clear. Now, they were packed with rickety carts and hundreds of people on foot. Men, women, and children were pushing and shoving one another, all trying to make their way up the ramps and onto the crawler.

'Reduce speed, tempestor?' Erdon asked.

'We haven't the time. Plough through. They'll move. Or not.'

Ulrich had risen from his seat beside the cylinder and made his way to the front. He peered through the front window slits at the tumultuous crowd. 'Use your smoke launchers,' he said. 'They'll scatter.'

Erdon said nothing, but simply thumbed a series of switches on the control panel before him. From either side of the vehicle, there came a soft chuffing sound. Metal canisters bounced into the crowd and began spewing thick clouds of choking grey smoke. Gasping, the people drew back.

The Taurox ascended the ramp, and turned onto the winding street that led to the landing field. This too was filled with people. They poured out from the patchwork buildings and gathered on the low rooftops, pointing up to the sky where fiery black streaks now fell like rain.

The mob only worsened as they approached the field. All around them were people laden with bags and cases, or bundles of clothing and provisions wrapped hastily with plastek cords. They were shouting and crying. Many of them were pressed up against the metal fence that cordoned off the landing field from the rest of the hab-crawler. On the other side of the chain-link, the

Battle Sisters had established two semi-circular barricades with three women behind each. An additional pair of women stood just inside the single entryway.

Erdon did not slow the Taurox at all until they came to the gate. Chavis spied a few weapons in the crowd: long, barbed poles, spearguns, and even a few of the kinetic bullet rifles the governor's guard had used. He could also hear something of what the people were shouting. They were screaming at the Sisters to save them, or to do something, or to let them come in and board the shuttle. The two Sisters rolled the gate open, and shut it once more as the Taurox passed.

The Canoness emerged from the doorway of the control tower, flanked by two Battle Sisters armed with storm bolters. The three of them walked with determined strides directly into the path of the Taurox. Erdon brought the vehicle to a screeching halt just as the front grille of the engine housing touched the Canoness's chest plate. She stared up into the front viewing slits with a look of indignant fury.

Ulrich felt a twinge of anxiety. 'Here are your orders, gentlemen,' Ulrich said, loud enough for all of the Scions to hear. 'I want the containment cylinder taken aboard the lander at once. Then, contact our ship in orbit and tell them that we will be returning within the hour. Do not let Canoness Grace or any of her Sororitas get in your way, or attempt to slow you down. This is our mission. Not theirs.'

He exited through the rear ramp, pausing for a moment to rest his hand on the cylinder. The tentacle within had long since stopped moving. It was regrettable, he thought. A living specimen would have been a much more impressive prize than a deceased sample.

When Ulrich stepped onto the landing field, the Canoness and her two charges came around the side of the Taurox and blocked his path. 'So,' she said sternly, 'I see you have returned.' Her eyes flashed down to the blackened metal plating behind the repaired quad tracks.

'Indeed, Canoness,' Ulrich said. His tone was cordial with a touch of venom. 'You'll be happy to know that my mission was a success. I'm sure you've been praying for me.'

Canoness Grace watched as Thieus, Brandt, Savdra and Devries exited down the ramp and fell in behind Ulrich. 'Where is Sister Margene?'

Ulrich met the Canoness's withering gaze and said simply, 'She died.'

Canoness Grace lifted her chin slightly. 'How?'

'Heroically.' Ulrich could tell that she was waiting for him to elaborate, but he said nothing more. Neither of them blinked. At the gate, the crowd grew louder. Several more of the meteors streaked across the sky.

Erdon and Chavis began to bring the containment cylinder down. The sight of it caused Canoness Grace to speak at last. 'What is that?'

'That,' Ulrich said, 'is the concern of the Inquisition, and not the Adepta Sororitas.' He turned his back to her and walked away to join Chavis and Erdon.

'Inquisitor Ulrich!' she shouted. 'I know that you are here conducting the business of the Ordo Xenos. If that container has anything to do with an alien life form, I demand to know about it!'

Ulrich whirled around, incredulous. 'You demand? Did I not just say that this was no business of yours?'

Canoness Grace pushed her way past the four Scions before her. 'Everything that takes place on this world is my business. I am in charge of all operations on Lysios.'

'Then I am happy to inform you that I am leaving Lysios.'

The Canoness thrust a finger at Chavis and Erdon. 'You two, open that container for inspection.'

The two Scions exchanged a glance, but did not stop.

Ulrich couldn't help but smile when he saw the Canoness's face go livid. 'Gentlemen,' he called to Savdra, Thieus, Devries, and Brandt, 'time to go.'

The four Scions started moving towards the lander's boarding ramp. Ulrich gave the Canoness a curt nod, and turned his back to her once again.

The inquisitor and the Scions were at the foot of the lander when all eight of the Canoness's command squad moved in and blocked their way. Their boltguns were in positions of readiness. Chavis and Erdon stopped, and set the cylinder down. Ulrich slowed his pace and turned around to find Canoness Grace glaring at him.

Chavis caught the eyes of his men. Slowly, he lowered his hand to hover above the butt of his bolt pistol. Erdon and the others gave nods that were almost imperceptible. The moment this degenerated into a firefight, they would be ready.

'Tell your Sisters to clear out of our way,' Ulrich said to Canoness Grace.

'Show me what you have in that canister,' she replied.

Ulrich grasped the pommel of his sword. 'No.'

Chavis heard the sound of something striking a metal surface. He glanced around, certain that one of the Battle Sisters was responsible. They were standing perfectly still, filled with tension. The noise, he realised, had come from inside the containment cylinder.

'If you won't open it,' the Canoness said to Ulrich, 'then I will.'

Chavis saw movement behind the glass. He opened his mouth to speak when suddenly, the tentacle slammed itself against the container. It twitched, and its cilia started waving. Its skin glowed from within as it drove its consciousness like a thunderbolt into Canoness Grace's mind.

CHAPTER NINE

Dessecran was a night world. For ten months out of the year, the tiny planet lay in the shadow of two gas giants. For the other three months, however, the sun shone bright and clear. None of this mattered to Magda Grace, though, because she was underground where the day would never break.

The sewers ran for kilometres in all directions. Some of them were big enough to drive a tank through, while others could barely accommodate a single person. What they all had in common were the constant drip of water, the flickering lumens built at even spaces along their length, and the monsters.

Grace was thirty-two years old. She was a humble Battle Sister, and her hair was still as black as pitch. She stood ankle-deep in raw sewage, but the stench didn't bother her. She had been down here for so long that she was immune to it now. In her hands she cradled a storm bolter with double clips and a halogen light strapped to the top. Eight more magazines dangled from her belt. To her left and right, the bodies of nineteen fellow Sororitas bobbed in the mire. She was the lone survivor.

The monsters had arrived months before, raining down from the sky in bloated, slime-coated pods. At first, the people of Dessecran had thought that it was a meteor shower, but they were soon proved wrong. The pods cracked open, releasing millions of horrors that bit, and scratched, and slaughtered, and fed.

Dessecran was being invaded by tyranids.

Rumours persisted that the Imperial Navy was on its way. Any day now, people said, a flotilla of starships would arrive in orbit and several million Imperial Guardsmen would liberate the cities. Those rumours had been circulating for eight months now. Grace doubted they would ever come true. So, the defence of Dessecran was left up to the Sororitas of the local convent. She, and others like her, were the only ones holding things together on this world.

The creature Grace was stalking was a specialised member of the warrior caste. The xenobiologists, before they had all been killed, had called it a lictor. These beasts could move swiftly and soundlessly through nearly any terrain, and were excellent at hiding. They liked to stalk individual prey, corner them, and then devour their brains. No one on Dessecran was certain why this was, but rumour had it that by eating the brain, the creature stole the memories of the person being killed. It was certainly not beyond reason. The tyranids had displayed all manner of strange and hideous abilities since they first made planetfall. Some of them, it was said, even used sleeper agents to corrupt and take over religious enclaves.

Grace had been pursuing this particular creature for some time now, ever since it had ambushed her Canoness and devoured her brain. Every member of the convent had sworn revenge. Although it had been wounded many times, every Sister who had gone after the beast was now dead.

She wheeled around just in time to see the lictor drop from somewhere up above her. She fired her weapon. A cluster of bolts struck its chest. Bits of chitin and soupy blobs of pus exploded outward. It made a gibbering sound that might have been a cry of agony, and lashed at her with its claws. Grace tried to move aside, but the water slowed her down. The armour plates around her right shoulder were broken clean away. Ceramite fragments flew up into her face. She squeezed her eyes closed, but when she opened them again, her vision was obscured with blood. The skin above her eye and on her cheek felt as if it were on fire.

Above the lictor's shoulders sprouted a pair of segmented, serrated spikes. It drove both of them down at her. By all rights, Grace should have been ripped into three vertical sections. But her armour held fast. She thanked the Emperor, and struck the beast again in the face with her hefty storm bolter. Once more, her efforts seemed in vain.

The lictor's claws flashed across her chest like giant scissors. Grace staggered back with the impact. She glanced down, expecting to see her guts push their way out of the lacerations and spill like discarded waste into the sewer water. Instead, her breastplate was barely scratched.

'*Blessed is He who is my shield,*' she recited. '*Truly, the Emperor protects those who call upon Him.*'

Seconds went by with neither one of them able to inflict damage upon the other. Grace began to get the impression that the lictor was becoming angry and frustrated, if such a thing were possible.

The lictor lunged at her. She twisted to one side, and jammed the barrel of her storm bolter down against the side of its face. She pulled the trigger. The sound was deafening in the enclosed space. The dead bulk of the thing dropped into the stinking wet. She looked down at herself in awe. Her armour was torn in multiple places, but only her shoulder plate had given way. The side of her face burned like hellfire, but she considered it a blessing. From this day forward, as long as she lived, she would venerate the Emperor who had blessed her armour to such a degree, and she would eradicate the tyranid threat wherever it dared to show itself.

The Canoness staggered backwards, clutching her head. It took a moment for her to remember that she was an iron woman of eighty-three, not a thirty-two year old novice, and that she was on Lysios, not Dessecran. She touched the scar that ran along the side of her face. The creature in the containment chamber had used some kind of mental power on her, violating her thoughts and memories. The attack had taken only a heartbeat, but in that flicker of time, they had been linked.

'Inquisitor,' she said, 'order these Scions to step aside. This specimen of yours has got to be destroyed.'

'I'll do no such thing,' Ulrich said.

Grace exhaled, well aware of the chain reaction that she was about to start. She pulled the plasma pistol from her holster and aimed it at the containment cylinder. In a blur of motion, Ulrich had his own pistol in his hand, levelled at the Canoness. Chavis drew his weapon. The Battle Sisters hoisted their bolters. The five Scions raised their lasguns.

'Put down your weapon, Canoness,' Ulrich said slowly. 'This canister is coming back with me to Terra.'

Grace blanched. 'To Terra? Are you mad? That would mean the end of everything. Don't you know what this thing is?'

'Proof of a legend. And the start of a new future for me.'

'No. No, I cannot allow this.'

Just as she began to squeeze the trigger, her weapon was knocked from her hand. She blinked. The inquisitor had dashed forward and disarmed her far faster than she had ever expected. She drew her sword. Ulrich jumped to avoid the blade as it left her scabbard.

The Canoness charged, ducking low. She slammed her entire weight into Ulrich, and sent the man tumbling. His gun clattered to the ground. He rolled, and sprang back to his feet. His own blade was out.

The Sisters and the Scions regarded one another, and backed away. By some unspoken consensus, they formed a rough circle around their respective champions. Both the Canoness and the inquisitor were wielding power weapons, and both of them were highly skilled fighters. The matter would be settled very quickly, and with at least a semblance of honour. There was no need for them to become involved.

Ulrich thrust at the Canoness once, twice, and a third time. She managed to parry the first two attacks, but the final one got past her. He lunged and then withdrew. For a second, she wasn't sure that she'd been wounded at all. But as he danced backwards, sword held straight out before him, Grace could see blood dripping from his blade. She hadn't even felt it bypass her armour and its blessed wards.

Grace swung at Ulrich again, hoping to lop off his legs. Instead, her blade edge stopped millimetres away from his flesh, and bounced away. There was a slight rippling around the area, like sunlight playing over water.

Grace scowled at his use of a personal force field. 'A bit dishonest of you to use a refractor in a duel,' she said.

Ulrich shrugged, and charged forward. He and Grace collided again in a flurry of slashes and parries. Sparks flew as their weapons touched. Then they were apart once again, surveying one another coldly.

The Canoness was panting, which she thought odd. She was in excellent shape for a woman of her age. She glanced down at herself to see that Ulrich had rent her armour just below her collar bone. She snarled.

Ulrich, for his part, shot the Canoness a look of pure, undiluted hatred, and then toppled to the ground. His chestplate was slashed clean through from left to right, and blood began to gush through the rent. He gave a grunt of disbelief, dropped his sword, and clasped both hands over the wound.

Grace sheathed her sword, and went to collect his pistol from where it had fallen.

'Scions,' Ulrich croaked, 'kill them.'

Grace froze, kneeling over her gun with hand outstretched. Slowly, she lifted her face.

Across the landing field, the people pressed against the fence screamed and tried to scatter. A groundcar ploughed through them at top speed, sending bodies flying, and smashed its way through the gate. The Scions recognised its make. It was exactly like the ones they had encountered earlier in the day.

The car barrelled straight towards them. Without a word, the Scions and the Sisters turned their weapons on it. Sister Fayhew's heavy bolter spat out round after fist-sized round. Erdon's volley gun tore three of the passengers apart. Superior Cairista and Sister Paniece, the newly-promoted bearer of the flame, covered it with gouts of promethium flame. Within seconds, the car crumpled under the combined firepower and exploded. Flaming pieces of metal radiated outwards.

Through the collapsed gate, a wave of bodies began to pour onto the field. Grace saw that many of them were dressed in the blue robes and modified diving gear of the Shelsist cult.

Grace picked up her pistol. 'Sisters, kill the heretics!' She glanced back at Chavis.

'Scions,' he shouted. 'Autonomous fire! Push them back!'

Erdon and the others rushed forward, firing their lasguns. They were joined by the Battle Sisters, who advanced on the breach with a storm of bolter fire. Yet the cultists did not break or flee. They flew apart and crumpled and turned to ashes, but onward they came, pouring through the breach. Their resolve was insane.

Two more of the disgraced governor's groundcars came flying through the collapsed gate. They skidded to a halt, and from each of them, eight figures leapt out. They might have once been human, but they were obviously no longer so. Some of them had hands that were tipped with elongated claws. Others had an additional set of arms sprouting from their ribcages. Their skin all showed varying degrees of mutation, and all of it appeared aquatic in nature: scales, shells, and tentacles covered them in haphazard places. They began to sprint forward.

Grace's sword was in her hand, still stained with the inquisitor's blood. Las-fire and bolts flew all around her, glass and flaming debris crunched beneath her heeled boots.

The mutants came at her with their claws bared. With rapid swipes, they cut at her face and chest. She lopped the head off of one of them, and impaled a second one through the centre of his chest. They attempted to surround her, so that she couldn't hope to stop them all, and pounced. Grace kicked and shoved at them. Something struck her on the top of her head and opened a wide gash. She flipped her sword around and thrust it into the soft belly of someone behind her.

There were too many of them, she realised, and their awful, hybrid nature made them faster than she. She calmly accepted the possibility that this was going to be her final fight. Then, through the blood that smeared her face, she could see that the Scions had joined her. The six of them fought with powerful, exacting moves, blocking the attacks of the mutants until they spied an opening that they could exploit. They kicked, and stamped, and used the bulk of their firearms to bash in skulls. It was a style of fighting completely different from any the Sororitas used, but in that moment, Grace was thankful for it.

From the sky came a deafening screech. A fireball plunged down from the heavens and impacted the hab-crawler very near to the landing field. The plates beneath their feet shook with the impact.

'Meteor,' Chavis yelled.

The Canoness shook her head. 'Those are no mere rocks. They're a sign. Something terrible is about to come upon us.'

As if to illustrate her point, another dark object slammed into the Taurox with a terrible velocity. The transport crumpled and detonated. The shockwave knocked everyone from their feet. Fire and smoke obscured everything.

The object in the centre of the flames cracked along one side. Thick mucus gushed out, bubbling in the heat. Another crack appeared. One entire side of the massive egg-shape gave way, and a dozen alien shapes spilled out onto the field. Through the burning haze, Chavis saw that the Canoness was correct. The things falling from the sky were hollow pods, not solid hunks of rock. The things inside were half as tall as a man, with long tails and scythe-like talons in place of hands. Their heads were bulbous, with tooth-crammed, oversized mouths. Armour plates covered their backs. They stretched their jaws wide, and made guttural, utterly inhuman noises.

A group of twenty or more Shelsists seemed to catch their glinting black eyes. The creatures darted off towards the cultists, leaping up to slash them with their bony, bladed front limbs. Compared to their attackers, the Shelsists reacted with glacial slowness. Their spears and tridents were knocked aside with ease. The creatures pounced on them, knocking them to the ground with a combination of speed and body weight. Then they hacked the Shelsists to pieces and rabidly began to eat the remains.

The roar of turbines drowned out the world as the lander's engines began to cycle up. Grace and Chavis simultaneously looked at the place where the inquisitor had been lying. He was gone, along with the canister. The engine bells began to glow. They had only moments before the lander lifted itself skywards, and they were all vaporised by its rocket exhaust.

'Get up!' Chavis yelled. 'All of you, on your feet.'

Grace pointed to the control tower. Several of the Sisters nodded and stumbled towards it. Chavis helped Erdon and Devries, and the three of them ran for the control tower doorway.

Everywhere was madness. The Shelsists continued to pour through the fence. They fired harpoons and spears at the lander. Another meteor impacted near the hab-crawler, destroying one of its treads. The entire community shuddered and ground to a halt. Steam pipes and fuel lines burst, spewing geysers of fire and water into the air.

The Scions and Sisters scrambled into the control tower. Chavis slammed the heavy blast door shut. The space was small and cramped. A staircase spiralled upwards. Outside, the Shelsists were being torn to ribbons by the scythe-limbed monstrosities.

Seconds later, the lander's engines ignited and bathed the field with superheated clouds.

They made their way up the stairs. At the top of the tower was a circular control room. A single door led out onto the roof of an adjacent building. Chavis and the Canoness ran out through it. The landing field below them was littered with corpses and smouldering craters. The scythe-limbed aliens were nothing now but blackened husks. At the gate, a fresh wave of Shelse's followers began running towards the control tower door.

In the sky above, the lander continued to rise on a plume of rocket exhaust, taking the inquisitor with it.

The Sisters and the Scions joined their respective leaders. All around them, their enemies' numbers grew and grew. The small rooftop was becoming an island inundated by a murderous sea.

'What are your orders, Canoness?' Chavis said.

Grace touched her forehead, her chest, and hilt of her sword. The Sororitas mirrored her.

'We fight, of course,' Grace said.

Chavis nodded grimly and pointed down at the mass of cultists, mutants, and renegade soldiers. 'Scions,' he shouted, 'directed firestorm sanctioned!'

Grace raised her blade above her head. 'Emperor, grant ascension! Sisters, strike them down!'

Together they attacked the horde before them with las-fire and bolt, while all across the hab-crawler, meteor pods continued to impact, crack open and vomit out their murderous cargo into the streets and buildings.

CODA

The canister had been a considerable load for two Tempestus Scions to carry between them. It was nearly impossible for Damien Ulrich. The exertion of dragging it up the lander's boarding ramp was causing him to bleed out, he knew. His wounds were covering everything with a slick film of blood. His vision began to swim. Still, he refused to give up; not when victory was close at hand.

At last he managed to reach the top of the ramp. He slammed his fist into the door controls, and staggered to the cockpit as the ramp slowly closed behind him. He sat down heavily in the pilot's chair, activated the launch sequence, and then reached under the control board. It took him two tries to open the emergency medi-pack. As the engines began to come to life, he grasped a thick hypodermic injector, squeezed his eyes shut, and stabbed himself in the stomach with it.

The elixir within the syringe flowed into his wounds like liquid fire. He pushed his head back into the seat's deep cushions and gasped with pain. Outside, the lander's engines ignited. The landing field was consumed in clouds of burning gas. The lander shook violently all around him.

Something clipped the lander as it rose into the air, sending it spinning wildly. Ulrich's eyes shot open, and for a moment his agony was forgotten. He grasped the controls and steadied the craft.

Outside the viewports, the skies of Lysios were choked with dark, misshapen objects. They rained down surrounded by wreaths of fire, and impacted on the surface below. Ulrich knew exactly what they were. He was of the Ordo Xenos, after all.

The atmosphere outside began to thin from blue to black. Ulrich put his head back again, and gave a weak laugh.

'The Shattered World,' he said aloud, knowing now what the Emperor's Tarot had been trying to tell him.

As the pain began to abate, exhaustion took over. Well, no matter, he thought. Very soon, he would dock with the ship that had brought him here, and he could relax all the way back to Terra. His chin sank down to this chest. He did not hear the tentacle banging against the inside of the containment cylinder, nor did he hear it smash its way free. He was too busy dreaming of the fine reception that would no doubt await him upon his return, and of the rewards he was sure to reap.

DEVOURER

JOE PARRINO

CHAPTER ONE

Anrakyr the Traveller was caked in the blood of men. The organic liquid dripped across his skeleton, red and glistening. He could still hear the screams of the dying creatures, still hear them begging and pleading. They shouted prayers with their meat-voices to some deific being.

It was a waste of breath and a waste of their final moments. Nothing awaited them after death. Anrakyr cared nothing for their prayers or their begging. He merely watched as the humans aspirated blood and the life drained from their weeping eyes. His unblinking visage of death gazed upon them without mercy.

Anrakyr the Traveller, would-be overlord of the necrons, descended upon Kehlrantyr in an orgy of death. He brought order. He brought certainty.

Kehlrantyr was infested. It was infested with grey buildings and grey people.

'What dull creatures, living in their own filth,' Anrakyr mused. No response met him. The sentient necrons within his forces were out of range, venting their fury upon the humans. Only the dull-witted warriors surrounded him, marching through the streets and avenues of Kehlrantyr's human stain.

Necron phalanxes smashed through those buildings and those people. Necron warriors turned gauss weaponry on fleeing masses of humans. Bodies carpeted the roads. Fires broke out, sending smoke into the turquoise sky.

Resistance began lightly. Isolated bands of humans fired primitive laser rifles upon marching steel. Then their resolve stiffened. Machines, armoured boxes on wheels, rolled out to fire weak shots into colossal monoliths. Obsidian flanks chipped, but ultimately the human artillery affected nothing. The necron forces rolled down the broad avenues of the human settlement, tearing up the poured stone that served as road material. Human soldiers advanced alongside.

Anrakyr sprinted into them, the metal of his feet clinking against the stone. The Traveller stabbed his lance through the crew compartment of one of the vehicles, laughed as eldritch energies tore the humans sheltering within to dripping hunks. Something exploded inside, some rough human ammunition touched off by the actinic fury of his warscythe. The vehicle broke into millions of pieces of metal and fire. Anrakyr was propelled back, slamming into one of the grey buildings. He flew through the walls, past crying and weeping animals, hiding in their dens.

The Traveller pulled himself to his feet. He could hear bellowing outside.

The sounds were deep, registering low on the human wavelengths. Anrakyr spared no glance for the cringing organics that ran screaming away from him, deeper into the building. Paintings and human pictoglyphs covered the walls. Metal rusted. Grime gathered.

'Filthy, filthy animals,' Anrakyr cursed. He strode back into the sunlight, skirts of chain-linked metal rustling about his legs.

Rubble shifted beneath his feet as he emerged into the bright light. Already, curious necron warriors, led by dull glimmers of guiding instinct, were pulling themselves into the buildings. Static blurted from between their clenched jaws.

Standing outside were the three triarch praetorians who followed the Traveller.

'Space Marines,' said Khatlan.

Dovetlan added, 'There are human Space Marines active on this world.'

'How did you come by this information?' asked Anrakyr.

They provided no answer. They stood, smug and silent. 'Odious constructs,' he hissed. Again they offered no response. Spies of the Silent King posing as his emissaries to the Pyrrhian overlord, they assured Anrakyr that they served the glory of the necron race. Perhaps that was true. But where did they judge that glory to lie?

A renewed bout of screaming came from behind Anrakyr as he set foot upon the concourse again. Warriors were striding into the hole after him.

Vehicles burned all around him, casting deep palls of smoke into the bright blue sky. Necron warrior phalanxes and hovering destroyers faced something through the smoke. They waited, filled with the patience of the grave.

Cylindrical objects fell on parabolic arcs into the necron mass, and bounced off warrior chassis, unnoticed. Anrakyr was already running, casting orders for the warriors to disperse and spread out their forces. It was too late. The warriors, dull-witted, lobotomised by the c'tan's bargain, began to react, but too slowly.

Fire and shrapnel erupted, tearing through milling warriors, breaking sentient necron commanders into shards of spinning metal. More of the objects exploded. More necron warriors fell.

Bullets came tearing out of the smoke, smashing into struggling necrons. Gauss rifles responded, firing into the veil of darkness. A brace of night shrouds roared overhead, setting the smoke to roiling, dropping death spheres down onto whatever lurked beyond Anrakyr's vision. The anti-matter laden munitions consumed the smoke, annihilating the carbon particles and tearing through reality.

The Traveller pumped his warscythe into the air, signalling the advance for his scattered and reeling forces. Implacable as the tide, the phalanxes reformed and marched forward.

Grotesquely armoured meat-creatures, the human elite, came sprinting through the smoke and rubble.

'Space Marines,' Anrakyr cursed. The triarch praetorians had been right.

They cannoned into the necron line, weaponry buzzing and screaming. A spearhead had barrelled through his phalanxes, driving a wedge into the advancing necrons. Explosives tore struggling warriors apart. Humming swords carved through the necron bodies in showers of sparks.

A knot of giant necron immortals, prized soldiers in Anrakyr's army, the remnants of lost Pyrrhia, met the human wedge. They anchored Anrakyr's line, blunting the assault on his phalanxes. Their gauss blasters punched through the armour, tearing into the flesh beneath. Humans faltered and fell, torn into steaming pieces by the disciplined fire of the immortals. One of the hulking warriors toted a tesla carbine. Lightning cascaded from the weapon, tearing through multiple bodies.

A flight of Space Marines dropped from the sky, fire ripping from their backpacks. Axes hammered at the immortals, punching through their chassis and breaking their metal bones.

Anrakyr waded towards their position, knowing that if the immortals were defeated then his warriors would be hard pressed to achieve victory here. Frustration flowed through the Traveller. His warscythe rose and fell with economical movements, cracking through the green armoured shell of the animals. Before he could reach the immortals, the human leader showed itself. It was coated in ornate armour, wrought in green and gold. The motif of a skull and star was repeated across the plates.

Organic gibbering emerged from the animal's throat, a screed of imprecations and unintelligible words, far deviated from the corrupt 'Gothic' that the animals usually spoke. Its intent was clear, however. Calm descended around the two as necron warrior protocols ensured that their leader was given a wide berth.

Bright eyes twinkled in a ruddy face. The animal smiled and then raised its sword in some sort of salute.

Anrakyr ignored it, merely standing still and silent. He was above the petty motivations of these beings. The animal's sword snaked in while the weapon it held in its other hand spat crude ammunition at the overlord.

Economical swings of his warscythe deflected the shells, driving them off with a high, sharp pinging noise.

The animal proved difficult to kill. For hours they fought, beneath the gentle blue sky of Kehlrantyr. For hours they fought, the centre of a melee that swirled around them. Anrakyr was fuelled by frustration, angered at the momentary denial of his destiny. He had come to Kehlrantyr expecting to find a tomb world to draw into his sphere of influence. Instead he had found an infestation of humans. He exorcised that frustration and anger on the animal.

To give it credit, it battled on long after it should have fallen. Blood dripped from between the plates of its dark green armour. Sparks showered from torn cabling.

Anrakyr was implacable, an elemental force. Dents and nicks marked his chassis where the creature had struck him, but they were few.

'Surrender,' Anrakyr demanded. 'Submit to order.'

The animal snorted a laugh. Its twitching features, hidden beneath sweat, blood and its armour of green and gold, jabbered in its organic tongue. It was slowing, strength ebbing with every movement.

Anrakyr grew tired of the animal. As it heaved in great breaths, the overlord shoved his warscythe through its abdomen, driving deep into its spine. He lifted the human, met its dying eyes with his deathless gaze.

'Filth,' he muttered. He threw the animal away, casting it to lie broken against the ground. Crypteks scurried after it, driven by curiosity to examine its physiology. With its death, human resistance on Kehlrantyr crumbled.

It awoke to utter darkness. It tried to take a breath that would not come, that brought no oxygen, no relief; a juddering breath that existed only as a sound-bite, a piece of manufactured noise.

Panic. Its mind clawed at the emotion. A consciousness stirred and coalesced around a physical form.

Its fists were raised, beating at the sarcophagus that kept it bound, kept it trapped. Obsidian walls enclosed it. No escape. No movement. Cables snaked from the walls towards its body, disappearing into interface ports, driving along its limbs and into the limits of its spine. It was omnipresent, its consciousness undifferentiated between sarcophagus, cable and skeletal body. It saw through the body's sensors, disoriented by seeing as the sarcophagus, the body and, in some remote sense, the circuits of the tomb world.

It felt the miles and miles of cables and crystalline lattices that stretched through the depths of Kehlrantyr. It was dimly aware of the cousins that walked upon its world above and the dwindling infestation of life that stained its surface.

It saw, in a blink, half glimpsed and little remembered, sixty million cycles of unchanging constancy. Sixty million cycles of unbroken silence and infrequent change.

Then the view was gone, battered into its subconscious. Events became localised, drawn through the cables snaking into the metal of its body.

Fog and smoke whirled around it, drifting through its vision. Green lights blinked. Indicators chirped and demanded attention. Its mouth opened in a silent scream. It writhed, trying to stretch, trying to break open its prison of metal and stone.

Slowly its identity returned, dripping through the feeds that connected it. A name. An existence. A life. A person. *Valnyr.* Memories joined the name. Identity flowed through her limbs, brought the panic away. Female. It was a she, a female, when such biological distinctions had mattered, during the Time of Flesh, before biotransference. When her race had strode the stars with bodies of meat and bone, before they had been deceived by Mephet'ran, the Messenger, the golden-tongued star god.

A laugh, a shrieking mad cackle, left her, vocalised in the synthetic sound that served her as a voice. The sound reeked of unknowable hunger, of desperation and fear.

Breath. Oxygen. Valnyr was beyond such needs, had been past such requirements for uncounted millennia. She would have smiled, were the skull that served her as features to allow such a gesture.

The panic bled away, the momentary distractions of awakening. Half-remembered preparations and theoretical constructions mumbled in some part of her consciousness.

Trepidation. Concern. These emotions cascaded through her limbs, setting her skull ablaze. The lack of clear memory set her to panic in a way the lack of breath could never equal. The fear of death, the erosion of identity: was this how it began?

Valnyr shuddered. That fear ran through every choice her race had made, the terror of mortality, the grasping jealousy of the overlooked and the passed over. It had led them, in their pride, to war with the old races. It had led them to the abandonment of their very lives.

Twinned emotions had driven her to this place and to this moment: vengeance and the fear of death. The latter, though perhaps not as easily admitted by the proud, was more influential than the former. *Frailty and mortality.* Easily deceived by the promises of the accursed star gods, these things had driven her entire race into the arms of hubris and made them easy prey to the blandishments of false, vampiric gods. In the end, it had broken their glory. Bereft of the vigour of the living races, Valnyr's kin had stagnated.

Valnyr mused on what had brought her here, considered the paths her life had taken. Vague memories of mortality, the hint of an identity she no longer coveted, haunted her.

Her sarcophagus shook. Momentum and rushing wind battered the ancient box. Light burned through as the wall facing her became translucent. Quartz-eaten caverns flashed past, marked with lurid green. Metal spread along the caverns, adorning the stone like mould.

Indicators flashed from red to green. A chime beeped. She cancelled it with a thought, banishing the noise. Gravity shifted. Her weight settled on her skeletal feet. Steam whistled and, with subtle pops, the lid to her prison disengaged. Air wafted in, the lifeless sterile atmosphere of the tomb world of Kehlrantyr, tinged with the dust of uncounted ages, utterly empty and devoid of movement. Perfect.

Valnyr, High Cryptek to the Kehlrantyr Dynasts, stepped from the sarcophagus and onto the obsidian floor. She resisted the urge to stretch. Valnyr had gone to the Great Sleep in glory, in a chamber rich with carvings and light. She awoke from that sleep in the same chamber. She emerged from her sarcophagus into ruins.

The walls were broken, caved in by seismic shifting. Neglect, nearly tangible on the still air, ate into everything. Tarnished metal shot through the cold, lifeless rock.

She looked down, her hands outstretched. Her chassis had taken on the form of a skeleton, bones formed from subtly rippling living metal. A strange drift from how she had looked prior to the Great Sleep.

She exhaled, steam vapour leaking from between her clenched jaws. Cracks ran through the chamber, fissures driving deep where unmarred obsidian had once echoed. Quartz crystals sprouted from the fissures, glowing slightly against the darkness. Swooping curves and crossed lines glowed green in the gloom, marking ancient devotions to the c'tan. Name runes whispered prayers, titles and devotions that the necrons had broken and betrayed. Her eyes focused on the symbol of the Void Dragon, the being to whom Valnyr had once bowed.

'Never again,' she vocalised. The words hung in the still air, the sound vibrations nearly visible to the vision granted by her metal chassis. Some unknown emotion gnawed at the pit of her being.

Floating on anti-gravitic suspensor fields, an attendant canoptek spyder hovered into Valnyr's field of vision. Its head, a blocky thing coated with gently blinking lenses, cocked to one side. Curiosity engrams, pre-programmed aeons ago, drove the construct. Sensors winked and scrutinised. Probes extended, tasting the air, examining the electromagnetic fields her skeletal body generated.

She needed to awaken the Dynasts, the overlord and her kin. That was her function. That was her task.

Valnyr started to move, but sensation fired along her neural links. Her mouth cracked open, but no sound emerged. She doubled over, her knees crashing into the stone. Seizures laced through her, jerking her body in random motions. She could hear a buzzing, low and deep.

The sensation passed. Something whispered at the back of her mind. With the moment's passing, more panic lanced through her. She despised the lack of control, feared any erosion of her authority. Anxiety kicked into life, driving along the synaptic cables that laced through her body. Sensation dimmed. Her eyesight grew dark as the panicked emotion drove away her senses.

In the wake of the fit, a new question emerged.

The Great Sleep had clearly ended, but what had prompted her awakening now? Vague memories of necrons striding across Kehlrantyr came to mind, but there was no time stamp associated with them.

The same unknown feeling flashed through her, bright and malignant. She doubled over, clutching at the unmoving canoptek spyder with fingers of living metal. Her vision blacked out completely. Valnyr lost all control over her motive functions. The canoptek machine compensated, its only reaction a rotation of its head, slow and deliberate.

Sensors stabbed from where its jaws would be. She staggered back. Static emerged from between her jaws, static and panic. Her mind fuzzed, overwhelmed. She felt hunger. Scrabbling, horror mounting, Valnyr surged back to her feet. She could hear a faint buzzing noise.

'No!' Valnyr commanded.

Denied its ability to test, to assure purity, the machine drifted away and awaited further orders, looking somehow chastised. Granted a degree of autonomy not usually seen among the constructs of the necrons, the canoptek spyders were responsible for the maintenance of the necrons in their sleeping state. Granted incredibly resilient and robust processors, they had even mimicked independent intelligence.

She appreciated the efforts of the machine in the same way that a person would appreciate an unthinking tool. If there were issues with her awakening, Valnyr would rather test them herself than rely upon the canoptek spyder's probing senses. Corrections could be made without the constructs' in-built programs accidentally detecting anomalies and prescribing eradication as the only possible solution. Worry gnawed at her, but she reasoned away the malignant fit as a side effect of the awakening process.

Doors of polished obsidian cracked open. Valnyr left her chamber, canoptek spyder following on her heels, and strode off into the silent tomb world. She entered into a far vaster chamber than the one she had awoken in. On obsidian walls, resplendent in unbroken glory, carved and shaped by the whims of her long-dead people, phalanxes of Kehlrantyr's most fabled heroes marched.

The skeletal shapes of necrons warred with the lithe alien eldar. Stylised and wrapped in stygian shadows, the carvings were a thing of wonder. Evidence of the pride of Kehlrantyr, its legions of fierce warriors marched across the walls, bound for the glorious wars that served as her history.

Bulwark of the War in Heaven, defender of the dead and doom of the living. This was the reputation Kehlrantyr had earned in ages past. The walls were pristine, kept serviced by scuttling scarabs. They betrayed little of the entropy that had greeted her in her awakening chambers. But the silence was a melancholy thing, thick and turgid in the air. It spoke of ages lost, of time slipped by unremembered and unmourned. The Great Sleep smothered Kehlrantyr.

She stopped in a vast, circular room. Warrior friezes, twelve in all, stared out from the walls. Valnyr walked towards one of the figures and rested her hand on the cheek of the warrior's skull.

'Shaudukar,' she whispered. The name helped dispel the disquiet she felt, driving it to the back of her mind. Then she stepped back, moving towards the centre. The canoptek spyder merely hovered, waiting, probes extended.

An infrasonic buzzing vibrated her metal bones, emanating from the circuitry that laced the walls. Cracks sounded and vapour shot from new fissures. This was no sudden onset of the passage of eons, however. Valnyr adopted the pose of restful relaxation and waited.

Sections of the walls, each marked by a single stylised warrior, pulled away from the rest of the obsidian panels and floated. Slots opened in the floor and the blocks ground into the depths of Kehlrantyr. Vapour hissed with greater intensity. Cruciform shapes resolved from the white steam, and caskets, similar to the one she had recently stepped from, were carved with the images of those who slumbered within.

Her left hand indicated a smile, while her right began the pose of greeting.

Shaudukar's, fittingly, was the first casket to open. The lychguard was her friend from the time before biotransference. Armoured in thick plates of metal, spine overarched to shelter her head, Shaudukar was a fearsome sight.

Poblaaur's casket opened next, followed by ten more, until her lychguard surrounded her. They hung, crucified in the sleep of eons. Cables and circuits were attached all over their bodies, snaking through their metal bones. Green lights flickered around them, shining through the steam. The canoptek spyder behind her chattered and broadcast the frequency of awakening.

The bodies jerked in their cradles.

Valnyr awaited their resurrection with excitement. She looked forward to the reunion, eager to hear the voices and thoughts of her guard. Their bonds had been forged in the turbulent days of war against the treacherous and hateful eldar. Those bonds had only been strengthened by conversion as loyalty engrams had rewritten portions of the lychguards' personality to ensure devotion beyond even that which they had exhibited in their mortality. These lychguard were Valnyr's wardens, gifts from the Dynasts.

The green lights gave way to arcs of corposant that juddered between the limbs and along the spines of the lychguard.

Emerald balefires flashed in Shaudukar's eyes, winking with intelligence programs being brought back online. She awoke, the first to do so. Shaudukar, oldest and truest friend of the cryptek called Valnyr. Shaudukar, leader of her lychguard. She fell from the casket. The others followed, some crunching to their knees. Shaudukar's fist crashed to her chest plate in the old salute. The others echoed her scant seconds later, except for Poblaaur.

Shaudukar said nothing as her sentience resumed control of her body, as she shrugged off the Great Sleep. She reached for her weapons from behind her casket, arming herself with her warscythe and shield. No nonsense and no fuss, as she had been in life. Valnyr felt relief to see her unchanged by sixty million years of dormancy.

Poblaaur kept his eyes dim, facing towards the wall.

'My mistress,' Shaudukar said. She stared at her hands.

Valnyr approached her, standing nearly uncomfortably close. For the status-obsessed necrons, where distance often indicated hierarchy and respect, it was an expression of great affection.

'Shaudukar,' Valnyr whispered the name. 'I am glad you are awake.'

The lychguard leader inclined her head. 'I am too. Is there a reason for our awakening?'

'No. Not so far as I can tell, at any rate.'

Shaudukar nodded. 'Your orders?' She never removed her gaze from her hands. Her fingers continued to flex. 'Do these... Do my fingers seem longer?'

Valnyr's head cocked to the side. Her right hand adopted the position signifying confusion.

'We do as the programs dictate. We awaken the Dynast and her kin.'

This was her sacred duty, her charge and purpose. While the lesser, mindless creatures of Kehlrantyr awoke, it was her duty to ensure the Dynast had weathered the ages and awoke in comfort, attended by a cryptek of her calibre.

The other lychguard waited in patient silence.

Poblaaur's mouth clacked open, drawing Valnyr's attention. Then he began to scream, the noise screeching and static-laced. The lychguard collapsed, clattering into a pile of awkwardly laid bones. He placed his hands beneath his shoulders and began to rock back and forth. Crackles sounded from his metal bones. Spikes erupted all along Poblaaur's body, along with hooks and wicked edges. He juddered along the floor, sending cracks crazing through the obsidian with mindless blows.

The infrasonic buzzing increased in pitch.

Valnyr retreated, hands held out in warding. Her other lychguard placed themselves between her and Poblaaur. Their loyalty engrams ensured that they would defend their cryptek even when doing so contravened their natural instinct of self-preservation.

The light in Poblaaur's eyes twitched. He stopped shuddering. His hands had lengthened into talons. Erratic madness betrayed his every motion. The intelligence that should have governed his movements, made them economical and precise, was nowhere to be seen. He stood. Static spilled from his mouth, pulsing in time with the buzzing. His fingers flexed.

Disgust and panic warred in Valnyr's mind. She recognised the signs, believed she knew the affliction clawing through Poblaaur's soul.

'What is happening?' demanded one of the lychguard.

'The flayer curse,' Valnyr whispered, her voice filled with horror.

What had begun as the merest whisper of calamity was now confirmed before her eyes. The flayer virus. A curse from a broken and vengeful god.

'How did it come to Kehlrantyr?' asked the lychguard, Othekh.

Valnyr answered, 'The refugees.' Her mind was distracted, latching onto the implications and the possibilities. 'To survive so much and to lose it all, to preside over... and then to lose it all to the witless afflictions and hunger of an ancient curse.'

She was muttering, the words emerging thick and fast. They flew, along with her thoughts, racing down paths that she had no desire to consider. The implications flashed through her mind. How deep did the taint run? How far had the words of accursed Llandu'gor reached?

The thought was horrifying. The sudden loss of identity, personality and memory flooded beneath the inescapable and inevitable hunger for flesh and blood. The desire, the *need*, to profane the body with the fluids and fibre of organic life. That was what the rumours had said, brought by distant necrons fleeing such existential horror on their own tomb worlds.

Some amongst the Khelrantyri had argued for the immediate destruction of such brothers and sisters, that they carried the flayer virus like an unwitting plague host. Cooler heads had prevailed. Sympathy, and a form of patronising dynastic arrogance, had ruled and the Dynasts allowed the unfortunates to strike the sigils of their original tomb worlds from their chassis and to anoint themselves with the glory of Kehlrantyr.

But perhaps that had been wrong. Perhaps they had been blinded by their sympathy. In the eons while they slept, when personality codes had been duplicated by necron artifice and back-up systems, the infection might have spread, leached into the core processes of the tomb world. Even now, the legions that faced awakening might be irretrievably afflicted by the flayer virus.

Horror such as Valnyr had rarely known flowed along her nerve-bundles. Personality fail-safes, designed to prevent the erosion of her mind by strong emotion, enacted themselves and calm slipped into her limbs, even as Poblaaur screamed his transformation before her eyes.

The necrons watched, unable to move, unable to act.

The canoptek spyder barrelled into the flayer-touched lychguard, knocking the still-screaming necron to the ground.

But the contact was enough. The green lights running along the tomb spyder flared, then dimmed. The construct spasmed. Spikes erupted from its back and the thing blurted out static and screams.

Most of the lychguard remained immobile, waiting for their moment to strike, confusion reigning as they assessed threats and friendly targeting prohibitions prevented them from assaulting one of their own. The lychguard were designed to be patient, designed to judge the best moment to strike, but they were also limited by ingrained assurances for loyalty.

Valnyr gripped her scythe and canted activation protocols. Time froze. Poblaaur, locked in a snarling hunched shape, was unable to move. Sound ceased. The buzzing ceased. Valnyr strode forward, feeling as though she were moving through mud.

The energy necessary to stop the passage of time was prodigious, the effort – especially so soon after her awakening – draining. She waded forward, buying each step with a silent grunt of pain. The green lights that played through her circuits dimmed, power drawn away to propel her motive functions against the flow of time.

Supplemental energy flowed from her staff of light, augmenting her power reserves. She approached Poblaaur one stubborn step at a time. Placing herself equidistant between the corrupted lychguard and the tomb spyder, she lowered her staff and fired.

A beam of incandescent fury began the slow crawl out of the head of the staff as the passage of time started to reassert itself.

Reality snapped back. Poblaaur launched himself to his feet while the canoptek spyder continued to spasm and writhe, viral programs rewriting the construct's processes.

Fire shot from Valnyr's staff and speared the struggling tomb spyder through the head. Another beam took Poblaaur through the chest as he stumbled to his feet, carving the necron in two.

The lychguard's torso collapsed, hissing and screaming. Poblaaur clawed his way towards Valnyr, mouth stretched open and teeth sharpened to fangs. Another beam burned away his skull and the room descended into silence.

'What just happened?' Shaudukar demanded.

'The flayer curse.'

'It is real?'

'So it would seem.'

'But how?'

Valnyr had no answer. Around her, screams reverberated from the darkness, similar in pitch and timbre to Poblaaur's. More necrons were awakening to the dreadful hunger, to the loss of identity and the erosion of all they had been.

CHAPTER TWO

Anrakyr's army marched through the human settlement, culling the living from the face of the world. A curious destroyer called Armenhorlal hovered near the Traveller and hummed to himself.

The trio of praetorians emerged from the smoke, covenant rods held across their chests. They took up station behind Anrakyr as he paraded through the dying settlement.

As he left the burning, broken concourse behind, Anrakyr toyed idly with a cluster of stones hanging from his neck. Marked with the curving, looping rune-script of the eldar kind, they had been recovered from the snow-coated fields of Carrh-enn-Derac.

Carrh-enn-Derac, the last battlefield he had walked. Carrh-enn-Derac, butchered by the eldar tongue into Carnac in the sixty million cycles the necrons had slept. It was now the site of their latest conflict, another battle in the War in Heaven that still raged. The last tomb world graced by his presence.

Anrakyr could not discern the purpose of the stones, but their ubiquity among the fallen foe, the way the eldar had screamed as he stole them, spoke to their value. At times, as now, the necron overlord believed he could see glimmers in their depths, could catch the faint whisper of torment from within.

Anrakyr had vented his displeasure on the eldar's world spirit, a rudimentary collection of utility programs and personality repositories that crudely mimicked the majesty of the circuits that cradled a necron tomb world. Such ramshackle attempts at technology were an affront, a reminder of the failures of lesser races. The bruised construct had been given to Trazyn the Infinite in fulfilment of the bargain that had secured the eldar defeat.

Now he came to Kehlrantyr to awaken the tomb world's fabled legions and welcome them into his growing empire. Hope had flared in his breast, enough to override his distaste at dealing with the worms that were the Kehlrantyr Dynasts. Renowned equally for their flippant arrogance and the limitless numbers of their population, the Kehlrantyri were a necessary evil. Anrakyr found it curious they had yet to awaken, that they had yet to stride forth from their tombs.

The Traveller dropped one of the subtly glowing gems and stabbed it with the edge of his warscythe. He expected to feel something, some emotion or some sense of action. He analysed his responses, examined the tactile sensations of the breaking gem, the change in structure of the stone as it went from whole to shattered, but the metal chassis of his body conveyed no feelings. No emotions welled within him, just empty nothingness: calm, assured, ordered. Only a mild curiosity remained, dissatisfied by the petty experiment. He left the other stones in his hand, dangling from chained wraithbone. He could not see why the eldar invested so much value in the stones, but then, the reasons behind so much of what the living races did escaped him.

Clutching the rest in shining digits, stained by the blood of human animals, Anrakyr tried to ignore the insidious hiss of the organic liquid that dripped down his spine. He clicked together the fingers of his other hand, let the relief at the gesture calm him, let lightning arcs crawl over him and wash away the taint of life, abrading the stain with puffs of burned smoke.

Gravel crunched beneath his feet as he moved through the burning human settlement. Warriors scuttled around him, and the hum of anti-gravitic motors set his skull to vibrating. The metal skirts he wore rustled around his legs.

Movement caught his gaze, drawing the fell fury of the Traveller's attention. A knot of warriors, their gauss weaponry abandoned, were feasting on the bodies of the slain creatures.

Meat ripped. Blood flashed in the afternoon air. They stuffed flesh down the empty caverns of their mouths. Anrakyr watched, annoyed, angry, as the organic matter dripped down through their chest cavities to flop into the dusty gravel at their feet.

'Sickness. Accursed,' Anrakyr said. Disgust flared through him. Without turning, he gestured to the floating destroyer that shadowed him. The flayer-touched had been a constant problem on Kehlrantyr. Normally they followed Anrakyr's forces in small numbers, cowed by the threat and majesty of the overlord's presence. Kept confined to their nightmare realm in the aptly named Ghoul Stars, lorded over by the whispered name of Valgûl, the flayed ones were a plague that rarely troubled Anrakyr. Until coming to Kehlrantyr, that was. Something about this tomb world was corrupting his warriors, drawing the flayer curse to rewrite their already damaged souls and psyches.

'Attend,' the Traveller ordered. 'Cull the flayer-touched. Purge those beholden to the dead words of Llandu'gor.'

It was no longer strange to utter the true names of the c'tan. He and his kind had shed that taboo when they broke the c'tan into shards, when they turned gods into servants. Thus they displayed their mastery over the beings to whom they had once owed fealty. Mephet'ran, Llandu'gor, Hsiagn'la. Others existed, lost to the half-forgotten mythologies of the necrons.

The destroyer cackled. His own madness, the nihilism that so gripped his kind, flowed through the laughter. Light crackled along the necron's spine as it sucked in power, drawing it from the atmosphere in a microscopic siphoning of energy. The heavy barrels of the gauss cannon that was Armenhorlal's arm flashed blindingly green.

Malignant energy unleashed, chain-whipping into the pack of unwitting flayers and wiping them from existence. Their shadows stretched for a moment, dark against the bright green. The spreading virus of vengeful Llandu'gor manifested more and more among those who walked beneath the Traveller's banner. All who succumbed would share this fate.

Armenhorlal cooed to himself, a childish sound and a holdover from his mortal existence. Anrakyr knew the destroyer's mind to have been fractured by some malfunction during his conversion, but it mattered little. For the moment the skimming destroyer was useful. He floated about Anrakyr in looping circles, each flash spinning faster and faster. The overlord shot out a hand.

'Enough. Cease your motions.'

Anrakyr's voice cracked into Armenhorlal's dented head, reaching into the destroyer's battle-damaged psyche. He slowed to a halt.

'So many. So many of the damned packs of the accursed. Why? What draws them to this place? These meat-creatures offer little sustenance. Especially not to such as us, who have passed beyond the petty concerns of mortality.' Anrakyr kicked one of the feebly struggling bodies at his feet, barely noticing as it cried out in unreasoning animal pain. For a moment, Anrakyr thought he could see the cunning gleam of intelligence in the creature's eyes, some evidence of sentience.

Primitive structures clustered around him, little more than enclosures against the elements. Decorated with bird wing motifs, tiled in grey and black, the buildings were crude. Warriors battered at the walls with single-minded belligerence. More intelligent necrons had sensed lurking humans within and ordered the warriors to deal with them.

That organic beings should so taint Kehlrantyr brought anger to surge through Anrakyr. The jewel of one of the ancient dynasties of his people, populated by savages, reclaimed by the life that had once been extinguished and purged beneath the marching benevolence of the necrons. Life always struggled against order. That was its nature. But just once, Anrakyr wished that he would see organisms submit and accept the gift and honour he brought.

A trio of destroyers flew overhead, followed by flyers. In the distance, a monolith patrolled, its black flanks glistening obsidian-wet in the light of the sun. Phalanxes of lesser warriors, their identities eroded by the epochs since their conversion, marched through the human settlement. They were beneath the pity of Anrakyr and Armenhorlal.

The three triarch praetorians trailed after Anrakyr and the destroyer. They were silent, darkling things, just like their master. They rarely offered commentary or condemnation. They observed. They waited. They *served*.

Despite the decades they had followed Anrakyr, the trio of necrons had never offered him their names. Anrakyr had first been annoyed by this wilful defiance. Then he had taken to calling them Khatlan, Dovetlan and Ammeg. The names weren't particularly clever, merely the first three numerals in the necron counting system. The praetorians never questioned his choice. Sometimes they even answered to the names.

The servants of the Silent King had been known to cow even the most recalcitrant phaerons into obedience. That they followed him, that they observed and marched alongside him, filled the necron overlord with trepidation. Why were they here? What did the last ruler of the Necron Empire want with Anrakyr?

That these creatures had refused to submit to the Great Sleep, that they had stridden the stars for sixty million cycles acting on the orders of the Silent King, beggared Anrakyr's mind. He could have done the same, he reasoned. His will was no less strong. But these triarch praetorians *had* walked the stars, shaping the mortal races, witnessing events and observing, silent as deathless gods. The evidence of those years lay on them. They were hunched, shamed-looking creatures. The metal of their bodies was tarnished, bronzed edges pitted and shadowed by weapons fire. Yes, they were unimpressive to look at, but what they represented and the havoc they could wreak more than made up for their outlandish and decrepit appearances.

Red-painted human helmets dangled from Ammeg's elbows. Belonging to one of the warrior caste of that despicable race, the things were crudely constructed but martially impressive. They were broken and pitted, lifted from some battlefield. She too wore eldar spirit-stones, older in provenance than Anrakyr's looted gems. The tattered robes of some infesting species drifted about her while a fungal reek suffused her metal bones.

All of the triarch praetorians bore some token of the warrior humans. Khatlan's back was studded with the sickle boxes the humans discarded as they made war. They formed rows of three spines rising from the praetorian's back and lent the necron the disgusting reek of the propellant the humans used to fire their crude weapons. Other odds and ends from scattered races and cultures coated the triarch praetorian.

Dovetlan had elected to place steel knives in a fan around her face. Stamped and marked by rough human artifice, the weapons were crude and technologically inferior. A winged teardrop of blood decorated each blade.

The praetorians refused to elucidate the circumstances of their acquisition of the human artefacts, nor why they wore the trophies as marks of pride. Each inquiry was met with the same blank stare and infuriating posture as any other. A fruitless endeavour, so Anrakyr could only guess their provenance. When the praetorians spoke, they stated only the obvious.

Humans burst from a side building, led by several of their males. Anrakyr recoiled, annoyed and wary that some of their tainted cells might besmirch his chassis.

Armenhorlal did not have time to spool up his gauss cannon before pinprick lasers ate at his chassis. The destroyer started to giggle, then laugh. Armenhorlal began thrashing, clubbing several of the fleeing humans.

Khatlan and Ammeg stepped into the sky, propelled by their gravity displacement packs. Dovetlan placed herself before Anrakyr while the Traveller watched and observed.

The universe groaned as scything waves of light emerged from the praetorians' covenant rods. Weeping humans, eyes and mouths wide, desperation spewing from their wretched faces, erupted into clouds of burning ash. Other bodies were dragged out of buildings by unthinking, unfeeling warriors and lined up in rows for incineration. It was endlessly fascinating, Anrakyr mused, that life always followed the same paths. They were fleshy and pink or brown, all colours drawn from the same palette. Some were tall. Others were short. Female and male. But they all followed the same template.

Two legs. Two arms. One head. How unbelievably common. The universe tried to impose order, from the eldar to the necrontyr to these human dregs. Two by two. A curious coincidence or evidence of some great plan? That it all led to entropy and disruption, to *chaos*, was an eternal shame. Only the necrons had refused such predestination, electing to take a different path rather than walk down the road that led to destruction.

Only under the eternal hegemony of the Necron Empire would the universe finally achieve the order and certainty it so obviously craved. Anrakyr bent his eternal life towards that goal, towards uniting his kind beneath his own banner and conquering all the lesser races.

Khatlan and Ammeg fell back to the ground, crunching into the poured stone. They resumed their place behind Anrakyr as he walked through the human settlement, stalking behind the overlord with silent threat.

Armenhorlal trailed behind them with scattered fires burning about his body. The destroyer crooned to himself.

They waded through piles of ash while fuel bowsers exploded and necron warriors systematically dismantled the signs of human habitation.

The gentle breeze, swaying trees, even the soft light of the sun angered Anrakyr, brought a rage deep to what he considered his soul. It all stank of life, of a time that he wished he could forget. Bodies were gathered and fed to waiting canoptek spyders. Bound for the monoliths and the pyres burning within, the traces of organic life were slowly being cleansed from Kehlrantyr.

The sun that glowed above, driving through the turquoise depths of a cloudless sky, was a pale thing, weak and dying, fed upon by a c'tan in the ages before the Breaking, leeched by the star gods in their desperate hunger before the discovery of the sustenance of souls.

Scourged by the necrons who called this place home, life had crept back, perhaps borne on the stellar winds, perhaps brought by some far-reaching traveller as vermin.

Kehlrantyr had not suffered the eons well.

Change brought anger. Death was an unceasing thing, a constant, and a known quantity. And there was nothing that brought pleasure to Anrakyr like that which was known, that which remained unchanging.

Metal crunched on stone gravel, the footsteps furtive. A cyclopean eye met Anrakyr's fell gaze. A cryptek. It chattered, its body hunched in a posture that screamed excitement. It wrung its hands together, digits flashing in complex formations that conveyed the emotions that its skull-like visage never would.

Excitement. Relief. Obeisance.

Anrakyr waved the cryptek into stillness. 'Your news?'

'We have aligned the maps and the portents, my lord. The approximate entrance location has been found.'

'Then where are my legions? Where are the phalanxes of this world?'

Profound regret. Unwelcome news. 'It seems a mountain range has arisen during the Great Sleep. The doors are buried.'

Anrakyr took the news well, surprisingly so.

'Open the doors. Dig them out. I will have my legions.'

Gratitude. Alacrity. 'Of course.'

The cryptek left, scurrying away.

Pressure pushed down from above as a shadow passed over Kehlrantyr's fitful sun. Atmospheric displacement caused the wind to howl. Anrakyr could hear a faint buzzing noise. He turned to the triarch praetorians in confusion. They merely stared back.

A ripple passed through his warriors. They all stiffened. Questions passed between the necrons that still possessed intelligence.

Deathmarks stepped from hidden pocket dimensions. Consummate spies and patient assassins, they were odious creatures, underhanded constructs whose methods were distasteful. They had their uses, however, and Anrakyr permitted their presence within his army, unlike the accursed flayers whose virus was known to spread to others. Still, the overlord flinched at their sudden appearance.

One of their number pointed above. Anrakyr looked up to see a sky pierced with swarming bone and red. From horizon to horizon descended hordes of insectile alien things.

He knew them, knew the creatures that came to feast on Kehlrantyr. Anrakyr wanted to spit curses. His body subconsciously adopted a pose of extreme anger with the subtle inflection of utter disappointment.

Known to the mortal races as the tyranids, he had fought the creatures on several occasions, each nearly disastrous. Their sheer numbers proved a vexing irritation that overwhelmed his mindless hordes. That they dogged him on Kehlrantyr, that they dared to disturb his plans, was unconscionable.

The tyranids were a threat to the necrons. They were life unfettered, anarchic, predictable only in their insatiable hunger. Their consumption of the lesser races proved problematic in the establishment of necron dynastic rule and the eventual goal of the imposition of lifeless order against a galaxy teeming with Chaos.

And now they were here, on Kehlrantyr.

Even as he watched, streaks broke through the sky, flaring with friction fire. Bio-ships, massive organisms, dropped into low orbit.

Already necrons were reacting.

Green lightning started lancing from the drifting monoliths, but there were too many descending objects to knock from the sky. The warrior phalanxes did not react at all. They slouched where they stood, unheeding, oblivious to the tyranids that filled the skies.

CHAPTER THREE

Jatiel was not an introspective man. Stolid, dependable, reliable, he was a sergeant in the Blood Angels Second Company. Proud of the red and gold he wore and the position he occupied, he had earned the rank some hundred years previously, fighting against the orks on Lared VII. He would hold the position until his death, never destined to rise higher.

Beatific cherubs stared down at the gathered Space Marines, watching over the bridge of the frigate *Golden Promise*. The entire room was a work of art, painstakingly crafted by generations of Blood Angels. Not all of the darkness in the souls of Sanguinius's sons could be brought to light upon the battlefield, and so the making of art was encouraged. Jatiel himself had carved the throne on which he now sat, taking rad-blasted wood from Baal and creating an artefact surpassing the work of any mortal craftsman. Gilded in red-gold, hand-painted, it dominated the bridge. As he reclined, alabaster angel wings framed his head.

The alabaster had been mined from the deep crust of Baal Prime. When Jatiel leaned back as he did now, if he wore his helmet, the sight echoed the sigil that all Blood Angels and their serfs wore upon their shoulders and worked into every aspect of their armour: the winged teardrop of their beloved primarch.

Pretentious, but no less so than his position demanded. All of his warriors' armour was marked by the winged teardrop, with details picked out in gold. They were encouraged in this, to modify their battleplate with approval from the Chapter's forgemasters.

Only Emudor's armour was mostly devoid of ostentation and grandeur. His artistry was subtler. Filigreed loops and whorls were carved into the curved plates, creating a trail of shadows that lessened his profile, broke it up and added to his talent for stealth. It suited his temperament; he was a brooding, dark and gently sarcastic soul.

Jatiel's soul, as the saying went, was sanguine. He was fine with this, content to live and serve his primarch and the Emperor in this position. The sergeant knew that he lacked the inspirational quality and the glory that some of his brothers hungered for, that others from the Chapter looked down on him and his squad. The thought brought a fang-bared smile to his craggy, careworn face. He had no desire to rise further. He served where he excelled, at the squad level.

That didn't make his current duty any less onerous.

'When have so many enemies fallen upon a single system like this?' he asked, gazing out through the oculus. The question was rhetorical, Jatiel barely conscious of asking it. He received an answer nonetheless. Ventara, studious, curious, bright and quick, provided it.

The battle-brother's eyes shone green, bright as the emeralds that studded his chestplate. 'Armageddon.'

'No.' This from Asaliah, grizzled, older even than Jatiel. 'You're wrong, lad. Armageddon was bad, mark me. I won't denigrate the warriors who fought and bled for that world, who do so still. But not near such as this.'

Asaliah spoke from experience. Along with the red and gold of his armour, black and silver also served. The skull, crossbones and stylised 'I' of the Deathwatch proudly glared from his left shoulder pad. The veteran had served two terms with the alien hunters, sworn never to speak in specifics of his time with the Ordo Xenos. But the experiences he had gained, the horrors he must have seen, were etched into his face. Every gesture of his hooded eyes evoked far-off sights, glories and darkness. He served as Jatiel's right hand, a pillar of knowledge and experience.

The veteran scratched the dusky beard scrawling across his lower face, diving through the peaks and valleys of scars and wrinkles left by a lifetime of war and secrets in service to hidden masters. 'Say what you like about the damn orks. They bring numbers. Always have and always will. But a *hive fleet*.' Asaliah nearly shuddered. 'That's numbers beyond counting, beyond even beginning to count.'

Jatiel thanked the winged primarch that Asaliah had never lost himself to the melancholia that so often afflicted the returned veterans of the Deathwatch. Indeed, many lost themselves to the Black Rage before they could impart their valuable experience and knowledge to the Chapter they returned to.

Asaliah's deep rumble ceased, the bass tones of his words echoing through the bridge. Silence descended over the room, taking malignant station in creased frowns and worried glances. It lived among the carved cherubs staring down with painted glass eyes.

The hiss and crackle of vox-access disturbed, yet did nothing to dispel the silence. The slack-jawed servitor mumbles of lingua-technis joined it.

War had come to the Cryptus System, war such as the Imperium had rarely known. Doom, blood and bile. Crawling horror. And Jatiel was missing it.

Somewhere out there, the Imperial Navy were fighting to hold back a swarm of hive ships, and the soldiers of the Astra Militarum prepared to face the onslaught on the ground when the fleet inevitably failed. Soon, the Blood Angels would arrive and lend their aid, determined to stop the aliens here before they could strip the system bare and move on, threatening Baal itself.

But Jatiel? His squad and the *Golden Promise* had been sent ahead of Lord Dante's forces to monitor the battle and watch over the dead world of Perdita. It wasn't for Jatiel to ask why. The Space Marine knew his duty. But the order chafed.

Jatiel's attention drifted down to the planet gently rotating below. Perdita was worthless, broken by calamity, or spawned stillborn in the system's formation.

Ventara broke the silence again. 'Why are we guarding this virus-bombed waste?' Another question lurked beneath. Jatiel knew it well enough, because he kept asking it himself. Why weren't they fighting alongside their brothers? Why weren't they taking the *Golden Promise* and joining the line?

'Trust in the Chapter Master,' Asaliah answered. Steel lurked in the veteran's voice.

Ventara wasn't willing to let it lie. 'Who even bothered to virus bomb Perdita in the first place?'

Another of the squad, newly joined Cassuen, asked, 'Do you think this was one of the battlefields of the Great Heresy?'

'It's too old,' said Ventara simply. 'Think millions of years, boy, not thousands.'

Cassuen's smile dipped. 'The eldar breeds, then?'

'Perhaps, but I've never known them to scour a world like this,' Jatiel said. These ethereal, blasphemous creatures rarely lowered themselves with such systematic destruction. Their methods tended far more to hit and run attacks or piratical squabblings.

Blocks of xenos material floated by, obscuring their view of the distant fleet. Circling one another in slow, complex orbits, the weaving constructs seemed at times almost to spell out runes, and at others to take on intricate polygonal shapes. Massive constructions of carved xenos bone, they appeared, at first, to belong to known eldar materials. However, these curious stones, stones that the Inquisition had taken a great deal of interest in, were engraved in some other alien runic script.

Silence descended again. The squad sat on the command deck with weapons drawn. Jatiel cradled his mace across his knees, the ornate golden head resting gently on the carved splendour of his command throne.

An air of stymied impotence and impatience suffused the deck. The serfs scurried with downcast faces.

Shadows danced at the edge of Jatiel's vision, shadows from another age. His fangs bared and he felt the ghost of pain dance through his limbs.

'No,' he muttered. 'Not now.'

Naskos Ventara offered his sergeant a concerned glance. 'Sergeant?'

'Nothing. It's nothing.' The sergeant pointed back to the viewscreen. 'Watch.'

The ship's astropath, Amanther Kidrun – a woman who had been muttering for weeks, wracked with visions of chittering horror and sentient darkness – started to scream. Her shrill cries echoed around the bridge.

Kidrun descended into a seizure, heels drumming against the gilded deck, boots carving scuffs into the murals that featured there. 'The Great Devourer!' she cried. 'The swarms, the ungodly swarms. They descend upon us. They will consume us!'

Alarm spread through the serfs as morale plummeted. Jatiel could feel the fear leach from them all, could smell the foetid animal reek of terror taking root in the souls of his crew. He surged to his feet. A storm cloud passed over his craggy features, drawing his grey brows down over his blue eyes.

'Enough!'

Asaliah and Emudor dragged the struggling woman from the bridge. They returned moments later and resumed their seats. All eyes returned to the screens.

Swarms of colour arrived at the edge of the map, soon blotting the entire screen like bruised fruit. Grim looks stole over the Space Marines' faces.

'Holy Throne,' someone murmured. It became a litany, over and over, descending into madness. Then screaming.

Jatiel's armoured fist thundered into the arm of his command chair, sending a crack shivering through the wood. The serfs jumped, but no one looked chastened or chagrined. The sergeant realised the oath had come through the vox, the echo stealing from some Navy captain or officer.

'Shut off that noise,' the sergeant ordered.

'Compliance.'

The waiting was the worst. The trillions of men and women who called Cryptus home would be waiting on their home worlds, each having to shoulder weapons to defend their way of life. Ranks of Astra Militarum would bolster their lines, serving as the core of the defence. They faced untold trillions of tyranid organisms, each designed for death and consumption.

His teeth gritted with duty. Perdita offered no sustenance to the xenos and was likely to be overlooked. Frustration thundered through Jatiel's veins. But he had his orders, so the *Golden Promise* continued to orbit Perdita. Swarms of the xenos passed the world, streaming towards the heavily populated core worlds.

Frustration and fear drifted through the bridge. The *Golden Promise*'s shipmaster, a rad-scarred, formidable Baalite woman by the name of Dabria Korbel, flinched at each flash of light, as each ship died. She stood before Jatiel, clad in the red, black and gold uniform of a Chapter-serf.

'The swarms are too close for my liking, my lord,' she spat.

They were not close enough for Jatiel, but he nodded. 'There's nothing we can do about it.'

Emudor said, 'We can move to the other side of the planet.'

'With respect, lord,' Korbel said, 'we can't. They'll see our engine flare. And to make matters worse, auspex shows them just as thick coming around the other side.'

'We hold to Lord Dante's plan,' said Jatiel. 'We wait in orbit and...'

Well, he wasn't sure of the 'and'. The Chapter Master had merely said to hold Perdita. Quite how Jatiel was supposed to do that, he wasn't aware.

Asaliah heard the hesitation. 'We hold the world or we die in glory.'

'Simple,' said Ventara.

'But it will not come to that,' predicted Emudor. 'We present no real threat to the tyranids and Perdita holds nothing of interest to them. Until our brothers arrive, we will remain in orbit around the dead world.'

A uniformed serf approached Shipmaster Korbel with a data-slate. The movement attracted Jatiel's eyes, but the sergeant ignored the pair. It was a scene that repeated often on the *Golden Promise*.

The humans conferred for two minutes before the serf rushed back to his station. Korbel approached Jatiel's throne. Her eyes were wide, eyebrows arched. Wrinkles stood out on her forehead, pushing up at the black and grey hair. Concern was writ large on her face.

She gave the data-slate to the sergeant, retreated five paces and crossed her arms. Her booted foot tapped at the deck-mesh.

'What is this?' he asked, glancing at the data scrolling across the slate. He knew the answer, but he wanted to hear the shipmaster's appraisal.

'Inbound ship signatures, my lord.'

One of his eyebrows arched. 'Xenos?'

'No,' she said. 'Size and signature point to human origins.'

'And they're on an approach vector to Perdita?'

'Their current speed and direction indicates so, my lord.'

The other members of the squad clustered around the shipmaster. The buzz of active power armour filled the bridge.

'Any indication of who they are, sergeant?' Ventara asked.

The sergeant looked to the shipmaster. 'Nothing yet, my lords,' she said. 'We have attempted to hail the ships. No response.'

'But why head to us? Who even knew we were here?' asked Ventara.

Jatiel ignored the speculation that ensued. He preferred to deal with facts. 'How long until they intercept us?'

'Twenty-four hours, my lord.'

This was a complication that their mission did not need. The ships, whatever their motive, could draw the tyranids to their position, instigating xenos interest in the dead world.

An idea flashed. 'Have the approaching vessels made any significant course corrections since their launch?'

Korbel stared at the data-slate, brow furrowed and lips pursed. 'Three registered, my lord.'

She pointed out the times.

'And competency of those manoeuvres?'

'The first indicates standard Imperial Navy competency, perhaps a touch out of place. Their route also indicates that they were bound for one of the front-line planets.'

She frowned. 'The second reeks of desperation and attention seeking. Engine output also flares and then drops at this point. Something went wrong aboard those vessels.'

Since first registering the course corrections, the data had almost become lost beneath a screed of other orders, information and concerns. Jatiel had not forgotten, but Shipmaster Korbel had been forced to. A frigate did not cease functioning while it tried to evade detection.

While they remained a single ship hidden against the backdrop of a massive world that stealth was made moderately easier. Korbel kept the ship's systems running at the bare minimum. The engine was cool and the ship's machine-spirit drugged into a haze by the lack of power.

Frost crept across the doors leading away from the bridge, a testament to the low priority currently granted to life-support systems. Chapter-serfs were confined to quarters and only essential personnel were left to man their stations.

Only the bridge retained a modicum of full function. Stale air and stale breath drifted through the room, masked only slightly by the mingled scents of body odour and incense. Air scrubbers wheezed from behind hidden panels, barely coping with the stagnant atmosphere.

A communications officer began yelling, drawing attention to his station. They all believed the moment had arrived that they both dreaded and half hoped for, that the tyranids had caught notice of their ship, drawn against the backdrop of dead Perdita.

The communications officer's words, seconds later, dispelled concern. Jatiel could hear over a dozen serfs letting slip a sigh of relief.

'One of the ships has opened a channel. They're attempting to hail us.'

Korbel looked to Jatiel. The sergeant nodded.

'Put it through,' the shipmaster ordered.

Static assaulted their ears, suddenly loud with the background noise of the universe's birth pangs. Then a voice, hunched and whispered, filled with unremitting fear.

'*Please,*' it whispered. '*Please.*' Sobbing filled the bridge. '*Please help. They've taken the ship. The convicts...*' Jatiel heard laughter, a deep burbling sound hissed through consumptive teeth. '*Throne of Terra!*' The feed washed back into static.

A new voice came on, the source of the laughter. '*Please.*' A man's voice. He sounded pleading, as desperate as the previous person had been, but Jatiel caught the ripe undercurrent of fear driving through the word. '*Let us go. We're leaving this system. We ain't done nothin'.*'

A servitor began to mumble, spouting binaric cant.

Korbel cocked her head to the side, deciphering the lingua-technis, an augmetic ear translating the language of the Adeptus Mechanicus into Gothic.

The colour drained from her face. 'My lord,' she began. 'Multiple targets inbound.'

The convict's voice and the approaching Imperial vessels were forgotten. A pregnant silence descended on the bridge. Mortals held their breath. An acrid, metallic taste suddenly danced on Jatiel's tongue. He knew his pupils were dilating, knew it as the lights stabbed into his suddenly hypersensitive vision. Breath heaved in and out from his chest. Adrenaline pounded through his veins. Chemical signifier scents wafted from the Blood Angels. Manic light gleamed in all their eyes.

Cassuen and Emudor both bared their teeth in feral smiles of anticipation. The sergeant could feel his own fangs piercing through his gums, suddenly painful and uncomfortable.

Blood, sacred blood, shared with the primarch Sanguinius, pounded in his ears. His armour's machine-spirit sensed the rising kill-lust in the sergeant, dampening some less desirable aspects and bringing clarity and thirst to the fore.

His mouth and throat felt dry.

'Helmets,' the sergeant growled. It would bring no balm to the mortal serfs to see the thirst painted across their masters' faces now. The squad complied, shutting the bridge away behind red masks.

The presumed convict's voice washed away. All vid-screens became occupied by a singular view. The vid-feeds switched to display near space. The feed was no longer on a scale of millions of kilometres, now it was simply thousands. Point blank in void-war terms.

Fleet markers were tagged, although they showed no friendly notifiers. There was just the *Golden Promise*, held in close orbit to Perdita. The Blood Angels vessel, marked in the red and gold of the Chapter, tried to lose itself against the colossal bulk of the dead world. It should have registered as no more than a mere speck against the drifting snow and ash of Perdita's landscape.

But with the other human ships drawing closer, somehow having found the Blood Angels vessel, the cluster of life, the heat wash from burning engines, drew the attention of whatever malevolence served the tyranid breed as intelligence. A choice target, canisters of meat and biomatter to fuel the swarm.

Simulated by a marked river against the black of the void, screen overlays brought meaning to the situation. Jatiel ignored the overlays, stepping beyond them, moving to one of the many observation windows that studded the bridge. At first, all he saw were stars against the field of utmost black. But now, just becoming visible at the extremes of his genhanced vision, were pinpricks of light.

They looked to be stars. They were not. The tyranids were now aware of the *Golden Promise*. And they were coming.

The anxiety aboard the bridge deepened, rancid fear-stink filling the room. Jatiel could not fault them. Despite being serfs in service to one of the most glorious Chapters of the Emperor's own warriors, they were mortal, after all.

'With your permission, sergeant?' Korbel asked.

'Granted.'

A klaxon broke out wailing.

'All hands to battle stations,' Korbel commanded into the ship's internal communication networks. Jatiel knew that serfs and Chapter slaves were being roused from their bunks, life-support systems increasing by the barest of notches. What had been running on almost uninhabitable was now bolstered to the merely uncomfortable.

Gun batteries opened along the *Golden Promise*'s flanks. Torpedo tubes in the ship's armoured prow yawned. Crew began shouting firing solutions, plotting out projected movement patterns and void shield capacities.

'Fire,' Korbel whispered. The ship shuddered and torpedoes, loaded as the ship achieved a stable orbit around Perdita, raced forward. Forged on Halfus, half a segmentum away, the torpedoes acted like frag grenades.

Halfus-pattern torpedoes were notoriously effective against tyranid swarms, originally seeing use on Deathwatch vessels. Since that world's fall to the Tau Empire, the torpedoes were rare and precious things. The *Golden Promise* only carried four.

All were launched within twenty minutes of detecting the approaching tyranids.

There was no visible change as the torpedoes left visual range. Tags on the overlay watched their course while Adeptus Mechanicus adepts blessed their passage in lingua-technis.

Lance strikes speared out moments later as those weapon systems kicked in. Then the torpedoes detonated, massive bursts of razor-sharp metal that stretched over kilometres of space.

A ragged cheer moved like wildfire through the bridge as the Master of Sensors detected several vessel kills. A drop in the ocean, even against this merest splinter of the hive fleet assailing Cryptus.

More lance strikes stretched into the void, eating millions of kilometres in the blink of an eye.

The winking stars came closer and increased in multitude, Cryptus's sun shining off the iridescent chitin of the tyranid bio-ships.

'The other vessels are attempting to hail us again,' a comms officer said.

'Deny them,' Shipmaster Korbel ordered.

Jatiel watched as the convict vessels continued to make for the desperate protection of the *Golden Promise*.

'What are they doing?'

Korbel ignored the sergeant, concentrating on the encroaching xenos.

Jatiel could almost see them now. They manifested as a cloud of bright colour against the depthless black of the void.

Mortals kept glancing up from their consoles at the vid-screens. Sweat broke out against pale skin. Fear, nervousness and anxiety once more created a heady stench in the bridge. The carved and gilded cherubs continued to stare down impassively. They had gazed on countless such scenes in countless wars. That they still had a bridge to guard was evidence of the *Golden Promise*'s resilience.

Void shields shimmered as probing tyranid weapons fire impacted. The *Golden Promise* shuddered under the kinetic blowback. Point defence cannons streamed their fire into the void as tyranid fighter-analogue organisms, having slipped past the ship's auspex, ducked through the void shields and attempted strafing runs on the Blood Angels vessel. Jatiel could feel miniscule vibrations through the arms of his throne as the ship shuddered beneath the tyranid onslaught.

'Shipmaster, my lord,' a robed serf announced from the sensorium. 'Sensors detect energy build-up from the xenos structures.'

Jatiel's mind was awash with tactical inlays. A reprieve or a new threat?

Asaliah gripped his own chair with manic concentration, gauntlets eating grooves into the smooth Baalite marble. He loomed forward, leaning over the table.

'Brother?' Jatiel asked.

Asaliah opened and closed a vox-link multiple times. 'I cannot speak,' he finally growled. 'The oath.'

'It matters little now. We may have to face whatever threat emerges from here in the next few moments. Oath or no, the Inquisition no longer has claim over you, brother. We must seize whatever advantage we can.'

'Necrons,' Asaliah spat eventually. 'It could be the necrons.'

'What can we expect?' asked Cassuen.

'Nothing good,' came Asaliah's grim reply.

'But they allied with us once,' said Jatiel.

'Because it suited them,' Emudor replied. 'I was there on Gehenna. I fought alongside the xenos, but they did not ally with us out of kindness.'

'Is there anything to suggest they would do the same here?' Korbel hissed.

Asaliah shook his head. 'Not that I can see. These aliens are not like the eldar. We have nothing in common with them.'

'Then we will prepare for war with them as well,' Jatiel said. 'Asaliah, you will advise Shipmaster Korbel of any noteworthy weaknesses and tactics the xenos may try.'

Asaliah laughed. 'There are few enough of those, but I will do what I can. The aliens are masters of the void. On the ground, they can be countered, but they owned the stars once, if what the Inquisition says is true. They will hammer us with weaponry not fired since before life began on Ancient Terra. Or they will ignore us. But my knowledge is at your disposal, shipmaster.'

'Why would they come here?' Korbel asked.

Asaliah shrugged.

'Watch the structures,' Jatiel ordered the sensorium officer, his words dripping with finality. 'But we must focus our efforts on the tyranids. Deal with the immediate threat now. We will face the necrons when, and if, they arrive.'

CHAPTER FOUR

Valnyr and her lychguard moved with purpose through the darkness of the awakening tomb world. Canoptek constructs watched from shadowed alleys, letting them pass. Scrabbling sounded from the cracks in the obsidian walkways. Stalactites loomed from the darkness, the result of countless cycles of dripping fluid trickling from the planet's surface.

They made their way down a memorial processional, an arterial that ran through the entirety of Kehlrantyr's interior. The ceremonial route of kings and phaerons, it would once have been lined by the living. Now it was a thing of empty shadows and forgotten grandeur. Scarabs scuttled down the walls, attempting to repair yawning fissures through the carvings. All around them towered immense friezes depicting the necrons of Kehlrantyr at their height of glory, figures from countless tomb worlds bowing before the might of Kehlrantyr's Dynasts.

Silence, broken only by the clack of their footsteps, surrounded the necrons. A dull green glow emanated from scuttling scarab lenses. Valnyr took heart at the silence. Silence meant order. Silence meant assurance.

At times the road became a statue-lined bridge. Below, in rank upon silent rank, Valnyr could see the legions of Kehlrantyr. The bulk of the planet's population, personalities and identities removed, waited in the darkness. Once, these had been the ordinary citizens of the Necron Empire. Once they had been artisans, children, mothers, fathers, farmers, writers, artists and merchants. The *nonessential*. Mephet'ran's deception saw them converted into mindless creatures, their entire existence erased and burned away.

Valnyr almost felt sorry for them, almost felt remorse at what became of the vast populations of the empire. But better that they lose their identity than her. She shuddered at such a fate, could barely understand an eternity of unwitting and unwilling servitude. They were abhorrent things, a reminder of her race's glory and its decline. They represented her deepest fears, the violation of all that she was, the erasure of everything that made her an individual, deleted in order to create an unthinking, unreasoning construct no better than the scarabs that serviced the tomb worlds.

Metal rasped along stone. The flickering sparks of talons screeching through the obsidian echoed down a side route, followed by running footsteps. The lychguard readied their weapons.

A group of warriors emerged, eyes shining in the darkness. They were altered, gripped by the same changes that had afflicted Poblaaur. Red lights played along their bodies, while their hands stretched into talons. Bent double by unnatural, insatiable hunger, they stalked forward, muttering and screeching at random. Valnyr could hear buzzing, low and subsonic.

'Flayed ones,' said Shaudukar.

The lychguard formed a shield wall, once more placing themselves between the corrupt and their cryptek. Dispersion fields activated on their shields, repelling the shambling flayers into the obsidian walls. Three lychguard held the broken necrons in place, while the others approached.

Their warscythes flashed down, crunching into the corrupted warriors' skulls. The light in their eyes immediately died, while the bodies collapsed to the floor. The warscythes struck once again, severing the flayed ones' torsos from their legs along the vulnerable spine section.

The lychguard pulled back in lockstep, resuming their guardian position around the cryptek. More hissing came from the shadows. More red lights blinked as corrupted warriors shambled forward, mouthparts clicking open and closed. Their chassis were tarnished by ages uncounted. They spat static at the party of sane necrons.

'Mistress?' Shaudukar asked over her shoulder.

'Through them.'

The lychguard leaned behind their shields and advanced. The flayer-touched flew backwards, propelled by the dispersion shields.

Valnyr and her lychguard rushed through the depths, passing through the decrepit majesty of Kehlrantyr, leaving the flayer packs behind. Kilometres separated them from their goal, the sleeping chambers of the ruling dynasty. Kilometres filled with slumbering warriors and ages-old chambers.

Ruin crept in the closer they came to the crypts of the Dynasts. Fissures lanced from the ceiling, cracking deep through carved walls. There was greater activity in this place, scarabs swarming in the darkness. Canoptek wraiths and other constructs flittered about, attending to pre-programmed tasks, running the same routines for presumably millions of years, guarding for intruders that would never come and enacting repair protocols on damaged regions that could never be fixed.

'How much have we lost while we slept? How far has our glory fallen?'

'Mistress? I do not remember.'

Valnyr was shocked to find herself saying, 'I do not either.'

Some of her memories were gone. She could feel the gaps, the aching wounds in her psyche that were filled with some malignant emotion that recoiled at her scrutiny.

Weak sunlight drifted from fissures, descending from miles above. They walked between the beams and Valnyr felt a moment's flush of pleasure at the sight.

Something shrieked, something that sounded horribly organic. The screams approached, moving with fierce rapidity. A creature landed in front of them, black eyes staring with malign intelligence. It was bone-white and red. Tendrils stretched from its head, waving like worms or snakes. Great spiked limbs descended from its shoulders, arching over. A tail whipped through the air behind it. The tentacles around its mouth reached out and vile ooze dripped from its pores.

The necrons froze. Green light played out from their eyes, scanning and analysing.

The creature fixed its gaze on them. It sucked in great breaths, betraying its disgusting organic origin. It shuffled forward, moving in quick hops. Bioluminescence rippled along its fleshy skin, tracing out complex patterns. Parts of the creature's body blended in with the stone surrounding it.

As it drew near to the lychguard, the beast turned its head from side to side. Its tendrils reached outwards. Then it screamed. Hooks shot out from its chest, clattering off the lychguards' shields.

'What foulness is this?' someone asked.

More screeches sounded from far above as the lychguard bulled forward. The creature leapt over the necrons' heads, twisting in midair. Spiked appendages slammed into one of Valnyr's guardians and wrenched him apart. He continued to attack, even as he was torn in half. The fallen lychguard used his warscythe and shield to crawl forward, still moving stubbornly towards the source of the attack.

But the creature was already moving out of the way, darting towards Valnyr. The cryptek held her staff out, beginning to summon the energy to freeze the animal in time, to halt it in its tracks. She knew, even as she did so, that it was too fast.

'No!' she yelled. 'I will not die here!' Panic flew through her. Buzzing overwhelmed her senses.

Shaudukar grasped the creature by the spine. It stalled and mewled in pain, still reaching for the cryptek. The tendrils around its head fluttered as it breathed out. Shaudukar ripped out the beast's spine with a wet meat *thunk*. The creature collapsed and flopped against the floor, obscene, pallid flesh glistening against the obsidian.

Blood spilled out in a pool. The necrons gathered around it, curious. It was the first glimpse of organic life they had seen since beginning the Great Sleep. It screamed as it died, still writhing.

More screams answered. Creatures swarmed down the fissures. Buzzing clouds of scarabs met them. Arcs of green lightning stabbed from tiny jaw-gripped weapons. Greater canoptek creatures fired whining streams of energy. Gouts of alien flesh rained down on Valnyr's head, but the tide was too strong.

There were four-armed beasts, gaping maws filled with sharp teeth. More of the larger beasts with the tentacled faces followed. All moved quickly, scuttling with disgusting living motion, blue and red and purple, flying through the gloom in blurs faster than Valnyr could track. Whirring winged organisms engaged the scarabs in miniature dogfights.

Valnyr could only stare, overwhelmed by the revulsion that swept through her. She suddenly felt hungry, a half-remembered sensation that ghosted through her. The lychguard were frozen, gazing up at the descending animals.

Valnyr knew they were considering, adapting, planning an assessment of the encroaching aliens. But there were too many and they were too slow. They would be overwhelmed.

More canoptek constructs were advancing down the processional. For a moment, Valnyr was distracted, seeing the advancing tide of burnished metal as a mark of the lost glories of her people, the processional reasserting its previous function this one last time.

Flayer-cursed appeared, clambering down walls from hidden crevices, climbing up the bridge with talons spearing into the cracks of the stone.

'Move,' she commanded. 'We must find a way to neutralise these threats.'

Her words echoed, slicing through the static-screams of the flayer-cursed and the organic sounds of the alien organisms. Beneath it all, she could hear the laughter of the necrontyr, almost mocking.

An idea came to her. 'Halt,' she commanded her lychguard. 'Listen.'

Aliens sprinted for them. With a grunt of effort, Valnyr froze them in time, pausing the organisms mere metres away.

All around them, quiet and distant, came the noises of a bustling city, the sounds of the long dead and the long forgotten. She could hardly hear them through the ever-present buzzing. She focused, concentrated, and pinpointed the hall the echoes originated from. A new plan began to crystallise. It was desperate, but what other hope did she have?

'We move down there!' she yelled.

They fled through empty dwelling places, marked with sigils proclaiming the habitation of early necron scientists. Aliens and flayers poured after them, some drifting into eddies of battle and the shrieks of hunger.

Valnyr knew this district. She had served here in life. Its emptiness disquieted her, but desperation urged her on. Legs that would no longer tire drove her forward, fear adding to her flight. She outpaced her lychguard, the larger necrons fighting a desperate rearguard against the twin threats that pursued them.

Valnyr heard a faint cry and glanced back. She saw one of the lychguard pounced upon by flayers and torn apart beneath a metallic mass of flashing blade limbs.

She turned down a side passageway and her lychguard followed. Dwellings were replaced by defunct laboratories. The sounds, louder now, screamed all around them, keening with horror and loss. They were thick with the noise of some calamitous event. Valnyr ignored them, focusing only on the origin point.

At the end of the passageway, carved into the obsidian darkness, stood an open laboratory. Half-seen shapes moved through the gloom, pale and translucent. Valnyr burst through them, sparing no glance for the time-dilated ghosts of her lost kin. She emerged into a vast chamber and the sounds of a battle waged in the unimaginable depths of the past. Her lychguard stumbled in moments later.

'Defend the entrance,' she told Shaudukar. 'Buy me time.'

The lychguard nodded and took up position. They hefted their shields and prepared to serve their cryptek. Valnyr cast them from her mind and tried to ignore the sounds that surrounded her: the ululating cries of the aliens, the static-laced screams of the flayers and the time-wounded echoes of her lost kin. Panic and fear drove her. Through her mind, in some dark corner of her being, some facet of her demanded in increasingly shrill tones that she survive.

She knew this chamber, knew what it represented. This had been a room where the early chronomancers practised their art. Here they had perfected the sciences that Valnyr used. She knew the theory behind what had been accomplished in such a place.

She began to chant, activating long dormant protocols in the laboratory. Rock rumbled and lights flickered on. Ancient scenes of glory from the history of the necrontyr looked down from the walls, an inspiration to those chronomancers who would have worked within. The panels slid down, exposing blinking sensors and whizzing gears.

Valnyr recited names, placing exception commands on her and her lychguard. There was no time to fine-tune what she attempted.

Echoes rose around her, sounds of battle and loss, mixing with the looping static of the flayers and the keening of the interloping aliens.

'Let them through!' she snarled.

The lychguard did not question her words. They tumbled back, some driven to the ground by organisms or flayers.

Valnyr backed up, running towards the wall. A grim carving showed eldar and necrontyr forces fighting one another above her. She stumbled and an alien dived onto her, four bladed and clawed arms stabbing at her chassis. She raised her staff to ward it away.

There was no time to consider the consequences of what she attempted, no time to replicate perfect conditions. She had to act now. Valnyr shouted the activation command.

Light flashed. Sounds stretched. The buzzing grew louder.

Then the light faded and silence engulfed the chamber.

The aliens and the flayers were gone. So were three of her lychguard, although Valnyr found that she could no longer remember their names.

A new panel on the walls caught her attention. Necrontyr forms battled what could only be altered necrons and stylistic representations of the nameless organisms. A new event in the history of Kelrantyr, but one that, now, had always happened. Such was the power of her art.

'Mistress?' asked Shaudukar, shaking her from her reverie.

'We make for the Dynasts, as before.'

Already they could hear the static cries of more flayer packs and the mindless screaming of the organic beasts.

CHAPTER FIVE

Anrakyr's anger rose. His plans were rapidly being thwarted, lost amid the swarming tyranids.

His already depleted army, comprised of necrons from dozens of tomb worlds, faced countless aliens. That the swarm diverted to consume the oozing remains of the humans offered little consolation. Already the warrior-beasts were probing his lines, already they were attacking his necrons. His deathmark spies, kept hidden in their pocket dimensions, reported massive feeder tendrils descending into the oceans. Crypteks said that the planet's orbit was destabilising as colossal volumes of liquid were funnelled into orbit.

A monolith dived for the ground, coated in flapping, gnawing creatures. Careening into a wall, it carved a swath through battling necron phalanxes of warriors and scuttling, clawed things.

While it allowed his army to face the uncounted numbers of aliens, they were still vulnerable to attack from the sky. Monoliths anchored the line, but they were slowly being overwhelmed.

A gap opened before him. Necrons were flung into the air. Warriors were broken. Destroyers were rent asunder by clawing, shrieking animals. Huge, towering tyranid beasts sprinted towards him and his sentient attendants.

A great creature, towering three times Anrakyr's height, came rumbling from the swarms of its lesser brethren. Great scythe arms were brandished to the sky, while a brutal call emerged from its mouth. It barrelled towards Anrakyr, mouth gaping open and oozing ichor.

Anrakyr met its charge, driving a wedge of sentient necrons, immortals and the like, into the tyranids. The huge warrior-beast threw itself upon him, trying to crush his skeletal chassis beneath its bulk.

The Traveller fell. He landed awkwardly, spear stuck beneath his bones. The mass of the tyranid creature cracked down, pushing him into the stone. Anrakyr struggled to get his hands beneath him, to gain leverage against the hulking beast. Blood dripped from above, staining his body and eating into the necrodermis. The living metal reacted, repairing the damage as quickly as it was wrought.

He realised the blood's source: the axehead crest of his Pyrrhian overlordship. He sawed his head back and forth, carving into the blubber and flesh of the creature above. It roared in pain and fury. Anrakyr carved a space for himself, and soon he was able to push himself to his knees and retrieve his spear.

Blood dripped down his body, pitting the pristine metal, and Anrakyr tried to ignore the cloying disgust that threatened to drown him. More space was opened. He could see green lightning flickering and hear the screams of dying tyranids through the quivering flesh of the beast. He swung the spear, hitting something vital, and a great torrent of acid-blood and viscera gouted out from the animal. Its movements slowed and it ceased breathing.

Anrakyr continued to pull himself through, bursting through the skin, bones and chitin of the monster. He clambered up, stood upon the vast bulk of the tyranid beast and surveyed the battle.

Tyranid creatures milled as something like shock passed through the swarm. Warriors and other slow-moving necrons punished the animals, reaping and killing.

He hoisted his spear into the sky, stabbing out towards the occluded disc of Kehlrantyr's sun. A cheer emerged from those battered sentient necrons that surrounded him.

Behind him, at the far end of the defile, his crypteks, broken warriors and programmed constructs chewed their way into the mountain range. Beneath, behind, below, lurked his entire reason for coming to this planet. The tombs of the Kehlrantyr Dynasts. Legions of warriors. Enough to drown these aliens, and not just these, but the paltry humans that grew like scabs of bacterial life across planets once belonging to the necrons.

But he must wait to secure them. He must survive long enough.

The tyranids threw themselves at his line, unheeding of the casualties they suffered. Necron warriors endured the onslaught. Anrakyr watched as warriors were pulled beneath thrashing tyranids, dragged beneath rending claws that beat futilely at metal forms. They stood, seconds later, shrugging off the beasts with a stubbornness bred out of ignorance.

What went on within the skulls of Anrakyr's warriors, he could not even begin to guess. Did they still think? Did they know that they fought? In the end, it mattered little to the Traveller.

Anrakyr threw himself into their midst, stood shoulder to shoulder with the barely cognisant, the dull-minded warriors who made up the bulk of his host and his race. Vast jaws gaped towards him, hissing and spitting acid. One scrabbled over a warrior to his fore, spiked limbs flailing. Its jaws crunched into his head. Diamond-hard teeth punched through the metal of his skull. Something akin to pain flashed along artificial synapses. A thick, glistening tongue slapped against his face, trying to find purchase. Bladed limbs scrabbled against his body, getting hooked into the gaps between his ribs. The jaws tightened. Anrakyr grabbed them. He began to pull.

The creature struggled, desperate and panicking. Something tore in the hinges of its jaw and Anrakyr continued to pull. The head came apart, ripped down the centre. Wriggling worms fell from within and more acid-blood sheeted over the overlord. But there was no respite, yet more creatures already careening into the necrons.

More of the scrabbling, blade-armed organisms sprinted forward, jumping at the last second. Anrakyr skewered one of the mewling beasts, sending ichor erupting out of its chitin-armoured back along with his spearhead.

Great creatures, amongst the few tyranids that seemed capable of independent thought and decision making, marshalled their lesser brethren. They stood amidst the swarm, smaller creatures breaking around them like a sea of flesh and bone.

Destroyers targeted these, bracketing the great beasts with concentrated fire, catechisms of hate spewing from their mouth speakers. The nihilistic necrons cast their spite towards the largest synapse monsters. Armenhorlal led the destroyers.

Beetles fired from flowing schools of tyranids bounced off their necrodermis, smacking with chitinous crunches from the metal. One of the beetles hit something vital in a destroyer, chewing through the necron's spine. Critical explosive failure followed as the drive skimmer core separated from the commanding section. Shards of metal studded out, thudding into the other destroyers floating around it. Incapable of experiencing pain, none of them even noticed, continuing to fire into the advancing swarms.

A monolith exploded in the sky. Green lightning expanded in a ball, eliminating the flapping tyranids that had proven the construct's doom. Anrakyr watched it all, noting everything, watching the ebb and flow of the battlefield. His warriors were holding, but barely. While their metal bodies and tireless forms were proof against much of the tyranids' wiles, they were outnumbered. With every passing second warriors were being pulled beneath shrieking waves of dead-eyed horrors.

Warriors to either side of Anrakyr were torn down by claws and, in horrific squeals of stressed metal, rent asunder. Some stood seconds later, green lightning playing about their joints as the metal that formed their bodies repaired itself. But most never stood back up, buried under a wave of flesh, reanimation protocols unable to activate.

The tide of tyranids receded. Blasted creatures that towered over their lesser kin locked eyes with Anrakyr, and then scuttled back into their ranks. The eyes were appraising, considering. Anrakyr met them.

Marks of green light flickered over the larger creatures' heads as deathmarks stained their targets.

A new sound arose alongside the shrieking and baying of the tyranids, a deep whuffling noise, followed by rhythmic shudders of earth and stone. Rock cascaded down from the sides of the defile, crunching into unwitting necron warriors. Dust rose and pebbles bounced and danced beneath Anrakyr's feet.

A number of hulking tyranids came screaming down the defile. Their throats were massive sacs of swinging flesh. The creatures stood nearly as tall as the ravine itself. Anrakyr struggled to divine their purpose, what the tyranids meant to accomplish. He understood, seconds before it was too late.

'Block the mouth! Kill the creatures!' he screamed.

The remaining three monoliths arced down, anti-gravitic fields straining as they crashed into the ground, blocking the monstrous beasts from Anrakyr's view.

A great retching sound filtered through to the necrons, then a steaming hiss as viscous liquid spilled forth. Smoke began to rise from the monoliths almost immediately. A tide of bio-acid spilled around the flanks of the slab-sided constructs, filling the defile in a great, hissing flood. Entire phalanxes of warriors dissolved beneath the slurry, denuded down to nothing.

Displacement field shielding erupted belatedly as crypteks stepped into the air and added the weight of their science to the conflict. More and more were streaming away from the digging project to reinforce Anrakyr's failing line.

With the monoliths down, the skies were left unprotected. Spores fell from overhead bio-ships, landing behind the necron line. They erupted with a sickening vent of gases and the reek of scorched flesh. Tyranid warrior forms made straight for the necron line.

'Retreat!' Anrakyr rumbled. Synaptic relay processes enacted in the dull minds of the embattled warriors. More autonomous constructs, necrons that had survived biotransference with a degree of sense and sanity intact, began to stream back.

The mindless warriors retreated in slow lockstep. Many were lost beneath the slavering claws of the tyranids, pulled down and gnawed upon by mindless beasts that were yet to realise there was no bio-matter to be had from them. The ripped-fabric sound of gauss weaponry grew ragged and inconstant.

A necron retreat was a measured thing, devoid of panic and mindless fear. While Anrakyr's higher processes may have been capable of approximating such biological responses, he had long since disabled any debilitating emotions.

Instead, the Pyrrhian overlord was filled with rage. His eyes flared while the axe blades on his head quivered with subtle vibration. Lights pulsed all up and down his chassis. Anrakyr raised his left hand, fingers outstretched into the gesture of *hesitant decision* and *anticipation*. His body deactivated as power was siphoned to a small weapon embedded in his wrist.

Sentient necrons wailed in sudden terror of what was to come, while the triarch praetorians stationed themselves before the Traveller. Green lightning played about his gauntlet. Then a tiny object, a sliver of Anrakyr's own necrodermis, launched from his wrist. Part of Anrakyr, a tiny fragment of all that he was, flew with it, leaving a curious buzzing sound in its wake.

Reality itself shrieked as it was violated. But this was no phenomenon born of the warp, like the unearthly powers of the eldar or a crude human starship travelling beyond celestial bodies. This was necron science at its finest, the laws of physics and the material universe exploited to their utmost.

The tachyon arrow gathered mass to it like a thunderclap, manufacturing matter from the air in an alchemical transmutation. It hit the tyranid front, slicing through several of the larger creatures before impacting with the ground. The world broke. Rocks fell. Tyranids died in their hundreds. His own warriors were ripped to pieces or buried beneath tonnes of rock.

Anrakyr saw none of it. His systems were momentarily offline, drained of all power by the needs of the tachyon arrow. They rebooted as he was being thrown back by the blast.

Something felt wrong. Something always felt wrong after the tachyon arrow's deployment. It was a last resort weapon, a choice only made in the direst of circumstances.

A fraction of him was missing, nearly as intangible as the sliver of his necrodermis used to form the tachyon arrow. A fraction of what made Anrakyr the Traveller, of what drove the great necron overlord, had been denuded away and lost to oblivion. It ached, the void, but he could not identify what was gone.

The prospect of losing himself terrified Anrakyr, the idea that he might lose his personality, become as blunt and worthless as Armenhorlal, or, horror of horrors, a lobotomised drone like one of the warriors that marched in his legions.

Dust drifted, while tyranids hesitantly crawled over the gently glowing fused-glass wreckage of the tachyon arrow impact. They sickened rapidly, broken by the unnatural radiation leaking from the site.

But more were pouring across, hesitant and confused. The tyranids seemed aimless, as if the guiding intelligence that governed them had been weakened. It was a start.

CHAPTER SIX

Alien organisms whirled and left Valnyr's fleeing party alone, focusing on the larger threat of the flayer-touched. Whatever intelligence motivated them, whatever shreds of cunning and cleverness worked away behind their dead-black eyes, knew enough to recognise a greater menace. The creatures shrieked as one and moved forward, as eerily coordinated as the marching necrons.

Flesh hit metal as the party left the tide behind them. More alien creatures were shrieking their way into the fray, some fanning out to infiltrate deeper into the tomb world.

A scattered few of the beasts followed, hissing and drooling. Light stabbed from Valnyr's staff, obliterating the aliens. Her vision dimmed as her internal power source was temporarily drained.

Then they were moving again. Two of her lychguard peeled off at a narrowing in the processional. Her last sight of them, peering over her shoulder, was of the two hunched necrons crouched with shields and warscythes ready.

The surroundings gradually grew more ornate the deeper into the tomb world they fled. The walls were no longer cut obsidian, but burnished metal as well. The carvings moved with clockwork precision, telling of the glories of the Kehlrantyr Dynasts.

One room displayed a colossal hologrammatic galactic map. Every tomb world was marked and spun about in its orbit. Through some lost science, the map updated in reaction to events out in the universe. Valnyr saw how far things had come in sixty million cycles, how many tomb worlds had been lost, how decrepit the once great empire looked.

Massive gates of metal barred their way, inscribed with gently glowing runes describing the names and deeds of all of Kehlrantyr's Dynasts stretching back to the Time of Flesh and the emergence of the necrontyr. The gates loomed large, towering into the darkness. Time-etched facial features showed how the Dynasts had once looked.

Green light flashed from the open mouth of the founding Dynast, scanning them from feet to head. Grinding noises sounded from deep within, followed by a rhythmic clunking. The scarabs ceased their scuttling and flowed into the gate's joints as it rumbled open, splitting down the middle of the largest carved face. Light shone from the revealed chamber, the largest they had yet seen.

Valnyr was assailed by memories of the time she had spent sealed away in the ancient city-within-a-city. Forbidden to the masses of necrontyr – and later necrons – only the favoured of the Dynasts were allowed to walk its depths.

She had once conducted experiments within. Yet while her status within the hierarchy of the tomb world had been high, it had not been enough to warrant her entombment within the rarefied depths of the dynastic palace chambers. Even despite her mandate to awaken the Dynasts, she was forced to suffer the processional as a symbolic reminder that she lacked the former genetic grandeur and the splendour of a dynastic name.

The group entered through the yawning portal. It slowly slammed shut behind them, cutting off the shrieking xenos and the awakening tomb world.

The necron warrior phalanxes continued marching backwards in lockstep. The defile narrowed as they retreated from the tyranids. Rock walls crowded in, dun-coloured and stratified, testament to the ages that had passed while the Kehlrantyri slept. Soon their backs were to a rock wall, cut and carved by working necrons and their constructs. Already Anrakyr could see threads of obsidian lacing through the stone of Kehlrantyr's crust.

Anrakyr left the battlefield front behind, sweeping towards the furiously working crypteks. 'Where are my legions?' he demanded.

'We are still digging, my lord,' the lead cryptek answered.

'The tyranids come on my heels. They will be running over us soon. "Still digging" is *not* an acceptable answer.'

The lead cryptek bowed, knowing better than to respond further, too wise to offer excuses to Anrakyr the Traveller.

A green flash split the sky and an immense noise rumbled through the cloud layers. Tyranid vessels, sickening blends of meat with mechanical purpose, erupted into expanding clouds of flame. Internal combustion gases must have been touched off. The green flash signified something deeper to Anrakyr. His ship, his fleet, dying in the void, destroyed by the tyranids. A setback such as he had never before faced. How many resources had he just lost? How far had this set back his dreams of a reunified Necron Empire?

His ships, his legacy, destroyed. He swayed on his feet, internal processes struggling to compensate for the sudden surge of negative emotion. Dampeners kicked in, settling his psyche. They were burst nanoseconds later, drowned beneath an ocean of spiralling darkness. Desperation spooled in Anrakyr's central processes. It gnawed at him, ticking away at his thoughts. A screaming whine built in his vocalisers, a petulant hiss of escaping sound vibrations. Anger and rage joined the sound. Behind it lurked the certainty that some core aspect of himself was missing, shed along with the tachyon arrow.

Personality, memory, the knowledge that some indefinable portion of himself was gone, shivered at his centre. This was the true reason why he rarely fired that weapon, though its efficacy was undeniable. Anrakyr had contemplated mounting it on one of his subordinates in the past, but could not bring himself to place such a massive level of trust in another being.

Intelligent necrons were sent scrambling, redoubling their efforts at an unspoken command. None wished to stand before the Traveller now. None wished to become the object of his wrath. They would rather face the tyranids.

CHAPTER SEVEN

A calm machine voice broadcast across the *Golden Promise* as violent tremors afflicted the venerable frigate. 'Stand by to repel boarders,' it stated, repeating every thirty seconds.

Red lights and alarm klaxons flashed across the bridge. Servitors mumbled damage reports and sparks showered from blown-out consoles, broken by feedback and sympathetic damage.

Jatiel's warriors stood with weapons ready and girded their souls for imminent conflict.

The walls of the spaceship, hidden by paintings of grand Naval warfare, popped open on steam-driven hinges. Shotguns and low-beam lasweapons waited, shiny and wrapped in plastek. They had never been called upon before, still sitting pristine in their original packaging.

Non-essential crew were gearing up, grabbing reinforced armour and assorted weaponry. Ratings brought rifles to enthroned officers, who were engrossed in the battle that they still fought, in order to destroy as many of the tyranid boarding pods as they could before they could breach the *Golden Promise*'s hull.

'Your gunnery crews have reaped a fearsome toll on the aliens,' said Jatiel. 'That is a worthy achievement. You have my compliments, shipmaster. We could not have asked for more.'

Korbel accepted the praise stoically. Her face was pale and etched with stress. 'It has been an honour, sergeant,' she said. Finality undercut every word.

Jatiel knew that the situation was dire. He could see it on every one of the screens within the bridge. The *Golden Promise*'s primary batteries were still culling the tyranids that reached for them, but the swarm was everywhere. Point defence guns, smaller turrets mounted on the hull, spat at approaching tyranid organisms.

His hearts pounded, pulse beating behind his eyes. It formed almost a migraine, a painful pressure that mounted and mounted. Four drums thrummed in time with the beats of his hearts. His mouth was dry and yet thick with acidic drool, the prospect of battle bringing the Red Thirst to the fore.

His warriors, all four, watched the oculus screens. Emudor spotted it first. 'They will break through amidships,' the Space Marine calmly announced over the inter-squad link.

The ship endured a manic bout of shaking. Gravity generators failed and the mortal crew locked themselves into their seats. Jatiel watched them shoot nervous glances towards the massive adamantine doors that guarded the bridge.

'Shipmaster,' Jatiel said. He cocked his bolter. 'We *will* repel the xenos from this vessel.' His words were not impassioned. They were delivered with a resigned tone. 'Cassuen, you will guard the bridge.'

The young Blood Angel nodded his assent, the gesture nearly imperceptible.

'Shipmaster Korbel, die well,' Jatiel said.

The high tombs of Kehlrantyr's ruling Dynasts displayed the forgotten glory of necron civilisation. The decay so evident throughout the rest of the tomb world was nowhere to be found here. It was pristine. Perfect.

Gold warred with obsidian and other precious substances. Rippling curtains of chained metal partitioned the great chambers, forming complex runes announcing the majesty of the sleeping occupants. Glorious sights, beautiful reminders of the technology and mastery her race possessed, but rendered mundane by their familiarity.

Necron constructs swarmed everywhere, filling the tomb in massive numbers. Scuttling motion broke the great silence as the mechanical creatures conducted their tasks with mindless diligence. Gravitic pulses removed accumulated dust while swooping scarabs snatched the offending particles from the air.

The chamber itself was long, shaped like the runic symbol for Kehlrantyr, an announcement of mastery that was not lost on Valnyr. Complex and perfect, the same symbol adorned her chassis and those of her lychguard, making the same declaration of ownership that this chamber did. The message was clear: they belonged to Kehlrantyr, which, in turn, served at the pleasure of the ruling Dynasts.

One long corridor with many branches swooped out to either side. Each led to the resting niche of the ruling family. Subtle green lights ran through the walls, flashing in arrangements of runes that spelled the planet's history. Gaps showed where devotionary words had once spoken the praises of the c'tan. They had been excised, but not neatly.

The lesser chambers crowded towards the gate, the most easily accessed. Carved first, when the tomb world had still served as a necropolis to house the truly dead, these chambers lacked the impossible artistry of the others. They betrayed an earlier, cruder age. These were the tombs of the false necrons, the beings whose personalities had only been approximated with artificial intelligences, rather than converted. Advanced programs mimicked them as they were said to have been. Bodies had been constructed, made of the same living metal that Valnyr and the true necrons used for motive functions. But no real intelligence motivated them. Only artificiality acted behind the eyes.

They were the ones who had died during the Time of Flesh, whose mortality had prevented them from seeing the true glory of the necrons. These were the fallen leaders of necron society, those who gasped out their last as cancers destroyed their bodies, politicians assassinated in their prime and generals culled in the ages-long wars against the Old Ones and their servants. They were the ones deemed worthy of remembrance and reconstitution.

Nuensis, who had led the necrontyr in battle. Gevegrar, inventor of great and terrible technological marvels. Maantril, one of those who had opened negotiations with the c'tan. Names and beings she had heard stories of when she herself had walked Kehlrantyr in the flesh. Heroes. Luminaries. Now their simulacra would be awoken to advise the Dynasts.

But they were just complex machines, no better nor worse than the tomb constructs that the necrons created to serve their purposes. In such ways was the wisdom of ages preserved and brought to immortality. Valnyr could hear them already stirring, restless in their tombs, locked away behind curtains of rippling scarabs.

'We will awaken them soon,' Valnyr said. 'Our focus must be the ruling Dynasts. They will lead us through this crisis.'

They moved through the Dynasts' necropolis, hissed at by tomb constructs curious about these interlopers but which withdrew after recognising their authority and legitimacy. A cloud of flowing scarabs buzzed before them, tiny jewelled wings and humming ripples of anti-gravitic fields fluttering in the gloom.

The corridor, wide with marching symbols and friezes, ended in one large looping circle. At the centre of the ring, rising in a stepped ziggurat, was the tomb of the ruling Dynast, Phaerakh Nazkehl.

A statue of the formidable phaerakh stood guard over her tomb, hanging from the ceiling with one hand clutching an ornate weapon and the other cradling a map of the galaxy. Its eyes were dead, black pools, while its skeleton bore the telltale signs of circuitry. Valnyr's escort took station around the chamber, each standing equidistant from the others.

Recessed niches in the wall hinted at Nazkehl's own lychguard, where they slumbered away the eons. Valnyr paid them no attention. They would be the last to be awoken. Their services were not required yet.

The cryptek stepped forward onto the dais. Colours inverted as ancient programs scanned everyone in the room, searching for interlopers and tomb robbers. Horns blared. She began to recite the ritual of High Awakening, the words flowing in time to the instruments. Every step she took was marked by green lights in the glassine obsidian.

A sarcophagus rose from the highest tier, pitched vertically. The front was transparent, revealing the ornate chassis of Nazkehl. She was still clad in ancient wisps of frayed fabric. One hand clutched the sceptre of her authority while the other crossed over to hold a recurved sword.

Glass slowly hinged open and lights played along the phaerakh's chassis. Her mouth yawned open.

She screamed.

Valnyr and her lychguard recoiled back. They knew the sound. They'd heard it before. It was the same static-laced cry of the necrons whose minds were corrupted and controlled by the flayer virus.

'The phaerakh is cursed,' cried one of the lychguard.

Nazkehl fell to her knees, cables detaching from her body, hissing and flapping with escaping vapour and energy. Long-fingered hands, tapered with rippling necrodermis talons, clawed at the stone of her ziggurat. The corrupted phaerakh snaked her clawed hand around Valnyr's shinbones. She looked up, met the cryptek's horrified gaze. The static-scream echoed from her open maw.

Valnyr panicked, her mind seized by indecision. Loyalty protocols warred with the instinct for self-preservation. Self-preservation won out and Valnyr's staff slammed down into Nazkehl's skull, crunching the metal, driving it into the stone with a deep crack. Her vision blurred. Pain danced along her limbs as punishment engrams crackled through her circuits. Hunger blazed through her again, but it was momentary, drowned beneath the agony.

Shaudukar dragged Valnyr away from the spasming phaerakh.

'Corrupt, my cryptek. We must leave. The tomb world is lost.'

Valnyr heaved, lost in momentary panic as her mind struggled to remember that she no longer lived. 'How deep does the contagion extend? Some of the Dynasts must surely be pure.'

'Where will we go?' one of her lychguard asked.

'I don't know,' Valnyr said. 'I don't know.' Her thoughts fled. No plan of action existed. 'What contingency could exist for such as this? How could we anticipate and plan against such horror?'

Emptiness filled her, along with a hollow, grief-stricken fear. Emotions burbled that her existence could not countenance or express. What posture could she adopt to say that she had just killed the being she served? What gesture could announce that her people were corrupted, irredeemably so?

'The gates,' Valnyr said. 'We make for the gates. We go to the surface and find...' What? What would they find outside the tomb? Refuge? Relief?

It did not matter. She needed to move, to escape this horror. Her lychguard waited, patient, loyalty programs ensuring that they would accept her every command. But they offered no opinions or ideas of their own. They stood, silent and still as statues.

She hated them then. She hated the responsibility they gave her, hated the mockery they made of the beings she had known in life. These slaves, these unquestioning constructs, were no better than the false necrons or the ranks of warriors. A reminder, as if she needed any, of the doubts that plagued the cryptek.

More static-laced screams emerged from the darkness, mocking her. Her lychguard readied their shields and hefted their warscythes. They left the phaerakh's chamber behind.

Automatic processes awakened more of the ruling Dynasts. The static-screams revealed the state of their sanity. Flayer-touched highborn crawled from their tombs, exiting niches in the walls where their metallic chassis had lain for millions of cycles.

Warscythes flashed down and killed the ones who had once ruled over

Kehlrantyr, the ones whose minds and bodies had been remade by the vengeance of one of the gods of her people. They died, flailing and broken, destined to be forgotten at the heart of their former glory.

Constructs sought to halt them, confused at the sight. Necrons fighting necrons was inconceivable to their programming. They hovered, gravitic repulsors pushing them from one side to another. In the end, their programming motivated them to attend to the fallen bodies of the exterminated Dynasts.

Valnyr and her lychguard were nearing the end of the chamber when a gang of lesser lords from late in Kehlrantyr's history sprang upon them. One of the lychguard pushed Valnyr out of the way and was pulled to the ground by the cursed highborn. Screaming his own curses, the lychguard was subsumed by flashing metal limbs and pulled to pieces.

Bright light skewered the lords seconds later from Valnyr's staff. From behind her, lightning flickered and killed other hunched, flayer-touched necrons. Lychguard heads turned to identify the new threat.

The false necrons marched from their tombs, ornate weapons flashing as they obliterated the flayed ones.

'Cryptek,' said the warlord Nuensis. He inclined his head in respect and greeting. 'We have been waiting to remind the tomb world of our worth.'

'Your intercession is appreciated, warlord.'

'What afflicts these Dynasts?'

'The c'tan.'

'Such slavish devotion to the star gods,' said Nuensis, his eyes shifting to regard the hunched and hiding figure of Maantril. Several of the false necrons began to make sigils of obeisance to the star gods before ingrained engrams prevented the motions from completing.

'It is beyond that,' Shaudukar said.

Valnyr added, 'They are afflicted by the curse of Llandu'gor.'

'We should relieve them of this affliction,' Nuensis said without hesitation. He hefted a great, curved sword. He sketched the posture for *bloodthirsty* and *anticipation*. He was clumsy and awkward, lacking the poise of a true necron. He had never needed the postures and poses in life.

'There is no time,' Valnyr asserted. 'The world is lost to this curse.'

'Your plan, cryptek?' asked Maantril.

'We head for the surface, to find succour or relief.'

The false necrons shared knowing looks. 'What of the Dolmen Gate?' one asked.

'No,' said Valnyr. 'Such technology was fickle in its prime. After all this time, to trust that it would still function is madness.'

'For all we know,' added Shaudukar, 'the eldar still haunt the twisting paths. They were mighty of old and while they are frail compared to the strength of our kind, we lack the comfort of numbers. The eldar are cunning creatures.'

'How do we know the eldar linger into this age? Perhaps they have earned their final extinction,' insisted Maantril.

Nuensis hissed a laugh. 'I wish that it were so, but they were persistent creatures. It is equally likely that they rule the galaxy now. Have you had access to updated knowledge since your awakening, cryptek?'

'No,' said Valnyr. Her thoughts were distracted, still lingering on the option presented by the Dolmen Gate. Further technology granted to them by the wiles of the c'tan, the Dolmen Gates had been stolen from the Old Ones and their eldar servants. There too lurked tricks and turns not anticipated by the naïve necrontyr. Like the biotransference that had ensured their unending half-life, the Dolmen Gates offered the unexpected and the unwelcome. They were access points to the webway, a means of travelling across vast distances at great speeds and without touching reality. But to move so close to the nightmare dimensions of the otherrealm, to tempt the beings that dwelled therein, was madness.

'A last resort, then,' said Maantril. 'I may be no more than a simulation, but I have no wish to face the darkness of the real grave.'

Valnyr surveyed the gathered necrons. She nodded. 'A last resort.'

Nuensis grunted his agreement. 'We make for the surface. We shall stride Kehlrantyr once more.'

CHAPTER EIGHT

Bioforms in their shrieking millions dived into the necron line, mindless beasts driven to the slaughter. But for every ten, twenty thousand cut down by the mindless discipline of the necron warriors, hundreds of thousands took their place.

Anrakyr's back was to a wall, metal scraping against stone. There was more evidence of necron artifice now, the great gates of Kehlrantyr. Storied things, they were said to have once been carved with colossal friezes of the ruling Dynasts. A waste of time and resources, evidence of too-obvious arrogance. Crypteks and canoptek constructs sawed through the carvings, reducing them to atomised ash.

Chronomancers surrounded the Traveller. Each faced the wall, humming harmonics that disrupted the flow of time and space. They projected a field of slipped time. The necrons caught within the field moved at a greatly enhanced pace, allowing work that would take hours to take minutes.

Still, it was too slow; the tyranids felled too many necrons, and too few were reanimating to wreak mindless revenge on their killers.

Nimble creatures dropped from the sky, accelerated through the time field and impacted into geysers of unwholesome flesh. More fell, cratering into the rock floor. One of the tyranids knocked into a working canoptek spyder, denting the construct and dropping both to the earth.

An idea germinated in Anrakyr's skull. 'So simple,' he said. 'Three of you,' he bellowed to the working crypteks. 'I require three of you.'

Three of the crypteks detached themselves from their efforts at the wall, moving like blurs until they reached the edge of the time dilation fields. They approached Anrakyr with bodies posed in *anxiety* and *subservience*.

'How may we serve, my lord?' they chorused. Their chassis featured ornate markings and esoteric runes scrawled over every surface. A single, cyclopean eye stared from each cryptek's forehead, the lens nictitating. The markings of Anrakyr's own tomb world, Pyrrhia, featured heavily. They were of the tattered few, Anrakyr's original servants. Forces from other tomb worlds made up the bulk of the Traveller's forces now. His own sub-phaerons and lords from Pyrrhia had been allowed a degree of autonomy, striding the stars to issue Anrakyr's proclamation of empire and begin the diplomatic process.

The Traveller grabbed one of the working crypteks by the shoulder and roughly shoved it around.

'Join the front line. Employ your chronomancy for my warriors. Let time serve as our ally to enforce the harvest. These tyranids offend my sight.'

The three crypteks bowed. If they felt any trepidation, any fear, at taking their place in the line of their mindless brethren, Anrakyr did not care, nor did he notice. They departed, moving with alacrity.

The triarch praetorians stepped down from the sky. Vapour wafted from the ends of their covenant rods. They surrounded Anrakyr the Traveller.

'This will fail,' said Khatlan.

Dovetlan added, 'This world will give you nothing.' As if to punctuate the praetorians' words, a doomsday barge detonated in an expansive cloud of green-tinged fire.

Anrakyr waved their words away. 'Be gone,' he said. Inwardly, he was disquieted. These praetorians were proving to be prescient. 'You are a chorus of the unwelcome.'

The praetorians remained where they stood, eyes boring into the Traveller's. 'This will fail,' asserted Khatlan again.

'You already said that,' Anrakyr growled. 'What do you know? What will happen here?'

Ammeg shrugged. 'There are too many tyranids.'

'What of the legions that slumber below?' asked Anrakyr.

'Worthless,' said Dovetlan. 'You will find them to be useless.'

'You will need allies,' said Khatlan.

Anrakyr laughed. He knew their game now. In his desperation, he was supposed to call on their master. 'The Silent King will answer? I suppose all I must do is pledge my eternal fealty.'

'No,' said Ammeg.

Anrakyr was taken aback. That was not what he expected them to say. 'Then who?' he asked.

They paused, glancing at one another. 'You will need allies,' repeated Khatlan.

'How do you know this?' Frustration bled through Anrakyr's voice.

'Orikan the Diviner revealed this to the last triarch long ago,' said Ammeg.

'And you only tell me this *now?*'

Their heads jerked up. Something in the front line had caught their attention. They stalked forward, hunched forms moving awkwardly.

'We will speak more on this later,' said Dovetlan over her shoulder.

The insolence of these enigmatic servants of the Silent King set Anrakyr to fuming. He followed the praetorians, wading through the acidic blood that flooded the battlefield. Their pace increased as a screeching wail sounded from the tyranid swarms.

Flapping creatures streaked overhead, darkening the skies. Warriors angled their gauss rifles towards the sky, firing streams of lightning up above. Smoking corpses fell like rain. The ground shook as they marched forward.

Power reserves, generators supplied by clouds of linked scarabs, swirled around the crypteks. As the art of the chronomancers took hold, scarabs fell, sparks consumed by the hungry science of necron technology. The effect took moments to begin.

It started small, hardly noticeable. A slightly increased tempo in gauss shots from the necron warriors betrayed the effect of the time meddling. Then the true apocalypse began. Where before, disciplined volleys had lashed out at the flowing tides of tyranids, now came sheets and sheets of green lightning. The fabric-tearing refrain of gauss weaponry increased to become a deafening, constant sound, like the crash of rocks falling, but magnified and made constant.

Anrakyr stepped into the field of increased time, marvelling as the tyranids before him slowed. Creatures swarmed towards him, moving like they were wallowing through mud. Anrakyr laughed. This was necron technology functioning as intended.

But some creatures, already monstrously fast, charged forward heedlessly. Numbers pushed them beyond the deadly volleys of the necron warriors and into the field. The ground shook violently beneath them.

Clumsy warriors fell over, made unstable by the tremors. Rock cracked and exploded upwards. Five metres to Anrakyr's right, a wormlike tyranid with six pairs of grasping limbs spat acid and pulled warriors down. These creatures were bursting all amongst his battleline.

Anrakyr ran towards the burrowing animal, but it retreated down its hole before he drew close. Then it exploded back up, just below the Traveller. Anrakyr cursed as he was thrown up, legs caught in the organism's jaw.

It started to twist, to rend and bite, trying to pull the overlord beneath the earth. Anrakyr flailed, thoughts and plans flashing through his mind, but instinct took over, honed in a time he could barely remember. His spear stabbed down, diving into the top of the creature's head. It exhaled a carrion wind, spewing the cloying reek at Anrakyr. His blow carved a furrow through the chitin that guarded the organism's braincase. Blood oozed, but the creature continued to live.

Grunting with effort, it continued to drag the overlord below ground. He dropped his spear and grabbed at the lip of the hole, trying to find purchase. But he failed, drawn inexorably backwards in convulsive motions.

'Assist me,' Anrakyr yelled. No one answered him.

Light flashed, and the creature that held him exploded into clouds of ash.

Dovetlan and Ammeg stood at the lip of the hole. They offered no words and Anrakyr offered no thanks. He retrieved his spear and took up his place once more in the line.

He returned to find the time field failing, overwhelmed by the sheer number of actors moving through it. It failed and the tyranids ran forward, no longer impeded by the constant sheeting of the necron gauss volleys.

The necron line was in shambles, broken up by the tyranid subterranean assault.

Something screamed, setting his skull to shivering. Through occluding mists of boiled tyranid blood came a lumbering form. A crescent shaped head swept from side to side. The animal was the size of one of the huge human war machines, trundling forward on bladed limbs. A spiked tail lashed behind it. Scurrying along its flanks were lesser organisms, still fearsome, each easily the height of a necron.

Everything about the creature displayed its importance in whatever passed for a tyranid hierarchy. It screamed again, sending the tyranids running forward with renewed vigour. Mandibles waved around its jaws, wickedly hooked. Other organisms fell dripping from orifices in the animal's body, newly born and already hunting.

Anrakyr looked around him, trying to find some means of killing this new threat. There was little help around him, merely dully moving warriors.

Already the emboldened tyranids were breaking the necrons, pushing them back to the gate. There was no time to find a better weapon.

Anrakyr hefted his spear and charged forward.

Surprisingly, the triarch praetorians followed. Their rods of covenant blasted a hole for him through the guardian creatures.

He slipped in the blood. Things swam in it, wormlike organisms and other, less identifiable creatures. They popped beneath his strides.

Anrakyr cast his spear, lancing the weapon deep into the organism's head. The animal slowed with a trilling squeal. He tried to sprint forward, but the blood slowed him. He managed a run. Then he leapt, fingers punching into the beast's side.

Other tyranids continued to spill from holes in its side, but Anrakyr ignored them. Thin blood oozed from the small wounds he punched in. He clambered onto its back and ran forward.

It bucked and trembled, trying to dislodge the necron overlord. Anrakyr nearly lost his footing, only just avoiding falling from its side to be trampled beneath its thrashing claws. An orifice opened before him and a hissing thing climbed out. Anrakyr's fist took it through the skull, punching through chitin and bone, popping the brain.

His spear gleamed where it was lodged in the greater creature's skull. It beckoned, like a flag. He wrapped his hands around the haft of the spear and thrust down, driving it through the braincase of the beast. It screamed one last time before it collapsed.

Anrakyr leapt clear, ploughing through the pooling tyranid blood. He paused a moment, letting the sense of victory flow through him, but it felt hollow. The tyranids lost their coordination, milling in confusion.

The overlord left the colossal corpse behind and rejoined the main body of his necrons.

The tyranids were thrown back, carved to pieces at the molecular level. Steaming chunks of dead alien collapsed into the rock. Their glutinous, acidic blood washed up the defile, unable to drain down through the solid rock, rolling in thick waves like the sap from millions of cut trees.

The bio-acid hissed and spat, creating foul-smelling, chemical steam, as it slowly ate into the shins and feet of the embattled necrons. Tyranids continued to charge forward, driven by unspeakable hunger and abominable intelligence.

Some of the smaller creatures could barely slog through the remains of their fellows. They thrashed and screamed as they drowned, sucked beneath the waves of their own species' blood.

The assault faltered. Only the largest creatures were able to navigate the rising tide of blood. Those that approached were torn apart by concentrated gauss fire as coordinated targeting protocols activated in the empty-shelled skulls of the necron warriors. Scarabs fell in carpets as their energy was completely drained.

A reprieve had been bought.

Elation flooded through Anrakyr as further good news arrived. A rush of air fluttered the tattered, ancient fabric that draped his chassis. Jubilant, synthetic cries came from the canoptek creatures. The worker crypteks surrounded the Traveller. All of them bowed.

'Kehlrantyr is open,' they chorused.

Anrakyr turned away from the dead tyranids. The great gates of Kehlrantyr, the carved obsidian portals, had been levered open. Air pressure differentiation gusted out as the tomb world opened on to the surface for the first time in countless years.

Tyranid blood already spilled in, rushing in little rivulets past Anrakyr's legs. Green lights played in the stygian darkness of Kehlrantyr's interior. It seemed the tomb world had still to awaken, even with the tumult that engulfed its surface.

'So it is,' Anrakyr said. Had he been able, he would have smiled.

Shaudukar was the first to notice the pack of flayer-cursed that hunted them.

'We are being followed, my cryptek,' she whispered.

Valnyr sighed. 'The reprieve is over. I suppose it was too much to hope that our path to the gate would leave us unmolested.'

Static followed her words. It sounded like the buzzing she kept hearing.

Numerous side passages branched from their path. Rotten air gusted from statue-carved niches flanking them.

'What are your orders, Valnyr?' Shaudukar asked.

'I don't know.' Every fibre of her being demanded that she run, but she remained where she stood.

Footsteps echoed down one of the side passages. Lockstepped, disciplined, they sounded like metal on stone. Lychguard and false necrons readied themselves to face whatever this new threat might be.

The flayers hissed their static from behind, breaking into an ungainly run. A ragged volley of gauss fire and more esoteric weapons slowed them. But it was not enough. The flayers advanced, faster and faster, eager to share their hungry curse.

The mysterious footsteps grew louder and louder, bouncing off the stone, echoing from the statues. Valnyr prepared herself for the worst, diverting her attention away from the flayers. She held her staff ready. The cryptek gathered the threads of time, prepared to do what she could to survive for minutes longer. Green light flickered down the passage.

The flayers faltered as they drew level, stunned and broken by the thunder of gauss weaponry that exploded outwards. Warriors marched from the passage with near mindless belligerence. At their front stood a sentient necron. Valnyr recognised the leader as a necron of high stature, judging by the ornate carvings of his chassis and the crown that stood proud from his skull. She did not know the sigils that marked his allegiance, but she was thankful to see him.

She fell to her knees, elated. Then hunger burned through her once more. Her world went dark.

Strongpoints were being set up all across the ship, manned by armed serfs and combat-tasked servitors. Plates in the floor, walls and ceiling angled out on hydraulic pistons, creating cover and barricades.

Jatiel caught the telltale scent of smoke moving through the ship's atmosphere.

'That is not a good sign,' Emudor said.

'No, it isn't,' agreed Ventara.

They rushed through corridors of preparing serfs, through strobing fields of blood-red light and alarm klaxons. The ship shuddered around them, wracked by palsied tremors. A tech-adept directed them through the vessel, routing them towards the likely ingress point for the tyranid boarders. Serf shock troops, encased in bulky void-suits, were caught up in the Space Marines' wake.

Great screams of tortured metal overwhelmed the alarms. Localised atmosphere died. Serfs fell, pulled through sudden holes in the hull and out into vacuum. Tentacles erupted through the breaches, questing, reaching and writhing. Asaliah was the first to react, to open fire. The Deathwatch veteran's bolter coughed, popping frozen blood blisters out of the crimson and bone tyranid limbs.

Jatiel pushed himself forward. Through the vacuum and zero gravity, the Blood Angels sergeant flew towards the hole. He brought his mace down with a thunderous crack, pulverising chitin, flesh and bone. A fine mist of blood droplets sprayed outwards and then quickly froze.

Boltguns fired, the sound muted, and rounds impacted into more of the tentacles, detonating and blowing more chunks from alien flesh. Ventara yelled into the vox as one of the grasping tentacles, coated in bone hooks, rasped along his armour. Vapour shot out from the compromised battleplate, but the Space Marine fought on.

Genestealers flowed in, clambering along the tentacles like jungle predators. They jinked and danced through the hail of bolter fire. One leapt towards Jatiel, face leering with a dead-eyed smile. His mace caught it under the jaw, pulling the head and attached spinal cord off and out.

'There are too many!' the sergeant yelled.

Grenades sailed past him in response. The sergeant kicked off a tentacle, pushing himself back into the embrace of the *Golden Promise*. Shrapnel erupted before his eyes, breaking through the tentacles and running genestealers.

He saw a squid-like organism behind them, mouth open wide, vomiting forth the genestealers. Bolts flew through the void around him, impacting into the grasping organism's body.

As he floated backwards, Jatiel reached for the krak grenades at his belt. He primed and flung them. Tentacles caught the grenades and pulled them greedily into the grasping organism's mouth.

Jatiel smiled as they detonated, breaking up the creature's head. Genestealers were caught in the explosion, pulled apart by bone and chitin fragments.

But Jatiel had misjudged the explosion. He was caught on its edge, flung back towards the ship and cracking into its gothic skin. His armour's auto-senses warned him of breached integrity. Cold spots flushed against his skin and he could hear a rush of air as his armour's atmosphere escaped.

Then Asaliah was there. 'Up you come, sergeant.' The veteran grabbed Jatiel and dragged him back inside.

The ship's vox-network intruded. Tyranid creatures flooded her, boarding at multiple locations.

'The xenos are making for the bridge and the enginarium. This ship is lost if we do not hold those locations,' Ventara said. Already more squid-like creatures were swarming towards this breach.

'Asaliah, you and Ventara will go to the enginarium. Secure and hold. I will take Emudor to reinforce the bridge.'

CHAPTER NINE

Valnyr awoke before the great gates of Kehlrantyr, borne upon the shoulders of her lychguard. The atmosphere was tense. She could hear an argument between Shaudukar and the false necrons.

'The cryptek is afflicted,' said Nuensis.

'No,' asserted Shaudukar with weary finality. Her tone indicated she had been repeating the word for some time.

'I am... well,' Valnyr said. 'Let me down.'

The great gates of Kehlrantyr lay open. Green glyphs continued to glow, announcing the impeccable glory of Kehlrantyr and her unassailable hosts. The irony was not lost on Valnyr.

Their numbers were greater than they had been. Other necrons had joined the party, marked with symbols the cryptek didn't recognise. A brace of destroyers, cackling in their own dark tongue, flew overhead, out of reach of the flayers. Canoptek constructs, summoned by the desperation of the necrons, swarmed to them. Valnyr's fleet splashed through liquid. The acidic fluid pitted her legs, hissing and drawing clouds of dissolved metals into the air.

'Blood,' said Shaudukar. There was an edge to the lychguard's voice. Valnyr glanced over, her posture indicating *concern*. The cryptek resisted the urge to fall to her knees and lap at the organic liquid with a tongue she no longer possessed. She shuddered. Where had that thought come from?

Sunlight streamed in from beyond, dispelling the gloom that afflicted Kehlrantyr's interior. More unfamiliar necrons rushed inside, while Valnyr could hear the distinctive wail of necron weaponry from outside.

The Kehlrantyri drew up in a protective circle, hunched in shadow, ready for whatever came at them. Aliens hissed from behind them, joining the static-screams of the flayer-touched. One hundred necrons of Kehlrantyr, perhaps the last left sane of their fabled world, greeted their kin from elsewhere.

'A paltry display,' boomed a voice. 'But a welcome one.' The other necrons advanced on them, nigh on a thousand of them. 'I was concerned that the tomb world was not yet awake and I am heartened to see that Kehlrantyr stands ready to greet me.'

'Yes, my lord,' Valnyr said. Best to err on the side of caution, she thought. Crypteks, distinctive and easily recognised to Valnyr's practiced gaze, split from the main advancing group and took station beside the great gates. Already the vast portal was humming closed, driven by the cants of these foreign necrons.

'Your words and presence indicate that this tomb world is awake. Yet your posture states that you wish it were not so.' The speaker halted. 'What has happened here?'

One of the bizarrely ornamented necrons that accompanied the speaker whispered, 'You were warned, Anrakyr.'

Valnyr said, 'The dead words of Llandu'gor afflict us.'

Curses streamed from the speaker. A great thud sounded from the gate, a bruising organic sound as something large charged into the obsidian doors. He shouted to his crypteks, 'Seal the gate!'

Valnyr watched them comply, watched the telltale glow of chronomancy centre on the great edifice. 'A null field?' she asked, unable to keep the words contained.

The necron lord turned to face her, hands clenched in the sign of *profound disappointment*. Lightning played over the overlord's body, abrading away the blood and gore that covered him. A dry circle of stone surrounded him, kept clean by flowing scarabs. 'Yes,' he answered.

Such a display of skill, such unsurpassed knowledge of the ancient time science. To seal the doors in a field where time no longer held sway, a permanent region of stasis. They would open no more. They would never again face a progression of time. But to do so would drain the crypteks, using their power to channel the field. The implications were staggering.

She groaned, 'What comes behind you?'

'The tyranids swarm on this world, cryptek.' He spoke slowly, enunciating his words as if to a child.

'Tyranids?' asked Maantril. 'What manner of beasts are these?'

Nuensis blurted the equivalent of an exasperated snort. 'The aliens that have infiltrated our tombs.'

'We are trapped, then,' said Maantril. Other nobles took up the cry. 'We are trapped and there is no way out.'

The newcomers advanced. One of their number, a floating destroyer, said, 'What of the tomb's Dolmen Gate?'

The overlord registered surprise to hear such a question come from the dent-skulled destroyer. 'You must have a route out.'

The three triarch praetorians flanked the overlord, rods of covenant prepared to compel an answer.

'We do,' Valnyr said. 'We did not wish to use it.'

'Where does it lead?' asked one of the praetorians, its skull-visage surmounted by a fan of broken knives. The others chorused the same question.

'Zarathusa,' answered Valnyr.

The overlord groaned. 'Of course it does,' he muttered. 'There is no time to waste. You,' he indicated the Kehlrantyrian necrons, 'will lead us to the Dolmen Gate.'

* * *

The buzzing came first, low and subsonic. It lanced through the darkness, gliding on static wings and setting the metal bones of her chassis to vibrating. Hunger followed. Valnyr's mouth opened and static joined the screams already echoing from the dark chambers. These were the static-screams of the lost, the haunting cries of those rewritten by the flayer virus. Valnyr could almost hear the tortured personalities, the ghosts of those who had endured so much, who had let bitter jealousy and the fear of death drive them into a bargain in a now forgotten age. Her family, her kin, all those she had known, lost to the creeping vengeance of a broken god.

Necrons recoiled around her. Her fingers tapped against her staff in a restless rhythm. The fit passed.

'You are afflicted,' said one of the praetorians.

'The dead words of Llandu'gor ride your soul,' said another.

Shaudukar and her lychguard bristled. 'Our mistress is fine,' said the lead lychguard. Valnyr could hear a crackle beneath her words, a hint of static and buzzing.

Weapons were drawn, turned upon one another. The old divisions showed themselves. Fear and buzzing, static and horror, branched through hurried conversation, past accusation and understanding.

The tyranids were forgotten, pushed aside as a problem that could be dealt with later.

'Enough,' said Anrakyr, steel lashing all the others into silence. Valnyr noticed that the overlord kept his spear levelled, ready to stab out at a moment's notice.

Two camps were forming. Kehlrantyri and Anrakyr's foreigners faced one another. They stopped marching to the Dolmen Gate. They stood, immobile, shoulders hunched, faces impassive but with upraised voices echoing through the darkness.

Flayers chose that moment to assault, sprinting in their jerking movements, shambling into momentum from darkened streets.

Lightning lanced out from the unafflicted, punching through clumps of the flayers. Crackling sheets of green light, chained and shackled to the near-mindless necron warriors, stabbed out. Other, more esoteric weapons added their voices to the hue and cry as sentient necrons, gifted with weaponry of ancient science and provenance, fired.

But on the flayers came, talons reaching, mouths stretched wide to taste non-existent flesh.

Valnyr forgot the division between Kehlrantyri and foreigners, between her kin and her accusers. All was subsumed beneath her desire to survive and the dreadful buzzing.

Time slowed, but this was no expression of her science – this was the stress-filled moment of collision, the do or die of combat. She slammed her staff forward with nerveless grace, ramming it into the chest cavity of a hissing flayer. She grunted as she lifted the flayer. It slid towards her down the haft of her staff, hands and talons outstretched, reaching for her head.

The buzzing grew, louder and louder. She yelled, screaming into the flayer, matching the buzzing with her own vocalisations.

Then the flayer's head was gone, chopped away by Anrakyr the Traveller. 'Less panic, more restraint,' he hissed. The melee swept him away.

Valnyr watched as knots of warriors were subsumed, dragged down by the frantic motions of flayers. She channelled energy, stealing atoms from the stale air of Kehlrantyr, converting them to heat and power. It coalesced at the head of her staff and blasted outwards with a thunderclap of noise, shattering flayers into pieces of stinging metal.

Shrapnel expanded in a cloud of flickering metal and smoke, pinging off the chassis of nearby necrons. An unlucky false necron was caught in the blast, flung to pieces.

Valnyr felt a moment's pity, but it was drowned with the instinctual scrabbling for continued existence. Flayers threw themselves with mindless belligerence onto the shields of Valnyr's lychguard.

Everywhere she looked there were flayers, stumbling from shadowed doorways, lurching out from dark streets. With them came the static, growing and growing and growing. The sound numbed her, broke her mind apart. The cryptek could scarcely stay standing.

All was confusion. All was broken. The world died around her, not with a bang, nor a whimper, but drowned beneath screams of static and buzzing.

A flayed one broke through the cordon of her lychguard, still clad in the finery of a necron noble. Its mouth stretched open, broken metal teeth glittering in the green light. Talons stretched, scraping for her throat. She stumbled back, but fell into a lychguard.

The flayer scrabbled after her.

Valnyr spat a word. Time froze in a small bubble. It enclosed just the two of them, an intimate moment between flayer-cursed Dynast and cryptek.

The flayer scrabbled on four limbs, prowling like some predator. It skittered and jumped, jaws distended. All the while it announced its terrible hunger. Something in Valnyr's breast answered, but she shoved it away. She levered her staff, keeping it at bay. It snapped at her, jaws clacking.

Time began to resume. She shoved the bladed end of her staff through the flayer's skull. Energy swirled down the weapon, blew through the skull and erased one of her lychguard in the blast. Again came the guilt, momentary and fleeting, and again it was smothered beneath self-preservation.

The flayer tide receded, but the buzzing stayed behind.

Valnyr could hear words, faintly through the noise, old and lost to time in a dialect she could scarcely remember. *'To those who have turned their faces away,'* she could hear in the buzzing and the static. *'To those who are faithless and wretched in their jealousies.'*

She stood still, head cocked to the side. The words echoed from all around them, driven through the shadows and the gloom.

'Do you hear that?' she asked Shaudukar. The question echoed through the forgotten halls of her home.

'To those who have denied us. To those who have denied me. I will wreak vengeance. I will wrench your souls and break your bones. I will cast hunger

through your accursed existence. Down the eons, you will not forget. I will grant you this gift from love turned aside and make you like me, break you in my image as you have broken me. I shall cast the fear of myself into you and all of your kind. I am Llandu'gor. I am the hunger. I am the flayer, and from this moment, you shall be too.'

'I am Llandu'gor,' announced one Kehlrantyrian necron. The chorus rippled everywhere, bouncing from the dead walls.

The division came back with a sound like fire. The necron who spoke the c'tan's name was annihilated by one of the triarch praetorians, reduced to its constituent atoms by a covenant rod.

Confusion reigned.

'Enough,' Anrakyr bellowed. 'This bickering solves nothing. Cryptek, where is the entrance to the Dolmen Gate? Are we near?'

'Yes,' Valnyr answered, tearing her attention away from the buzzing and the half-heard words. 'We are close.'

By the time Valnyr was aware of the betrayal, she was already bisected. Anrakyr's spear stabbed through her spine, carving her body apart. The Traveller's expression was impassive. How could it not be? His face, his features etched themselves onto Valnyr's memory.

She opened her mouth to question, to ask why he had done this, but all that emerged was a scream. It sounded like static.

'I am sorry,' he said in a tone that implied nothing of the kind.

Shaudukar and Valnyr's lychguard charged the Traveller, warscythes raised, angry and belligerent. The triarch praetorians turned them to ash with rapid blasts from their rods of covenant.

'You are afflicted,' continued Anrakyr, as if nothing had happened. 'And that is why I am honoured by your continued insistence that you serve.'

Already flayers were emerging from the shadowed ways, lurching out from the darkness. The stunned Kehlrantyrian necrons answered with desperation, or fell to their knees and joined them.

Her mind sought purpose, searching for some utility, some artifice that could salvage this situation. She reached towards Anrakyr, trying to summon the presence of mind to repay his betrayal. Nothing answered, nothing except the frenzied screaming of the flayers.

The foreigners punched free, heading towards the Dolmen Gate and the ship that would take them from this place, take them to safety and freedom. Valnyr could only watch, inching towards her fallen staff. Already lightning played about her severed spine, metal flowing and stretching towards her sundered lower body.

But it was too slow.

Flayers were everywhere now, surrounding the doomed remnants of their kin. A chorus arose, three words repeated over and over from those still with minds and those already broken.

'*I am Llandu'gor,*' they chanted.

A snapping crackle saw her sundered body reunited. Valnyr stumbled to her feet and grasped her staff. She fired at the flayers and her kin. There was no finesse here, no discrimination and no mercy. She killed so that she would not die. She killed so that she could deny the hunger that burned within her.

One flayer attacked, clad in markings she ought to recognise. She punched her hand through its chest, reaching its spine. She tore at it, dropped her staff and reached in with both hands.

She failed. Flayers bore her down, hungry mouths open, eager to share, to welcome her into their curse.

The buzzing swelled, until it was all she could hear. Gone were the words. Gone was her identity, her science, her personality, her artifice.

With the buzzing bloomed hunger, ever-present, but now all-consuming.

The necron once known as Valnyr, High Cryptek to the Kehlrantyr Dynasts, vented its screaming hunger to the darkness, joined by the rest of her doomed kin.

CHAPTER TEN

Through the faded shadows of Kehlrantyr they moved. Down processional avenues, watched over by the great legions that once called the tomb world home and who would now wander the halls as corrupted revenants of the glory they once possessed. Kehlrantyr's people doomed to suffer a fate worse than the true death. Their mortality surrendered only to find their personalities erased and their purpose futile and corrupted.

'A tragic loss,' insisted Armenhorlal, shockingly lucid. 'This world is dead. Its people are dead.'

Anrakyr offered no response. The destroyer cooed to himself with an idiot's sincerity.

The deeper they moved down into the tomb world, the greater the decrepitude of the surroundings and rampant technology became. Machines rumbled. The floor and walls vibrated to a hidden hum, just on the edge of their hearing. Green sigils stood out everywhere, warning signs marked by canoptek constructs. Each announced broken quarters of the tomb world, submerged or stolen by collapse.

Turning a corridor, they found transparent observation windows studding the processional they advanced down, offering a vista into a cavernous space. The centre of the world, the hollowed-out core of Kehlrantyr, gaped to their left, the ceiling arcing away impossibly far until it faded into itself.

A bizarre, thrumming hum coated the air. 'The warp,' Armenhorlal said, voice quavering slightly.

A cry went up from the front of their force. Anrakyr prepared himself for the worst. What he saw instead would have brought a smile to his face, had he been capable. Ships floated, still hanging suspended in their docks, over the world-chasm below.

Sentient necrons broke ranks and watched from the windows. Lights activated at their presence, dispelling the darkness at the heart of the tomb world in a wash of brilliance. At the very centre of the world, suspended by sciences lost even to the oldest of crypteks, floated the Dolmen Gate, and before it the great crescent blade of a Cairn-class tombship.

**

Derelict and desolate, the webway was a truly alien place. Colours that had no basis in reality and sounds and echoes broke all around them, shifting and dazzling. Some comforts were to be found, some anxiety balms. Here and there glowed the bright green of necron technology, eating into the walls, veining through the twisting corridors.

Small spider-like constructs flowed in their wake. The command tomb of the necron vessel was a tense place. None of the necrons spoke. They all stood at their stations, silent in their thoughts, ruminating on the paths that had led them astray, that had lured them to this desperate moment.

The near presence of the warp weighed heavily on their souls. Anrakyr felt observed, as though the eldar were watching.

As if reading his thoughts, Armenhorlal turned to him and asked, 'Where are our old foes?'

Anrakyr, caught, collected himself, laughed. 'Fading. They are a shadow of what they once were. Their empire was broken by their own hubris, and they have entered the twilight of their species. Their threat is past.'

'So why do we hide here? Why not move at full speed?' asked the destroyer.

Anrakyr provided no answer, merely toyed with his cluster of eldar stones.

'You will need allies,' announced Khatlan, apropos of nothing. The praetorian's tone was conversational.

'You have already said this,' said Anrakyr, watching the swirling utterly alien colours of the webway pass.

'You will need allies,' repeated Dovetlan. The praetorians moved to surround the Traveller. Their message was clear, but Anrakyr grew tired of their sudden upsurge in communication.

'We know where you will find them,' said Ammeg.

'Where?' asked Anrakyr, his frustration rising.

'Where we are already bound,' answered Dovetlan.

'The Zarathusans?' asked Anrakyr.

'Yes,' said Khatlan.

'No,' said Dovetlan.

'Probably,' finished Ammeg.

'They will help,' began Khatlan. 'But you will need more assistance to defeat these tyranids. You cannot rely upon the Zarathusans to stand firm against these foes.'

'We know of others who will assist.'

'Who? The Silent King?'

'No,' said Ammeg. 'The living.'

Anrakyr laughed. 'Why would the living accept our help?'

'For the same reason you would seek them out. They are desperate. *You* are desperate.'

'Desperation does not cause beings to take leave of their wits, nor does it ignore history,' Anrakyr growled. 'After what we have wrought here, after what we have wrought all over their "empire", why would they agree to assist us?'

'Because they have done so before. These tyranids create strange alliances.

Their threat is monumental in scope. The Silent King knows this and has allowed for a loosening of the old prohibitions.'

'You have hinted at this alliance before. Your *decorations* betray an organic taint,' Anrakyr said.

'We fought alongside the humans at the Silent King's command once before. The alliance was convenient and ensured his victory there,' said Ammeg. 'We wear these decorations as a mark of honour and a reminder.'

'Tell me more,' said Anrakyr.

The bridge was destroyed, open to the void. Shipmaster Korbel was dead, erased in a wash of bio-acid. A wing of tyranid fighter organisms had made directly for the vital nerve centre aboard the *Golden Promise* and broken it open. That the organisms were eliminated scant seconds later by point defence turrets offered no consolation.

The ship was now dead in the void, while secondary systems and strongpoints were still struggling to come online. They had held for three hours, a valiant, desperate effort. A number of tyranid bio-ships lay crippled around them, a testament to Shipmaster Korbel's command of void war. Killed in long-range duels, or broken by point-blank broadsides, they oozed frozen blood and escaped gases into Perdita's orbit. But they had been overwhelmed by sheer numbers, surrounded by ever increasing hordes of the twisted creatures.

The convict ships had fared worse, isolated and torn apart before they could reach the perceived safety of the Adeptus Astartes vessel. Their burning hulks already painted Perdita's skies, carved by the maws of tyranid leviathans and cast down to be rent asunder by atmospheric entry.

'Asaliah, what is your status?' Jatiel asked as he drove his mace through a twitching termagant.

'We cannot hold the enginarium, sergeant,' Asaliah grunted. 'Too many creatures swarm this location.'

Frustration filled the Blood Angels sergeant. Duty drove him, sustained him. 'We must abandon the ship. Head for the ventral hangar bay.'

The hangar sat roughly equidistant between the Blood Angels. Jatiel knew that this was a lost cause, that he would likely not survive making it there, let alone launching a Thunderhawk. But he was a Space Marine, and he was stubborn besides.

The sergeant and Emudor rushed through the gothic steel innards of the *Golden Promise*. Crew warnings and propaganda stared down at the red-armoured giants, admonishing service and praising diligence.

Bulkheads sealed, dropping down on magnetic hinges, directing the Space Marines. One to their right, sealed and shut, exploded. Acid swamped out, followed by swarming tyranids.

Emudor fell to his knees, a spar of metal skewering his helmet. The Blood Angel sank below the acid.

Jatiel pushed his way through panicking serfs. He fired over his shoulder, trusting in muscle reflexes to target the tyranid swarm behind him. Twenty thousand souls aboard the *Golden Promise* went about their duties. Some fled from cored and voided sections of the ship, bound for others where their skills could still be useful.

Explosions constantly rocked the ship now. Void shields were down. Jatiel could smell the actinic blowback. Smoke filled the compartments. Screaming, too. Jatiel knew it for a bad sign. 'The ship's air scrubbers are down,' he hissed. Crew recoiled from the Space Marine stalking through their panicking masses. Red-robed magi, tech-priests from the Chapter's Adeptus Mechanicus allies, swung censers and mumbled binaric prayers over sparking service panels as the *Golden Promise* died.

Threat identifiers painted every face that spewed past Jatiel's vision, his helmet locking him away from the hue and cry. Vital signs for each of his squad members showed elevated heart rates and the chemical spill of combat hormones. One flickered where nothing should be, the battle-brother Jatiel had left stationed on the bridge. Cassuen. A ghost return, an imaging artefact. A taunt from his damaged armour.

A channel opened. Jatiel stopped moving. The request for contact, a haunting reminder of casualties presumed.

'Sergeant,' Cassuen's voice hissed.

'Brother, you live? What of the bridge?'

Cassuen let out a cough that was thick with phlegm. A juddering, sour breath sucked in through lungs rendered consumptive by fluid. 'The auspex–' Cassuen began. Another horrific, laboured breath. 'The auspex still functions.'

It broke Jatiel's hearts to hear such pain and such belligerent honour, to know that his brother was so near to death, and yet still clinging to duty without succumbing to the perennial curses of the Blood. 'Sergeant. Sergeant, they have arrived. The xenos. The gate. It is open.'

One more wrenching breath, one more exhalation and then a long, gurgling rattle. The link remained open, but no more sound came through. Cassuen was dead, his warning delivered. His words heralded a great tremor through the cracking ship, shivering it down to its bones. Serfs staggered and fell, flung against walls and bulkheads. The emergency wailing took on an even more plaintive quality.

Disturbing screams filtered down the broad corridors. Shadows filled with hissing, although Jatiel knew that to be escaping atmospherics as compartments were opened to hard vacuum.

Closed bulkheads, sealed to all but the Adeptus Astartes command codes, opened as he approached. The sergeant could hear the distinctive pop-whine of firing shotcasters hurling non-standard ammunition. The weapons fired low-grade plasteks and rubber at tremendous speeds to prevent hull breaches.

Alien cries of pain and hunger met the noises. More tyranids were aboard the *Golden Promise*, swarming and boiling through the proud vessel's veins.

A sudden clang was the only warning he had before spikes of super-dense bone chewed through the hull section next to him. Bright blue gas flooded in from the holes in the hull. Nearby serfs started coughing, then spasming as the gas-induced seizures. Their flesh melted seconds later.

Paint abraded from Jatiel's armour, but the self-sufficient nature of Mark VII plate ensured the gas did little more.

The alien bones flexed and with a sound like hawked spit, the sheared-off section of bulkhead cannoned into the opposite wall. More gas flooded in. Hissing creatures leapt from the darkness, bringing with them cold, trailing vapour from an imperfect seal.

Jatiel's boltgun barked and a stream of high-velocity, high-calibre rounds cut down the first emerging ranks of tyranid organisms. He fired one-handed. Those that slipped past were met by the sergeant's power mace. The golden, inverted teardrop of blood crunched into an alien's misshapen head, blowing out its brains against several more. His return stroke struck them down in turn, breaking bones, shattering bodies, culling meat.

'For the Emperor and Sanguinius! For the Angel!' he snarled, helmet vox-casters set to maximum, throwing his cry of belligerence and rage at the invading xenos.

Ventara and Asaliah joined him in the age-old war cry, running into the chamber. The pallid xenos creatures recoiled, sensitive aural organs nearly overwhelmed by the wall of noise. Bolts scythed them down as the two other Space Marines culled them.

'The hangar is no longer a viable option,' said the Deathwatch veteran.

Errant shots cut into the boarding organism that had delivered the tyranids onto the *Golden Promise*, prompting mewling cries of pain.

More creatures emerged from within the boarding pod, vomited out in a slurry of viscera and sickening liquids. These were four-armed organisms, each limb ending in a deadly claw.

'More genestealers,' Ventara spat. The aliens jinked and danced, flickering out of the way of fired bolt shells. Nimble and deadly monstrosities loped through the fug of blue smoke and squelched into the slurry of dissolving serfs.

One got inside Jatiel's guard before Asaliah's hurled combat knife skewered its head. It aspirated blood as it died, gurgling as dripping chunks of jellied brain oozed from the hole in its skull.

Beetle creatures whirred through the blue smoke, latching on to the front of Jatiel's armour. They started chewing, spitting acid onto the ceramite and cutting in. He swiped them off, desperate to remove the creatures before they damaged something vital.

More termagants flowed around the genestealers, firing beetles from obscene organic rifles. The Space Marines were pushed down the corridor, retreating in the face of the tyranid onslaught.

'There are too many of the xenos!' Ventara yelled.

'We need a defensible position,' Asaliah agreed.

Jatiel had a map already overlaying his visor. His eyes rolled over the options, but there were precious few and none nearby. He spat curses into the vox.

They passed from one section into another, vaulting over a trough in the deck. All the while they fired their boltguns. All the while tyranids died. But it was not enough, nowhere near enough.

Asaliah stopped firing, wheeled and slammed his fist into the wall. A bulkhead dropped down, pounding through squealing tyranids.

Silence and smoke filled this section of the ship. Fires burned from within habitation quarters. Life pods sat quiet and empty in their cradles, waiting for serfs too filled with duty and obedience to ever use them. Drooling servitors patrolled the area, sweeping for dust and particulates. Some had fire crawling along their organic flesh.

The distant crackle of lasweaponry echoed through the corridors. The Space Marines followed the sound. Halfway down the *Golden Promise*'s length, they entered an observation deck.

Armourglass windows stared out into the vacuum. Tyranid creatures, some ray-like, others attached with the mindless insistence of molluscs, glared down from the windows. More organisms swooped past.

But something else dragged at Jatiel's attention. Beyond the tyranids sucking on the glass, beyond the hive ships, the sergeant could just see a green glow emerging from the ancient structures that orbited Perdita. Lightning stabbed out from a sudden rift in reality. Then a crescent-shaped ship appeared, hanging in the darkness.

'As if one xenos wasn't enough,' Asaliah spat.

The newcomer's movements were slick, sliding between the grasping tyranid ships. Sheet lightning broke from random surfaces. Each blast terminated a bio-vessel, breaking it to bleeding pieces.

Then it slid past, bound for Perdita's surface, punching through more xenos hive-ships.

Something critical died in the *Golden Promise*. Jatiel watched a surge of fire sweep from the bow of the ship, back towards the engines. Secondary blast doors slammed shut. A serf was carved in two by the descending portal. He set up a shrieking wail, agonised and horrible.

Ventara ended him with his gold-encrusted power sword.

Localised gravity failed as the ship began to spin, pushed by the explosion back into Perdita's orbit. The Blood Angels snapped their maglocked boots to the deck.

Horror dawned in Jatiel's soul. He knew what was coming. 'All hands, brace for impact!' he shouted. He was still bellowing the order when fire danced along the *Golden Promise*'s battered hull, erasing encrusted tyranids vomiting warrior organisms into her decks, when the storied ship entered Perdita's atmosphere, on an inexorable course for the dead planet's surface.

CHAPTER ELEVEN

Jatiel awoke to a pain such as he had never known. Something felt wrong in his head, as though something had come loose. He opened his eyes, saw through the green lenses that stared from his helmet. He thanked the primarch that the systems were still functional. He lay over a melting puddle of ash and snow. That should have brought meaning and understanding to where he was, but his mind refused to focus.

The Blood Angels sergeant braced his hands beneath him. Servos whined as he tried to push himself up.

He toppled and fell, overbalanced. Blood pooled beneath him, the deep and rich red of Space Marine vitae. Jatiel tried to push himself up again, grunting and heaving out breath that burned like fire. Something felt wrong, terribly wrong. His vision blurred. The ash and snow was gone, replaced by star-filled blackness. The two images wavered, fading into one another.

'No,' he cried.

A weight settled on his back. A calming voice, Adeptus Astartes deep, spoke. 'Easy, sergeant. Easy.'

His backpack whined as something clicked. Power thrummed through his armour as it reactivated. 'Up you come,' said Asaliah, an echo of his words on the *Golden Promise*.

Jatiel was pulled to his feet. 'Took a beating, Jatiel,' said Asaliah. The Deathwatch veteran's face, left bare to the feeble atmosphere, was a mask of pain and gritted teeth. Furrows had been carved in his flesh, rocks studding it from where he must have slid. Jatiel couldn't tell whether Asaliah referred to himself, the sergeant, the *Golden Promise* or the situation in general.

Asaliah shot Jatiel's right side a pointed look.

Jatiel glanced down and saw the reason why he couldn't push himself up. His right arm was gone. His prized power mace was missing.

Jatiel's gaze drifted away from Asaliah and he saw the *Golden Promise* burning. 'The serfs?' he asked, working his jaw, stretching his wrenched muscles. He used his left hand to crack his jaw back into place.

'No unarmoured mortal would have survived that crash. We are lucky we were in the observation dome. We were thrown free from the ship when it fell. Your head preceded us, sergeant. Truly, you are blessed with a thick skull.'

Asaliah hazarded a smile, and then winced in pain.

Jatiel barked an ugly laugh. 'What of Ventara?' he asked after a moment.

'I've yet to find him, sergeant. I did find this, however.' Asaliah offered Jatiel Ventara's bolter. 'We should be armed.'

'Acknowledged, brother.' Jatiel cocked the boltgun, awkwardly cradling it with the stump of his right arm. 'This will take some getting used to.'

Asaliah grinned. 'I suspect you'll manage.'

They picked their way out of the rubble, moving away from the burning *Golden Promise*. The ship groaned as it settled into Perdita's crust. Jatiel saw that the great vessel had carved into the planet's depths.

'What lies beneath us?' he asked.

'Some sort of cave network.' Asaliah shrugged. 'The tactical briefings never hinted at their existence.'

'We should ascertain if a threat is here, try to find the xenos that appeared in orbit.'

Asaliah nodded. 'As you say.'

The pair descended awkwardly through the treacherous footing. Spars of metal stabbed from Perdita's surface, relics of the crash, offering handholds and a precarious route down.

Obsidian replaced granite the deeper into the crust they moved. Great metal cables snaked through the rock, sparking and stabbing out from broken ends where they had been snapped by the *Golden Promise*. Melted adamantium, ablated and super-heated by the ship's disastrous entrance into Perdita's orbit, dripped past them in sizzling streams.

Jatiel was breathing heavily. An insistent rune in his helm-display announced that he had a fractured skull. Shadows swooped, shadows that Jatiel knew had no basis in reality. He blinked the rune away.

As they neared the bottom of the hole, Jatiel slipped and fell. Without a right arm to stabilise him, the sergeant clattered and slid down into the darkness. He knew that Asaliah would be following as quickly as he dared.

The sergeant slipped over an edge, body cartwheeling as it encountered empty, stale air. Jatiel's thoughts deserted him as he fell the last metres.

Cables snapped at him, violently arresting his momentum. They held for microseconds, then broke in showers of sparks and lightning. He hit more and more, until he neared the bottom of the chasm. The last held and the sergeant was stuck, gently swaying in the darkness.

Liquid dripped from above, pattering across the blood-red plates of his armour. He blinked. The runes asserted that his skull was fractured. They announced that his brain suffered from oedema, swelling in its case, punished by trauma. Strain was placed on his psyche. The cracks in his mind widened further. He ignored the insistent bio-readouts.

'Sergeant,' a voice called.

Jatiel knew the cadences of the voice, recognised them, but could not match a name or a face to it.

'It's Asaliah,' said the voice. Asaliah. Of course. 'I am going to cut you down. Hang tight.'

Jatiel nodded and then laughed, the sound echoing. 'Hang tight,' he said. The words and the situation were absurd. He could see Asaliah's face highlighted in the darkness, pale and worried.

The report of a boltgun echoed, suddenly loud and bold. Sparks flew and Jatiel fell.

Fifteen metres down he hit the smooth, polished planes of the floor. Stone and ribs cracked. Ceramite fractured. Jatiel blacked out with the pain.

Asaliah was there to help him up. 'My thanks,' said Jatiel.

Lights clicked from Asaliah's armour, splitting the gloom and cutting away the strobing darkness. The broken hulk of the *Golden Promise* pressed down from above, shifting and creaking in the darkness. Small fires still burned on her. Blood and ichor dripped from cracks in the hull, the last remains of the serfs that had called her home and the xenos that had broken her.

Jatiel pushed out a breath, laboured and wheezing. It emerged as a snarl from his helmet's vocalisers. A groan replied from the darkness. The two Space Marines' bolters snapped up, hunting in the darkness. 'Xenos?' Jatiel voxed.

'No,' said Asaliah. 'That was human.'

Asaliah's light pierced the gloom, but barely broke into the obsidian-walled depths. Strange carvings reflected the light back at them, tinging it green. Skulls, great metre-high reliefs, watched from the black, shadows lingering in their sockets.

The groan came again, a wet cough of pain, thick with blood.

Asaliah's light shone, illuminating the space just below the *Golden Promise*.

A metal spar had stabbed into the floor, then broken free from the wreck. Impaled on that spar, pierced through his groin and abdomen, was Ventara. The Space Marine hung, blood drooling down the metal. His armour, with all its beautiful decoration, was cracked and broken.

Jatiel and Asaliah rushed to his side, both hobbling as fast as their abused bodies allowed. 'This looks grim, sergeant,' said Asaliah.

'It does. We'll have to pull him off.'

Asaliah nodded. With a grunt, the Deathwatch veteran stepped below the impaled Space Marine. Jatiel took up position beneath Ventara's backpack. They shoved, inducing pain-born stars to dance in Jatiel's vision.

Ventara groaned again, chemically numbed, voice thick with drool. He barely moved, sliding up the glistening length of broken metal. Asaliah grunted and they shoved the wounded Space Marine off the spar.

Jatiel heard scrabbling from above, claws snicking against the adamantium hull of the *Golden Promise*. Screeches came from the upper darkness, filled with alien hunger. Jatiel caught glimpses of bioluminescence, of bone and red chitin.

He opened fire, trying to track the aliens, to follow their movement patterns. The sergeant hit something. Blood spattered against the broken hulk of the frigate. A headless body fell, crunching grotesquely into the stone beside Jatiel.

The fallen creature writhed on broken limbs before exhaling a noxious breath and dying.

Asaliah added his own fire to his sergeant's before Jatiel's bolter clicked dry. He dropped the clip and pulled a new one from his belt, but it would not fit. It had been dented by his fall, wrenched out of shape. He had no time to find another.

Genestealers swarmed towards the Space Marines, hissing their vile hunger. Four-limbed monstrosities leaped forward.

Jatiel missed his mace as they came close in the blink of an eye. Bereft of the beautiful weapon, Jatiel resorted to using the empty bolter as a club. The weapon proved effective as a blunt instrument of death as he broke through a genestealer's chest cavity. Organs were blown out of the mauled xenos's back. It flew back into more of the beasts.

Others danced and jinked, moving inhumanly quick on long limbs. They scrabbled and clawed.

Ventara opened up with a bolt pistol, slurring litanies of fury and thirst through his chemical haze. Asaliah's bolter fire was expertly timed. Each bolt broke through one xenos, breaking out in a spray of blood and bone fragments, to find a home in another.

The horde of genestealers thinned.

'My–' Jatiel began. A xenos slipped through his guard, past the bolter, past his armour. Its clawed limb reached out. He ducked, trying to get out of its way. He tried and failed. It knocked into his helmet. A horrible pain blossomed in his skull. He blacked out.

Jatiel awoke to find Asaliah and Ventara surrounded by the broken and bleeding corpses of genestealers.

Ventara shared a worried, knowing look with Asaliah.

'I am fine, brothers,' said Jatiel, seeking to allay their concern.

'As you say, sergeant,' Ventara replied. The Space Marine clutched at the horrific wound that carved through his centre. It continued to bleed, a bad sign to one blessed by the gene-seed of Sanguinius. That the wound would not clot, that the Larraman cells and leucocytes of his advanced biology could not repair the injury, did not bode well.

With the combat over, the xenos dead – this wave at least – Asaliah sprayed synthetic flesh over the horrific injury. Ventara removed his helm. His pupils were large, dilated to account not just for darkness, but for the chemicals that raged through his system.

'Your orders, Jatiel?' Asaliah asked.

The sergeant cradled Ventara's bolter, reloading it awkwardly with one hand. 'As before. We ascertain the threat these xenos pose. We find a way to warn Lord Dante.'

His brothers nodded, but he could see disquiet in their eyes. Their situation was dire. Without a ship, how would they warn their Chapter Master? With the tyranids consuming this system, how would such a message even reach him before he brought the strength of the Chapter here?

Jatiel shoved the doubt aside. It served no purpose here. Questions had never suited him. Only duty. Only ever duty. 'We go deeper.'

So they did, through the darkness, weaving between massive chambers, black as the void. They moved past xenos carvings that glared with mindless, empty hunger. Sounds echoed behind them, the scrabbling purchase of claw against smooth stone, the scrape and susurrus of xenos breath.

The Space Marines ignored the noises, letting the sounds wash over them. They had a mission, and nothing else mattered.

Green lights swam through the gloom-filled depths. A hum suffused the air, setting dust to floating. Jatiel was no expert in xenos blasphemy, but even to him it was apparent that something here was awakening.

Little beetle machines watched from cracks in the wall, Asaliah's torchlight winking off micro-lenses and metal carapace. All around their reflections were thrown back at them, bouncing off the smooth obsidian of the walls. Carved reliefs displayed skeletal xeno-forms battling against what Jatiel thought appeared to be eldar.

'What are those?' Ventara asked, his voice blurring through the gloom, slurred with pain and chemical pain-suppressants.

'Eldar,' answered Asaliah simply, his voice grim.

Noise came from above, a subtle clicking sound, like gears shifting or a pen tapping.

Asaliah's light illuminated the ceiling. Green lenses stared down.

Ventara bellowed, 'Contact!'

Jatiel opened up with his boltgun as the alien construct descended on millipede callipers from the ceiling, hovering like a Land Speeder. It screeched at them in a machine burble.

Light played about the large lens that served the construct for a face. Energy coalesced. The chattering boltgun threw rounds into the construct's body, glancing off rippling alien materials. Sparks flew. As it moved, the construct phased in and out of existence, bolts passing through the now translucent body. Each phased effort brought the alien machine closer.

Lightning spat from its eye, barely missing Jatiel. His armour blackened, paint abraded into ash. He could feel intense heat flash-burning his skin.

Asaliah's bolter barked again, joined by Ventara's pistol. But the creature faded, dropping into the darkness.

The clicking of its calliper limbs surrounded the Space Marines. Pain punched through Jatiel's left leg. A metal forelimb erupted through his thigh.

Asaliah dropped his bolter and grabbed the sergeant as the machine started dragging him backwards, pulling him into the darkness. Jatiel bellowed as more limbs gripped his leg, and pressure and pain mounted.

The construct stopped moving. It phased out of existence, leaving holes in Jatiel's leg. It reared back into reality above Asaliah and Jatiel, energy coruscating about the eye lens.

'The eye!' Asaliah yelled. 'Take out its eye!'

Bolts hammered at the construct, pinging off the metal as Ventara fired his pistol. A well-placed shot blew out the construct's eye in a wash of actinic lightning. Micro-explosions studded the alien construct, travelling along its length as circuits were consumed by energy blowback. Anti-gravity engines failed and the thing fell to the floor with a clatter of metal.

More tapping came from deeper in the tunnel. A curious looping speech sounded as well, harsh and full of consonants and machine burbles.

The Space Marines moved back, clustering closer to one another. Jatiel hurried to reload his bolter. Ventara and Asaliah readied their close combat weapons.

Lights burst into being all around them, emerging from the walls, eating the darkness. The reliefs seemed to march and writhe, alien figures making war once more.

Screeching sounded from behind them, the unmistakable hiss of questing tyranid organisms. Ventara turned to face that direction. In his hand, he hefted a number of fragmentation grenades, primed and ready for throwing.

'It seems we are caught between one threat and another,' Asaliah said. 'As usual.'

Jatiel barked a dark, sad laugh. 'We were lucky to survive this long. We lived through the crashing of a starship. Every breath since has been a gift from the Emperor and Sanguinius.'

'Your orders, sergeant?' Ventara asked.

'Die well,' answered Jatiel. 'Die well, my brothers.' The Blood Angels sergeant sighted down his boltgun. He breathed out words, ages old. They felt smothered by the darkness around them, but not by the situation. 'For the Emperor and Sanguinius.'

Asaliah handed his sergeant a bolter magazine and took up the words, belted them out with all three of his lungs, and expelled them at the foe. 'For the Emperor and Sanguinius! By the Blood of our primarch!'

Footsteps arched towards them, the sound slightly off as it echoed, as if it were produced by legs that did not match the proportions of the human frame. The cadence was different, and therefore wrong. Synchronised stamping signalled the double-step of a marching phalanx. Green lights sputtered from ahead of them.

Scuttling claws came from behind, scrabbling and hurried, like rats crawling through the walls of a house, hungry, searching.

The first aliens came into view, skeletal and vile. Jatiel opened fire, boltgun blazing and clawing chunks out of the advancing phalanx. They did not answer back. They withheld fire, weathering the storm of righteousness. Xenos fell, spindly skeletons toppling to twitch in the dust of their dead world. Lightning played about their limbs and they staggered to their feet seconds later, lifeless skulls glaring without malice at the Space Marines.

Still they came on. Still they withheld their fire. Why? The question formed in Jatiel's mind before being shunted away. The question served no purpose. All that mattered was that he yet drew breath and that the enemies of mankind surrounded him.

Behind him, he could hear the savage movements of Ventara as the Space

Marine fought off sprinting tyranids. Creatures vaulted overhead, and soon a sea of hissing, screeching organisms surrounded the Space Marines. Claws extended, hooting and spitting xenos rushed forward in a mad scramble, dead-eyed with mouths twisted by unknowable hunger. Acidic drool pitted the obsidian floor. The ambient temperature rose as the press of bodies grew and Jatiel turned to face the tyranids. If the necrons weren't going to fight back, the organic aliens were the more pressing threat.

Jatiel's bolter, emptied of ammunition, became a club once more. He used it with savage efficiency, laying into the tide of genestealers. Bones broke and flesh split. Alien ichor flew from shattered jaws and cloven skulls. The strength of his blood sustained him, driving him to feats that would be considered heroic even by the genhanced standards of the Adeptus Astartes. He was an avatar of fury, an angel of death. His fangs cut into his lips, driving from his gums and drawing his own blood. His fractured skull, his injured brain, were forgotten in the purity of this moment.

But the genestealers were quick things, bouncing and jangling. They slipped through the sergeant's guard, punching claws into his armour like knives through paper. Blood streamed freely from his many wounds. Already he felt cold, lost blood being barely replaced by synthetic chemicals.

By Jatiel's side, Ventara's skulls and sliced off limbs. Adrenaline cast off the sluggishness of the chemicals and medicines that flooded his body. He chanted litanies of death and devastation, hymnals to a secular understanding of the founder of the Imperium and His primarchs.

They fought back-to-back, killing and somehow avoiding death. They moved as one, each action followed by another, anticipated and anticipating. Their boots squelched in the rapidly growing pool of blood and ruptured organs. But they did not slip. They did not fall. They were the Emperor's finest, none better. They were sons of Sanguinius, the Emperor's Own Angel.

Wounds were carved, rents made in their armour. Transhuman blood spilled, dripping to the floor, mingling with spilled tyranid perfidy. The wounds were ignored, lost beneath the killing haze. The red thirst of battle gripped their souls, consuming them, filling them with an unquenchable thirst. A low, howling moan slipped through Jatiel's lips, channelling his pain and rage, expelling it outwards in time with every blow he landed.

The Space Marines fought on, flesh hanging from them in ribbons, bodies torn and bleeding. But no mortal blows fell. They fought with the fury of their primarch, the consummate poise and skill of that angelic being.

Shadows descended over Jatiel's vision. He heard a scream in his mind, a voice far deeper and more beautiful than his own could ever be. The Blood Angels sergeant blinked the darkness away and turned as he heard a sigh slip through slack lips.

Ventara was the first to die, decapitated by the bladed limbs of a lictor. His body fell, cast aside and dashed against the rock walls. He shattered into a frieze, breaking an eldar warrior-figure and a necron overlord. The body, no longer housing the immortal soul of Naskos Ventara, slumped to the floor with a wet meat thump. It danced and jerked as neurons continued to fire, the flesh not aware that the animating force was gone.

All the while the skeletal ranks of necrons watched and waited, as silent and still as the dead things they resembled. They saw the Space Marines' heroism, observed Ventara's death. Their gaudy leaders, covered in ornate trappings, watched with cocked heads.

Through the screen of flickering tyranids, Jatiel saw a skeletal limb flash up and then down. It was obviously an order given.

Green lightning sheeted into the tyranids, slaying the creatures. Skeletal forms waded into the melee, culling and scything down the beasts. The reprieve was entirely unexpected. His brain began to form a question, lost in the distraction. And so, Jatiel was entirely unaware of the chance to save Asaliah's life, the opportunity to buy the Deathwatch veteran a chance to fight on for a scant few seconds more.

A genestealer lunged forward, four killer limbs outstretched, mouth wide and the filthy, crawling horror of the creature's ovipositor distended from between drooling jaws. It danced past Jatiel, passing inches from the sergeant. He could have reached out, could have battered the creature, thrown himself before it. But he did not, lost in wonderment at receiving aid from the necrons. The genestealer latched onto Asaliah.

Asaliah, the brother who had served twice with the Ordo Xenos, the brother who had fought horrors beyond counting in both the black and silver of duty and the red and gold of honour, right hand and friend to Jatiel, fell, vivisected into steaming sections by the alien.

Jatiel could have saved him, could have intervened. He could have lashed out with his elbow, knocking the creature away. But he was distracted, and Asaliah paid for his laxity.

Jatiel's psyche flew apart. The duty that pulled at him, that shaped and guided him, was drowned beneath a tide of blood. The angelic exterior that should have guided every son of Sanguinius fell away, revealing the beast that lurked within.

The sergeant flew at the crouching genestealer that had torn apart his friend. He dropped his bolter and pummelled the alien. It mewled in sudden pain, but he ignored its sounds, as he ignored the claws that ripped at him. All that mattered was that this creature die, that *all* of these creatures die.

He broke the genestealer, shattering its spine upon his knee. Jatiel tore after the others, seeing only red. In the back of his mind, he could hear the repeated discharge of the necron weaponry, could hear the strange sounds of language coming from the aliens, but he was lost to anger.

More tyranids fell before him, torn apart by his fury. A genestealer landed on his back, hissing and spitting. Its grasping claws tore away his helmet, baring his senses to the foetid reek of blood and spilled viscera. He could feel his fangs carving through his lips.

He was alone and surrounded. The tyranids glared at him with their dead eyes. Then they swarmed him as one. Jatiel fell beneath a mound of the creatures, borne down by claws and bladed limbs. Barbs and spikes shot into his flesh.

His world was filled with hissing, buzzing pain. The red haze lifted from him, beaten into submission by his impending death.

Then came a reprieve. The mass of wriggling, biting tyranids was pulled from him by aliens with expressionless skulls. A blade lanced through a genestealer that crouched on top of him, the tip nearly punching through the aquila that stood proud on Jatiel's chest. Metal hands gripped his pauldrons, hefting him into the air.

The sergeant looked down.

A skull's unblinking visage, proportions noxious and alien, met his gaze. The head was cocked to the side, a curious regard. More of them crowded around this overlord, bedecked in tattered gold and tarnished metal. Axe blades crowned its skull and it opened its mouth to speak, to craft words in a halting and unfamiliar accent. The xenos's skeletal hand stretched up to his throat, grasping at the soft point where the helmet interfaced with the breastplate.

'I am called Anrakyr the Traveller,' it said in machine-mimicked language. 'I wish to offer assistance in your time of trials.'

Jatiel's mind struggled to comprehend the situation, struggled to make sense of what was happening. 'By the Blood,' he said, the oath slipping past his lips unbidden. 'Why?' he asked, his voice full of wonder and growling rage. 'Why would you help us, xenos?'

The necron shifted where it stood, placing Jatiel down almost gently. 'You assume that we think and behave on the same twisted wavelength that you filthy humans do. You assume our reasoning follows the same paths that your stunted minds take. We wish to help because it is in our interest to aid you here. Be relieved that we offer our assistance. Now, come with me as I awaken this tomb world. Know that you are privileged to witness this. Take it as a mark of respect, for your skill in fighting these things.' He gestured to the dead and dying tyranids.

'And then?' asked Jatiel. 'After you have awoken this world?'

'Then,' said Anrakyr, 'you will take me to your leader.'

THE WORD OF
THE SILENT KING

L J GOULDING

More, my Lord Anrakyr? You would know more?

Better than this, we will tell you *everything*. Perhaps then you will understand. After all, you will need allies.

Long have we known of the Devourer. While the majority of the necron race slept away the aeons, his great majesty Szarekh, the Silent King, journeyed far and wide beyond the borders of this galaxy. Such unspeakable things did he witness as cannot be adequately articulated in our noble language, nor any other.

The most dire of all these extragalactic enemies were the tyranids.

For countless cycles he has sought to repel this threat. In his wisdom he has observed them, studied them and committed them to oblivion in all but the final, decisive deed. He has brought them to battle on a hundred worlds, ravaged their slumbering fleets out in the cold, measureless void, and even united the more fractious, warring dynasties so that our mutual interests might be protected.

What, you ask, has this to do with an alliance between the living and the dead?

We will tell you everything, my lord. Perhaps then you will understand.

The world's name is not important. Not to us. To the humans, though, it seemed to be paramount. For a species that would see themselves as the undisputed masters of this galaxy, they place so much emphasis on names, and the paradises and damnations that they imagine for themselves.

This, then, becomes a tale of angels and of devils, to use the crude, ancient terms.

The bloodiest of angels, fighting upon the Devil's Crag.

And we were there. The three of us – Khatlan, Dovetlan and Ammeg, if you will – and so many more. So many, many more.

While you travelled the stars, seeking tithes and tribute, we answered the call of our true master. The Praetorians can move in great numbers, quickly and quietly, when the attentions of the dynasties fall elsewhere for a time. So it is that we return to the court of the Silent King whenever he would wish it, to bring him new word of the Great Awakening. To the rest of the galaxy, we are his eyes and ears, as we are his right hand, and his only voice.

He does not speak. He will not speak. Not to you.
Not yet.
But he may, in time, if you prove worthy.

They had us, brothers. We were done for.

We had fought them hard. On Gehenna, those clanking mechanical xenos seemed to be without number. For three weeks, Dante had led the Third Company against their Legions – we in the Assault squads would strike and fall back with the commander, over and over, while Captain Tycho directed the long range engagement. It was a dry, dusty grind. The only blood that fell upon the barren wastes was ours.

That felt wrong. There was nothing to slake our thirst, no glorious crimson to bathe the armour of the damned.

Tycho was the Master of Sacrifice. That title seemed appropriate. We felt sacrificed.

Gehenna is nothing if not an altar upon which such offerings can be made, though the myriad alien races seem forever drawn to test the Imperium's right to preside over it. A million souls more hallowed than ours had passed on the hive world's plains, over the millennia. What more noble endeavour, what more glorious calling can there be than to defend such a place from the hordes of the restless xenos dead?

And so defend it we did, with every last ounce of our company's strength.

We fell from the grey-streaked skies, the crimson of the Ironhelms Assault squads like a bloodstain upon the pristine gold of the Sanguinary Guard. Commander Dante was ever at the front, the tip of the blade thrust into the necrons' flanks. The Axe Mortalis hewed left and right, cleaving through metal bodies as easily as it might through living flesh on any other battlefield, and in Dante's divine shadow we were inspired. I led my squad in a freefall drop, the weight of our charge like the hammer of Sanguinius's own wrath against the enemy, their dully glowing eyes turned upwards in those last heartbeats before we were in their very midst.

No towering necron lords swathed in fuliginous silks, no insectoid sentinels lashing us with electrum whips. These were the poorest stock of the Legions that we now faced, the meagre revenants that seemed almost without number and whose only tactical use seemed to be that they *absolutely would not die*.

Exhorting my battle-brothers onwards, I drove into the necron warriors with my blade held before me. Speed, we had found, was the key – they simply could not track us quickly enough as targets if we kept moving, and they seemed incapable of firing their gauss weaponry without first taking careful aim. And so we struck them down by the dozen, taking heads and limbs and blowing out armoured torsos with point-blank pistol fire, and stamping their remains into the dust beneath our boots.

Yet for every necron we tore apart, three more would trudge forwards to take its place; or else the supposedly dead warrior would simply rise up again once we had passed by, wounds reknitting under whatever baleful technomancy powered them.

Green flashes cast the seemingly endless horde in silhouette, and I looked up to see more of the great, gravitic monolith structures gliding ponderously down the slopes from the crags beyond. Their energy matrices cast thumping charges into the melee, scattering golden-armoured Blood Angels like leaves in the wind. Maddening, squealing static cut through the inter-squad vox-channels, and suddenly we were cut off from Dante's command entirely.

And more necrons came. And yet more.

The press of cold, lifeless bodies around us become entangling, and the warriors began to jab at us with their hooked bayonet blades. Brother Jophael tried to free himself from the horde's grasp by launching back into the air, but metal claws pulled him down, jump pack and all, beneath the ambling tide. His agonised screams were mercifully brief.

I planted a boot into the chest of the closest necron warrior and sent it sprawling backwards with a pair of frag grenades for its trouble. The blasts hurled a score more of them aside, but all that bought me was the space to truly see the inevitability and futility of our assault. We were outnumbered by hundreds to one, and hovering ark-transports would gather the xenos dead right out from beneath our feet to send against us once more. And on, and on, until we were buried.

We *had* been sacrificed. I did not know if Commander Dante had planned it that way, but I could no longer even see his Sanguinary Guard amidst the throng.

There would be no resurrection for us. Once fallen, the Angels of Death do not rise from the dead. There is purity in that – something that the necrons have failed to grasp in their eternal pursuit of... eternity.

Two more of my brothers fell. Then a third.

I don't remember what it was that I screamed in that moment – likely it was something ignoble and suitably defiant. I struck a necron down with every swing of my blade, until it seemed that I could no longer even find room to draw it back between blows.

My pauldrons began to catch on the press of metal limbs. Unfeeling fingers clamped around my wrists, and my neck. My sword was pulled from my grip, and my plasma pistol too. I realised that I was being dragged over backwards, and I was no longer even screaming real words.

That's when it happened.

The pause. The *stutter*.

As one, the necrons faltered. Just for a fraction of a second, their eyes dimmed.

Then, again as one, they put up their weapons and turned to withdraw. I crashed to the ground on my back, before scrambling free of my jump pack harness to see ten thousand immortal xenos warriors striding away from us as implacably as they had been advancing only moments earlier.

I snapped my pistol up and put down nine of them without thinking. I shot them through their retreating backs, hot plasma dashing their mechanical innards onto the ground. Others did the same, in futile impotent rage. Our blood was still up, and the wounded remnants of the front line squads harried the enemy with frustrated battle cries still upon our lips. Necrons fell, and still the Legions did not pay us any more regard that day.

It was as though we had simply ceased to exist.

It made no sense at the time. Why would they suddenly give up, with certain victory within their unfeeling, iron grasp?

The answer was the result of cold, mathematical logic. It would come to stun us all, and most especially Commander Dante.

We had misjudged them. We misjudged them so badly.

You understand, lord, that the angel-humans were never our real foe in this. Mere happenstance it was that placed them in opposition to the Silent King's plan. That, and their characteristic unwillingness to admit that they know nothing of the true nature of the universe.

For as much as the human empire considers itself the height of evolution and the antithesis of the tyranid race – if you can believe such a thing! – they are perhaps more alike than either of them can know. Dovetlan once likened the humans to insects. They swarm. They cannibalise. They live without real thought for the future or the past, beyond the propagation of their own brood.

And they build hives. Literally.

Teeming with human vermin and other, even more degenerate life forms, their settlements agglomerate around the points of industry and resource, openly abusing their worlds to feed the wasteful cycle of war and procreation. Even their ruling classes may live out their entire organic lifespan within a ten-kilometre area, such is the self-contained and parochial nature of the hive cities.

In all our time, we have rarely witnessed such edifices constructed by a sentient race. They are stockpiles of humankind, in all its stripes. Concentrated cells of organic filth.

Bio-mass.

Bait.

It was a fortuitous coincidence that placed a world such as this in the path of the Silent King's quarry. After his great victory over the tyranid beasts in the dimensional anomaly at Anjac, he pursued a splinter fleet through the void entirely undetected for almost three cycles. He observed their movements. He studied their reactions to external astral stimuli.

And then he began to calculate ahead.

None but he, in his majestic wisdom, could have accomplished such a feat – but even the magnificent Szarekh could not deny the providence that brought them hence afterwards.

Our cold bodies hold little interest for the Devourer. At best, they might be drawn to the more physical power sources utilised by our technologies, or defend themselves when we strike them. But fodder for their living ships, we are not.

The hive worlds of the humans shine like beacons in comparison. The tyranids are drawn to such banquets with a singular, predatory hunger.

The Silent King knows this.
The beginnings of a plan began to form in his mind, as he later told us.
He would lay a trap for them, and he would bait it with the humans.

The seven of us stood around the hololith table – the five surviving squad sergeants, battered and bloodied, shielded from the worst of the commander's wrath by our noble captain Erasmus Tycho. Though he was similarly armoured in golden plate, the two of them could not have appeared more different in that moment.

'Answer me this,' Dante growled. 'How did they know? How can the necrons scan the interstellar void more accurately than the long-range sensors of the *Bloodcaller*?'

The Chapter Master had set his death mask upon the surface of the table, and I could scarcely take my eyes from it. The play of light over the angelic, sculpted features of our Lord Sanguinius lent the helm an even more numinous aspect, beyond even the polished golden halo that encircled the crown.

From behind his own half-mask, Tycho spoke carefully.

'I'm not sure they can, commander. It is possible that they already knew the tyranids were approaching before the hive ships crossed the system's heliopause. Our sensorium officers' report did cite multiple objects "of unknown origin" in their initial tactical sweeps, but you and I both bid them turn their full attention towards the necrons. We simply perceived a greater threat on the ground.' The corner of his mouth flickered with an involuntary tic. 'We were watching the pageant when we should have been scouting the hall.'

Dante glowered up at his protégé, gauntleted palms resting on the table's edge, and a grim smile creased his dour features. 'Aye, perhaps.'

Between the two of them, the lambent silhouette of Gehenna Prime turned slowly in the tactical hololith projection. The planet was bracketed by the battle-barge *Bloodcaller* and the twin strike cruisers *Melech* and *Fratrem Pugno* at station in high orbit. Of the necron cairn-ships that had apparently retreated from the system more than a month earlier, there was still no sign.

Instead, from the galactic southeast had come the tyranids.

Xenological identifiers marked them as a splinter of the defeated Behemoth fleet, or possibly cousins of little-known Dagon. Regardless of their origin, the four great hive ships had already spawned a veritable multitude of lesser craft and begun to move into a splayed formation that bypassed the outer worlds entirely. Tiny numerals rolled down the hololith next to each sensor contact as the telemeters updated their distance and relative speeds.

There was no mistaking it – this was a standard xenos attack vector. The tyranids had set their ravenous gaze upon Gehenna Prime.

'What would you command of us, my lord?' asked Phanuel, turning away from the dire tableau. The Devastator squads had been furthest from the necrons' front wave, and so were the least mauled by the weeks of attrition that the rest of us had suffered.

Dante gestured to the approaching hive ships. 'We are about to be caught between our chosen foe on the ground and a new one in the heavens, brother-sergeant. Our victory over the necrons was already far from assured. Now we face an even more overwhelming force – one that could take an entire world on its own.'

The weight of that truth hung in the silence for a moment. Tycho nodded slowly, presumably at the prospect of a swift and glorious end for his battle company. 'The presence of the tyranid fleet does at least go some way towards explaining why our astropathic calls for reinforcement seem to have fallen upon deaf ears, Chapter Master,' he offered with a shrug. 'Nonetheless, the Ironhelms are with you to the very last.'

Before the commander could reply, the hololith flickered and a shriek of white noise cut through the embedded audio feed. We all recoiled, startled but ready to react.

Then the display blinked out, along with every visual feed, lumen and powered system in the strategium chamber, plunging us into darkness.

'Generatorium!' Dante roared. 'Restore the—'

Static seeped through the dead channel, bleeding in and somehow multiplying in the air before us. Motes of greenish light ran upwards from the table's surface, though this time it cast no reflection in the Death Mask of Sanguinius.

The rasping un-sound built upon itself, pulsing in strange, eddying waves.

'Listen to that,' whispered Gaius, reaching for his bolt pistol but finding the holster empty. 'It's a voice.'

I spat, my hands bunching into fists as I scanned the room for any threat. 'That's no voice. It's artefacting from an incompatible signal source. Nothing more.'

The motes of light began to swirl and gather above the centre of the table, blocking out some new shape in the space where Gehenna had previously hung. The emerald glare grew in intensity, rising with the crackling, maddening howl of the—

'HUMANS. PROSTRATE YOURSELVES BEFORE OUR MAGNIFICENCE.'

Turning slowly in the shimmering field, a gaunt necron visage with a high crest stared out at us, its eyes blazing almost white and casting tiny arcs of energy before them. Tycho and two of the others moved quickly to place themselves between Dante and the xenos avatar, but the commander barged them aside, a look of disbelief upon his face.

'I AM THE JUDICATOR-PRIME. I AM CHARGED WITH SECURING YOUR COOPERATION. YOU WILL NOT RESIST.'

With a snarl, Phanuel drew his combat blade and slashed at the thing's face, but the weapon passed cleanly through and left him only with a tracery of greenish sparks dancing over his gauntlet and vambrace. The necron either did not notice, or did not care.

'WHOM AMONG YOU HOLDS AUTHORITY?'

Dante scowled, and stepped forwards. 'I am Dante,' he said from between clenched teeth, 'Master of the Adeptus Astartes Chapter the Blood Angels. Who are you to address me and my officers in such a manner?'

The avatar regarded him with its blazing white eyes. '*I AM THE JUDICATOR-PRIME. I AM CHARGED WITH SECURING YOUR COOPERATION. YOU WILL NOT RESIST, DANTE OF THE BLOOD ANGELS.*'

Reaching out to the table controls, Gaius warily mashed the keypad with his palm, hoping to sever the connection. It did not have any effect. Commander Dante looked back to the Judicator.

'Cooperation in what, xenos? Until mere hours ago, our forces were locked in mortal combat. Now you are fled to the empty plains, awaiting our inevitable vengeance. There is no matter in which we or you will ever cooperate.'

'*YOU ARE INCORRECT. OUR SUCCESS HAS ALREADY BEEN CALCULATED. THE CONFLICT BETWEEN US WAS AN ERROR.*'

Rage boiled up inside me at the thing's brazen insolence. I bared my teeth and bellowed back at the projection. 'Silence! Let us end this on the field of battle. You will not strike at the worlds of the Imperium and then run for cover when a greater enemy rears its foul head!'

The Judicator's gaze swept over me. '*THE CONFLICT BETWEEN US WAS AN ERROR,*' it repeated.

Tycho raised his voice, then. 'Who decides that? You?'

'*NO. IT IS THE DECISION OF MIGHTY SZAREKH, LAST AND GREATEST OF THE SILENT KINGS. PROSTRATE YOURSELVES BEFORE HIS MAGNIFICENCE.*'

An uneasy silence fell over the seven of us. I turned to my brothers, unsure how to react.

Dante narrowed his eyes. 'The Silent King... *The* Silent King?'

'*MIGHTY SZAREKH, LAST AND GREATEST OF THE SILENT KINGS.*'

'The Silent King is... here, on Gehenna?'

The Judicator's head twitched. '*I DO NOT UNDERSTAND THE SIGNIFICANCE OF "GEHENNA". BUT THE SILENT KING IS HERE, NOW. HE WOULD TREAT WITH YOU, DANTE OF THE BLOOD ANGELS, IN THE FACE OF OUR COMMON ENEMY.*'

More motes of light spun out to create a topographical map in the projection, with a specific ridgeline highlighted in a brighter green from the rest.

'*SEND YOUR EMISSARIES TO THIS LOCATION AND MIGHTY SZAREKH, LAST AND GREATEST OF THE SILENT KINGS, WILL RECEIVE THEM.*'

With a sudden flash that left blooms of colour on our retinas, the necron avatar vanished. After a single heartbeat of silent darkness, the lumens and hololith stuttered back into life and left us blinking in the pale light of the strategium once again.

I spun to face Tycho. 'My lord, I know where they want us to go.'

Though Commander Dante still stared at the now empty space above the table, the captain's expression was stern. 'Speak, Brother-Sergeant Machiavi. Where is it?'

'It's where my squad landed in the last assault – the Devil's Crag.'

Szarekh would have it known by every phaeron of every dynasty, that he is a just and noble ruler. Before the Great Sleep, he realised his failings and vowed to atone for them. He is humble enough to learn from his own mistakes. The necrons will rise once more, and he will lead us into a new and glorious age as the preeminent masters of creation. Not because it is his right, but a privilege that he would first re-earn.

Yet, his benevolence has its limits.

It is not to say that he harbours the humans any particular malice. Simply, their supposed destiny is incompatible with our own. Perhaps if they had ascended more powerfully in an earlier epoch, then they might have claimed this galaxy out from beneath the slumbering dynasties while the Silent King still dwelt in self-imposed exile.

And perhaps not. Their propensity for self-destruction is... troubling.

The tyranids are anathema to all life, and life is what the necrons require for supreme domination. So too, then, is the primal destiny of the Devourer incompatible with our own.

The humans create.

The necrons maintain.

The tyranids consume.

There can be no lasting symmetry in that triumvirate. One must fall. The great Szarekh has decreed that it shall be the tyranids, and none can refute the word of the Silent King.

It is unlikely that the humans see things as clearly as we do, Lord Anrakyr. Ironic, is it not, that they gnash their teeth and cry out at the injustice of a new alien race polluting 'their' empire with brash, unwitting conquests? We have seen this before, and doubtless we will see it again. When all of this is but a footnote in the annals of our great triumph, who will even remember the name of a dead human Emperor, or the ignorant miseries doled out in his name?

The court awaited the humans openly. There could be no suggestion of deception. We had returned to the ridge where last the Dante-Angel had resisted us.

Beyond the unnumbered ranks of common warriors and the Immortal Legions, a full *nine hundred* of the Triarch Praetorians stood sentinel before the Silent King's throne. Not in the living memory of the Imperium would such a gathering of our order have been witnessed by any human, and likely it never will be again. Our Judicator-Prime attended noble Szarekh at his right hand, and the High Chronomancer, whose techno-magicks had so confounded the humans, stood at his left. Beyond were arrayed the seven phaerons who had sworn themselves to the Silent King's purpose in secret – each of them wearing a bronzed mask to hide their identity from all but their own household guardians.

The first we saw of the humans was a haze of chemical fumes and plains dust kicked up by their primitive transport. It trundled over the terrain on wheeled treads, its bulky armour caked in red paint and crude, winged glyphs. As it drew nearer, the Judicator-Prime descended the polished steps of the courtly dais to bar the humans' path.

At Dante's command, the hastily installed servitor driver brought the Rhino as close as possible to the necron herald. The engine idled for a moment, then cut out. Cooling metal on the exhaust stacks ticked and clicked in the dismal morning sun, but aside from that the silence felt absolute. Though we could see the necrons standing in their uncounted thousands, not a sound did any one of them make, nor was there any hint of movement.

I peered out through the forward viewing block, scanning the grand dais for sign of our host.

It was absurd – a monolithic ziggurat, easily forty metres at the peak, dropped onto the surface of Gehenna Prime as a monument to xenos vanity. Cast from some achingly black, polished metal, it was edged with glinting golden runes and glyphs that ran in interconnecting patterns up the long flight of steps to the summit. Upon its tiers stood the more elite warriors of the necron horde, elevated above their kin and presumably enjoying the prestige of greater proximity to their monarch. Gleaming statues of alien deities towered at the cardinal points of the structure, and the two greatest of them held their arms out to form an arch over the peak of the dais, heads bowed in symbolic supplication.

This was a king, their posture said, that had once held even the gods in his thrall.

And this was his court that travelled wherever he went.

I glanced back into the darkened interior of the troop compartment. Captain Tycho reluctantly put up his combi-melta in the overhead stowage, and edged around the tarpaulin-covered bulk in the middle of the floor. He had pleaded for the honour to undertake this endeavour alone. Nay, he had almost *begged* for it. It was his right, and he had insisted. His privilege. His duty. But Dante would not hear of it.

The commander's face was set, almost as serene as the golden mask that he held so carefully in his gauntlets. It was the face of a man who knew that destiny had smiled upon him, no matter what the cost of that fortune might ultimately prove to be. How like our father Sanguinius he seemed in that moment.

'Brothers,' he said calmly, 'let us go to him.'

I eyed the open palm of my gauntlet warily – it felt so heavy – and tried to keep my voice low.

'My lord, is this necessary? We are here. We could–'

Tycho silenced me with a hand on my pauldron. 'This isn't about tactical positioning, Machiavi,' he muttered, squinting at me sidelong through the eye of his half-mask. 'This is about respect. No matter how much we may despise the xenos, the Chapter Master would at least meet this Szarekh face to face. No one else will ever get this chance again. We have to at least see him with our own eyes.'

Dante nodded. Tycho managed a wry grin, and reached for the rear hatch controls.

'Besides, I think noble Dante wants to hear the supreme ruler of the necron race beg for our help, first.'

The ramp opened on powered hydraulics, and the three of us stepped out onto the dusty ground at the foot of the ziggurat, defiant in the face of the ten thousand enemy warriors who watched from all sides.

The Judicator-Prime stood before us, a tall ceremonial glaive held rigidly in both hands. As well as the high crest of his office that had been visible in the hololith projection, he wore a mantle of smooth metal links that hung from his shoulders like a cloak. He regarded us coldly for a moment before inclining his head in a condescending gesture that we should follow him.

My hearts began to hammer in my chest. I could taste the acrid tang of xenos energy weapons in the air, feeling the dead gaze of the machines upon us as we ascended the steps. I walked to the commander's left, Tycho to the right. The captain glared, but said nothing.

Dante simply followed the herald, the mask of Sanguinius held in the crook of his arm.

We reached the summit and passed beneath the archway of the god-statues. Beyond, shimmering silk drapes fluttered in the breeze between ornate electroflambeaux that cast the various necron lords of the court in an even more eerie light against the Gehenna sun. I looked to each in turn, wondering which of them was *him*...

Without warning, the Judicator-Prime halted, and whirled around. Reflexively, the fingers of my gauntlet closed, but I managed to catch myself before it was too late.

'Kneel, humans,' he commanded. 'Kneel before mighty Szarekh, last and greatest of the Silent Kings.'

The visible half of Tycho's face appeared unimpressed. He rested his thumbs at his belt, and tilted his head. 'We will not. He is not *our* king.'

The Judicator-Prime bristled, but did not repeat himself. Instead he turned solemnly and sank to one knee. The move was echoed first by the masked nobles, then by their retainers, and then by every other necron warrior upon the dais and beyond. Again as one, they knelt.

Except for one figure.

He was taller than the rest, yet not as tall as I had imagined he might be. His mechanical body was a work of unspeakable xenos artifice, more finely wrought than any I had ever seen upon the field of battle. Where they might be skeletal, he was lithe. Where they were animated with grim, unyielding purpose, his every movement possessed an undeniable vitality. His form spoke of musculature and clean-limbed strength, perhaps touched by the divine, and his finery was simple and yet impossibly elegant.

His face, though...

Brothers, I can scarcely put into words what I felt in that moment. What all three of us must have felt. It was not reverence or awe, I can tell you that much.

It was closer to hatred.

Framed by a cowl of shimmering light and the traceries of his intricate collar, Szarekh – heralded as the last and greatest of the Silent Kings, and undisputed overlord of the necron race – wore a golden mask fashioned into the likeness of our Lord Sanguinius.

A rank blasphemy, indeed.

* * *

The humans were surprised. Their flesh-forms took time to process what they were seeing, though it clearly stirred their indoctrinated racial hatreds at a fundamental and subconscious level. The Judicator-Prime was the first to rise, transmitting a sub-ethyric signal to the Praetorians to be ready. No matter that they had sent the Dante-Angel and the Tycho-Angel, their most respected battle leaders, as a gesture of good faith. The human warrior castes can be unpredictable and nihilistic when pressed, and may act illogically in the face of insult or overwhelming adversity.

We may speak more of this later, Lord Anrakyr. After all, you will need allies. Learn their strengths as well as their weaknesses, and turn all to your advantage.

Wise Szarekh knew this. He saw the truth of it when first he encountered the humans squatting upon the tombs of the dynasties and the ruins of the eldar empire. They believed that their stars were in the ascendant, and that they would soon conquer the galaxy. Of course, this was not to be. It will never be. It cannot be.

It is curious what the humans choose to know of their past, and what remains unremembered. They do not heed the lessons that they have already learned, because they often elect to forget them. Perhaps, had he not fallen to illogical and prideful infighting, their Sanguinius-Angel might have steered them towards a more enlightened destiny.

Certainly, he would have made a more amenable emperor than a preserved witch-corpse.

If ever there were a human to be mourned, noble Szarekh would say that it was him. That alliance – the *first* alliance, perhaps? – might have ended the threat of the Devourer before it ever surfaced. At least, the tyranids might never have been drawn to this galaxy in the first instance.

Like the humans, the Silent King was blind to this possibility at the time.

But unlike the humans, he is humble enough to learn from his own mistakes. The High Chronomancer's temporal mastery merely afforded him the insight that he required, and the opportunity to prepare a new truth for them.

The Chapter Master's grip tightened around the golden helm in his hands, and he quaked with a barely suppressed fury. This time I saw Captain Tycho's fist clenching, although he too managed to restrain himself. We had to see how this would play out before doing anything premature.

Dante looked from his own mask – the Death Mask of Sanguinius, holiest relic of the Chapter – to the benign, alien representation of the primarch worn by the Silent King. The similarities were astonishing, brothers. Though elongated and curiously more androgynous, the features were mournful and angelic in the way that every Blood Angel knew and recognised even from the first day of their Adeptus Astartes induction. The proud and noble brow. The suggestion of tumbling hair swept back from the face. Even the stylised halo crowned Szarekh just as it did the commander.

But where Dante's mask was crafted into a defiant, righteous battle snarl, this was Sanguinius at his most benevolent and peaceful.

The face of a king. A ruler supreme.

More beautiful, perhaps, than any sculpture or cast had any right to be that was not the work of human hands, though it pricked at my soul to admit it.

Dante's blood was up. Finally, he found his voice.

'How... *dare*...'

Ignoring the commander's outrage, the Judicator-Prime spoke again in his strident and uncaring tone. 'Dante of the Blood Angels, the Silent King bids you welcome. None among us shall harm you while you respect the sanctity of this court.'

Captain Tycho's eyes widened, and he looked to me in disbelief. The Silent King remained still, regarding us all with the eyes of our primarch.

Through gritted teeth, Dante cursed.

'Your Silent King had best learn to speak, and explain to me why he insults us with this... this... *mockery* of our Lord Sanguinius. It is a travesty, and I shall not suffer it! If he thinks to make his demands more pleasant by skinning them in the face of our holy founder—'

'This is not so, Dante of the Blood Angels,' said the herald. 'Mighty Szarekh, last and greatest of the Silent Kings, honours your angel-father and the accord that we wished to strike with him in ages past.'

Numbness spread through my chest at these words. Even Dante twitched.

'That is a lie,' he murmured. 'Our gene-sire would never have treated with xenos filth.'

'The Silent King cannot lie, Dante of the Blood Angels, for he does not speak. He will not speak. Not to you. But your angel-father would have seen the wisdom in this alliance, and we hope that you will also. The tyranids are coming, whether you or we choose to remain, or not. The conflict between us was an error. Our success has already been calculated.'

I was very keenly aware that the Chapter Master held his gauntlet loosely at his side, with the palm wide open. Both Captain Tycho and I followed suit, trying to keep the movement as surreptitious as possible and hiding it from the passing gaze of the necrons. All three of the human emissaries kept their right hands open. It was a curious gesture, likely some measure of deference offered to the majestic Szarekh as their natural superior.

Ammeg later postulated that it signified they were unarmed. I am not so certain.

Regardless, the alliance was soon agreed.

The ignorance of the humans is easily turned to our advantage.

Unable to take his eyes from the Silent King's mask, I watched Dante consider the herald's words.

'Why, then? Why seize this world, and defend it from us when we came to reclaim it?'

'The conflict between us was an error. Mighty Szarekh, last and greatest of the Silent Kings, did not seize this world. He meant to defend it from the Devourer.'

Another long moment passed. I regarded the various necron nobles of the court – where living beings might betray their true intentions with subconscious body language or barely perceptible movements, these machines were unreadable. Instead, I wonder if I projected something of my own thoughts onto my perception of them, in their perfect ambiguity. The Silent King continued to gaze plaintively at us. I shuffled uneasily.

For the first time ever, in all my days, I felt a tremor of *pity* for the necrons. Had we, in fact, misjudged them?

The Judicator-Prime raised a hand. 'The error was yours, Dante of the Blood Angels. But you were not to know, and we did not take the time to make it known.'

'Oh, blood of Baal...' Tycho whispered, realising the full extent of what was being implied.

Dante let out a long, measured breath. 'And in fighting us, you have lost significant forces that might have assured your victory over the tyranids.'

The Silent King nodded slowly, but it was his herald that spoke.

'Correct. There is no more time. We must form the alliance that mighty Szarekh would have pursued with your angel-father. Join us, and we will save this world for your Imperium.'

The Chapter Master's brow furrowed, just slightly. 'What do you care of the Imperium and its people?' he asked in a low voice.

The Judicator-Prime swept his arm out to encompass all of the assembled necron Legions. 'Regardless of what you might believe, Dante of the Blood Angels, we are most concerned with the survival of the human race. There are greater matters at stake here. Perhaps one day these lesser differences can be reconciled.'

With great solemnity, Commander Dante handed his helm off to me, and I took it carefully in my free gauntlet. Then he stepped forwards, holding out his left hand to the Silent King.

'I cannot speak for the Imperium, and I cannot speak for what my blood-father Sanguinius would or would not have done in my place. But my warriors will lend their numbers to yours, if you truly mean to save this world from the Great Devourer.' He paused, and his expression became more fierce. 'And then you and I will speak of the future, King Szarekh. We will speak of what may be, if this alliance is honoured to its end.'

The Silent King reached out and grasped Dante's wrist in a remarkably Imperial manner.

Then he leaned in with an alien grace that should have been impossible for a machine, and whispered something into the Chapter Master's ear.

I speak the truth. The Silent King spoke to him. Tycho and I both strained to hear, but the words were lost to the breeze. Dante recoiled slightly, his face a picture of shock and confusion. Then he composed himself, and nodded to Szarekh.

And so the alliance was accepted.

* * *

Calm yourself, my Lord Anrakyr. The great Szarekh did not need the humans in order to defeat the tyranids.

Consider the facts. Our fleet had transitioned out of range of their primitive sensors, but were at full battle readiness throughout our engagement with the Dante-Angel's forces as well as afterwards. Similarly, we outnumbered them by many hundreds to one on the ground. A thousand or more, by the end, since it was they who made the greater sacrifice in battle against the tyranids.

Consider the wisdom of noble Szarekh. He allowed the humans to believe that they alone held void-superiority over the hive fleet, and so they alone took damage in engaging the alien vessels as part of the allied offensive. Our ships remained safely out of the conflict. He also allowed the humans to mount what they considered a valiant and righteous defence of the larger city-structures – a manoeuvre that held little tactical merit or advantage, and a much higher likelihood of attrition. He maximised the effectiveness of the alliance entirely in favour of the necron forces, by giving the humans just enough hope for a brighter future, and just enough of the truth to commit them to our cause.

Doubtless, they would have turned on us if the opportunity had presented itself, later. Most especially if they had learned the whole truth. That was a risk that wise Szarekh could not take.

Even so, it was hard not to admire the conviction with which the humans fought. They may come to recognise in time the threat of the tyranids like we do. For that, we wear these trinkets and adornments to commemorate their sacrifice. We honour their dead, even if we do not mourn their loss.

If you would review the specifics of the battle that the magnificent Szarekh fought that day, then I will bring you the accounts from the Praetorian archives. They are exhaustive.

Do not be like the humans, my lord. Learn from the past.

You will need allies if you are to prevail. Maximise the effectiveness of your alliances, and turn them entirely to your advantage.

Prove yourself worthy in this, and the Silent King may speak to you as well. In time.

It was only after the Gehenna Campaign was concluded that we realised how completely we had been deceived by those thrice-accursed xenos. But it was difficult to be truly bitter when we had intended to betray them from the start.

When Commander Dante, Captain Tycho and I had returned to the Rhino to leave, we had carefully removed the remote triggers from our gauntlets, and disarmed the detonators under the tarpaulin. As I said, this had all been Tycho's idea, and he had wanted to carry it out alone. He would have become the Master of Sacrifice, indeed.

When Dante had realised that the Silent King – *the* Silent King – was present on Gehenna Prime, our duty to the Imperium was clear. This was the supreme ruler of the necron race, a being so legendarily elusive that even the most informed members of the Ordo Xenos doubted whether or not he even existed in a literal sense.

We had to kill Szarekh, no matter what. He could not be allowed to leave this world.

Concealed beneath the tarp inside the troop compartment was the warhead from a cyclonic torpedo. It had been carefully and painstakingly removed from the magazine on board the *Bloodcaller* by our company Techmarines, shuttled down to our encampment and hidden within the Rhino at Dante's command.

It was a planet-killer. An Exterminatus-grade weapon, the use of which could only be sanctioned by the Chapter Master himself.

Each of us held a trigger in our open, gauntleted palm, and any one of us could have fired it in an instant. At ground zero, the nucleonic blast would have annihilated everything on the planet's surface within a five hundred kilometre radius. The Silent King, the three of us, every single necron construct stationed at the Devil's Crag, every last member of Third Company who remained in our own encampment, and the common citizenry of at least two major hive cities – all would have been evaporated in the space of a few heartbeats.

It was a sacrifice worthy of Erasmus Tycho's title, and his ambition.

Dante, however, had refused to let him go alone. He schooled us in his reasoning around the strategium table.

It would arouse the suspicions of the necron lords if the Blood Angels suddenly withdrew from the surface, leaving only a single, nihilistic warrior to approach their master. We could not risk ordering an orbital strike without first making visual confirmation of Szarekh's presence, lest the necrons realise our duplicity with the bare, vital moments that they needed to pre-empt us.

It had always been a desperate scheme, with only a slim chance of success.

But for that slim chance, Dante was willing to sacrifice himself.

I claimed the honour of the third position within the emissary group. My familiarity with the local terrain made me the obvious choice.

It was only Szarekh's mask, and the insinuation that Lord Sanguinius himself might have once been on the verge of an alliance with the necrons, that stayed Dante's hand. Was it even true? Had Szarekh ever looked upon the face of our primarch? It did not appear to matter.

As the Rhino had bumped and rolled over the plains back to the encampment, Tycho had voiced the question that was at the forefront of my mind, too.

'So we are taking his... *word*... for it, my lord? We will knowingly and willingly enter an alliance with our hated xenos enemies, with the view to some possible future reconciliation?' He rubbed at his good eye. 'No one will believe this. Chapters have been excommunicated for less.'

Dante narrowed his eyes. 'We serve the Imperium. We protect its people when they cannot protect themselves. If we do this, then we will save at least a portion of Gehenna Prime. If we do not, then the world will fall to the tyranid advance, and the nucleonic fire of Szarekh's murder.'

Before Tycho could reply, Dante had raised up the Death Mask of Sanguinius and gazed into its lifeless eyes. Appraising. Reconsidering.

'And when the war against the tyranids is won, I will slay Szarekh myself.'

It had seemed like the perfect solution: we would use the necrons to ensure an Imperial victory first and then strike down their king once we had secured his confidence. But we had misjudged them. We misjudged them so badly.

They had deceived us.

As the campaign against the foul hive-spawn drew to a close, we began to notice strange things – the bodies of our fallen brothers were being looted, our supplies raided. Was it the tyranids, you ask? Unlikely.

We realised that fewer and fewer of the necron lords and elite guard were making each successive rendezvous with us as planned. We had not heard from the Judicator-Prime or his Praetorians in days.

We were being frozen out of the final stages of our combined victory.

By the time we stood upon the killing fields in the shadow of Hive Sendeep, our rent armour and notched blades caked with more xenos blood than we could ever ask, we were reduced to a handful of survivors from the Ironhelms and the Sanguinary Guard. The *Fratrem Pugno* had been gutted by plasma fire, and it would be many more months before she was warp-capable again.

Wounded, Captain Tycho had instead been evacuated up to the *Melech* to coordinate the last stages of the void-war. It was I alone who stood at Dante's side, and the grim realisation came upon us both as our battle-brothers led teams of ragged local militia in heaping up the bodies of slain tyranids for the cleansing pyres.

He leaned heavily upon the Axe Mortalis, his breath coming like a gasp through the gaping mouth of the Death Mask.

'We haven't seen any necrons in over twelve hours, my lord,' I muttered. 'Szarekh isn't coming back, is he?'

Dante did not answer, but stared hard at the setting sun over the distant mountains. His rage was spent. It was the same for all of us.

I wiped xenos foulness from my combat blade, and sheathed it at my hip. 'Do not concern yourself with this, Lord Dante. I will have the official records amended to state that you allowed the xenos to depart as a gesture of respect for their unexpected assistance in the campaign. We will catch him eventually, and you will have vengeance.'

At this, the Chapter Master shook his head, and pulled his helm free.

'No, Sergeant Machiavi. We will never have this chance again. I doubt whether any warrior of the Imperium will ever again lay eyes upon the Silent King.' He sighed. 'If that is even who he was...'

We remained there for another hour or so, watching in quiet contemplation as the pyre flames began to spring up in the dusky twilight.

I thought back to the moment that we decided to spare Szarekh from the fire, and I am ashamed to say that the most impertinent question sprang unbidden from my lips. In fact, brothers, I am still amazed that this moment of indiscretion did not cost me my eventual succession to command of Third Company.

'What did the Silent King say to you?'

Dante's weary gaze rolled to me, and he stiffened slightly.

'He said... something that I no longer think I understand.'

The commander paused. I waited expectantly, almost now dreading to hear the answer.

'He said, "They are the rising storm, and you must become the shield".'

DREAD NIGHT

NICK KYME

I wait in the shadow of Saint Agathena for night to fall. At night, the beasts disengage. From my studied observations, I have determined that the darkness makes them more or less quiescent.

It does not, however, make them any less dangerous.

The collapsed amphitheatre is cold, and the place I currently inhabit is narrow. There is barely room enough for my shoulders and every time I move, the armoured guards scrape against stone.

There is blood here too; I smell it on the hot breeze coming from the east where the city of Vanarius once stood and the last great battle of this world was fought.

And lost.

The hunters I am hiding from do not seek out this blood. It is old and any violence that once imbued the ancient rock of this temple has long since faded. They seek different prey now, a beast that is their equal.

When the shadow of Leviathan came to this world, that beast found them.

A faint but insistent pulse thrums gently against my chest. It is the transponder Dagomir gave me. I have been following it for three days, ever since my brothers and I became separated. It was after Vanarius, after we lost this world.

'Brothers find me...'

If I will it hard enough, perhaps it will become true. I seek a reunion with my fellow paladins but I must cross an ocean of damnation and torment to reach them.

The last light fades in the blood-bleached sky, setting like ink in water. It paints my silver armour in ruby red. I wonder if the light will rise again. It is my sacred charge to ensure that, that one way or another, it does.

I am Siegus Mortlock of the Grey Knights of Titan and this is my final testament.

With darkness shrouding the barren wastes beyond the temple, I ease from my hiding place into the former arena. It is a sandy, rubble-strewn plain that yawns open to the sky like a wound. As I emerge, my armour's servos growling, I realise I am not alone.

It is humanoid, its flesh the colour of viscera and sizzling like cooking meat. Iron-hard skin clothes a muscular form standing tall on reverse-jointed limbs that end in hooves, not feet. It is horned, this foot soldier of the aether, and clenches a dark blade in its clawed fist. It snarls as it sees me, a long serpentine tongue lathing the air as if to taste my soul.

I mutter three canticles of warding, the words trickling from my lips in a strong and certain cadence. To show weakness of faith before a hellspawn of the warp is to invite death and the rending of your soul.

This one is not alone as it stalks towards me, snorting and braying as if it were a beast of nature and not some abomination. Seven others join it. They hunt in packs of eight.

I will show them they should have brought more.

Donning my helm, I let the optics normalise and adjust to the retinal display that overlays my vision. The force halberd in my fist resonates as I grip the haft. It is time to do the Emperor's work.

'I am the hammer,' I bellow loudly in challenge. 'I am the tip of his sword!'

The hunters come for me, quickly breaking into a loping run. Three peel off to the left, another three to the right. Two more remain in my frontal arc.

A hard *clank* of its loading mechanism indicates my storm bolter is ready.

I advance as my enemies advance, quickly overcoming inertia and driving my body into a punishing charge.

'I banish thee, daemons!'

The storm bolter roars and a tempest erupts from the muzzle, turning two of the hunters into mist.

'Let His light incinerate!'

A sigil of daemon killing that burns as it touches cursed flesh is engraved onto every one of my silver-tipped and thrice-blessed shells.

Six daemons remain and I feel their strength ebb as I reduce their unholy number further. I swing around the storm bolter and unleash a second burst. They are wiser to its bite this time and two of the hunters avoid destruction by darting behind one of the amphitheatre's ceremonial columns. The third reacts too slowly and meets the same fate as the other two I have just banished.

Six become five. As I come to the clash of arms, I hope the few I have killed turn the scales enough and that my steel and momentum will overcome what daemons still remain.

I lower my shoulder into the charge, colliding with the foremost hunter, and feel the resistance of warp-forged muscle and sinew. Nonetheless, I press with all the mass and augmented strength of my power armour. The daemon is lifted up, braying as I crush its ribcage, raking ineffectively with its claws, its dark blade failing in the air. The sheer force of my momentum carries the daemon further than the initial impact and it becomes a distant memory as I watch it catapult in my peripheral vision. Smoke rises from its slowly dissolving form.

Sparks rain from the haft of my halberd, the runes upon the blade flaring brightly as it comes into contact with the daemon's sword. The blow from the second hunter is stronger than I expected, and it drives me onto my back foot. With a shout and the exercising of Emperor-given strength, I throw the beast back and carve it down the middle with my return cut.

Two more are despatched, but it has left me vulnerable to the two that remain.

First there is heat, agonising and pure as primal anger. Then comes the cold, bone deep and numbing. My left leg has a chunk of Chaos-wrought iron sticking out of it. Only the wardings on my armour have saved it from being completely severed.

A glancing blow jams the storm bolter mounted on my wrist as I level it to fire. The dull thunk of a fouled mechanism sounds almost like a death knell.

I barely parry the third weapon thrust. Its edge skids off the blade of my halberd and grates down the side of my war-helm. For a few seconds the optical feed crazes and cuts out. When it returns, I am already fighting blind, fending off the twin onslaught of the hunters. They attack intelligently, one inducing a defence as the other seeks to exploit a weakness in my guard.

The halberd becomes a blur in my hands, more a staff now than an axe blade. I am conscious of the fact that I am giving ground too easily, trying to prevent them from circling. Warning icons flash across my retinal feed as I take damage. The aegis of my armour is keeping me alive but it is not inviolate. Neither am I.

Like a third heart beating in my breast, the transponder gives off a steady pulse and I am reminded of the duty to my brothers. I must find them and reach salvation.

But I am tiring, still weary from the last great battle. Something about this world, it is hampering my ability to heal. It could be the poison in the air or the overwhelming taint now present on this world. It does not matter. The fact remains that I am dying. Determination and willpower have got me this far but they will not avail me here...

'We die together, hellspawn,' I promise them, eliciting a cruel smile from both that parodies a uniquely human reaction. The perversity of it turns my mind towards righteous wrath.

Knowing it will be suicide, I am about to thrust my force halberd into one of the daemons and expose my defence when I catch the faint echo of something scuttling against a stone arch above me. There is a momentary pause in the melee as the daemons also detect it before a horde of chittering, chitinous creatures spill down from the arch. Diminutive but numerous, they swarm the hunters, biting and stinging as they bring them down. I feel them scratching and clawing at my armour, but it is tougher than daemon flesh and I endure where the hunters do not. I behead one and impale another through the mass of smaller creatures, the hunters' screams damning me in a language I understand but would never utter.

With the last daemonic corpses denaturing before my eyes, the fight becomes a brawl as I stab, bludgeon and stamp free of the horde, their vile alien blood gumming up my servos and riming my armour in a heliotrope crust.

I smash my gauntlet against a ceremonial column to clear my jammed storm bolter and am rewarded with the hard metal report of shells slotting into my weapon's twin barrels.

'Machine-spirits be praised...'

The storm bolter speaks again, and its words send the chittering swarm creatures to their deaths.

It is over in seconds, the aliens clustering on instinct and tactically inferior to the daemons. Their demise drains my clip and I slam the last remaining reload into the empty breech with an ominous clack.

In spite of the darkness, the skirmish will almost certainly draw others to the arena. I leave quickly, making egress through a gaping fissure in the boundary wall.

On my retinal feed there is a topographical representation of the region. Flashing dully in the lifeless monochrome rendering is the locator-signal of the beacon linked to my transponder.

On foot, it will take me almost an hour to reach it.

Shadows deepen beyond the amphitheatre's border. They hiss and whisper and harbour the grunting calls of beasts as they are stirred from slumber. The very landscape undulates, reshaping and twisting, and I realise not all of it is 'land' and what little earth remains will be forever changed.

I make haste and hope there are enough of us left to reach salvation.

It was a fortress once. Buttressed walls wrought into a high escarpment of rock, I can see why Dagomir would have chosen this place to take refuge in. As I stand before it, I look up at the razor wire that crowns the summit of a single, lonely tower. There are gun emplacements, murder slits, a redoubt raised around the foundations. It was formidable... but now the gate lies open, a forbidding invitation.

Alone and standing before the shadow of this ferrocrete colossus, I cannot linger. With little choice, the transponder pulse now drumming out what feels like a warning, I make for the entrance.

Inside, the signs of what fate may have befallen my brethren are no better than the ruined gate through which I entered. Psychically, the atmosphere is deadened, though I detect a pressure against my skull that threatens from afar. Not the spoor of my brothers. It is something else. Not a daemon, either. I would know if I felt one. This is altogether unique and wholly disquieting.

Engaging the prey-sight filter of my retinal lenses, I venture into the darkness and soon find myself travelling downwards.

At the end of a broad stairwell, I discover the fortress catacombs, ancient beyond my reckoning. I make out baroque columns in the shadows and the glaring statues of long-dead lords. Some stand upon daises, clad in stone finery, while others are wrought into the lids of tombs in grim repose.

I also find corpses.

Dagomir is amongst them, eyes wide but sadly dead. I am heartened at least to see his force sword still clenched in his unyielding fist.

'Ave Imperator, brother,' I mutter, the tremor in my voice betraying my grief. 'Only in death...'

Unlike the others, he stands upright, having wedged his body into a narrow alcove that now holds him fast.

Merek has been impaled. A long spear of dark iron is thrust through his chest. Terrowin lies supine, apparently unwounded until I notice the burnt out sockets of his retinal lenses. Radulf is on his knees, staked by swords to the stone flags where his blood has pooled. His beaten posture prompts a pang of sudden sorrow in me.

Others have been felled in similar fashion. I recognise them all, Leofrick and Berinon, Argonus and Longidus. I have to still my temper to stop from crying out in ambivalent rage and anguish.

My brothers are fallen around the catacombs, and none shall be borne to the Dead Fields, for there are none but I to carry them. The only salve to my grief is that a great reaping lies scattered around them. Daemonic forms lay cleaved, more hunters and tallymen, hounds and the shattered remains of winged furies. Whatever evil now permeates this place, it is strong enough to prevent daemonic dissolution.

It is almost too much to endure and I fall to one knee, the weight of my force halberd a heavy burden. I had hoped some would have survived, but I know now I am the last of us. The last knight of Titan on this world.

I rise – perhaps it is the eyes of my dead brothers upon me that force me up – and approach Dagomir. As soon as I touch his face to close his staring eyes, a hololith hazes into being, projected from the Justicar's armour and triggered by my presence.

'Here then marks the end,' utters Dagomir's monochromatic simulacrum. He is battered, bloody, and his armour badly rent. 'These are my parting words for any Grey Knight who yet lives on this world. If you are seeing this, I am slain and our brotherhood stands defeated. Nothing could have prepared us for what we face here. We are the grist caught between the monsters of two worlds.'

The image flickers and for a moment I fear it will fade before Dagomir can impart his entire message but the machine-spirit endures and the Justicar goes on.

'A last hope still exists. The salvation of a hundred million souls. My brothers...' he says as a locator signal flashes up on my retinal display and my transponder is repurposed by a data-burst hidden in the hololith. He continues, 'only you can reach salvation now. Ave Imperator, and may the Bell of Lost Souls ring out for all of the Em–'

The image flickers and dies at last, a fitting omen perhaps.

Several leagues lie between this sundered fortress and the salvation Dagomir spoke of. Alone and injured, my fate appears sealed until the faintest shaft of light, penetrating through the crack in the stone above, although from what source I cannot fathom, alights upon a statue glowering at me from the near pitch dark.

As I draw closer, I recognise it – Brother Sedric, our Librarian. Dried blood cakes his upper lip, his nose and ears. I do not need to be a psyker to recognise the mind-death. It grieves me to see him slain as I raise my eyes to meet his but the armature clad around him is the divine providence I need to achieve Dagomir's mission.

A Nemesis Dreadknight stands before me, an immense skeletal armature that encases Sedric's body in an unyielding adamantium frame. It is a relic, armoured and armed with the deadliest weapons of our order. In the hands of a worthy paladin, it is capable of killing greater daemons. I must use it to cross the barren lands to salvation.

Muttering a benediction, I release Sedric from his cage, catching his falling body and gently bearing it to the ground. There is nothing more I can do for him or the rest of my slain brothers, so I climb aboard the Dreadknight in Sedric's place and see if I am worthy of it.

I lock the stabiliser harness over my shoulders, and as I grip the twin stick controls in either fist I feel the charge of the plasma reactor waking. A sense of invulnerability fills my heart, despite the odds levied against me. Both weapon mounts are functional and I dry spin the gatling barrels in a self-indulgent moment of belligerence. On the opposite side, attached to an immense adamantium power glove, the dulcet burning of my incinerator's ignition flame is a whisper of the vengeance to come.

With a grunt of effort, I set the giant armature in motion, each slow and heavy footfall drawing cascades of dust motes from the settled stone.

As I set my sights on the stairwell, the chittering I had heard in the arena returns. I am wrenched from thoughts of grief and vengeance and reminded of what comes for me.

I take three steadily more confident steps as the sound intensifies, detecting scuttling against the spiral stair that drills down into the catacombs where I await.

A deluge of tooth and claw erupts from the mouth of the stair, spilling over the steps in a cataract of pale, carapaced bodies and clacking mandibles.

With a bellow, I unleash the gatling silencer. It is the daemon's bane but will serve well enough to vanquish these creatures, whose forms are mutilated by my fusillade.

'Back unto whatever pit whence you crawled, filth!'

I spit the words, though my prey will not hear them above the roar of the cannon. With one foot thrust forward, I release the incinerator to wash the flagstones and the remains of the xenos beasts with purifying promethium.

'Lo! Such is the fate of all abominate creatures! Burn in righteous fire!'

I step into the blaze, heedless of its flame, and grind the xenos into offal.

More are coming – I hear them shrieking and baying from the summit of the stairwell. They sound like larger beasts, the masters of these dregs.

I snarl and mount the landing, my armature still wreathed in fire as I climb.

A beast surges at me. Reverse-limbed, hoofed and chitin-laden, it stands almost to my waist. Its head is large and bulbous, plated by organic armour, and two of its four arms end in arcing bone scythes. The monstrosity would dwarf even a son of Titan but I am clad in holy armour and catch its frenzied attack, seizing the creature's throat in my power glove.

I fend off its raking claws, the Dreadknight more than their equal.

Two more of the beasts come bounding for me, armed with long, ossified blades. I eviscerate one with a burst from the gatling mount, simultaneously shredding the creature clenched in my fist. Its flung corpse is a missile that trammels the third beast. It has barely regained its footing when I immolate it.

As it dies screaming, I advance, knowing that haste must be my companion now. At the stairwell's summit, I meet a swarm of lesser creatures. The act of slaying them is not unlike wading knee-deep into a diseased ocean. As I despatch them, the distant throbbing in my skull, the psychic siren-call, grows ever louder. Another alien caste, I am sure of this now.

I breach the gate, the killing almost metronomic in its regularity. Xenos blood has turned my armour a viscous purple hue.

In my wake, I leave behind a massacre and a growing horde hunting down the last living mortal of this damned world.

Night still holds but there is blood and violence on the air that has woken both beasts. Images assail my mind, of great tentacles unfurling, of a deep and fanged maw gaping to swallow the world. I feel the collective consciousness of both the alien and the daemonic pressing against my psyche, slowly thinning the membrane between sanity and madness.

I hear them clashing over distant, broken cities, feeling the malevolence of their gaze fall upon me.

'I am Mortlock!' I roar at the hills that writhe in the manner of something sentient. 'I defy the will of dark gods! I defy the xenos! This world is not yours to claim!'

On the breeze, I swear I can hear laughter.

With my weapons auto-loaded, I set off at a brisk pace. Less than a few hours of night remains and I still have far to travel. The transponder guides me, its thrum insistent, desperate. By the dawn, I must reach salvation else all will be lost.

My last hope, and the last hope for this world, sits upon a barren crag of rock. *Salvation.* Though I cannot see it, the transponder in my armour tells me it is there. My armature is battered, the incinerator gone, ripped free in a previous encounter, and the gatling has long since run dry. I have my faith and my will alone. It must suffice.

The nascent light of the last dawning of this world is just breaching the final vestiges of night. Exhausted, grieving and near broken, I urge myself to one last effort.

Nearby, I can hear the crash of the oceans... before I realise there are no oceans left.

The great tide of abominations, daemonic and alien, has reached me.

I turn and see them, sweeping, baying, shrieking and killing. In their murder lust, they have not forgotten me. I suspect I am a trophy to them, something to be savoured, a symbolic victory.

I shall deny it to both.

I barrel up the scree slope of the crag, kicking up dust and rock. I fall to my knees in the armature, scrambling now with power gloves digging into the dirt, scratching for purchase so I might stand and at least meet my end on my feet.

The tide washes up to the foot of the crag. As I look back, I see the rock I crawl upon has become an island in an ocean of monsters. Still, they bite and gnaw at one another. A vast daemonic lord with great, ragged wings is locked in a deadly duel with an immense alien tyrant. Overhead there are flocks of furies and flying xenos engaged in aerial battles, and all the while the swarm creeps closer.

'Salvation.'

It is the second to last word I will ever utter. I see it inscribed upon the metal outer casing.

The device looks innocuous enough. A lozenge-shaped capsule, it is barely half the size of my broken Dreadknight. I disengage the harness and fall from the armature, its use expended now. Finding my helmet stifling, I wrench it off and let it fall. Foulness assails me, the tainted air of this world. Crawling, I reach the edge of the device, aware that the horde is coming.

The overwhelming chatter of their voices is deafening, their foul musk suffocating, but my will holds and as I release the panel and key in the manual activation sequence, all I can hear are the words of my Grand Master, giving benediction before battle. All I smell are the votive candles of my brotherhood's chapel back on Titan.

In my mind's eye, I am standing in the Dead Fields surrounded by a legacy of heroes.

I am Siegus Mortlock of the Grey Knights of Titan and this is my final testament.

Judging from the device's control panel, it has misfired, its arming mechanism thwarted by some twist of fate, but I can realign its machine-spirit.

As I feel the first daemonic breath upon my neck, as the psychic presence that has been oppressing me since the fortress emerges from the horde in all its alien horror, as the dawn rises and bathes my wounded body in the light of a bloody sun, I speak the last word that will save this world from damnation and ignite the bomb.

'Exterminatus...'

There is light... There is glory... There is–

ABOUT THE AUTHORS

Guy Haley is the author of the Siege of Terra novel *The Lost and the Damned*, as well as the Horus Heresy novels *Titandeath*, *Wolfsbane* and *Pharos*, and the Primarchs novels *Konrad Curze: The Night Haunter*, *Corax: Lord of Shadows* and *Perturabo: The Hammer of Olympia*. He has also written many Warhammer 40,000 novels, including the Dawn of Fire books *Avenging Son* and *Throne of Light*, as well as *Belisarius Cawl: The Great Work*, the Dark Imperium trilogy, *The Devastation of Baal*, *Dante*, *Darkness in the Blood* and *Astorath: Angel of Mercy*. For Age of Sigmar he has penned the Drekki Flynt novel *The Arkanaut's Oath*, as well as other stories included in *War Storm*, *Ghal Maraz* and *Call of Archaon*. He lives in Yorkshire with his wife and son.

Josh Reynolds' extensive Black Library back catalogue includes the Horus Heresy Primarchs novel *Fulgrim: The Palatine Phoenix*, and three Horus Heresy audio dramas featuring the Blackshields. His Warhammer 40,000 work includes the Space Marine Conquests novel *Apocalypse*, *Lukas the Trickster* and the Fabius Bile novels. He has written many stories set in the Age of Sigmar, including the novels *Shadespire: The Mirrored City*, *Soul Wars*, *Eight Lamentations: Spear of Shadows*, the Hallowed Knights novels *Plague Garden* and *Black Pyramid*, and *Nagash: The Undying King*. He has written the Warhammer Horror novel *Dark Harvest*, and novella *The Beast in the Trenches*, featured in the portmanteau novel *The Wicked and the Damned*. He penned the Necromunda novel *Kal Jerico: Sinner's Bounty*. He lives and works in Sheffield.

Braden Campbell is the author of *Shadowsun: The Last of Kiru's Line* for Black Library, as well as the novella *Tempestus*, and several short stories. He is a classical actor and playwright, and a freelance writer, particularly in the field of role playing games. Braden has enjoyed Warhammer 40,000 for nearly a decade, and remains fiercely dedicated to his dark eldar.

Joe Parrino is the author of a range of Warhammer 40,000 stories, including the novella *Shield of Baal: Devourer*, the audio dramas *Alone*, *Damocles: The Shape of the Hunt* and *Assassinorum: The Emperor's Judgement*, and the short stories 'Witness', 'The Patient Hunter', 'Nightspear', 'In Service to Shadows' and 'No Worse Sin'. He lives, writes and works in the American Pacific Northwest.

L J Goulding is the author of the Horus Heresy audio drama *The Heart of the Pharos*, while for Space Marine Battles he has written the novel *Slaughter at Giant's Coffin* and the audio drama *Mortarion's Heart*. His other Warhammer fiction includes 'The Great Maw' and 'Kaldor Draigo: Knight of Titan', and he has continued to explore the dark legacy of Sotha in 'The Aegidan Oath' and *Scythes of the Emperor: Daedalus*. He lives and works in the US.

Nick Kyme is the author of the Horus Heresy novels *Old Earth*, *Deathfire*, *Vulkan Lives* and *Sons of the Forge*, the novellas *Promethean Sun* and *Scorched Earth*, and the audio dramas *Red-Marked*, *Censure* and *Nightfane*. His novella *Feat of Iron* was a *New York Times* bestseller in the Horus Heresy collection *The Primarchs*. For Warhammer 40,000, Nick has written *Volpone Glory* and the Dawn of Fire novel *The Iron Kingdom*. He is also well known for his popular Salamanders series and the Cato Sicarius novels *Damnos* and *Knights of Macragge*. His work for Age of Sigmar includes the short story 'Borne by the Storm', included in the novel *War Storm*, and the audio drama *The Imprecations of Daemons*. He has also written the Warhammer Horror novel *Sepulturum*. He lives and works in Nottingham.

YOUR NEXT READ

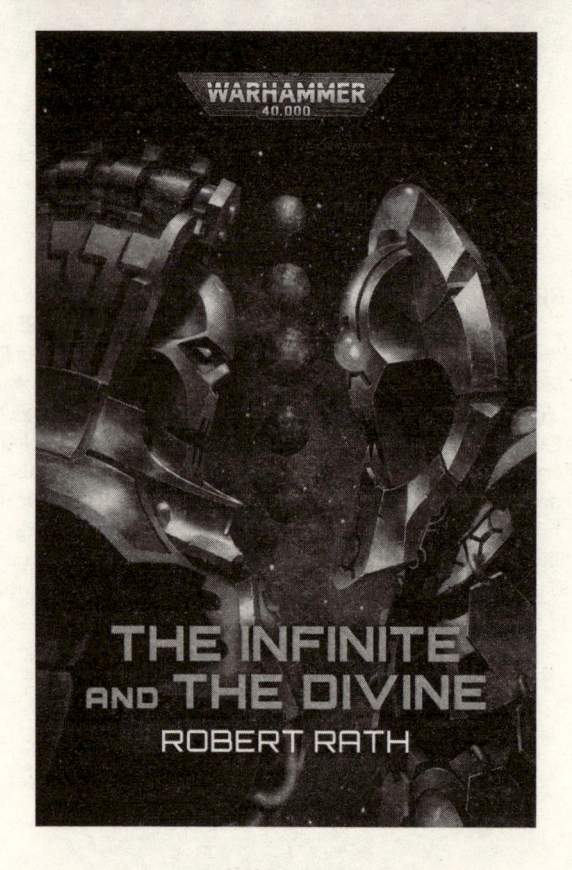

THE INFINITE AND THE DIVINE
by Robert Rath

Trazyn the Infinite and Orikan the Diviner are opposites. Each is obsessed with their own speciality, and their rivalry spans millennia. Yet together, they may hold the secret to saving the necron race…

For these stories and more, go to **blacklibrary.com**, **games-workshop.com**, Games Workshop and Warhammer stores, all good book stores or visit one of the thousands of independent retailers worldwide, which can be found at **games-workshop.com/storefinder**

YOUR NEXT READ

BRUTAL KUNNIN
by Mike Brooks

When Ufthak and his orks attack the forge world of Hephaesto, the last thing they want is to share the spoils with the notorious Kaptin Badrukk. But with armies to defeat and loot to seize, Ufthak's boyz might just need Badrukk's help – though that doesn't mean they can trust him…

For these stories and more, go to blacklibrary.com, games-workshop.com, Games Workshop and Warhammer stores, all good book stores or visit one of the thousands of independent retailers worldwide, which can be found at games-workshop.com/storefinder

YOUR NEXT READ

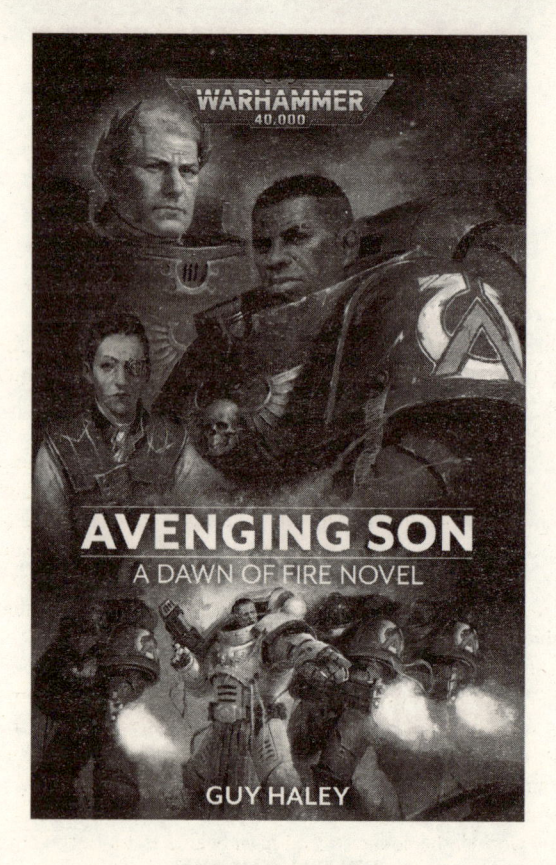

AVENGING SON
by Guy Haley

As the Indomitus Crusade spreads out across the galaxy, one battlefleet must face a dread Slaughter Host of Chaos. Their success or failure may define the very future of the crusade – and the Imperium.

For these stories and more, go to blacklibrary.com, games-workshop.com, Games Workshop and Warhammer stores, all good book stores or visit one of the thousands of independent retailers worldwide, which can be found at games-workshop.com/storefinder

An Extract from
Avenging Son
by Guy Haley

'I was there at the Siege of Terra,' Vitrian Messinius would say in his later years.

'I was there...' he would add to himself, his words never meant for ears but his own. 'I was there the day the Imperium died.'

But that was yet to come.

'To the walls! To the walls! The enemy is coming!' Captain Messinius, as he was then, led his Space Marines across the Penitent's Square high up on the Lion's Gate. 'Another attack! Repel them! Send them back to the warp!'

Thousands of red-skinned monsters born of fear and sin scaled the outer ramparts, fury and murder incarnate. The mortals they faced quailed. It took the heart of a Space Marine to stand against them without fear, and the Angels of Death were in short supply.

'Another attack, move, move! To the walls!'

They came in the days after the Avenging Son returned, emerging from nothing, eight legions strong, bringing the bulk of their numbers to bear against the chief entrance to the Imperial Palace. A decapitation strike like no other, and it came perilously close to success.

Messinius' Space Marines ran to the parapet edging the Penitent's Square. On many worlds, the square would have been a plaza fit to adorn the centre of any great city. Not on Terra. On the immensity of the Lion's Gate, it was nothing, one of hundreds of similarly huge spaces. The word 'gate' did not suit the scale of the cityscape. The Lion's Gate's bulk marched up into the sky, step by titanic step, until it rose far higher than the mountains it had supplanted. The gate had been built by the Emperor Himself, they said. Myths detailed the improbable supernatural feats required to raise it. They were lies, all of them, and belittled the true effort needed to build such an edifice. Though the Lion's Gate was made to His design and by His command, the soaring monument had been constructed by mortals, with mortal hands and mortal tools. Messinius wished that had been remembered. For men to build this was far more impressive than any godly act of creation. If men could remember that, he believed, then perhaps they would remember their own strength.

The uncanny may not have built the gate, but it threatened to bring it down. Messinius looked over the rampart lip, down to the lower levels thousands of feet below and the spread of the Anterior Barbican.

Upon the stepped fortifications of the Lion's Gate was armour of every colour and the blood of every loyal primarch. Dozens of regiments stood alongside them. Aircraft filled the sky. Guns boomed from every quarter. In the churning redness on the great roads, processional ways so huge they were akin to prairies cast in rockcrete, were flashes of gold where the Emperor's Custodian Guard battled. The might of the Imperium was gathered there, in the palace where He dwelt.

There seemed moments on that day when it might not be enough.

The outer ramparts were carpeted in red bodies that writhed and heaved, obscuring the great statues adorning the defences and covering over the guns, an invasive cancer consuming reality. The enemy were legion. There were too many foes to defeat by plan and ruse. Only guns, and will, would see the day won, but the defenders were so pitifully few.

Messinius called a wordless halt, clenched fist raised, seeking the best place to deploy his mixed company, veterans all of the Terran Crusade. Gunships and fighters sped overhead, unleashing deadly light and streams of bombs into the packed daemonic masses. There were innumerable cannons crammed onto the gate, and they all fired, rippling the structure with false earthquakes. Soon the many ships and orbital defences of Terra would add their guns, targeting the very world they were meant to guard, but the attack had come so suddenly; as yet they had had no time to react.

The noise was horrendous. Messinius' audio dampers were at maximum and still the roar of ordnance stung his ears. Those humans that survived today would be rendered deaf. But he would have welcomed more guns, and louder still, for all the defensive fury of the assailed palace could not drown out the hideous noise of the daemons – their sighing hisses, a billion serpents strong, and chittering, screaming wails. It was not only heard but sensed within the soul, the realms of spirit and of matter were so intertwined. Messinius' being would be forever stained by it.

Tactical information scrolled down his helmplate, near environs only. He had little strategic overview of the situation. The vox-channels were choked with a hellish screaming that made communication impossible. The noosphere was disrupted by etheric backwash spilling from the immaterial rifts the daemons poured through. Messinius was used to operating on his own. Small-scale, surgical actions were the way of the Adeptus Astartes, but in a battle of this scale, a lack of central coordination would lead inevitably to defeat. This was not like the first Siege, where his kind had fought in Legions.

He called up a company-wide vox-cast and spoke to his warriors. They were not his Chapter-kin, but they would listen. The primarch himself had commanded that they do so.

'Reinforce the mortals,' he said. 'Their morale is wavering. Position yourselves every fifty yards. Cover the whole of the south-facing front. Let them see you.' He directed his warriors by chopping at the air with his left hand. His right, bearing an inactive power fist, hung heavily at his side. 'Assault Squad Antiocles, back forty yards, single firing line. Prepare to engage enemy breakthroughs only on my mark. Devastators, split to demi-squads and take up high ground, sergeant and sub-squad prime's discretion as to positioning and target. Remember our objective, heavy infliction of casualties. We kill as many as we can, we retreat, then hold at the Penitent's Arch until further notice. Command squad, with me.'

Command squad was too grand a title for the mismatched crew Messinius had gathered around himself. His own officers were light years away, if they still lived.

'Doveskamor, Tidominus,' he said to the two Aurora Marines with him. 'Take the left.'

'Yes, captain,' they voxed, and jogged away, their green armour glinting orange in the hell-light of the invasion.

The rest of his scratch squad was comprised of a communications specialist from the Death Spectres, an Omega Marine with a penchant for plasma weaponry, and a Raptor holding an ancient standard he'd taken from a dusty display.

'Why did you take that, Brother Kryvesh?' Messinius asked, as they moved forward.

'The palace is full of such relics,' said the Raptor. 'It seems only right to put them to use. No one else wanted it.'

Messinius stared at him.

'What? If the gate falls, we'll have more to worry about than my minor indiscretion. It'll be good for morale.'

The squads were splitting to join the standard humans. Such was the noise many of the men on the wall had not noticed their arrival, and a ripple of surprise went along the line as they appeared at their sides. Messinius was glad to see they seemed more firm when they turned their eyes back outwards.

'Anzigus,' he said to the Death Spectre. 'Hold back, facilitate communication within the company. Maximum signal gain. This interference will only get worse. See if you can get us patched in to wider theatre command. I'll take a hardline if you can find one.'

'Yes, captain,' said Anzigus. He bowed a helm that was bulbous with additional equipment. He already had the access flap of the bulky vox-unit on his arm open. He withdrew, the aerials on his power plant extending. He headed towards a systems nexus on the far wall of the plaza, where soaring buttresses pushed back against the immense weight bearing down upon them.

Messinius watched him go. He knew next to nothing about Anzigus. He spoke little, and when he did, his voice was funereal. His Chapter was mysterious, but the same lack of familiarity held true for many of these warriors, thrown together by miraculous events. Over their years lost wandering in the warp, Messinius had come to see some as friends as well as comrades, others he hardly knew, and none he knew so well as his own Chapter brothers. But they would stand together. They were Space Marines. They had fought by the returned primarch's side, and in that they shared a bond. They would not stint in their duty now.

Messinius chose a spot on the wall, directing his other veterans to left and right. Kryvesh he sent to the mortal officer's side. He looked down again, out past the enemy and over the outer palace. Spires stretched away in every direction. Smoke rose from all over the landscape. Some of it was new, the work of the daemon horde, but Terra had been burning for weeks. The Astronomican had failed. The galaxy was split in two. Behind them in the sky turned the great palace gyre, its deep eye marking out the throne room of the Emperor Himself.

'Sir!' A member of the Palatine Guard shouted over the din. He pointed downwards, to the left. Messinius followed his wavering finger. Three hundred feet below, daemons were climbing. They came upwards in a triangle tipped by a brute with a double rack of horns. It clambered hand over hand, far faster than should be possible, flying upwards, as if it touched the side of the towering gate only as a concession to reality. A Space Marine with claw locks could not have climbed that fast.

'Soldiers of the Imperium! The enemy is upon us!'

He looked to the mortals. Their faces were blanched with fear. Their weapons shook. Their bravery was commendable nonetheless. Not one of them attempted to run, though a wave of terror preceded the unnatural things clambering up towards them.

'We shall not turn away from our duty, no matter how fearful the foe, or how dire our fates may be,' he said. 'Behind us is the Sanctum of the Emperor Himself. As He has watched over you, now it is your turn to stand in guardianship over Him.'

The creatures were drawing closer. Through a sliding, magnified window on his display, Messinius looked into the yellow and cunning eyes of their leader. A long tongue lolled permanently from the thing's mouth, licking at the wall, tasting the terror of the beings it protected.

Boltgun actions clicked. His men leaned over the parapet, towering over the mortals as the Lion's Gate towered over the Ultimate Wall. A wealth of targeting data was exchanged, warrior to warrior, as each chose a unique mark. No bolt would be wasted in the opening fusillade. They could hear the creatures' individual shrieks and growls, all wordless, but their meaning was clear: blood, blood, blood. Blood and skulls.

Messinius sneered at them. He ignited his power fist with a swift jerk. He always preferred the visceral thrill of manual activation. Motors came to full life. Lightning crackled around it. He aimed downwards with his bolt pistol. A reticule danced over diabolical faces, each a copy of all the others. These things were not real. They were not alive. They were projections of a false god. The Librarian Atramo had named them maladies. A spiritual sickness wearing ersatz flesh.

He reminded himself to be wary. Contempt was as thick as any armour, but these things were deadly, for all their unreality.

He knew. He had fought the Neverborn many times before.

'While He lives,' Messinius shouted, boosting his voxmitter gain to maximal, 'we stand!'

'For He of Terra!' the humans shouted, their battle cry loud enough to be heard over the booming of guns.

'For He of Terra,' said Messinius. 'Fire!' he shouted.

The Space Marines fired first. Boltguns spoke, spitting spikes of rocket flare into the foe. Bolts slammed into daemon bodies, bursting them apart. Black viscera exploded away. Black ichor showered those coming after. The daemons' false souls screamed back whence they came, though their bones and offal tumbled down like those of any truly living foe.

Las-beams speared next, and the space between the wall top and the scaling party filled with violence. The daemons were unnaturally resilient, protected from death by the energies of the warp, and though many were felled, others weathered the fire, and clambered up still, unharmed and uncaring of their dead. Messinius no longer needed his helm's magnification to see into the daemon champion's eyes. It stared at him, its smile a promise of death. The terror that preceded them was replaced by the urge to violence, and that gripped them all, foe and friend. The baseline humans began to lose their discipline. A man turned and shot his comrade, and was shot down in turn. Kryvesh banged the foot of his borrowed banner and called them back into line. Elsewhere, his warriors sang; not their Chapter warsongs, but battle hymns known to all. Wavering human voices joined them. The feelings of violence abated, just enough.

Then the things were over the parapet and on them. Messinius saw Tidominus carried down by a group of daemons, his unit signum replaced by a mortis rune in his helm. The enemy champion was racing at him. Messinius emptied his bolt pistol into its face, blowing half of it away into a fine mist of daemonic ichor. Still it leapt, hurling itself twenty feet over the parapet. Messinius fell back, keeping the creature in sight, targeting skating over his helmplate as the machine-spirit tried to maintain a target lock. Threat indicators trilled, shifting up their priority spectrum.

The daemon held up its enormous gnarled hands. Smoke whirled in the space between, coalescing into a two-handed sword almost as tall as Messinius. By the time its hoofed feet cracked the paving slabs of the square, the creature's weapon was solid. Vapour streaming from its ruined face, it pointed the broadsword at Messinius and hissed a wordless challenge.

'Accepted,' said Messinius, and moved in to attack.

The creature was fast, and punishingly strong. Messinius parried its first strike with an outward push of his palm, fingers spread. Energy crackled. The boom generated by the meeting of human technology and the sorceries of the warp was loud enough to out-compete the guns, but though the impact sent pain lancing up Messinius' arm, the daemon was not staggered, and pressed in a follow-up attack, swinging the massive sword around its head as if it weighed nothing.

Messinius countered more aggressively this time, punching in to the strike. Another thunderous detonation. Disruption fields shattered matter, but the daemon was not wholly real, and the effect upon it was lesser than it would be upon a natural foe. Nevertheless, this time it was thrown backwards by the blow. Smoke poured from the edge of its blade. It licked black blood from its arm and snarled. Messinius was ready when it leapt: opening his fist, ignoring the sword as it clashed against his pauldron and sheared off a peeling of ceramite, he grabbed the beast about its middle.

The Bloodletters of Khorne were rangy things, all bone and ropey muscle, no space within them for organs. The false god of war had no need for them to eat or breathe, or to give the semblance of being able to do so. They were made only to kill, and to strike fear in the hearts of those they faced. Their waists were solid, and slender, and easily encompassed by Messinius' power fist. It squirmed in his grip, throwing Messinius' arm about. Servo motors in his joints locked, supplementary muscle fibres strained, but the White Consul stood firm.

'Tell your master he is not welcome on Terra,' he said. His words were calm, a deliberate defiance of the waves of rage pulsing off the daemon.

He closed his hand.

The daemon's midriff exploded. The top half fell down, still hissing and thrashing. Its sword clanged off the paving and broke into shards, brittle now it was separated from its wielder. They were pieces of the same thing, sword and beast. Apart, the weapon could not survive long.

Messinius cast down the lower portion of the daemon. There were dozens of the things atop the wall, battling with his warriors and the human soldiery. In the second he paused he saw Doveskamor hacked down as he stood over the body of his brother, pieces of armour bouncing across the ground. He saw a group of Palatine Sentinels corner a daemon with their bayonets. He saw a dozen humans cut down by eldritch swords.

Where the humans kept their distance, their ranged weapons took a toll upon the Neverborn. Where the daemons got among them, they triumphed more often than not, even against his Space Marines. Support fire rained down sporadically from above, its usefulness restricted by the difficulty of picking targets from the swirling melee. At the western edge of the line, the heavy weapons were more telling, knocking daemons off the wall before they crested the parapet and preventing them from circling around the back of the Imperial forces. Only his equipment allowed Messinius to see this. Without the helm feeds of his warriors and the limited access he had to the Lion Gate's auspectoria, he would have been blind, lost in the immediate clash of arms and sprays of blood. He would have remained where he was, fighting. He would not have seen that there were more groups of daemons pouring upwards. He would not have given his order, and then he would have died.

'Squad Antiocles, engage,' he said. He smashed a charging daemon into fragments, yanked another back the instant before it gutted a mortal soldier, and stamped its skull flat, while switching again to his company vox-net. 'All units, fall back to the Penitent's Arch. Take the mortals with you.'

His assault squad fell from the sky on burning jets, kicking daemons down and shooting them with their plasma and bolt pistols. A roar of promethium from a flamer blasted three bloodletters to ash.

'Fall back! Fall back!' Messinius commanded, his words beating time with his blows. 'Assault Squad Antiocles to cover. Devastators maintain overhead fire.'

Squad Antiocles drove the enemy back. Tactical Space Marines were retreating from the parapet, dragging human soldiers with them. An Ultramarine walked backwards past him, firing his bolter one-handed, a wounded member of the Palatine Guard draped over his right shoulder.

'Fall back! Fall back!' Messinius roared. He grabbed a human by the arm and yanked him hard away from the monster trying to slay him, almost throwing him across the square. He pivoted and punched, slamming the man's opponent in the face with a crackling bang that catapulted its broken corpse over the wall edge. 'Fall back!'

Mortal soldiers broke and ran while Squad Antiocles held off the foe. Telling to begin with, in moments the assault squad's momentum was broken, and again more bloodletters were leaping over the edge of the rampart. The Space Marines fired in retreat, covering each other in pairs as they crossed the square diagonally to the Penitent's Arch. The mortals were getting the idea, running between the Adeptus Astartes and mostly staying out of their fire corridor. With the fight now concentrated around Squad Antiocles, the Devastators were more effective, blasting down the daemons before they could bring their weight of numbers to bear upon Antiocles. Sporadic bursts of fire from the retreating Tactical Marines added to the effect, and for a short period the number of daemons entering the square did not increase.

Messinius tarried a moment, rounding up more of the humans who were either too embattled or deaf to his orders to get out. He reached three still firing over the parapet's edge and pulled them away. A daemon reared over the parapet and he crushed its skull, but a second leapt up and cleaved hard into his fist, and power fled the weapon. Messinius pumped three bolts into its neck, decapitating it. He moved back.

His power fist was ruined. The daemon's cut had sliced right through the ceramite, breaking the power field generator and most of the weapon's strength-boosting apparatus, making it a dead weight. He said a quick thanks to the machine's departed spirit and smashed the top of his bolt pistol against the quick seal release, at the same time disengaging the power feeds by way of neural link. The clamps holding the power fist to his upper arm came loose and it slid to the floor with a clang, leaving his right arm clad in his standard ceramite gauntlet. A century together. A fine weapon. He had no time to mourn it.

'Fall back!' he shouted. 'Fall back to the Penitent's Arch!'

He slammed a fresh clip into his bolt pistol. Squad Antiocles were being pushed back. The Devastators walked their fire closer in to the combat. A heavy bolter blasted half a dozen daemons into stinking meat. A missile blew, lifting more into the air. Messinius fell back himself now, leaving it to the last moment before ordering the Assault Marines to leap from the fray. Their jets ignited, driving back the daemons with washes of flame, and they lifted up over his head, leaving four of their brothers dead on the ground. Devastator fire hammered down from above. Anti-personnel weapons set into casemates and swivel turrets on the walls joined in, but the daemons mounted higher and higher in a wave of red that flooded over the parapet.

'Run!' he shouted at the straggling human soldiery. 'Run and survive! Your service is not yet done!'

The Penitent's Arch led from the square onto a wall walk that curved around to another layer of defences. His Space Marines were already making a firing line across the entrance. A gate could be extended across the arch, sealing the walk from the square, but Messinius refrained from requesting it be closed, as the humans were still streaming past the Adeptus Astartes. Kryvesh waved the banner, whirling it through the air to attract the terrified mortals. The Space Marines fired constantly into the mass of daemons sprinting after them, exhausting their ammunition supplies. Shattered false bodies tumbled down, shot from the front and above, yet still they came, overtaking and dismembering the last warriors fleeing away from the parapet.

Squad Antiocles roared through the arch, landing behind their brethren. Messinius passed between them. For a moment he surveyed the tide of coming fury. Endless red-skinned monsters filling the square like a lake of spilled blood, washing over a score of brightly armoured Space Marine corpses left behind in the retreat. Several hundred humans lay alongside them.

He opened a vox-channel to Gate Command.

'Wall batteries three-seven-three through three-seven-six, target sector nine five eighty-three, Penitent's Square, western edge. Five-minute bombardment.'

'On whose order?'

'Captain Vitrian Messinius, White Consuls Chapter, Tenth Company. I have the primarch's authority.' As he dealt with gunnery control, he was also data-pulsing a request for resupply, and checking through layered data screeds.

'Voice print and signum ident match. Transponder codes valid. We obey.'

The far side of the square erupted in a wall of flame. Heavy cannon shells detonated in a string along the rampart. High-energy beams sliced into the square, turning stone and metal instantly to superheated gas. The approaching daemons were annihilated. A few bolt-rounds cracked off as the last daemons nearing the Space Marine line were put down.

'Company, cease fire. Conserve ammunition.' Nobody heard him. Nobody could. He re-sent the order via vox-script. The boltguns cut out.

Penitent's Square was a cauldron of fire so intense he could feel the heat through his battleplate's ceramite. The ground shook under his feet and he considered the possibility that the wall would give way. The noise was so all-consuming the idea of speech lost relevance. For five minutes the Lion's Gate tore madly at its own hide, ripping out chunks of itself in a bid to scrape free the parasites infesting its fabric, then, as suddenly as it had begun, the bombardment ceased.